BLAZING ~~TALES~~ TAILS
OF THE BLAZAR BITCHES

A Spanking Space Pirate Adventure

By Clarine Klein | Leila Hann

http://clarineklein.com

PRAISE FOR BLAZING ~~TALES~~ TAILS
OF THE BLAZAR BITCHES

"Robots! Spaceships! Bruised butts! The sci-fi stands by itself as a rollicking good yarn, the sexy spanking scenes are the icing on the cake. This is the queer spanko pirate space opera I didn't know I needed!"

- Pandora / Blake, Dreams of Spanking

"This book has everything I want in a spanking story: a well-written, exciting plot, memorable characters, and even a little bit of humor. Saucy spanking space pirates being gay and doing crimes? What's not to love? One thing's for sure, though - Phera's not going to be doing much sitting!"

- Jillian Keenan, Author of Sex with Shakespeare

"Hot spankings and high-speed sci-fi - what more can you ask for? Phera's bratty adventure is exhilarating, hilarious, and adorable."

- Elysia Daye, Better Dayes Erotic Fiction

"This book brings together two of my favorite things: science fiction and good, hard spankings!"

- J.J. Rose, Author of Baker's Dozen and other Spanking Erotica

"This is so much fun between the space adventure, the protagonist's brattitude begging for a spanking, and the hot space pirates trying to keep the girl in line."

- Alex Bridges, author of I'm Not a Little Girl (Really)

ISBN: 9781733935074
Imprint: Studio Bebop Inc.

- Cover Illustration by Cul Lector -

https://www.patreon.com/CulLector
https://twitter.com/CulLector

- Chapter Illustrations By -

Cul Lector
https://www.patreon.com/CulLector
https://twitter.com/CulLector

Arkham-Insanity
https://www.patreon.com/isadoraarkham
https://twitter.com/ArkhamInsanity

Mitch After Midnight
https://www.deviantart.com/MitchAfterMidnight
https://twitter.com/MitchAMidnight

Being a pirate is hard when you're the one with all the booty!

For Phera Sinclair, life aboard a remote asteroid mining facility is nice and predictable. Sure, she might be a corporate slave working to pay back student loans that will never actually go away, but at least she has a job, right?

That all changes when she's caught up in a shipjacking by the Blazar Bitches!

After an explosive (and erotically-charged) first encounter with the gruff and frustratingly attractive space pirate, Straya, Phera finds herself being press-ganged into the crew. Free of the chains of her old life, she's able to use her PhD in robotics to help rob megacorporations blind in between learning firsthand just what being a horny brat among a crew of spank-happy space pirates means for her and her way too jiggly backside in this hard sci-fi adventure with even harder spankings!

CHAPTER ONE

CHARGES ACCRUED

Willful Destruction of Company Property

Phera Sinclair was not having a good day.

Granted, there really weren't all that many "good" days to be had on Binary Star System Asteroid Mining Facility F6C-8 (aka. The Bin), but somehow things had found a way to go from their usual baseline of mind-numbingly boring but at least predictable, to downright punch you in the gut and take all your stuff shitty in the blink of an eye.

"Strap in or get out, Red, we're pushing off!"

"Wha-?"

"I said move it or lose it!"

"Ow! *Hey!*"

Levering herself out of the boring laser assembly she'd just been shoved headfirst into (ruining all of her meticulous recalibration work in the process), Phera whirled around in time to see Sergeant Ember barreling into the cockpit of the shuttle she'd been performing maintenance in for the last three hours. Between the bland, company-approved but at least fast and energetic music she'd been blasting inside the flyer's hold and the haze of hallucinographic status readouts and reference schematics she'd been awash in, she hadn't even noticed him boarding until she'd gotten a faceful of ore excavator.

"All right, let's do this!"

"Wait, what? Do what?"

Ignoring her entirely, the sergeant brought the shuttle's engines online and began uncoupling them from The Bin's outer docking ring.

"Oh shit!"

Mind catching up all at once with what was happening as the soles of her boots began to levitate off the deck with the sudden loss of the minimal amount of gravity she'd been enjoying up until that point, Phera scrambled to strap the drone she'd been working on down to her workbench along with any loose tools she could see that might double as improvised missiles at high acceleration. That taken care of, she then made a lumbering, null-grav dive for her vacsuit helmet before it could get away from her. Immediately regretting it when the heavy-duty, braided cable tethering her brain and its neural interface to the ore crawler she'd just secured was violently yanked out of its socket beneath her ear, sending a blinding cascade of electric shocks up through her sinuses and down through her arms and legs.

"E-Ember, what the fuck is going on?" she managed to croak through the haze of pain clouding her mind, terror blossoming inside her spasming chest as she fumbled blindly with her helmet before finally managing to drag it down over her tight bunches of red curls and lock it into place with the rest of her suit.

"Pirates!" the other man called back as he keyed in a safety bypass to bring the engines up to full power all at once, gleeful voice muffled by her helmet since he wasn't bothering to use the local comms channel. "The outer perimeter picked them up a few minutes ago, and I'm about to go blast their sorry asses back to particles."

"*Particles?*"

As far as Phera knew, the clunky flyer only had a pair of tiny point defense lasers mounted on swivel pods along its underside that were meant for clearing debris, not ship-to-ship combat.

"Are you kidding me? We don't have that kind of-"

"Hang on tight. Engaging in ten!"

Whatever else Phera had been about to say was cut short by a sudden burst of hard acceleration that sent her caroming off a bulkhead, knocking the breath from her lungs even through the thick material of her vacsuit.

"Come on, you motherfuckers, it's go time!" the small mining station's chief of security whooped, oblivious to the roboticist's plight as he put the flyer through several more evasive maneuvers, bouncing her around the hold like so much living flotsam in the process.

"Ack! Shit! Fuck!"

Head throbbing and stomach lurching as "down" continued to shift at random with the unrestrained acceleration, Phera managed by some small miracle to grab onto a handhold with her third ricochet. Clinging to it for dear life, she slapped blindly at her boots until their maglocks engaged, securing her in place just as the flyer made another sharp banking maneuver that nearly wrenched her free all over again. Her boots held tight, though, and, chest constricting with panic as her inner ears continued to register their protests with her static-addled brain, she dragged herself down into a squat to make herself as small a target as possible for any loose tools still bouncing around the hold while she fumbled out her emergency tie-down kit from the pouch at the side of her hip.

"G... Gods damn asshole..." she slurred inside her helmet, fighting hard not to throw up against her faceplate as she strapped herself into place with hands made boulder heavy by all the accel Ember was pulling, wedging herself in tight between a wall and the side of her workbench.

Anchored in place, she was finally able to take a moment to catch her breath (or at least try to, at any rate). Her back and left shoulder were both throbbing dully from their repeated impacts against seemingly every hard edge and surface the damn flyer had to offer. Her vacsuit had managed to absorb the worst of it, but she knew she'd still be sore for a day or two. Assuming, that is, she didn't die in the next few minutes. On the bright side, the pink-tinged signal noise that had been flooding her optical nerves while her neural implant struggled to recalibrate itself after its sudden disconnect was finally starting to recede. Not that that really did much to make the absolute clusterfuck of a situation she found herself in any better, but now she could at least *see* how fucked she was.

KUH-THUMP!

And feel it too, apparently.

"What was that?" she yelped into her comm, heart managing to somehow climb even higher into her throat.

Even with Ember's borderline-deadly flying, something had still managed to impact against the side of their shuttle with a bone-rattling shake that made Phera's teeth slam together so hard that she was surprised she hadn't just cracked a molar.

Oh gods, oh fuck, please don't tell me that was a missile and we're about to explode...

She was pretty sure those were supposed to detonate on impact, but that was just going off of what she'd seen in vids and games. She'd never actually been in real space combat before (and had been hoping to never be, as a matter of fact). Some divinity must've decided to get off its lazy ass and throw her a bone, though, because a handful of heartbeats later it occurred to her that they were still in one piece, and she let out a shaky exhalation.

An exhalation which immediately got sucked back up again in another startled yelp as an ominous *THUNK-THUNK-THUNK* started reverberating through the hold above her.

"For fuck's sake, Ember," she snapped into her comm, irritation starting to override her initial panic now that the sergeant had stopped treating their modest shuttle like his own personal space fighter. "What the hell is going on out there?"

"Power armor on the port side hull!"

Ember was at least on the local comms channel now, but still sounded way too excited for Phera's liking.

"Get ready, kid. They're overriding the airlock controls and will start boarding any second now."

"Get ready?" the engineer squeaked, tensing where she crouched in her emergency harness a few meters away from said port side airlock. "What the hell does *that* mean?"

As if on cue, warning claxons indicating that someone was pressurizing the airlock without confirmation from the pilot started blaring inside the cramped confines of the cargo hold.

"That's right. Come get some, you bastard..."

Once again, Ember was completely ignoring her, having apparently decided that the best course of action was to take up a position on the other side of the airlock, weapon drawn and legs braced. Phera could see the manic grin on his sweaty face through his helmet's illuminated faceplate as he waited for the inner hatch's bolts to finish drawing back so it could swing open, and she found herself *really* hoping that all that time he'd bragged about putting in on the station's shooting range was about to pay off.

"Just a little more… A little more… Eat shit, you pirate scum!"

PING-PING-PING-PING-PING!

Only, when the security chief cut loose with a spray from the prized coilgun rifle Phera had so often seen him toting around during his station patrols, rather than showering their assailant in a deadly fusillade of magnetically accelerated projectiles, the sergeant's ordinance instead ricocheted off a semi-transparent shield that had been wedged into the opening of the airlock hatch; perforating his chest and helmet in at least six different places and very nearly taking Phera out in the process. It was only by sheer dumb luck that she'd wound up in cover behind her workbench, its storage cabinets exploding in a hail of detritus as they absorbed the errant gunfire and prevented her from being killed alongside the overeager idiot who'd been channeling his inner action vid star.

Just then, though, she was way too busy screaming to really notice.

"All right, listen up. If there's anyone else in there thinking about pulling some tough guy shit, just drop it, yeah? I'm coming in, and I'm not in the mood for a fucking firefight. Just throw out your weapons and surrender and I promise you'll be fine. Your friend here fucked his own shit up, but you don't have to end up the same way."

The tinny voice coming from an external vocaster inside the airlock sounded gruff and feminine, and sent a fresh surge of dread cascading down Phera's hunched spine as she remained frozen in place. But, again, whether it was dumb luck, divine intervention, or just the fact that she'd been crouching out of sight when the three meter tall suit of power armor eventually pushed its way out of the airlock and into the cargo hold, the terrified engineer managed to go unnoticed as its back panels split open and the pirate that had been operating it slipped free.

"Oh fuck, oh shit… Ember, you asshole," Phera moaned in a voice that was barely more than a strangled whisper, eyes cast up toward the ceiling in supplication as they tracked the lazy arc of a loose ribbon cable.

As dire as her situation was, though, the loss of the sergeant didn't bother her nearly as much as she thought it might. He'd been a bully who'd used his mandate to "maintain order" over his little fiefdom of Panorama Corp. station to make any time she wanted to take a flyer out for drone collection or maintenance an absolute nightmare of invasive security scans and paperwork. To say nothing of how he'd taken it upon himself to personally open and inspect every single message and package she'd sent or received that didn't come directly from the corporation itself.

Besides, it had all happened so fast. If anything, she was more shocked by just how abrupt and one-sided the "firefight" had been than she was at seeing a dead body in person for the first time. One moment Ember had been alive and all but salivating at the opportunity to finally use his favorite toy on an actual person, and the next he wasn't. Simple as that. The man had always been an obnoxious ass, and even through her haze of panic as she watched the pirate stow his body in a storage locker and push off in the direction of the shuttle's cockpit, she still couldn't help but agree with her that the security chief had definitely brought his fate down on himself.

Still, it would've been nice to have at least *someone* on her side just then.

For several heart-pounding, lung-clenching seconds all Phera could do was stay right where she was, doing her best not to move so much as a millimeter lest she draw the shipjacker's attention as she settled in at the helm. But, as those seconds began to stretch into minutes without her being discovered, she started to breathe a little easier. That is, until she felt the telltale tug of acceleration toward the back of the engine compartment that indicated they were underway once again.

Uh-oh...

The pirate wasn't flying anywhere near as aggressively as Ember had. But, even so, Phera knew that with every moment that passed they were getting further and further away from The Bin and any hope she might have of a rescue. Which, given the fact that the person who might've led such an effort was currently very much dead, kind of made that a moot point.

No, if she wanted to get out of this without being taken prisoner or getting herself killed, she was going to have to do it herself.

Somehow.

Even with that knowledge, though, it still took her another solid minute or two of deep, deliberate breathing before she was finally able to push through her fear paralysis to release her tie-down kit and start making a beeline toward the engine compartment.

"Oh fuck, oh shit, oh fuck, oh shit!"

Hauling ass when "down" was what was usually your "forward" was a lot trickier than the engineer had been expecting it to be. Panorama had only given her the bare minimum amount of null-grav training required to pass her basic safety certification when she'd first been hired. And, up until that point, she'd never really had a reason to put any of it into practice. The Bin's grav, while slightly less than a full one G thanks to all the hyper dense osmium-titanium alloys that made up the bulk of the asteroid it was carved into, had at least been consistent and made sense. But, avoiding being kidnapped, murdered, sold, or whatever it was that pirates did to pretty roboticists made for a powerful motivator, and she managed to make it into the engine compartment and pull the hatch closed without being noticed.

Probably.

"Shit, shit, fuck, shit, fuck, fuck, shit..."

Alternating between those two four-letter words with a randomness that might've been interesting to plot out had she not been so busy freaking out, Phera cast her panic-addled violet eyes about for something to help put an end to this shipjacking in progress. Well, actually, she already knew what she was going to do. Cutting the control lines to the engines was really her only option outside of maybe trying to steal Ember's weapon and attempting to take the shuttle back by force. But, actually *doing* that without killing both herself and the pirate in the process was a smidge trickier.

As far as plans went, it definitely needed work. But, just then, she was willing to make do with what she had.

"Okay, okay, you can do this," she breathed, trying (and failing spectacularly) to shove her jackhammering heart rate back down to something more reasonable as she pushed off toward a likely looking spot near the engine housing's status readout screen. "It'll be thick and insulated, and probably maroon, or maybe yellow. Now, let's see…"

The engine compartment was a lot warmer than the hold had been, and as Phera started digging around among the trunk lines and other cables clamped against the wall (doing her absolute best to avoid anything that looked like it might be pressurized, high-voltage, or explosive in the dim yellow glow of the overhead lights) she could feel an itchy sheen of sweat starting to break out across her fretfully furrowed forehead and all along her lower back. It took all of her self-control not to stop what she was doing to deal with that, but, eventually, she managed to find the densely packed fiber-optic bundle she'd been looking for. And, after taking a deep breath of stale vacsuit air to steady her nerves, she cut the whole thing clean through (well, *clean-ish*, it took a couple tries) with a pair of flush cutters from her toolkit.

BANG!

And was unceremoniously thrown ass over tea kettle once again as the engines cut off with a *lot* more accel-shift than she'd been expecting.

"Ugh…"

Groaning to herself in the resulting silence, Phera groped for the nearest handhold in the cramped compartment she could find and reached back to rub at where her plump ass had just been violently bounced off of one of the rounded (but still way too pointy for her taste) corners of the engine housing.

"Would it kill them to buy suits with at least a *little* bit of structural reinforcement? I don't need armor plating, but something besides just a kevlar weave would sure be nice."

Her latest bout of vertigo and potential bruises quickly became the least of her worries, however, when she began to feel a brand new series of vibrations carrying through the inner hull to where her tender backside sat pressed against what was usually the "ceiling" of the flyer in more objective gravity.

Clonk. Clonk. Clonk. Clonk.

Slow, heavy footsteps, brought down with the unnatural cadence of magnetized vacboots with a *lot* of armor around them. She felt more than heard them draw closer and closer, until finally they were just outside the hatch to the engine compartment. Right above (or below, if you prefer) her head.

Once again Phera's litany of uncreative cursing picked up speed, before just as quickly being quashed. The palms of her vacsuit gloves making a sharp, plastic-on-plastic *clack* against her faceplate as she hurried to silence herself.

Shit, shit, shit!

She really hadn't planned this far ahead, she realized with a start. She'd figured that… Well, if she was being honest with herself, she'd been hoping that the pirate would call it quits once the ship stopped responding to the helm.

"Shoot, darn, dang, butter cakes!" she'd say, and then get back into her power armor and evac back to whatever shuttle she'd come in on.

But noooo.

Shaking her head to clear it as she realized that those very heavy-sounding boots weren't going anywhere now that they'd stopped just outside the hatch, she frantically cast her gaze about for something, anything, she could use as a weapon. Only problem was, highly pressurized lines of fuel and coolant didn't tend to occupy the same space as anything explosive or impactful on a shuttle.

So, she improvised. Snatching up an aerosol can of lithium grease from its hook on her tool belt, she reoriented herself to face whoever might be about to come for her, feeling her pulse pounding in her sweaty fingertips as they flexed in her gloves around the can. There was nowhere to hide inside the tiny engine compartment, and she was realizing now that she *really* should have set up some sort of barricade before cutting the control lines. Still, she could at least try and bluff her way out of this. Who knew? Maybe she could make the pirate slip on a patch of deck plating and bang their shin really hard on something that would make her decide she wasn't worth the effort of killing or capturing?

Or maybe she could just throw the damn thing at her and hope for the best.

Again, not a great plan, but beggars couldn't be choosers.

The silence continued to drag on for several more long, interminable moments, reaching the point where Phera was ready to initiate the confrontation herself just to get it over with. Then, the hatch slid open and any feelings of bravado the engineer might've been harboring evaporated in a fresh burst of panic. Behind it, she saw a massive bulk of white armor and insulated joints, covered in a haphazard mess of weld marks and hastily applied patches. It dominated the doorway, and its blazing red optical sensors were staring right at her.

"Oh gods-!"

Phera felt her breath quite literally catch inside her chest at the sight. She'd been expecting an angry pirate, not an angry pirate in *power armor*, and it took several small eternities before she was finally able to strong-arm her lungs into getting back to work.

The ship itself hadn't ever really felt "big", but with an optical array glaring (could optics "glare"?) right at her, it felt positively minuscule. But, on the bright side, that went both ways. The stupid armor wasn't about to get inside the engine compartment any time soon, not unless the pirate wanted to bust out a plasma cutter. Which, given their proximity to the engines, would be even more dangerous than what Phera had just done.

So, hefting her can and willing herself to believe it was a weapon, she did her best to look as intimidating as possible as she took aim at the lens in front of her. Then, remembering that she was still wearing a vacsuit, she blinked at her suit's heads-up display to activate her vocaster.

"I don't know who you are, but unless you want a faceful of pressurized acid, I'd back off!"

"Acid. In a plain aerosol. Right."

That same gruff female voice from earlier came from somewhere outside the hatch, and it did not sound the least bit amused.

Wait, what the...?

Why did it sound like her voice was coming from *behind* the power armor? Were there actually two pirates? Gods! How many boarders could they have possibly landed on such a tiny shuttle in mid-flight?

The answer to her question came a moment later, when a tall, stocky figure wearing a vacsuit not unlike Phera's own (except with a *lot* more armor) came whipping out from between the power suit's massive legs and skimming along the ceiling right toward her. The armor suit, meanwhile, remained completely motionless. Sensors left on and glowing, but not actually moving.

She'd been tricked!

Frozen in place by a perplexing mix of shock, terror, and a surreal disbelief that this was really happening to her, Phera just barely managed to snap back to reality right as the pirate's hand came into contact with the front of her helmet. Letting out an undignified squeal of terror through her still active vocaster, she jerked her aerosol spray up and pulled the trigger as hard as she could, nailing the woman dead center in her opaque faceplate with a healthy dollop of grease just as she went toppling backward.

Propelled adorable ass over tea kettle for the second or third time in less than an hour thanks to the combined forces of her aerosol spray and the pirate's push, Phera went tumbling further into the compartment. Though, thankfully, this time around she didn't carom off of anything at high-speed and instead was just left slowly spinning, bouncing gently off the engine housing and back toward her assailant.

Not that that was really all that better.

"FUCK!"

Phera heard only a tiny blip of sound, like a televised shout with the volume turned almost all the way down, as the pirate woman roared inside her helmet without vocasting it.

She'd lost most of her initial velocity by then, and was left drifting in the middle of the compartment. Too far away to grab onto anything to stabilize herself with, she continued to spin helplessly while her arms and legs pinwheeled uselessly out to either side of her. With one rotation, she caught a glimpse of the pirate yanking off her grease-covered helmet. With the next, the tiniest hint of thick black hair. Before she could spin a third time, however, a strong body slammed into her side, knocking her to what passed for the floor just then and straddling her sideways against the deck.

With a sharp *SMACK* of teflon on metal, one of the pirate's palms magnetized to the plates beside Phera's shoulder, while the other wrenched the aerosol out of her grip so hard she feared for her fingers.

"Ow, ow! Okay!"

Struggling to look back at her assailant, she was met with a glowering, olive-skinned face framed by curly hair cropped low-grav short and a scar running along its right cheek.

"WHAT THE HELL DID YOU DO?"

The voice was no longer muffled and distant, and the venomous glint in its owner's iron gray eyes had Phera feeling like she'd just missed a step on her way down the stairs. (A sensation made no less gut-wrenching even with their current lack of gravity.)

"L-Lithium grease," she wheezed, tentatively flexing her fingers to confirm they were all still attached.

It wasn't exactly an explanation, but it was the only thing that came to mind at that moment, and it seemed like a really good idea to at least say *something*.

"I mean what did you do to the helm, *idiot*!"

The woman's arm twitched, and Phera heard her grease can bounce off the deck and then the ceiling again at a frighteningly high velocity.

"Oh."

Wincing, she tried to think of the best way to break the bad news to the pirate, before then remembering that she was, in fact, a pirate, and wasn't actually her supervisor. So, with a very small amount of defiance sparking in her chest, she spat, "I cut the control lines to the engine!"

She would've scoffed for good measure, but between the pressure on her side and the rapid-fire staccato of her heartbeat, she just didn't have it in her.

"Figured."

The woman scowled as she spoke, and it occurred to Phera, just for a moment, that she might have a pretty face if it weren't for the murderous expression she was currently wearing. And the scar.

Actually, scratch that, the scar was pretty hot.

"Well, you'd better reconnect them, or else we're in for a rough landing."

The big woman's weight shifted off of her then, and Phera felt herself start to float away as she swung her body free of the straddle and planted her boots on the deck where her hand had just been magnetized.

Long, flexible, split-toed boots, she couldn't help but notice. This pirate was an actual spacer then.

"Get up," she ordered, still helmetless as she loomed menacingly over Phera (who was still drifting several centimeters off their current "floor"). "And work fast!"

With more arm and leg flailing than she would've preferred (she'd been hoping to maintain at least *some of her* dignity with her captor), the addled engineer managed to get her magboots locked back to the deck. And, head still spinning, was about to tell the pirate to fuck off and fix the damn engines herself if she was in such a hurry, when what she'd just been told started to sink in.

"Wait. We're heading *toward* something?" she demanded, a fresh surge of panic welling up inside of her.

She immediately turned back toward the dislodged bundles of trunk lines she'd been ferreting around in earlier, bouncing nervously on her toes (which sent her drifting up toward the ceiling again) as it occurred to her that "fixing" a completely severed series of control lines wasn't something she could just do right away.

But, then again, maybe she wouldn't have to?

Even with Ember out of the picture, hangar control at The Bin could still remotely call the shuttle back so long as they were within range. She'd been fine-tuning the finicky remote piloting software long enough over the last few months (Panorama wanted to cut out hiring shuttle pilots for routine maintenance runs altogether), and she knew for a fact that it worked. Mostly. She'd just need to figure out some way of bridging the severed engine lines to the ship's comm array since the helm was out of commission. Yes... Yes! She could totally make this work!

First, though, she had to somehow incapacitate her hijacker. Which, it occurred to her half a heartbeat later as her eyes were drawn back toward the glaring optical array of the bigger woman's power armor, she might actually be able to pull off with a little help. And so, drifting toward an out of the way corner of the compartment while doing her best not to look suspicious, she pulled up her rudimentary drone control software on her wrist comp (beyond grateful just then that the cheap vacsuit Panorama had supplied her with at least had passthrough support built into the gloves) and brought the mining unit she'd been working on back when this whole mess had started to life out in the cargo hold. With a little luck, she'd be able to steer it into the compartment with her. *Then* they'd see how things went.

She was sure her new pirate friend wouldn't be nearly so scary once she had a boring laser aimed right at her dumb, stupid, kinda pretty face. Granted, there was no way Phera would have the stomach to actually *use* said laser on her. But, she didn't have to know that.

"The hell are you doing?"

The pirate dragged out that last word as she frowned, giving Phera an ominous look.

"Um…" she replied, trying to keep her voice level as she briefly met the other woman's eye before looking back at her status display. "You know… Just running a diagnostic and, uh, stuff."

Risking another glance back at her wrist, she surreptitiously poked and prodded at it with the suddenly much too big and clunky fingers of her vacsuit gloves as she attempted to navigate her now active drone through the hold using only the minuscule projection on the back of her hand as a guide.

How are you literally banging into every single thing in there you stupid idiot? I thought I programmed you for collision avoidance?

Never mind the fact that she was manually overriding those protocols just then.

Glancing up, she did her best to look both harried and helpful.

"Give me a sec to figure out where the, uh… the cut is, yeah?"

At that, the scarred woman took a big, menacing step toward her. Eyes narrowing as she pulled her boot free of the deck and let it slam back down again.

CLOMP!

"What do you mean 'figure out'?" she demanded. "You just cut it yourself a second ag-"

With one final flick of her fingertips, Phera brought the crawler charging forward between the empty armor's legs. Only, her pathfinding wasn't quite as precise as it should've been, and it ended up clipping them and scratching its knee joints in the process as it noisily jackknifed its way into the compartment.

"Son of a-!"

Immediately whipping around at the motion, the pirate kicked off the deck to avoid the drone. Though, she really needn't have bothered. Its course had already been knocked askew by its graze with her armor. And, before Phera could stop it, it had streaked across the compartment and right into another bundle of fiber optics. There then came a brief flash of green light, a harsh whine of metal sawing through plastic, a distressing amount of smoke as sensitive components heated up and burnt out, and then a spray of severed cable ends bloomed around the half-entangled spider in a halo of ruined electronics.

"Oh crap."

"*You.*"

Floating near what counted as the ceiling just then, glove gripped tight around a coolant intake pipe, the pirate's head swiveled very, very slowly back to Phera.

"Uh…"

With even more panic settling in on top of her already overflowing supply, the cornered engineer hurriedly issued a shutdown command to the crawler before it could do any further damage, holding her breath and hoping against hope that the sudden pressure she felt squeezing her heart was just the pirate's smoldering glare and not atmo venting or something pressurized and explosive flooding the compartment. But, since said smoldering pirate was still smoldering and they hadn't both been blown to pieces, she assumed she hadn't just destroyed anything all *that* vital.

Which freed her up to start panicking properly.

"Fuck, shit, fuck!" she babbled, whipping her head around in search of her lithium grease.

It wasn't actually caustic, but the pirate seemed to hate it the last time she'd gotten a faceful of it. Maybe she could use it to temporarily blind her or something so she could get free and…

Well, she'd figure that part out later.

Deciding to just pick a direction and go, she pushed off the deck as hard as she could and made a lunge toward the engine compartment hatch.

"Oh no you don't!"

Phera made it all of a third of the way toward her goal, when she heard a loud, animalistic growl (an actual growl!) from somewhere behind her that froze her heart and sent her stomach lurching. The next thing she knew, the pirate was flinging herself off the pipe she'd been clinging to and back at her. She didn't quite manage to land on her this time, but as her long-toed feet slapped against the deck and kicked off again, she grabbed hold of her suit and spun her around to face her.

"What."

The pirate held Phera's arms pinned painfully hard against her sides while she glared acid directly into her faceplate.

"Just."

"Got."

"Cut?"

"Um-" Phera squeaked, wriggling in the woman's vise-like grip.

Geez. Why bother with the power armor when you're this strong already? Talk about overkill.

Managing to get a look over her shoulder at where her would-be rescuer now lay amid a ruin of mangled cables and shattered electronics, she squinted.

And then winced.

"Uh... Nothing major," she ventured tentatively, looking back toward the other woman and failing to meet her eye. "Just some auxiliary sensors..."

The pirate gripping her as they slowly spun in place started to look slightly relieved. That is, until Phera added under her breath.

"And comms."

"Comms."

Her face hardened then, before going ashen.

"We're adrift," she repeated, slowly, deliberately, voice quiet but starting to rise. "And now we have *no comms*?"

"Yeah, so?" demanded Phera, a sudden, giddy spike of adrenaline making her mouth run far, far ahead of her thoughts as she continued to wriggle uselessly in her captor's clutches. "Who cares? It's not like we can't be... rescued..."

Trailing off, her face likewise paled.

"Oh."

Adrift they might be. But, adrift after pulling the kind of Gs they'd been doing back when the pirate had taken control of the helm (to say nothing of the massive burst of acceleration that had occurred when she'd severed the engine's control lines), more or less guaranteed they'd left The Bin's sensor range behind long ago.

And she'd just (accidentally) destroyed their comms.

"Shit."

Without something to broadcast their transponder ID, they would have for all intents and purposes disappeared into thin air (or lack thereof in this case) as far as The Bin or anyone else was concerned. Unless someone had already been actively tracking their vector the entire time since being boarded (which, again, was highly unlikely considering the person who was *supposed* to be in charge of operational command in situations like these was currently perforated with whatever low-velocity, but apparently still lethal, ordinance he'd packed his weapon with) they were well and truly on their own.

In a ship with no engine control or comms.

"Think you can fix that wiring?"

The woman's voice was tight. Tense. Barely controlled.

This time it was Phera's turn to glare. Somewhere between her attempt at escape and realizing how dire their situation had become, she'd forgotten just how scared she was right then.

"Probably," she confirmed, dragging the word out with all the annoyed disdain she could never bring to bear against her Panorama superiors lest she find herself confined to quarters on mandatory "stress leave" for a week (accruing unscheduled vacation day penalties all the while, of course). "That is…"

"That is…?"

This was all such bullshit. They never would've been in this situation in the first place if this woman hadn't decided to hijack the flyer. And so, giving in to the urge to be petty, Phera lashed out at her with her boots.

"That is if you'd let me go, *asshole*!"

"Oh, I'll let you go!"

The pirate started to raise her voice again, not intimidated by Phera or her flailing legs in the slightest.

"Just as soon as I've made sure you won't try any more of your brilliant 'strategies'!"

She released her grip around her upper torso then, only to grab her by the material of her suit at her waist and flip her around and upside down so that her head was angled toward the engine monitoring station, directly opposite the pirate's own orientation. An instant later, the bigger woman's armored thighs clamped down tight around her soft midsection, once again trapping her arms in place against her sides. She was straddling her again now, though this time from behind.

As her legs squeezed painfully and the engine room slowly spun around them, her hands started grasping roughly at Phera's waist. Phera, though stunned by this sudden turn of events, still nevertheless recognized the hand motions. The lifting of the velcro flap over the mag release, the manual drawcord for the insulation separation, and then both of the pirate's hands were seizing hold of the hem of her vacsuit's lower half as it became visible.

"You have absolutely *earned* this, you little brat!"

"What?"

Wriggling and squirming with renewed vigor, Phera tried to free herself. Except, floating as she was, being gripped between thighs that clearly saw routine exercise in actual grav and with nothing to use as leverage, she was left helpless as could be as she heard and then felt a *pop-hiss* around her waist as her vacsuit's seal was broken and her pants came free from her top. Under any other circumstances, being pinned beneath a woman with muscles like the pirate's while she tore at her clothes would've been nice. But, the acrid stench of ozone and melted plastics that rushed in to fill Phera's nostrils as her suit separated, coupled with her adrenaline spiking into overdrive, kinda spoiled the mood.

"I-I don't know what you think you're doing, but you'd better knock it off right now or else I'll... I'll..."

She tried to reach her wrist comp in an attempt to summon more of the crawlers then. But, with her arms trapped, all she could do was flail her comp in the general direction of the hold while profoundly regretting not getting around to setting up subvocalization commands for her drone controls.

"Oh, *hell* no!"

Noticing what she was up to, the pirate bent forward and reached between Phera's flailing thighs to snatch up her right wrist. With a grunt and a thrashing motion that got them spinning even faster, she forced the hand with the computer attached to it under her strong, thick thigh, and then tightened her legs again around Phera's stomach. Imprisoning the hand that had the closest thing to a weapon on it against her body where it couldn't do any (more) damage.

Then, curly black hair bouncing as they continued to wrestle in the null-grav, she grabbed hold of the waistband of Phera's vacsuit pants and yanked the thick, reinforced plastic up (or down, from the engineer's still rotating perspective) and out of the way. She had to pull very hard and very roughly to get them past her bulging hips, for the exact same reason that it always took Phera forever to get them on or off in the first place. (One size fits all was an absolute lie in her case, she'd found.) But, some five seconds later, the pirate had managed to aggressively and not at all comfortably for the young woman who'd been wearing them, get the pants down to her thighs, where their once constricting waist now floated free and loose around her still frantically kicking legs.

"Oh my gods, you-!"

Despite the confusion and panic still strangling her heart, part of Phera couldn't help but be relieved to finally have the way too tight material off of her. The (relatively) cool air of the engine compartment a blessed relief on her sweaty, lab-pale thighs.

And, her ass, apparently.

"Eep!"

In the pirate's haste to enact what she could only assume was a slapdash plan to disable her vacsuit so she couldn't use one of her drones to punch a hole through the hull (not that she'd ever be so cruel as to attempt to suffocate the other woman) she'd somehow managed to work the snug pair of hip-hugging boyshorts Phera had on beneath her vacsuit halfway down her full cheeks.

"Okay, okay, you've made your point!" she hurriedly conceded, rolling her hips in a desperate move to coax the waistband of her panties back up to where it belonged while adding under her breath. "Whatever the hell that was."

Her underwear wasn't cooperating, though, and a moment later she was forced to breathe out an exasperated sigh and crane her head back to address the curly black bunches and broad shoulders towering above her.

"Hey, uh... friend, isn't piracy kinda silly sometimes?" she asked with as much good-natured camaraderie as she could muster, face flushing with a heat that had absolutely nothing to do with their proximity to the engine as goosebumps broke out across her half-exposed seat. "You, um... Ahem. You think you could maybe give me a hand with my underwear real quick?"

"I'll give you a hand all right."

The other woman's reply was cross, but at least sounded slightly mollified. Either from Phera's humorous comment, or the sight of her surprisingly bare ass blooming out almost right in her face.

"Piracy may be 'silly', but it's still nowhere near as silly as SETTING US ADRIFT AND CUTTING COMMS!" she exploded without warning then, yanking Phera's boyshorts the rest of the way down her thighs before cracking a rigid, teflon-reinforced palm against the center of the blushing engineer's pale and very naked left buttock.

SPLAT!

The loud, fleshy report echoed around the tiny engine room like a gunshot, and the force of the pirate's descending hand slowed their spin toward Phera's back.

"Ah! What the-?"

SPLAT!

Pain like a cord cutting loose and lashing against her skin lit up across her right cheek this time, and was followed almost immediately by another right below it, this second handprint partially overlapping the first.

SPLAT!

"Ow-! *Fuck*!"

Bottom clenching on reflex, she tried to flex the pain from the trio of still smoldering swats away, but only succeeded in making her generous bottom wobble all the more.

"Not what I-!" she started to grate through clenched teeth, shallow breaths fogging up the inside of her faceplate as the pirate's hand attempted to maglock itself to her other cheek this time.

SPLAT!

"Ack! Meant!"

SPLAT!

"Owie!"

"Do you ever do what you *meant* to do?" the pirate scolded, not quite shouting anymore, but voice still raised.

She didn't stop the motion of her arm as she lectured, bringing her heavy hand back up behind her head and down *hard* through the weightless air.

SPLAT!

Over.

SPLAT!

And over.

SPLAT!

And *over*!

SPLAT!

Both of Phera's cheeks felt like she'd backed them into a live wire now, and it was only getting worse as the glove impacted again and again and again. Its owner barking out a single word with each full-armed swat.

"No. More. Funny. Business!"

They'd stopped spinning toward her back, and were slowly starting to rotate forward instead, propelled by the air resistance against the bigger woman's palm.

SPLAT! SPLAT! SPLAT! SPLAT! SPLAT!

"You're going to do *exactly* what I say!"

SPLAT!

"Exactly when I say it!"

SPLAT!

"You got that?"

SPLAT!

"I- Ack! I...!"

SPLAT!

"Wrong answer!"

If someone had told Phera that she'd wind up spending the latter part of her workday being *spanked* by a gods damned (and admittedly pretty attractive, if you could get past the whole shipjacking thing) *pirate*, she would've had a small heart attack and demanded to know how you'd gotten access to her browser history. in that moment, however, unable to do much more than scissor her ankles back and forth behind her in a useless attempt to kick her stupid captor in her stupid head (which only succeeded in working her too tight vacsuit pants a few centimeters further down her legs), she was way too busy finding new and creative ways of expressing her pain and discomfort to really care about the odd particulars of her situation.

SPLAT! SPLAT! SPLAT! SPLAT! SPLAT!

"Okay, okay, okay!" she finally squealed, her defiant streak shattering under the force of a rapid-fire burst of extra-hard swats to the extra-sensitive undercurves of her naked cheeks.

SPLAT! SPLAT! SPLAT! SPLAT! SPLAT!

"FUCK! Fine! I get it-!"

SPLAT!

"I *get* it. Geez!"

"What do you get?" the woman grunted as she raised her arm and brought it back down with just as much ruthless force as all the times before. "Be *specific*!"

SPLAT!

The glassy-hard palm of her glove was starting to split through the layer of burning heat she'd painted across the squirming engineer's bare bottom and was now creating another, even worse, one beneath it. One that would stick with Phera long after this surprise spanking was over, keeping the deep tissue of her cheeks tender and sore, and making trying to sit down an absolute nightmare.

SPLAT! SPLAT! SPLAT!

"*Well*?"

Before the woman could continue (very literally) hammering out her frustrations against her defenseless, throbbing ass, Phera allowed her muscles to go slack beneath the pressure of the firm thighs around her. And, face once again flushing with a heat not all that dissimilar to the one radiating from her backside just then, pushed out a flustered breath through her nostrils and grit out.

"I get that you're pissed."

Then, letting go of her own agitation before it could end up adding any more accel to the free-spin she and the other woman were still in, she added more amiably.

"Look. Neither of us wants to be stuck out here. I don't get paid enough for this shit, and I'm pretty sure that drone's coming out of my paycheck."

The drone, the workbench, and probably the repair costs for the flyer too.

"I think I can probably fix the comms, but it's going to be kinda hard to do that if you keep wailing on my ass, yeah?"

She'd read somewhere back in college that negotiations were best carried out from a position of strength. And, while the pirate might outclass her in physical strength, *she* was the one with the engineering degree. That had to count for something, didn't it? She wasn't really sure what she was going to do once she got the comms back up and running again, or how she was actually going to *do* that precisely (though, she had some ideas), but saving her butt (both literally and figuratively) was a proving to be a powerful motivator.

SPLAT! SPLAT! SPLAT!

"Owie, owie-! Hey, come on!"

The pirate landed a few more slaps (even more painful now that Phera had relaxed her muscles), but then stopped when the younger woman didn't start trying to escape again.

"That's *better*," she huffed instead, clearly satisfied.

"Glad you think so," deadpanned the engineer around a wince.

"Mmhmm..."

A gloved hand pressed itself against either swollen, agonizingly hot and stingy cheek then. Applying a steady pressure and making their owner's ankles scissor back and forth even faster above her head as she let out a breathy hiss that was only partially a pained exhalation.

"So, if I let you go, you're not going to try to kill me again and end up cutting life support this time, are you?"

"Kind of a moot point given the circumstances," grumbled Phera, cheeks flexing against the other woman's palms in a transparent attempt to co-opt their thermal conductor properties to cool her sizzling seat.

Then, realizing that might not be the smartest thing to lead with, she added quickly, "I mean, nope! Nope, nope, nope. I don't know about you, but I *like* being alive. Soul-crushing megacorp contract notwithstanding."

"Soul-crushing, eh?"

The pirate's muscular legs relaxed around Phera's midsection as she spoke, not quite letting go, but at least loosening enough to be more comfortable while her voice grew slightly mocking.

"Are you sure you're not just saying that?"

A derisive snort erupted from Phera as the bigger woman's hands at last withdrew from her bare and glowing bottom.

"Are you kidding me?"

It struck her as funny then how, even red-assed and face burning while trapped aboard a nearly dead ship adrift in the cold and the black, her contempt for her employer still far outstripped any ill will she bore toward her captor. With her no longer threatening or yelling at her, the pirate's brassy alto was actually kind of nice.

"Panorama suckered me in by saying they'd pay off my student loans if I signed a contract to come work for them after I finished my PhD."

Shaking her head, her self-loathing at her own stupidity having long since withered to little more than a dull ache in the pit of her stomach, she rolled her eyes.

"They paid them off all right. Only, thing is, they then rolled that debt over into a new loan I owed *them*."

"Shit. That's rough."

"Tell me about it. I don't know how much compound interest you deal with in your day-to-day life as a pirate, but take my word for it when I say it's absolute bullshit."

"Yeah. No. We tend to pay up front or right after."

The woman's legs finally unwrapped themselves from around her torso then, and she reached out with one foot to grab hold of a clump of torn fiber optics with her long, agile toes. Bringing their spinning to a gentle halt and turning the sore and exhausted engineer right side up relative to herself by the hips once again.

Phera's vacsuit pants and flattering underwear were still bunched up around her thighs, but the pirate didn't seem to pay much mind to that. Which was probably for the best considering she was undeniably wet just then and not at all prepared to have *that* particular conversation with her captor.

Get it together, this isn't a date. You're being kidnapped. Well… Shipjacked. Same difference.

The pirate let out a long, slow breath then, no longer looking angry or aggressive. Agitated and stressed, sure, but not glowering or grimacing. It really was too bad they'd met this way. With the scar on her cheek, her lips were perpetually quirked up on one side in an almost half-grin that had Phera longing to discover what they tasted like, and that short haircut lent her a powerful butch energy that was very much her type. If she had to guess, she'd say she was probably somewhere in her late thirties, assuming she hadn't opted for any particularly good rejuvenation treatments, that is. Which, given her line of work, didn't seem likely.

All in all, she had to admit she was frustratingly close to the sort of rough and tumble pirate rogue she'd so often fantasized about whenever she'd been by herself late at night in her quarters.

Oh my gods, Phera, masturbate after you've figured out how to fix the comms. Geez!

Ugh. She seriously needed a vacation.

Only two more years...

"Okay. Sorry about your friend in the storage compartment," the pirate said, interrupting her wandering train of thought. "There was nothing I could do. He shot me right in the shield and got hit by his own ricochet. We really do try not to kill people who we don't know deserve it."

Distracted as she was with righting her clothes while her hips remained gripped in the older woman's firm clutches, her words didn't quite sink in for Phera at first. But, as she released the latches around her helmet and yanked it off once she was decent (or close enough, there was no way in hell her vacsuit pants were coming back up until her seat shed about a thousand more degrees of heat), she shook out the shoulder-length auburn curls that confirmed for the pirate she was indeed a natural redhead, and shivered slightly.

"The sergeant and I weren't friends."

The answer came automatically, and Phera felt her face warming once again to match her hair and buns as it occurred to her that she maybe should've sounded more upset about his demise. But, again, she had to admit he wouldn't be missed.

"Is that right?"

Raising her dark eyebrows as she took her in with renewed appraisal, the pirate nodded to her left, changing the subject.

"You said you can get the comms back up, yeah? And, when you do, I can trust you not to send out a general SOS or a Panorama panic code?"

"Not much point in that now. I'm sure they'll get me back eventually…"

Giving her head another shake to break away from that particularly depressing train of thought, Phera somewhat reluctantly reached behind her and gently pushed off the wall toward where her drone lay tangled.

"Uh… Okay, let's see… Depending on whether or not the comms in the cockpit caught a back-surge of current when Number Seven here tried to rescue me, it might take me a couple more hours than I'd prefer. But, hmmm… Yeah. We'll be fine. The antenna array is all passive, so it's not like *that* could fry."

I think.

Pushing aside a few trunk lines and frayed bits of fiber optics, she attempted to haul the drone out of its nest, only to lose her grip on its smooth chassis and send herself tumbling back with the force of her yanking.

"Whoa there!"

One of the pirate's hands caught her by the shoulder, helping her back down toward the deck. Her other hand then tucked itself beneath the folded over back-to-crotch-level material of the pants currently floating around Phera's thighs and hit the switch there to reengage her magboots for her. Leaving her standing with her red bottom bulging out of her boyshorts in the space left between the top and bottom parts of her vacsuit while she stood perpendicular to her, feet gripping some more engine components.

"Forget the drone for now and focus on the comms," she ordered, voice firm and authoritative. "If you need a hand with something, I can probably help. How much air does this thing have left?"

Noting once again the obvious biomodding that had been done to the pirate's feet, it took a supreme effort of will on Phera's part not to reply with, "I think you could offer four."

"Um… Good question."

Running her violet eyes along the still intact control and component lines around her, she nibbled at her lower lip while she attempted to ping the ship's internal status report system through her wrist comp. Only, apparently "comms" in this case also included the internal wireless network.

Shit.

Prying one maglocked boot off the deck and letting it *clomp* back down in an approximation of a frustrated stomp, Phera took in a long, deep breath and then sighed.

"Well, good news is that it doesn't smell like stale air in here."

She didn't at all like being that vague with her assessments, but the pirate had managed to light a proverbial fire under her ass, and results seemed like something she'd appreciate just then.

"Since we've still got temp control and lights, I'd say the scrubbers are probably still working, but I'm not a ship tech and I wouldn't want to stay here any longer than we absolutely have to."

Clomping her way back over to her drone, she shoved aside more cables and pulled as many of its arms free as she could while she searched for one end of the trunk line that ran from the actual comms systems of the shuttle to the antenna array. Finding it, she gave it an experimental sniff and then pulled back just as quickly as she caught a strong whiff of ozone and something acrid that probably wasn't super healthy to be breathing in.

"Uh... Yeah. So, bad news. We fried the onboard comms."

"*We* fried it?"

The pirate flashed her a sardonic and slightly judgmental smirk at that. Though, it cleared away quickly as her eyes flitted down to the well-rounded cheeks and taut pair of panties being aimed at her, replaced by something slightly more satisfied and appreciative.

"All right, fine. Anything burned out that you don't have a spare of? Maybe in one of the drones?"

Choosing to ignore the other woman's sneer (after all, *she'd* been the one hijacking the flyer, Phera had just been defending herself), the redheaded roboticist pushed her lips out into a thoughtful pout.

"Hmmm... No, not really. I've got them configured to form a short range peer-to-peer mesh network to coordinate extraction. It uses less power that way."

The suggestion managed to spark an idea, though, and turning back to take in the still glaring power armor blocking the entrance of the engine compartment, her lips quirked up in an excited smile.

She'd never gotten her hands on something like *that* before.

"I bet your friend there might, though," she said, gesturing at the armor.

Immediately, the pirate's eyes narrowed to dangerous slits.

"Uh-uh. That's not replaceable."

Then, a moment later, she seemed to remember what was at stake and her suited arms folded beneath the generous swell of her armored chest.

"Well…"

She gave a reluctant sigh.

"What exactly do you need? Specifically?"

Tucking away the stray thought of what it might be like to lay her head back against the other woman's breasts before it could drive her to distraction, Phera drew herself up from her hunch, dusted off her front, and cleared her throat. Adopting the same tone and posture she used during staff meetings when proposing a new project or giving a status update.

A look which was only slightly undercut by the vacsuit pants still bunched up around her thick thighs.

"If I'm guessing right, and I probably am," she added before the skeptical pirate could become any more skeptical. "That armor looks like the real deal."

Even if it is a couple decades old.

She vaguely remembered seeing combat armor like that being used in some of her textbooks back in school when they'd covered the last major Cilaran civil war.

"Which means that it's got a full comms package, just like our ship does."

Part of her wanted to correct her slip-up as soon as she made it. It wasn't *her* ship, and it certainly wasn't the pirate's. Though, to be fair, that last point seemed fairly academic just then.

"Its antenna array is just smaller is all," she went on instead. "I'm sure if I could get inside and poke around a bit I could find some place to jump its comms to the flyer's antenna. It's not like the primary data wavelengths are any different between ship-to-ship and armor-to-armor. With a decent enough amp assembly and a little luck, I should be able to get us a mildly underpowered radio up and running."

It would probably drop packets like crazy, and wouldn't at all be viable for any lengthy communication. But, so long as it *worked*, then that was good enough for Phera.

With another long-suffering sigh, the other woman hung her head, looking very much like she thought she might've stopped spanking her just a bit too soon.

"What about our suit comms?" she eventually suggested. "Any way you could try using those first?"

She looked back at the armor standing in the doorway with a strained, sad expression. The pain on her face wasn't just that of losing property. It looked deeper than that.

"Or... Would trying that waste too much time and run us out of oxygen?"

"Oh. Suit comms. Right."

Face falling with disappointment, Phera tore her gaze away from where she'd been staring longingly at the power armor and glanced down at her partially removed vacsuit. Her gloved fingers soon made short work of the seals running up and down along her front. And, half a minute later, she was squirming out of her torso piece, leaving her in only a pair of boyshorts, a snug sports bra to keep her own well-endowed chest in check, and a pair of mostly still on plastic and kevlar pants.

"Here. Hold this, would you?" she asked, thrusting the chest piece at the pirate and giving it an expectant wiggle.

She took it, looking extremely relieved, and as Phera got to work, she slowly righted herself from the wall to the floor; clamping her magboots to the deck.

"You really wanted a look at my suit, didn't you?"

She wasn't quite smiling, but her face had softened more than Phera had seen it yet.

"Got someone who's willing to pay for schematics?"

She quirked an eyebrow. Not judgmental, so much as inquisitive.

"Um, maybe?"

Reaching for the small toolkit affixed to the left thigh of her vacsuit, only to realize said left thigh was somewhere around her left knee right then, Phera wriggled and squirmed to reach the box and unlatch it. She hadn't really understood the woman's question, but her grip was steady, and leaning in as close as she was to dig around the interior of her suit's torso cavity in search of a promising access point gave her the opportunity to breathe in the musky scent of her. She smelled of oil, sweat, and some spice or combination of spices that she couldn't quite put her finger on. It was actually pretty soothing. Especially now that the flaming heat in her bottom had subsided to a dull throb.

"I'm sure there's someone out there interested in suit plans, yeah. I mostly just wanted to look inside yours and see what makes it tick. I've never gotten to play- I mean, *work* with something like that before. The station has some cargo lifters, but none of them come with targeting packages or infantry shields."

Glancing up from her work after managing to wedge a screwdriver beneath a likely looking panel and prying it open to reveal the components she'd been searching for, she jerked her head toward the armor.

"What's that shield made of anyway, graphene?"

"Close. It's a layered nanotubule polymer sheet. Not as flexible, but a lot stronger and way less permeable."

Something almost like an actual smile ghosted across those weary-looking lips then.

"You're a munitions engineer? What the hell did they have you doing out here?"

"No, no, I'm a roboticist. But, you'd be amazed at the amount of overlap there is between combat engineering and engineering for asteroid mining," replied Phera, the corners of her own lips shooting up well past the other woman's as she broke into what felt like her first genuine smile in weeks. "The corp always wants things done faster, cheaper, and more efficiently."

She waved her screwdriver in a negligent circle beside her since she was too busy parsing out what was and wasn't useful to properly roll her eyes.

"Which, when it comes to mining, means lots and lots of controlled explosions and hyper-precise laser boring."

Casting her eyes about for a useful work surface to set her screwdriver on and finding none, Phera gripped the tool between her teeth as she continued to talk with her mouth full.

"I don't get to work with anything all that fun since my bosses are cheap bastards. I'd absolutely *love* to get my hands on a spool of nanotube filament for our printer back on station, though."

Scoffing to herself at her own wishful thinking, she brought a pair of fine-tipped probes up to the circuits she'd just exposed. And, after a few seconds of poking and prodding at obnoxiously tiny traces, found what she'd been hoping to and let out an excited cheer, dropping her screwdriver in the process.

"Oh my gods, I think this might actually work!"

Plucking the screwdriver from the air with her free hand, following Phera's movements with her eyes, the other woman said, "Huh. That was fast."

Releasing the partially disassembled vacsuit top to let it float free, she stepped around beside her and looked down at what she'd removed.

"Just need that screwed in place? I can help you set the cables if you handle any programming it might need."

Again, that hard-bitten almost smile flitted across the pirate's scarred face.

"I'm not an engineer, obviously, but I've had to learn some basic things about jury rigging."

She paused then, looking back down at the disassembled suit radio components and then back at the curvy young redhead in the bra and boyshorts.

"I'm Straya, by the by."

Still elbow deep in her suit, Phera looked up at her.

"Nice to meet you, Straya," she said on reflex, only stopping to reflect a moment later that it really hadn't been.

Well, at least not at first, anyway. She wasn't exactly bad company now.

"I'm Phera."

Again, reflex took the lead and she made as if to shake the other woman's hand. Between her planetside upbringing and the amount of time she'd spent around company officers, it was second nature for her by now. But, realizing that she still had a handful of components that she wasn't exactly sure were the most structurally sound pieces of electronics, she opted for an abbreviated spacer's bow in the form of a nod instead.

Then, using her hips to gesture vaguely in the direction of where drone Number Seven still lay, she added.

"You mind helping me move all this over there? I don't want to let go of anything before I can set it down on something relatively sturdy, and I've still got some soldering to do."

"Sure."

The pirate took an armful of parts as Phera passed them to her and smirked.

"Gotta say, it's nice meeting a pretty girl like you in a crummy place like this."

Before patting her firmly on her still tender backside with her free hand.

"Now, let's get to work."

CHAPTER TWO

CHARGES ACCRUED

Aiding and Abetting Armed Robbery, Grand Theft

It turned out that getting the components she and Straya managed to salvage from her vacsuit (cannibalizing most of it in the process) actually bridged to the flyer's antenna array was slightly more complicated than Phera had originally anticipated. But, on the bright side, that at least gave her an opportunity to spend more time half-chatting and half-flirting with the pirate while they worked to bypass traces and piggyback power regulators.

Phera knew she should probably be more scared of her than she was, but she just didn't have it in her. She'd already resigned herself to being a hostage and eventually ransomed back to Panorama, and with that acceptance had come a loosening of the knot her stomach had tied itself into when Ember had taken off all those lifetimes ago. Straya could have easily killed her if she'd wanted to, and the fact that the worst she'd done was (justifiably) light her seat on fire for her attempt to weaponize an ore crawler against her made it surprisingly difficult to be all that resentful of her captor. Besides, she was actually kind of nice in a scary sort of way once you got past all the kidnapping and spanking stuff.

The latter of which, if Phera was being totally honest with herself, really wasn't doing anything to make her any less attractive in her eyes. She hadn't caught a an ass blistering like that since college, and she was *still* riding high on the resulting endorphin rush as she finished up the last of her soldering.

"Comm array looked like it was mounted up top," Straya said, breaking the comfortable silence they'd fallen into over the last few minutes as she pointed toward an access hatch set into the upper part of one wall in the engine compartment. "So, no need to open the cockpit and vent more air. That's good."

"Better safe than sorry, right?"

Straightening up from where she'd been doubled over her makeshift comms package with a cheeky grin, Phera reached behind her to knead her lower back. Inadvertently thrusting her generous chest out toward her new pirate friend in the process as she did so.

Despite her sassy reply, she had to admit Straya did have a point. The air scrubbers inside the shuttle were still chugging along as far as she could tell, but between her non-standard emergency engine shutdown and the power surge from Number Seven's violent introduction to the wall, she didn't want to risk taxing any of the enviro subsystems any more than she absolutely had to. Which, unfortunately, meant wedging herself into a wiring conduit meant for maintenance bots and hoping that she didn't get stuck.

"Guess I'm dressed for it at least," she sighed, sifting her fingers through her sweaty copper curls and wishing that she'd thought to bring a hair tie with her when she'd clocked in that morning.

"Mmmm... No complaints here."

The low purr that accompanied Straya's words as her dark eyes danced along the curves of her backside and breasts did absolutely nothing to help with Phera's internal body temperature problem. It was already way too hot inside the cramped space of the engine compartment, and the heat thrown off by her soldering iron and the physical exertion required to free some of the more stubborn pieces from her vacsuit had made it positively stifling. She'd stripped off her useless vacsuit pants only a few minutes into her comms surgery project in an attempt to cool off, and stood now in only a pair of clunky magboots that looked totally at odds with her practical sports bra and significantly more stylish boyshorts. If ever there was a time she was going to fit inside a tiny conduit, it was now.

Probably.

"Right!"

Clapping her hands against either side of her face hard enough to make her wince, Phera let the sudden sting help her focus on the task at hand.

"Let's get this done."

Snatching up her custom comms package, its umbilical of repurposed wires trailing in the null-grav back to her discarded helmet's mic and speaker assembly, she released her magboots' hold on the deck and pushed off toward the access hatch.

As she tugged it open and wriggled her way inside, Straya settled back against a wall to watch her work. Still dressed as she was in a full vacsuit (minus her helmet), she was sweating even worse than Phera was.

"So, a PhD, huh? How old are you? Thirty?"

In response to her question, there came the muffled sounds of hair much longer than her own being spat out of a mouth, followed by, "Twenty… seven? Wait, no. Twenty-eight."

The engineer's round hips wobbled invitingly with her cramped shrug inside the conduit they were spilling out of.

"Time kinda starts to run together once you've been on The Bin for a while."

"Sounds delightful," deadpanned Straya. "Can't imagine why you'd hate it there."

"Right?"

Phera's hips started up their wriggling again as she tried to work an arm back behind her, before eventually giving up with an annoyed huff.

"You mind passing me my signal probe?"

She bobbed her right magboot in the general direction of where she'd been working earlier.

"It should be next to the socket wrenches."

"Sure."

Snatching up the toolkit she'd tied to her discarded vacsuit pants so she wouldn't lose it, Straya unclipped a small, flower-shaped device.

"Here, catch."

Hoisting herself up the various trunk lines still clamped to the wall, she parted the younger woman's thighs with the top of her close-cropped head and threw the little tool like a dart down the narrow gap between her belly and the bottom of the conduit. She almost made it to her hand too, but an unexpected bounce of the engineer's heavy chest as the pirate gave her left cheek a sharp pinch caused it to go slightly awry and hit a rather sensitive spot.

"Ack!"

Grunting at the unexpected jab of pointy carbon through the thin material of her grimy, sweat-soaked bra, Phera's hips jerked on reflex, producing a surprisingly cute squeak from their owner as her thighs momentarily clamped around Straya's face before letting go just as quickly.

"Oops, sorry!"

"Damn. Buy me a drink first, why don't you?"

Wincing sympathetically at Phera's abused nipple, Straya nevertheless reached up and flicked her lightly between the legs, earning herself yet another adorable (and decidedly breathy) squeak in the process.

"Don't you have a job to be doing?"

"Um, yep! Right! On it!"

"Take your time and do it right," the pirate chided lightly, helping to "steady" the younger woman by reaching up and around her soft thighs to grip an equally soft cheek in either hand.

"Yes ma'am!"

Straya left her to her work then, occupying herself with enjoying the silhouetted charms outlined by the engineer's formfitting underwear before eventually speaking up again.

"How long have they had you out here anyway?"

"Uh…"

After a bit of muffled cursing and the occasional *beep-beep!* of her signal probe, Phera spat out another mouthful of hair.

"Three-ish years now? I know I'm supposed to review my contract in a couple more months. They said they want me to renew early."

There came some more beeping, followed by an audible (and undeniably bitter) grumble.

"Not that I'd be able to do anything else."

"Right. The debt transfer."

"Yeah. *That.*"

"Well, if we were headed deeper into B-Sys I'd ask the captain to drop you off at the little loop. You know, if you wanted. Pretty sure most collectives that side of the primary don't care about hiring Alpha-side contract breakers."

The Beta System or Proxima sector, the collection of celestial bodies that orbited the lesser of the system's two suns with but rare entrapments by the Alpha star remained largely non-signatories of most of the later corporate extradition treaties, and was the perfect place to disappear from "civilized" space if you knew what you were doing.

"Don't think that's happening any time soon, though. Sorry."

There came a deflated sigh from Phera at that. Even if she'd never set foot outside of A-Sys, by this point in her go-nowhere career, she was more than willing to take a crack at striking out on her own in some seedy nowhere station.

"Oh well. Thanks anyway, I guess…"

A minute or so later her probe let out a long, continuous chirp as she finally found the spot she'd been looking for.

"Yes!"

Her quiet noise of triumph brought a relieved look to Straya's scarred face.

"You got it?"

"Yep! Well… Probably. If I start jerking around uncontrollably, drag me out, yeah?"

"Excuse me-?"

In reply to Straya's half-formed question, there came a series of blue-tinged flashes of light and sparks, followed by the thick stench of ozone a couple moments later.

"Phew. Yep, okay, that *was* the low voltage rail. Good."

Phera gave her slapdash comms bridge a fond couple of pats as she spoke, blinking away tears from the acrid fumes that had arisen as she'd melted back the wire insulation she'd needed to splice it in.

"All right, give the mic on my helmet a couple taps, would you? If I did this right, it should get passed along to the amp here."

Nodding, Straya used her long-toed feet to shove off from the wall and float her way over to Phera's helmet, giving its half-exposed mic a couple of experimental flicks.

"Testing."

This time the wriggling coming from the conduit had a distinctly celebratory air to it.

"It's actually working! Yes!"

Straya's brows dipped down into a frown at the implication of the engineer's words, but she seemed to decide not to press the issue since she'd managed to pull it off in the end.

"You can use the controls in the helmet to set the frequency."

Phera's voice was still muffled as she bobbed an ankle in lieu of gesturing with her hands.

"The amp from my suit isn't nearly as powerful as the flyer's, but hopefully your friends will be close enough to hear us."

There came yet more wriggling from the conduit then as she tried to work her way free. But, the wiring channels in the shuttle hadn't been designed with someone of her voluptuous proportions in mind, and she found that she was well and truly stuck.

"Uh…"

Wriggle, wriggle.

"You mind?"

"Hmm? Mind what now?"

Looking up from the helmet she'd been in the process of adjusting the settings on, Straya's lips gave a slight upward tilt. Phera's stomach was definitely a bit on the chubby side, and a cluster of thickly-insulated wires that had been pushed back out into the engine compartment by her hips were now drawn taut against her bare belly and the lower part of her thighs.

"I'm, uh… Ahem."

Phera cleared her throat with as much shabby dignity as she could muster and bobbed an ankle up toward her cheeks.

"I'm kind of stuck here."

"I can see that."

Eyeing the skintight boyshorts and the twin crescents of dark pink cheek spilling out the bottom of them, Straya gave a small snort and shook her head.

"Probably for the best considering your habit of breaking stuff when left to your own devices."

"Oh my gods! I already said I was sorry for that, didn't I?"

"Actually, no you didn't, but that's fine. Let me just get this message out first and then I'll help you do the same. If my crew's on the far side of the asteroid right now, waiting for them to get a reply back could bring our air supply well into the yellow."

She started inputting a code then.

"You're sure we're on low-powered projection, right?"

She looked back up again from the keypad they'd mated to the helmet and smirked at the part of Phera that was visible.

"Not readable past a light minute?"

"Uh…"

There came a few more sparks and another puff of ozone from the conduit, followed by two prolonged beeps before Phera spoke again.

"*Now* we are, yeah. Also, um… How bad is 'yellow' exactly?"

She was seriously starting to regret not paying more attention in her ship safety training course.

Straya, meanwhile, grinned toothily at her nervously flexing cheeks.

"Not critical, but could become so if something goes wrong on their end."

She left the helmet looping a tap code that should catch her crew's attention, and then pulled herself back up to the tight opening Phera's lower body was protruding from like a particularly attractive house plant. For a moment, it seemed that she was tempted to pick up where they'd left off before their little science project. *Very* tempted. But, Phera did still have her hands on the jury-rigged connection, so she restrained herself.

For now.

"Hold on a sec."

Grabbing the hatch handle in one foot and a coolant intake pipe in the other, Straya slipped her hands in along the younger woman's sides, right above her hips.

"Let's see…"

She moved her palms around her soft sides, searching for the best spot to grip.

"Suck in your stomach."

"R-Right."

There came a clattering of tools as Phera hurriedly gathered them up. Then, with a deep breath that betrayed to the pirate behind her that she wasn't the biggest fan of tight spaces, she sucked her stomach in.

"Okay!" she grunted, voice tight with the effort of doing as she'd been instructed.

Straya grabbed the thinner of the two wire clusters Phera was tangled in, and half-rolled, half-forced it down over the younger woman's still slightly tender right flank and just barely inside the lip of the entrance. There was a short squeal of pain from her at this, and she quivered with the effort of holding her breath. Thankfully, though, she wasn't left to wait for long as Straya then took a firm hold of each appropriately named love handle, and with a low grunt, yanked her free.

"Oh thank gods!"

With a gasp of relief, the auburn-haired engineer came tumbling end over end back into the engine compartment. Her curly hair was matted down on one side with sweat and grease, and her brief outfit looked like it would need a couple cycles through the washer to get it back to its original crisp black and gray, but she nevertheless exuded triumphant self-satisfaction. She even managed to catch herself as she bumped against the bulkhead next to the entrance to the compartment, locking her boots against it and beaming at Straya.

"Am I good, or am I good?"

"I don't know," the other woman teased. "But, I think I'm leaning toward good."

Straya was finally letting herself smile now. Actually smile. Not grimacing, not smirking, and definitely not that predatory sneer she'd leveled at Phera when she'd started spanking her. The shorter engineer's bright exuberance was contagious, it seemed.

"And, yeah, that should keep looping. We'll hear from them when they're in real-time range."

She locked her own boots to the deck and looked up at the ceiling, sighing in relief. Eyes closed. Lips hanging slightly open.

"Signal's out. They'll be here. Probably in thirty minutes or under."

Phera wasn't sure if this last bit was for her benefit or not. Judging by the way the other woman's shoulders had just sagged as she mumbled, though, she thought it best not to comment.

Straya took in another deep breath then, blindly detaching her gloves so she could scrub at her suddenly exhausted looking face with clean, bare skin.

"Let's get out of here," she said, slowly opening her eyes once again. "It's cooler in the hold. We'll hear the ping when they get close."

Her suggestion reminded Phera just how hot and sweaty the cramped engine compartment was, and she nodded quickly.

"Good idea."

Then, looking over to where the pirate's armor still blocked the entrance, she frowned.

"Uh... That thing wouldn't happen to have remote control, would it?"

"It wouldn't. Hang on."

Disengaging her boots, Straya grabbed one of her power armor's ankles and levered herself between its legs and out into the cargo hold with its payload of diverse drones and drilling modules.

"You could come out the way I did, but I think we've learned our lesson about you and tight spaces."

She was being mean, but Phera could hear the note of playfulness in her voice and chose not to hold it against her. Though, she *did* stick her tongue out at the optical array still glaring at her.

While she did that, Straya inserted a key she produced from a pocket in her vacsuit into an access point on the armor and pressed her fingertip against the little strip that emerged from the vehicle's back. When it split open along the "spine," she reached inside and hit the quick maneuvering pad, riding the suit's back as it took two clumsy, blind, magnetized steps directly backward before taking her finger off the button and closing it up again.

"There we go. Open sesame."

"Oh, wow..."

Any annoyance Phera might've still been harboring toward the other woman's dig at her talent for getting stuck had melted away as she'd watched the armor move out of the way for her.

"That is *so* cool."

Eyes still glued to the armor as she came to a stumbling, magboots-assisted halt just in front of it, she grinned from ear to ear. The temperature inside the hold was easily ten degrees cooler than it had been inside the engine compartment, and it felt absolutely amazing on her bare legs and sweaty back.

"So," ventured Straya, climbing down off her power armor and planting her foot and toe pads firmly back on the deck. "We've got at least twenty minutes to kill, probably more."

As she spoke, she drew in closer and closer to Phera until her simultaneously intimidating and flattering chest armor dominated the majority of her vision.

"They'll probably just hook us up airlock to airlock and get going immediately."

"Awww, what's the rush?"

Swallowing a sudden surge of giddy nervousness, feeling inexplicably like she was back in college flirting with an upperclassman she'd somehow caught the attention of, Phera forced herself to drag her gaze up to meet the looming pirate's hard-edged, yet wryly-amused eyes.

They really were a lovely shade of gray.

"Your boss have a hot date to get to or something?"

Please don't tell me you do.

"Not quite. Your friends managed to get an SOS off back when we first breached your perimeter, which means there's some unpleasant company headed our way."

"Who, InterSec?"

"Got it in one. Good job."

"Oh! I, um, well…"

Twirling some of her copper curls around a finger, Phera did her best to project an air of nonchalance while her lower abdomen fluttered at Straya's praise and her heart hammered against her ribs at the prospect of finding herself in yet more space combat.

"I don't think I've ever been in a high-speed chase with the police before. That could be… fun."

"The idea is to *avoid* the high-speed chases," Straya corrected, rolling her eyes but still smirking. "For now, though, we've just gotta wait."

"I think I can handle that."

"Uh-huh."

Brows arching as she eyed Phera appraisingly, Straya began making a slow circuit around her.

"That was some good work you did back there, you know."

"Heh. Um, thanks."

Phera blushed, and one grimy hand rose up to tuck a free floating copper coil back behind her ear. It drifted away almost immediately, but the gesture still made her feel better as she did her best not to squirm under the pirate's scrutiny.

"Pretty sure slowly suffocating to death out here in some shitty megacorp shuttle would've ruined both our days, so I'm glad it worked out."

"Noooo kidding."

The corners of Straya's mouth drew up in a fresh grin as she paused to linger behind her, her look turning wolfish as she took note of the good three or so centimeters of deep crevice visible above the slightly askew waistband of Phera's boyshorts.

"So then, what oh what should we do to pass the time until they arrive, I wonder?"

She left that question hanging open, sending a cascade of tingles down Phera's fidgeting body as she drew back around to stand in front of her, waiting for her to reply.

"Um, let's see, uh, until then..." echoed the younger woman, managing to resist the urge to step back as Straya's sharp eyes caught on the pair of pebbled nipples pushing out against the stretchy material of her bra. "We could..."

She could practically feel the words, "What do pirates do for fun?" taking shape on her lips, but swallowed them and asked instead, "Since we've got time and I'm not really going to be able to go anywhere once your friends get here, what with me being your, uh... you know, your captive?"

She put enough questioning emphasis on that last word to make Stray smirk as she nodded.

"Mind if I take a peek inside your armor?"

"Er... Inside my ulfsark?"

Clearly taken aback, the pirate looked like she was about to say no, but some of the raw, unabashed enthusiasm beaming off of Phera like sunlight off a thermal shield must've gotten through to her. Because, after drawing in a deep breath through her nostrils and letting it out as a resigned sigh, she nodded.

"All right, fine. You can take a look," she conceded. "But, *no touching* the internals."

She hooked a thumb over her shoulder with a wince that carried with it a genuine hint of remorse.

"This thing is barely holding together as it is."

"Don't worry, I'll be careful!"

Before she'd even finished speaking, Phera was already on the move, *clomp-clomp-clomping* her way over to the armor and running her hands lovingly along its scratched and pitted frame.

"Wow, this is…"

Tracing her fingertips in exploratory circles around the side of one armored thigh, she gave it a thoughtful rap with her knuckles and gasped.

"These plates are a ceramic composite! I thought for sure they'd be tungsten. And, hmmm… Is that some sort of mesh weave embedded in them?"

She paused to scratch her fingernails against where she'd just been rubbing and nodded to herself.

"Oh yeah, *totally*."

Giggling in pure, nerdy delight, she hurriedly half-jogged, half-stumbled around to the back of the hulking armor, releasing her boots' maglocks as she did so and drifting up to get a better look at its top side.

"Eeee! Oh my gods, this is so *cool*!"

At the sight of a slanting line of five-centimeter indentations, though, she paused to frown thoughtfully.

"Uh… What're these for? Air drag?"

Wait a minute, there's no drag in space. Maybe for atmospheric combat then?

"They are now," answered Straya, mouth twisting in disgust. "Little souvenir from some low-yield explosive rounds back during Midway."

She trailed after Phera and continued to stare at the row of dents for a few more moments, before letting out a distant sigh.

"He was trying to knock me out an airlock. And succeeded."

Folding her arms in front of her as she shifted her own respectable hips out to one side, she watched the curvy engineer's delicate fingers play along the rims of the row of craters.

"Long time ago now."

Her explanation took some of the fun out of Phera's exploration, and she drew her hand back with a grimace. The reality that the armor wasn't just a fun experiment in engineering, but was in fact a tool meant for actual combat and violence, coming back to her all at once.

"Oh, I... I see."

Looking away from the dents, to Straya, and back again, she did her best to reassert her earlier smile.

"Well, I, uh, I hope you were okay. That doesn't sound... Uh, yeah. That definitely sounds like something you wouldn't want to do twice."

"If I wasn't fine then, I wouldn't be now either," pointed out the pirate, her sardonic grimace returning full force to her scarred face. "Didn't even notice the damage until I was cleaning aerosolized dickhead out of the joints after I got picked up. But, yeah, only one surprise involuntary spacewalk so far."

She shook her head, and grimaced a little harder.

"Though, the way I've been going lately, that probably won't last."

Phera's own grimace returned upon hearing that. Though, this time it was more commiserating than startled.

"Yeesh. Being a pirate sounds rough."

Then, realizing that that was probably another fairly obvious thing to say, she added quickly, "Well, I mean, I guess it kind of *has* to be since your job is literally to steal stuff. But, uh... For what it's worth, I hope your luck holds. Getting tossed out into the cold and the black sounds like it would fucking suck."

Deciding that it would probably be better to change the subject, she started to awkwardly shimmy her way up the armor using the maglocks on her boots for support. Forgetting for the moment that they were still in null-grav and she could have just as easily floated up instead as she scurried along its back with its old battle scars and patched-over bullet holes to the head of the unit.

"What kind of sensor package does this thing have for optics? You've got to at least have one of those chaff particulate analyzer things, yeah?"

It'd been a long while since she'd done any sort of research on military hardware for fun. (Gods, had secondary school really been that long ago?) But, she assumed the power armor's optical array had to at least be capable of punching its way into the x-ray spectrum. Though, judging by its age and general wear and tear, she couldn't totally be sure.

"Not as much as it used to have," Straya admitted, rubbing at the back of her neck as she traded out her grimace for a wince instead.

She seemed like she was about to explain further, but then caught herself before she could and shook her head.

"Most of that damage happened before I was a pirate, actually."

"Before, huh?"

Shuffling around to get more comfortable atop the armored dome of the ulfsark's head, Phera propped her elbows against its antenna pod and cupped her face in her palms.

"Heh. That's funny. I kinda just figured you were born with a coilgun in hand, kicking down doors and slapping pretty girls on the ass while you stole their ships."

"That so?"

Straya looked like she couldn't decide if she should be flattered or offended.

"Well, no, not quite. I used to be military," she said by way of explanation, not elaborating any further than that as she directed her gaze up to where the engineer's ample cheeks squished out and down behind her (the hem of her boyshorts riding another centimeter lower). "These things aren't exactly easy to come by, you know."

Moving back around to the ulfsark's front, Straya laid a hand almost tenderly along the curve of one of its wrists, just above where it coupled to its carbon-lined shield.

"So, I've been making it last as best I can."

"You don't have an engineer maintaining this?" gasped Phera, looking aghast at the armor she was straddling. "Oh my gods, that's really dangerous! An actuator or something could give out without proper maintenance, and then who knows what might happen?"

She wasn't so sure she actually knew the answer to that question herself, but her look of concern mingled with professional indignation was entirely genuine. Slipping off the top of the unit, she let her magboots pull her back down to the deck where Straya stood, before rising up onto her tiptoes to inspect the joint the other woman was caressing for herself.

It *seemed* fine. Scuffed and pitted in a couple spots, but otherwise fine.

"I do have someone taking care of it, yes. But, even actual engineers don't know everything."

Straya shook her head a little, letting out a slow breath.

"The one we've got does pretty well, considering she'd never seen an ulfsark in person before we met."

She shrugged.

"My old pal here would have fried me or broken me in half years ago without her, so I guess I can't complain."

She rapped her knuckles against the suit's side armor and looked back at Phera with a wry smile.

"So, you're 'gods', huh? You from somewhere around Yaara? Or is that just a phrase you picked up in college?"

"The latter," admitted Phera, the tension in her shoulders easing as the fear of catastrophic joint failure dwindled inside of her. "I dated a girl sophomore year whose family was big into Daziqir, and I guess some of it must've stuck. I got more than my fill of religion while growing up back on Cilara, but I liked the multiple gods thing. Plus, those worship halls were really pretty. Way better than the whole 'grace through humility' thing the Church of Harmony goes for."

She was moving on autopilot now, keeping up a high-speed stream of off the cuff chatter as she prodded at the small, interlocking plates that sheathed the control lines routed through the armor's elbow joint.

"She and I did the festival of colors once. That was lots of fun. I kept my hair purple for most of that semester."

Circling back behind the armor, trailing her fingers along the dented and scratched plates there, she noticed what looked to be an embedded touch sensor. And, holding her thumb there for a couple seconds, there came the distinct *click* of an unlatching somewhere near where the unit's left leg joined with its hips.

"Oooh, redundant limb control circuits!"

'Well, I wasn't just assuming you were Daziqir. Just from that general neighborhood-" Straya was still replying, before finally noticing that the manual override controls had just revealed themselves to Phera. "Whoa, hold up! What are you doing there?"

"Just checking out the gait auto-balancers," the redhead supplied in a tone that showed she was only half-listening as she squatted down to tap at the newly exposed controls, causing the ulfsark to take a smooth, gyroscopically-controlled step forward toward the engine compartment. "Oh my gods, *yes!*"

"Okay, nope. That's enough for you, kid!"

Straya's magboot clamped down so hard on the deck next to Phera that it made her jump mid-excited-clap as she seized hold of her by her thick copper curls and dragged her back to her feet.

"Ack! Heeeey!"

"I said look but don't touch, didn't I?!"

Her face a mask of fury and exasperation, Straya yanked on her fistful of hair, forcing the shorter woman to meet her eye.

"*Well?*"

"Ow! Fuck! What's your deal?" she hissed, caught between Straya's ruthless grip on her hair and her boots' grip on the deck. "I wasn't touching the internals."

Huffing out an affronted breath through her nostrils, Phera rallied her defenses as she met Straya's glare with one of her own.

"It's just maintenance mode. Why are you freaking out? It wasn't like I was trying to make it dance or anything."

The way she said that last bit left a big, fat unspoken "yet" floating in the air between them, that did absolutely nothing to diminish the pirate's anger.

"What's my *deal*?"

Releasing her hair, Straya moved to plant herself firmly between her ulfsark and Phera, hands balled into fists on her hips.

"Oh, let's see. How about what happened the *last* time I saw you control a walking unit?"

"I-! That's not-!" spluttered the engineer, cheeks flushing with renewed warmth.

"And what did I have to do to make you stop then, hmm?"

"I…"

Phera knew the answer to that question all too well.

"I, um…"

Bottom clenching while her face darkened to match her hair, her mouth worked itself up and down for several more seconds before she finally managed to get actual words to come out of it.

"Oh come on! That was, like, the heat of battle or whatever."

Channeling all of her embarrassed indignation into outright annoyance, she jabbed one bare finger at the taller woman's armored chest.

"Besides, I'll have you know that if *you* hadn't been tackling me, that drone would've totally kicked your ass!"

Much of Phera's fervor wilted with this last declaration. Straya's earlier comments about aerosolized dickhead sending a visible shudder through her as unpleasant visions of what said drone might've actually done to the other woman asserted themselves unbidden in her mind's eye.

"Look. I'm sorry, all right?" she huffed after another moment, crossing her arms beneath the swell of her breasts, pushing them up as she half-turned to grumble at a bit of floating detritus next to the pirate's right elbow. "I promise I won't make your armor walk again."

"Yeah. I think you won't be."

Straya, sounding slightly mollified by the earnest apology (sass not withstanding), and seeming to understand that Phera hadn't realized what she'd been about to do with her drone earlier, leaned over and pushed the access panel back into place on her ulfsark.

"That does remind me, though," she continued, a mixture of emotions in her voice coming together as she straightened back up to loom over the blushing engineer once again. "There's something I wanted to talk to you about. From earlier."

"Um... There is?"

"Uh-huh."

The smile that Straya leveled at Phera then was not a friendly one.

"So, there's probably another good fifteen minutes until pickup."

She threw a glance back toward the engine compartment where the helmet was still cycling its low-powered transponder code.

"And letting you look at my suit isn't on the activity list anymore."

Still smiling, she laid a heavy, calloused hand on either of Phera's nearly bare shoulders. She still had on most of her vacsuit, but without the gloves her arms were exposed up to the elbow, and the younger woman couldn't help but notice that the muscles there were distressingly thick and well-defined.

"I already taught you a lesson for trying that drone trick. But, you just reminded me that we still haven't addressed you nearly getting us both asphyxiated out in the middle of fucking nowhere."

Watching the emotions that flitted across Phera's face with that pronouncement almost certainly confirmed for Straya that she was an absolutely atrocious cards player.

"Hey now, come on," she protested, a pleasant little tremble working its way through her stomach and down between her thighs as she opened her mouth, closed it, and then opened it again. "That was at least sixty percent your fault. I'm not the one who was trying to hijack a flyer that doesn't belong to me."

"Well, that doesn't-"

Suddenly there came a series of harsh clicking sounds from the helmet floating on the wire clusters in the engine compartment, accompanied by a rush of static.

"Oh, thank god!"

The two of them said it in unison. Phera's exclamation came with an extra S on the end of it, while Straya pressed a hand to the chest of her vacsuit and sighed in relief.

"Twelve and a half minutes on average," she murmured, voice so low Phera was only able to hear because they were standing so close. "From that distance they might even make it in twelve..."

The tension and fear that hadn't quite released Straya up until that point finally let her shoulders loosen and wiped the angry half-glower, half-smirk from her face.

"They heard us! We'll be picked up in less than a quarter hour."

"That's fantastic!" exclaimed Phera, the confirmation that someone was actually coming to rescue them likewise lifting a weight she only realized she'd been carrying by its absence.

"Yep. And, by the time they arrive," the pirate continued with the languid ease of a predator who'd just cornered its prey, her toothy grin reappearing with less (but still undeniably present) anger behind it. "*You* are going to regret a *lot* of things you shouldn't have done today."

Her arms shot out quick as a pair of missiles in the void then. One hand seized hold of Phera by the upper arm just below her shoulder while the other wrapped itself around the engineer's soft midsection. And, without so much as a grunt of effort, she hauled her up off the deck.

"Wait, Straya, no!"

Phera's whiplash from sagging relief to disbelieving panic as she flailed her one free arm and both her legs was enough to draw out a bark of grimly amused laughter from the bigger woman as she easily grappled with her in the null-grav.

"Afraid so."

Straya had somehow managed to toggle the locks on Phera's magboots off while she'd been grabbing her (those extra-long toes were apparently good for more than just holding onto things while floating around, it would seem) and with *her* feet the only ones anchoring them to the deck, it was beyond easy for her to carry her over to a nearby workbench and thrust her face first across its smooth surface.

"Oh come on! This isn't fair!"

"Yeah, pretty sure the technical term for your situation is 'tough shit'."

"But... But..!"

"And," she continued, voice triumphant as she licked her lips at the sight of the round and very full bottom perched over the edge of the workbench before her. "You do *not* get to keep these on this time either!"

Shoving down against Phera's lower back with her left forearm, Straya pinned her roughly to the table while giving her other arm more room to work with (much more than it'd had back when they'd been tumbling through the air in the engine compartment). And, planting one maglocked foot behind the auburn-haired engineer's ankles to trap them in place and prevent her from kicking, she snatched up the waistband of her oh-so-flattering boyshorts and yanked them unceremoniously down to their owner's knees, leaving two pinkened cheeks floating high and free in the cool air of the hold.

"Yep. *Much* better."

"Hard disagree!"

"Don't care. You've absolutely earned this, and I'm going to enjoy every single second giving it to you."

Suiting actions to words, Straya brought her right hand up well past her shoulder and then sent it soaring back down against the pinned younger woman's left cheek in a full-armed, shoulder-powered *SMACK!*

"Ah!"

In response, Phera's voice ratcheted up an entire octave higher as her bare hips bucked roughly against the chilly workbench in front of her.

"Oh my gods! Straya-"

SMACK!

"Owie!"

"Mmhmm, that's right," replied the pirate, adding another handprint to Phera's right cheek this time.

SMACK!

Its outline flashed white for a split-second with its initial impact, before filling in a delicious shade of dark pink in time with the flighty girl's yelp.

"Straya, come onnnn!" she moaned, copper curls bobbing to and fro as she shook her head and hissed. "I said I was sorry!"

"No," corrected Straya without missing a beat. "You're *starting* to be sorry. You'll *actually* be sorry right about the same time my crew gets here."

SMACK!

Another sharp, air-splitting report of palm ricocheting off sensitive flesh echoed around the hold.

SMACK!

Followed by another.

SMACK!

And a third immediately after that.

SMACK!

Red handprints piling up on top of the faint, rosy hue left behind from Phera's previous spanking.

"Think this should pass the time okay?"

SMACK! SMACK! SMACK!

Straya started swinging her arm faster (though no less hard) then, making a different cheek flatten and splash out each time her palm struck home.

"Don't you wish you could still be looking at that suit?"

SMACK! SMACK! SMACK!

"Yes-!"

SMACK!

"Ow! *Yes*! Let's do-"

SMACK!

"Ack! That!" gasped Phera.

SMACK!

"Nope. I already told you, that option's off the table."

SMACK!

"And that's all your fault, isn't it?"

Straya punctuated this largely rhetorical question with a whirlwind of extremely hard swats to the undercurves of Phera's cheeks where bottom met thigh.

SMACK! SMACK! SMACK! SMACK! SMACK!

"Ow! Ack! Fuck-!"

"I asked you a question, you little brat!"

SMACK!

"Speak up!"

"We don't have to be- Ah! Doing this!" Phera protested in response to Straya leaving a particularly vivid handprint on the back of her left thigh, followed by about half a dozen more for good measure. "We could- Oh! We could just call it- Erk! Call it even and go back to- Owie, owie, owie! To show and tell!"

Her voice held a distinct mixture of pain and panic coupled with a thick helping of deliberate, taunting challenge to it that was all but begging Straya to keep spanking her.

Well, that and the way her cheeks kept jiggling in the null-grav.

"Show and tell?"

Only too happy to oblige it seemed, Straya kept her hand pistoning up and down without mercy.

SMACK!

Again.

SMACK!

And again.

SMACK!

And again!

SMACK!

"Well, you're certainly showing me plenty right now."

Unable to keep the grin off of her face, Straya cinched her arm around Phera's full waist and started planting her next twenty or so swats all across the swollen undercurves of her plump and blushing buttocks. Making them splash with incredible drama as the layered handprints there started to blend together into a deep, angry red that would keep her from sitting down once she was back under gravity for a long time to come.

"But, I guess it's my turn to bring something new to the table, huh?"

With an even more sadistic, toothy grin, the pirate moved her right hand down to where she'd hooked her teflon-coated, kevlar-lined vacsuit gloves to her utility belt for safe keeping. And, with practiced ease, detached one from its partner and held it by the wrist, its empty fingers trailing semi-rigidly out in front of it.

"Heh."

This was undoubtedly cruel, but Phera *had* just been begging for it.

Straya swished the glove through the air a couple of times then, giving the engineer and her sizzling seat ample opportunity to hear and realize what a fiery end these few moments of reprieve she'd been enjoying were about to come to.

"Eep!"

As rigid fingertips grazed along her crack, Phera actually squeaked!

She'd forgotten all about those damn gloves from earlier. She'd gotten so used to only having her magboots on, that it hadn't really clicked for her that the other woman was still wearing most of her vacsuit.

"Um, now... Okay, hold on," she hemmed, stomach sinking even as her heart fluttered in anticipatory dread. For as much as this all hurt, she'd be lying if she said she wasn't enjoying herself at least a little bit (or a lot). "I think I'm starting to see where you're coming from here, Straya. And, um, those are some very nice gloves you have, but, uh… Maybe you should put that one back so it doesn't get lost?"

"As soon as show and tell is over."

Leaning in so that her lips brushed feather-light against Phera's *very* pink ear while her armored chest dug into her largely bare back, Straya cut loose with a throaty chuckle that sent a bolt of arousal directly between the engineer's squirming thighs.

"Sweet cheeks."

SNAP!

"Aieee!"

Phera's scream as Straya's glove impacted against her right thigh without warning was truly a work of art, and the whimper that followed after even more so.

Prompting her to repeat the treatment against her left thigh.

SNAP!

And then her right.

SNAP!

And then her left.

SNAP!

Right.

SNAP!

Left.

SNAP!

Red hand, wrist, and fingerprints splattered out across jiggly, formerly pale skin like cracks on a sheet of glass. Each impact of the deceptively heavy glove, jerking Phera's hips forward against the hard edge of the workbench and causing her to wish very much that she'd kept her vacsuit pants on. Straya would've just taken them down before they'd started, but it was the thought that counted just then as the pirate continued to bring her glove down against her with vicious, forearm-powered swats.

SNAP! SNAP! SNAP!

"Okay, okay!"

Breath shallow and frantic as she squeezed her eyes shut against the first beads of null-grav tears bubbling up at their corners, Phera tried yet again to bargain for her bottom.

"You've made your point! I *swear* I won't accidentally cut the comms ever again!"

"And?"

SNAP!

"Owie! Um..."

SNAP!

"Ack! And I won't touch your suit controls without permission!"

Phera was rapidly running out of things to promise, and she very much hoped at least one of them would work.

"Oh, I know you won't," the pirate replied with an unconcerned shrug, still grinning wickedly. "I'm making sure of that."

"But-!"

The flailing palm and fingers of the glove streaked down again, this time biting into the thoroughly spanked, wobbling globes of Phera's buttocks.

THWACK!

"Owie, owie, *owieeee!*"

Dark crimson blossomed over what was already an extremely red sit-spot, keeping it jiggling for a full three seconds while another whipping glove-slap struck its twin.

THWACK!

Followed by even more, spaced out every couple of seconds.

THWACK...! THWACK...! THWACK...!

Providing the howling engineer with more than enough opportunity to fully wrap her mind around the initial breathtaking bite of each impact before it flared out into a deeper, lingering ache that would be sticking with her long after the furious burning in her bottom had dissipated.

THWACK...! THWACK...! THWACK...!

"Ack! Owie! Oh my gods!"

Teeth gritted tight and unable to stomp out even a little of her overwhelming agony with her legs pinned beneath Straya's much stronger calf, Phera was able to at least take some solace in the fact that the pirate had stopped smacking her thighs. Unfortunately, her bottom wasn't exactly all that much better of a target. It had more padding, true, but that just meant she was free to swing as hard as she wanted to without fear of doing any serious damage.

At least she wasn't swatting as fast as she had been back when she'd been using her *actual* hand.

THWACK...! THWACK...! THWACK...!

That was little comfort, though. And, as more tears continued to swell and break free to float around her head, Phera found herself finally having to admit that this woman was more than a match for her. That, as much of a smartass as she might be, and how good she was at adjusting the variables of a situation to make it clear she hadn't done anything (that) bad, it didn't matter. Straya had her pinned in place and was taking all of her reckless decisions (and probably a good deal of her own worries and frustrations) out on her ass, and there wasn't a damn thing she could do about it.

"Oh my gods, Straya, *please*!" she begged, tears flowing freely around her in a miniature, shimmering galaxy of crystallized remorse and pain.

"Just. One. More. Minute!"

Straya's voice had a crowing singsong to it as she punctuated each word with another *THWACK!* of her glove. Phera's lower bottom cheeks were both streaked with a livid carmine that bordered on purple now in addition to their neon crimson, and had swollen up so that they were even bigger than before.

Shifting her aim back down, the pirate gave each thigh a couple more swats for good measure.

SNAP-SNAP! SNAP-SNAP!

She was just starting to bring her arm down for another round, when suddenly there came more static and clicking from the improvised comm interface inside the engine compartment.

"Ah. Just a second, I'll be right back."

Patting the lower-inside of Phera's left buttock, feeling for herself just how hot and taut the flesh there had become (as well as how wet the engineer was despite her sobbing), Straya let her go and clomped back toward the tethered helmet, glove still in hand.

"Hello, yes, it's Straya! Yep, I'm fine, no damage. I've got the whole package, and... an extra. Tell the captain to be ready for a guest."

From the other end of the line, a staticky voice asked, "Corporate?"

Straya nodded, though no one could see her do so besides Phera.

"Sorta. Don't think she'll be toooo much trouble, though. And, yeah, no, I can't slow us down, sorry. My new friend will explain why once we're on board."

Letting the helmet go, she stepped back over to the workbench from which Phera had started to drift away.

"You should probably put something on," she smirked. "Wouldn't want anyone to get the wrong idea."

Straya's words managed to pierce through the hazy swirl Phera's thoughts had been subsumed by as she'd rubbed at her throbbing bottom.

"Wha-?"

"Our ride's here."

"Oh crap! Right!"

Still floating a meter or so above the workbench, she spun and flailed in place as she struggled to gather up the boyshorts that had slipped down to her ankles Hissing through clenched teeth as their elastic waistband rasped over her thighs

"Ack! Shit. Ow."

Phera thought she'd already endured the worst of Straya's spanking, but she was oh so wrong. While her thighs were decidedly tender and more than a little swollen, her ass was easily twice as bad. Her panties had already been pretty snug to begin with. They'd had to be, given how tight the bottom of the barrel vacsuits Panorama bought were on her. Which made pulling them up over her bruised and aching cheeks absolute agony.

And did some things to her between her thighs that she unfortunately didn't have the time to enjoy just then.

But, somehow, she still managed to make herself presentable (relatively speaking, at any rate). Anybody looking at her would be able to tell immediately what had happened, but that quickly became the least of her worries as the heavy *THUNK-THUNK-WHIRR!* of a new ship mating itself to their partially mangled airlock echoed through the hold.

Phera swallowed.

"Oh boy, here we go…"

Straya, meanwhile, had put her gloves and helmet back on, and was currently in the process of fitting her legs back into their analogue control cavities inside her ulfsark. As the pirate ship docked with them, she took one last look at the struggling, levitating Phera over the vehicle's shoulder and grinned at just how much swollen red meat was puffing out from under those ill-fitting panties. Still, she had a job to do, and brought her head and torso back inside the power armor, extended her arms into place, and pulled the switch to close it up in back again just in time for her personal comm to crackle to life.

"Hey there, Stray," crooned a welcomely familiar male voice. "Blazar Bitches interstellar taxi service at your, well, service."

"Obette, you beautiful son of a bitch," laughed Straya, beyond relieved. "I could fucking kiss you, you know that?"

"Save it for later, sugar lips. InterSec is five minutes out, and the captain wants us gone yesterday."

"Right. We're on our way."

CHAPTER THREE

CHARGES ACCRUED

Unlawful Disclosure of Proprietary Information,
Evading Arrest, Breach of Contract

As the airlock hatch in front of her finished cycling open and she stepped out onto the umbilical passthrough linking the pilfered Panorama flyer and the pirates' ship together, Phera had to actively stop herself from reaching back to rub at her still throbbing bottom. You only got one chance at a first impression, and the last thing she needed was to give a bunch of brutish pirates ideas on how to deal with her if she got too mouthy for their liking. Well, that, and she didn't dare slow down with Straya *CLOMP-CLOMP-CLOMP*ing right behind her in her power armor, presumably keeping close enough to discourage her from trying anything clever.

Not that she need have bothered. Operation "Escape the Shipjacking Like a Total Badass" had gone up in flames right about the same time that her panties had gone down her thighs. Nope. For better or worse, she was at the mercy of her captors for the foreseeable future, and she knew it was in her best interests to be on her very best behavior until she was ransomed back to her employer.

If she didn't think about it *too* hard, it was almost like a vacation.

Almost.

I'm wearing about the same amount of clothes as I would on an actual vacation, at least...

Floating into the new ship's surprisingly spacious cargo hold, doing a passable job of getting her magboots to lock to the deck without stumbling more than a couple steps, Phera was greeted by a knot of armed and armored (though, thankfully, not *power* armored) pirates. Most of whom had the cold, dark muzzles of their coilguns pointed straight at her!

"That's far enough!" a woman with broad shoulders, a barrel chest, and wide hips in the most muscular version of an hourglass figure Phera had ever seen barked as she came to an awkward halt. "Drop your weapons and put your hands on your head."

She stood with her legs braced a shoulders' width apart in some sort of vaguely military looking shooter's stance next to a lean and lanky woman with bright white hair and dark shadows under piercing, amber eyes. That, given the distressing amount of armament being aimed at her just then, still somehow managed to capture all of Phera's attention. There was something undeniably *gravitational* about the way she carried herself, and it wasn't just that the stylish undercut she wore her hair in did a fantastic job of highlighting the elegant lines of her swanlike neck and perfect collar bones. There was also the fact that she was the only one *not* holding a weapon. Though, to be fair, the cool half-grin she wore as she took her in with an amused once-over made it pretty clear to the engineer that she didn't have to.

She had people for that.

"I said drop your weapons!" the muscular woman barked again, jerking Phera back to her present predicament with a startled squeak.

"I don't have any!" she yelped, hands flailing in front of her in a frantic attempt to draw attention to the fact that they were completely empty. "Don't shoot, don't shoot!"

Her stomach was clenched so tight at that moment, that she was surprised it hadn't formed a singularity. But, considering the fact that she was still an outie (something which everyone in the hold could see for themselves since she was still very much in just her underwear and a pair of heavy magboots), she decided to add on in a tiny voice.

"Um… Please?"

She'd never been held at gunpoint before, but an extra bit of politeness seemed like it'd go a long way toward the whole not being shot thing.

"You really think I'd keep her armed?"

Straya's voice projected from her towering power armor as it stomped forward to take up a position behind Phera.

"Been one of those missions, huh, Lem?"

The big woman, who Phera assumed must be Lem, scowled a little at the ulfsark. But, a sideways, mocking grin from the taller woman beside her had her looking down, clearly embarrassed as she holstered her coilgun; the two other pirates to either side of her following her lead and doing the same.

"Gang, Phera," Straya continued as the suit's massive hand nudged the half-naked engineer forward into the midst of the semicircle of pirates. "Phera, gang. She's handy with comms, but not so much with shipboard safety."

"Um, hello…" ventured Phera with a brittle wave. "Pleasure to meet you all."

She'd almost added, "thank you for having me," but just managed to catch herself in time. Mangling the words in a sudden coughing fit instead.

"Uh-*huh*."

The woman with the half-grin and no visible weapons took a long, graceful step toward her then as she finished pretending to clear her throat, dipping her chin to meet her violet, gene-augmented eyes.

"Phera…" she repeated slowly, languorously, rolling the engineer's name over her tongue as if trying to decide whether or not she liked the taste. "Straya does like them thick, doesn't she?"

Phera's forehead flushed.

"I… I wouldn't know."

Prompting the woman to wave a negligent hand in response to her apparent discomfort.

"Never mind, hon. Just thinking out loud."

Nibbling at her lower lip, she angled her head to the side as if trying to get a side-on view of the obviously intimidated younger woman.

"So then, what's your story, hmm?"

"Um, well, that is…" stammered Phera, skin going tingly as her heart hammered in her chest just as hard as that first time Straya had attacked her in the engine compartment.

Suddenly, she wished she'd thought to prepare a speech ahead of time or something. Though, as her bottom flared in protest at her reflexive, full-body clench, it occurred to her that she *had* been kind of busy.

"Ahem. I'm a robotics engineer for… for Panorama," she started to explain, half-turning to gesture back toward the airlock without actually lifting her boots from the deck. "I was performing maintenance on the drones in the flyer when, uh…"

She wanted to say, "When your attacked us and stole it," but the lingering ache in her sit-spots and thighs coupled with the coilguns still within easy reach of the people around her had her picking her words very carefully.

"When Straya arrived," she went with instead. "We kind of got into a bit of a tussle after the engine control lines got cut, and then into *more* of a tussle when the comm lines also got cut. And, well, uh… Yeah. Now I'm here."

Swallowing a nervous lump in her throat, Phera plastered on a shaky smile.

"Thanks for the pick-up, uh… Ma'am?"

The taller woman seemed like she probably had a naval title of some kind, but she wasn't about to start guessing and risk insulting her.

"*Ma'am.*"

Chuckling, the pirate looked back to the bigger woman at her side, receiving a tight half-smirk in return.

"Usually, it's 'Captain'," she continued, directing her attention back to Phera with a wink. "But, I'm nothing if not flexible."

From behind Phera, Straya's vocasted voice snorted out, "Yeah, the engine lines got 'cut' all right."

None of them could see her face just then, but they could all hear her rolling her eyes inside the armor.

"This little gearhead thought it would be a good idea to cut off the helm mid-takeoff."

The ulfsark's heavy hand made surprisingly gentle contact with said gearhead's sore seat as she added with just a hint of mockery.

"Don't worry, though. She's learned her lesson."

"We noticed," purred the captain.

"Wait, wait, wait," Lem interrupted then, saving Phera from having to dwell on the snickers and roaming eyes of the pirates around her angling for a better look at her backside. "You said you were doing *drone* maintenance?"

There was a gratifying (and intimidating) stir from the gathered crew at her question, and Phera nodded.

"Uh-huh. That's right."

Doing her best to ignore the color rising in her cheeks, she threw a glare at the power armor behind her and mouthed, "It worked didn't it?"

She *had* managed to stop Straya's hijacking, after all.

Sort of.

Well, okay, impede it.

Same difference.

Turning back to address the outrageously muscular woman with the hard stare and the impressive hips, Phera hooked a thumb over her shoulder and tried to summon up some semblance of professional confidence.

"The job I was hired by Panorama to do, among a bunch of other things because my contract has a lovely little clause about 'additional duties' in it, was to maintain those drones and increase efficiency wherever possible for greater yields."

Gathering steam now, grateful to be on familiar territory once again, her lips began to tip up at the corners with a sense of genuine pride.

"I've actually been developing a decentralized operations protocol that a group of crawlers on a short-range mesh network can utilize to coordinate drilling positions and dynamically adjust boring laser focal lengths to avoid creating stress fractures and unexpected mantle splits from pressure build up caused by one or more units outpacing the others. It's-"

She was rambling now, she knew, but the captain hadn't told her to shut up and she didn't look mad (just appraising, which Phera hoped was a good sign). So, she just kept on going since it was far easier to talk about her passion for systems development and robotics, than face up to the reality that she was a pirate captive who may or may not be mostly responsible for totaling the shuttle said pirates had been trying to steal.

As she started in on her projected yield increases versus power consumption ratios, Lem turned her broad face back toward the Captain with an intrigued expression that Phera wasn't sure she liked.

"Synchronized drilling, huh?"

The others all seemed intrigued, while the captain just stood very, very still, the half-grin dropping away from her face to be replaced by something flat and measuring.

"Yes… Huh," she agreed thoughtfully. "Huh, indeed."

She took a slow, deliberate circuit around Phera as she spoke, almost vulture like in her appraisal while her face remained disconcertingly blank.

"Phera," she eventually continued in a voice that was low and coaxing, hooking a finger beneath the engineer's chin and tipping it up to lock eyes with her. Her neutral expression cracked into a wicked grin then, and her amber gaze sent a fresh wave of tingles rippling over the shorter woman's mostly exposed skin. "Why don't you come with me back to the hab cylinder? I think I'd like to talk with you a bit more while the girls start unloading."

Two of the pirates, a distant part of Phera's suddenly fuzzy mind noticed, looked to be presenting much more masculine than feminine. But, they seemed to take the plural noun in stride as they moved to follow their captain's unspoken order to get to work.

"You might be interesting."

"I, uh…"

Phera swallowed, resisting the urge to look away as the taller woman's gaze bored deeper and deeper into her.

"I might?"

"Mmhmm."

With that, the captain turned on her heel and started striding away toward the floor-to-ceiling spinning tube set into a wall at the far end of the cargo hold, armored magboots clanking against the deck plates as she called back without looking.

"This way now. No lollygagging."

"Uh… Right. Yes ma'am!"

Stomach twisting with fresh anxiety, Phera winced. The captain had so far been nothing but even-handed and cordial with her, but there was still something about the eerily calm way the woman carried herself that made her feel like she should be extremely careful around her. But, with little choice other than to follow, the engineer clomp-turned to wave goodbye to the power armor she'd been admiring earlier (and the pirate inside of it) as she pushed off the deck and drifted toward where the captain had retreated.

"See you later, Straya?"

Her goodbye came out in the form of a question and sounding much more nervous than she would've preferred. But, in that moment, it was hard for it *not* to when she was literally leaving behind the one thing she was even slightly familiar with in this situation.

Straya didn't seem to mind, though, and instead just lifted one gigantic, metal and ceramic arm (the one not currently busy holding onto an infantry shield) in farewell.

"Watch out, she bites."

"Um, I'll keep that in mind!"

Well now, that was certainly an odd way to wish someone luck, Phera couldn't help but think to herself with another wince. However, she didn't have much time to dwell on whether the pirate was being serious or not, as only a moment later she was latching back down onto the deck just outside the entrance to the hab cylinder where the captain stood waiting for her.

The lean woman had her hands stuffed into the pockets of the flattering long coat she was wearing, and with a nod, she turned and began leading her through the rotating spindle corridor ahead of them. After a few meters of walking along in silence, the two of them dropped down from the ceiling, one after the other, and into the donut-shaped grav acclimation tunnel that wrapped around the inner hab cylinder.

"Up here, second door on the right," instructed the captain, gesturing down the spiraling corridor with its bare steel walls and floor panels, dented and stained here and there from years of wear and tear, and toward a propped open hatch ahead of them.

"Ugh. I always hate this part."

"Planetsider, eh?"

The captain didn't sound particularly sympathetic as she looked back and noted the strained look on Phera's normally friendly features.

"Uh-huh…"

"Well, hold it in. I don't need you throwing up on my floors."

Swallowing hard, Phera nodded.

"Y-Yes ma'am."

The weight of the centrifugal force gradually starting to pull down more and more on her as she and the other woman clomped along was more than a little jarring for the engineer. After spending the last few hours in null-grav, it felt like her guts had suddenly gotten ten times heavier, and she had to fight down a fresh bout of nausea with every other step as they settled back into place inside of her. Before too long, though, they were through the worst of it without any unplanned stops from Phera, and the captain ushered her up a much more traditional hallway and through another set of hatches that led out onto the habitation cylinder proper.

Unlike the cavernous cargo hold, the habitation cylinder had discreet sunsim panels set at regular intervals along the curving ceiling overhead that lit the corridor and its cream colored walls and dark gray deck plates with warm, diffuse light as they walked. Just then they seemed to be set to late afternoon, which matched the time on Phera's wrist comp. And that, combined with the reassuring tug of a proper one G and the rhythmic thrum of oxygen scrubbers and engines just on the edge of hearing, lent the ship a surprisingly comfortable air of homeyness that helped put the still slightly green around the gills engineer more at ease.

Honestly, it was pretty cozy for a pirate ship.

Mimicking the captain's example, Phera squatted down and demagnetized her boots before then following after her under her own power up to one final hatch about a dozen meters down the hall. A hatch, which opened up on what appeared to be… Well, a completely ordinary office.

Huh.

Oh, sure, it was perhaps a little messier than most. A trio of mostly empty coffee cups sat clustered next to a touchpad and monitors turned every which way, and there was a respectable smattering of crumbs and snack wrappers cluttering up most of the available desk space. But, other than that, it really wasn't all that dissimilar to her own boss's office back on The Bin.

As the door hissed shut behind them, the captain stopped in the middle of the slightly cramped room and turned back to address Phera, face once again looking both assessing and like she knew the punch line to a joke that had just gone over the shorter woman's head.

"So, how long with the company?"

Trusting herself to speak now that it was clear she wasn't about to puke all over the pirate's floor, Phera cleared her throat and said, "Oh, about three years now give or take a couple months."

Then, as it occurred to her that she really ought to make herself seem like someone worth the effort of ransoming instead of tossing out an airlock, she quickly added.

"They recruited me during the final year of my PhD program. My dissertation apparently caught their talent scout's eye, and I was on my way to The Bin- Er, I mean, Asteroid Mining Facility F6C-8, three days after graduation."

To cover up the resentment she still harbored over not getting a proper post-grad vacation before unwittingly signing herself over into corporate indentured servitude, she finished by saying with a shrug.

"I've been with them ever since."

"Anything to drink?" asked the captain, abruptly changing the subject.

"Oh! Um, uh, yes please," replied Phera on reflex, feeling like she'd somehow missed something obvious but not sure what it could've possibly been. "Some coffee would be just wonderful right about now."

The bruises on her bottom throbbed with her in agreement as she spoke, and it was all she could do not to reach back and massage them. The captain's almost certainly augmented eyes seemed to be taking in her every move, and the last thing she wanted to do was draw any *more* attention to what Straya had done to her poor cheeks.

"It's been kind of a long day."

She knew the taller woman had most likely already gotten at least an eyeful or two of Straya's handiwork. Phera hadn't seen her own reflection lately, but she could still feel that her lingering tenderness reached down well past the brief area her boyshorts covered. However, if the captain didn't bring it up or acknowledge it, then neither would she.

"Coffee. Sure. Still have some, I think."

She spent a moment or two tapping at a machine perched on the side of her desk, and a second later it started burbling as it began to heat its watery contents.

Then, just as casually, she shrugged out of the jacket she'd been wearing up until that point and tossed it onto the chair behind her desk. It made a surprisingly heavy *thunk* as it landed there (apparently, it wasn't just stylish, but also armored), and while her chair swiveled and spun, she reached up to her throat and began stripping off her vacsuit top. Undoing the clips there and pulling down the zippers hidden beneath, the top split apart to reveal a slim, dark chocolate belly and a smooth, lightly muscled chest swelling up into an orange crop top.

"It'll take a minute to heat up."

Saying this, she released the latches around her waist and stepped out of her vacsuit's pants as well. Under them she was wearing skintight short-shorts, not unlike Phera's own underwear, in a dark navy blue. Only, *hers* actually managed to cover her entire ass and most of her thighs. She let both parts of the heavy vacsuit drop unceremoniously to the deck at her feet as she slipped out of her magboots, and then turned her attention back to Phera, face still serious and inquisitive.

"Repeat that story again, would you? Sorry, I wasn't paying attention."

Knocked off guard by the pirate captain's surprisingly casual attire (she'd been expecting something with more ruffles), Phera dragged her gaze away from where it had been tracing the faintly visible curves of the other woman's abs. She wasn't particularly muscular, but the engineer had a sneaking suspicion that she was still more than capable of kicking her ass and then some.

"Ahem."

Looking down to her much softer stomach, a now very flustered Phera pretended to pick at a stray bit of lint on her bra while she used her hair as cover for her warming cheeks. Somehow, the captain being about as (un)dressed as she was only made her that much more intimidating. But, finding her voice once again, she managed to repeat her story while doing her best to trim it down where she could in case she was being boring.

"I've been with Panorama for three years, Captain, ma'am. They recruited me while I was finishing my PhD, and I've been doing drone work and whatever else they decide to add, ever since."

"Where'd they have you before the station?"

As she spoke, the captain turned back to regard the coffee maker, her halter top silhouetting her breasts in a way that made them look like ripe oranges. And, preoccupied as she was with her own generous backside just then, Phera couldn't help but notice that the woman was sporting an enticingly full ass of her own that was only just barely starting to be weighed down with age.

Guess I know where all those snacks seem to be going on her...

"Also, when are they supposed to move you off?" added the pirate, interrupting the engineer's drifting train of thought.

"Oh! I, uh..."

There was something about the captain's unpredictable cadence (and her undeniably attractive appearance) that was tripping up Phera and making it hard for her to focus.

"Nowhere before The Bin," she answered quickly, starting to feel more than a little tongue-tied as she added. "Well, I guess *technically* speaking, I did do my orientation on a company ship while they were transferring me. But, other than that, I've been on The Bin the entire time. And, as to your other question, um... I'm not really sure."

Suddenly feeling like she'd forgotten all her notes for a staff meeting, Phera racked her mental logs of the last few messages she'd received from her manager and HR.

"My contract is supposed to renew next year, and HR said they wanted to talk about getting that taken care of sometime in the next few weeks, but that's about all I know."

Then, deciding to take a shot at easing some of the tension still coiled tight around her stomach with a joke, she gave her best commiserating scoff and rolled her eyes.

"Believe it or not, Panorama isn't exactly super big on clear and open communication."

Before adding under her breath with bitter irritation.

"Or disclosure of debt structures."

"A PhD on that station, *really*?"

The captain drew herself up to her full height and glared down her nose at Phera, a knowing, victorious smirk starting to dawn ominously across her hawkish face.

"Yeah, okay, honey. I know."

"Um... Know?"

Tilting her head in confusion, Phera tried to meet the captain's smirk with a smile of her own, but the corners of her lips suddenly seemed to be stuck.

"Know what?"

"I know..." the captain purred, her expression growing predatory as she drew in uncomfortably close to tower over Phera. "All about your little '*project*'."

The amount of disdainful emphasis she put behind that last word hit the engineer like a sharp poke to the chest.

"Y-You do?" she gulped, taking an involuntary step back, only to discover that the door behind her wasn't opening.

The captain was a full head taller than she was, and even with the distance she'd managed to put between them, she still had to look up to meet her eye.

"But... But how? Who told you?"

The captain didn't answer, instead making the space between them smaller and smaller.

"I think," she said, voice low and dangerous. "You'd better start sharing details. *Now*."

"Ah!"

A sharp gasp escaped from Phera as her bruised backside butted up against the hard metal door behind her without warning, nearly sending her toppling forward into the pirate hemming her in.

"Details?" she squeaked, part of her resenting the captain demanding she hand over the specifics of the project she'd been working so hard on for so many months now, while the rest of her brain fought to push down the shapeless, animalistic fear threatening to overtake her just then.

Whatever. It's not like Panorama wouldn't own the rights to all of it anyway... she tried to tell herself, forcing her lungs to take in a long, deep breath that did very little to calm her rapidly racing heart and roiling stomach as the captain continued to glower at her like she'd just caught her red-handed trying to steal her ship.

"I am not in the habit of repeating myself."

The captain's voice had gone ice cold and razor sharp, and Phera found herself surrendering all at once.

"All right, all right! The drone's mesh network primarily exists to make sure all of them stay in contact with their control monitor while they're out in the field, but I figured out that with a custom comms package and some firmware tweaks, I could piggyback off of that same network to facilitate a distributed index of unit positions and geological data that could be used to more effectively control laser burst timings via-"

Words were flying out of her at high speed now, and she wasn't sure how clear any of them were since she hadn't paused to take a breath since the start of her explanation. But, so long as the captain was still looking at her like she'd cornered her in a dark alley, she wasn't about to stop.

As she babbled, though, the captain seemed to gradually start to relax, and she eventually settled her shapely bubble butt down on one corner of her messy desk, giving Phera some much-needed breathing room. Her expression had changed too. Now back to the confident, bemused half-grin she'd worn while in the cargo hold.

"Sorry, hon. Different project," she dismissed with a negligent wave when Phera finally had to stop to catch her breath or pass out. "I must've confused you for someone else."

Seeming not the least bit perturbed now, she swiveled her torso around and poured a steaming cup of instant coffee from the little machine the panicking engineer had all but forgotten about. She took a sip from it, nodded to herself in satisfaction, topped it off, and then held it out to Phera with one corner of her mouth still slightly quirked.

"You can keep telling me about it, though," she added, eyes crinkling at the corners like she'd just heard another punch line Phera had missed. "This is all *very* interesting."

"Um, thanks," mumbled a now thoroughly drained Phera, accepting the reassuringly warm cup of coffee and starting to sag with relief before remembering her proximity to the way too hard door behind her and taking a step forward.

Taking a long pull from the hot liquid to steady her nerves, she licked her lips and cast her eyes around for some sugar or cream. Right now her drink was a lot darker than she preferred, but she wasn't about to go poking around the pirate's stores without permission.

"Well, uh, yeah. So, basically, the mesh network gathers and shares geo data and borrows the optical sensors on the crawlers to keep an eye on fractures and the like and each unit adjusts accordingly."

Though she'd attempted to arrange her expression into something at least approaching confident and steady, her words still poured out of her hesitant and shaky. And, powered now by adrenaline and caffeine, rather than an abstract fear of the captain, Phera continued to outline her pet project in meticulous detail. Honestly, it was kind of nice. None of her coworkers ever seemed to care about what she was working on, and her manager had just been interested in the yield percentages.

The captain, on the other hand, seemed to actually be paying attention.

Phera wasn't sure if perhaps she'd been an engineer before she'd started stealing things for a living, but it was still nice to be able to talk about her work with someone who wasn't also actively trying undercut her for a chance at advancing a couple rungs up the corporate ladder for a change.

"I like it."

The captain's grin had broadened again, only this time it looked like it was sharing a secret with Phera rather than preparing to eat her.

"No milk, by the way," she added, apparently reading her mind (or just taking an educated guess based on her curvaceous frame). "Also, we're rationing sugar until we get back home."

She tilted her head a little to one side and then leaned back with both hands resting on the desk behind her. Phera noticed the little bit of metal poking out from beneath the hair on the left side of her head with the change of angle, and idly found herself wondering if the captain had opted for an internal comms implant.

"All right, you're in," she declared. "I'll have Straya find you a bunk."

"Um... In?" echoed Phera, the emotional whiplash of the last few hours really starting to make her head spin. "In what?"

"The gang, swabbie."

The captain winked at her this time as her broad grin gained a couple more bright white teeth.

"Specifically, you'll be an assistant to our current engineer as well as our drone specialist. We were going to need someone to help with that haul anyway, and since you already know those units inside and out, it saves me the trouble of having to go head hunting."

She stood up from her desk again then and advanced on where Phera still stood awkwardly sipping at her coffee beside the door.

"You're probably tired from your fun with Straya, so you can take it easy for the time being while the rest of the crew finishes taking inventory."

One taloned hand reached up then and glided through Phera's copper curls. It was gentle, but at the same time promised not to be as she locked eyes with her and licked her lips.

"Just this once."

"Th-Thank you..."

Phera, unable to break away from that hypnotic, amber stare, shuddered as some rather pleasant sensations stirred between her suddenly weak legs.

The captain giggled at that. Actually, straight up, honest to gods, giggled.

It was a decidedly very non-piratey noise. But, coming as it was from this woman who'd very nearly made her wet her pants just a few minutes earlier (and was making a damn good effort at it in an entirely different way now), Phera couldn't help but feel that it was somehow appropriate.

"Anything else you'd like to tell me before I go keep the girls out of mischief?"

She'd leaned in when Phera hadn't been paying attention, and her breath was a hot rush against her ear.

"Uh..."

Phera seriously felt like her brain was short-circuiting or that she'd missed some crucial bit of conversation. Of all the ways this interrogation slash interview could have ended, this had definitely not been what she'd expected. In fact, if she didn't know any better, she'd say it sounded a lot like she'd just been offered a spot (or more accurately, press-ganged) on a pirate crew. That, and the captain of said crew was about half a heartbeat away from getting inside her pants.

"So, um…"

Swallowing again, Phera made an attempt to put some distance between herself and the woman currently only a handful of centimeters away from her.

"You mean you're *not* going to ransom me back to Panorama?"

"Now why would I go and do something like that, sweetness? If they thought you were worth half as much as I do, they wouldn't have sent you out here."

The captain chuckled then, and her grin was all teeth and taunt as she let Phera sidle away.

"Or would they?"

"I mean…" stalled the engineer, skin going tingly once again with a mix of relief and excitement (along with a healthy dose of fear). "Okay, yeah, fair point."

Reality was starting to push past the surreal nature of this whole situation. Helped along in no small part thanks to a particularly tender spot left behind by Straya's vacsuit glove making itself known with a sharp twinge of discomfort as her weight shifted from one hip to the other.

The captain was right, though. Panorama had never respected her, or treated her like they'd promised. Still, they'd at least paid. Even if that was more of a theoretical thing considering the absurd amount of debt they'd saddled her with at the start of her employment.

"So…"

Phera had never been good at these sorts of conversations, but she knew she had to make herself ask even so. Especially with all her possessions at the moment amounting to a pair of too tight magboots, a dirty set of boyshorts, a bra, and a company-issued wrist comp she'd probably have to toss out in case they used it to track her.

"This *is* the kind of position that comes with pay, yeah?"

"Nope."

The captain shook her head.

"It comes with room, board, and a share. Just like me and the other chicas."

"Isn't that basically pay?" pressed Phera with a smirk, unable to resist teasing the woman just a little bit.

It wasn't like she was going to fire her right after hiring her, was she?

"Or is everyone coming away from your operation today with a pet ore crawler?"

"Not quite."

The captain's head shake this time around carried with it a distinct note of indulgence to it.

"Your little friends are collective property now. We'll see about 'basically pay' once we've got a price tag on that death trap Straya brought you home in."

She snorted.

"Assuming I can actually find someone willing to go through with buying it after the damage you did."

"I mean, technically speaking, Straya is the one who made me do it," Phera found herself harrumphing as she did her best not to think too hard about how much of a pain in the ass (literally and figuratively) that whole shipjacking incident had been for her.

Suddenly, she was very glad not to be working for Panorama anymore.

Although, she was going to miss her plants.

Maybe Istrid will adopt them?

Shaking her head to clear it, Phera adopted her most professional smile and bowed toward her new boss.

"Thank you very much for your generous offer, Captain… Captain, uh…?"

It occurred to her then that she hadn't yet learned her new employer's name.

"It's *just* Captain," the other woman replied with another wink, putting enough emphasis on the first letter of the word to make it abundantly clear that it wasn't just a title. "And, you're welcome."

With that, the door to the office unlocked and slid open behind Phera seemingly of its own accord. Only, that wasn't possible, so the engineer reasoned it must've been triggered by that cybernetic implant embedded in the side of the other woman's head.

Geez. Wiring your brain directly to the ship like that seems pretty risky, she mused. *But, well, pirate. I guess.*

"You just wait right here in the hall," the Captain ordered, plucking Phera's half-drained coffee cup from her hands and ushering her back out into the slightly curved corridor. "I'll have your BFF Straya right over before you know it. Oh, and don't go trying to open any doors until then, or else you and I are going to have problems."

Underscoring this last statement, the Captain's hand lashed out to deliver a really needlessly hard *SMACK!* across Phera's right buttock, snapping her fingers right over the dark red and purple lower chub swelling out of her panties.

"Eek!"

The yelp that escaped from Phera as the door sealed shut behind her once again echoed all along the corridor in every direction. But, luckily, it seemed that she was alone just then as her hands flew back to cup her reignited cheek and its less smoldering fellow. It was perhaps not the most piratey way to start this new chapter in her career, but she wasn't about to start complaining. She was finally off The Bin. And, even if she only had some clunky magboots and her underwear to her name, that was just fine with her.

She could make it work.

Although, it occurred to her as the chorus of an ancient folk song bubbled up to the surface of her mind, she was definitely going to need to invest in some extra-thick pants if she was going to keep working around Straya and the Captain.

"Oh well... Yo ho, yo ho, looks like it's a pirate's life for me."

CHAPTER FOUR

With the delightfully high-pitched squeal of her latest acquisition still ringing in her ears, the Captain strode over to her coffee maker and topped off the curvy engineer's cup. She spared a moment to savor the simple act of inhaling the rich aroma of the steaming brew, and then took a long pull from it. Despite the minor hiccups with the flyer's engines, she couldn't have asked for a better conclusion to this phase of their current operation.

Striding around to the other side of her desk, she plopped down into her swivel chair and let its adaptive foam mold itself to her curves as she brought the myriad displays in front of her to life with the tap of one elongated, spacer's toe to her touchpad.

"Now then, where are you...?"

Straya's ulfsark was back inside its docking cradle in its usual corner of the hold, and Kelt was already fussing over it. Good. The aging unit seemed to have collected a few new scratches during its outing, which was less so. However, the damage appeared to be shallow enough not to affect its performance, so she set the observation aside as unimportant and began cycling through security feeds in search of the armor's pilot.

Soon enough, she spotted her familiar head of tight black curls emerging from the airlock umbilical mating the Mayhem to their new flyer. She was carrying what appeared to be a worse for wear ore crawler, and the sight of it caused the Captain's brows to quirk up ever so slightly.

"Well, at least she'll have something to keep her busy come tomorrow."

With a thought, she opened a connection to the comm embedded in the half-undone collar of the other woman's vacsuit.

"Oh Straya…"

As usual, her surprise susurrus in the raider's ear didn't produce so much as a twitch. She just tapped a button on the inside of her collar with her chin, and her brassy alto replied, "Here, Cap. What's up?"

"I just finished having a chat with that cute little stray you brought home."

"Oh yeah?" she grunted as she shoved the half-mangled crawler onto a workbench near the far end of the hold and strapped it into place so it wouldn't drift away. "How'd that go?"

"Surprisingly well, as a matter of fact. I learned a lot of very interesting things about sympathetic refraction resonance and distributed pressure analysis through heat mapping."

"Sounds complicated."

"Complicated *and* profitable," the Captain corrected with a sleek, vulpine smile, taking another sip of her coffee. "I've decided to keep her, by the way."

She made a vague gesture with her free hand as she spoke.

"Phera, I mean."

Straya let out a low chuckle at that and rolled her shoulders.

"Thought you might."

"Mmhmm. She's got the goods and motivation to be an asset," mused the Captain, her grin turning predatory. "Not to mention the assets to be good for crew morale."

Judging by the 7% reduction in stress indicators she'd observed in Straya since her return, she was already having a positive influence.

"No arguments here," agreed the former soldier, rolling her eyes good-naturedly. "Kelt is just going to *love* her."

"Yes, well, as to that… I think we'll avoid giving her any assignments that require directly interfacing with the Mayhem's subsystems for the time being. At least until the chief engineer decides she's safe enough to leave unsupervised."

"A decade isn't that long, I guess."

"Now, now," chided the Captain with a mock-pout. "I'm sure she'll be able to win her over in half that time."

She gave her coffee a lazy swirl, watching the light from the sunsim panels dance across its turbulent surface.

"Well, that, or Kelt's poor arm will completely give out and she'll have no other choice but to let her help. Either way, our new roboticist's skills are *very* promising."

"If you say so. That's all a bit a bit above my pay grade."

"Oh please, don't go selling yourself short. You did an excellent job salvaging things after they went tits up out there."

Unlike when she'd been interrogating Phera, the Captain's purring voice held no mockery to it now. She was a firm believer in positive reinforcement for her crew, and Straya *had* done well.

"Thanks," huffed the other woman, sounding just as awkward as she always did whenever someone paid her a compliment, before a twitch of apprehension flattened her lips. "But, uh… You sure this is a good idea? I like the kid and all, but she could still sell us out to Pano."

The Captain just shook her head, bemused.

"You don't seriously believe she'd do that, do you?"

"Well…"

She watched as Straya put off answering that question by scrubbing a hand through her close-cropped hair and breathing out a long sigh.

"No, not really. That shit the corp pulled on her would be more than enough to get me to turn on them the first chance I got."

"Agreed. Besides, with how easily she folded when I started turning up the heat during our little interview, she's either a terrible liar, or the best I've ever seen."

The Captain would still have Obette pull the woman's records from Panorama and monitor her net access for the next few weeks just to be sure, but she wasn't particularly worried about her being a corporate spy. She'd had plenty of time and a large enough dataset to refine her ability to assess people's motivations and character over the last couple decades, and everything she'd observed so far indicated that Phera would be a perfect fit for her little crew of misfits.

"Turned up the heat, huh?"

Straya snickered.

"Already breaking in the new cabin girl, Cap?"

"Oh dammit, that's a way better title than assistant engineer!"

Aggressively dunking a cookie into her coffee, the Captain popped it into her mouth with an annoyed huff.

"That's not an answer, you know."

"Well, I'd be lying if I said I wasn't tempted."

Chuckling, she crossed one bare ankle over the other atop her desk, easing back into a comfortable slouch.

"But, no, she was already wound up so tight. I was worried she might snap in two if I decided to avail myself of that truly wonderful backside of hers."

"How magnanimous," deadpanned Straya, the shit-eating grin on her face crisp and clear in the surveillance feed trained on her.

The Captain felt her lips quirk up to mirror it.

"Watch it, swabbie, or I might just decide to make up for that missed opportunity with *your* perky little ass."

Rather than be intimidated like their new roboticist would've no doubt been, Straya just gave a derisive snort and rolled her eyes once again.

"Uh-huh."

Even so, the Captain was pleased to note that the hue saturation in her cheeks had shifted 3% toward red, and she let her stew for a few more moments while she swished around another cookie.

"She's waiting outside my office now," she eventually said around a mouthful of some of Adryel's finest work to date. "Get showered and changed, and then find her somewhere to sleep, would you?"

"Aye aye, Captain."

Mocking formality practically oozed from the words as Straya said them, but she nevertheless immediately turned and pushed off in the direction of the hab cylinder.

"I'm on my way."

"Good girl."

CHAPTER FIVE

CHARGES ACCRUED

Misdemeanor Assault

Phera was left waiting outside the Captain's office for what felt like an excessively long time after her door hissed shut behind her. Her sore ass and antsy demeanor conspired together to make her feel like she was back in secondary school and had been sent out to stand in the hall after getting caught talking during class one too many times. Worse still, not having anything to do and being explicitly told not to go poking around was making the minutes drag by at an excruciatingly slow and tedious pace. Even so, she did her best to while away her time alternating between trying to affect a casual air of indifference as she leaned against the cool metal wall behind her to soothe her tender backside, and shifting away from it with a grimace whenever her cheeks' complaining became too much for her to ignore.

Holy shit. Am I seriously trying to kill time on an honest to gods pirate ship?

With a shaky laugh, Phera cast her gaze left and then right in an attempt to confirm that this was indeed real life and she wasn't just trapped in some particularly painful and sexually charged daydream.

There's a lot less skulls and crossbones than I would've imagined. But, yeah, I guess I am...

Her head was still spinning from the emotional whirlwind that had been the last few hours, and nothing felt quite real for her just then.

Not the fact that she'd escaped Panorama and their soul-crushing corporate debt. Not the fact that she was apparently a *pirate* now (that one was especially hard to fathom considering the turbulent way she'd been "recruited"). But, even with the artificial grav weighing her down, she still felt like she could hover off the deck at any moment.

"Yes, yes, yes!" she cheered quietly enough that it hopefully wouldn't carry into the Captain's office as she pumped her fists in triumph. "Hell YES!"

She was free!

She was free, and she had a brand new career that was sure to give her ample opportunity to stick it to Panorama and every other shitty megacorp like them that ground people's lives to dust beneath their heel in their relentless search for higher and higher profits.

Her parents would absolutely freak.

Wonder if I can get away with shooting them a quick message? she mused to herself, thumbing her wrist comp to life with an unpleasant smirk. *Dear Mom and Dad, I decided to quit that job you said I was just soooo lucky to have and became a pirate. Fuck you, Phera <3*

She didn't actually have network access just then, but it was the thought that counted, she supposed. However, even with all her hype over her new job and the imagined looks of horror on her shitty, buttoned-up parents' faces to keep her company, waiting for her orientation escort to arrive was proving to be difficult.

And boring.

Phera was just about to start pacing down the hall to see what she could see without actually *opening* any doors, when she finally heard the steady thud of bootheels approaching from the direction she and the Captain had come down earlier.

"Oh! Hey, Straya!"

Straightening up from her slouch and brushing off the front of her sports bra in an attempt to make herself more presentable, Phera gave the pirate a little wave.

"'Ello there."

She'd stripped off her vacsuit in the intervening time since Phera had seen her last, and now wore a loose white shirt and a pair of dark sweatpants. She'd also swapped out her armored magboots for heavy black ones that looked like they'd be more at home on a hiking trail than a climate-controlled hab. Which, the engineer had to admit, seemed like a slightly odd choice given the rest of her casual attire.

Then again, if you need to be ready to kick someone's ass at a moment's notice, you might as well be wearing the right shoes for it.

"So, you made the cut then, did you?"

"Heh. Apparently so."

Suddenly bashful, Phera attempted to cover her awkwardness by tucking some of her curls behind an ear as she looked up through her lashes at the taller woman.

"Didn't even realize I was being interviewed until I got the job."

"Cap can be a little much, yeah."

Straya cocked a brow at her then, favoring her with one of her rare, genuine smiles.

"Well, I'm glad she decided to keep you. You seemed like you'd be a much better fit with us than those shitheels back at Pano."

Hearing an actual pirate (who she liked very much, despite her way too heavy hands) say that made the slightly embarrassed smile on Phera's face go full on supernova.

"Awww, thanks!"

It still felt odd that this was her life now, but she was starting to get used to it. And, more to the point, she *liked* it.

"So, uh... What happens now? Do we just cruise around and see who we can rob or something?"

Phera had no idea what exactly she could bring to a ship-boarding party quite yet, but she was determined to think of something. The Captain had said she was qualified to be one of them, and she fully intended on proving that to her as soon as possible.

Straya just snorted, though.

"And leave a trail of hits for InterSec to follow? Nah. Maybe if we had a lot more ships and some big, fuck off lasers to go with them..."

She trailed off then, eyes rolling.

"Maaaaybe don't tell Cap I said that last bit," she continued with a wince. "She's about had it with my suggestions on where we should be taking our operation."

"I don't know, I happen to think big lasers sound like a great idea," teased Phera. "But, don't sweat it. Your secret's safe with me."

"It had better be."

Straya's tone held an edge of flat warning to it, which combined with the grim smirk on her scarred face made the shorter engineer's knees go wobbly for a split-second. Then, with a sigh and a visible effort, she seemed to put aside some long-held frustration and continued on more conversationally.

"But, yeah. Right now we're headed home. Once we get there, you should have ample opportunity to show off what you can do. We've still got to modify your crawler friends before we can use them for the payday we've got coming up, after all."

At the mention of her drones (really, the only thing she'd cared about back on The Bin), Phera's mind shifted away from trying not to stress too much about being caught by InterSec while simultaneously imagining what the Captain's version of "had it" might look like, and her face lit up in a bright smile once again.

"Yeah, no, totally. I can absolutely do that," she said quickly, not exactly sure what "that" might entail quite yet, but still confident that she could reconfigure the crawlers for whatever daring bit of thievery her new boss might require of them.

"Great."

With that, Straya laid a hand on one of Phera's largely bare shoulders and began steering her away from the Captain's office.

"So, wait, 'home'? Do you all not just live on the ship then?"

Pausing at the question, that almost smile ghosted back across Straya's lips again.

"We *do*, but... Yeah. Guess she didn't show you the frame at all, did she?" she asked, nodding back toward the office behind them.

At Phera's answering shake of her head, she made a broad, sweeping gesture with her free hand that took in the ship as a whole around them.

"Okay then, here's the short version. Right now we're on a Marathon Class II hauler named the Mayhem. It's had plenty of custom work done, so it's fast as hell and has some pretty good shielding to boot, but that still doesn't make the hab cylinder any bigger, yeah?"

"Uh-huh…"

"Right. So, in our particular hab, we've got two crew cabins. And, cozy as those are, they're basically just bunks and a couple of storage lockers."

Straya started walking again then, hand still resting on Phera's shoulder as she continued explaining.

"We tried setting up some better beds in out of the way corners of the ship, but there just aren't enough of them to make that work. So, until that changes or Shi gets his hands on one of those space-time folding cube things from that book he and Steph keep telling me about, we've got to dock every couple of weeks or else we all go crazy."

One corner of Straya's mouth quirked up with that last bit.

"Well, *crazier*."

"Heh."

Phera couldn't help but match the other woman's smirk, one hand drifting back to cup a cheek through her boyshorts.

"Yeah… I think I can definitely see the benefits of you not getting too stir crazy."

Being a pirate had to be stressful. Phera hadn't been one for more than half an hour, and already the potential of getting caught loomed in the back of her mind as an ever-present dread, making her stomach twist if she thought about it for too long. She could only imagine what someone like Straya, who actually went on boarding missions, must feel like.

No wonder she'd gotten so spank-happy back on the flyer. Geez.

"Just two cabins, huh?"

Phera tried to recall how many people had been pointing coilguns at her earlier when they'd docked. Counting hadn't exactly been a priority for her then, and her brain had just defaulted to "a lot", so she did her best to try out her own version of a sardonic pirate half-grin.

Judging by the way Straya quietly snorted in response, it needed work.

"Is there going to be room for me, or am I going to have to make do with one of those out of the way corners that there aren't enough of?"

"Nah, you're fine. There's just the eight of us along for this ride, including Cap and Lem who've got officer accommodations, so you've got your pick of whichever roommates you want for the next few days."

"Oh. That's, uh... good. I guess."

Phera hadn't had a roommate since college (there hadn't been that many people on board The Bin, so she'd had her own quarters), and the prospect of picking roommates suddenly made her feel more than a little stressed. How the hell was that even supposed to work anyway?

Hey there, total strangers. Don't mind me, I'm just going to be sleeping in your room from now on. I don't snore, I promise.

"What about the cargo hold?" she found herself asking. "I know null-grav sleeping is kind of awkward, but there's enough space in there for at least a dozen people to spread out and get comfortable."

"Cargo hold's for holding cargo."

Straya gave a bemused shake of her head.

"Can't have people taking up valuable space when there's perfectly good bunks in actual grav."

Her features softened slightly then, and she added with a reassuring wink.

"Don't worry, sweet cheeks. The Captain runs a respectable gang of scoundrels. Nobody's going to take advantage of you without your permission, I promise."

"Oh, good!"

The sound of the nickname on the other woman's lips sent an arc of excitement through Phera, making heat blossom in her cheeks as she let out an embarrassed little laugh.

"Actually, I, uh... Wasn't really worried about that."

Though, it was still nice to hear.

"Sorry," she went on with a chagrined wave of her hand. "Just working my way through some anxiety at meeting new people is all."

"No worries."

The hand on her shoulder gave a quick squeeze as Straya shrugged.

"Like I said, we've got a good crew here. I'm sure you'll fit right in."

"Thanks. But, now that you mention it," continued the engineer, eager to push past this latest bit of awkwardness with her new crewmate. "If we're not picking off targets of opportunity as we go, then what's all the cargo space for?"

"I told you already, didn't I?" replied Straya, starting to sound just a little annoyed at having to repeat herself. "The cargo hold's for holding cargo."

Then, seeing the look of confusion on Phera's face, understanding dawned behind her dark eyes.

"Ah, sorry. I see what you're getting at now. In between the more exciting jobs like today's, we usually just haul goods for people who can't afford corporate rates or who need something dropped off in a particularly nasty part of B-Sys."

"Wow, really? That's... Surprisingly normal."

"Mmhmm," agreed Straya, ushering her through a hatch and back out into the central corridor of the habitation cylinder. "Gotta keep the lights on in between the big scores somehow."

"Guess that makes sense."

"Plus, it helps keep InterSec off our asses."

"Wait, really?"

Now *that* was a surprise.

"Don't tell me they have a policy of forgiving past crimes for good behavior?"

The taller pirate scoffed at that, but her amusement seemed genuine enough that Phera smiled right along with her.

"Not really, no. But, taking on legitimate work helps keep us from drawing too much attention or getting on the shit list of anyone important. Out of sight, out of mind and all that, yeah?"

"Ahhh, gotcha."

"Uh-huh."

The look on the Straya's face seemed to say she doubted that, but that was just fine with Phera.

It was only her first day, after all.

"Okay, so over here we've got the head, rec room, engineering, and the workshop."

She pointed out each door as they passed them by, and then further along the hall and to their right where two more were set into the wall a few meters apart.

"Over there are Cap's and Lem's state rooms. Don't go poking around there unless you're itching for more of what you got earlier."

Straya let her hand drift down from Phera's shoulder to squeeze her seat with this admonition, making her jump.

"Ah! Threaten me with a good time, why don't you," the auburn-haired engineer laughed around a yelp.

"It's your funeral, newbie. Lem's got the meanest swing on the crew, and the Captain's no slouch either. Don't go biting off more than you can chew."

The pirate's fingernails dug in just a bit harder as she added with a wicked grin.

"Or, if you do, let me know in advance. I wouldn't want to miss the show."

Phera's answering pout did absolutely nothing to diminish Straya's amusement. And, letting go of her bottom, she gestured back toward a pair of doors set into the opposite wall a few meters past the officers' quarters.

"Crew cabins are over there. You can pick your bunk now if you want, or we can head over to the mess. I don't know about you, but I could use a bite."

At the mention of food, Phera's soft stomach rumbled, and it occurred to her that all she'd had to eat so far that day was half a cup of coffee in the Captain's office and a blueberry muffin at breakfast.

"I guess I can pick a bunk later."

Shrugging, she nodded at her current ensemble (or lack thereof).

"It's not like I've got a lot of stuff to move in or anything."

Then, feeling a pleasant flutter in her still rumbly stomach, she added.

"There wouldn't happen to be an open bunk in *your* cabin by any chance, would there?"

She might not have to worry about having anything stolen from her, but it would still be nice to know at least one of the people she'd be sharing a room with.

"Might be."

Straya gave her a wry, sideways look.

"Why do you ask?"

As the engineer's cheeks flushed with fresh color, she led them on to the next pair of doors past the crew cabins and put her hand on the pad by one of them to open it.

"Oh, well, you know…"

Twirling some of the curls at her shoulder around a finger, Phera found herself suddenly much more tongue-tied than she was used to being while talking to an attractive woman. The pickings had been slim back on The Bin (a couple of her coworkers had been pretty cute, but hooking up could lead to all sorts of headaches when it came to securing advancement in the company), and she'd apparently gotten rusty.

"It's nice to have a friend in new places, and I think you and I hit things off pretty well, all things considered."

She smirked at the unintentional double entendre, but decided to roll with it as she gave the taller woman a friendly hip check.

"Some of us more than others. But, hey, I'm not about to hold a grudge."

Doing so with Straya seemed like a dangerous idea anyway.

"I guess we'll just have to wait and see how you feel after you've had to live with me for a while," guffawed the pirate in response to that.

She gave Phera an only sort of joking split-second smirk, the kind she was so good at that made it hard to tell if she was being self-deprecating or making a threat, and then nodded as the door they were standing in front of slid open.

"This is the mess hall, by the way. Don't let the name fool you, though. Cap might be a slob, but make a mess in communal territory and Lem is *not* going to be understanding."

"Wasn't really planning on it," quipped Phera. "But that's still good to know, thanks."

The floor looped up in front of them as Straya led her into one of the hab cylinder's annular segments. Inside, three metal tables with bench seating had been spaced evenly across the floor that gradually became a wall. Someone had also taken it upon themselves to affix a handful of small projectors to the base of the curve, creating several makeshift "windows" that looked out on what had to be live feeds from the Mayhem's exterior.

"Oh, wow…"

Again, it was a surprisingly homey touch for a pirate ship. Plus, they offered a pretty spectacular view for eating your meals by.

"About damn near had a heart attack the first time I saw those things after Kelt put them in," chuckled Straya. "Thought for sure I'd just walked straight into a hull breach."

In addition to the tables, just before the wall cut out of sight behind the spindle that served as the ceiling for the room, there was also an open kitchen island with an induction cooktop, storage drawers, and a small oven. And, a meter beside that, stood a door leading into what Phera assumed had to be food stores and protein recyclers.

All in all, it was a pretty relaxing place to catch a meal after a long, hard day's work of piracy, she decided. And, apparently, she wasn't the only one who thought so too, because there was already someone in there who looked over to them as they marched inside.

"Hi there," Phera waved, deciding to push past her fresh burst of social anxiety and take the lead on introducing herself.

The person had broad shoulders and was about as muscular as Straya (though, perhaps a little shorter), with close-cropped dark hair that showed off a wicked scar tracing along most of the right side of their head. They were currently leaning against the edge of one of the tables, slurping up a mouthful of noodles from a steaming cup they held in one hand. And, given what Straya had just told her about the ship's crew complement, Phera was pretty sure they'd also been one of the people in the welcome party the Captain had arranged for them when they'd first docked.

The holstered coilgun strapped to their thigh definitely looked familiar, at the very least.

"How's the,. uh… noodles?"

Sidling in just a bit closer to Straya as she spoke, Phera pressed the side of her hip against her firm thigh in an unconscious bid for reassurance. The last time she'd seen anyone else from the crew she'd been a captive, and she didn't want them thinking she'd somehow been caught in the middle of an escape attempt.

Rather than raise the alarm, though, this new pirate just looked at her skeptically for a long couple of seconds before directing their attention over to Straya with an open question on their scarred face.

"Adri, this is Phera, our new engine bitch. Phera, this is Adryel, my fellow boarding bitch."

Adryel looked back at her then, and their liquid, dark brown eyes narrowed a little.

"Oh, right. The corp girl."

Phera's lips pursed at the "corp girl" label. Even if that's what she was (well, had been), it still rankled. "Engine bitch" wasn't that much better, but the way Straya said it made her want to forgive her anyway.

Ignoring her visible irritation, Adryel raised a hand and waggled their fingers (the longest of which, Phera noticed with a wince, was missing) at her none too enthusiastically.

"Nice job with those engines."

It wasn't a compliment.

"I like to think I'm fast on my feet when I need to be," she sniffed, deciding that she needed to work on emphasizing her budding pirateness. "It could have gone better, maybe. But, for an on the fly decision, it wasn't bad. It certainly got the job done."

"Uh-huh. Sure."

Phera's facade of confidence cracked beneath the other pirate's deadpan, and what the Captain had said earlier about trying to resell the flyer came rushing back to her all at once, coiling her insides with renewed dread.

"You don't think it'll be too hard to fix, do you?"

"You'd better hope not," answered Adryel, looking grave. "Lem is going to be *pissed* if we have to scrap that thing."

"But, I mean... It wasn't my fault! I-"

Before she could well and truly panic, however, Straya interrupted the two of them by loosing an exasperated sigh.

"Give it a rest would you, Adri?" she said, rolling her eyes at her fellow pirate before turning a half-grin on the shorter woman beside her. "Don't mind them, Phera. They're just pissy because I got to have all the fun today while they were stuck on cleanup duty here."

Adryel snorted into their noodle cup at that.

"You're out of your damn mind if you think for a second I'd let Cap launch my ass at a moving shuttle like the system's most attractive lancer missile."

"Pussy," taunted Straya.

"Psycho," fired back the other raider without missing a beat.

Both of them were grinning now, though. And, despite her annoyance at Adryel's earlier dig at her on the fly wiring work, Phera felt the corners of her mouth starting to pull up ever so slightly as well. Truth be told, she couldn't help but feel a small stirring of kinship with the grumpy enby. There was something about them that made it hard to not want to smile at least a little bit when they weren't being a jerk. And, given their particular choice of pronouns, they'd apparently grown up planetside like she had (the lack of biomodded feet were also a pretty good indicator), so the two of them at least had that in common.

Though, judging by the scars crisscrossing their well-toned forearms and the missing finger, their upbringing appeared to have been a good deal more turbulent than hers had.

"Ahem."

Clearing her throat and turning to cover a fresh stirring of awkwardness, Phera stepped over to the storeroom door and palmed it open in search of something tasty.

"Are there any more noodles?" she called back to Adryel, not quite managing to meet their eye, and instead focusing on the absolutely chiseled obliques dipping down into the distractingly low rise of their cargo pants.

Even without bronze muscles to distract her, there were a *lot* of different foodstuffs and supplies stacked neatly on shelves set into the back wall next to a large refrigeration unit. And, while she was sure there were probably noodles hidden somewhere among the various dry goods she could see, it still seemed like it would probably be better to just ask instead of poking around in unfamiliar places. Especially with the organization system someone clearly had going on in the little storeroom.

"Top shelf," supplied Straya, smiling at the engineer's barely covered hips and buttocks as she bent over to inspect the lower shelves, before then jerking a thumb over to the island almost as an afterthought. "Hot water's on the red nozzle."

"Ah, thanks."

Easing up onto her tiptoes and spying her target, Phera suddenly found herself very much missing null-grav as she planted her feet on the bottommost shelf and hoisted herself up to reach her noodles.

"Well," Adryel spoke up again, slurping their own snack loudly as they too took in their fellow raider's handiwork with a smirk. "Looks like Stray already gave you the talk about what you pulled, at least."

"Wha-? Oh!"

Realizing with a start just how much of a show she was putting on for the two pirates with the way her boyshorts were riding up between her currently eye level, lightly bruised, and still faintly pink cheeks as she groped around half-blind for her food (she'd gotten so used to her current "outfit" that she'd completely forgotten how much skin it showed off), Phera went rigid and very nearly lost her balance on the shelf she was standing on.

"Uh, yeah," she managed to answer dryly after catching herself, face warming to match her hair once again. "She made how she felt pretty clear back on the flyer."

Adryel snickered.

"Seems like she made herself 'pretty clear' about a few dozen times by the looks of things. What'd you use to get those little splotches around her thighs anyway, Stray? Tie-down strap?"

"Vacsuit glove," corrected the other woman with a shrug, as if the two of them were discussing a game they were playing, and not the monumental butt blistering she'd given the new recruit while they'd been waiting for their ride. "The gearhead here decided she wanted to get cute after I already had her bent over, so I got creative instead."

"Hah. Nice."

Letting out an irritated, embarrassed harrumph, Phera threw a venomous glare back over her shoulder at the two pirates, before attempting to cover the move by locking eyes with Straya and nodding back toward the shelf.

"You want anything while I'm up here?"

Straya just shrugged, the engineer's annoyance rolling off of her with ease.

"Sure. I could go for some noodles."

Shotgunning the last of their own soup, Adryel pushed themself up from the table they'd been lounging against and moved to join Phera in the storeroom, tossing their empty cup into the cleaner as they went.

"I'm still kinda hungry. You want me to warm up the rest of that borken?" they called back to Straya, pulling open the door to the refrigerator box and starting to poke around inside for something else to eat.

"Oooh, hell yeah! I forgot we still had that."

"Me too until about half an hour ago. It's going to go bad in a couple more days, so we might as well use it to spice up some soup while we can. There's not enough for a proper crew meal, but it'll make a decent snack, at least."

Bumping the refrigerator closed with a knee, Adryel straightened up and snatched the noodle package Phera had been about to grab.

"Here, I'll make it. Just go wait with Stray, yeah?"

They spoke without looking at her face, but instead eyeing her well-roasted cheeks where they swelled out of her boyshorts.

"I'll be sure to let you know if I need any tomatoes," they added with a wry chuckle. "Though, by the looks of things, these ones are already bruised."

The pirate's smug amusement and Straya's snort of laughter instantly shifted Phera's mood from mildly annoyed to properly miffed.

"Gee, thanks," she grumbled, grabbing another noodle package and tossing it at them with maybe a bit more force than was strictly necessary. "Here's an extra."

Distracted as they were with her elevated hips, it caught Adryel completely unaware. Bouncing off their stubbly head and onto the shelf in front of them, making them yelp in a decidedly un-piratey way.

"Oops."

Hopping down from the shelves, Phera turned to go with a very satisfied smirk on her lips, fully intending on swaggering her way out of the little storeroom with every ounce of smug self-confidence she could muster.

"Sorry."

At least, that had been the plan up until she made the mistake of looking back for one last bit of gloating.

"FFFF-"

Rounding on her with a look of furious disbelief, Phera blanched at the thin trickle of blood dribbling down from a small cut just above Adryel's left eyebrow.

"What the hell, kid?!"

Immediately, her badass pirate swagger wilted under the heat of the *actual* pirate's glare.

"Oh gods, are you all right?" she gasped, caught in the door frame of the storeroom and torn between whether she should try and find some sort of rag, or just flee for cover behind Straya's reassuring bulk.

"Yeah, I'm just *peachy*."

Adryel's left hand (the one with all its fingers still) shot out and seized a fistful of her sports bra then, yanking her in close.

"What in the ever-loving fuck-?" they started to demand, face contorting in a rage that sent a comet of ice punching through Phera's insides, before being cut off just as quickly by a sharp reprimand from Straya.

"Hands off, Adri," she ordered, voice firm and eyes flinty as she stepped in between the two of them and shouldered Phera back a step. "She's my responsibility just now, not yours."

"But she-!"

Pinching the bridge of her nose and holding up a hand to forestall the other raider's tirade, Straya let out a long, exasperated sigh.

"Look. I know. You can have one of my cupcakes once we're finished, all right?"

"Fine, fine..."

Adryel heaved out a sigh of their own then, blowing away the rest of their fury with it.

"You drive a hard bargain, Stray. But, I think I can live with that."

Straya's lips twitched ever so slightly.

"Thought you might be able to."

Phera herself was just starting to relax as well, knees still a little shaky from her almost fight with the bigger pirate, when Straya turned back to her and grabbed a thick handful of copper curls.

"Ow! Hey!"

"Right then," she continued, completely ignoring her cries of discomfort as she started dragging her back out into the mess hall proper. "You cook the noodles, and I'll cook the brat."

"Works for me," chuckled Adryel, vindictive mirth loosening their scowling features into a grim smile.

"Fuck! Ow! Come on, Straya, that was an accident! It just slipped out of my hand is all."

Half bent over and scurrying to keep up with the taller woman's long, purposeful strides, Phera's mouth continued to move on autopilot as adrenaline-fueled panic spiked inside of her.

"Besides, it's not *my* fault they weren't paying attention! Aren't you all supposed to be good with reaction times and stuff?"

Looking back to Adryel over the struggling engineer, Straya cocked an eyebrow in silent question, receiving a very firm shake of their head in response. Not that she really need have bothered. An accidentally knocked over package of noodles wasn't going to bloody someone's face.

"Have you seriously not gotten any better at excuses since you were six?" she scoffed, almost laughing at the sheer brazen silliness of Phera's protest.

"Um... Yes?"

"Well then, I guess it's a good thing for you we don't plan on getting caught, huh?"

Adryel snorted.

"No kidding."

Jerking Phera past the island and over to the nearest table, Straya shoved her face first across it with great force and very little grace.

"Oof!"

The protests that she could be plenty sneaky when she felt like it were knocked right out of the plump engineer as her stomach and breasts came into rough contact with the metallic table in front of her. The thin material of her bra did absolutely nothing to shield her sensitive (and frustratingly erect) nipples from its cold, smooth surface. And, as she felt her waistband start to draw back from her cheeks, she found herself flabbergasted that Straya was about to spank her for a *third* time that day.

"Look, I said I was sorry!" she blurted out in a rush, only to realize half a heartbeat later that she hadn't actually. "Er, I mean- I'm sorry, Adryel!"

Pushing up onto her tiptoes in a desperate attempt to keep her boyshorts right where they were, she threw a pleading look back at Straya.

"Isn't there, like, some sort of conflict resolution exercise we can do instead?"

She doubted these pirates had an HR department, but it was still worth a shot.

"Sure is," said Straya as she tore her panties down past her already swollen cheeks. "This is it."

"Mmhmm," agreed Adryel.

They'd emerged from the storeroom by now, and were in the process of filling a pot with water as they watched. Dish towel pressed to their forehead, and mood already greatly improved.

"And *you*," continued Straya with a growl that would've almost sounded playful if it weren't for the steel of her grip pinning Phera to the table. "Are seriously starting to wear out my arm!"

With another hard yank, she finished dragging the boyshorts down past her thighs (stretching out the already overtaxed material even further and popping several stitches in the waistband in the process), and immediately landed one of her by now familiar full-armed, cupped-palmed swats directly against the center of the engineer's right cheek.

SMACK!

"Ack!"

Before adding another just below it, right on her bruised sit-spot.

SMACK!

"Owie!"

Her attention then shifted to Phera's left cheek, and her swatting started to pick up speed.

SMACK! SMACK! SMACK!

"No-! Ow! I'm sorry- Ow!"

Though the sensation of Straya's rough palm meteor-striking her bare ass was no longer new to Phera, that didn't make it any less painful. The tall raider had done an exceptionally good job spanking her back on the flyer. And, even if she were getting tired now, Phera's pre-tenderized and lightly bruised skin was more than making up the difference for her.

SMACK! SMACK! SMACK!

And then some.

"Ack! Ow! SHIT!"

As Straya's palm drifted back to her right cheek, making it compress and jiggle just as impressively as the left one had, Phera's dancing feet began shifting her sideways in an attempt to escape the other woman's wrath.

"If your- Ow! If your arm hurts so much- Ack! Then give it a rest!" she half-demanded, half-begged, managing to twist her hips around to put the her bottom against the rounded-over edge of the table.

Which also gave the two pirates an unobstructed view between her parted and trembling thighs in the process as her poor, abused panties slipped further down to her ankles.

"You're not even the one I was throwing stuff at!" she added indignantly, glaring so hard at Straya that it made the other woman smile.

Truth be told, she didn't want Adryel to be spanking her either. Not with arms like those. But, with her bottom throbbing like it was just then, she was willing to pursue any tactic that might save her seat from another Straya sizzling.

"You know, Stray, she's got a point there," agreed the enby as they poured borken shreds into the boiling water. "You really should go easy on that arm."

With a broad grin, Adryel picked up a long-handled, metallic spatula from next to the stove and tossed it through the air. It spun four times as their practiced aim compensated for the diagonal pull of the hab cylinder's artificial grav, and smacked right into the open palm of Straya's outstretched right hand.

"You're just the sweetest thing, Adri," she crooned, shoving Phera back onto her stomach as she swished the lethally taut and shiny spatula behind her. "You're still only getting the one cupcake, though."

"Yeah. Just *so* sweet," gritted Phera, cheeks clenching and feet shifting, further tangling her boyshorts around the hard angles of her clunky magboots. "Thanks a lot. Seriously."

"Any time, newbie."

Heaving out a shaky breath, Phera adjusted her stance to something slightly more stable and looked back to Straya with a hopeful expression.

"I don't suppose you and I could make a deal by any chance?"

That spatula looked like it was a lot lighter than the other woman's vacsuit glove had been, but her engineering background had her painfully aware of just how much force the business end attached to that long, flexible handle would be able to strike with.

"Make it quick."

Straya gave the spatula a flourish and then pressed it into Phera's left buttock, delighting in the sight of the red and mottled skin bulging out between its slats.

"Well, uh... L-Let's see..."

Those damn slats were making it surprisingly difficult for Phera to focus, and the sensation of them rasping along her bottom was sending little ripples of pleasure directly between her legs.

Focus!

"I could, uh... Give you a back rub? Your shoulders are probably pretty sore by now, yeah?"

Phera threw a petulant harrumph over at the thoroughly amused Adryel and added.

"Shouldn't you be making sure nothing is burning?"

"Shouldn't you?" they shot back with an undisguised grin.

Straya, meanwhile, seemed to actually be considering her offer.

"Damn. A back rub *does* sound pretty nice..." she admitted with a tired huff.

"Right?" agreed Phera, pressing her advantage, only to be cut off by Adryel as they off-handedly shook out two different seasonings into the simmering soup without looking.

"I've got your back, Stray. Don't sweat it."

"What? No! But that's-!"

"Sorry, sweet cheeks."

Shrugging, Straya pressed the spatula down a little harder

"You've been outbid."

Then, with a fluid grace belied by her heavily muscled frame, she raised the spatula up past her shoulder and brought it sailing back down again in a smooth arc that exploded against the middle of the pinned pirate recruit's already throbbing right cheek.

SWISH-THWAP!

"Aieee!"

With lots of good, quality atmo inside the Mayhem, Phera's high-pitched howl was able to travel far and wide as both her feet left the floor in a literal jump of surprise and pain. The spatula's lack of kevlar and teflon might've made it lighter, but that just meant Straya was able to send it crashing down even faster.

Fucking Newton, you godsdamn asshole! she growled to herself as she rasped in a frantic breath through clenched teeth, fighting back a sudden sob.

She was pretty sure she'd been able to feel every single individual slat of that stupid spatula as it had bitten into her. And, had she been able to see her own backside just then, she'd have to agree that it had left behind a rather impressive triple-line welt.

The kind that just *begged* for another.

SWISH-THWAP!

"Ah! Ah! FUCK!"

Straya and Adryel, meanwhile, had no such problem, and were able to openly admire the taller woman's handiwork.

SWISH-THWAP!

"Strayaaaa!"

And, of course, the oh-so-abundant jiggle of Phera's extremely well-endowed bottom.

"Okay, yeah, this is pretty great."

The spatula whistled down again against Phera's left cheek this time.

SWISH-THWAP!

"Ah! Please!"

Then again, right on the exact same spot.

SWISH-THWAP!

"This is-! Ack!"

Then higher.

SWISH-THWAP!

"*So* mean!"

Then back down on the exact same spot once again, air hissing evilly through its slats as it cut through like the sword of an avenging goddess.

SWISH-THWAP!

"Aieee!"

"Don't care."

Grinning from ear to ear, Phera's howling apparently having helped her catch her second wind, Straya repeated the process on the engineer's right cheek this time.

SWISH-THWAP! SWISH-THWAP! SWISH-THWAP! SWISH-THWAP!

"Ack! Ah! Owie! Ouch!"

Before transitioning into a high-speed, random assault on both of her bruised, swollen sit-spots and upper thighs.

THWAP! THWAP! THWAP! THWAP! THWAP!

Straya had a lot of area to work with, and seemed dead set on making sure every square centimeter of Phera's broad hips and thick thighs got at least a taste (or six) of the spatula. Imprinting bright white slat patterns that swelled into puffy red welts with slightly bruised edges all up and down their length, ensuring that the newly minted pirate would forever associate spatulas and noodles with not being able to sit down for a long, *long* time to come.

THWAP! THWAP! THWAP! THWAP! THWAP!

The muted, metallic report of the shiny spatula echoed off the hard walls and curving ceiling of the mess hall, mingling in vicious harmony with Phera's ever increasingly frantic yelps and cries. Straya clearly wasn't holding back in the slightest despite having already spanked her twice that day. Which, given what she'd done to deserve this particular punishment, Phera couldn't really blame her for.

"Oh my gods, Adri, I'm sorryyyyy!" she sobbed into the hands she'd buried her face in, thoroughly spent, red-eyed, and above all else, prepared to do just about anything her crewmates told her to as she writhed beneath the implacable gravity well that was Straya's hand bearing down on the small of her back.

It really had been a jerk move to throw those noodles at them. They'd just been tired and a little grumpy, and she'd totally overreacted.

"Eh, I'd say you're *almost* sorry," corrected the enby from their post in front of their bubbling pot.

Well, amended Phera to herself as she looked back and noted through bleary, tear-streaked eyes the way they were grinning as they took in the sight of her wriggling carmine ass and thighs appreciatively. *It had been a jerk move to throw them quite so **hard**. Humph.*

At least it was just the three of them in the mess hall. Having a bigger audience just then would have been...

Well.

Phera's thighs shifted together beneath her, confirming for her that the corners of her eyes weren't the only things that were wet just then.

Yeah. At least it was just the three of them.

THWAP! THWAP! THWAP! THWAP! THWAP!

When Phera's cheeks were at last a many-layered patchwork of grid lines and rectangles from crown to crease, Straya's swatting began to gradually slow before coming to a halt.

"Yep. I think you're just about sorry now," she declared, allowing the engineer several long moments to attempt to collect herself while she admired the view.

"Gods, I sure fucking hope so," sniffled Phera, dragging a forearm across her watery eyes and laughing shakily.

SWISH-THWAP!

"Watch it..."

"Ah! Yes ma'am!"

"Hah! Ma'am. Right," snickered Adryel.

"Hey, if Cap can be a ma'am, then so can I," protested Straya, feigning indignation as she set the spatula aside and began massaging her forearm. She'd apparently not gone quite as light as she probably should have, and her arm seemed like it really was killing her now.

Well, at least she had a massage coming after they were finished eating.

She rolled her shoulders and popped her neck, and then took another assessing look at the puffy purple cushions bent over the edge of the table beside her (swollen even larger than they had been before), along with their whimpering owner and her glistening cheeks.

Oh yes. The look on Straya's face made it abundantly clear that any amount of muscle pain she was experiencing just then was more than worth it.

Phera was absolutely toast.

"Done cooking?" she asked Adryel, looking back to them with a wink.

"Not as well done as your own little recipe, I'd say. But, yep. Bringing it over now."

They were grinning from ear to scarred ear, the pain from their no longer bleeding eyebrow seemingly forgotten, as they carried the borken noodle soup over to the table Phera was still sprawled across.

"Oh gods..." she groaned.

A pleasant aroma chased through the air ahead of them, barging its way in past her clogged sinuses and drawing her slowly back onto an unsteady pair of legs.

"That smells *amazing*."

Her panties were still tangled around her ankles. They'd been stretched all to hell between her magboots while she'd been thrashing and kicking, but she was sure they were probably (hopefully) still fine. Either way, she was way too sore, tired, and hungry to actually care just then. And so, after making a brief attempt to bend over and pull them back up, which just resulted in her taut and tender skin being pulled and compressed enough to touch off a fresh wave of agony in her spatula marks, she decided they were fine right where they were for the time being.

It wasn't like either pirate hadn't already gotten several dozen good looks at her nakedness. And, really, food was much more important than preserving the literal scraps of her remaining modesty.

"Thanks for cooking, Adri."

"You are more than welcome," Adryel chuckled at her, managing to juggle the steaming pot along with three bowls and a handful of spoons as they nodded toward the table. "Stray, I need some room. Also, top marks on the attitude adjustment."

"I do what I can."

Had her attitude not been so thoroughly adjusted, Adryel's quip about it would have no doubt drawn some sort of snappy comeback from Phera. But, Straya was nothing if not thorough, and she wisely chose to keep her mouth shut.

"And, yeah. Sorry about this one."

With a low, dark chuckle of her own, the taller woman steered her away from the table by her shoulders. Thanks to all her earlier squirming, the exhausted engineer's top had slipped off of one shoulder, leaving her left breast hanging out almost entirely. She hadn't actually noticed this yet, though, preoccupied as she was with her throbbing bottom and the other raider's delicious smelling food. Straya nevertheless decided to take pity on her and adjusted the strap for her as her lips drew back in a wickedly self-satisfied grin.

"Let's sit down, shall we?"

Giving Phera's swollen, purple-gridded bottom a firm pat that made the younger woman hiss adorably, she plopped herself onto the bench opposite where Adryel was settling in and drew Phera down onto her lap. Making her roasted, puffy bottom cheeks flatten and smoosh out across her muscular thighs. Drawing out a fresh yelp from her new lap warmer in the process.

"Ah, geez!" Phera laughed despite the sudden surge of pain, attempting to assume as dignified a position as she could with her feet several centimeters off the floor and her panties tangled around her ankles. "Uh, thanks, I guess…"

Well, on the bright side, at least she didn't have to endure the raised ridges of the bench. That, and Straya had opted for sweatpants instead of something with lots of thick stitching and buttons like Adryel had. Her well-toned thighs felt like they were made of warm tungsten just then, though.

Actually, it was kind of nice now that new marks weren't being piled on top of her already existing collection.

Painful? Yes.

Tender? Absolutely.

But, also nice.

So, she didn't let herself grumble as she leaned forward to ladle soup into her and Straya's bowls before drawing them toward her and offering one to the other woman.

"Here you go."

This evoked simultaneous "awww"s from both pirates, Adryel's sour attitude in particular seeming to have been effected even more than Phera's had.

"Thanks, sweet cheeks."

Taking up her bowl, Straya passed the sniffling woman on her lap a spoon. Then, with that taken care of, her free hand settled back down along the gentle curve of Phera's hip, giving it a surprisingly affectionate squeeze as she did so.

"Now, I don't know about you two, but I am fucking starved."

"Gods, me too."

"Fuck yeah, let's eat!"

CHAPTER SIX

Though sitting through it was anything but comfortable, Phera couldn't deny that the meal she shared with the two pirates was an enjoyable one.

Adryel and Straya's wry, genially combative back and forth was a lot of fun to listen to, even if she could only participate in it occasionally. In a lot of ways, it reminded her of the cantina chitchat she'd overheard while she'd been on The Bin. Albeit far less guarded, and neither of them seemed like they were angling to screw the other over for a promotion. Plus, she'd already found out firsthand that the dangerous swagger the two of them carried themselves with was entirely genuine, as opposed to the posturing all the station sec staff Panorama had hired liked to affect, which made them all the more exciting to be around.

If perhaps just a *bit* scary.

As it turned out, Adryel wasn't just a raider, but also the crew's cook. Or, as they put it, "I like to think of myself as a cook who *happens* to be a raider, rather than the other way around. I got my fill of the violent shit back on Senacan."

They held up their heavily scarred right hand then and wiggled the stump of their missing middle finger, making Phera grimace.

"Uh... Senacan?" she asked, eyes wide as she tried to picture what sort of life or death scenario could push a pirate into semi-retirement. "Where's that?"

"Oh, just a little hab out Proxward."

Adryel winked.

"You wouldn't have heard of it."

"Uh-huh," deadpanned Straya. "You are so full of shit, Adri."

Which prompted the crew cook to press the hand with the missing finger to their chest in mock-outrage.

"You wound me, *ma'am*!"

"Not likely."

Leaning in to prop her chin atop Phera's curls, Straya's lips curved up in a malicious grin.

"Senacan is a bar back on Marcos that we got into a brawl at a few months back," she explained. "Don't let the missing finger fool you, kid. Adri here's got some of the best blade work I've ever seen, and they're more than happy to put it to use whenever the Captain says."

"Awww, love you too, cupcake."

The kiss Adryel blew Straya managed to draw out a giggle from Phera, earning her a pinch beneath the table from the bigger woman for her trouble.

"Speaking of brawls, though," they went on, showing off just how dexterous they could be as they twirled their spoon back and forth between their fingers while their fellow raider found a comfortable spot to stroke along the inside of Phera's left thigh. "This one time, Cap sent Stray and I out with Lem for a meetup on some shady as fuck hab in the middle of nowhere, and there were these..."

Beyond being someone that Phera absolutely never wanted to be on the wrong side of during a fight, she also quickly learned that Adryel had no small supply of funny (though often harrowing and annoyingly cheek-clenching) stories to share about past raids and other misadventures the crew had gotten up to over the years. And, as she drained the last of her broth and scraped the few straggler noodles and bits of meat into her mouth with the edge of her spoon while they took her through a play-by-play reenactment of the time the Mayhem had almost gotten boarded by InterSec, Phera could honestly say that she liked both of her new crewmates very much.

She just hoped the feeling was mutual.

"I don't know what asshole was feeding them their intel, but somehow those idiots hit the docking berth *next* to ours, and we were able to hightail it out of there before they realized they'd fucked up."

"Blew out the port side power coupler doing it, though," added Straya with a wicked chuckle. "Pretty sure Kelt had Shi making the entire return trip to Marcos standing up."

"Wait, the *entire* trip?" pressed Phera, feeling her own cheeks tingle in sympathy for the pilot.

"Six and a half days straight," nodded Adryel. "Kelt was *pissed.*"

"Made breakfast lots of fun, though. That lady is real mean when she hasn't had her coffee yet."

"I know! That was great."

"Seriously."

"Ugh. Speaking of not being able to sit down," interjected Phera, throwing in the towel on her attempts at stoicism as she adjusted her position on Straya's lap in a futile attempt to get more comfortable. "Are there any ice packs around here I can borrow?"

Setting her bowl back down on the table in front of her, she pushed her lips out into a pout.

"Maybe like six of them? And about thirty pillows to sit on while they do their work? I'm pretty sure my ass and thighs are one big bruise right now."

Adryel cut loose with a booming laugh at that, while Straya just snickered a little. Neither of them sounded particularly sympathetic.

"The freezer's right back there," they said, gesturing toward the storeroom. "You're gonna have to find your own ice, though. I've learned better than to show you around the pantry."

"Humph. Baby."

"That's some pretty big talk coming from the girl who'd been bawling her pretty little eyes out just a bit ago. Are you sure you wanna start-?"

"So..."

Straya's voice grew a few degrees more serious as she spoke over whatever witty rejoinder Adryel had been about to fire back at Phera with.

"That reminds me, Phera. I told Cap I'd bring you by to see the crew doc for screening as soon as we weren't starving. Steph should be in the medbay right now, and if not I'll go drag ver out of the rec room. Either way, ve'll probably be able to give you something better than ice."

"Oh crap, that's right! Orientation. I'd completely forgotten that's what we were doing."

Moving to get up, the hearty meal warming her stomach and the prospect of something to help her aching bottom granting her a fresh burst of energy, Phera discovered that she was trapped. The table they were all sitting at was bolted to the deck, along with the benches. (Nobody wanted heavy furniture flying around if their pilot had to start pulling serious accel, after all.) And, perched as she was on top of Straya's lap, she was more or less pinned between the pirate's thick, muscular thighs and the bottom of the table.

Which meant that she was going to have to work extra hard to get herself back on her feet.

"Oh gods dammit…"

Squirming around, Phera fought to extricate her magboots out from under the table and onto the bench beside her.

"Sorry, Straya, I'll be out of your way in just a sec."

"Grind away, sweet cheeks. It's been way too long since I had a good lap dance."

"Oh hah-hah."

Harrumphing, Phera redoubled her wiggling efforts while Adryel snorted out another laugh and waved toward the exit of the mess hall.

"Be sure to tell Steph hi for me when you get there."

There was something in their expression as they spoke. Some coy, suppressed gloating quality that Phera couldn't quite put her finger on. As if they were in on a joke she wasn't. But, just then loaded smirks from the crew cook were the least of her worries as she rasped her bare cheeks against the bench's cold, unforgiving raised edges, hissing and moaning as her hands balled themselves into fists to either side of her.

"I'll walk her over," Straya volunteered once she'd finally managed to regain her feet, easing up after her and casting a significant glance at the shorter woman's ankles. "You should probably pick on or off for those, by the way."

Following her gaze down to her tangled boyshorts with an air of exasperated disgust, Phera let out an explosive huff that devolved into a groan.

"They were hard enough to get back on the last time," she complained, hating the whining edge that crept its way into her tone. "Pretty sure they're not going to fit at all now. Plus, they're kind of the only ones I have left. They could probably use a break from being stretched to the breaking point."

"It's your call," shrugged Straya. "Either way works for me."

"Ditto," added Adryel with a friendly leer.

"Gee, thanks. Really."

Face blossoming into a blush almost as red as her hair, Phera shuffled around to the head of the table and leaned against it for support as she bent down and raised her feet one at a time in as dignified an attempt to slip off her panties as she could. Only problem was, her magboots were way too bulky to let that happen without one hell of a fight that she just didn't have the energy for right then.

"Ugh! Damn it..."

"Problem?" prompted Straya, hands on her hips as she took in her struggle.

"No, no, it's fine."

Waving her off with false-levity, Phera gave up on her original plan and instead leaned further down to unlatch her boots so that she could slip her feet free of them and her panties all at once without accidentally face-planting into either of her new coworkers.

"Just, uh... Give me a sec."

"You keep waving that thing at me like that, and I might just have to keep you bent over for a bit longer," warned Straya with a sinister smile, reaching out and helping to steady her with a hand on the small of her back.

"No thanks!"

As Phera stretched and struggled to reach the release latches at her ankles, she could feel her plump and plum-shaded cheeks naturally starting to part. Showing off more than a hint of the puckered opening and swollen labia that lay hidden between, and causing the warmth in her face to climb all the way up to the roots of her hair as a phantom current of climate-controlled air caressed along her parted crevice.

"I know there's a pirate booty joke to be made here," she attempted to deadpan as her stomach lurched with fresh embarrassment. "And you both have my sincerest thanks for restraining yourselves."

Adryel's grin turned slightly wolfish with that, their scars lending the look an extra hint of danger that sent a not altogether unpleasant shiver down Phera's spine as she met the cook's upside down gaze between her knees.

"Oh, I can think of a few different spots I wouldn't mind marking X on, if you know what I mean."

"Looks like she's got plenty of those already," grinned Straya, poking mercilessly at a particularly vivid crisscrossing of welts.

"C-Cute."

"Right back at ya, Red."

Adryel cocked a brow at Phera then.

"Or should I call you Purple?"

"Neither if you don't mind, actually," she huffed in return, straightening back up and dragging her hair into a loose ponytail that sprang free as soon as she let it go. "All the station sec assholes back on The Bin used to call me red, and I fucking hated it."

"All right, all right. Fair enough."

The crew cook raised their hands in mild surrender before winking again.

"Sweet cheeks."

"Heh. That, uh…"

Sparing a moment to tuck some of her loose curls behind one sizzling ear, Phera's gaze fell back to the abandoned clothes on the deck in front of her.

"That works."

Still blushing, she hurriedly scooped up her boyshorts and boots. Then, using them to shield her naked front, looked from Straya, to Adryel, and back again.

"It's not *too* far, yeah?"

"Not too far for what?" asked Adryel, looking impish.

"It's just back up the spindle," Straya answered for them, echoing the other pirate's smirk as she laid a hand on the small of Phera's back and began steering her new favorite shipboard diversion back out into the hall. "Also, don't worry, you'll get tired of booty jokes about an hour after we dock with the next civ port, trust me. Now, come on."

"Remember to say hi to Steph for me," Adryel called after them, watching Phera's thoroughly swollen cheeks roll and heave behind her like they had their own tidal forces as Straya ushered her away. "Oh, and I'll be back in the cabin whenever you're ready, Stray."

Looking back over her shoulder, Straya's tired smile grew just a bit brighter.

"Great. I'll see you there."

"Bye Adri," added Phera, waving. "Thanks again for the meal."

—

Padding along on bare feet through the hab cylinder's inner spindle was *so* much easier than having to clomp around in magboots, Phera found. Which was good, since she was doing her absolute best to strike an inconspicuous balance between outright sprinting and moving as silently as possible on her tiptoes as Straya led her back toward the Captain's office and docking access.

Please don't let her see, please don't let her see, please don't let her see…

By some small miracle, they managed to reach the medbay without incident. And, shifting her grip on her boots and boyshorts to hold them in one hand, Phera reached up, cleared her throat, and gave the heavy, metal door three hard knocks with the side of her fist.

Straya, for her part, just rolled her eyes and put her hand on the pad next to the door. Making it swish open to reveal yet another pirate sitting at a desk with one foot crossed over a knee and their eyes glued to a slate.

"Hey, hey, don't just go barging in here!" ve started to protest before looking up and seeing who it was who'd interrupted ver and immediately changing ver tune. "Oooh, you're the new girl?"

Setting aside ver slate, ve sprang to ver feet and rushed over to greet them properly.

"I was just about to go looking for you. Come in! Come in!"

Steph was the first crew member so far that didn't have at least half a dozen centimeters on Phera. In fact, ve was just a little under her height, with a thin, wiry build and a dark blonde pixie cut accentuated by shiny silver earrings. Well, that, and a giant, almost too wide grin on ver narrow face.

"Love the outfit, by the way."

"Heh. Thanks."

Despite the enthusiastic frankness with which the slender doctor took in her near total lack of clothing, Steph was just too bubbly to be annoyed at.

"I'm Phera, by the way. It's nice to meet you."

Dipping her chin in an abbreviated but respectful spacer's bow (Steph had the same biomodded feet as Straya and the Captain, so it seemed like a safe bet for making a good first impression), she crossed the medbay threshold and adjusted one of the straps on her bra so that it framed her generous chest slightly more evenly.

"Oh, and before I forget, I'm supposed to tell you that Adri says hi. So, uh, 'hi'."

"Um…"

Steph cocked her head to the side and blinked at her, apparently not quite following.

"Tell them hi back? I think?"

"She's all yours," Straya said, saving Phera from further digging her foot into her mouth as she winked at Steph over her shoulder. "Take good care of her, yeah?"

She then gave the engineer a friendly pat, and added.

"Behave now."

Before turning and swishing her way out of the room, leaving Phera alone with the crew doc.

"So, you're our new sort of engineer, right?" Steph asked. "Like, I mean, you're a roboticist, I think they said?"

"That's right!"

Looking back from where she'd been mockingly mouthing "behave now" to the closed door (there was no way she was going to risk being that brazenly bratty while Straya was still within earshot), Phera met the shorter enby's biomodded mother of pearl gaze with her own altered violet one.

"I'm not really sure what my official job title is yet," she admitted with a bashful smile. "The Captain sort of sprung this whole change of employment thing on me out of the blue. But, yeah, my PhD is in robotics. Specifically systems development, though I'm pretty capable when it comes to the mechanical engineering side of things as well."

"Oh wow, another PhD? Yay!"

Beaming revealed a pair of dimples on Steph's face that gave it a distinct edge of mischief Phera immediately took a liking to as she watched the doctor clap excitedly.

"I was a coroner before joining the Blazar Bitches, but I'm pretty good at working on people who are still alive too. So!"

Absolutely overflowing with effervescent energy, ve bounced up onto ver low-grav elongated tiptoes.

"The Captain ordered a full physical, *and* blood and tissue tests!"

"Works for me," replied a slightly bemused Phera. "Just tell me what you need me to do."

"For starters, you can finish getting undressed. I'd offer you a gown, but, well..."

Steph's grin took on a slightly embarrassed bend to it.

"I sort of ran out after the whole bone wasp incident."

"Um... Bone wasps?"

A twinge of worry coiled its way around Phera's insides at that, and her bottom gave an involuntary clench.

"Oh yeah. You should've seen it!" giggled Steph, ver bright mood not diminished in the slighted by the engineer's obvious discomfort. "Lem was soooo mad, it was amazing. It wasn't that bad, though. Adri and Stray got to have target practice, and in the end we all learned a valuable lesson about the importance of pre-screening shady cargo *before* we take it on board."

Ve swiveled to look at a terrarium next to a clear-doored storage cabinet then, sighing wistfully.

"And *I* got a cute new pet."

"Sounds like a blast," snickered Phera, very glad that she'd missed that particular bit of fun, before going rigid as she did a double-take at the terrarium. "Wait, pet?"

Squinting, she saw with a stab of panic that it housed what appeared to be a half-meter long larva that was 90% wriggling, pointy legs and whip-like feelers.

"Wh-What kind of pet?"

"Bone wasp larva," answered Steph with an easy shrug. "Don't worry. Cap won't let me give it access to all the nutrients it needs to reach maturity, so it's perfectly harmless. Well, harmless unless you're ticklish. Ve likes to climb around on people."

"I, uh… I see."

Looking from the love-struck doctor to the captive larva, Phera supposed she could see a sort of exotic charm to it. The lack of wings, armor-piercing stinger, and small-arms repelling carapace sure helped a lot.

"Cool, cool, cool," nodded Steph absently before jerking out of whatever winding trail ver thoughts had started to wander down and turning back to her, all business. "Now, like I said, we don't have any more gowns. So…"

Ve made a twirling gesture with one of ver fingers.

"Ditch the bra and we can get started."

"Can do."

Glancing down at her grimy sports bra and much less grimy torso, Phera winced and set her boots and boyshorts aside and started to peel it up. Gods, did it ever feel good to get the damn thing off. She would've probably agreed to let Straya take her vacsuit glove to her ass right there and then all over again if it meant she'd be able to get her hands on a fresh change of clothes.

Mmph.

In response to that mental image, Phera's bottom gave an unpleasant twinge.

Or… Maybe not. Let's come back to that in a week. Maybe two.

Even so, the thought of the tall raider and her heavy, calloused hands with their long, confident fingers sent a momentary tremble through the engineer, and her thick thighs pressed themselves together as she broke out in goosebumps.

"Say, uh, Doctor…?"

Trailing off, Phera realized that she didn't actually know Steph's surname. She wanted to phrase her request for help with her backside in as respectful a way as possible, so she paused with her bra still in hand and turned the last word of her lapsed sentence into a question that would hopefully convey just how seriously she took the enby's role on the crew.

"Just Steph is fine. I'm not all formal like the Captain."

Ve tore ver gaze away from where ve'd been unashamedly appraising her newly exposed breasts and their erect, peach-colored nipples, and met her eye.

"Yeah?"

Relaxing somewhat, Phera let the still warm bit of elastic and microcotton drop onto her boots beside her. But, with nothing left to occupy her hands, it suddenly dawned on her that she was completely naked in front of a total stranger. And, though Steph was a professional and surely would've given her a gown if ve'd had any (and she'd basically shown Straya and Adryel just as much already), she still couldn't stop one arm from rising up to cover her chest while the other slipped between her thighs as she turned to angle her wide hips toward the crew doc.

"I, uh… Don't know if you can tell," she began, doing her best to level a wry smile at ver over her shoulder. "But I've kinda gotten on Straya's bad side a couple times today, and I could really use a hand with, you know…"

She blew out a bashful exhalation and dipped her chin toward her very, *very* well-spanked backside.

"All this," she finished lamely. "If you don't mind, that is."

Steph's blonde eyebrows shot up as ve properly took in Phera's swollen seat for the first time, almost disappearing into ver hairline as ve let out an impressed whistle.

"*Wow.*"

Stepping in closer, ve crouched down right behind her to inspect the injured area.

"Your ass is *huge.*"

"Ugh, I know," moaned Phera, stomping a foot for added emphasis and making her chest and cheeks jiggle in a way that had Steph's biomodded eyes going wide as ve licked ver lips. "That lady doesn't hold back when she decides she's going to make a point, does she?"

"Hah! Well, I meant more like in general," teased Steph, reaching out and giving her right cheek an exploratory squeeze. "Like, obviously you've got a lot of inflammation going on back here, but you had plenty for the blood flow to work with."

This time, Phera let herself pout to her heart's content. Though, she had to admit, the crew doc's small hand felt surprisingly nice.

"Do you think you can help?" she pleaded. "I can't get my panties back on, and it hurts just *thinking* about sitting down right now."

"Hmmm…"

Letting out a musing hum, Steph's other hand found purchase on Phera's left cheek and ve gave them a thoughtful wobble, followed by a firm squeeze as ve pulled them apart to expose her anus.

"Eep!"

Making the auburn-haired engineer squeak a full octave higher than she'd just been speaking.

"Topical anti-inflammatory ought to take care of most of this," ve murmured, grip tightening to prevent her from getting away. "Don't think Stray would be too happy with me if I gave you a painkiller, but I can at least get the swelling to go down."

Giggling, ve let her go with a firm pat to both cheeks.

"I'll bet those panties look great on you. So, yeah. I'd like to see them back on before someone eventually takes them down again."

Bouncing back to ver feet, ve pointed toward a lightly padded exam table with an antibacterial flash cleaner embedded into its sturdy base.

"Lay on the cot and we'll get started."

"Sure thing!"

Moving with a renewed spring in her step at the doctor's forthright compliments, Phera strode over to where ve'd indicated. She loved her wide hips and heavy breasts, and knew she looked damn good in a pair of boyshorts.

Still, it was nice to be appreciated.

Reaching the table, she turned to plop down onto it, and just barely managed to catch herself right as her hips were about to make contact. Casually dropping all of her weight onto her ass just then would *definitely* be a bad idea.

"Heh."

Smirking in self-deprecation, Phera turned and crawled stiffly up onto her hands and knees on top of the exam table (well, it was really more of a cot like Steph had said, but it was hard to change the vocabulary in her head) before easing down onto her stomach and turning her head to look at the enby.

"You know, Straya doesn't *have* to know if you give me some painkiller," she wheedled, watching ver shrug into a white lab coat as ve sauntered toward her. "I promise I won't tell if you don't. Besides, I'm pretty sure she'll make up the difference sooner or later."

She made a show of grimacing.

"And then some."

SLAP!

"Ah!"

The doctor's little hand wasn't all that strong, but it was snappy and bony. And, delivered as it was with great speed and zero warning to the interior side of Phera's very swollen left buttock, it was more than up to the task of wringing out another high-pitched yelp from her.

"That's enough of that," ve admonished, though without dropping ver smile. "People around here tend know things, trust me."

Spine arched and bare breasts wobbling from her impromptu push up, Phera looked back to the grinning doctor with a much more genuine pout this time.

"If you say so," she harrumphed, collapsing back onto the cot with her forearms folded in front of her. "You'd think doctor-patient confidentiality would cover that kind of thing, but noooo."

"Oh please. If I cared about the rules, I'd be on another ship," snorted Steph, wriggling ver hands into a pair of teal disposable gloves that matched the stripes on ver stockings.

SNAP! SNAP!

Giggling again, ve drank in the sheer dismay evident on the engineer's pouting features.

"Well, here. Let's just... Hmmm. You know what? The physical is a lot more critical to crew safety than sorting out your sore seat, so I think we'll do that first."

Ve gave a very unprofessional wink then as Phera's dismay turned a good deal more accusatory.

"But-! Can't we just-?"

To which Steph clucked ver tongue, wagging a gloved forefinger at her.

"None of that now," ve chided lightly. "Think of the anti-inflammatory as a reward at the end, 'kay?"

Much as she might've wanted to, Phera found it pretty much impossible to stay miffed at the doctor.

"Yeah, yeah," she conceded, feet idly kicking up and down behind her. "You've got a point about crew safety and all that, I guess. Though, my last company physical was only a few months ago."

Phera couldn't help but snort out a laugh.

"But, yeah. If it'll get me some anti-inflammatory, I'll do whatever you say, Steph."

"Oh...? *Whatever* I say?"

Stopping in place where ve'd been reaching for a biochem kit, the doctor slowly looked back to her with a silent, expectant mischief.

As their eyes locked, Phera realized how what she'd just said must've sounded. But, rather than backpedal, she did her best to imitate one of Straya's wry little half-grins and nodded. Steph was nice, and fun, and after how tightly she'd found herself wound up by her time with Straya, she was more than ready to see where her new attitude as a devils may care pirate might lead her.

"You're the doc," she pointed out, feeling a frisson of giddiness that she hadn't experienced since college. "Whatever you say goes, yeah?"

"Oh... Oh shit."

Steph raised ver thin hands to ver cheeks, looking suddenly overwhelmed and anxious.

"Someone is giving me total power over them without adult supervision? Oh god... No... No stop. I'm not supposed to let myself be in this situation..."

Ver trepidation soon gave way to a wicked glee, however, and Phera felt her bottom clench on reflex. Fortunately for her, though, Steph was still a professional. If also apparently a sadist.

"Um. Okay. Physical! Um... Let's see... We'll do the biochem, then sonar..."

Plucking up a tissue sampler from its charging base on the wall, ve shuffled quickly back toward the cot near Phera's head.

"Say ah?"

Ve held up the sampler, giving it an expectant wiggle.

"Sure thing."

Bemused by the doctor's animated reactions (Steph was definitely cute with the mad scientist vibes ve was putting off, and something told her they were going to be fast friends), Phera opened her mouth wide enough to accommodate the sampler and made the requested noise.

"Ahhhh…"

The device in doctor's deft hands clicked and beeped several times as ve scraped it along the inside of her left cheek, and then beeped again as ve drew it across her soft palate; managing to avoid triggering her gag reflex as ve collected ver samples.

"Oh… Kay."

Withdrawing the sampler, Steph gave the readings on its screen a cursory glance.

"You can close it now," ve added as an afterthought, making Phera flush.

"Oh, uh, right. Thanks."

There came a few more beeps then as Steph tapped at the sampler, and then ve looked up at her again with a nod.

"Nothing tripping any known alarm bells so far, but the full results won't be in for another twenty-four hours. You know the drill, I'm sure, hehe."

Phera shrugged.

"Waiting's fine with me, doc."

"Cool, cool… So, back to before, you've been doing networked ROV stuff for basically years now, right?"

"Yep!"

Surprised by the sudden shift in topic, Phera was nevertheless more than happy to talk about her field.

"Like I said, my specialty is systems development, so I was doing a lot of stuff revolving around optimizing drilling subroutines via data sharing and distributed analysis with the crawlers Pano was using."

"Neat! I kiiiinda had some ideas related to that, actually. But, we haven't had an expert onboard until now. Like, you've probably heard about that project they're doing on Mukpeh, yeah? The one with the surgical drones?"

Steph took out a little flashlight as ve spoke.

"I'm just gonna shine this for a second in each eye. Follow my finger, okay?"

"Right."

Doing her best to keep her head steady while she tracked the doctor's gloved fingertip (she didn't know if excess movements would give a false positive for eye worms or something equally as horrifying), Phera found a fresh surge of excitement welling up within her.

"And, yeah, I *did* see that project!" she exclaimed, feet bobbing up and down behind her. "The hab I was on before was way out in the middle of nowhere, so it took absolutely forever to send and receive data bursts, and I'm pretty sure the corp was censoring our feeds on top of that which didn't help with latency at all either, but I still managed to get my hands on the white paper they put out. Aren't those organic micro-servos just the coolest thing ever? You could cut the amount of time it takes to do a neural lattice graft in half, not to mention eliminate a ton of the risks at the same time if you could get that system up and running properly."

After Steph was done checking her vision, Phera blinked hard several times in an attempt to get rid of the neon spots now clouding it.

"I got mine when I was twelve," she added, lightly tapping the metallic data jack mounted just below her right ear. "Pretty sure I didn't sleep the entire week before the surgery. I just kept thinking about what would happen if the surgeon's hand slipped on the controls and they, like… I don't know. Poked my gray matter with a scalpel or something, you know?"

Phera shivered.

She sometimes still had nightmares about that day, actually. Getting her implant had been a requirement for the kind of highly-specialized systems development work she'd wanted to do after she finished secondary school, but it still hadn't been easy. Especially not with her dad screaming at her about her trig grade the morning of.

"You got any fun mods?" she asked with a somewhat brittle smile, trying to purge memories of crying in that hospital room from her mind.

"Heh. Um. A few. I wasn't always this cute."

Steph gestured at the pair of small breasts pushing out from beneath the front of ver lab coat, as well as the gentle swell of ver hips beneath ver skirt, before sweeping ver hair aside to reveal a hypodermic port in the side of ver neck. The kind someone wanting their hormone replacement medication to bypass their liver might use. All of the transgender friends Phera had had back on Cilara had preferred to take their hormones via oral capsule, but she supposed it made sense that someone living on a station or ship would want a more long-term delivery method that didn't require periodic access to a medical printer.

"Oh! I've also got a haemoelectric coupling."

Pushing up ver right sleeve, Steph turned to show off the circular, plex-covered port embedded in ver arm just a little below ver shoulder.

"I know, I know… These went out of style most places years ago, but it's *really* handy for powering stuff when we need to run silent."

Ve grinned.

"It's also pretty great for weight loss. Not everyone carries it quite as well as you do."

Giggling, ve gave the engineer's well-endowed rump an appreciative pat.

"Heh. Thanks."

Tossing her hair, Phera grinned just as broadly as Steph. The bubbly doctor had some serious tech packed inside of ver petite frame, apparently, and she couldn't help but be impressed.

"But, yeah," ve continued, shifting conversational gears once again. "If we can get the materials to tinker with it, do you think we could try and steal their research? I'll bet Cap would be down."

"Oh. My. Gods. *YES!*"

Phera's smile grew so wide that it was starting to hurt her cheeks.

"I would absolutely *love* to steal cutting edge medical research from a pharmaceutical megacorp with you, Steph. Do you think the Captain would let us make it open source? I mean, I guess we've gotta get paid too somehow, but it would still be nice to twist the knife on them like that, you know?"

"Dunno. Figuring out the money is Cap's job. I've never really cared about that stuff."

Setting ver handheld devices aside, Steph bade Phera to hold still a minute for the sonar scan. Then, once that was done, ve strode over to ver desk and gave the projected three-dimensional display that popped up above it a couple of spins and a hard look.

"I'm not really a pirate, exactly. Or, I mean, I guess I technically am?"

Ver narrow shoulders rose and fell in a shrug, rustling the hem of ver lab coat.

"I'm just here because I like the people, and Cap lets me experiment. As long as I get paid enough to do the things I want, I don't really pay attention to how much it is, you know?"

"That's... Surprisingly liberating."

"Mmhmm," absently agreed Steph, leaning in closer to the projection and starting to frown. "Wow, your vitamin D is really low."

"It is?"

"Yep. Like really, *really* low. I'm honestly kind of impressed."

"Uh, thanks?"

"Any pre-existing conditions that wouldn't show up on the initial biochem scan I should know about?"

"Er... I don't think so."

Wincing, Phera surreptitiously flexed her fingers.

"Are my bones going to be okay? The grav on The Bin wasn't a full G, but I assumed they at least had sunsim."

All the light panels had changed their brightness with the time, but apparently that was *all* they'd been doing.

I swear, if I break a fucking leg or something because Pano wanted to save money on energy costs, I'm going to-

"Let's see..."

Oblivious to her inner grumbling, Steph swiped aside the graph ve'd been looking at and dragged over a different one.

"Bone density is a little low, but nothing too serious yet. Looks like we caught it just in time."

Banishing the display with a careless, backhanded swipe, ve turned and strode back to Phera's side, regarding her with a surprisingly reassuring smile.

"Adri's cooking and the *actual* sunsim on the Mayhem ought to sort things out for you soon enough. But, just to be safe, I'll take another reading in a couple weeks. If your levels are still too low then, I can put together a supplement package for you, all right?"

Leaving over, ve gave one of the puffy cheeks pouting up at ver a friendly pinch.

"Wouldn't want our new roboticist passing out over her work, now would we?"

"Owie! Th-Thanks!"

"No problem. Okay now, let's have a look-see at your neck."

Stepping in closer, Steph's small, energetic hands rested themselves on Phera's forehead and shoulder, gently turning her head one way and then the other as ve ran a fingertip over each lymph node, feeling the texture and assessing the skin coloration there. Evidently satisfied, ve then dragged a pair of fingertips up along the gentle curve of the engineer's neck and cupped the side of her face.

"Looks good," ve declared, Phera's own dimpled cheek pushing against ver caressing thumb as a mischievous smile stretched across ver glossy lips. "Now, push yourself up a little higher so I can get a look at those breasts."

"Whatever you say."

Matching the doctor's smile with a wink, Phera gathered her hands beneath her and pushed herself up. Arching her back and stretching her spine with a prolonged groan that thrust her impressive chest forward. It honestly felt really nice to just lay there after all the running around and bending over she'd been doing, and stretching her tired muscles was even better.

"This work for you?"

"Yep! Now, hold still, cutie."

Leaning in, Steph cupped both hands underneath Phera's right breast. Slick-gloved fingers then began to probe and slip their way up and around it, feeling for protrusions. Finding none, ve then lifted it up against the pseudograv and traced a fingertip around the soft pink areola.

"Okay. Other side now."

Grinning toothily down at Phera as she gnawed at her lower lip, eyes half-lidded, Steph abruptly released her breast and moved around to the other side of the cot to repeat the process.

"E-Everything... Feel all right there, doc?"

The slim enby's deft fingers were making their second or third pass around her left areola now, sending pleasant tingles all along her skin and down to her aching clit as she let her head lull back and closed her eyes fully. It was good to know that her new doctor was so thorough, but ver touch was also making it *extremely* difficult to stop herself from moaning.

"Yep, just peachy!"

Steph shifted ver grip to put a hand on each of Phera's breasts.

"Or, really, more like grapefruit-y, I suppose."

Before suddenly giving each hardened nipple a sharp pinch.

"Ha- Ah!"

Phera's snort of amusement at the dumb joke was transformed partway through into a startled yelp.

"Geez. Warn a girl would you?" she grumbled, whipping her hair in the general direction of the doctor's face in retaliation as her palms shifted on the cot beneath her. "Aren't you supposed to say something like, 'Now this might sting a little'?"

"I already told you. If I wanted to follow the rules, I'd be somewhere else."

Beaming, Steph looked not the least bit apologetic.

"Plenty of sensitivity, it looks like. That's a good sign."

Ve gave each nipple another pinch as if to underscore the point.

"Ready to move on?" ve asked pleasantly, fingers still clamped tight around the engineer's nipples and starting to twist.

"Ah! Y-Yes vir!"

"Great!"

Letting her breasts go all at once, Steph straightened up and started gently gliding a set of gloved fingertips down along the valley of Phera's spine until they reached the patchwork of purple and crimson at her buttocks. There, ve idly traced the pattern of ruptured blood vessels curving across her left hip, before finally coming to a stop at her thigh.

"Gonna need you to lift this up now."

Ve gave the welts on the back of her thigh a gently commanding pat.

"If you insist," snickered Phera.

Shuffling her knees forward, she gradually shifted her seat up until she was once again on her hands and knees on the medical cot. Her, swollen purple-hued cheeks now at eye level with the blonde doctor.

"Like this?"

"Perfect."

With another pat, Steph finished meandering along to the end of the cot and put a hand on each of Phera's thighs, just below the parts Straya had so thoroughly abused.

"Now then, let's see..."

Gripping a fistful of thigh in either hand, ve pulled her legs further apart to get a better look at her groin.

"How much fun have you been having back on that station or wherever?"

"Oh! Well, um..."

The engineer's post-punishment arousal had largely subsided while she'd been eating with Straya and Adryel. The need for food and the pirates' stories had been enough to distract her from the feelings the woman whose lap she'd been sitting on had so thoroughly (and literally) whipped up within her. But, all of that had returned with a vengeance as soon as Steph had started examining her. And, shifting her knees further apart to accommodate the doctor, she could feel that it showed.

"Not much, I'm afraid," she admitted with an embarrassed chuckle, thanking every god she could think of that she was facing away from ver just then as her face went supernova. "It was pretty slim pickings back on The Bin. Me and an IT girl hooked up one night after a company-mandated morale boosting party, but our schedules just never seemed to want to line up and we kinda just gave up on trying for something more. I wasn't really in a good headspace for it anyway, to be honest. That place pretty much drains the life out of you."

"Awww, that's too bad. Though, it does make this part easier at least."

Steph's fingers very gently took hold of one labium and then the other, pushing them aside as ve leaned in to inspect everything more closely.

"Happy to help," answered Phera with a snort, a fresh shiver coursing through her at the sensation of warm breath against her glistening folds. "Incidentally, I can promise that I'm plenty sensitive there too."

"I noticed."

A gloved fingertip poked her right in the clitoris.

"Th-Thought you might."

"Birth control?"

Steph's fingertip shifted from poking to rubbing as ve waited for her to reply.

"Biomod," the engineer managed to answer around a gasp, referring to the process of having her genes augmented to prevent her body from being able to fertilize eggs. "Got it done back at the start of college. Perks of having a scholarship."

"Good, good. Now, you just stay right there."

Stepping away from her, Steph strode back over to the counter where ver terrarium with its bone wasp larva sat, and picked up a long-stemmed thermometer. Ve spared a moment to examine it, making sure that all was in order, before pulling it out of its airtight sheath and pressing a button near the head that squeezed out a thick dollop of lubrication.

"I really probably should have done this earlier," ve admitted with an unconcerned shrug, using a gloved thumb and forefinger to spread the lube around the distressingly bulbous head of the blinking device. "But, like I said, informal!"

"Um... Is that... I mean..."

Swallowing the first few responses that sprang to mind, Phera winced.

"Couldn't we do this orally?"

Steph, in turn, just blinked at her, clearly confused.

"Well, yeah. But that would taste *awful*."

Sashaying ver way back behind her, ver grin just a little too eager for Phera's liking, the giddy doctor cocked an eyebrow.

"Is that going to be a problem?"

"I, um..."

Phera could feel yet another flush creeping its way up her chest and into her face, warming the tips of her ears beneath her bunches.

"I guess not?"

"Then quit your whining, you big baby."

SLAP!

"Ah! Okay, okay, okay!"

Hissing in a breath, Phera's toes fluttered furiously against the lightly padded cot behind her as Steph leaned in and rested a hand between her ample cheeks, spreading ver thumb and forefinger around her tiny pucker.

"Hold still, please," ve ordered conversationally. "As much as I enjoy being rough on a cute bottom, I'd hate to damage my probe."

"W-Wouldn't want that," agreed Phera sarcastically. "Ah! Cold, cold!"

The insistent press of the oily thermometer against her anus drew out a sharp gasp and a shudder from her. But, even so, she found that she couldn't stop herself from smiling. Steph was a *lot* more attractive than her last physician had been. And, truth be told, she'd always had a thing for doctors.

Well, doctors and pirates.

A pirate doctor? Now that was a hard combination to beat.

"Why am I not surprised this is the kind of thermometer you have on hand?" she teased, toes curling and uncurling behind her.

"Oh, I have other options," admitted Steph, swiveling the tip of the probe around in a screwing motion as ve worked its slick shaft deeper and deeper into her. "But, this one suits you. Now, relax."

"H-Hah!"

Panting, Phera willed her bottom to cooperate.

"You have noooo idea how tempting it is to say 'make me' right now."

"I mean, you don't *have* to do as I say. At least, not right away. It'll just be less comfortable for you if you don't. Either way works for me, though, sweet thing."

Pushing the thermometer all the way in up to its boxy head in one swift thrust, Steph gave its status monitor screen a few more spins just for fun. Which had the very entertaining effect of setting the auburn-haired pirate recruit's hands and feet to fluttering as she sucked at her lower lip.

"Right then, while we're waiting for that to do its job," ve crooned, choosing to ignore the fact that thermometers hadn't had a waiting time for over three hundred years. "I think you've been good enough to earn yourself not only that anti-inflammatory, but also a mitotic stimulant treatment as well."

"Awww, no lollipop?" teased Phera, deciding that if ve wanted to make ancient medical jokes, then she could too. "And here I was looking forward to something sweet."

"Ran out of those a while ago, sorry," Steph said with a mock-scowl. "You wouldn't believe the sweet tooth on Lem."

Popping over to a small refrigeration unit, ve pulled it open and selected a large squeeze bottle of something clear and viscous from one of the shelves inside, glancing back to assess Phera's swollen cheeks as ve did so.

"Straya really did a number on you, didn't she?"

Visibly gloating, ve bumped the unit shut with a hip as ve sauntered back behind Phera's raised hips. Tucking the bottle against ver side as ve pulled off ver gloves and stuffed them into ver coat pockets.

"Ugh. Pretty sure she worked out a whole ass vector calculus proof, actually."

"Oh, I dunno. Seems like she managed to get your thighs pretty good too."

Highlighting just what ve meant, Steph gave one of the more prominent welts on Phera's upper left thigh a quick pinch.

"Ack! Hilarious."

Rolling her eyes, but still maintaining a lopsided grin, Phera heard a squelching sound from somewhere behind her as Steph squeezed out a generous measure of thick gel into ver cupped palm. A moment after that, a gasp of shock (followed by a profoundly relieved groan) escaped her lips as ve started slathering the ice-cold substance all across the upper edge of red and purple welts marring the backs of her thighs.

"So, what'd you do anyway?"

As ve spoke, Steph's nimble fingers continued to spread out the gel. Rubbing it in with surprising tenderness as ve slowly began working ver way up toward her buttocks.

"Well, uh… That's a bit of a long story."

Shivering both from the temperature shock and the fact that Steph was extremely good with ver hands, Phera heaved out a sigh that was mostly just for show since Straya *had* technically been in the right on all three occasions she'd spanked her.

"Let's see. First there was the whole shipjacking incident," she said, ticking off a point on one of her fingers. "After she'd breached the airlock and the dumbass station sec pilot had taken himself out with his own ricochets, I made the executive decision to cut off the engines from the helm… While they were still at full power."

This last bit came out as a mumbled admission from Phera. Lips twisting into a grimace as it once again dawned on her just how much worse things could have gone for the both of them.

"What? Are you serious? I thought Kelt and Adri were just bullshitting. You actually did that?"

"Yeah…"

Steph snorted.

"You got off pretty light then with just Straya burning your butt, and not reentry heat."

To which Phera couldn't help but snort right along with ver.

"Tell me about it."

Having reached the top of her cheeks, Steph began to spread the soothing gel back downward. Rubbing ver hands in slow, meandering circles around each swollen buttock, making them bob and jiggle. After a while, ve stopped to dollop on more of the chilly fluid directly atop their proffered centers, now working to spread it out wider and deeper in earnest.

"Oh gods, that feels *soooo* good."

Reveling in the ache the slender doctor's questing fingers produced, Phera sank down onto her forearms with a contented sigh and let her eyes drift closed as gooey fingertips started to venture into her crack and toward the thermometer protruding from her anus. Despite Straya not having actually done any damage there, she nevertheless appreciated the attention to detail.

"I'm glad to hear you like it. This is my own special blend, actually."

Steph chuckled.

"It's a surprisingly valuable commodity among this crew, believe it or not."

"Gee," deadpanned Phera good-naturedly. "Can't imagine why."

"Really?"

The doctor's hands paused mid-squeeze at that, ver voice sounding confused and more than a little hurt.

"Joking, joking," the engineer quickly amended, sensing that her new crewmate might have a hard time picking up on certain social cues and sarcasm. "I'm sorry, Steph. This gel is absolutely amazing. You have my sincerest thanks for sharing it with me, really."

"Oooh! Okay, gotcha. Yeah, no problem."

Shrugging off the misunderstanding, Steph's fingers resumed their work with gusto.

"You're lucky actually. You're getting the really good stuff. The mitotic stim I mixed into this particular batch helps speed up tissue recovery," ve explained, further parting Phera's cheeks and gliding ver thumbs up and down along their insides. "So, those bruises shouldn't last nearly as long as they otherwise might."

"Wow, really? That's wonderful!"

"Mmhmm. Hence why it's a valuable commodity. Now then..."

With another giggle, more of the gel was squirted out into the doctor's hands, and this time they were applied to Phera's magnificently swollen undercurves. With slow, methodical care, Steph worked ver fingers and palms back and forth across the crease of her sit-spots. Kneading the homebrew cooling gel deep into the bruise and welt mottled skin there, before turning ver attention toward the engineer's extra-sensitive thighs.

"Ah! Oh! Erk!"

Despite the soothing relief it brought with it, the application of the gel itself wasn't exactly a painless process. Especially not with the way Steph kept rasping the pads of ver thumbs up and down along the length of her welts. But, Phera wasn't about to start complaining. Not if it meant she could avoid having to put up with a bruised backside all the way until they reached the pirates' home port.

"But, uh... yeah," she eventually continued, picking up where she'd left off in her breakdown of the day's events. "Straya definitely wasn't happy about losing engines, and even less so when I sent one of the crawlers after her. Which was *before* she found out that we lost comms."

"Wait, I thought you said you only cut off the engines?"

"Well, I mean, *technically* yes I did..." conceded Phera, wincing. "That one was on purpose, at least. Number Seven plowing into that conduit and shredding all those trunk lines, on the other hand? That one was an accident."

The shiver that ran through her this time around had much less to do with Steph's roughly fondling hands, and more to do with the all too vivid memories of kevlar-reinforced teflon exploding against her bare bottom and thighs.

"Straya absolutely let me have it after I'd finished rigging up a bridge with my suit comms. I don't know if you've ever gotten spanked by a vacsuit glove before, but it's, uh… It makes an impression."

"I, um… I might have to rethink my joint research proposal."

Pausing a moment to stare at her in incredulous disbelief (which from where ve was standing, basically just amounted to letting ver eyes dance over the pleasantly plump curves of her raised ass), Steph added more gel to Phera's sit-spots and renewed ver efforts to massage away her bruises and welts. Then, after repeating the process against her soft and tender thighs one last time for good measure, ve slipped ver oily fingers deeper inside her partially parted crack once again; working them up and down around the head of the thermometer there, grinning.

"Swelling is starting to go down already," ve observed, lips pursed in professional assessment while naked satisfaction danced behind ver mother of pearl eyes. "Bruises… Well, that'll mostly depend on how long it usually takes for you to heal up from those. But, this should cut the recovery time in half."

Steph managed to dodge the obvious next question that declaration led to about ver own experiences on the receiving end of this magnificent concoction of vers by suddenly remembering that the thermometer had finished doing its job.

"Okay, uh, temperature! That's…"

Ve paused to wake the protruding device back up from its auto-shutdown.

"Thirty seven degrees on the dot! Nice!"

With the word "dot", ve tapped the face of the thermometer's display quite a bit harder than ve really had to. And, with "nice", ve gave it another couple of swivels.

"G-Glad to hear it," Phera managed, hips squirming behind her in a futile attempt to escape the doctor's teasing touch. "I was honestly a little worried after how hot Straya had managed to get me with that stupid spatula Adri gave her…"

A breathy giggle bubbled up around her gasps then as her unintentional double entendre occurred to her.

"Those two are a bad influence on each other."

"Awww, I like Adri."

Steph chuckled.

"Just for that..."

Face lighting up with malevolent glee, ve pulled the thermometer free with one hard, smooth yank.

"Eep!"

Wringing out a high-pitched squeal from Phera in the process, her hips jerking forward on reflex and her face flushing to match her hair at the audible *POP!* that accompanied its sudden egress.

"Okay, okay, Adri's not bad!" she surrendered quickly. "They're actually really nice. I like them a lot."

Humiliated and exhilarated, riding high on endorphins and a sudden surge of adrenaline, Phera huffed out an embarrassed laugh and finished her list of offenses by saying.

"Although, they definitely weren't a fan of getting clocked in the face by uncooked noodles. You'd think a pirate would have better reaction times, but noooo."

She put enough sarcastic self-deprecation into that last word to make it abundantly clear that she did, in fact, feel bad about that last bit of brattery in particular.

"Wait, wait, wait!"

A torrent of disbelieving, manic laughter welled up from Steph then, and ver entire body tilted to the side to look her dead in the eye past her still elevated bottom.

"You what?! Seriously?"

Phera smirked.

"Okay, so, it *seemed* like a good idea at the time," she prefaced her story by saying. "They were in a really grumpy mood when Straya and I got to the mess, and were acting all smug about how red my butt was under my boyshorts while I was climbing up a shelf in the storeroom to grab some noodles. Soooo, I thought maybe I'd just 'accidentally' drop some of those noodles on top of them when they made a wisecrack about my tomatoes being bruised or whatever, but I kiiiinda, maybe, sort of threw them just a bit harder than I should've."

Phera shivered again at the mental image of Adryel's snarling face, and gave her hips a hopeful wiggle, wordlessly pleading for Steph to make doubly sure there weren't any spots ve'd missed while applying the gel.

"They got a front row seat while Straya roasted my ass, though, and even helped her out by giving her that fucking spatula that left all those fun marks back there. So, I think we're even. They didn't seem mad after it was all said and done, at least. Also, they make some absolutely killer borken noodle soup."

Having to explain the whole situation had Phera suddenly feeling extra bad about it, and she resolved to find some way of making it up to the burly, kinda grumpy pirate later.

"You know, something tells me I'm going to be seeing you in here a lot."

Shaking ver head in disbelief, Steph returned ver attention back to her glistening cheeks, idly rubbing ver palm along one large curve and down the other.

"I don't think I'll mind, though."

As ve said that, ver other hand ventured between Phera's thighs and played in a tauntingly feather light circle around the edges of her labia.

"Mmph! O-Oh gods..."

Huffing and puffing with pent up need, the by now extremely horny roboticist pushed her hips back against the doctor's hand without an ounce of shame or hesitation.

"C-Count on it, doc."

She wasn't actually *planning* on stirring up any more trouble for her new crewmates, but it was still nice to know she had somewhere she could retreat to if need be.

"Well, if that's going to be your attitude..."

Steph's voice took on a playful edge to it then that had Phera suddenly all too aware of the vulnerable position she was still in as she felt something round, slick, and smooth press itself against her slightly gaped anus.

"How about some more, just in case?"

Not actually waiting for her to respond, Steph pushed the tip of the bottle just a fraction of a centimeter inside of Phera and then clenched ver hand shut tight. Sending the remainder of its ice-cold gel squirting up through her lower intestines at a velocity that made her squeal easily as loud as she had back in the mess hall.

"Oh my gods, oh my gods! Cold! *Cold*!"

Pushing herself back up onto her hands and knees, arms shaky with surprise and humiliated delight, she took in several shallow, ragged breaths as the tingly gel settled in along her insides. The sensation definitely wasn't unpleasant, but coming all at once and without warning as it had, it was a lot to take in. Both literally and figuratively.

As her breathing started to settle, though, her heavy chest swaying beneath her, nipples diamond hard and at the mercy of every phantom current in the little medbay, a broad grin spread across the new recruit's face.

"Y-Yes vir, whatever you say. I hear and obey."

"Hah!"

Tugging the nozzle from Phera's now chilled and tingly anus, Steph wiped the former very thoroughly with some disinfectant scours as she continued to tremble and giggle on her hands and knees; keeping her bottom clenched as hard as she could to avoid any humiliating leakage. Her giggling came to an abrupt halt, however, when Steph solved that particular problem for her by picking up a disposable rubber beaker-seal from a nearby counter and spreading her cheeks one last time before stuffing it into place with another spinning motion. Plugging her up tight and making her yelp all the more as she shot up to a kneeling position with her hands clamped tight over her slick, and now significantly less swollen, bare bottom.

"Well, that's that then. See you at dinner," ve declared, taking a step back and wiping off ver hands on the front of ver lab coat.

Thoroughly pleased with verself, the doctor swiped a wispy lock of platinum hair out of ver face.

"And... maybe at bedtime too, if you want. There's a spare bunk in my group's cabin."

"Humph. I seriously don't know what you mean about not being sure if you're 'really' a pirate or not," pouted Phera, her petulant glare lacking anywhere near the amount of actual indignation required to be genuine as she climbed ever so carefully down off of the exam cot. "You're definitely more than ruthless enough, *trust me.*"

"Hmmm. Maybe."

SLAP!

As if to confirm her assessment, Steph turned in a surprisingly graceful pirouette and landed a full-body swat directly against the center of Phera's tingling right buttock.

"Off you go now, sweet thing."

Though her bottom was significantly less swollen, it was still splattered with dark pink rectangles and faint welts. Moreover, the gel had softened her skin quite a bit, making the doctor's casual slap sting all the more.

"Owie, owie, OW!"

It was a good thing the hab cylinder had full grav like it did, otherwise she would've been bouncing around even worse than she had back on the flyer. Instead, Phera just hopped forward half a meter, clenching down tight on the beaker seal between her buns, and landed in a half crouch next to her discarded clothes and magboots.

"Which crew cabin are you in, by the way?" she asked in an attempt to change the subject before the enby could show off any further, pulling her semi-soiled clothes back on and grimacing at the feel of the decidedly much less snug waistband of her boyshorts as they settled into place around her hips. "I was kind of planning on bunking in Straya's."

"Guess you'll just have to choose between me and her then."

Sticking out ver tongue, Steph skipped over to the control panel for the medbay door and palmed it open.

"Anyway, test results tomorrow. Try and behave yourself until then, yeah? Much as I might enjoy getting my hands on that butt of yours, that gel takes time to cultivate, you know."

"Heh. I'll try my best."

Smiling fondly at the crew doc as she slipped past ver on her way out the door, Phera placed her hand over her heart and winked.

"No more noodle missiles or impromptu system surgeries until we make it to port, I promise."

CHAPTER SEVEN

Later, Phera would remember the rest of that first day in fits and snatches. After fleeing the medbay and sorting out Steph's oh-so-thoughtful parting gift, she'd briefly considered tracking down where the crew had transferred the ore crawlers to so that she could get to work on fixing up Number Seven. But, that plan lasted all of four steps toward docking access before she decided to let it go until tomorrow. It had already been an extremely long day, and the Captain *had* said she could spend the rest of it resting. So, she opted to take advantage of her kind offer instead.

After all, she was nothing if not an obedient pirate.

—

Limping back to the crew cabins, a heavy magboot hanging by its fastening latches from either wet noodle arm, Phera picked one at random and keyed its door open with her elbow. As luck would have it, the one she picked just so happened to be Straya and Adryel's (the latter of whom seemed to be in the middle of arguing that their fellow raider's hips counted as part of her "back" when the door swished open).

She'd waved hello to the pair of them with a boot, tossed it and its fellow onto the deck before the only bunk that didn't have any sort of personal flare or rumpled sheets, and collapsed face first onto it. The pillow was soft and cool, and as her face pressed into its gel-infused surface, she let out an exhausted but contented sigh. Passing out just as Straya was shoving the crew cook onto their bunk with orders to ditch the cargo pants.

—

"Come on, get up. It's chow time."

"Mmph. Wha…?"

Blinking dazedly, Phera levered herself up from where she'd been drooling into her pillow and propped her head on an elbow. For a few sluggish moments, she found herself wondering what had happened to the small armada of succulents she kept in her quarters, but then everything came rushing back to her all at once and she let out a prolonged yawn.

Right. She was a pirate now. She was on board the Mayhem, and The Bin was nothing but a distant, bitter memory.

"Chow? As in, dinner?" she echoed, rubbing at one bleary eye with the back of her hand as she idly wondered where the blanket that slipped down her front to pool around her hips had come from. "Didn't we just eat?"

"Yeah, like three hours ago."

Shrugging, Straya held out a hand to help her up.

"Cap says she wants you to circulate. So, up and at 'em, sweet cheeks."

"Three hours? Seriously?"

Yawning again, Phera staggered gracelessly back to her feet with the taller woman's help, kicking over one of her magboots in the process.

"Uh-huh."

Straya's usual sardonic half-grin blossomed across her scarred face then as she took in her rather severe case of bedhead and the creases left behind on her cheek by her pillow.

"You were passed the fuck out. Slept all the way through me fucking Adri sideways and everything. Now, you coming or not?"

"Yeah, yeah. Let me just…"

Still a bit groggy, Phera cast one look down at her magboots and then rolled her eyes, deciding to stick with going barefoot for the time being. It wasn't like they were doing anything to help preserve her nonexistent modesty just then anyway.

"Oh, never mind. Yeah, I'm good."

More than good, if she was being totally honest with herself, actually.

That soothing gel Steph had been so thorough with had absolutely done its job while she'd been asleep. The pain in her bottom and thighs had receded to a blunt all over ache that was oddly comfortable, like she'd just finished running a marathon. Which, she supposed, in a way she technically had. She'd certainly given Straya enough exercise for one day.

Smirking, Phera swept a hand toward the exit hatch of their cabin.

"Lead the way, *cupcake*."

SMACK!

"You've already got Steph beat for the most spankings in a single day, you know. Do you seriously want to lap ver again?" the older woman asked, propelling her new cabinmate forward with a firm swat to the seat of her slightly sagging boyshorts.

There was a glint of amusement in her iron gray eyes, though. And, rather than be annoyed, Phera just sped up enough to put her still mildly tender backside out of swatting range as she turned back to stick out her tongue.

"No time for that, Stray. Best not keep the Captain waiting."

—

Dinner ended up being an extremely filling rice and hydroponic vegetables dish served in a spicy sauce that vaguely reminded Phera of her Daziqir girlfriend back in college, and which she absolutely adored.

The meal itself passed in a quiet interlude of scraping utensils and slurping drinks amid the low buzz of casual conversation and the occasional bit of laughter. It was a quiet, relaxingly subdued affair, and the new recruit allowed herself to be carried along by the ebb and flow of chattering and joking around her as she unhurriedly worked her way through two servings of rice and then a bowl of sorbet one tiny spoonful at a time. The sorbet in particular was some of the best she'd ever had, and not just because the meal selection Panorama had offered had been so appallingly bland.

Apparently, the crew's absolutely yolked first mate had a talent for making tasty treats as well as eating them.

Sucking on her spoon while she watched Adryel perform a dramatized reenactment of Straya's taking of the Panorama flyer for

Lem and an older woman with a boy who looked to be in his early twenties on her lap, Phera reflected that as far as fresh starts went, she really couldn't have asked for a better one. She'd only been on board this ship for half a day, and already it was starting to feel like home.

"Hello there, Phera."

The sound of scuffing soles on the deck beside her drew Phera out of her idle contemplation of the frozen citrus swirls in front of her as a pair of bright orange ship slippers slid into her peripheral vision.

"Oh! Uh, hello, Captain."

Dragging her eyes up from the incongruously fuzzy slippers to the lean face of the woman wearing them, Phera was profoundly relieved to see that she was smiling. Granted, it was that same hungry, predatory smile she'd been wearing back in her office. But, the engineer was starting to suspect that might just be her usual look.

"Seems like you've had yourself an eventful first day."

The Captain's amber gaze flitted briefly to the faint traces of fresh bruises peeking out from the sides of her bare thighs and back up to her face, her grin widening.

"I'm so happy to see that you've been *fitting in* so well with the crew."

"I, um..."

There was something in the way she phrased that last statement that instantly had Phera's cheeks warming.

She might know about what went down with Adri, but there's no way she could possibly know about what happened in medbay, right? Not unless Steph told her...

She had no idea how the doctor's improvised plug would come up in a medical report or casual conversation, though, so she did her best to tamp down on her embarrassment as she spoke up again.

"Yes ma'am."

Oops.

She hadn't meant to tack on that "ma'am" part, but it just came so naturally for the Captain that it was out of her mouth before she'd even realized she was saying it.

"Everyone has been really nice so far," she continued, pointedly ignoring the growing grin on Steph's face. "Thanks again for taking me on."

"Mmhmm…"

The Captain's attention seemed to have wandered in the intervening seconds while Phera had been trying to form a response. Her expression had gone blank and her gaze unfocused. But, just as the engineer had noticed it, her smile returned in full force and her left hand shot out to snatch a fistful of a passing man's sleeveless top. Dragging him around to stand beside her.

"Have you met our systems infiltrator yet?"

"Sort of…" hemmed the new recruit somewhat hesitantly, caught off guard by the abrupt change in topic. "We talked a bit over dinner."

Extending her hand without pausing to consider if the silver-haired pirate would find the gesture rude or not, Phera flashed her most friendly professional smile.

"Hello, officially. I don't think I actually introduced myself properly yet. I'm Phera. It's nice to meet you."

"Obette," replied the man smoothly, clasping her hand just as firmly as any native planetsider might before sweeping it up and leaning in to plant a kiss on its back with a wink. "Welcome aboard, Doctor Sinclair. I was perusing through the data on you that we pulled from that station you were on, and I must say it's an honor to have such a lovely and talented roboticist such as yourself joining our merry band of misfits."

"Oh, um, wow. Really?"

Obette's dashing grin only grew wider as Phera's cheeks flushed with fresh color.

The Captain, meanwhile, just rolled her eyes at the man's shameless flirting, making no move to hide her open assessment of his shapely ass while he was bent over getting cozy with Phera.

"Absolutely. I *also* noticed that you and I happen to be cabinmates, and I must say that I am very much looking forward to getting to know you better. Perhaps we could-"

"Yes, yes, lay your moves on the new girl later," the Captain interrupted, laughing all the while as she gave Obette's perfectly positioned posterior a pinch. "I didn't call you over here to try and get into her lack of pants. Check her comp already, you slut."

"Aye, aye."

Unlike Phera, whose face was positively radiating heat now, the man just smirked at the Captain and flashed her a sardonic, two-fingered salute before straightening back up with an elaborate flourish.

"If you'd be so kind," he said, holding his palm out to Phera. "I just need it for a moment. Security scan and all that. I'm sure you understand."

"Uh, yeah, of course."

Dragging herself out of the gravity well of the suave pirate's emerald gaze, Phera slipped her hand out of her fingerless comp glove and passed it over.

"Here you go."

"Many thanks, my dear."

Fishing out a small slate from his back pocket, Obette ran a thin cable from it to the access port on her comp and began rapidly typing out commands.

"Anything interesting?" the Captain prompted half a minute later, cocking a brow.

"Nothing more than the usual megacorp fare. Some basic keylogging and a shadow proxy they were probably using to keep an eye on what she got up to online."

Obette kept his attention fixed on his slate as he spoke, watching as lines of status readouts scrolled up its display.

"There's some fun browser history here too, and I think she might be able to give Shi a run for his money on puzzle games. But, that's about it."

Knowing all too well just what sort of browsing history the infiltrator was referring to, Phera kept her mouth shut tight as her entire face did its best to blend in with her hair. Mercifully, though, he made no other comment about what she liked to look up in her off hours. And, after receiving a nod from the Captain, passed the glove back to her.

"There you go. I've gone ahead and cleared out the spyware for you. We'll be reaching real-time network access range soon, and you should be safe to browse to your heart's content. Just make sure you stay off socials, yeah? Straya isn't the only one who can whip a mean ass, you know."

He gave the dark belt cinched around his trim waist a meaningful tap then, and Phera cast a chagrined smirk in her erstwhile disciplinarian's direction. Left hand wandering down to the side of her hip for a quick rub.

"Guess I got pretty lucky she didn't have an actual belt on hand at any point today, huh? She's more than scary enough with her hand."

"And a vacsuit glove, and a spatula," the Captain added sotto voce.

While Obette just snorted.

"She is indeed a force to be reckoned with."

"Are you kidding me?"

Her hungry grin widening, the Captain swept her gaze from her latest recruit to her infiltrator and back again.

"Straya could skull fuck the pair of you with her hands in her pockets without breaking a sweat."

"Hell yeah she could," agreed Steph as ve passed them by, sounding not the least bit intimidated by the idea.

From across the table, Straya rolled her eyes, but Phera couldn't help but notice she sat up just a bit straighter.

"She's not the only one you know," pointed out Obette, making a show of flexing one exposed bicep.

It wasn't anywhere near as bulky as Straya's or Adryel's (and didn't even come close to Lem's own laser canons), but it was at least well-defined and there was enough of it there to make a good showing.

"Awww, you're so cute when you try acting all tough," crooned Steph, reaching up to patronizingly pat the infiltrator on the cheek, earning verself a scowl from the man in the process as he looked back to the Captain.

"Will that be all, Cap?"

"Hmmm?"

The Captain's mind had apparently gone wandering again, but her gaze snapped back into focus at Obette's prompting.

"Oh. Yes, yes," she dismissed with a flick of her fingers. "That's all I needed."

"Great, thanks."

Turning back to Steph then, his face settling into a determined (albeit playful) snarl, the infiltrator hunched forward and, with a grunt of effort, scooped ver up and over one shoulder.

"How's *this* for acting tough?" he laughed, stalking away somewhat unsteadily with his captured physician while ve let loose with a prolonged "Whee!"

The Captain, meanwhile, took advantage of Phera's momentary distraction to pluck up her sorbet and spoon from the table.

"I don't have anything immediately important for you to do until we get back to port," she said around a mouthful of dessert. "But, do try and make yourself useful until then."

"Of course, ma'am!" answered the engineer with a hurried nod, only catching her repeated title slip-up when Adryel and Straya both snickered.

Covering her embarrassment by shifting some of her hair out of her face, Phera shot a sidelong glare at her two cabinmates before returning her full attention to her new boss.

"I was planning to start repairs on Number Seven first thing tomorrow morning, along with any other units that might've sustained damage during the, um… turbulence. That, and maybe start redocumenting that distributed communications protocol I was telling you about since my original write-up is back on The Bin. While I'm doing that I can also-"

Rather than let her continue rattling off all the ways she could be a valuable asset to the crew, the Captain instead pushed a spoonful of sorbet into Phera's mouth and grinned at her with a measure of rough affection.

"Very good, hon. Now…"

Clucking her tongue, she plucked at one dirty strap of the eager engineer's sports bra, nose wrinkling.

"Why don't you go take a shower while these take a cycle or two through the wash?"

She phrased it as a question, but Phera could tell it was one she ignored at her own peril.

"Yes Captain, I'll get right on that."

Hastily pushing herself back to her feet (gasping as the raised ridges on the bench that had been digging into her tender skin while she'd been sitting were yanked free all at once), Phera did her best to straighten out her dirty top as she fought down the urge to salute.

"Good girl. I won't have my latest acquisition looking like she's been crawling around in vents all day. We have a reputation to maintain, you know."

SMACK!

"Right then, off with you, swabbie."

"Ah! Yes ma-! Er, I mean, aye aye, Captain!"

CHAPTER EIGHT

CHARGES ACCRUED

Unauthorized Modification of Company Property, Unlawful Disclosure of Proprietary Information

Phera had been hoping that the Blazar Bitches (a name Obette had been thoughtful enough to provide her with as she'd been turning in the night before) were the sort of pirates she'd seen in vids while growing up. The kind who drank all night and slept all day before finding some attractive and scantily-clad long haulers to seduce and pillage. But, while her new crew more than lived up to her expectations with regard to the whole pillaging thing (at least as far as her backside went), come 0800 that following morning, Lem was rousing everyone out of their bunks with orders to get ready to greet the day.

Well, her exact wording was, "Get your lazy asses out of bed before I do it for you!"

But, Phera was pretty sure the first mate meant it in a fond sort of way. She'd certainly been smiling when her barking command had sent her toppling naked onto the hard and unforgiving deck with a startled yelp, at any rate.

As jarring as it might've been, that wakeup call was still an extremely effective way to get Phera up and moving. And, the next thing she knew, she had her single blanket neatly folded and tucked beneath her pillow, and was wriggling back into her all too skimpy sports bra and way too loose boyshorts.

Which was right about the time something soft and warm hit her in the side of the head, sending her stumbling back into her bunk.

"What the-?"

Shaking out the improvised missile, she saw that it was the loose white shirt Straya had fallen asleep in the night before.

"You're distracting," the older woman said by way of explanation as she fastened the clasp of her dark bra behind her back, giving Phera ample opportunity to admire the intricate and vaguely military-looking insignia tattooed a few centimeters above her left hip.

She was just about to ask her about it, when Straya broke her from her reverie by pulling a formfitting top down over her tattoo and turning to grin at her with just a hint of that dangerous swagger she always seemed to carry herself with.

"Put that on before today winds up being another cardio day for me."

This order produced simultaneous groans of disappointment from both Obette and Adryel, but Phera dutifully pulled the proffered garment on and flashed the other woman a grateful smile.

The hem of the pirate's hand-me-down only came to just below where her boyshorts ended, leaving a tantalizing (and still slightly bruised) pair of bare crescent moons peeking out from beneath it, but the engineer couldn't have cared less. It sure as hell beat the crap out of walking around in nothing but her underwear for another day. And, as a happy bonus, it smelled like Straya. All in all, she thought it went quite well with her clunky magboots and partially sagging boyshorts ensemble.

It wasn't *quite* the pirate chic look she'd been hoping to cultivate, but it was definitely a start.

"Thanks, Stray."

"Uh-huh," the other woman grunted. "Just try and stay out of trouble, yeah?"

Face lighting up with unapologetic mischief, Phera performed an elaborate spin to show off her new top before coming to a stop with a sloppy salute.

"Ma'am, yes ma'am! Whatever you say."

Straya's right hand actually twitched at that.

"You're lucky I'm not a morning person," she sighed, scrubbing that very same hand through her sleep-tousled curls as she shook her head.

Prompting Phera to blow her a kiss.

"So, annoy you before lunch? Duly noted."

Before making a beeline for the exit of their cabin before Straya (or Adryel, or Obette) decided to put off breakfast in favor of doing something about her sass.

"See you later!"

———

Lingering over a bowl of oatmeal and a glass of juice in the mess hall after everyone else had left to do whatever it was that pirates spent their mornings doing, it occurred to Phera that she really didn't have a proper supervisor to report to anymore. The lack of a direct superior to hold her accountable for how she spent her time was definitely an odd sensation for a native-born Cilaran like her, who'd been raised to believe that setting and tracking goals coupled with reporting and analyzing her performance to those above her were two of the highest virtues a Daughter of Harmony could possess. Still, as freeing as it was to have more or less full autonomy over what she did with her time, that didn't mean she wasn't expected to pull her weight, she reminded herself. So, bidding a fond farewell to the habitation cylinder and its artificial grav, she made her way through the acclimation tunnel and back out into the cargo hold in search of the crew's newly-acquired collection of ore crawlers.

She quickly found them in an out of the way corner of the hold not too far from where Straya's ulfsark stood in its docking cradle. Seeing the power armor, proud and powerful even with its dents and dings, it took a great deal of the auburn-haired engineer's willpower not to spend at least a few minutes poking around it. But, between the sharp glare from the woman in coveralls currently wrist-deep inside one of its actuator assemblies, and a particularly timely twinge of one of her few remaining bruises, she decided that it would probably be better to stick to her more immediate tasks rather than try and sate her professional curiosity.

At least for the time being.

She could always bring it up with Straya in a few days after her bottom had had a chance to fully recover.

So, sparing a moment to give the grumpy looking woman a friendly wave, Phera pushed off toward where someone had been thoughtful enough to strap down Number Seven to a workbench for her, magnetized her boots to the deck, and got to work.

—

It was only as she was settling down with a hot plate of leftovers for dinner later that evening that it occurred to Phera that she'd completely forgotten to stop for a midday meal. After finishing most of her repairs on the damaged ore crawler, coming up with a few potential performance improvements along the way while she'd been at it, she'd spent the rest of the day floating weightless in the hold. Lost amid a haze of hallucinated schematics and performance analytics as she went about redocumenting the distributed communications and environmental adaptation protocol she'd told the Captain about the day before.

It was still a little hard to get an accurate read on the older woman, but she'd seemed to be genuinely interested in the project when she'd been interviewing her, so Phera made doubly sure to detail everything in clear and concise terms and to include as many reference charts and illustrations as she could to ensure that her report would be understandable to both engineers and non-engineers alike. She'd still need to take a few more passes through her write-up before it was ready for review, but she was feeling pretty confident that she'd have something truly stellar to show off to her new boss by the time they reached the crew's home port in a few more days.

That could wait until tomorrow, though. Just then she was off the clock, and she fully intended on enjoying herself as much as she could. Which, given her new profession, involved a fair bit of alcohol.

—

"Oh come on!"

After she'd had her fill of rice and veggies and had dumped her dishes into the mess hall's ultrasonic cleaner, Phera met back up with Straya and Adryel in their cabin. And, over the course of the next two hours, they'd worked their way through a bottle of spiced rum the crew cook had stashed away beneath their bunk as they played ever increasingly loud and competitive rounds of a racing sim Straya had produced some time halfway through their second glasses.

Perhaps not surprising to her new crewmates, Phera was pretty good at the game. There hadn't been much to do back on The Bin as far as recreation went unless you were really into weight lifting or long walks on a low grav treadmill, so she'd whiled away more hours than she cared to admit playing games alone in her quarters.

But, good as she was, Straya was better.

"This is some *bullshit*."

Jumping to her feet, face and belly pleasantly warm as her mouth twisted into a scowl, Phera jabbed a finger at Straya and snapped.

"I had you that time!"

Well, she *had* had her at the start of the race, but then Adryel had spun her out near the tail end of the second lap and she'd come in at a distant third.

"We can go another round if you want," Straya offered.

While Adryel interjected with a smug, "I can't promise I won't do that again, though."

"Well, duh. It wouldn't be fair if you can target me but not the gearhead, now would it?"

"True, true. I'm an equal opportunity ass kicker."

The crew cook's teasing did absolutely nothing to ease Phera's scowling.

This was serious!

"You stay out of this," she huffed, shifting her jabbing finger to the muscular enby with far more assertiveness than she would have had she been completely sober, before reorienting said finger back to Straya. "And *you*!"

Pushing out an annoyed breath through flared nostrils, Phera's face screwed up into a mask of intensely-focused concentration.

"I *know* I can beat you if we're playing fair. I want a rematch. Just the two of us."

"What? Now I can't play because Phera's throwing a tantrum?" whined Adryel, chucking a pillow at the glaring engineer and sending her spilling onto her mattress.

Straya, meanwhile, just took another sip of her rum as a conspiratorial grin drew up the corners of her scarred mouth.

"Oh, I think I can make her conditions worth your while, Adri."

Sensing that something was afoot, the crew cook's eyes narrowed.

"And how's that exactly?"

"Easy. When I beat Phera fair and square, she has to suck your cock."

The alcohol flush in Phera's cheeks grew several shades darker at this suggestion, but that didn't stop her from replying immediately as she sprang back to her feet.

"Deal!"

"Just like that?" asked a mildly surprised Adryel.

"Just like that," she nodded.

It wasn't like it was a particularly difficult decision to make. She liked oral, and all the spankings she'd been on the receiving end of over the last day or two had put her into a servicey sort of mood. Besides, the crew cook *was* pretty cute.

It was just too bad for them that she wasn't planning on losing.

To cover her total lack of even pretending to stop and think about Straya's wager, Phera cut loose with another harrumph.

"Also, for the record, I am *not* throwing a tantrum. I'm simply... enthusiastic."

She sniffed then, nice and haughty.

"So, Straya, what am I going to get when you lose worse than you've ever lost in your entire life?"

"Beats me."

Rather than be intimidated, Straya just shrugged her broad, muscular shoulders and took another swig of her rum.

"You can choose Adri's cock too if you want. I don't mind."

Adryel, meanwhile, grinning in embarrassment, stage-whispered, "Gods. I feel so objectified."

"You know I'm the one who literally got stolen yesterday, right?" Phera teased, her pout melting into a wry smirk as one hand drifted back to rub at the phantom twinges of vacsuit glove swats along the seat of her boyshorts.

The very same boyshorts that had once again managed to work themselves halfway down her hips while she hadn't been paying attention. Between Straya's angry yanking on them and her frantic flailing while they'd been tangled around her magboots the day before, the elasticity of their waistband was all but ruined, forcing her to have to constantly pull them back up. And, though she at least had the other woman's borrowed shirt for partial cover, having her bare bottom suddenly come into view among this particular crew seemed like a recipe for disaster.

It *did* give her an idea, however.

Pivoting back to Straya, Phera crossed her arms beneath the swell of her currently unsupported breasts, causing them to spill over her forearms as she regarded her coolly.

"All right, fine. When I win, I want to get inside your pants," she declared with as straight a face as she could muster.

Prompting Adryel to snort out a disbelieving laugh.

"Specifically, I want to get inside some pants of yours that fit me. Or, that at the very least come with a belt or something."

At her clarification, both pirates affected disappointment (Straya in particular).

"Heh," snickered the crew cook. "Are you sure you want to go asking Straya for a belt? Might want to word that a bit more carefully, newbie."

"Oh please."

This time it was Straya's turn to snort.

"As if I need permission for that."

She leveled an even stare at Phera then, who was doing a very poor job of hiding the excited flutter this ominous dismissal had sent through her stomach.

"Clothes you can wear, huh? Sure, I can do that. I'll just get Shi to fork over those resizables he was wearing the other day."

"Oh, wow! Are you sure he won't mind?"

Straya's face split into a malicious half-grin.

"Not if he knows what's good for him."

"Well, geez, in that case…"

Lighting up at the prospect of getting even more than she'd been hoping for, Phera grinned right along with her cabinmate, completely oblivious to the way Adryel was pinching the bridge of their nose as they shook their close-cropped head. She'd been fully prepared to spend the next however long it took for the Mayhem to dock somewhere with a textile printer she could beg the Captain to cover the access fee for wearing pants that she had to roll the legs up on five or six times. If she'd known that she could have just asked that sweet pilot boy she'd made small talk with at breakfast earlier that morning for something to wear this entire time, she would've done so way sooner.

Still, a bet was a bet. And, honestly, the clothes were more of a secondary bonus at this point. She needed to show these pirates who was boss!

Snatching up her glass from where it'd been sitting miraculously unspilled on the deck by her bare feet, Phera downed its entirety in one prolonged swig that she hadn't had cause to show off since sophomore year.

"You're on!" she half-gasped, half-winced, dropping heavily back onto the edge of her bunk and snatching up her controller. "One v one. Three laps. Three races. Let's do this!"

—

Standing off to one side, arms crossed over their firmly toned chest, Adryel watched the unfolding competition with interest. Well, half-watched. They mostly seemed to be taking a clinical assessment of Phera's soft pink lips as they tensed and twitched with the ebb and flow of the races.

The first of which, she won handily. Happening to catch up with Straya at the perfect moment to send her ship spinning off into a whirling tornado with a small tap in just the right spot. It took her nearly five seconds to get free of the twister. And, by then, she wasn't able to make up the difference.

"Fuck yeah! How you like that?"

"Not bad. Not bad."

Straya's face remained neutral as the highlight reel from their first race played out in front of her, seemingly indifferent to the way Phera had her tongue sticking out at her as her projected ship spun off course again and again.

"Hope you don't think I'll fall for that feint a second time, though."

"Oh, don't you worry. I've got plenty more tricks where that came from."

"Uh-huh. We'll see."

Despite Phera's boasting, round two proved to be a lot closer. Both racers were constantly pushing each other off the course, though neither was able to drive the other into any major hazards. In the end, it looked like it would go to Phera. But then, at the literal final stretch of the last lap, Straya twitched her ship to the right just in time to pick up a speed boost that sent her rocketing off toward the finish line. Leaving the engineer spun out and eating her dust.

"One, one," announced Adryel helpfully, looking almost as pleased as their fellow raider. "Last one wins it all, ladies."

Phera remained undaunted.

"Yeah, Straya. Get ready to lose!"

"Pretty big talk, sweet cheeks. You ready to put your money where your mouth is?"

"She'd better be," chimed in the crew cook with a wicked grin, causing Phera's face to flush even brighter as she doubled down on her trash talk.

"Bring it!"

"With pleasure."

If their second race had been close, this third one was welded together at the seams. Phera and Straya mirrored each other move for move, each taking the same precise line through the course. Neither managed to snag a power up, nor knock the other into a hazard. And, in the end, they crossed the finish line together.

"What? You have got to be kidding me!"

Caught somewhere between laughter and disbelief, Phera shot to her feet to glare at the results, hoping that if she could see them from a different angle they might somehow change. No such luck, though. The projection showed each of their times, and they were identical down to a hundredth of a second. If one of them had beaten the other, the game wasn't showing them enough digits past the decimal point to prove it.

It was a tie, pure and simple.

"Wow, I didn't even know you *could* tie in this game," marveled Straya, settling back onto her palms against the mattress behind her.

"This is so dumb. We can't have tied!"

"Says 'draw' right there on the screen, can't really get any clearer than that."

"Yeah, but-!"

"So, uh..."

Setting down their glass with deliberate care, Adryel locked eyes with Phera as whatever drunken argument she'd been about to make petered out.

"You're going to be all dressed up for my blowjob then, I take it?"

Straya guffawed a little at that.

"I wasn't really sure how we should call this," she admitted. "But, yeah. I think that sounds about right."

Shutting off the game, she grinned at Phera.

"Of course, you could just pay up now since we're all here. I can go get you your clothes after the show."

Stomach fluttering at the predatory look on the older woman's face, Phera glowered.

"Or you could stop trying to chicken out and play me again!" she challenged, one hand tugging up her boyshorts as she rounded on Adryel, swaying slightly with the sudden movement. "If I'm going to suck your cock, it's not going to be on some stupid technicality."

"Yeah, well."

Standing up, Straya rolled her shoulders and popped her neck.

"I'd prefer not to miss out on seeing you fix those shorts again on a technicality either, but them's the breaks."

"Oh come on!"

Whirling back to Straya, Phera pushed her cheeks out into an indignant pout.

"If we're taking the matches as a whole, I totally won!"

"You did?"

Raising a half-gone eyebrow at her, Adryel tilted their head.

"Not sure I quite follow that last bit of logic there."

"It's obvious, isn't it?"

Phera was very much enjoying rounding dramatically on her cabinmates with each exclamation she made.

"Cumulatively speaking," she went on with exaggerated hand gestures, panties slipping halfway down her thighs with her vehemence. "My lap times were way better than Straya's."

Whirling back to address the older woman then, she jabbed an accusatory finger at where her left breast pushed out against the flattering material of her top.

"And I wouldn't *have* to keep fixing these," she said in a voice positively oozing with undiluted sass as one hand absently scrabbled to restore her underwear to its proper place. "If *you* hadn't been so rough with them yesterday. So *there*."

Straya just smirked.

"Nope."

"Um... Nope?"

Blinking in confusion, Phera looked to Adryel, who just shrugged.

"Your lap time," the other woman clarified, her smirk turning vicious. "Is about to be a *lot* longer than mine."

She gave Phera a couple seconds to let the implications of that fully sink in through her alcohol haze. Then, the moment she saw comprehension dawn and defiance turn to dread, she seized hold of her by both shoulders and dropped to the deck, taking her with her.

'Wait, no, hold on-!"

Phera was definitely not a grappler, and went down about as easily as the rum she'd been enjoying all evening as Straya crossed her legs and dragged her across her thighs.

"Okay, okay, it can be a draw!" she hurriedly backpedaled, caught between laughter and panic as the heavily-muscled weight of the older woman's left arm bore down against the small of her back, tugging her in close against her firm stomach.

"Huh. That's odd. Wonder what changed between now and a few seconds ago?"

Feigning a bemused grimace, Straya flipped up the back of the oversized t-shirt her pinned pirate cabinmate was wearing, and yanked her half-ruined boyshorts the rest of the way down to her knees.

"Her total lap time, obviously," taunted Adryel, likewise smirking as they took in the still slightly pink and yellow cheeks pointing in their direction. "If I remember right, I think it was… four? No, no, *five* minutes longer than yours."

"Sounds about right to me."

"Oh my gods, you two are the worst!" protested Phera, also grinning even as she struggled to get her knees back under her so that she could buck up off of Straya's lap.

"Adri, you mind?"

Still grinning, Straya nodded toward where the engineer's hips were squirming.

"I suppose if I must…"

Kneeling down behind Phera with a long-suffering sigh, Adryel took hold of her legs, pinning her ankles to the floor and leaning in to put their broadly beaming face within a mere forty centimeters of the coming action.

SMACK-SMACK-SMACK-SMACK-SMACK!

And action it was!

With Straya holding Phera's upper body, and Adryel her legs, her thoroughly well-rounded rump had absolutely nowhere to go as the by now familiar palm of her cabinmate was sent plummeting down against it again and again.

SMACK-SMACK-SMACK-SMACK-SMACK!

Positioned as she was, Straya couldn't quite swing her arm as far or as hard as she would've perhaps preferred, but she was able to more than make up for that with sheer speed and drunken horniness. Going for quantity over quality as she set the younger woman's hips to bouncing and jiggling while she cried out a distressed accompaniment to the sharp percussion of hard hand on soft bottom filling their tiny cabin.

"Ah! Oh! Owie! Fuck! Shit!"

SMACK-SMACK-SMACK-SMACK-SMACK!

Phera's bottom was still mildly tender from its misadventures the day before. Little spots here and there along her generous curves ached whenever she (or anyone else) poked at them, but they were doing markedly better than they had been the last time Straya had gotten her hands on them. Still, that didn't stop the near constant barrage of swats from touching off fresh fires back there!

"Oh my gods, oh my gods!"

Pinned as completely as she was (Adryel and Straya were at least 70% hard muscle as far as she'd been able to tell while she'd watched them changing that morning), the only part of her that was able to really move just then was her hips, which was no help at all. She was easily just as drunkenly horny as Straya was, and the sensation of her cheeks rippling beneath her pistoning palm was doing absolutely nothing to help with that situation.

"Five minutes, seriously? I can't believe you'd be so- Ack! So mean to Straya!"

Throwing a glare back at the crew cook in between short yelps and the occasional hiss, Phera stuck out her tongue.

"Ah!"

Pulling it back in almost immediately as a particularly harsh set of swats lit up her sit-spots.

"I know she- Owie! Sucks at racing, but she's not- Oh! *That* horrible."

"Horrible? Really?"

"What? It's the truth, isn't it?!"

"You know..."

Glancing up at Straya, expecting to see her giving the younger woman a "challenge accepted" sort of look and not being disappointed in the slightest, Adryel couldn't help but cringe just a bit in sympathy.

"I'm starting to think you might actually enjoy this, Phera."

Pulling the new recruit's squirming legs apart nice and wide by her ankles, their suspicions were confirmed as they exposed her absolutely sopping pussy to the cool air of the cabin.

"Well, what do you know?"

"Adriiii!"

Squealing in abject mortification, Phera tried and failed to bring her legs back together, succeeding only in working a thin rivulet of glistening arousal down the inside of her straining left thigh.

"Whaaaat?" replied the crew cook in a mocking falsetto as Straya's long fingers caught the extra-sensitive insides of the furiously blushing engineer's undercurves.

"This isn't fair!"

"Hah! So?"

"So- Owie! It's... Ack! It's not fair!"

"Tough shit, sweet cheeks, we're pirates."

"Yeah, we don't *do* fair. That's basically our whole thing."

Adryel and Straya's twin guffaws of amusement only added further fuel to Phera's humiliation, nearly making her come right there and then as she tossed her hair in frustration, teeth gritted.

"Oh my gods, you both- Ack! Suck- Owie! So- Ugh! *Much*!"

"Nah, that's your job, remember?" taunted Adryel, wringing out a pained laugh from the auburn-haired recruit in spite of her discomfort.

"Oh, go fuck yourself," she gasped.

"Again, your job," they countered smoothly, before turning a faux-concerned look to Straya. "She does have a mouth on her, doesn't she?"

"Yes, she does. But I think I've got something to sort that out before you stuff it."

Cutting loose with a low growl that produced an absolutely adorable squeak from the engineer, Straya snatched up one of her slippers from the deck beside her and brought it down in quick succession.

THWOP! THWOP! THWOP!

"Ow, ow, owie!"

Like the Captain's, its interior was soft and fuzzy. But, as Phera quickly discovered when three long, red ovals blossomed up and down along her left cheek, its rigid sole packed one hell of a punch.

THWOP! THWOP! THWOP!

A fact that was confirmed for her in triplicate as three more ovals exploded across her right cheek this time.

THWOP! THWOP! THWOP!

Before Straya repeated the process on her left.

THWOP! THWOP! THWOP!

And then her right!

"H-Hey! That's not- Ow! Not fair!"

With each heavy, semi-muted *THWOP!* of the pirate's slipper against her rapidly-reddening seat, Phera's hips jerked forward and back against her lap, propelled ever onward by Straya's swats and the reflexive need for something, *anything*, to grind against. Unfortunately, she lacked both the necessary leverage and position to find purchase on the pirate's firm thighs, and was left to complain loudly as her frustration (and pain) continued to mount.

"Strayaaaa- Owie! I said you *weren't* horrible!"

At least Obette was off somewhere else just then.

With Adryel holding her legs splayed apart, each gyration added an additional dimension of humiliation to her jiggling cheeks, parting and joining to reveal hints and peeks of her puckered anus as she shifted desperately up and down by the scant few centimeters her crewmates' grip on her allowed.

THWOP! THWOP! THWOP!

Straya wasn't taking her bait or bothering to lecture. Instead, just enjoying herself as she continued to roast the new recruit.

THWOP-THWOP!

THWOP-THWOP!

"Aieee!"

Startling an even higher-pitched squeal out of her as she bounced the sole of her slipper off of either thigh twice in quick succession.

"So."

THWOP!

"Ready to exchange prizes yet?"

As she finished speaking, Straya held the slipper up by her shoulder. Not quite prepared to let it go just yet as she retained her grip on Phera's now sweaty midsection.

"Humph. Maybe," pouted the engineer, bottom clenching and unclenching behind her as she took in slow, deep breaths and savored the renewed warmth radiating from her cheeks. "Are *you* ready to admit I'm technically better than you at racing?"

She knew cracking wise just then was a gamble, but she just couldn't help herself.

These two brought it out of her!

Shaking her head in mock-exasperation, Straya let out a long sigh.

"Your turn, Adri."

"Why, I thought you'd never ask."

Crawling forward to straddle the backs of Phera's parted knees while her torso remained pinned in place over Straya's lap, they took up the proffered ship slipper as their lips curled up into a lascivious smile.

THWOP! THWOP!

"Ack! Hey-!"

Where Straya might've been preserving her strength, Adryel seemed content to leverage their current position and its added swinging room to bring the slipper down hard enough to ratchet Phera's yelps up a full octave higher.

"This wasn't part of the deal!"

"New deal," Straya chuckled, giving the crew cook a thumbs up before tightening her grip on her wriggling cabinmate. "You say that we tied fair and square and that you're just a sore loser with a sore booty, and *then* we can get around to you putting that whiny mouth of yours to work on our first deal."

As she outlined her demands, Adryel punctuated every couple of words with a resounding *THWOP!* of the slipper. Beating out a steady, vicious rhythm against the auburn-haired younger woman's hypnotically rolling cheeks.

"Ack! Ah! Hah!"

Sore and horny and wound up as tight as she was, Phera broke down into uncontrollable, gasping giggles. Adryel's swats burned like pure engine thrust. The textured, no-slip tread of the slipper rasping across her bare bottom wringing out another yelp with each rippling impact. Still, her breath came in shallow laughs and high-pitched squeals as they continued to turn up the heat and she all but drowned in a sea of endorphins and adrenaline.

THWOP! THWOP! THWOP!

"Okay, okay, okay!"

Sufficiently motivated to agree to just about anything then, she babbled the word over and over again, far outstripping the muscular enby's measured pace.

THWOP! THWOP! THWOP!

"Owie, ow! Come on Adri-!"

She'd assumed that once she'd agreed they'd stop, but apparently they had other plans.

THWOP! THWOP! THWOP!

"I said okayyyy!" she howled, hair tossing to and fro as she threw a fresh glare over her shoulder.

"Okay, and...?" prompted Straya, giving her partner in punishment an expression that signaled for them to continue.

"And...!"

THWOP! THWOP! THWOP!

Gasping and giggling, squirming and yelping, it took perhaps longer than Phera would have preferred to admit to catch on to what Straya was expecting from her.

Though, to be fair, she *was* pretty distracted just then.

"And-!"

THWOP!

"Ah!"

Gritting her teeth and cheeks in an effort to marshal the ragged shreds of her composure enough to speak more than a few broken words at a time, she managed to squeeze out in a hurry.

"We tied fair and square!"

THWOP-THWOP!

Adryel helped punctuate that declaration with a pair of particularly ruthless swats directly between her partially parted cheeks.

"Aaaaand?"

Straya narrowed her eyes at Phera and gave her fellow raider a slight nod.

Catching her drift, they used their free hand to spread the engineer's swollen cheeks, before then bringing the slipper down (just as hard!) at an angle that caught the especially-tender insides of her parted cleft.

THWOP-THWOP-THWOP!

Delivering a trio of near FTL swats that gnawed at both her inner cleft and her twitching back door before releasing her buns and once again turning their attention to her pinned thighs while Straya continued to wait patiently for the younger woman to fully surrender.

"Aieeeyowie! Okay, okay, OKAY!"

Feet flailing behind her as much as they could (which, with Adryel straddling her wasn't much), Phera let out a petulant harrumph and spat out a mouthful of red curls.

"I'm a sore-" she started to drone, rolling her eyes, but unable to quite suppress a smirk.

THWOP!

"Ow! Loser."

THWOP!

"Ah! With a sore-"

THWOP!

"Owie! Oh come on, Adri, that one was way too hard!"

A final pair of ***THWOPS!*** on either thigh finally choked the "-booty!" out of Phera's babbling lips. And, with another nod from Straya, the crew cook stopped.

"Oh thank gods!"

All tension flowing out of her at once, Phera melted across the bigger woman's lap. Her bottom, still sizzling red and burning, felt like the surface of a dwarf star just then, and she couldn't have been happier.

Well, I guess Adri's living up to their title at least... she mused wryly, flexing her cheeks and groaning in a mixture of exhaustion and bone-deep satisfaction. *I'm pretty sure I'm about as well done as you can get.*

"Soooo..." the crew cook ventured tentatively, setting aside the slipper and shifting off of Phera's legs.

"So," Straya repeated.

"So," echoed Phera, sighing in relief as Adryel's weight lifted from her.

With nobody pinning her down, she was able to gather her hands beneath her chest and push herself up onto her hands and knees. Arching her back over Straya's thighs, she held that position for several lazy seconds while she caught her breath. Her borrowed shirt clinging to the valley of her spine and hanging down in front to give Adryel a clear view of her naked breasts as they swayed gently beneath her with her breathing.

With one last huff to recenter herself, Phera eased back into a kneeling position facing away from the enby, immediately thought better of it when her bare heels pressed into her tender hips, and then shot back up onto her knees as she shuffled around to face the pirate she owed some hard-won oral.

"Now?" she asked with a teasing chuckle, pushing back some of her unbound hair as her eyes drifted toward their lap and the visible outline of a hard shaft straining against their pants. "Or would you rather bank this one for later?"

"Not on your life, sweet cheeks."

Adryel shook their head with a half-eager, half-embarrassed grin.

"You won me fair and square."

Levering themselves back up to their feet, they reached for their pants, unclasping them in front and letting them sag as they spread their legs to catch the waistband around their knees. Then, with a repeated hand motion, they pulled down their dark olive briefs as well, letting an *extremely* rigid, nicely thick shaft of taut, dark brown flesh bounce up and outward.

"Besides, I think Stray's earned herself a show by now, wouldn't you agree?"

Eyes following the bouncing head of the penis in front of her, Phera smirked.

"A show, huh?"

As she spoke, she drew her violet gaze away from Adryel's cock to direct a largely endorphin-fueled wink at the other pirate behind her, before taking hold of the hem of her borrowed shirt where it rested just below her scalded cheeks.

"I think that sounds like an excellent idea."

Peeling the sweaty garment up and over her head, she tossed it in the general direction of her bunk as she turned back to the enby with an easy shrug.

At this, Adryel's eyes widened just a bit, and Straya had to bite back a comment. Settling instead for an appreciative up and down of the engineer's nude form.

"It needed to dry off anyway."

Still on her knees, Phera shuffled her way forward toward the crew cook as they settled down on the edge of their bunk; making themself nice and comfortable. Pulling her hair back into a loose ponytail, she reached Adryel and leaned forward to press soft breasts and hard nipples into their knees as she took hold of their

warm thighs and parted them, making room for her to shuffle in a bit closer. The base of their fully erect cock was clean shaven, as were the hard stomach muscles above and nicely curved, earthen colored thighs and scrotum below. Surface veins stood proud along its length, and the tip of the head gleamed with just the smallest bit of precum as it twitched with their heartbeat.

It looked delicious.

Licking her lips in a mostly unnecessary move to moisten them, Phera opened wide. Then, because she was still feeling sassy in spite of (or, more accurately, because of) the throbbing ache in her bottom, went "aaaah-omph!" as she wrapped her pink lips around the head and first quarter or so of Adryel.

Almost immediately, they were gasping, twitching their head back with a low moan. One hand went to a bare knee to steady themself, while the other rested atop Phera's curly red hair as she took a moment to accustom herself to the pirate raider's mouthfeel. Prize or penalty, it really didn't matter to her at that moment. It had been far too long since she'd had a chance to enjoy herself like this, and she fully planned on wringing every last drop of fun out of the situation (and her fellow crewmate) as she could.

Running her tongue in slow, lazy circles around the underside of the crew cook's head, tasting each vine and using the tip of it to probe their open mucosa, Adryel started to shiver, gasping again. They were smooth, slick, and just the perfect width to fill the engineer's mouth comfortably.

"Damn," observed Straya, watching Phera's gently bobbing head and very loudly presented, beet red buttocks with open fascination and more than a little surprise. "They must *really* be missing you back on that station."

Humph. Yeah, right.

Gliding her mouth up and down along Adryel's length, not quite managing to take it all in at once but getting the majority of their shaft nevertheless, Phera felt almost two years' worth of pent-up sexual frustration start to come free all at once. It had started to loosen yesterday with Steph, and especially with Straya (though, her attention at the time had been much more punitive), and that slippering just now and this cock in her mouth brought it all crashing free.

Being a pirate was proving to be a *lot* of fun.

Maintaining an even pace, one of her hands worked its way up the raider's inner thigh as she continued to alternate between bobbing and drawing nearly away to lash her tongue against the head of their cock just as eagerly as they had with that slipper against her ass not too long ago. Soon, her hand reached their scrotum and, squeezing gently, she ran the pad of her thumb along the tendons surrounding its base. And, while that hand was busy, her other snaked down between her legs to trace tight circles around her swollen lips and aching bud.

"Ohhh damn…" Adryel whispered through their gasps as Phera all but attacked their erect cock with her tongue and lips.

Seated on the bunk behind her, Straya's own eyes had grown wide as accretion discs. Clearly she hadn't expected quite this much enthusiasm.

Close as she was, Phera was able to hear all of the raider's feedback just fine over the sounds of her saliva-slicked lips slurping up and down along their rigid flesh, and she giggled.

"Hehe."

The vibrations of which sent a sharp spasm ripping through the pirate that she felt through their cock. And, sensing that she'd stumbled onto something extra effective, Phera started humming to herself. Working her way through a nameless tune she made up as she went while swaying her carmine hips from side to side in time with the beat as she continued to idly toy with her clit.

It took only a few stanzas of humming before Adryel's feet drummed out a staccato beat of their own against the deck plates to either side of Phera's knees. Jerking back, their left hand shifted away from their knee to seize a handful of blankets for stability as a low groan rumbled up from deep within their taut belly. As the noise reached its crescendo, there came another hard twitch, and then hot, salty liquid was exploding all across the engineer's soft palate.

"Umph!"

Phera had felt Adryel tensing right as they were about to come, and her first instinct had been to pull back and take it on her face and chest, using her borrowed shirt to clean it up afterward. But, with that well out of reach, and their fingers threaded tight through her curls, holding her right where she was, she opted to just swallow it instead.

It wouldn't have been the first time. And, honestly, it made clean up a whole lot easier.

"Oh god, Pheraaaa…"

As molten semen rushed into her mouth and down her throat, she tightened her grip on the crew cook's scrotum and continued to bob her head. She knew that at that moment Adryel's head would be hyper sensitive. And, though she might not be anywhere near as strong as they were and wouldn't normally be able make them call uncle, she could at least do her darndest to make the gasping pirate tap out before they collapsed onto their bunk.

Plus, she'd settled into a nice rhythm with her cock sucking and clit rubbing, and she was way too close to coming herself to stop now.

What Phera didn't expect at that point, however, was for Straya's own fingers to join hers between her legs.

"Ahfth!"

Stroking her as they curled and uncurled gently along the insides of her parted labia while her fellow raider's head lulled back, breath coming fast and heavy as they trembled under the engineer's relentless ministrations.

It was a race now. Could Phera make Adryel surrender before Straya ruined her concentration?

Guess we're having that rematch after all.

Phera had already been close to coming before, but with Straya's help while she continued to work her clit, she was now redlining toward an orgasm at what felt like borderline dangerous speeds. Her earlier humming having been replaced by muffled gasps and sharp in and out breaths through her nostrils, she wanted nothing more than to hold out to the end, to make Adryel admit defeat. But, in less than half a minute of pumping, the older woman had shoved her (almost literally) into coming harder than she had in months.

"Oh godsth!"

Contracting around Straya's skilled fingers, Phera's bobbing motions jerked and stuttered before coming to a halt altogether. Adryel's cock still deep inside her mouth while she panted through her nose.

Straya, just as merciless as she'd been with the slipper, kept working her fingers for several long, agonizingly blissful seconds after Phera had finished coming. Smugly rubbing in her victory as Adryel slumped sideways on the mattress, their hands moving defensively over their deflated crotch as the younger woman finally let them go.

"See? You could have just skipped the painful part if you hadn't been such a brat."

"Wh... Where's the fun in that?"

Her pirate captor stopped twitching her fingers then, pulling them free without warning and giving Phera's proudly presented ruby rump a really unnecessarily hard pair of swats across either cheek.

SMACK-SMACK!

"I'll go get you your clothes now. Don't do anything too mean to Adri while I'm gone, yeah?"

'Take... Take your time..."

Easing back onto the blessedly cool deck behind her, Phera dragged an exhausted forearm across her mouth and grinned.

"I don't think I'm going to be needing them for a while."

CHAPTER NINE

Late that following morning found Phera in the aft engineering section's workshop, on her hands and knees beneath the Mayhem's primary 3D printer overseeing its material feeders and ensuring that the auto-levelers were calibrated correctly. Though she'd woken up nursing a pretty decent hangover, she'd nevertheless been eager to get the ball rolling on implementing all the exciting new improvements to the ore crawlers that she'd thought of the day before. And so, after powering through breakfast and the hour of mandatory exercise Lem had ordered her to get in on the treadmill in the rec room, she'd headed straight to work on her new project.

She still had no idea what (if anything) the Captain planned on doing with the gaggle of ore crawlers the Blazar Bitches had stolen from The Bin. Phera very much doubted that the lean and scary woman had a secret osmium mining operation she hadn't yet told her about. But, regardless, she fully intended on making sure each and every unit was in tiptop shape for whatever came next.

At least, that was the plan at any rate.

"Ahem."

BONK!

"Ack! Shit!"

Startled out of her energized humming and hip bobbing by the sound of a throat being cleared from somewhere behind her, Phera jerked up in surprise and cracked her head on the underside of the workbench the printer had been bolted to. She'd been so engrossed in her work that she hadn't even heard the door to the workshop swish open.

Grumbling a string of swear words under her breath as she rubbed at the back of her smarting head, she double-checked that the spool of graphene she'd set up to feed into the printer's auxiliary extruder was still turning properly, before wriggling her wide hips back and out from beneath the table. Rolling her shoulders as she pushed herself somewhat unsteadily back onto her feet, she looked back to see who had startled her and felt a small burst of excitement at the sight of the woman who'd been working on Straya's ulfsark the day before.

"Oh! Good morning, Kelt."

She gave the petite engineer a friendly wave and then leaned forward to dust off the front of the stylish and very comfortable new pants Straya had gotten for her the night before. Then, noticing the haggard look on the other woman's face and the vaguely Captain-like dark circles under her eyes, she flashed her a commiserating smile.

"I didn't see you at breakfast earlier. Long night?"

"Very."

Kelt had her salt and pepper hair pinned up in a smart bun that morning. A few strands of which had popped loose to frame her tired, almond eyes and the stern line of her mouth.

Taking a long pull from a steaming thermos she held in one hand, she gave the younger woman a cool, appraising once-over.

"Nice outfit."

"I know, right?"

Straightening up, Phera kneaded her lower back with her knuckles, arching her spine and proudly thrusting her chest and its snug, matching top out in front of her.

"I won it from Straya last night."

She felt her ears go red with this last bit of information, memories of Adryel's thick cock in her mouth rushing back to her all at once as she chuckled awkwardly and turned to face her fellow tech.

"Sure beats wandering around half-naked, that's for sure."

"Yes. I'm sure that must be *great* for you."

The corners of Kelt's mouth dipped down into a scowl as she spoke.

"What are you doing in here anyway?"

"Oh, you'll like this!"

Brightening, Phera beckoned the grumpy engineer over to the printer. She knew all too well the misery of pulling late hours and not getting enough sleep, but she was sure her design improvements would be enough to help pull her out of her funk.

"Okay, so," she began to explain, all but dancing in place as she dismissed the status screen from the display attached to the printer and pulled up a rendering of the part it was currently working on instead. "While I was repairing the damage to Number Seven yesterday, it occurred to me that I could totally ditch the nanoweave mesh in its over-casing for a graphene lattice like what Straya's shield uses instead. It'd make it about four percent less dense, and would still be just about as strong. These things aren't built for serious impact anyway, so as long as it can shrug off minor flying debris and the occasional micrometeor, then it's fine, right? Plus, with a lighter frame it'll be more power efficient, and I bet I could even rearrange some of the internals to fit in a…"

Phera was fully into show and tell mode now. Pulling up cross sections of the part she was printing and drawing Kelt's attention to where additional components could potentially be seated, along with the oscillating, self-supporting infill braces she'd come up with for the underside of the piece.

"They're designed to flex with impact torsion and guide kinetic energy out through the manipulators, rather than the internals. See?"

Dragging her finger along one of the braces, she traced out the path she was describing, complete with sound effects.

"It might take a little longer to print, but once it's done, it's done, and it *shouldn't* need to be patched all that often. Well… probably. I'll still need to actually field test that last bit to be sure, but I'm pretty hopeful. My simulations all looked promising, at least.."

"Amazing," Kelt said dryly, taking another pull from her thermos before capping it and setting it on the workbench beside her.

"Isn't it, though?" Phera preened, face and smile bright as a supernova.

The other woman was perhaps a bit less impressed with her clever design work than she would have preferred. But, that was fine. Maybe she just wasn't the kind of person who could easily visualize things.

I'm sure she'll get excited once she sees the final product in person.

Kelt, meanwhile, leveled a flat stare at the printer as she folded her arms in front of her.

"So, when can I print my fiber optics?"

"Uh…"

Deflating somewhat, Phera occupied one of her hands with tucking a loose curl behind an ear.

"Fiber optics?"

"Yes. Fiber optics," came Kelt's acerbic reply. "Specifically, the ones I was *planning* on taking care of as soon as I got into the shop this morning. When can I print them?"

"Goooood question," replied Phera, dragging out the word with several additional Os as her chest tightened with the first inklings of an all too familiar workplace anxiety. "Um, let's see…"

Dismissing her cross-section, she hurriedly pulled back up the print status screen and felt her stomach twist with a sudden burst of accel-shift. 3D printing always took so much longer than she expected. Which, given the fact that the machine was literally extruding her new part out a fraction of a millimeter at a time, was kind of a given.

"It's at about three percent right now, so…"

She did some quick mental math based on the percentage remaining and how much time had elapsed so far.

"I'd say somewhere around twelve or thirteen more hours?" she offered apologetically, before rushing on in a hurry as if somehow she could bury that bad news under enough other words to make it better. "It's a pretty big part, you know. I actually had to print it an angle just to get it to fit onto the build plate as one single piece. Trimming away all that support flashing later is going to be a pain. But, hey, at least this unit has multiple extrusion, yeah? The one back on The Bin only had a single nozzle, and it was *such* a pain getting new pieces built up."

"Uh-huh."

Kelt made an exasperated noise in the back of her throat as she turned her full attention back to the partially out of breath roboticist.

"It's Phera, right?"

"Uh, yep, that's me," confirmed the new recruit in a somewhat brittle singsong, trying to ignore the prickling feeling raising the hairs on the back of her neck as she waved a pair of jazz hands at the older woman. "The Captain hired me after the uh... The Panorama raid."

"I'm aware."

Crossing over to the machine, Kelt glared down at its rapidly shifting build plate with an air of distaste before turning her attention back to Phera. Despite being half a head shorter than the younger woman, she still somehow found a way to tower over her.

"Haven't really had a chance to talk to you much yet. Sorry."

"Oh, hey, don't worry about it," Phera was quick to reassure her, doing her best to quash the sudden, irrational feeling that *she* was somehow at fault for their schedules not aligning until just then. "I'm sure you've been busy. It's a pretty big ship."

'Yes. Yes it is," agreed Kelt with a single, curt nod.

As she spoke, she laid one olive-tan hand on the printer console next to the display, drumming her fingers against the ceramic composite as she peered down the slope of her nose at Phera.

"Incidentally, did I say that you could use my printer?"

"Um... *Your* printer?"

Phera's violet eyes darted back to the precisely shifting extrusion nozzles beside her, cheeks coloring slightly.

"I kinda figured it was, you know, the crew's printer? The Captain mentioned earlier that the drones were now crew property, so I sort of just assumed that engineering fell under that same umbrella."

Part of her wanted to reach out and pause her print. But, stopping now would only lose her over an hour's worth of progress and waste valuable material.

"Um... Does it not?"

"It does," conceded Kelt, sounding no less annoyed as she continued to pin her in place with a cold, assessing stare. "But, don't you think the ship's *engineer* ought to be informed before you go tying up our one and only heavy materials printer for half a day?"

Drawing her hand back from the display, she took a purposeful step toward Phera, lips tight and eyes sharp.

"You know, since there are some projects that keep the ship from falling apart en route, and others that can easily wait until we're docked?"

"Well, when you put it like that..."

Backing up a step in sync with the other woman's advance, Phera winced.

"I mean, if it makes you feel any better, I was going to ping you about this at breakfast. Shi said you were still asleep, though, so I figured it'd probably be fine."

"Shi."

The mention of the pilot seemed to only further sour Kelt's mood. Maybe they'd had a fight?

"Um, yep, that's right."

Then, face going pale, Phera cast a worried look around the workshop.

"We, uh... We don't have something that's falling apart en route right now, do we?"

For as much attitude as she'd given Straya about it earlier, their near brush with death on board a stalled ship with no comms and gradually failing enviro had definitely made an impression on the would-be pirate.

"I don't know, Phera. *Do* we have something falling apart en route?"

Kelt took another step forward, backing the younger woman into the workbench behind her, hard gaze going all the harder.

"You seem to be pretty confident that we don't. Which is honestly rather amazing considering you only just got here two days ago. So, tell me, just how did you go about making sure of that, hmmm? Have you been reading over my maintenance logs? Or do you just have a sixth sense for hull stress I wasn't aware of?"

"Well, I uh..."

Looking abashed, Phera focused her attention on a very interesting bit of curving ceiling just beyond Kelt's right shoulder.

"I kinda assumed that since there weren't any, you know, blaring alarms or people panicking or anything like that, that it was probably fine."

She almost added "Don't look at me, I'm just the roboticist," but decided that might not be the smartest idea just then. Kelt had nowhere near Straya's bulk, nor the Captain's ominous, looming aura of knowing what you were thinking, but there was something in the iron filings of her gaze that had Phera standing up straighter as she fidgeted with her new top.

"*Assumed*, huh?"

"Er... Yep."

Trying to cut through the sleep-deprived woman's dour mood, she quirked a self-deprecating, mocking grin and shrugged.

"It's recently come to my attention that I'm a lot better at causing those kinds of problems than finding them. But, um, if you want to point me at one, I'd be more than happy to take a crack at it for you while we wait for my print to finish. I'm not too bad at rigging up holdover fixes, you know."

"Yes. I saw that."

Rather than crack a smile, Kelt continued to maintain her position, giving Phera a severe, static look.

"Though, now that you mention it," she eventually continued several awkwardly silent eternities later, shoulders finally relaxing a fraction. "There actually is something I can point you at."

Raising her arm, she directed a slim finger toward another workbench that had some free space on one side and a pile of power cell cartridges on the other.

"Oh, great!"

Eager for any excuse to escape the gravity well of the tiny woman's wilting stare, Phera scurried over to where Kelt had indicated and picked up one of the cells at random.

"So... What's up?" she asked, holding it a few centimeters from her face and narrowing her eyes, inspecting it for faults. "These need to be tested?"

"Other side of the table, young lady."

Kelt stepped up beside her as she spoke. Hands on her slim hips, looking no less stern.

"Go on now, hurry up."

"Oh, um, gotcha," replied Phera automatically, setting the power cell back more or less where she'd found it and sidestepping to her left. "Here?"

"That's right. Now lean over and reach toward the back."

"Uh... Are you sure?"

Doing as she was told while squinting hard in an attempt to see what the other woman could possibly be talking about, Phera was starting to feel more and more like she was missing something really obvious. As far as she could tell, the table was clear all the way to the other side, but she wasn't about to turn back and imply that her new senior engineer might be mistaken. She was looking grumpy enough as is and, besides, she'd spent the last two and a half decades of her life having it drilled into her that you do *not* question your superiors. So, instead, she planted her hands on the rounded over edge of the workbench in front of her and used it to hoist herself up off the floor, levering herself forward and craning her neck to see if something had rolled out of sight and was caught in the gap between the workbench and the curving wall.

"I'm seriously not seeing anything back here."

"Oh no, you've definitely got it, hon. Trust me."

Smiling viciously at the raised curves stretching taut the seat of the size-adjustable pants being presented to her, Kelt shifted her feet about a shoulder's width apart for stability and took aim.

"Now, as for taking a 'crack' at it."

Raising her left hand high and pivoting back for extra leverage, she landed as cruelly hard a slap as she could right where Phera's right bottom cheek looked to be the softest and most sensitive.

SMACK!

"Ow! What the-?"

Before following it up with three more that were just as cruel in half as many seconds.

SMACK! SMACK! SMACK!

Making sure to twist her hips and put her whole body into it with each impact in order to deliver the maximum amount of force possible.

"Ack! Geez!"

Jerking in surprise, Phera collapsed across the table, mashing her generous chest roughly into its cold, smooth surface as Kelt grabbed hold of the stretchy waistband of her brand new pants and yanked them down to her thighs in one smooth, practiced motion. Revealing that the new recruit hadn't bothered to wear any underwear that morning.

"Heh. Guess that saves me a step."

"Oh my gods! Wait, Kelt, please-!"

Kelt was having none of it, though.

"No, I don't think I will."

SMACK! SMACK! SMACK! SMACK! SMACK!

"But- Ah! Come on!"

Had the older engineer not been so thoroughly spanking her already, Phera would have absolutely been kicking herself just then. In retrospect, it was painfully obvious what she'd been angling to do, but she honestly hadn't expected this short, no-nonsense woman to be so… Piratey.

"Okay, okay, I'm sorry about the printer!" she yelped, sounding anything but as one hand attempted to push herself up from the workbench, while the other hurriedly flailed for her pants.

"Oh no you don't!"

Kelt was ready for her, though, and shoved her roughly back down onto the workbench with her right hand, using it to pin her in place.

Well, that and give her better leverage to increase the force of her swats.

"You and I are going to have a nice, long chat about how things work around here, little girl."

"We *really* don't have to do that, ma'am!" insisted Phera, the title slipping free on reflex as the older woman's fingers tightened around the material of her top at the small of her back.

"Oh, but we do," countered Kelt. "We really-!"

SMACK!

"Really-!"

SMACK!

"Do!"

SMACK! SMACK! SMACK! SMACK! SMACK!

"You see, I was *going* to spend the next ten minutes getting this project started, but now I can't thanks to you."

As she spoke, she continued to slap Phera's bare buns as crisply as her small hand would allow. Making them bounce and wobble in time with their owner's increasingly frantic foot flailing.

"So, now we're doing this instead."

"But... but...!"

SMACK! SMACK! SMACK! SMACK! SMACK!

"But *what*, Phera?"

It took half a dozen more swats to the center of auburn-haired young woman's right cheek before it dawned on her that she was actually expected to answer that question.

"This isn't fair!" she eventually whined, unable to think of anything more articulate just then with each sharp starburst of pain echoing around the room constantly derailing her train of thought.

"I'll tell you what isn't fair," fumed Kelt, shifting her aim to Phera's gyrating left cheek. "What isn't fair, is not being able to finish the job I was up all night working on because some bratty little roboticist barely out of college thinks she can just waltz in here and tie up valuable ship resources for her pet projects without clearing it first!"

SMACK! SMACK! SMACK! SMACK! SMACK!

"Hey-! Owie! It's not just a pet project!" protested Phera, hands balling themselves into fists beneath her rolling torso. "The Captain hired me specifically to maintain those drones!"

"She did," Kelt agreed mildly as she began bombarding the central divide between the squirming younger woman's bouncing buns. "But your official title as she explained it to me is *assistant* engineer. Which means that you do what *I* say. Is that understood?"

"But... But you didn't actually say I couldn't use the printer!"

"So?"

"So... um..."

"Did I say you *could* use the printer?"

"Well, no, but-"

SMACK!

"Owie!"

"Children these days, I swear..."

Kelt paused in her swatting just long enough to loose an oddly maternal (albeit exasperated) sigh.

"I already told you. If I can't use the printer, then this is what we're going to do instead."

She left the rest of that sentence hanging silently in the air between the two of them, but the implication was loud and clear to Phera. It was either take her spanking, or else Kelt would toss out the beginnings of her drone plating and make her start over tomorrow. Which, considering the fact that her bare cheeks were still mottled by little pinch welts from the tread on Straya's ship slipper, and that Kelt wasn't showing her even the slightest bit of mercy, made her seriously consider making the sacrifice.

SMACK! SMACK! SMACK! SMACK! SMACK!

Graphene wasn't cheap, though, and she *really* didn't want to run the risk of running out of material just because she caved over a little spanking. Besides, if Kelt was annoyed with her now, she could only imagine how she'd react if she had to explain to her that they'd ran out of their presumably only spool of high-grade nanoweave graphene only 70% of the way through her second attempt at a print.

"Ack! Oh! Ow!"

But, on the other hand, Kelt was spanking surprisingly hard for a woman of her diminutive size!

"Owie, owie, owie!"

"I take it that hurt, young lady?"

"Ye- Ack! Yes it did!"

"Good. That means I'm starting to make an impression."

"L-Lucky me."

"You are lucky indeed, my dear. You'd be a far more contrite little girl by now if I had my hairbrush with me."

"Eep! No thanks! Hand is fine!"

"Uh-huh."

SMACK!

"I thought you might say that."

SMACK!

Phera was rapidly developing an intimate knowledge of the subtle differences between her crewmates' spanking techniques, and the analytical side of her brain was hard at work cataloging Kelt's particular idiosyncrasies. Her palm, for instance, didn't impact with nearly the same amount of *oomph* as Straya's or the Captain's did, but she more than made up for that with sheer determination and a methodical attention to detail born from years of working as an engineer.

SMACK! SMACK! SMACK! SMACK! SMACK!

She also seemed to really enjoy attacking the same damn spot over and over and *over* again. Demonstrating that she had a ruthless streak just as deep as Straya's by constantly going for where Phera was clearly the most tender from her slippering the night before.

"Are you- Ack! Really sure this is- Owie! The most effective use- Oh! Of your time?"

Even if getting her cute, jiggly backside spanked silly by an attractive older woman in a lab setting had been an idle fantasy she'd indulged herself in on more than a few occasions while she'd been back on The Bin, the reality still definitely hurt a lot more than she'd have preferred.

"No."

Kelt kept working her hand in two tight circles, right where Phera would have to rest her weight when she sat down later. Five on one side, then ten on the other, then thirteen back on the first. Making each sit-spot feel like it would split open at any moment just before switching.

"But, it at least helps me feel better."

SMACK! SMACK! SMACK! SMACK! SMACK!

Three or so minutes had already managed to drag by, and probably at least a couple hundred cruel slaps, with absolutely no signs of the petite woman slowing down in the slightest.

At least, that was Phera's estimate. She'd lost count somewhere around eighty-three. Besides, just then she was far too busy being caught up between staring desperately at her wrist comp, willing time to move faster while clenching her teeth and hissing out sharp yelps and the occasional grunt of pain as she writhed atop the workbench. Unfortunately for her, said bench was absolutely the perfect height for someone of her stature to bend over. Low enough to be comfortable (relatively speaking), but high enough still to necessitate balancing on the balls of her rapidly shifting feet.

Worse still, Kelt's straightforward manner and sizzling lecture had completely left her at a loss for words. So, rather than try to argue with her more, she defaulted back to bratting instead. That, at least, gave her mind something else to focus on besides how stupid the passage of time was and how much trying to sit down for lunch that afternoon was going to hurt.

"You know, I feel like you're- Urk! Really- Oh! Leaving some options on the table here," she protested, lips pushing out into a pout for a split-second before more yelps wiped it away. "Fuck! Geez, you know there's more to my ass than just the sit-spots, right?"

Huffing and puffing, she grumbled out through gritted teeth.

"Also, you're really going to be kicking yourself- Oh! When your shoulder is- Ack! All tired- Oof! And you have to come crawling to me- Owie! To do everything for you. Humph!"

"You offering your services to me already, young lady?" prompted Kelt, pausing to glide a pair of fingertips between the pinned pirate's legs.

"M-Maybe?"

Phera felt her face all but burst into flames as the senior engineer parted her labia with a brief caress before drawing back as she chuffed out a low laugh.

"I'll admit the idea of having you at my beck and call *does* have its appeal. Especially after what I heard about your... Ahem. *Talents* from Straya."

Ten more hard swats exploded against the vermilion undercurves of Phera's upturned bottom then, catching her utterly by surprise.

SMACK! SMACK! SMACK! SMACK! SMACK!

"But, you're right. It really would be best not to tire out my arm so early in the day."

With one final *SMACK!* for good measure, Kelt took a step back and began rolling her left shoulder in its socket.

"Oh thank gods..."

Phera allowed herself to go to jelly atop the workbench for several blissful moments, before starting to push herself back up.

SMACK!

"Stay in position!" snapped Kelt. "I didn't give you permission to move, did I?"

"No, but I-"

"Just be glad I'm not making you give those pants and shirt back to Shi, you little brat."

SMACK!

"Just be glad I'm not making you give those pants and shirt back to Shi," Phera mimicked under her breath in a sudden burst of sass.

"*Excuse me?*" pressed Kelt, eyebrows rising dangerously.

"I *said...*"

Huffing out a petulant harrumph, Phera threw the dirtiest look she could back over her shoulder.

"That I won these clothes fair and square."

She gave the currently inside-out resizable pants tangled around her knees a little wiggle for added emphasis.

"And if you've got a problem with that, you can take it up with Straya."

Prompting Kelt to roll her eyes, and Phera to turn her head back with a haughty sniff.

She was glad for the reprieve, however, assuming that she'd finally managed to talk some sense into the other woman. Or, maybe, just that she'd actually gotten tired. Either way, she was more than willing to stay bent over with her bottom out for the time being. The cool caress of the air circulation system felt absolutely wonderful on her sizzling skin, and anything that prolonged having to pull up her formfitting pants over her swollen backside was more than all right with her. Plus, if she was being totally honest with herself, it was actually pretty fun to be bossed around by this petite pirate.

She'd definitely need to think of some way of making it up to her for borrowing her printer without asking, though. After all, she knew all too well how frustrating having to delay starting a project could be.

"Hmmm... Speaking of Straya, that reminds me."

As Phera continued to pout, refusing to meet the other woman's eye, Kelt slipped a slate out from one of her pockets and snapped a few quick pictures of the bent, bared, and blazing buttocks sticking out over the workbench and above the stolen pants in front over.

"There. That ought to cheer Shi up."

"Pardon?"

"Oh, never you mind."

Tucking her slate back into her pocket, Kelt affected a sharp glare.

"You just tell Straya that if this happens again, I'm using *her* clothes as water pipe insulation."

Phera couldn't help but snort at that.

"Yeah. I'm sure that would go over suuuuper well."

Actually, that particular head-to-head would be a lot of fun to watch, now that she thought about it.

Her sardonic eye-rolling was cut short, however, when Kelt took up position beside her once again. Quickly transforming into heart-hammering worry as she felt the light *tap... tap... tap...* of something long, flexible, doubled-over, and wrapped in protective insulation with a metallic core. It sure felt a whole lot like Kelt had decided to improvise a strap out of one of the cables next to the power cells on the workbench. And, given the older engineer's admirable preoccupation with ship safety, said cabling was probably *very* durable.

"Um…"

Swallowing against her rapidly rising panic, Phera threw a fretful look over her shoulder at Kelt, having her suspicions confirmed for her in the worst possible way.

"Oh dear."

That cable looked to be both heavy and extremely flexible.

"You know, I'm pretty sure that's not an appropriate use of equipment."

"You're going to start lecturing *me* on appropriate use of ship equipment now? Really?"

Tap... Tap... Tap...

"I… um… Yes?"

"Little brat!"

Without warning, Kelt brought her makeshift implement exploding down in a whizzing arc across both of Phera's bare cheeks.

SWISH-SNAP!

"Aieee!"

Branding a thin, continuous line of white hot fury right along where they were the fullest.

SWISH-SNAP! SWISH-SNAP!

Before carving out two more atop the twin maroon circles she'd worked so hard to paint across her sit-spots.

"FUCK SHIT OW!"

Properly howling now, Phera pushed herself halfway up off the workbench as she started to dance from foot to foot.

"My goodness, you have quite the mouth on you, young lady."

SWISH-SNAP! SWISH-SNAP!

"I have half a mind to wash it out."

SWISH-SNAP! SWISH-SNAP!

"N- Owie! No thank you!"

SWISH-SNAP!

"We'll see."

SWISH-SNAP!

Phera was pretty sure she could actually *feel* new welts starting to blossom up and down along the undercurves of her cheeks in real time. Joined by ever more as Kelt continued to ruthlessly *SWISH-SNAP!* the flexible length of cable against her frantically gyrating seat.

"Oh my gods, oh my gods, oh my gods!"

But, even though it hurt like crazy, the thought of trying to flee from her crewmate's wrath never so much as crossed her mind. Although, she *did* continue to sass, if for no other reason than to prove that she could. (But even that was rapidly losing its appeal.)

"I've had a change of heart, okay?" she gasped, just as tears began to prickle at the corners of her eyes. "I promise I'll fill out a resource allocation request in triplicate and file it with you twenty-four hours ahead of time from now on, all right?"

It was a very stupid thing to say, she knew. But, it was either that or cave and start pleading. Which, if this kept up for much longer, was about to be her next course of action whether she liked it or not.

"Triplicate? Really? That's what you want to say to me right now? No wonder Straya has had to discipline you so often."

SWISH-SNAP! SWISH-SNAP! SWISH-SNAP! SWISH-SNAP!

"Then again, I can certainly see the appeal. You've got quite a bit more jiggle than I'm used to. Heh."

Four more searing lines blossomed across Phera's lower cheeks, leaving them more welt than not. Then, the cable started slashing further down. Biting across the backs of her plump thighs.

"Here's some news for you, kiddo," huffed Kelt as she continued to thrash the younger woman with even, vicious strokes of her improvised strap. "I'm not doing this for what you promise to do in the future."

SWISH-SNAP! SWISH-SNAP! SWISH-SNAP! SWISH-SNAP!

"I'm doing it for what you already did."

SWISH-SNAP! SWISH-SNAP! SWISH-SNAP! SWISH-SNAP!

"And because it's fun to punish unruly brats. Shi's so well-behaved, I almost never get to properly discipline him these days."

"But... but... Oh!"

With the first explosion of Kelt's improvised lash against her relatively untouched thighs, Phera had collapsed against the workbench with a gasp that transformed partway through into a high-pitched squeal.

"Oh my gods, oh my gods!" she howled, clawing herself further and further up onto the table, grinding her ample breasts and sopping pussy against its smooth surface as she tried to flee through it.

It remained steadfastly immovable, however (being bolted to the deck tended to do that), and she was forced to take whatever her senior engineer decided to give her.

Which, as it turned out, was quite a bit.

SWISH-SNAP! SWISH-SNAP! SWISH-SNAP! SWISH-SNAP!

"I'm sorry, Kelt, I'm SORRY!"

She was finally sounding genuinely contrite now. Salty rivulets of molten tears running down her cheeks from where her eyes were screwed shut tight and onto the body heat warmed workbench beneath her.

Cracking one eye open, she stole a peek at her wrist comp, and then let out a plaintive moan metered by sniffling sobs as she saw through a blurry haze that she still had at least a minute left before the other pirate's self-imposed timer would finally run out.

Assuming she actually decided to stick to it, that is.

Oh gods! What if she doesn't stop?!

Phera could feel genuine panic starting to seize hold of her lower abdomen then. But, Kelt seemed to be able to read her mind, and quashed it before it could properly take root.

"Almost done," she grunted, her gaze just as cold and unyielding as hull plating as she continued to whip her arm up and down with single-minded precision. "I just need to make sure this lesson sticks before we wrap things up."

SNAP! SNAP! SNAP! SNAP! SNAP!

Shifting her aim further south, Kelt began to work her lash with even greater speed. Guiding it down Phera's dancing thighs and back up again. Layering them with another crisscrossing patchwork of vivid, red welts on top of her previous ones. Then, with ten seconds to spare, she turned her attention back to the weeping woman's sit-spots; spending her remaining time revisiting those with the same fervor as she'd shown her thighs.

"And…"

SWISH-SNAP! SWISH-SNAP! SWISH-SNAP!

"Done!"

Just as suddenly as it had started, Phera's spanking was over and Kelt was tossing her improvised implement back onto the workbench with the power cells.

"Now then, let that be a lesson to you, young lady," she admonished, sounding slightly winded as she waggled a forefinger at her in a surprisingly maternal gesture. "This might be the Captain's ship, but *I'm* the one who keeps it up and running. Which means that if you want to use so much as a screwdriver, you clear it with me first. Is that understood?"

"Yes ma'am, I promise!" blubbered Phera, now an incoherently sobbing wreck.

"Good girl."

Smirking in evident self-satisfaction at a job well done, Kelt snapped a few more pictures of her well-punished junior engineer before tucking her slate away once again.

"Also, I think I'll be taking these back."

Suiting actions to words, she knelt down behind Phera and started peeling Shi's (apparently) pilfered pants down to her ankles and over the spare slippers that she'd borrowed from Straya, knocking them to the deck.

"But... but... but..." the auburn-haired pirate recruit whined pitifully, pushing herself up onto a shaky arm as she furiously dragged a forearm across her red-rimmed eyes. "But I was wearing those!"

That wasn't exactly what she'd wanted to say. But, with the ladder of welts all along her bottom and thighs pulsing fresh fire in time with her every heartbeat, she kept her more heated protests safely locked away where they couldn't give Kelt cause to pick up her cable again.

"You were," agreed the older woman with an unconcerned shrug. "And now you're not."

Then, with another smirk, she rolled up the pants, gave each blistered bottom cheek one final squeeze, and turned to stride her way out of the room.

"Printer's all yours until your project finishes," she called back, pausing in front of the hatch that Phera was only now realizing had been left open that entire time. "Come find me after you've had lunch, and I'll put you to work. I really could use an extra pair of hands around here. Though, we'll be doing things properly from now on. No more improvised engine mods, yes?"

"Yes ma'am..."

"That's what I like to hear."

Heaving out an amused, tired groan as the workshop hatch slid shut behind her new supervisor, Phera shook out her sweaty curls.

"Well, I suppose that could have gone better..."

Still, as far as supervisors went, she found herself musing as she reached back to tentatively massage her burning backside with one hand while the other buried that evil, evil cable under a pile of power cells, Kelt wasn't all *that* terrible.

Perhaps a bit prickly, but not terrible.

She could work with prickly.

And, really, ship safety was important, wasn't it?

Glancing back to the printer quietly humming along on the project that had gotten her into this mess in the first place, Phera snorted out a laugh and rolled her eyes.

"Gods, I really hope my measurements were correct on that."

Doing her absolute best not to think about what Kelt might do if she had to tell her she'd tied up her heavy materials printer all day for nothing, Phera slipped her feet back into her borrowed ship slippers and padded her way toward the exit to the workshop.

"Now then, I'm off to see a cutie about some cooling gel…"

CHAPTER TEN

Tiptoeing her way through the hab cylinder, tugging down on the front of her top in an effort to coax an extra centimeter or two of coverage out of it (and mostly just succeeding in further exposing her ruby red rump and Kelt's extremely thorough handiwork), Phera was very much regretting not holding onto her boyshorts. After Straya had returned with her new outfit the night before, right around the same time Adryel had finished pounding her cross-eyed as luck would have it, she'd tried it on and immediately fed her poor, tattered underwear into the Mayhem's materials recycler. Which, apparently, had been a major tactical error on her part.

Seriously, though. Who held onto clothes that were falling apart?

"Not me, it would seem. Ugh."

Phera knew she'd need to figure out what to do about her now very much worse off wardrobe situation at some point in the near future, but just then she had much bigger fish to fry. Namely, finding some relief for her flash-fried rear end.

I know ve said ve was expecting to see a lot of me, but I was at least hoping to make it another week before proving ver right...

Reaching the medbay, she saw to her dismay that the hatch was locked. Bright, glowing letters projecting three centimeters from the smooth metal reading "IN USE".

Oh gods, I hope nobody's hurt, she found herself fretting, racking her brain in an attempt to recall if any of her new crewmates (the ones who'd bothered to show up, at least) had seemed off at breakfast that morning.

Nothing was sticking out to her as odd, though. Nobody had been hacking up a lung or looking like they were about to vomit, so she eventually decided there wasn't any harm in at least *asking* for some help with her terribly tender bottom. Worst case scenario, Steph would tell her ve was busy, and she'd just suck it up and go see if there was any sorbet stashed away in the mess.

"Then again…"

Shifting from foot to foot, Phera very nearly turned and scurried away. She didn't want Steph to think she only liked ver for ver medical supplies, after all.

Don't be silly, ve likes you! You know ve does. Now stop acting like a freshman trying to decide how long she should wait before messaging back and give ver a buzz already!

Gritting her teeth and giving the sides of her face a couple of light slaps to psyche herself up, Phera took a moment to straighten out her top and comb her fingers through her hair. Once she'd managed to make herself as presentable as she was likely to get, she took in a deep breath and pressed her thumb to the intercom switch next to the hatch.

"Hey, Steph. You got a minute?"

In response to her hail, there came the abrupt sounds of clanging and clattering from within the little laboratory.

"No! Not in there, you little-!"

"Um, is everything all right?"

"Yep!"

There came more sounds of tools and trays being knocked onto the deck with a metallic clatter.

"Shit! Ow!"

"I um… I can come back if this is a bad time."

"Be there in a sec!"

Frowning, Phera was just about to try and key the door open, when it slid aside on its own to reveal a slightly out of breath Steph. Looking perhaps a bit more frazzled than usual, but otherwise none the worse for wear.

"Sorry about that. You just startled me is all."

As the crew doc smiled up at her, a thin, whip-like appendage waved over ver left shoulder, the little mass of feelers clustered at the end of it thrashing around in Phera's general direction as if sniffing at her.

"So... What's up?"

"Oh! Um..."

Momentarily distracted from her initial goal by the unexpected inspection, Phera's eyes locked onto the waving feelers as the hand still gripping the hem of her new shirt tightened.

"You seem like you've got your hands full here, maybe I should just..?"

She nodded her head nice and slow at the bone wasp larva peering out from behind the doctor just in case ve wasn't aware of its presence.

"Hah! No, you're fine."

Giggling, Steph reached up to tickle the little appendage.

"I was just finishing up feeding Valiya."

At Phera's continued dubious look, ve gave her a wink.

"Although, if ve'd gotten hurt because of you startling me, now *that* would be a different story," ve continued, ver mellifluous voice turning playfully menacing as ver eyes took in her complete lack of clothing below the waist. "I might've even had to tell big bad Kelt on you."

Stepping aside, ve waved for her to join ver inside the lab.

"Anyway, what's up?"

As ve turned to escort her in, the creature clinging to the back of ver vest with its six pairs of legs flicked the long, whippy appendage on its tail back in Phera's direction. The antennae on it sniffing even closer to her skin.

"Well, it's funny you should mention Kelt, actually..."

Huffing out an embarrassed laugh, Phera trailed after the doctor, not quite sure how close she should allow herself to get with the critter on ver back so interested in her. She figured it was probably safe if Steph wasn't freaking out. Still, she found herself speeding up to overtake ver just in case.

"She and I kind of got into a bit of a disagreement over the proper procedure for reserving time with the Mayhem's heavy printer."

Steph's laugh this time was much more of a cackle.

"Oh, I was there in the corridor when you started howling, sweet thing. I saw."

"Y-You did?"

"Mmhmm."

The doctor's impish face cracked into a wicked grin then.

"You should *really* keep pissing her off. Your ass looks great like that!"

"Ah, well, I..."

Again, Phera felt her cheeks flush, but she couldn't deny that the prospect of someone witnessing her punishment did some rather enjoyable things between her legs.

"I was kind of hoping everyone would be too busy to have noticed," she admitted, scrubbing a hand along the back of her neck before stooping down to gather up a couple of the fallen tools on the floor as cover while she attempted to master her embarrassment.

"Oh, they were."

Watching her work, Steph's dimples grew all the more pronounced as ver smile deepened.

"Don't worry, though. I was able to record the entire thing."

"You were?"

Face going positively scarlet, Phera stiffened and nearly dropped the tray she was holding.

"Yep!"

Not the least bit perturbed by her reaction, Steph gave one of ver vest pockets a little pat.

"Obette said you color up even prettier than Shi does."

"I... That's..."

This news was doing absolutely nothing to ease the building need between Phera's suddenly wobbly knees. And, after failing to articulate any response that was more complicated than a single, half-formed word, she decided to just roll with it and snorted out a laugh.

"Send me a copy of that when you get a chance, yeah?"

"You sure you'd rather not just reenact it now?" teased Steph, waggling ver pale eyebrows as ve took the tools from her.

Phera felt herself grinning now.

"Sorry, doc," she snickered. "I think these cheeks are just about spanked out for one day."

Turning her back toward the reflective door of a storage cabinet, Phera was finally able to get her first proper look at her backside.

"Okay, yeah. Definitely done for the day."

She let out a low, appreciative whistle as she shifted her hips from side to side in the reflective surface. Her sit-spots were an angry shade of carmine, and the raised edges of her welts had gone a livid shade of purple. But, much as she might hate to admit it, Steph had a point.

Her ass really *did* look good like this.

"So, um…"

Dragging her attention away from her battered bottom after spending a few more delightfully aching moments rasping her fingernails across its myriad puffy welts, Phera met Steph's twinkling mother of pearl gaze and quirked a self-deprecating smile.

"I was sort of hoping that you might be able to help me out with all this."

She gestured back at her hips.

"That gel stuff was pretty effective last time, and I don't think Kelt would mind if you spared me a bit?"

She ended up phrasing this last statement more as a question, hoping that she wasn't being too presumptuous in asking. Kelt had put her in a mindset of not letting any ship resources go to waste, and she immediately started running through possible scenarios where disaster could strike because she'd used the last of the crew's topical anti-inflammatory.

"You know," giggled Steph. "If you're going to come crying to me every time this happens, you should at least try to let it happen less."

Setting ver instruments on top of the exam cot, ve crossed ver arms beneath ver modest breasts and gave Phera a very "you have nobody to blame for this but yourself" sort of smirk. As ve was doing this, ver bone wasp larva crawled up ver neck and settled atop ver blonde bob, feelers waggling energetically. Which, sort of ruined the authoritative effect ve was clearly going for.

That thing better not be trying to lecture me too, Phera silently harrumphed, while aloud she said, "Hey!"

Abandoning her attempts at holding down her shirt (allowing it to return to just below her belly button, showing off the neatly trimmed thatch of red curls above her glistening folds), she mirrored the doctor's pose, the built-in adaptive support in Shi's resizable top making her breasts bounce with the movement.

"I'll have you know that I haven't come crying to you *every* time this has happened," she sniffed with mock-indignation. "Straya and Adri spanked and slippered me last night, and I didn't complain to you even once!"

Granted, she'd been too busy on her knees after that spanking, and then too busy admiring her new outfit to focus on whining at the time, but the point still stood.

"Oh, wow, big girl. I'm soooo impressed."

Untangling the larva from ver hair, Steph strode over to the glass terrarium full of sticks and rocks ve kept next to the lab's refrigeration unit and lowered it back inside.

"There you go, nibble bug," ve cooed, snapping the enclosure's lid back into place and giving it a couple of fond pats.

Then, turning back to Phera, ver features softened into something more commiserating.

"Well, I do still have some of that topical anti-inflammatory. Though, at the rate you're burning through it, I'm going to have to start rationing it out until the new cell cultures I have going finish gestating."

Closing the distance between the two of them in three languid strides, Steph draped an arm around Phera's shoulders and leaned in close enough to tickle her ear with ver breath.

"In the meantime, how'd you like to come back to my place for some more *general* anesthesia?"

A lovely tingle cascaded along Phera's left cheek as Steph's lips brushed against her skin, and she smirked.

"'General anesthesia', eh?"

"Mmhmm..."

Pulling out a metallic hip flask from ver vest pocket, ve held it up and gave it a little waggle, making its contents slosh invitingly.

"You look like you could use a drink."

"Or three," Phera amended wryly, making Steph giggle again.

"Oh, you *are* fun."

Then, once again turning teasing, ve added.

"And, I suppose if you're reeeeally going to be such a big baby about a little smacked bottom."

Ve gave said bottom a *SMACK!* of ver own then.

"Owie!"

"You can have some of the topical stuff too."

Rolling ver eyes at Phera's overdramatic pout as she rubbed at the renewed sting in her backside, Steph strode over to the refrigeration unit next to ver bone wasp terrarium and pulled open its door to retrieve one of ver rapidly dwindling bottles of cooling gel. Bending over far enough to stick ver own round and compact bubble butt up for Phera's appreciative inspection as ve did so, and forcing her to exercise all of her self-control not to give it a pinch.

Much as she might've wanted to, she wasn't sure how such a move might be received. And, despite how she'd acted the night before, she wasn't quite *that* forward. At least, not without half a bottle of rum in her.

"Well..." she hemmed as the doctor turned back to her, pretending to give the matter some serious consideration as she stared off into space. "I don't have to report back to Kelt until after lunch, so... Okay!"

Meeting Steph's eye once again, she fixed ver with her most sassy smile. One she was fairly certain the doctor was capable of producing all on ver own.

"Also, I'll have you know that I am fully prepared to whine as much and as long as it takes to get you to hand over that gel."

"Careful..."

One platinum eyebrow rose as Steph sauntered back to her.

"Annoy me too much, and I'll have to go for the Kelt solution."

As if punishing her for her own unacted upon temptation earlier, ve pinched Phera's left sit-spot, sending her stumbling back out into the corridor with a startled squeak.

"No thanks! She's way too busy, trust me."

"Oh, I know better than to bother that lady when she's in one of her moods," Steph snickered as the two of them fell into step with one another and began making their way toward the crew cabins at an easy pace, one hand casually fondling Phera's tender left cheek as they went. "Don't worry, though. I'm fully capable of employing her methods myself should the need arise."

As if to demonstrate just what ve meant in case it wasn't already abundantly clear, the petite doctor gave Phera's bottom a hard squeeze that made her squeak adorably once again.

"Sure- Oh! Sure you are," she gasped, almost managing a deadpan until Steph's closely-trimmed fingernails began to dig in against her swollen skin.

"Careful, sweet thing," ve warned again in a menacing lilt. "You haven't actually gotten that cooling gel yet, you know."

"Y-Yeah, yeah…"

Despite the handful of surprisingly stingy swats ve'd sprung on her since they'd met, Phera had her doubts as to how effective the little doctor could actually be at delivering a proper ass blistering to someone who wasn't already thoroughly tender. With arms that thin and hands that soft, she suspected ve probably wasn't capable of doing much more than playing patty cake with a bratty backside.

Which, honestly, sounded like it might be kind of fun.

"I'm sure you're a very formidable spanker who's studied first-hand across the laps of Kelt, and Straya, and Ob, and Adri, and Lem, and the Captain, and-"

SMACK!

"Ack!"

"You're lucky you're cute, you know that?" Steph chuckled darkly, all impudent smirk and flashing mother of pearl eyes as the two of them drew up to the closed hatch of the second crew cabin. "Well, here we are."

Palming the door open, it slid back to reveal a room that was blessedly empty for the moment.

"So this is how the other half lives?"

Slipping inside, Phera performed a slow turn to take the cabin in more fully.

"Nice."

While its layout was identical to her own, each of the bunks had a little bit of extra flavor and personality their owners had added to them to make the cramped room feel like home. An extra pillow here. A colorful blanket there. Half-underneath the pillows of one particularly messy bunk lay a charcoal gray reading slate. While over another, stylized renderings of long extinct pre-colonization species native to the system peered out from their projections against the wall and ceiling.

"So, which one's yours?"

"Right here."

Flouncing over to the bunk with the slate peeking out from the pillows, Steph picked up the device and tucked it out of harm's way beneath the mattress.

"Best one in the room, right?"

Settling down on the edge of the bed, ve patted the spot beside ver.

"Gotta say, I absolutely love the view."

Phera winked then, making the doctor's pale cheeks color a delightful shade of coral as she settled stiffly down beside ver. Mostly managing to suppress a pained hiss as all of her weight came to rest atop her still throbbing sit-spots.

"Here," offered Steph, holding the flask out to her with a happy little snicker. "Drink up, me hearty."

"Yo ho!"

Giggling herself, Phera unscrewed the cap on the flask and gave its contents an inquisitive sniff before bringing it to her lips and swallowing a generous mouthful. It was smooth and nutty, and burned pleasantly all the way down to her stomach.

"Ahhh…"

Sighing contentedly, she looked back to Steph with an impish smirk.

"You know, it's been a pretty long time since I've snuck off to a friend's place in the middle of the day to share some booze. Your parents aren't about to walk in on us, are they?"

"Probably not," dismissed Steph with an unconcerned wave that made the glitter in ver nail polish sparkle in the sunsim. "Cap's in her office, so no worries there. As for Lem…"

Ver glossy lips pinched thoughtfully for a brief moment.

"Well, she might," ve admitted, before seeming to shrug the idea off entirely as ve stretched ver arms above ver head. "She's usually working out right about now, though, so I doubt it."

"Fingers crossed!"

Giggling again, Phera mirrored her words with the gesture and gave the contents of Steph's flask a little slosh before taking another sip.

She'd be lying if she said the idea of the crew's beefcake hotty of a first mate walking in on them just then wasn't a concern. She had biceps even bigger than Straya's, and Phera had a sneaking suspicion she probably wouldn't be too pleased with her and Steph's impromptu house call. But, on the other hand, she wasn't about to let that ruin her fun. Whatever happened, happened. And, worst come to worst, at least she wouldn't be the only one getting her ass knocked into orbit. Actually, now that she thought about it, the added hint of danger only made her private time with the crew doc all the more exciting.

Taking the flask when Phera offered it to ver, Steph knocked back a mouthful.

"Anyway, we should be docking back at Marcos sometime tomorrow," ve ventured somewhat tentatively, seeming to be at a loss for words now that they were alone in ver cabin. "I, uh... I'm guessing you haven't been out Proxward before?"

Ve was referring to the planets and other satellites held in semi-stable orbit by the system's smaller, secondary star, and Phera shook her head.

"Nope."

Shifting her weight onto the side of one hip, leaning into Steph's slight warmth for support, she kicked off her slippers and brought her bare feet up onto the bunk beneath her.

"I grew up planetside on Cilara."

Cilara was a major population center in the Goldilocks zone of the system's primary. Very stable, and very corporate controlled.

"Mom worked in a factory doing QA, and Dad did auditing for some corp or another."

At the mention of her father, Phera gestured for the flask.

"I forget which one. We never really talked much. He's kind of a huge asshole."

"Sorry."

Looking somewhat abashed, Steph handed over the booze.

"I'm guessing you'd rather I not ask for more details?"

"No, no, it's fine."

Waving away the doctor's concerns with only semi-forced breeziness, Phera took another, deeper, pull of the nutty liquor, seeking refuge in the warmth that settled in along the bottom of her stomach as she gathered her thoughts.

"It's not the worst story ever, I guess," she sighed. "We always had food on the table, and my parents' company insurance was able to cover stuff like my neural lattice graft. Dad was just one of those Head of Household types with all the capital Hs who loved to yell and throw stuff whenever he wasn't happy. And, well... Let's just say I wasn't quite the model Daughter of Harmony he'd been hoping for."

"Church girl, huh?"

"Oh yeah, big time. Dedication to Light when I was a year old, Baptism of Renewal at eight, regular visits to our local Temple of Reflection for ordinances for the dead all throughout secondary school, Blood Covenant at nineteen, the works."

"Wow, you weren't kidding," marveled Steph. "I'm surprised you didn't wind up in a convent."

"I definitely would've if they'd known about some of the stuff I was getting up to during secondary school," snorted Phera. "As it was, they really wanted me to spend a couple years doing missionary work after I graduated, but I managed to get out of that by being accepted into the University of Cilara with a scholarship."

"What about your other dad or mom or whatever? Were they just going along with all of this?"

Phera snorted a little at that.

"Harmony parents are always monogamous cishet pairings," she clarified. "And, yeah, Mom wasn't really much better than Dad. She never yelled, she just got '*disappointed*' and went along with whatever he said because that's what a virtuous helpmeet is supposed to do. She was just as strict as he was, though, and whenever Dad got into one of his moods, she always seemed to find something to clean in another room. Classic codependency bullshit mixed with a heaping helping of religious conservatism and corporate boot licking, you know?"

Steph grimaced.

"Can't say I've ever really experienced that firsthand. My dads and I all get along really well. That sounds rough, though."

"Living with those two was definitely a nightmare," agreed Phera with a bitter little laugh, buffing the surface of the flask with her thumb as long distant memories of cringing into the corner of the ugly, floral-patterned couch in their living room while her dad went ballistic about some thing or another came bubbling back to the surface of her mind like noxious gas in an ore refinery. "It's all good now, though. My college had a great therapy clinic on campus that was free for students, and my roommate in the dorms all but dragged me over there the first time I broke down sobbing after a call from my mom. I was there pretty much every other week all the way up until I finished my PhD, so I *think* I've managed to more or less work out my baggage with parents by now. Well... probably."

She gave a self-deprecating shrug at that.

"Either way, Dad and I haven't talked since I left for school, and that's been just fine with me."

"Sounds like it was for the best, yeah."

"Mmhmm. Totally was."

Coiling a copper curl around two of her fingers, Phera drew in a deep breath through her nose for four seconds, held it for seven, and then blew it out in a thin, steady stream through pursed lips for eight. Visualizing all of her anxiety and resentment blowing away with it as she did so, just like her therapist had taught her.

"Mom and I at least kept in touch for a while freshman year," she continued, somewhat more relaxed now. "She totally lost it when she saw these, though."

Phera gestured to her biomodded eyes and grinned with vindictive satisfaction as the memory of her strictly conservative mother's horrified face in her dorm's vidcomm drifted back to her.

"Got 'em done with a couple friends after our first midterms."

"Oooh, fun! I was around the same age when I got mine too," interjected Steph, taking back the flask and matching the curvy engineer swig for swig.

"Awww, eye buddies!"

Phera gave one violet-hued eye a wink.

"But, yeah. Once Mom figured out that I had no intention of coming back home for breaks or anything, those calls started to dry up pretty quick."

"Shit..."

"Yeah..."

Suddenly feeling like she'd brought down the mood, Phera blew out another sigh and forced herself to cheer up as she turned back to Steph with a sly grin.

"So, Proxima, huh? That where you're from? All the news reports back on Cilara made that whole system out like it's just one big mugging waiting to happen."

"Yep. And... Yeah, yeah that's about right, really."

Ve took another sip and let out a satisfied, burning exhalation that made ver shiny silver earrings sway in a way that had Phera biting her lower lip.

"I mean, they'll probably try to invade us again at the next B-Cluster conjunction, and it'll probably be even more of a mugging waiting to happen after that. But... yeah. That's home, I guess."

Shrugging, Steph passed back the flask.

"Dad's a doctor. My other dad *was* a doctor. And my other, other dad still is too. Mom's a Selentec III series gestation chamber. Think she got sold off to... Oh, either Taveria or Mylex tenish years ago?"

Leaning back on ver palms, Steph's grin turned mischievous.

"Never actually did full-on med school. Some classes here and there, but I mostly learned by helping Dad and Papa. Enough that I passed the exams when I took them alongside the university babes later."

"Wow."

Phera was genuinely impressed by that.

"That must've been a fun afternoon."

"Two days, actually."

"Even better."

Feeling pleasantly buzzed from both the liquor and the devastatingly cute enby beside her, she capped the flask and reached out to brush aside some of Steph's blonde hair to get a better look into ver mother of pearl eyes.

"I bet all those med nerds just *loved* watching you stroll up to kick their asses."

Shifting on the mattress, Steph wrapped an arm around Phera again and giggled into her approaching face.

"I, uh... Well, I didn't really kick any asses in those exams. I was sort of near the bottom of the curve for that group, actually. But, well, you know what they call the bottom ten percent of people who pass, right? They call 'em doctors."

"Damn right they do."

Grinning from ear to ear, Steph leaned in close and nibbled at the engineer's ear.

"Oh gods, that feels so fucking nice..."

Shivering in delight at the sensation of teeth on her earlobe, Phera's smile turned wicked as she leaned in to nip playfully at the crook of Steph's slender neck in mock-retaliation.

"So, doctor," she snickered, pulling back just enough to kiss the faint bite mark she'd left behind. "What job site did the Captain kidnap you off of?"

"An employment office on Darkside Station, actually. Didn't know what kind of independent hauler it would be, I just liked the crew."

Steph captured Phera's lips in a lingering kiss then.

Damn, ve's really good at this...

Reveling in the warmth of the doctor's soft and slightly fruity tasting lips on her own, Phera kept her mouth locked to vers for several long, blissful moments. Pushing her tongue in past ver lips to run along ver teeth as she laid her hands atop ver shoulders and used her greater weight to push ver onto ver back against the mattress.

It was nice being able to take the lead for a change.

"That's..." she said in a lazy mixture of disbelief and amusement as she drew back and moved to straddle ver slim hips with her hands on either side of ver head, red hair swaying down to form a curtain around the two of them. "Remarkably straightforward."

Who'd have thought pirates used recruitment offices?

"It's actually a pretty smart move, if you think about it."

Leaning into Phera's mouth for another kiss, Steph swiveled ver tongue around the engineer's as ve glided ver hands down along the curve of her arched spine to grip either of her roasted, striped buttocks. Squeezing them hard enough to make her buck forward.

"You don't want a ship's doctor to resent you, now do you?" ve taunted before kissing her again, more passionately this time.

"No- Ah! Kidding," panted Phera between smooches, the last word coming out as a grunt of pleasure at yet another hard squeeze.

While she put her tongue back to work wrestling with Steph's, she spread her legs further apart to settle her groin against the doctor's pelvis; eyes rolling up as she found some much needed friction to grind her aching clit against.

"I'd say I can be scary too," she teased breathily, gliding a hand up along ver vest.

Steph's lithe body tensed as her fingers found ver nipples through ver thin shirt. Ve wasn't wearing a bra just then, and was showing off two prominent targets for the engineer to tease.

"I mean, from what Straya's said," ve giggled just as breathlessly as Phera dragged the pad of her thumb in slow, clockwise circles around the silky material of ver top. "H-Having you on a ship unsupervised can be pretty scary, yeah."

Ve stuck ver perky little tongue out at her then, and instantly the engineer wanted nothing more than to kiss ver again.

So she did.

Hard.

"Hey now, scary can be fun," she protested, feigning a pout as she pulled back enough to sit up straight with her ample cheeks nestled around something ramrod stiff inside the doctor's dark slacks.

Naked below the waist as she was, this new position gave Steph a clear line of sight between her lasciviously parted thighs as she regarded ver soft white blouse and black vest with a keen, assessing eye.

"Besides," she continued in a low, teasing singsong, tugging Steph's shirt free of ver pants and slipping both hands beneath it and the vest. "I'd like to think my go-getterness is an asset."

Shifting her palms up along the doctor's smooth and delightfully warm skin as she leaned forward once again, Phera cupped a bare breast in either hand and gave them a firm squeeze as she caught their nipples between her thumbs and forefingers.

"Wouldn't you agree?"

"Different kind of- Ah!"

Grinning with a malevolence that would've made the Captain proud, Phera gave both swollen pearls a prolonged pinch that was just as hard as anything she'd experienced during her physical the other day.

"H-Hey!"

Steph's head twitched back, teeth gritted and eyes closed as ver body trembled.

"Mmmm... Yes?" she crooned, maintaining her grip as she flexed her palms around the doctor's chest and watched ver squirm with unabashed delight. "Go on, I'm listening."

"I... Ah! You-!"

Phera just nodded right along to the garbled, half-formed exclamations as if they were still having a casual conversation.

"Oh, I agree *completely*."

"Heh. My fault for getting you drunk," Steph eventually managed to pant as both ver hands clapped down hard against Phera's swollen cheeks.

SMACK-SMACK!

"Ack! Why you little-!"

Using ver captured chest for support (squeezing in retaliation, though not hard enough to actually hurt), Phera tossed her head back and hissed in air through clenched teeth as twin blossoms of pain bloomed along the outer curves of her hips.

"You still want that ointment?"

"I, uh... Ahem."

Blushing softly and clearing her throat, she eased her grip and sat up straight again, deliberately grinding her clit against the doctor's groin as she made herself more comfortable.

"Yes. Yes I do."

"Might want to adjust the angles then."

Steph stuck out ver tongue again, and gave Phera's poor cheeks another double *SMACK!*

"Good- Ah! Good point."

Wincing with the effort, the new recruit rolled off of the doctor and onto her stomach beside ver on the bunk. Giving her vermilion seat an inviting wiggle as she settled into place and sighed.

"If you'd be so kind…"

Steph was only too happy to oblige.

"Stars and void, Kelt really didn't hold back at all, did she?"

Sounding far more impressed than sympathetic, ve shifted up onto ver knees and straightened out ver top. Then, snickering at Phera's petulant harrumph, ve leaned forward and rested a hand gently on either thoroughly swollen and bruised buttock.

"Maybe she really should have Lem's job."

Ve paused for a moment then, before adding with a smirk.

"I mean, so long as I'm not aboard, that is."

Then, picking up the bottle of cooling gel ve'd brought with ver, ve squeezed out a generous amount into ver palm and began massaging it across both of Phera's incredibly abused sit-spots.

"Oooh gods…"

Phera's hips rose up on reflex to meet the doctor's touch as ve got to work, hot flesh breaking out into goosebumps as she shivered atop the comforter.

"I cannot tell you how good that feels."

Snatching up one of Steph's pillows from the head of the bunk, she pulled it beneath her chin as she turned her head to look back at ver slender profile.

"Wait. So, Kelt wants Lem's job? Seriously? She seemed like she was pretty happy with where she is now when I was talking to her earlier."

As Steph's fingers dipped between her cheeks, another long, deep groan escaped from her.

"Then… Then again…" she managed, eyelids fluttering shut. "Bossing everyone around might be right up her… up her alley…"

She smirked as she imagined Steph trying to pull off the same trick. Somehow, she just couldn't see Straya or Adryel getting out of bed at ver order.

"Hah! You haven't seen Lem acting as discipline officer yet, have you?"

Steph worked the tingly gel into both the masses of raised, overlapping ridges that technically constituted the drooling engineer's sit-spots, and then squeezed out more to give them another coating before spreading even more along the stripy expanse of her thick thighs.

"Kelt's... Hmmm. You know, I'm not actually sure which of them you want near your ass the least."

Steph emphasized the word "ass" by giving Phera's some more heavy-handed squeezes. Kneading the gel deeper into her welted cheeks as ve did so.

"Mmph!"

Grunting into her pilfered pillow, Phera felt her thighs parting to give the crew doc's clever fingers better access to anywhere they might want to wander.

"Haven't seen that, nope," she eventually managed. "Everyone I've ticked off so far around here has been h-hands on... with, uh... you know..."

Her words meandered and started to fall apart as Steph found a particularly tender patch of bruised flesh, and she gave her bottom a meaningful sway to finish the thought for her. Then, shaking her head, she let out a small snort.

"With biceps like those, though, I'd definitely be way more scared of Lem when she's in a mood to beat some ass."

Another not unpleasant shiver slithered its way down the valley of her spine and directly between her tender thighs as she gave that particular scenario some time to take shape in her mind's eye.

"That, uh... That doesn't happen often, does it?"

"Hah!"

Steph's guffaw was not reassuring.

"She's been in a pretty good mood thanks to this raid going better than she was afraid it would. Normally, I'd say Lem's responsible for, oh... at least thirty percent of the gluteal damage around these parts."

The doctor's skilled hands went back to rubbing Phera's thighs then, and this time crept deeper around their interiors. Moving in tight circles ever higher toward where little red hairs started to appear between them.

"You'll understand once you've seen her in a bad mood. Or, like, just a horny mood. It's not exactly fair."

Steph spent a few blissful moments rubbing more gel into the creases between sit-spot and thigh, and then started to wander back down and inward. Slowly closing in on Phera's drenched pussy.

"I'll have to- Oh gods... To keep an eye out for... for..."

The way she was starting to pant was making it extremely difficult to tell whether or not she'd actually be avoiding the first mate or not. The thought of her on the prowl for someone to have her way with wasn't without its charms, and Steph's teasing fingers were definitely swaying her toward being reckless as she shifted her hips subconsciously toward ver hand.

"I bet I know what you're thinking," giggled Steph, leering shamelessly. "Don't you worry, sweet thing. You'll get your wish soon enough, I'm sure. Though you'll proooobably wish you hadn't."

Ve immediately put the lie to those words by simultaneously probing into Phera's lower lips and tickling at her outer labia with ver gel-slicked fingertips.

"Either way, you better pray to all those gods you keep calling to that I've restocked on this stuff by then."

Steph nodded ver mop of platinum, pixie-cut hair toward the bottle resting on the mattress beside ver, not that Phera could actually see. Then, beaming, slipped ver middle and ring fingers all the way up to the knuckle inside of her and began pumping.

"Ah!"

The gasp that left Phera this time was both high-pitched and breathy, and was followed immediately by several more that were only partially stifled by her chewing on her lower lip as the crew doc's other hand found purchase on her clit. Random, disjointed thoughts and snippets of fantasies of being at the mercy of the crew's gruff and intimidating first mate in some vaguely formalized ship disciplinary setting were rushing through her mind at near FTL, sped along ever onward by Steph's fingers working her from behind.

"Oh... Oh gods, Steph... You're... You're..."

She was having a hard time stringing words together all of a sudden, so opted instead to express her appreciation of the doctor's skills by grinding her hips against ver cupped palm.

"I'm...?"

Steph seemed to actually be curious what she was going to say next, though ve kept ver fingers working as ve waited patiently for her reply.

"You..."

Pushing herself up so that she was trembling on her hands and knees, giving her hips easier leverage to ride against the doctor's hand, Phera drew her curtain of red curls out of her face and met the enby's gaze with an unabashed, lopsided grin.

"You are *very* talented."

Before letting out a startled squeak as Steph found just the right spot inside of her. Collapsing face first back against the mattress with her hips still in the air.

"And you're about to make me come. Oh gods, please don't stop..."

"Already, huh?"

"Wh-What can I say?" laughed Phera, adrift in a sea of endorphins. "It's been that kind of day."

"Is that right?"

Steph's fingers slowed their pace then, producing a pitiful whine from the sopping engineer as ve batted ver lashes at her teasingly.

"So what do I get in exchange for letting you come then, hmmm?"

"What do you want?" Phera managed to ask, keeping her hips poised high in a silent plea. "I'm not gonna lie here, you've kinda got me over a barrel, and I like you, so..."

She let that last word trail off and squeezed herself tight around the fingers still inside of her.

"What can I do for you, Doctor Hot Stuff?"

Steph grinned, victorious.

"Well, for starters, you can lift that ass up higher."

Ve straightened up onto ver knees then, and started working ver pants down. Underneath, ve wore a pair of tight white briefs that were bulging eagerly out in front. The sight of that grin and its accompanying bulge sent a fresh bolt of excitement directly between Phera's legs.

"Whatever you say!"

Giddy with anticipation, she shifted her knees further forward across the mattress toward her chest, arched her back, and spread her legs. Giving the slim crew doc clear and unobstructed access to her arousal-soaked, pouting lips, and just a peek of her puckered anus deeper in the cleft above them.

The sight of her had Steph grinning all the broader, and ve hurriedly shoved ver briefs down, letting verself bounce free and point directly at ver target.

"Right then, you naughty girl…"

Shuffling in behind Phera, ve began gliding ver fingers up and down along her labia again, using her arousal to lubricate the tip of ver cock. Then, just as ve was lining up to enter her, the cabin's door swished open and the petite pilot boy, Shi, stepped inside wearing a very comfortable looking pair of resizable pants that did not match his top in the slightest.

"Hey, Steph, you in-?"

The rest of whatever he'd been about to say got caught in the back of his throat with a surprisingly cute choking noise, and he jerked to a sudden stop only a few paces past the threshold. Eyes frozen on Phera's ruby red and gel-slicked backside, and the half-naked, fully erect Steph.

"Um."

He shuffled a little in place, cheeks brightening to match Phera's own.

"Cap wanted to see you, um, about the biocontainment bays. Says she wants it taken care of before we dock."

He bit his lip.

"Um… So, uh… Go fast, I guess?"

There was a brief, awkward pause before he spun on his heel and all but fled the room again. And Phera, who'd been frozen stock-still for the entire exchange, collapsed back against her pillow as soon as the door swished shut again.

"Oh gods," she groaned, red-faced but laughing in spite of everything.

Shi seemed like a sweet boy from what little interaction she'd managed to have with him so far, but that was…

Yeah.

"That was awkward."

Rolling over onto her side and propping her head up on an elbow, still blushing, she arched a brow at Steph.

"You need to get going, I take it?"

"Yeah… Mood's kinda shot."

Steph cleared ver throat, and wriggled ver pants and underwear back on over ver still very much erect penis.

"Well, you got your ointment, and I got my drink with a cutie. So, I guess things could've been worse."

Ve picked up the half-spent gel bottle and winked.

"You know, if you're not ready to give up just yet, you could always just stay like that and I'll send Shi back in to finish the job."

SMACK!

With a low chuckle, Steph delivered a properly hard swat to the center of Phera's glistening bottom, making both cheeks jiggle before getting up

"I…"

Phera wasn't really sure if ve was entirely joking or not, but she was desperate enough just then that she gave the idea some serious consideration.

"Heh. It's tempting, really. But, with my luck, it'd probably be Kelt who popped in next, and, uh… Yeah."

Actually, that wouldn't be the worst thing ever, now that I think about it.

Pushing herself back up onto her hands and knees, stretching with a long groan as she basked in the wonderfully tingly sensation of her cooled cheeks, Phera clambered off of the bunk and slipped back on her borrowed ship slippers; checking the time on her wrist comp as she went.

"We'll have to try this again sometime, yeah?"

"Definitely."

Leaning in, she kissed Steph on the cheek before making her way toward the door, waving dreamily over her shoulder as she went.

"See you later, Doc. I'm going to go grab a snack before Kelt comes looking for me. Have fun with your bio-what's-its."

CHAPTER ELEVEN

CHARGES ACCRUED

Indecent Exposure

True to Steph's word, the Mayhem and its complement of Blazar Bitches reached its home port late that following afternoon. And, while everyone else was ecstatic to get a chance to stretch their legs somewhere other than the ship's hab cylinder for a change, Phera was anything but. Oh, she was eager to see what a real life pirate port of call looked like for herself, but that enthusiasm was largely dampened by the fact that she'd been unable to come up with any sort of replacement for the pants Kelt had taken back from her the day before.

For *some* reason, all of her crewmates seemed to think it was hilarious that she was forced to walk around half-naked all the time, and all of the (increasingly desperate) attempts she made to barter clothes from them were summarily dismissed.

Well, mostly.

She was pretty sure she might've been able to get Shi to cave and hand over his resizables again if she'd had more time with him at breakfast that morning, but Kelt had swooped in as soon as she'd mentioned the word "pants" and put a stop to their burgeoning negotiations with a hard swat to both of their seats. Sending them scurrying out of the mess with orders to go make themselves useful while she and the rest of the crew snickered over their coffee.

In the end, with time running out and all other options exhausted, Phera finally worked up the nerve to throw herself on the dubious mercy of the Captain. Catching her just as she was leaving her office while Shi was beginning their final approach to the station's docking ring.

"Captain, *please,* you've got to help me out here. I can't go out like this!"

"Come now, Phera, I think you look great just the way you are," the older woman crooned, while Straya and Adryel stood a safe couple of meters further back behind their cabinmate, smirking.

"But... but..."

Completely at a loss for words and starting to really, truly panic now, Phera flailed a hand in desperation at the very visible patch of copper curls peeking out from between her firmly pressed together thighs.

"This shirt barely covers anything!"

"Oh, does it?"

The grin that split the Captain's face with that deceptively placid question exposed white, wolfish teeth that made Phera's knees go weak as she drew in close enough for her body heat to register.

"I hadn't noticed."

As she spoke, the Captain casually dragged the back of one knuckle along the curve of the engineer's cheekbone, making her shiver as her keen, amber eyes bored directly into her. Rooting her to the spot as she brushed aside a stray lock of hair. Then, still grinning, she snatched up a fistful of auburn tresses and used them to shove her roughly against the wall just outside the hatch to her office.

"Ack! Wait! What are you-?"

"What do you think, girls?"

Ignoring Phera's muffled protests, the Captain slid her lithe frame in alongside her generous curves. Then, head cocking to one side like a predator toying with its prey, she angled a nod toward the engineer's naked backside and the small of her back where she'd seized a handful of her top.

"Too exposed?"

"Looks good to me," answered Adryel, flashing the bare bottom and thighs in front of them two thumbs up. "Wouldn't change a thing."

"Ditto," agreed Straya, hard eyes twinkling with cruel amusement as she folded her arms beneath her breasts and settled back against the wall behind her. "People are definitely going to think she's your pet whore if you let her out like that, though."

"Oh, now *there's* an idea!"

Rather than be abashed, the Captain's grin only grew all the more wicked.

"Steph still has that collar and leash in ver lab. Maybe I ought to have ver go get them so we can complete the look?"

"Oh my gods, Captain! You can't!"

"Kidding, swabbie. Kidding."

The Captain's grip suddenly tightened on Phera then as she bore down on her back with her forearm, stretching her spine and pushing her hips further back and apart.

"But don't you *ever* tell me what I can and can't do aboard my ship."

SMACK!

"Ack!"

"Am I understood?"

While the Captain might've been joking about parading her around as her personal concubine, the swat she delivered to Phera's horror-stricken, goosebump-covered backside was anything but. Landing with a crisp, meaty report that echoed down the corridor and bounced her up onto the balls of her feet with the force of its impact.

"Yes ma'am! Sorry ma'am! It won't happen again, ma'am!" she blurted out all at once in a barely intelligible stream of panic-packed syllables as her heels thumped back down onto the deck behind her.

SMACK!

"Ah!"

Only to pop right back up again with another *heavy-handed swat.*

"Very good. I knew you were a fast learner."

Phera could hear the leering grin in the older woman's taunting cadence, and found herself nibbling at her lower lip despite herself as the Captain raked her amber gaze up and down along the robust curves at her mercy.

"Anyway, I *suppose* I can cut you a some slack if it's really that important to you. Straya, be a dear and let her borrow that top of yours from the other day, would you?"

"Awww. Are you sure, Cap?"

"She is! She is!" Phera quickly interjected.

SMACK!

Earning herself a third handprint that felt like it landed in exactly the same place as the previous two. Further defining its sharp outlines as it filled in with even more color.

"I am," confirmed the Captain, sounding only a little disappointed.

Then, seeming to reach some sort of decision in the intervening moments after saying that, her grip on the back of Phera's top tightened once again and she pushed down harder on the small of her back. Forcing the engineer to shuffle backward another couple of steps so that she was bent over at a near perfect ninety-degree angle.

"Take your time, though," she went on, free hand gliding up and down along each of Phera's soft, bouncy buns with a sensual, almost lazy smoothness; familiarizing herself with their topography before giving the leftmost one a hard, possessive squeeze and another *SMACK!*

"Owie!"

"We still have at least half an hour before Shi finishes docking, and I think I've just found the perfect thing to occupy myself with."

SMACK!

"Ow! Captain, wait, please-!"

SMACK!

"Hmmm? Yes, Phera? Was there something else you wanted to add?"

There was quite a bit, as a matter of fact. But, sensing that to protest further now would only make things worse for her (and feeling her brain starting to short circuit from the sharp spasms of pleasure every precisely meted out swat was pulsing directly between her thighs), Phera heaved out a chagrined half-laugh half-sigh and adjusted her stance to something a bit more stable as she blew a few loose strands of hair away from her nose.

"No ma'am. Never mind."

"See? That's what I thought. Now then, where was I?"

"I think you were about to get to work on her thighs," Straya offered dryly, while Adryel nodded in enthusiastic agreement.

"Don't forget the insides of her sit-spots too, Cap. She *hates* it there."

"Oh, you don't have to tell me, Adri, honey."

The Captain allowed her middle and ring fingers to slip between Phera's cheeks and glide along the spots the crew cook had indicated with an enigmatic chuckle that threatened to spill over into a malevolent cackle at any moment.

"I'm well aware."

SMACK!

—

While it was certainly better than nothing, Phera had to admit that Straya's oversized t-shirt left a lot to be desired in the modesty department considering its hem barely reached her sit-spots. A fact which was repeatedly driven home for her with little thrills of stomach-clenching terror and excitement each time she leaned forward just a bit too far or started walking too quickly and felt the invisible, trailing fingers of enviro-controlled air playing across her suddenly exposed skin.

Which, as it turned out, happened quite a bit.

In an effort to not die of embarrassment, she did her best to stay nestled snugly in between a knot of her fellow crewmates as they disembarked from the Mayhem early that evening and made their way through the docking ring at Marcos Station and out into the hab proper in search of some well-earned fun.

It didn't help.

"Hey hey, nova buns," called a greasy looking man selling equally greasy looking skewers of what appeared to be some sort of fried rodent just outside the grav acclimation tunnel leading from the dock. "You wanna come put that pretty mouth of yours around some of my meat? I bet you'd like it."

He accompanied this offer with an exceptionally loud wolf whistle that echoed harshly off the mostly well-lit, hard surfaces that made up the environmental enclosure around them. Drawing the attention of several more passersby and causing Phera's face to flush bright enough to match her unbound hair, while Straya made a show of cracking her knuckles one at a time; she and Adryel turning their heads to glare.

Only, instead of one of her cabinmates coming to her rescue, it was Lem who intervened.

"Shove it up your ass," she growled at the man, reaching out to roughly grope one of Phera's nova buns for herself. "She's busy."

"Ah, come on, lady. Red looks like she can take plenty of cock. Can't you, sweetheart?"

Several hands twitched toward holsters then, and Lem snorted out a derisive laugh.

"You'd have to be able to get it up for her first."

"Oh, I'm plenty hard enough for the both of you sluts," growled the man, making a move to step out from behind his stall.

"Doubt it," replied Lem, all levity draining from her voice as her big palm settled on the grip of an even bigger coilgun. "Especially after I break that fucking jaw of yours and piss down your neck."

She leveled a supremely frosty smile at the vendor then, one that just *dared* him to call her bluff. Wisely, he seemed to rethink whatever it was he'd been about to say next. And, suddenly finding his grill extremely interesting, looked away, thoroughly cowed.

"Um, thanks," Phera mumbled at the barrel-chested woman once they were well out of earshot of the greasy man and his friends, lips twitching up in a grateful smile.

"No problem, muffin," replied Lem with a level of affection the engineer hadn't been expecting, giving the seat she was still holding onto another firm squeeze before letting go and swiveling her head to frown at the Captain. "She's going to need a constant security detail if you let her keep wandering around like this, you know."

"Awww, but she's just so adorable!" countered the other woman with an unconcerned laugh, impervious to her first mate's disapproving stare as she grinned down at the very visible splashes of bright red fading to dark pink she'd painted along the undercurves of her new roboticist's ample cheeks. "Besides, you should've seen the way she was whining before we docked. She was all but begging me to let her wear that outfit. Isn't that right, Phera?"

Her blush deepening, Phera felt herself bristle at the implication that she was somehow (un)dressed this way on purpose. Idle bedtime fantasies were one thing, but even her surprisingly prodigious exhibitionist streak had its limits!

Still, she'd definitely learned her lesson about contradicting the Captain.

"Yes ma'am," she agreed as diplomatically as she could, making sure to keep her face pointed straight ahead as she rolled her eyes. "Uh… Thanks."

Before adding under her breath.

"I guess."

SMACK!

"Ah!"

Earning herself an open-palmed swat from the Captain that was hard enough to propel her forward in an ungainly, magboot-clomping bunny hop to the front of their group.

"You're welcome," she crooned, showing off that she either had *much* better hearing than Phera gave her credit for, or just really enjoyed making her squeak.

Honestly, with that head-mounted biomod she had, it could go either way.

"Oh fuck, look at that! Actual pirate booty," crowed a woman with an intricate tattoo coiling its way around her neck and up her face, pointing to Phera and cracking up with her partner as they passed by headed in the opposite direction. "Damn, and she's a hottie too."

"Yeah she is," agreed the other woman, licking her lips as she gave the suddenly shyly smiling engineer a lascivious once-over. "Hey there, cutie pie. Once you're done playing with the Cap, you wanna come join us for drinks? We'd be happy to show you around the station."

"Um, maybe later?" Phera offered weakly, not quite sure how to respond to that, but finding herself returning the flirtatious assessment even as several of her crewmates snickered behind her.

The woman who'd spotted her first nodded respectfully at the Captain then, before blowing Phera a kiss.

"No pressure, hon. We'll be at Tortuga tonight if you want some company. I promise we'll be gentle."

"Or not," her friend added with a coy wink that cycled her irises from jade to a deep, iridescent crimson as the two of them linked arms and disappeared around a corner. "Ciao."

"Captain…"

Lem's voice held a note of exasperation to it this time, as Adryel and Steph clapped Phera on the shoulder in congratulations.

"What? She's popular!"

"You *know* that's not what I mean."

Biceps straining beneath the sleeves of her top, Lem reached up to massage her temples.

"An unarmed, untrained, Alpha-sider with a figure like hers wandering around on her own out here is as likely to get herself robbed and dumped in a back alley, as she is to get laid. And that's *before* you take into account the fact that she's waving two bright red flags for everyone to see."

"Oh fine, I suppose you have a point," the Captain allowed with a huff. "I wasn't planning on letting her wander around without an escort, but if it'll get you to stop fretting about the cabin girl's moral fiber, I'll greenlight getting her some pants."

Lem snorted again.

"Gee, thanks."

"I dunno, Cap," Adryel chimed in then with a shit-eating grin. "Seems kinda hard to impugn the moral fibers of a material she's not actually wearing."

This minor bit of wordplay produced a round of groans from their fellow pirates, and a guffaw of pure delight from the Captain.

"My thoughts exactly. But, if Lem is going to pitch a fit over a little bit of skin…"

"God! Strip her naked and fuck her sideways for all I care," exploded the first mate, throwing her hands into the air in defeat. "Hell, I'll do it myself when we get back tonight if it'll get you jackasses to shut the fuck up. But when she's *outside* the Mayhem, she needs to be fully dressed."

'Um, that's not… You don't have to…" spluttered a now positively scarlet Phera, going completely ignored while her stomach lurched and her heart fluttered at the other woman's threatening promise.

Holy shit, my dance card is filling up fast. Talk about making up for lost time.

"Yes, yes, I defer to your better judgment, Lem, honey."

Though the Captain's tone was teasing, her look was sincere enough to mollify the other woman, whose broad shoulders relaxed as she gave a grudgingly amused scoff of her own. Then, tossing her hair and gliding her fingertips along the shorn sides of her undercut (briefly touching the mod anchored in the bone above her left ear), she looked back over her shoulder toward Straya and quirked one thin, perfectly plucked eyebrow.

"Take her shopping, would you? You can use the crew funds to get her sorted."

This time it was Straya's turn to frown.

"Can't Ob or Steph do that? I've got plans."

"Senacan can wait until later," the Captain chided, amber eyes hardening as she spoke. "This takes priority."

Phera could practically *hear* the unspoken "Don't make me tell you again" that accompanied that order, and for several long, tense moments she and Straya held each other's gaze in a silent battle of wills. Then, wonder of wonders, the raider blinked, and a very un-Straya like flush of warmth colored her olive cheeks.

It was gone just as quickly as it appeared, however, and she blew out a reluctantly obedient breath of assent as she dragged a hand through her close-cropped curls.

"Whatever," she groused, settling her weight onto one foot, making her high and tight, muscular backside pop rather nicely in the snug pants she was wearing as she rested her free hand on her hip with a long-suffering shake of her head. "Fine. I'll do it."

"Make sure you stick to essentials and keep it reasonable," Lem interjected then, while Phera's eyes lit up with excitement at the prospect of finally getting proper clothes that were all hers. "Boots, underwear, two pairs of pants, two tops, and a jacket. That's all. She can fill out the rest of her wardrobe to her heart's content *after* we all get paid."

"Uh-huh."

Rolling her eyes, Straya swept over to Phera's side and draped an arm around her shoulders, drawing her in against the outer curve of her breasts and steering her off in the direction of a branching stretch of corridor to their right.

"Don't worry, Lem. I'm not going to let the gearhead bankrupt us."

"Good."

"Yes, very good indeed," agreed the Captain with a pleased purr, smiling toothily at the pair of them as they went. "Have fun now, you two."

"I always do."

"Oh, and Straya?"

Phera could feel her cabinmate's body go stiff with the call, and her steps came to a sudden, cautious stop.

'Yeah?" she pressed, eyes hooded as she glanced back.

"Do make sure you find her something that'll look nice around her knees, as well as on the floor. I am *very* much looking forward to Lem following through on her promise later tonight."

"Hah!"

All of the tension that had been coiled in Straya's hard muscles unspooled all at once with that, and she shifted her grip down from Phera's shoulders to her waist, giving it a squeeze that shifted the hem of her borrowed shirt up a handful of centimeters.

"Whatever you say, Cap."

CHAPTER TWELVE

CHARGES ACCRUED

Lewd Conduct, Indecent Exposure

"Phera... Phera... Paging Doctor Sinclair..."

It was two nights after the crew had docked at Marcos Station, and Phera found herself being startled out of her meditative contemplation of the circuit board she'd been replacing capacitors on by a nutty brown hand waving in front of her face.

"Huh?"

Blinking a couple of times to bring her mind back to the present, the engineer looked up to find that the crew's systems infiltrator, Obette, was standing right beside her.

"Oh! Hey, Ob. What's up?"

Rather than answer her question, the exceptionally handsome pirate frowned at her in admonition.

"I'm pretty sure you were in this exact same spot when Kelt and I left the ship earlier this afternoon. Just how long have you been working today?"

"Uh..."

Slipping her soldering iron back into its cradle, Phera stretched on her stool. Popping her back as she drummed the heels of her brand new boots against the crossbar beneath them.

"I think I grabbed lunch around 1300? So... eightish hours? Maybe nine?"

"And have you had dinner yet?"

In response to this, Phera's stomach gave an audible rumble.

"I thought not."

Sighing theatrically, Obette tugged her up out of her seat by the elbow and began steering her out of the Mayhem's workshop.

"Come with me, young lady. You need dinner, and it's high time you put in an appearance at Tortuga."

"But-" Phera halfheartedly tried to argue, throwing one last, fleeting look back at her half-finished project.

"No buts."

Obette supplemented this reprimand with a friendly, and not particularly hard, swat to the center of where her cheeks filled out the flattering seat of her dark gray pants. Not succeeding in doing much more than making Phera's bottom jiggle, and the woman herself blush.

"Your work's going to suffer if you're too hungry to focus, and you can't keep hiding in here forever."

"I am not *hiding*!" insisted Phera, the deepening flush in her cheeks giving away the lie immediately.

"Uh-huh."

Obette's skeptical grunt was accompanied by an amused crinkling at the corners of his sea green eyes.

"You're fully dressed now, so I don't want to hear any excuses. People are still going to stare at your butt, Because, trust me, my dear, it's an outstanding butt."

At this, Obette's palm bounced off the engineer's seat with much more force than it had a moment earlier.

SMACK!

"But that shouldn't stop you from getting out there and seeing the station. Now, you're coming with me to Tortuga, you're going to eat some wonderful and overpriced bar snacks, get nice and tipsy, and you're going to like it. Am I understood?"

Though his voice was laden heavy with authority, the rakish grin on the infiltrator's face made it more of a teasing order between friends, rather than something more serious like Lem or Kelt might hand out. Still, Phera couldn't help but be just a bit of a brat.

"Oh yeah?" she challenged, not actually slowing her pace. "And what if I refuse, hmmm? Maybe I really do just want to stay home tonight and turn in early?"

"Well then, that's just too bad for you, now isn't it?"

Adopting a mock-scowl, Obette drew them up short just outside their cabin.

"However, if you simply *must* insist on arguing with me, we can always sort out your attitude first. I'd hate to have a sulky dinner partner, after all."

He cast a meaningful look in the direction of the hatch beside them, and Phera found herself giving the pirate's offer some serious consideration. A little bit of hand spanking from this suave thirty-something did sound pretty nice right about then, she had to admit. Especially on her still slightly bruised bottom. But, on the other hand, she actually was pretty hungry.

In the end, her need for food won out over her budding horniness, and she tucked an arm around Obette's waist. Escorting him away from their cabin before either of them could change their mind.

"There'll be no need for that, Ob. I'll have you know that I happen to be excellent dinner company. Now, stop dragging your feet and hurry up. I'm starving."

—

"Thank you!" Phera shouted to the approaching bartender, waving her arm and smiling extra wide in an attempt to convey her words just in case they were swallowed up by the bassy pulse of the music thrumming through the packed bar.

Accepting her third frozen, fruity cocktail of the evening from the woman, her gaze lingered on her extremely eye-catching subdermal LED body mods as she sauntered away, before then turning back to Obette and resuming their conversation.

"Are you sure it's okay we left Shi alone with the ship? I know he's part of the crew and all, but he doesn't really strike me as the valiant last stand type, you know?"

"Oh, he definitely isn't," agreed Obette, lips twitching up at the corners as he watched Phera's own purse around her straw with exaggerated concentration. "But, that's fine. Nobody's getting inside the Mayhem who shouldn't be with anything short of half a dozen heavy-duty plasma torches and a full on strike team."

"Mmmm… That's good to hear. I've got a really nice pair of slacks and a blouse in there I'd hate to lose."

Speaking around her straw, Phera's posture eased and she slouched down contentedly against her seat with her new drink. Though Marcos Station wasn't quite as lawless as she'd initially expected based on her childhood of after school specials wherein a promising young engineer escapes her impoverished Proxward life to found a successful corporation in the Alpha System, it still wasn't anywhere near as safe and orderly as she was used to back on Cilara.

Many of its corridors were dimly lit and more than a little on the claustrophobic side. Clearly, whoever ran the station's maintenance service had long since given up on dispatching drones to handle keeping things clean. As a result, several of the corridors bored into the asteroid that made up the station were dusty and grimy. Dusty and grimy, and packed with very visibly armed people who carried themselves with the aggressive (or, even worse, languid and unhurried) sort of swagger that seemed to say they'd be more than happy to kick your ass for you if you looked at them the wrong way.

In short, it was exciting and interesting. But, the sort of exciting and interesting that Phera would never venture out into alone, and that had her longing for the comfortable, clean familiarity of the Mayhem's hab cylinder almost immediately.

Well, mostly.

Tortuga was fun, she'd decided.

The drinks were strong, and tasty, and cold, and delicious, and tasty (and did she mention strong?), and they just kept bringing them to her. Plus, the pounding synth music from the dance floor reverberated so deep in her bones that she could practically *taste* them (or was that her drink?) as she tapped her toes along to the rhythm. It was too bad Straya wasn't there with them. She bet she'd be a really good dancer. And, even if she wasn't, Phera had a sneaking suspicion she'd still have a good time grinding against her as the two of them worked up a sweat in a sea of flashing lights and tightly-pressed together bodies, her hands slipping inside her waistband as she…

Oh well. Maybe next time.

Obette might not have the pirate raider's rough charm and intoxicating iron gray eyes, but he at least made her feel safe.

He'd been giving her the full rundown of the hab's history while they'd worked their way through their first couple rounds of drinks and appetizers. Explaining that Marco's Bountiful Windfall (now known just as Marcos Station by dint of being less of a pretentious mouthful), had once been a resource mining satellite not all that dissimilar to The Bin, though with far less automation and much more manual labor. The asteroid it had been built into had been completely stripped of its iridium and other dense metals some fifty years earlier. And, while the corp that had initially founded it had long since pulled up stakes and moved on, the people living in the small community that had sprung up around their operation hadn't.

Fortunately for them, being only a few hours off of one of the routes commonly used while traveling between several major habs in the Proxima sector had allowed the station to find a new lease on life in the form of a semi-convenient refueling port. As well as a decent spot to lay low and offload cargo of varying degrees of legitimacy.

Which, she supposed, explained why she'd seen so very little in the way of station sec while she and Straya had been out shopping the other day.

On more than one occasion, her escort had almost come to blows (and then one time to actual blows) with some of the station's more belligerent residents. Phera could still vividly recall the wet, crunching noise the nose of the one guy who'd groped her chest in passing had made when Straya had decked him. Laying him out flat on his back in front of his friends, who'd immediately scattered once they saw the look on her face. It had simultaneously been one of the hottest and most terrifying things she'd ever experienced in her relatively young life, and she'd stuck to her cabinmate like glue from that point on until they'd returned to the Mayhem later that evening.

At which time, Lem had peeled her away and proceeded to make good on her earlier threat. Mugging her in an entirely more preferable way while half the crew watched on in amusement. The Captain foremost among them with an actual bag of popcorn.

"Yoo-hoo..."

Obette, his face sporting a lopsided grin, poked her playfully in the cheek.

"Oopsie! Sorry about that, Ob."

Realizing that she'd completely zoned out while staring into her drink, Phera sat up straighter and got back to work on putting back as much alcoholic slush as she could before she passed out in her bunk later that night.

"Uh, yeah… I'm glad to hear that. I'd hate to leave poor Shi to defend the airlock all on his own," she said with a sheepish half-grimace, trying to recapture the momentum of their earlier conversation as she gave her slightly heavy head an extra-vigorous shake to clear it. "That sounds like a nightmare for the poor boy."

Obette snorted out a grim laugh at that and settled onto an elbow, watching her with an easy sort of amusement.

"A nightmare for whoever was stupid enough to try it, you mean."

Phera found herself mirroring his grin.

"Because Straya, Adri, and Lem would kick their asses when they got there?"

"No, because Kelt would," corrected the infiltrator, feigning a shiver. "That woman turns into an absolute terror whenever someone threatens her baby."

He winked at her then.

"And I do mean both the ship *and* Shi."

Which made Phera choke on her cocktail and very nearly topple out of her chair.

She didn't mind, though. Obette was wonderful company, and she was glad he'd managed to convince her to come out with him. Even if this bar *was* one of the crew's regular haunts, Phera always felt awkward in new places. So, it was nice to have someone who knew the lay of the land watching out for her. Plus, the way his keen eyes kept openly admiring her new outfit and the curves that filled it out was just the kind of confidence booster she needed.

"So, you think you're ready for this next run?" Obette asked, noticing that Phera's glass was nearly empty and pouring half of his own (still freshly refilled and barely touched) one into it. "Word around ship is that this is your big chance to prove yourself."

"Yeah, no, for sure, totally."

Phera's words came out in a slightly slurred, jumbled mess, and it took an effort of will to stop herself from babbling more and instead take a deep breath to recenter herself.

"Heh."

Obette just chuckled at her, though. Tilting his head to the side and letting his perfectly coiffed silver hair shift down across his neck.

It looked *so* shiny.

Phera wanted to smell it, and run her fingers through it, and-

"Don't sweat it, kid. You'll do great, I'm sure. Plus, you won't be the only one making an extra effort to earn their keep, either. I mostly just took up space on that Pano job. Cap had me pegged to handle the drones once we got them, but then you wound up coming along with them. So..."

He raised his glass and clinked his icy beverage against Phera's own with a wry grin.

"To being worth it."

"Cheers!"

Nodding perhaps a bit harder than she meant to, Phera drained most of her drink with their toast and found herself fighting down a sudden brain freeze.

"Ack! Fuck!"

Which just made Obette laugh all the more.

After her head had stopped trying to kill her, she attempted to cover her embarrassment by taking a more reasonable sip from her glass.

"The Captain's actually been pretty fuzzy on the details of what exactly she wants me to do," she admitted, licking her lips and trying not to let her budding nervousness take root. "Whatever it is, though, I'm sure I'll be able to do my part... Probably."

At Obette's quirked eyebrow, she plucked out the straw and tiny umbrella from her frosted glass and shotgunned the remaining slush in one go. Slamming the empty drink down onto the table.

"I mean, definitely! Drones are easy. It's not like I'm going to be kicking down any hatches or anything. That's all Straya and Adri's territory."

She found herself going in for another sip to bolster her confidence then, only to realize that there wasn't anything left.

Humph. They ought to make these bigger.

Obette reached out to pat the top of her hand reassuringly.

"Kicking down doors is the exception to the rule for crews of our size, actually."

"Awww, really?"

Phera felt an odd mixture of relief and disappointment upon hearing that. Straya had some truly magnificent thighs and calves, and it would've been fun to watch her put them to use.

"Yes, I'm afraid most of our swashbuckling takes place on board the ship *between* jobs. Though, I'm sure you've noticed that by now."

"You could say that, yeah."

Snickering, Phera unconsciously shifted in her seat as her still partially bruised (though rapidly healing) bottom clenched beneath her.

"Well…"

Favoring her with a knowing look, hand still on hers, the infiltrator took another measured sip of his drink.

"Personally, I just hope this next haul is as good as our last."

He gave Phera an appreciative wink then that warmed her already flushed cheeks considerably.

"Another glass?"

"Hmmm…"

Pinching her lips together, Phera made a prolonged humming noise as she dedicated the full force of her thinking power to whether she was good to go for another round or not. Her face was definitely hot, and she was definitely feeling a little giddy too. But, then again, she was pretty sure that had more to do with the topic of discussion and the pad of Obette's thumb playing across her knuckles than all the booze she'd been consuming.

"I think that sounds like a *fantastic* idea."

After all, when was the next time she was going to have someone at her beck and call that could make delicious frozen drinks for her? So, turning back to the bar, Phera started trying to catch the bartender's eye without being too obnoxious about it.

She might be a pirate now, but that didn't mean she didn't still have manners.

"Oh bartender!"

As if on cue, a familiar voice rose up over the din of conversation around them.

"If you might refill my friends at the end?"

Head turning toward the noise, Phera saw, with just a bit of a start, the Captain. Resplendent in tight pants that showed off her narrow curves, knee-high boots, and an ostentatious coat over a low-cut burgundy top that only partially hid a shoulder holster. She was standing in front of the bar with her hands on her hips and her eyes fixed on the iridescent woman behind it, nudging her head toward where she and Obette sat.

"When you're done bringing me my usual, and finishing up with them, that is."

She indicated the people currently ordering with an imperious wave of dismissal.

"Right away, Captain!"

The LED-underlit woman practically jumped to attention then and hurriedly finished her conversation with her current customers, before rushing toward her armada of liquor bottles. Snatching up a fresh glass and a bucket of ice along the way as she did so.

While she was busy doing that, the Captain sauntered leisurely over to Phera and Obette's table. Planting her hands palm down against its coaster covered surface and leaning forward so that her long hair tumbled across one shoulder in a silky cascade of white and gray highlights, exposing more of her cranial implant than Phera had seen up until that point.

Staring openly in alcohol-fueled fascination, the engineer found herself wondering what all it was capable of. It certainly looked beefy enough to pack some serious functionality behind it.

Gods, I'd love to get my hands on her sometime and just play with-

"This is our new roboticist's first visit to Tortuga, I understand," the Captain crooned, jerking the auburn-haired younger woman out of her contemplation of her body and the biomods embedded into it as her mouth quirked up into its usual half-grin. "Welcome."

"Oh! Um, thank you, ma'am!"

Despite the thrumming base all around them, the Captain's silken voice had no problems carrying, and Phera found herself sitting up straighter as she spoke.

When the bartender hustled over to her and Obette's end of the bar, she was grateful for the distraction and turned to nod at her with exaggerated thanks as she held out her empty glass to trade her. Then, turning back to the Captain, she tried to force herself to relax. Which was a lot easier said than done. Her amber eyes seemed to glow in their rings of smokey eye shadow, beckoning Phera closer and closer like the scintillating ghost lights that had supposedly haunted the forest around her university campus.

"You've, uh… You've got a real nice place here."

Gesturing with her drink as she spoke, Phera rolled her head around her shoulders to take in the dim and moody lighting with its splashes of alternating neons while Obette likewise traded out his empty glass for a fresh one. He'd mentioned something about how the Captain owned (or was it used to own?) this particular establishment while they'd been eating, and it suddenly seemed like a good idea to let her know how much she enjoyed the ambiance.

"Very… Piratey."

That felt so very, very lame coming out of her mouth. So, Phera immediately attempted to cover her awkwardness by taking a prolonged (though, slightly more measured to avoid another brain freeze) pull from her drink. Letting the taste of frozen berries and alcohol cool her warming face.

"Piratey?"

The Captain snorted.

"Going to need to redecorate then. Not a good look for a place that's actually, well, you know…"

Swiveling up from where she'd been leaning against the table, she plucked up her own glass from the bartender's tray and sent her along her way with a really unnecessarily hard *SMACK!* right across the center of the riotously lit woman's round bottom. Making her yelp in sync with the song that was playing and very nearly drop her tray.

"Off with you now, Sparkles. I've business to attend to with my crew."

"Yes Captain!"

Red-faced and rippling through multiple shades of pink and vermilion via her subdermals, the bartender scuttled as quickly as she could out of swatting range. Retreating to the safety of her polished metal bar, as several of her patrons chortled into their drinks.

"Awww, she's always so much fun to watch run away," the Captain sighed, giving her golden liquor an unhurried swirl before knocking back a generous swallow and smacking her lips. "I'm so glad Keller decided to keep her on."

The corners of her mouth still tilted up in a predatory grin, she turned back to regard Phera and Obette.

"Anyway, I was hoping I'd find you two here. There's been a slight change of plans. We're going to be casting off sooner than expected. Tomorrow at 1900."

"Hmmm?"

Phera had been rather preoccupied with staring dreamily at the self-lit bartender, admiring the way her purple and black painted lips pushed out into a pout as one hand drifted back to palm where the Captain had swatted her, to pay that much attention to what her boss was saying. Thankfully, Obette saved her from mirroring the bartender's pose by surreptitiously elbowing her in the side.

"Oh!"

Jerking in surprise, she sloshed a generous amount of her drink over the rim of her glass and onto the front of her brand new (and, thankfully, stain resistant) top.

"Um, did you say 1900?"

At the Captain's answering nod, she sat bolt upright and very nearly saluted.

"Right! 1900. Can do, Captain, ma'am!"

She relaxed just as quickly, however. Letting out a small breath as she favored the heavy-handed older woman with a sheepish grin.

"I didn't really have any plans anyway. So... yeah, that works just fine for me."

Before frowning thoughtfully (her pleasantly warm and fluttering stomach making her facial movements quite a bit more exaggerated than they usually were).

"This change of plans isn't a, uh..."

She made a vague, wiggly finger gesture with her free hand while she downed a mouthful of her frozen cocktail for courage.

"We're not, you know… Hiding from InterSec or anything, are we?"

These last few words came out in a tight rush that made her guts twist. Even though eluding authorities came with the territory of being professional lawbreakers, it still felt weird to imply that her boss might be running away from something.

At Phera's question, Obette looked pointedly away, and the Captain leaned in toward her until they were practically touching foreheads.

"Don't say the I-word so loud in here," she warned in a cool, commanding voice that only further tightened the knot in the younger woman's stomach. "You'll scare the customers."

She straightened up then, and dragged over a chair from a nearby table. Setting it across from Phera and the infiltrator and folding her tall, slender body into it with impressive speed and almost alarming suddenness.

"And, no, fortunately," she continued in a much more conversational tone. "If that were the case, we'd be laying low, not speeding things up."

She took another sip of her drink, the two large chunks of ice inside of it clinking softly against the glass.

"The ship we're supposed to rendezvous with cast off a day early from A-Sys is all. Which means it's going to take its pit stop a day early too. Follow?"

"Yep! Yep, tooootally."

Phera was absolutely lying through her teeth, but she was good enough with context clues to guess that their "rendezvous" with this mysterious ship probably wasn't one they themselves were aware of.

"That makes sense."

She busied herself with draining a third or so of her drink over the course of the next few seconds, letting the moment pass before meeting the other woman's eye again.

"Is there anything specific you want me to bring along for this, uh…?"

Pleasantly buzzed, but also now paranoid about saying the wrong thing loud enough for anyone else to hear, Phera leaned in until she and the Captain were actually touching foreheads this time and brought a hand up to cover the side of her mouth as she continued sotto voce.

"For the *raid*."

Judging by the wince that crossed Obette's handsome face with that last word, Phera had the sudden suspicion that she might've just made a mistake.

Then again, she'd made sure to whisper. At least, she was pretty sure she had. So, what was his problem?

Maybe he's more nervous about this upcoming job than I thought?

Surely, she couldn't be the only one whose stomach was threatening to swallow them up in a tidal wave of butterflies whenever they thought about the next time the crew would be seeing action.

"Phera."

The Captain didn't raise her voice as she drew back from her, but her look had suddenly sharpened to a razor's edge that sent a thrill of terror through the engineer's lower abdomen and had her hands tightening around her frosty glass.

"Um, yes?"

"What did I *just* get finished telling you about watching what you say in here?"

Had she been fully sober, Phera would've been able to pick up on the warning tone the Captain's voice carried and wisely chosen to back down. But, as many drinks in as she was, she instead found herself going on the defensive.

"What? Isn't this a pirate bar?" she demanded, waving both hands to encompass the semi-seedy drinking establishment and its packed dance floor around them. "It literally says 'Tortuga Cafe and Barrrr' on the sign outside!"

"Yes," agreed the Captain with what for her was remarkable patience as she continued to hold her gaze. "But not everyone here is a pirate, now are they?"

"I... I, um... I suppose not," Phera found herself allowing, frowning thoughtfully at the knots of people around them enjoying their drinks or dancing. "But-"

"And where do you think InterSec is most likely to send its spies?"

Phera blinked at the older woman a couple of times, expecting her to finish her thought before the answer dawned on her.

"Ohhh."

"Exactly."

Never breaking eye contact, the Captain plucked up a fried pepper from the bowl in front of her and popped it into the engineer's half-open mouth.

"So, make sure you watch what you say while you're not on board the Mayhem. Yes?"

Unable to reply with her mouth suddenly full of cheese and breaded vegetable, Phera just nodded obediently.

"Good girl."

Popping a pepper into her own mouth and somehow making the act of chewing look intimidating as all hell, the Captain settled back into her seat.

"Just remember, swabbie. 'Dead men tell no tales' is just as true today as it was back on the home planet."

Her lips pulled back into a savage grin then as Phera's face blanched, and she winked.

"And neither do blabby subs with gags in their mouths."

As she spoke, the Captain's foot found Phera's leg beneath the table, and she dragged the toe of her boot up along the inside of her calf and between her legs. Making the engineer choke as she attempted to swallow her pepper without chewing.

"Y-Yes Captain," she eventually managed to wheeze after Obette had given her a couple of hard thumps on the back, hoping very much that the molten heat she felt in her cheeks just then was the enviro's temperature control acting up.

Teeth flashing bright white in the neon, the Captain kept her foot right where it was, swiveling her toe as she watched the younger woman squirm.

"Kelt and I were going over your little thesis project earlier," she went on, changing the subject with careless ease as she drew back her foot and tucked it beneath her opposite thigh.

"You, uh… You were?"

Phera was a little surprised to hear that. She hadn't thought she'd sent that out to her boss yet. Had she maybe given Kelt an advance copy and just forgot?

Could be.

It *had* been a long day, after all.

"Mmhmm…" continued the Captain, tracing a fingertip around the rim of her glass as she leaned forward and propped an elbow on the table in front of her . "She and I had a couple of questions. But, just a couple."

She took another sip of her drink, and then suddenly her demeanor was totally businesslike. Back straight and gaze hyper focused as if Phera were speaking to a Panorama middle manager and not the cordially horny and violent pirate captain she'd been taken in by.

"The heavy excavators we took have Vertium 330 dendrites and a built-in Panorama thermal vibrodrill. Do you think the former will still have enough agility to carry out your networking behavior if we refit the heads with light Pendragon Gatecrasher modules? Also, will Panorama's software have any rejection issues with a resleeved drill head?"

The Captain's sudden shift, while unexpected, was at least familiar if mildly anxiety-provoking territory for Phera, and her face split into a wide grin that was only slightly (well, sort of slightly) tipsy. Explaining how she could solve a superior's problem with her skills was something she'd had plenty of practice at.

"Oh, wow. Gatecrashers?"

She flopped back in her seat, words slurring as she tilted her head to the side and stared off into space. Idly stirring the contents of her drink with her straw as she thought the problem through with the over-deliberate attentiveness that comes from being thoroughly buzzed.

"I've never gotten my hands on one of those before. They aren't in the purview of typical mineral extraction."

She actually winked at the Captain then.

Gods above, maybe it was time to slow down on the thermal freezers? How many had she had now?

Pushing that thought aside for later (her new boss was still looking at her expectantly, after all), Phera took another long pull, smacked her lips, and then shifted back up and leaned in enthusiastically.

"I'd need to double-check the data sheets for those if you have them, or else do a little bit of poke and prod with them to make sure they'll be compatible. *But-*"

She poured all of her professional weight into that last word as she held up a forefinger.

"Those excavators are specifically designed to be nice and modular just in case you need to swap out the drilling package. Power might be an issue, but... Hmmm..."

She plucked thoughtfully at her lower lip before draining the last of her drink. The sounds of sucking from her straw on the empty bottom of the glass audible for several moments before she realized what she was doing and set it aside.

"If you don't need them to operate for hours on end, which it kinda seems like you don't if you're wanting to put Gatecrashers on them, then that *should* be fine. You'd probably lose two hours of operating time from upping the voltage on the control matrices to compensate for the extra processing power required to handle the more complex modules, but... Yeah, no, it'll totally work."

She was back to grinning now, head swimming with mental notes, snippets of code, and visions of schematic sheets she'd need to pour over as soon as she could.

"For the sake of data parity you'd probably also want to include a redundant memory bank with ECC, but I suppose you could bypass that if you-"

Phera could hear her words tumbling from her mouth in a rush, but somehow managed to get ahold of herself as she said more evenly, though no less excitedly.

"If you've got those Gatecrasher things on board the ship already, I think I can have at least one or two manipulators refitted and ready for testing by tomorrow night."

She might be up all night doing it, but at least it would be fun!

"Will that be all right with you?"

The Captain gave her a crisp nod.

"If you're not sure of the specs, look them over tomorrow morning. If it's not going to work, we'll find a lighter replacement in the market and work around their limitations."

She took another drink then, draining most of her glass.

"Power for the drill modifications won't be an issue. Kelt has assured me that her additions there won't make them any hotter or heavier."

She put a dark brown finger to her implant, and her expression went blank. Just for half a second, though. Then, she was back to business, hyper focused and staring Phera down from across the table.

"Now, the crawlers that you introduced Straya to. I've seen their operational parameters, and I want you to tell me how much faster they can do a small hull decoupling project if I were to have this little cutie here..."

She leaned forward then and grabbed Obette's silvery hair, yanking him toward her and toppling him out of his chair to stand half-bent over beside her as she crushed his head affectionately against the side of her right breast.

"Wipe the cost-saving margin on their safety programming."

She was referring to the extra margin of caution that all Panorama drones had hard coded into their operational subroutines that capped off their drilling speeds to minimize wear and tear on the units. Tampering with which had been an instant firing offense back when Phera had used to work for them.

"Hmmm..."

Phera felt her professional grin go a little goofy as she drank in Obette's comical grimace and warming cheeks. He'd seemed a lot more suave and self-assured back when it was just the two of them, but the way the Captain handled him so effortlessly was... Well, it was pretty hot if Phera's happily drunken brain was being honest with itself.

Shaking her head as her own cheeks warmed just a bit more, she carefully gathered her thoughts while busying herself with scraping the last dregs of fluffy, boozy ice from the sides and bottom of her glass into a small pile that she slurped up.

"A hull decoupling, eh?"

She felt the corners of her lips twitch down ever so slightly at the idea of bypassing the drones' safety programming. For as overly-strict as Panorama might've made those margins, it'd be a real shame if one or more of the units were to fail catastrophically and go flying off into the cold and the black because of an unaccounted for explosion or something. But, then again...

"Barring anything, oh, you know..."

This time she looked to her left and right with exaggerated care before continuing in a voice low enough that nobody besides the Captain would be able to hear her (probably).

"*Military* grade, my dronies ought to be able to core their way through hull attachment and support struts in..."

She nibbled at her lower lip as she stared off into space again, brows drawing together as she ran some rough calculations.

"Twenty minutes if you want things done clean and safe, and probably around tenish if you don't mind needing to replace outer casings and maybe some minor components that end up overheating. Which... Huh. Now that I think about it, would probably not be a big worry with that new graphene casing I've been prototyping. It was holding up really well to the heat tests I was putting it through this morning."

At the memory of Kelt's thoughts on said prototype, she grimaced and shifted in her seat before nodding decisively.

"Yeah! Flood some aerogel behind that to fill in the gaps and insulate the components, and we'd be good to go. Ten minutes, tops. Maybe even eight if we can figure out some way of wedging a bigger power supply into them to overcharge the tapping drills."

"Power supplies," the Captain echoed as if making a mental note of her own. "You and Kelt can look into those before we leave tomorrow."

She retained her almost banal, businesslike tone and expression while Obette struggled against her arm and breasts, thoroughly trapped.

"Ten minutes is better than I expected. But, twelve should be fine if it means less repairs afterward."

With that, she released Obette. Who quickly withdrew and collapsed back into his seat, attempting to salvage his dignity as best he could as he caught his breath and fixed his mussed hair.

The Captain's businesswoman persona likewise melted back into her piratical half-grin.

"You're good, honey."

She winked.

"*Very* good."

Then, looking back over her shoulder at the bar, she shouted jovially.

"Bartender! Shooting Star on the rocks! And take this cup!"

She grinned back around at Phera and Obette.

"You two and Kelt are going to end up spending most of this upcoming trip in the workshop, so get ready for that."

"Oooh, that'll be fun! I haven't had the chance to do a proper collab since grad school."

Having someone else with her in the workshop along with Kelt also made Phera feel a lot better about spending multiple days with the strict woman and her grumpiness.

"You can count on us, Captain. We'll get those drones ready to kick the asses of whatever hulls you point them at!"

As the blinking bartender hustled over to the Captain with her new drink order in hand, Phera held up her own totally empty one.

"Would you mind bringing me another one of these when you've got a sec?"

She was probably going to hate herself in the morning. But, if she was lucky, Steph would have something that could help her out.

"Oh, and maybe a glass of water too while you're at it?"

Hydrate, Phera. College wasn't that long ago. Remember to hydrate.

The woman nodded yes, and took both hers and the Captain's empty glasses back to the bar while taking care to stay out of the taller woman's surprisingly long reach.

Pouting slightly, the middle-aged pirate consoled herself with her new drink.

"Looks like you've become a more careful clothes shopper," she chuckled at Phera after taking a long sip. "I like the top."

She rounded on Obette then.

"Get a matching one. That's an order."

Prompting the infiltrator to raise a silvery eyebrow.

"Already did. You know you're not the only one with a sense of taste, right?"

Beaming at the Captain's praise, Phera sat up a little bit straighter.

"Oh my gods, you should totally wear yours tomorrow!" she exclaimed, just managing to stop herself from bouncing in her seat. "Oh!"

This time she *did* bounce, though just the once.

"We should pick one up for Kelt too. Then we'd totally all be matchy-matchy. It'd be like we're our own drone racing crew!"

She threw a sly grin in the Captain's direction with that.

"You wanna sponsor an Olympia Circuit team, Cap-, uh... tain?"

She wanted to just say "Cap", but there was something in the other woman's demeanor that drew the full word out of her mouth anyway.

"No."

Though the Captain's answer was succinct, it wasn't harsh. Even so, Phera found herself suddenly tongue-tied again.

"Well. I have an engagement of my own I need to attend to."

Finishing his drink, Obette pushed his chair back from the table and rose to his feet, smirking down at his dinner partner as he did so.

"Also, Phera, I would absolutely *love* to pitch your suggestion to the crew and take whatever consequences that may come from command afterward. Let's spring it on them tomorrow at lunch, yeah?"

The Captain chuckled darkly at that, her catlike gaze fixed on the infiltrator as he shrugged back into his jacket and adjusted the holstered coilgun at his hip.

"You'd better watch it, cupcake."

"Worry not, oh Captain, my Captain. I shall."

With a flourishing bow, he bid the two of them another goodbye and then left. The Captain clucking her tongue after him all the while as she watched him go.

"Somebody needs a date with Lem."

She grinned conspiratorially at Phera, and the younger woman giggled.

"Now that's certainly one way to pass the time on our way to wherever we're going," she mused, nodding gratefully as the bartender returned with a fresh and frozen, pink and fruity cocktail for her, along with a tall glass of water. "Steph was mentioning something earlier about how she's a sight to behold when she's acting as disciplinary officer."

"What?"

The Captain raised her eyebrows in faux-outrage.

"You don't think she's a sight to behold even when she isn't?"

Her air was that of a defensive family member, and Phera broke down into a fit of giggles as memories of that first night in port came flooding back to her.

"You raise a good point there. That woman is absolutely *built*."

She smirked and sipped at her drink.

"Gods, it would be so much fun to watch her whip Straya and Adri's asses at an arm wrestling contest."

As she sipped again, more to occupy herself as it occurred to her that she was now sitting alone with her attractive new boss, another giggle welled its way up from deep within her.

"Or just whip their asses."

Now that would definitely be a fun change of pace.

"Bet I could find some mag gloves to let her borrow too."

"I've seen both. It was pretty okay."

The Captain stretched her arms above her head and then relaxed back against her chair, hands crossed behind her head and her boots propped up on the tabletop.

"Hmmm... You know, maybe Ob had the right idea for once. It is getting pretty late, and I know one cute little honeybuns in particular who has some important work to start on first thing tomorrow morning."

Drawing her feet back beneath the table, she eased her chair closer to Phera's and leaned in to run her long fingers through the engineer's hair.

"I guess that's true."

Another tipsy titter rang from Phera as the Captain played with her bouncy curls, a wave of tingles cascading along the side of her head as their eyes locked and her already flushed cheeks grew just a bit pinker.

"So, uh..."

She looked to her half-drained fifth (sixth?) cocktail and gave its contents a little slosh before flitting her eyes toward the bartender who was busy chatting up a pair of customers with knives prominently displayed on their hips.

"Is there, like, a crew roster thing I need to sign or something for her? Or can I just finish this off and go?"

"Crew roster?"

Angling her metal-flecked head down slightly, the Captain fixed Phera with a bemused look.

"That's for stuff we buy for the crew, honey. The booze we keep aboard, for instance."

She leaned back in her chair then, unconcerned.

"I've got my own tab. So does Ob."

"Oh…"

Phera's rosy face fell as it suddenly dawned on her that she'd been vastly overestimating her employment benefits all that evening.

"Crap."

Heart hammering inside her chest, her focus narrowed to a fuzzy point around the pastel slush in the bottom of her glass, and she tried to do the math on how much money she owed. Gods, she hadn't even looked at the prices! Just picked what looked the fruitiest, and sweetest, and most likely to get her nice and sloshed.

Fuck, shit, crap, fuck!

Pushing her glass further toward the center of the table to stop herself from accidentally taking another sip of the booze she had no money to pay for, Phera chewed fretfully at her lower lip and racked her slightly slow and hazy brain for a solution.

"You don't think maybe I could get, like, an advance on-?" she started to ask looking up from her contemplation of the tabletop to the Captain and letting the question die on her tongue.

The woman had done enough for her already as is between getting her away from her corporate servitude and footing the bill on her new clothes.

"Okay, no, that's fine. I'll, uh… I can think of something to get this sorted. Maybe she'll take an IOU until we all get paid? She knows you, doesn't she?"

The Captain just shrugged.

"It's not the sweet thing with the light show who's in charge. I sold this place to a handsome fellow who used to pilot the Mayhem for me a while back. I don't think he's here in person tonight to bargain with, though. Either way, I'm pretty sure Sparkles still wants her tip."

She put her hands together on the table then, and tilted her head forward as she regarded Phera in her half-grinning, feline way.

"I can get you for tonight, if you're willing to owe me for a few drinks. Plus your half of Sparkles's tip."

"Oh thank gods!"

Sagging in her seat, Phera pressed a hand to her racing heart and sighed in relief. She had *not* relished the idea of owing some mysterious ex-pirate on a seedy space station money. Especially not when Straya and Adryel weren't around.

"Sure. Absolutely. You've got it, Captain. Whatever you say!"

Throwing herself back up out of her slouch and to her feet, she reflected the other woman's toying grin with her most radiant smile as she leaned against the edge of the table to steady herself while the bar around her spun a little.

"I promise to get you absolutely plastered the next time we get paid, and will get you back for all this too. Just go ahead and take it out of my cut whenever we actually get our cuts, yeah?"

At that, the Captain shook her head.

"Don't worry about it. I know you can't access your old accounts without giving away our position, assuming Panorama even left anything in them in the first place. Plus, I'm not going to take half a dozen pretty expensive drinks out of your first cut when you've got nothing to your name."

"You're not?"

"Nope."

Phera could feel herself actually starting to tear up.

"That's... Oh my gods, that's so nice of you, ma'am!"

"Mmhmm."

The Captain spent several moments just watching her as she drummed her fingertips against the tabletop. The blunt, rounded over nails of her index and middle fingers serving as a muted counterpoint to the sharper *clack-clack-clack* of the pointed, purple talons on the rest of her hand.

"Right then, I won't make you pay me back for this. But, in exchange, I'd like to enlist your help with something."

"*My* help?"

"That's right."

Leaning further forward across the table, the Captain's predatory grin gained an edge of conspiratorial mischief to it that made Phera's stomach flutter as she was drawn inexorably in toward her like matter to a black hole.

"Something I'd actually prefer to take care of here before we turn in, as a matter of fact."

"For sure," nodded Phera eagerly, head movements exaggerated by all the alcohol she'd consumed.

She was genuinely touched by the Captain's offer. Gods only knew how her old employers would've had her paying those drinks off for the next four months with interest. So, eager to help her boss out, and remembering that drawing unnecessary attention to themselves (even here) wasn't something the other woman liked, she lowered her voice to a stage-whisper and asked.

"What do you need me to do?"

In response, the Captain reached up to push aside the thick red hair hanging over one of Phera's ears as she drew her in closer. Bringing her lips right up to it as she whispered.

"I need you to help me keep up my reputation."

Phera's whole body tingled as the Captain's warm breath and silky soft lips brushed against her skin, and something inside her stomach thrilled with the dangerous undercurrent that came with it.

"Uh, sure," she said, sounding only slightly hesitant as she darted her eyes around the room. "Are we, uh... Gonna rob someone, or something?"

She grimaced as she imagined trying to hold some stranger's arms behind their back while the Captain rifled through their pockets.

"Don't you think Sparkles will get mad if you start messing with her customers?"

A wicked chuckle reverberated up from deep within the Captain at this particular question.

"Oh, don't you fret. She'll be relieved. I promise."

She planted a tiny kiss on Phera's earlobe then. And, preying on the younger woman's alcohol-dulled reaction times as she shifted her weight toward her to meet an expected embrace, the Captain suddenly shoved her chair back from the table, seized a fistful of Phera's flaming hair in one hand and her soft midsection in the other, and yanked.

"Ah-! Oof!"

The engineer's startled yelp was cut short by a grunt as she landed heavily across the Captain's long, lean thighs, and it took her sluggish brain several more seconds before she realized what had just happened.

"Um… Captain?" she asked hopefully, doing her best to keep her voice as calm and casual as she could as she gathered her hair over one shoulder. "You're not about to-?"

Her words were cut short as all the blood that had drained from her face upon realizing that she had no money to cover her bill came rushing back all at once with the Captain snatching up her right wrist and preemptively pinning it against the small of her back.

"Guess again, swabbie!" she called out enthusiastically, causing several people to turn toward the commotion.

"Oh fuck, it's the Captain!"

"Hell yeah! Can't believe I caught the show in person this time."

"Wait a minute. Isn't that the hottie we met the other night?"

"It totally is! Ohhh fun! Hi there, cutie!"

Phera gave the woman with the neck tattoo and her partner an awkward wave, and then threw a pleading look over to the bartender. Hoping against hope that she might put a stop to what was about to happen.

She didn't.

Instead, true to the Captain's prediction, a relieved grin had spread across her pretty face while she absently twisted a rag inside a glass.

Humph. Traitor

An instant later, a brand new panic rose up to replace her earlier one as the first volley of sharp *SMACKS!* From the Captain began to land in a wide, slow circle around her ample, upturned seat. Full-armed, opened-palmed swats coming down hard and fast as a planetside heavy rain.

SMACK! SMACK! SMACK! SMACK! SMACK!

Instead of shifting from cheek to cheek as Straya and Kelt preferred to, the Captain kept her attention focused on largely the same area as she worked. Slowly moving her swats around in a gradual circle so that each and every handprint heavily overlapped the ones that came before it.

"Oh my- Owie! Gods!"

The dark gray material of Phera's stretchy, formfitting new pants did absolutely nothing to make her cheeks jiggle and splash any less under the Captain's high-precision assault. Instead, they kept them held nice and firm, as if offering them up to the older woman to punish at her leisure.

An offer which she accepted with extravagant showmanship.

"Pray all you want, my dear."

SMACK! SMACK! SMACK! SMACK! SMACK!

"There isn't a divinity around that's going to get between me and this criminally thick ass of yours!"

In less than half a minute, the wiry woman's arm had already made a full circuit of Phera's generous backside, leaving it a smoldering mass of wobbly flesh with sharp sunspots of more concentrated heat as she set in on another round of heavy-handed swatting. Painting a second coat of sharp, painful handprints that blended together to form one all-over burning sensation atop her earlier efforts. Before then reversing direction and starting over again from the beginning, all while the bar's patrons gasped and cheered, taunted and catcalled. Several of them drawing in closer, comp gloves up or slates out to record the auburn-haired engineer's half-suppressed cries of discomfort and adorable kicking.

"Who's a bad girl?" the Captain taunted, playing it up for her eager audience as they cheered her on.

SMACK! SMACK! SMACK! SMACK! SMACK!

"Ah! Ah! Ow! Come on- Oh! Captain!"

"Tell me!"

SMACK!

"Who's a bad girl?"

Even with her bottom still fully covered, the heavy-duty material of Phera's pants and the flattering pair of lace panties stretched taut over her buns beneath was feeling *mighty* thin right about then.

For a woman with such a lean frame, the Captain sure could pack a wallop!

*Was she... Was she going **easy** on me the other day?!*

The reports of the Captain's pistoning palm against her pants was far sharper and more pronounced than the dance beat still thrumming quietly around them was (had someone turned that down?), and their gathered audience of jeering onlookers was doing absolutely nothing to ease Phera's blushing.

SMACK! SMACK! SMACK! SMACK! SMACK!

"Is this- Ack! Really- Oh! Necessary?" she whined after the Captain had finished another full circuit of non-stop, burning fury around her bottom, boots stomping in protest one after the other against the floor behind her.

"That is *not* what I told you to say, young lady!"

The Captain's swatting came to an abrupt halt then, and her fingers were suddenly slipping into Phera's new waistband.

"Wait, no-! You can't!"

She was immediately proven wrong, however, as her pants and underwear were unceremoniously dragged down to just below the creases of her cheeks. Framing her bulging, still faintly striped from its previous encounter with Kelt, bare bottom between the dark fabric of her top and her pants.

There was a collective gasp from many of the bar's patrons, wolf whistles from a few others, and an explosion of applause from those who had been expecting this turn of events.

"Holy shit, just look at the way she jiggles!"

"I know, right? I just wanna bite her."

"Hell. I'd be doing a whole lot more than biting if I was in the Cap's boots."

"Some ladies get to have all the fun..."

"Awww, don't fret, baby. I'll whip your ass when we get home."

"Not what I meant!"

The Captain flashed a vicious grin at her audience, and then turned her attention back to Phera and the very visible impressions of panty lines she'd just exposed.

"Now," she growled. "WHO'S A BAD GIRL?"

She went back to spanking hard and fast then. No longer moving in slow, deliberate circles, but instead alternating cheeks with rapid-fire efficiency. The sounds of her palm's impact much louder and wetter against bare flesh.

"WHO'S-"

SMACK!

"A-"

SMACK!

"BAD-"

SMACK!

"GIRL?"

Gritting her teeth against a torrent of yelps and hisses threatening to escape as a result of the sudden increase in stinging pain coming from the Captain's tungsten palm, Phera tried to pull herself together. It was absolutely beyond humiliating to be bare-assed in the middle of a bar full of people with their eyes glued to her like this, and she found herself feeling extremely grateful that the Captain had only perfunctorily bared her bottom so that nobody could see just how much she was enjoying herself.

She knew she should be indignant at being treated in such a brusquely humiliating way. But, well… Maybe it was the alcohol. Or maybe it was the appreciative comments about her body and the way she yelped. Or maybe the way neck tattoo and her friend's wide eyes were riveted to her bouncing seat, all but drooling. Whatever the case might be, Phera found the words the Captain wanted her to say coming out with all the sass she could muster.

If the woman wanted to uphold her reputation, she was going to make her work for it, damn it!

"Oh yeah, no- Oh! Please, I'm *such* a bad girl," she deadpanned, almost managing to carry it off without hissing. "S-Seriously."

After all, she had a reputation as part of her crew to maintain too, didn't she?

"LIKE YOU MEAN IT, YOU LITTLE BRAT!"

SMACK! SMACK! SMACK! SMACK! SMACK!

The Captain's hand continued descending with very little change. Though, perhaps moving slightly faster after that last bit of sass. Handprints piling atop one another and darkening from a playful pink to an angry red that continued to smolder long after their initial biting sting had faded away.

"I *said* seriously!" Phera countered with an exasperated giggle borne along by a series of slightly more vocal yelps.

In response to this, the Captain grabbed her roughly by the hair and jerked her head around so that she was forced to meet her shining amber gaze.

"I'm really not getting through to you at all, am I?"

She looked like she couldn't have been happier.

Not waiting for a response, the Captain braced herself against her chair and dragged up on Phera's curls, forcing her to rise into an awkward half-crouch over her lap. Giving her room to slip out of her chair and stand them both up fully.

"You know this hurts you much more than it hurts me, right?"

There came another round of chuckles at this. Some nervous, others not. A few people cringed, though.

Phera among them.

The Captain shoved her face first over their table then, grinding her breasts against it and their abandoned snacks as she all but slid to a stop in place beside her mostly drained cocktail.

"Now, if you even *think* about trying to get up…"

The Captain's voice was a low, dangerous growl as she began to unbuckle her belt.

"Yeah, yeah…" sighed Phera with an over-exaggerated eye roll for the gathered crowd, deliberately pushing herself into a half-standing position hunched over the table and rubbing gingerly at where her hair had been grabbed.

"You know, most people just say 'bend over,' right?"

"Well then it's a good thing we don't have to count on 'most people' to give you what you deserve, you adorable slut!"

In a flash, the Captain whipped her belt free of its loops. Sending it whistling through the air with an evil hiss that made Phera squeak as she flicked it up and caught its other end in her hand. Forming a long, supple loop that had her new recruit's knees threatening to give out beneath her.

"Now."

SWISH-CRACK!

"WHO-"

SWISH-CRACK!

"IS-"

SWISH-CRACK!

"A BAD-"

SWISH-CRACK!

"GIRL?!"

SWISH-CRACK! SWISH-CRACK! SWISH-CRACK! SWISH-CRACK!

Each lash cut across both of Phera's cheeks, capped off with a particularly horrendous bite where the end of it flicked down against the far side of her right buttock, digging partially into the outer edge of her hip and making her hop and dance with its eye-popping fury.

"Oh fuck, oh shit, owie, owie, owie!" the engineer babbled in earnest now, hips waving from side to side in time with her frantically slapping palms against the tabletop beneath her.

As she danced, her pants slipped further down her thighs. Exposing the yellow and light brown of healing bruises from a couple days ago, and the embarrassingly wet muff of red hair between.

"Answer me!"

SWISH-CRACK!

Phera's arms were rigid, her teeth gritted, and her ass absolutely *blazing*.

It. Was. Wonderful.

"Is that- Urk! *actual* leather?" she found herself demanding, throwing a brittle, pouting glare toward where the Captain stood behind her.

Genuine leather goods were a lot less common so far out in station space away from planets with actual agriculture, but Phera was familiar enough with the feel of an actual belt against her bare bottom (both from her mother growing up, and a series of girlfriends in college) to tell the difference between the synth stuff and the real deal. And, if she hadn't been, then the lingering, burrowing heat left behind by the Captain's lashes that were even now *still* throbbing as they swelled into puffy, rectangular welts that spanned from cheek to cheek would've been a dead giveaway.

"That isn't your biggest concern right now!"

SWISH-CRACK! SWISH-CRACK! SWISH-CRACK! SWISH-CRACK!

The Captain continued to strap her squirming, rolling ass from the tops of her cheeks down to her lower sit-spots where she was still faintly striped and bruised. Then, to spread the love around even further, she quickly crossed over to Phera's other side and began lashing right-to-left.

"I hate it when one cheek is more swollen than the other," she huffed almost petulantly, as her roboticist's cries ratcheted up another octave.

SWISH-CRACK! SWISH-CRACK! SWISH-CRACK! SWISH-CRACK!

Phera honestly did as well, and part of her was grateful to the woman for her attention to detail. If she was going to be sitting (or, more likely, standing because sitting was seeming less and less viable by the second) sore tomorrow, she would at least like said soreness to be symmetrical.

That thought only took up a small portion of her mental processing power just then, however.

"Okay, okay, okay!"

The rest of her brain was far too busy trying to find some hitherto unknown combination of gasping and squealing that would diminish the sensation of supernovas exploding across her ass every other second.

"I'm a bad girl, I'm a bad girl!" she howled as loud as she could, practically jumping off the floor with every third or fourth lash.

This time, she was putting a great deal more genuine emphasis behind the words. Though, they were coming out so fast and close together so as to barely be intelligible.

"And, are you sorry for what you've done, you bad girl?"

SWISH-CRACK! SWISH-CRACK! SWISH-CRACK! SWISH-CRACK!

For a brief, terribly exciting moment, a suicidal, bratty, more than a little horny part of Phera was tempted to demand to know what she could have possibly done to deserve such an expertly administered strapping. But, then she noticed the bartender near the front of the crowd off to her right, LEDs cycling through pinks and purples as she watched her wide bottom bounce and jiggle under the Captain's lash with wicked glee.

Oh... Right.

She had to admit taking a thoroughly mean strapping was far more preferable to owing her boss money she didn't actually have.

A lot more fun too.

"Yes ma'am! Yes ma'am!" she squealed through clenched teeth, hair tossing to and fro as she stomped out the sting from a particularly low-landing swat along her sit-spots. "You have *no* idea how sorry I am, Captain. Seriously!"

"That's-"

SWISH-CRACK!

"Much-"

SWISH-CRACK!

"Better!"

SWISH-CRACK!

The lashes began to slow then.

SWISH-CRACK!

"Ack!"

Almost growing lazy.

SWISH-CRACK!

"Owie!"

Before finally coming to a stop altogether with one final *SWISH-CRACK!*

Then, with no further fanfare, the Captain unfolded her belt and started pulling it back through the loops at her waist as if nothing had just happened. Leaving the gasping, shivering, absolutely glowing-bottomed Phera collapsed over wet coasters and what remained of their snacks from earlier with her trembling legs spread wide. The flashing neon strobes above perfectly catching the faint, viscous string of arousal dribbling down from between her pouting labia.

"Now then. The next time I take you here, I expect you to be on your best behavior."

With that warning, the Captain directed a predatory smirk in the bartender's direction. Disrupting her gloating contemplation of the engineer's blazing buttocks with a visible shudder as her hands moved to cup her own seat.

"Wh... Whatever you say, boss," Phera panted, mostly managing to sound respectful.

Now that she no longer had the Captain's belt exploding across her still sizzling backside to distract her, she was starting to notice just how many people had gathered to watch the show. With that knowledge came a fresh blush to rival her seared buns, and the urge to pull up her pants.

But... Gods. Her ass was so sore!

Her pants were stretchy and had plenty of give to make them comfortable. But, that also meant pulling them up would require a *lot* of wriggling and rasping against her newly raised (and she very much hoped still visible once she was back on board the ship and could appreciate them in a mirror) welts.

"No brawls, no duels to the death. Just fruity cocktails and lots of flirting," she promised, still catching her breath and waiting for her seat to stop glowing quite as brightly as the blushing bartender's body mods.

"Nothing *too* sugary, though," admonished the Captain with a laugh, giving one bare cheek a sharp *SMACK!* with her open palm.

"Ack!"

"And don't you go flirting too much either. I didn't hire a tart!"

This second warning was punctuated by another, slightly harder, *SMACK!* to Phera's other cheek. Drawing out a fresh ripple of laughter from their audience.

"I think the ship's sailed on that one, Cap!" someone in the crowd called out, stirring up even more snickers and guffaws.

"I don't mind tarts!" another person chimed in. "I bet she tastes delicious."

"Humph," pouted Phera, pushing herself up to rub at the pair of handprints layered atop her welts and giving the people in front of her an unobstructed view of just how much of a tart she may or may not be as she stuck her tongue out at the Captain. "I thought pirates were supposed to be lawless hooligans who can't be tamed?

Guess I'll have to keep my loose ways and sweet tooth confined to the ship. Oh well…"

And, with that profoundly stupid bit of brattery, Phera was right back over the Captain's lap. Her hand flying faster and harder than it had up until that point. Laying into the already thoroughly sore bottom trapped across her thighs with the fury of an impromptu meteor shower.

SMACK! SMACK! SMACK! SMACK! SMACK!

A meteor shower made out of bombs.

SMACK! SMACK! SMACK! SMACK! SMACK!

Bombs that specifically hated cute engineers named Phera.

SMACK! SMACK! SMACK! SMACK! SMACK!

No scolding or theatrics this time. Just full attention, full energy, full breath devoted to turning as much biological energy as possible into as much pain as possible with maximum efficiency.

All of which was aimed squarely at the writhing engineer's much abused sit-spots.

SMACK! SMACK! SMACK! SMACK! SMACK!

"Aieee!"

Likewise, this time Phera's reactions were pure and unadorned. No sass. No bratting. Just the desperate, squealing howls of a disobedient young lady who'd let her mouth run away with her good sense, and who was now paying dearly for it.

"Ohmygodsohmygodsohmygods!" she blurted out in less than a second, arms and legs flailing at high velocity. "I'msorryI'msorryI'msorry! I'll do whatever you say, Captain! Aieee!"

"Oh, I'm sure you will."

SMACK! SMACK! SMACK! SMACK! SMACK!

The Captain was clearly satisfied that her contrition was genuine. But, after crossing the sass-threshold that she had, she was also just as clearly determined to spank her until her arm was too tired to continue.

Which was exactly what she did.

SMACK! SMACK! SMACK! SMACK! SMACK!

"Ack! Owie, owie-! Oh my gods!"

Unfortunately for Phera, the Captain was a woman who valued her cardio even more than Straya, it seemed. As a result, two long minutes passed with not a second going by without at least one sharp, ruthless *SMACK!* and an accompanying agonized, high-pitched squeal echoing around the thoroughly rapt bar.

Practically everyone had their comp gloves or slates up now. All of them trained on the hypnotic display of discipline and dominance going on before them.

"Please, Captain! *Please!*"

And Phera was playing her part to the absolute fullest. Sobbing in earnest as her bottom was obliterated with a single-minded fury of someone determined to burn into her mind just who was the one in charge.

SMACK! SMACK! SMACK! SMACK! SMACK!

When at last the Captain finally, mercifully let up and clutched at her bicep with a wince, Phera's bottom was a truly breathtaking shade of swollen, carmine red from the tops of her cheeks all the way to their full centers. Fading to a darker, more livid shade of purple from there to just below her sit-spots. No distinguishable handprints or welts from the wiry woman's leather belt remained to be seen anywhere. Just a flaming mass of distilled punishment that guaranteed that even the highly stretchable pants and underwear Straya had picked out for the engineer would have their work cut out for them.

And then some!

Breathing heavily, tears dribbling down her nose and Into the small puddle on the floor beneath her, Phera lay sagged with relief and an utter lack of energy across her Captain's lap.

She had wildly underestimated just how hard the woman could spank when provoked so brazenly. And, looking back with the benefit of hindsight, it had been an astronomically stupid idea to throw in that last bit of sass. But, even as she swiped at her tear-stained face with the backs of her hands, she couldn't quite bring herself to regret it.

"I'm sorry, ma'am," she huffed and puffed, shaking hair out of her face and spitting out a few stragglers who'd managed to work their way between her lips. "Very best behavior, not too sugary, and not too flirty. Can... Oh gods..."

She groaned and went just a bit more limp as her bottom gave a particularly vicious throb that threatened to crumble the faint amount of composure she'd managed to restore for herself.

"Can do."

"There we go."

Sounding thoroughly pleased with herself, the Captain reached out and snatched up a cup from the hand of an onlooker who'd wandered just a bit too close.

"*Much* better."

Then, without warning, half a glass of ice and fruity liquor was pouring down across Phera's smoldering ass. Splashing down into her crack and mixing with the arousal between her thighs before dribbling into the brand new pants and underwear still bunched up around her knees. Wringing out a shivering gasp from the woman herself, along with several others around the room, and an outraged shout from the man whose drink the Captain had just stolen.

"Put his refill on my tab," she said offhandedly, tossing the now empty glass to the bartender, who just barely managed to tear her eyes away from Phera's now literally and figuratively juicy ass in time to catch it before it hit the floor.

Then, grabbing hold of Phera by the hair again, she hoisted the sodden and dripping engineer back to her feet, along with herself.

"Right then, swabbie. Time to get you back to the ship."

Gasping, shivering, and groaning in equal parts, Phera stood obediently on shaky legs beside the Captain. Held up more by the woman's grip on her hair than her feet just then.

"Y-You are just... s-so mean," she managed to get out between chattering teeth as she fought to acclimate to the sudden chill between her cheeks and legs. "You know that, right?"

She was smiling, though, and she hoped to every god and devil that may or may not exist that her remark wouldn't be taken as more sass.

"You have no idea, my dear."

Snickering, the Captain leaned in and planted a lingering, possessive kiss on her cheek. Licking up some of the tears still clinging to her skin, before dragging her off in the direction of the exit. Not bothering to let her even attempt to right her clothing as the crowd parted before them.

"Now, come along. I need you up bright and early tomorrow morning. We've got a lot of work to do."

"Aye aye, Captain…"

Walking back to the ship was going to be an absolute nightmare. But, Phera couldn't say she hadn't had fun that evening.

Being a pirate was the best.

CHAPTER THIRTEEN

Meanwhile, that same evening.

Slate tucked under one arm and hands stuffed into his pockets, Shi strode through Marcos Station humming along to the song blasting out from a nearby food stall. Shore leave was always weird for him. The thing he liked most (aside from getting tucked in by Kelt) was flying, and being forced to stay docked for days on end made him antsy. Luckily, Steph had recommended a really good fantasy novel right before they'd landed, and he'd been able to keep himself occupied reading about a reincarnated trio of polyamorous wizards for the last couple days.

Kelt didn't like it when he stayed cooped up in their cabin reading all day, though. So, after finishing the chapter he'd been on, he'd gotten changed out of his pajamas and into proper street clothes, shot a message to her asking if she wanted anything while he was out, and left the Mayhem in search of something tasty. There was this little noodle shop somewhere on the entertainment mod that Adryel had taken him to the last time they were in port, and he'd really liked the spicy protein cubes there. He couldn't remember the exact name of the place, but he had a general idea of where it was at, and was willing to go on a little exploratory mission to find it.

Honestly, it felt pretty good to stretch his legs.

Well, at least for the first twenty minutes it did.

"I could have *sworn* we went through this corridor last time. Hmmm... Or was it the one over on the east side?"

"Hey there, hot stuff. Don't you know it's dangerous to go walking alone at this hour?" a low female voice drifted out from a narrower bit of cavern-exposed intersection off to his right. "There could be an extremely good looking mugger prowling around, just waiting to steal the pants right off of you."

"Wha-?"

Stumbling to a halt and nearly dropping his slate at the unexpected voice, Shi whipped around and narrowed his eyes at the alcove where the voice had come from.

"Oh, it's just you Straya!" he laughed a moment later, sagging with relief as his free hand rose up to cover his racing heart. "Geez. You nearly gave me a heart attack."

"*Just* me?"

Straya, clad in a black jacket, navy blue shirt, and tight pants, raised a dark brow at him from the shadows of the narrower corridor.

"That makes it sound like you're disappointed."

"Of course not!"

Coloring at the teasing tone in her voice, Shi waved a hand in front of him in a bid to reassure her.

"I was just-"

He realized as he was speaking then that he really didn't know what he was "just" doing, so cut that sentence off and instead forced himself to take a deep breath as he tucked his slate away in a jacket pocket.

Why was she so good at making him nervous?

Well, probably because she'd been wearing the exact same look a few nights back when she'd come to "borrow" the clothes he'd been wearing at the time.

"So, uh…"

Looking away from the muscular woman leaning against the exposed rock wall with her arms crossed, Shi shifted awkwardly on his boot heels.

"What're you up to? You out getting dinner too? I thought Cap sent you out shopping for parts?"

It was a lot of questions to ask at once, but the way she was staring him down had him wanting to fill the silence between them with anything he could.

"She did. I got the stuff. Then I got wasted and came stumbling out here looking for something, but now I forget what."

Straya rolled her eyes, looking a little disgusted with herself.

"But, I was also sort of hoping to run into you soon."

"You were?"

"That's-"

She hiccupped.

"That's right."

Shi took a couple of hesitant steps toward the raider then, unsure what he should do. She absolutely reeked of alcohol, and he could see a faint sheen of sweat plastering several of her dark curls to her forehead. But, then again, she also seemed to be maintaining her balance well enough. Well, well *enoughish*. She wasn't tripping over herself as far as he could tell, at any rate, but she was leaning pretty heavily against that wall.

"Soooo... What's up?"

He must not have been hiding his concern quite as well as he'd thought, because Straya let out a long, boozy sigh and dragged an aggravated hand through her hair.

"Don't worry, I'm fine," she grumbled. "I can still walk and talk and all that shit. Learned my lesson after last time."

As if proving that she could, she closed the distance between the two of them in two loping, only slightly unbalanced strides. Coming to a stop only a hand span away from him with a predatory leer.

"But, obviously, *you* didn't."

"I didn't?"

Unable to stop himself from letting out a nervous squeak, Shi tipped his head back to meet the much bigger woman's gaze. She was fully towering over him now, taking full advantage of the near two dozen centimeters she had on him.

"I don't think I've been hung over in months. Are you sure you're not thinking of Obette, maybe?"

Straya laughed with a harshness then that made Shi's lower abdomen tighten pleasantly, but which also shot his worry into overdrive as she gave the side of his face a couple of condescending pats

"Nothing to do with that."

Slipping in along his left side, she draped a heavy arm over his shoulders. Half leaning on him for support and half holding him in place so he couldn't get away.

"I *mean* that I told you to lay off the new girl," she explained with exaggerated slowness, as if this was a conversation the two of them had had many times before and he just wasn't getting it. "And what did you go and do the very next day?"

Straya shook her head and sighed heavily, making Shi's nose wrinkle as he got a strong whiff of the liquor she'd been drowning herself in that night.

"Yeah, sure, I stole your clothes and spanked you till you danced for resisting. But that was me, not her. Phera didn't know anything, didn't put me up to anything. I didn't even tell her the details afterward."

Her grip on his shoulders turned to tungsten then as she began steering him back up the way she'd come, across the metal walkway inset into raw stone and into a much less developed part of the station.

"But... but...! But I didn't do anything to her!" insisted the pilot, stomach flip-flopping with each step he and the raider took deeper into the side alley. "Kelt was the one who got those pants back from her."

His mommy-domme had been grinning from ear to ear as she'd thrust them at his chest the other day with gruff orders not to lose them again, but he'd just assumed Phera had agreed to give them back after Kelt had explained who they belonged to.

"You can't blame me for that!"

"Well, see, that's the problem."

Straya let out another drunken sigh and shook her sweat-sheened head as she pulled the pilot in a little tighter beside her.

"That's exactly what I told Kelt, and she goes and takes it out on Phera anyway."

They abruptly turned a corner then, stepping into a space that looked like it had once been cleared for a construction project that was never completed. Straya guiding him firmly through the gap in the crumbling wall and into the dark cavern full of old scaffolding, abandoned blankets, and empty drink containers beyond.

"And if *she* can blame Phera for what *I* do..."

Straya gave Shi a not quite apologetic look then.

"That means I'm at a tactical disadvantage unless I can punish *you* for what she does too. So, as far as that's concerned, you and her are basically the same person. Follow?"

"I... I... But!"

Fully spluttering now, Shi stiffened in Straya's grip and began looking for an alternate escape route that didn't have a muscular pirate blocking it.

"Oh, uh, hey look over there!" he said suddenly, mounting panic causing him to latch onto the first idea that sprang to mind as he pointed toward a spot off to Straya's left. "It's Kelt! You two should really work this out between yourselves, I'll just-"

Rather than finish that loose train of thought, he ducked out from under her arm and made a beeline back toward where they'd just come from.

He'd almost certainly catch hell from her later aboard the Mayhem once they were underway again (assuming she remembered this little encounter), but he'd long since learned that managing to evade immediate consequences was the best way to maybe save your seat in the long run among this crew. Heck, if he was lucky, maybe Straya would run into Phera first and take out whatever pent-up annoyance she had on her instead.

"Wha...? Hey, get back here!"

Straya was still more than a little drunk. As a result, Shi was able to make it five whole meters before she lunged into his back. Shoving him roughly up against the inside of a half-finished wall, one of her hands gripping his arm and twisting it behind his back while the other sealed itself over his mouth.

"Nuh-uh. Kelt needs to learn her lesson," she murmured huskily into his ear, voice low and utterly malicious as she molded her body to his against the wall.

They stayed like that for several long moments, Shi panting into her palm while the bigger woman huffed out tickling breaths against the side of his face; grinding her hips into the pert cheeks filling out the seat of his pants. Then, just as roughly as before, she started dragging him further into the construction site.

"Mmph! Mmph!"

Straya's hand over his mouth muffled all of his protests as it held him tight against her toned, biomodded-warm chest while they shuffled in awkward, stuttering bursts of partially off-balance steps. His slightly below average height combined with his soft (barely up to Lem's standards) physique made brute-forcing his way out of the pirate's grip all but impossible, and he found himself seriously regretting not buying those null-grav grappling vids he'd seen being advertised the last time they were in port. Still, he wasn't without options.

They weren't *good* options, but they were options.

Like, for instance, licking at the inside of the palm clamped over his mouth to startle Straya into letting go.

Come on… Ugh, she tastes terrible!

If she'd been sober, this would have almost certainly kind of bothered Straya at least a little bit. As it was, she didn't seem to even notice.

Shit.

Flopping down onto a foundation pylon that had never been built on, Straya surprised him yet again then by letting him go.

"Oh thank god-!"

His relief was short-lived, however, as Straya lurched forward, seized hold of his pants around his waist, and tore them and his underwear right down to his ankles in one fell (if slightly lumbering) swoop.

"Not so eager to run back out in public now, huh?" she taunted with a breathy laugh, leaning against his front for support.

Now *that* was one hell of an understatement.

"Oh come onnnn!"

Letting out the kind of high-pitched, startled whine that usually followed a particularly hard pinch from Kelt, Shi's priorities immediately shifted from escaping his spank-happy crewmate to preserving his dignity as best he could by cupping both hands between his legs as he stumbled back half a step. Even if it was just the two of them in this abandoned, half-dug-out construction site and she'd seen him naked plenty of times before, being pantsed so unceremoniously was enough to send a wave of plasma thrust shooting up his neck and across his forehead while his now bare backside broke out into mortified goosebumps.

"Straya!" he whined as the raider pulled him inexorably around to her right side, the pants and underwear tangled around his ankles forcing him to take shuffling baby steps so as to not lose his balance and wind up eating a faceful of foundation. "If you're mad at Kelt, take it up with Kelt!"

Even hobbled as he was, Shi still managed to stomp his foot as his knees bumped up against the side of Straya's thigh.

"Already told you, that's exactly what I'm doing."

"But, that's not-"

Amid a gale of protests, Shi found himself being toppled over the older woman's muscular lap with his hands still cupped protectively over his rapidly hardening cock. Landing with a grunt with his arms pinned beneath his own weight.

SMACK!

"Ow!"

"Look at you. Such a…"

SMACK!

"Good-"

SMACK!

"Little boy," cooed Straya facetiously, wrestling his frantically kicking legs underneath her right calf as she threaded her left arm around both his waist and his arms before he could work them free.

"Well, not good exactly," she corrected herself with another pair of swats, really putting her back into them this time.

SMACK! SMACK!

"Oh! Ack!"

"If you were *good*-"

SMACK!

"Then I wouldn't be spanking you-"

SMACK!

"Now would I?"

Teeth clenched and eyes already starting to tear up (he'd never been any good at taking a spanking without waterworks), Shi's toes curled and uncurled inside his boots as the raider's sloppily spaced spanks started to coalesce into a bright, all over burning sensation that suffused his compact seat.

SMACK!

"Would I?" Straya demanded again, voice starting to grow impatient.

SMACK!

"Answer me!"

SMACK!

"Owie, owie, owie!"

Shi knew full well that the answer to that question was very much an emphatic "yes!" Nobody on the crew had ever needed a reason to turn him over their knee before. Still, he wasn't about to start sassing someone who was already spanking him. So, instead, cheeks tensing in a futile attempt to dampen some of the pain from the bigger woman's rocketing palm, he did his best to make his voice placating and plaintive.

"No Stray-"

SMACK!

"Ack!"

"EXACTLY!"

Perhaps unsurprisingly, his attempts to appeal to the softer side of Straya's nature had the effect of only making her start spanking him faster.

Just as it so often did with Kelt.

SMACK! SMACK! SMACK! SMACK! SMACK!

Well, it was worth a shot.

Resigning himself to the fact that there was no escaping his fate until she wore herself out, Shi abandoned any pretense at acting tough and nonchalant about being ass up in the middle of Marcos Station and instead started to whine and yelp with each heavy-handed meteor strike of a swat.

"Ack! Owie! Oh! Please! I'm sorry!"

SMACK! SMACK! SMACK! SMACK! SMACK!

Drunk she might be, but Straya was still as strong as ever, and wasn't holding herself back in the slightest. Fortunately, with her pinning him across her lap with her right leg as she was, she was unable to really get at his thighs.

On the other hand, though, was the problem of, well... his hands.

SMACK! SMACK! SMACK! SMACK! SMACK!

His hands which were gripped around his fully erect cock.

SMACK! SMACK! SMACK! SMACK! SMACK!

His hands which had found the perfect angle to rub against his extremely sensitive head as his hips bucked and bounced with every single, cheek-scalding impact.

SMACK! SMACK! SMACK! SMACK! SMACK!

His hands, that were growing slick with small dribbles of precum as a low groan built up within him.

"S-Straya, please!" he panted, the hitch in his voice now having less to do with the fire being stoked in the hyper-sensitive undercurves of his sit-spots, and more with the rapidly building pressure he could feel mounting in his loins. "Y-You have to hold on! I'm going to… to…"

Something in his tone must've managed to pierce through the haze of alcohol and the visceral thrill of making his bottom bounce. Because, miracle of miracles, Straya's palm actually stopped swatting.

"What?" she demanded, sounding annoyed, but willing to make sure that he was okay before she continued making him feel much, much less so. "You cramping up?"

"Not quite…"

Teeth clenched and brain rattling forward and backward through all of the pre-flight safety steps he performed each time before taking the Mayhem out of port, Shi did his best to flex his fingers away from his twitching cock.

"It's just that- Well…"

Face warming to near supernova levels, he gave his hips a meaningful wiggle and gasped as a fresh spasm of delight shot up from where his head rubbed against his palms.

"Well…?"

Frowning at him, Straya bounced her leg. Which, in turn, drew out another shallow gasp.

"Oh!"

Rather than look embarrassed as understanding dawned, an evil grin spread across her dark features instead.

"Oh…"

"Um, yeah."

Caramel colored skin flushed a delicate shade of russet just barely visible in the gloom of the abandoned construction site, Shi grimaced and breathed out a sigh of relief.

"I didn't want to, you know... Get anything on you."

"How very considerate."

The taunting singsong that was Straya's voice just then did absolutely nothing to ease Shi's nervousness or embarrassment, but she did at least shift her right leg off of him so that he was finally able to wrench his hands free of his junk and flex some feeling back into his tingling fingers.

"Th-Thanks..."

"That's not going to get you out of your *punishment*, though."

Straya stuttered her way over the word three different times before finally managing to get it out without slurring.

"C'mere."

The next thing Shi knew, strong hands were seizing him by the shoulder and the side of his waist. Rolling him over and up into a sitting position on top of the pirate's left thigh.

He was just about to ask her what she was doing, when her spank-warmed, calloused palm took hold of the shaft of his still very much erect cock.

"S-Stray-ay-a..." he barely managed to get out, stumbling his way over the woman's name as her hand began to glide with smooth, practiced ease up and down his hairless length. "Y-You... You..."

"Hmmm?"

Halting mid-stroke around the trembling young man's head, Straya focused her slightly bleary iron gray eyes on his sweaty face with deliberate care.

"Is that a no?" she prompted in a lazy drawl, lips twitching up at the corners. "Just say the word and I'll stop. You know I'm not going to take advantage of a cutie without their permission, yeah?"

"N-No it's not a- Oh god!" Shi started to say, voice cracking as the other woman flexed her fingers around his cock, very nearly making hip pop off right there and then. "It's just... I mean... You don't have to-"

"Shut up."

Straya's tone, though commanding, was still a fond one as she playfully bumped her forehead into his.

"I know I don't have to. I want to."

Suiting actions to words, her right hand started moving again, drawing out more gasps and shivers from the bare bottomed young man as he squirmed atop her thigh.

"If Phera were here, I'd just have *her* suck your cock. But, since she's not, I guess I've got to take care of this myself. Oh well…"

Shi was barely paying attention now. His left hand was clenched into a fist at his side and his right was gripping the back of Straya's jacket for dear life as she ruthlessly and efficiently bulldozed her way through his attempts to stave off coming on her lap. He had his pride to maintain, after all, and she'd barely been going at him for a minute!

Still, he'd long since learned that there was very little to be gained in trying to go against the wills of his fellow crewmates. And, before he knew it, the tendons in his groin were tensing as a low groan bubbled up from deep inside of him.

"Oh god… Straya, I'm about to… to…"

Stars exploded behind his closed eyes as the twitching of his cock shifted into a hard flex as hot spurts of semen began to erupt from it in sporadic bursts.

"Mmmm… That's right, get it all out, you little brat," Straya purred into his ear, nuzzling her face into the crook of his neck and angling her right leg out of the way so that his cum landed on the ground between her boots.

Shi was nothing if not obedient, and he wasn't about to argue with her. He was far too busy groaning and writhing atop her rock solid thigh to really do anything else besides what he was told.

"Good boy."

Chuckling into his neck, Straya opened her mouth and bit down. Hard.

"Ah!"

Not hard enough to draw blood, but hard enough to leave a nice visible mark for Kelt to find later, and to make his writhing increase tenfold as she suckled at his skin, savoring the taste. All the while as she was doing this, her hand continued to stroke, milking him with a sort of lazy ruthlessness. With how hyper-sensitive his cock was just then, it was more than enough to have him whimpering in surrender as he collapsed into an exhausted puddle against her.

"There we go, *much* better."

As his cock began to deflate with the last dribbles of cum, Straya released her grip on him and his neck and straightened up enough to look down at him with a mixture of fondness and wry cruelty that was so typical of her.

"Y-Yep…" Shi managed to pant in response, feeling like he needed to at least say something to fill the silence left behind by his groaning.

Straya allowed him a minute to fully catch his breath, idly toying with his wavy, chestnut locks while she bounced her thigh beneath him. And, when at last he'd fully recovered and was sitting up straight on her leg again, she grinned. The wicked gleam in her dark eyes immediately had Shi's stomach turning somersaults.

"You ready now?"

"Uh… Ready for what?"

"Your spanking. Duh."

"But-! I mean-! You just-!"

"Mmhmm," the older woman nodded, taking his flustered half-sentences for the consent they were. "And now that you're not about to blow your load across my lap, it's time to finish what I started."

Without waiting for him to even try and mount a defense, she unceremoniously shoved him back over so that he lay jackknifed across her left thigh, and her right leg once again fell into place across the backs of his knees.

"Hang on tight," she crooned, left arm circling around his waist and pulling him in tight against her washboard abs. "I'm starting to sober up now, and I can't help but notice that you don't have your stun gun on you."

"Um…"

Fresh, genuine panic seized hold of Shi then, and his hands balled themselves into fretful fists on the hard-packed, dusty ground beneath him.

"Uh-huh. That's what I thought."

Straya's deadpan was practically oozing with cruel amusement, which was an incredibly bad sign for him.

SMACK!

"Ow! Geez!"

"Guess I get to cram *two* spankings in now. Lucky you."

"You really don't have to-" Shi found himself starting to say, before being cut off by a sharp pinch to his inner thigh and a full-armed, open-palmed *SMACK!* that took his breath away.

"Yes I do."

SMACK!

"I really-"

SMACK!

"Really-"

SMACK!

"Do."

SMACK!

"Now, take this like a good little brat, and *maybe* I won't rat you out to Lem and Kelt."

SMACK!

"Deal?"

SMACK!

"Ack! D-Deal!"

———

Enduring a long, drawn out, and extremely thorough punishment spanking right after an orgasm proved to be absolute torture for Shi. And not just because with Straya's gradually returning sobriety, she'd also caught her second wind and was able to swat even harder and faster than before. But because without the pleasant thrum of arousal to help distract him as his ass was reduced to a molten blast zone of superheated, swollen flesh, he had no other choice but to be present in the moment for each and every one of those devastating swats.

On the bright side, though, Shi found that he was starting to catch *his* second wind right around the same time she was wrapping up her eighth or ninth round of swats on his definitely bruised by now sit-spots. And, with it, he was able to swing back into enjoying the monumental butt blistering even as he sobbed himself hoarse.

When at last Straya's right arm finally ran out of steam, he was absolutely spent, floating along in a sea of endorphins, and voraciously hungry.

"You… You feeling better now?" he croaked.

Beating back the few remaining tears trickling from the corners of his eyes as he struggled to get his breathing back under control, Shi sniffled hard and wriggled around on Straya's lap to look back up at her over his shoulder.

"Yeah. I think I so," she sighed, looking somewhat chagrined, but grateful nevertheless for his understanding. "Thanks, kid."

"Heh."

Groaning as the pirate's calloused palms kneaded his sizzling seat like a baker with fresh dough, Shi let the last bits of remaining tension in his body ebb out with a long, exhausted groan.

"No prob, Stray. I'm sorry you were feeling shitty."

The raider had never opened up to him about what in particular always seemed to dig into her whenever she had too much time to herself and no task to work on, but he knew enough to understand that letting her blow off some steam here and there was one way that he could personally help her out. Therapy and a well-balanced regimen of antidepressants and anxiety meds would be way more effective (and infinitely less painful for him). But, until she was ready to make that move herself (or the Captain finally strong-armed her into committing to the help she needed), he was willing to be there for his fellow crewmate in this small way.

"So…"

Easing back onto his knees between Straya's legs and immediately shooting to his feet with a radiant blush when he felt his leg grind into something cold and viscous, Shi hurriedly began righting his clothes.

"Have you had anything to eat tonight that didn't come from a bottle?"

He knew he was taking his ability to sit comfortably for the next week (as opposed to just the next day) into his own hands with the undercurrent of sass that accompanied that question. But, thankfully, Straya just smirked as she watched him shuffle and hiss his way back into his briefs and then rasp his snug pants over his tender, swollen backside.

"Some pretzels... I think."

The raider's stomach contributed its own thoughts on the situation with an audible rumble, and the two of them laughed.

Rolling his shoulders and popping his neck, Shi returned her smirk.

"I was on my way to get some noodles when you and I bumped into each other. Wanna come with? It's my treat."

"Well, shit."

Straya's sardonic smirk blossomed into a genuine (albeit still mildly teasing) smile then.

"If that's the case, I ought to whip your ass more often."

She accepted Shi's hand and used him to pull herself back up to her feet. Looking a lot steadier on them now than she had at the beginning of their earlier tussle.

"Fair warning, I'm not actually one hundred percent sure *where* this place is exactly, so it might be a bit of a walk. You okay with that?"

"Sure."

Draping an arm around his shoulders once again, Straya began steering them out of the construction site and back toward the main pedestrian thoroughfare she'd snatched him from.

"It's that place Adri likes over near the nexus, yeah?"

"Mmhmm, that's the one."

"Great. I know the way. Just stick with me and we'll be there before you know it."

She accompanied this order with a firm squeeze to Shi's right cheek as she shifted her hand down to his back pocket, and he squeaked as adorably as she'd no doubt been expecting.

"Right!"

Allowing himself to be swept along by the older woman's strong grip, Shi felt a lopsided grin tug up on one corner of his mouth. One thing was for sure, he definitely wasn't bored on shore leave anymore.

Well, that, and he did not envy Phera in the slightest. Kelt would no doubt be sure to return the favor for Straya's antics this evening in spades, and that poor roboticist's absolutely amazing ass was going to be suffering the consequences for at least a week, he was sure.

Hopefully I'll be able to catch it in person this time, instead of just watching a recording after the fact.

Letting out a contented sigh, Shi shifted his weight a bit more into Straya's steady warmth.

Being a pirate really was the best.

CHAPTER FOURTEEN

CHARGES ACCRUED

Conspiracy to Commit Grand Theft

That following evening after the crew was underway in the Mayhem once again, belly's full of hot stew and soft bread courtesy of Adryel and their prodigious skill for selecting spices, the Captain called everyone into the rec room for a briefing.

"All right, girls, listen up," she began, addressing them as a whole once they were all settled onto either couches or stools (with the exception of Phera and Shi, who lingered on their feet doing their best to look like they were really just in the mood to stand and stretch after a big dinner). "I'm sure you're all eager to learn what I've picked out for our next target."

"Weapons cache?" asked Straya, half-smirking.

"Precious metals?" supplied Adryel.

"Come on luxury goods!" added Steph, making a show of crossing all of ver fingers and ver extra-long, biomodded toes.

"Ding-ding, we have a winner."

"Fuck yes!"

Rounding on Shi, Steph's face lit up with a hungry, flirtatious grin.

"Told you so."

Shi only smiled shyly in return and shuffled his weight from one foot to the other.

"Yep. I, uh... I guess you did."

Leaning forward to wrap ver hands around the pilot's girlish waist, Steph pulled him down onto ver lap, looking as pleased as Phera had ever seen ver. Steph's petite frame was largely dwarfed by Shi's broader shoulders and slightly taller body, but ve still somehow managed to make the arrangement work. Bouncing ver knees and shuffling around to prop ver chin on top of his left shoulder.

"You and I are going to have *so* much fun tonight."

"But, I um…"

Looking thoroughly worried (and a little excited), Shi's caramel colored features gained an adorable warmth.

"I think we're going to have to reschedule. I, um… I have the watch tonight. You know, plotting our course and all that."

"No you don't," countered the Captain, brushing aside the boy's flimsy excuse with a breezy wave of one lean hand. "It's a straight shot for the next seventeen hours. I'll keep an eye on the sensors for you so you and the doctor can resolve your wager."

"Gee, thanks."

Shi attempted to look annoyed, but he couldn't quite stop the corners of his mouth from quirking up ever so slightly.

"No complaining now, Shi. You took that bet, and you'll pay up like a good boy." chimed in Kelt then, face malevolently serene as she added. "We'll also be discussing your decision making *after* Steph is finished with you."

"Oooh, scary!"

Steph dragged out ver Os while wiggling ver fingers dramatically under Shi's armpits, making him squirm and laugh.

"You're welcome to join us if you want, Kelty," ve added. "He's got a mouth *and* an ass, you know."

"I am well aware."

The senior engineer leveled a tight, frosty smile at her boy toy and the crew doc, her even tone lending her sharp eyes a wicked gleam that Phera was simultaneously grateful and jealous wasn't being directed at her.

"And I'll be there, doctor. Absolutely."

"Yay!"

"Ahem."

The Captain cleared her throat loud enough to get everyone's attention, and the room fell silent once again.

"Before you all run off to fuck each other silly, perhaps we should finish our briefing?"

"Yes Captain," came a trio of replies from Kelt, Shi, and Steph in unison.

"Very good."

The Captain gestured, and the projection display beside her bloomed into life. Showing off the logo of a corp Phera knew very well from her youth on Cilara.

"Oh shit."

Though she'd only murmured her exclamation, the Captain's face still split into a wide, predatory grin.

"That's right, swabbie. We're going after one of the biggest food conglomerates on all of Cilara."

That was no understatement, Phera knew. Haven's Grove and their subsidiaries controlled all of the agriculture on an entire continent!

"Well," amended the Captain after allowing the engineer's mouth to hang open in disbelieving awe for a few more seconds. "To be more precise, we're going after one of their shipments."

The logo beside her transitioned into a three-dimensional rendering of a cargo hauler then. Though similar in size to the Mayhem, it had a much smaller hab cylinder, being little more than four engines at the back, a cockpit in front, and a series of clamping arms and support struts for holding onto a detachable cargo hold.

"This is the Altona. It left the Alpha System at 0400 today carrying just a little over one hundred thousand metric tons of top grade, planetside raised, meat. And we, my bonny lasses, are going to steal it."

"Have I ever told you how much I love you, Cap?" sighed Adryel, face positively beatific at the prospect of all that genuine, non-vat-grown food.

"We're only keeping a small portion of it for ourselves, cupcake," chimed in Lem, deflating the crew cook somewhat, though looking no less entranced by the prospect of getting her hands on non-recycled protein.

"Yes, I'm afraid we've already got a buyer lined up for it."

The look of bemusement on the Captain's face evaporated then, and her amber eyes and their perpetual sleep-deprived bags hardened as she became all business. With a flick of her wrist, the display transitioned again, this time displaying renderings of the Panorama drones they'd stolen over a week ago now.

"In exactly nine days, the Altona will be docking at Excaden Station on the outskirts of A-Sys to refuel. Before that happens, Phera, Obette, and Kelt…"

At this, she swept her gaze across the three techs, and they all sat up straighter.

"You three will have modified the ore excavators we acquired to use Pendragon Gatecrashers instead of their original vibrodrills. We will be docking at Excaden in *eight* days, and I expect those units to be retrofitted and ready to deploy by then."

"Um… Deploy?"

Phera, hand held up as if asking a question in school, looked remarkably worried. Especially with the way the Captain was cracking her knuckles.

"We're not going to, you know… assault the station, are we?"

This tentative question prompted the Captain to crow laughter long and hard at the curving ceiling while Straya, Lem, and Adryel all snorted.

"Oh, honey, no."

Wiping away a tear from the corner of her eye, the Captain sighed and smiled at her with a feline fondness that made the engineer's lower abdomen tighten.

"While I certainly appreciate your confidence in our muscle, they are in no way shape or form even close to well-armed enough to make a direct assault on a station."

"Yep," agreed Straya. "Sorry, sweet cheeks, I like being alive."

"Ditto," nodded Adryel with a wry grin.

"Could be fun, though…" added Lem, head tilted in thought. "We'd definitely need a *lot* more firepower to make it work. At least another ulfsark and some better personal armor. Some extra hands too."

"Lem, sweetie, please don't encourage them."

"Yes Captain."

"*Anyway.*"

Stretching her long arms above her head and making the breasts beneath her crop top bounce, the Captain strode over to her first mate and settled down onto her lap. Unlike Shi and Steph, she made it look imperious.

"In eight days, we'll load the modified drones onto that Panorama flyer we're still dragging around, and then Straya, Phera, and Obette will take it in to Excaden under the guise of collecting fuel for a larger corporate ship moored further out from station space. And, while you're collecting our fuel, because we *will* need to refuel by then so we might as well kill two execs with one shot, Obette will scramble the docking ring's local sensors to allow the drones to slip off the flyer and onto the station's hull. There, they will wait until our target arrives, and while *it's* refueling, will secret themselves onto their hull."

Lounging back against Lem's bulk, neck nestled between her heavy breasts, the Captain crossed one leg over the other.

"From there, all we have to do is wait for it to get back underway, and then intercept them at our leisure. When we're in range, I'll send a command signal, and the drones will then use their gatecrashers to sheer through the support struts on its cargo hold using Phera's distributed communication protocol to coordinate the process."

The Captain bobbed a foot at the projection display, and this time it played a simulation of what she'd just described.

"After that, we swoop in, snatch up the hold in its entirety, and then zip off to Marcos before anybody even realizes what happened."

"Sounds simple enough," nodded Straya, arms crossed and looking thoughtful before directing a semi-skeptical look in Phera's direction. "You sure your nerd shit is going to work?"

Phera herself was far too busy combatting anxious accel-shifts inside her stomach to bother being offended by the question.

"Of course it will!" she declared, mostly managing to sound convincing. "I've been modeling this sort of thing for months. Well, not *this* sort of thing, but coordinated drilling. I even managed to pull off a couple of limited field tests back at The Bin."

"And how'd those go?"

"One of the units blew out its processing assembly and melted half of its casing," she admitted, looking chagrined. "But that was a power issue, not a communications protocol issue. So long as the voltages are regulated properly and we use enough insulation, it'll be fine, I'm sure."

Kelt snorted at that.

"We'll see."

"Just try and avoid damaging the booty this time, yes?" put in the Captain then with a wink before Phera could snap back at the older engineer. "Otherwise it'll be coming out of *your* booty."

Straightening to her full height, her still very tender cheeks tensing enough to make her wince, Phera nodded quickly.

"Yes ma'am!"

"Very good."

Rising with liquid grace back to her feet, pulling Lem up after her to act as a wall of muscle for her to lean against, the Captain flicked her fingers in dismissal.

"That's all. Now, get to work."

CHAPTER FIFTEEN

CHARGES ACCRUED

Unauthorized Modification of Company Property

The next week was an absolute whirlwind of activity for the Blazar Bitches' tech crew. Phera, Kelt, and Obette wound up taking over the Mayhem's cargo hold to work on refitting the Panorama ore crawlers, while the workshop in the hab cylinder was converted into a miniature manufacturing plant that was constantly running with prints for various parts and other little pieces of tech.

But, though the hours were long and mentally taxing, Phera found that she was having an absolute blast.

For the first time since coming aboard, she was thoroughly in her element. She and Kelt drew up and refined schematics and blueprints for modifying the crawlers, with Obette chiming in every now and then with some bit of insight he'd gleaned from poking around in their control cores. Honestly, it was exactly the sort of working environment she'd been hoping for when Panorama had first recruited her back in grad school. It was fun, challenging, and above all else, collaborative. Well, collaborative with just a hint of danger and the ever-present threat of winding up over Kelt's lap if she annoyed her too much.

It was wonderful.

Despite their tumultuous introduction, Kelt in particular had really started to grow on Phera over the last few days. She'd quickly learned that her senior engineer, while snappy (especially in the morning when the caffeine in her coffee was still working its way through her system) was actually quite sweet once you got to know her. Her temper was no less short, and she was absolutely as ruthless as her fellow crew members when it came to discipline, but there was an undeniable current of maternal affection to her as well. Which, given her own rocky relationship with her parents, Phera found herself drawn to almost immediately.

Kelt was a stern taskmaster who did not abide sloppy work in the slightest. But, when Phera did well, she made sure to tell her so. And, when she couldn't figure something out, she might roll her eyes, but she still took as much time as was needed to show her how to do it properly. She was easily the best supervisor the young roboticist had ever had, and she found herself opening up to her more and more as they spent hour upon hour elbow-to-elbow in the cargo hold.

Their fields overlapped enough that Phera *finally* had someone she could discuss designs and theory with who actually understood what she was talking about, and who could make meaningful contributions that didn't just amount to "and how much is that going to cost?". Plus, the older woman was someone she could unload to about her life growing up in corporate-controlled space as well as her near three year stint as an indentured servant to Panorama.

Kelt, she learned, had grown up on a station in the Alpha sector, and spent the first decade of her career working as a junior engineer aboard a megacorp freighter. A freighter whose chief engineer had been a total ass who'd apparently only gotten his position because his father was on the company's board of directors, and who'd offloaded all of his responsibilities onto her.

"I tried reporting that idiot to HR for years, and was always dismissed out of hand. Then, low and behold, one day while we're making a run out toward Yaara, we blow a fucking seal around the airlock because *he'd* been lying on his maintenance reports," she'd fumed while Phera and her were disassembling one of the articulation motors on an excavator. "The hold gets blown out from explosive decompression, and who do you think gets the blame? Him?"

"Um... No?"

"Smart girl."

Kelt had given a friendly tap on the shoulder with her wrench then.

"Nope. Shit rolls downhill, and I was right at the bottom. I got blamed for that numb nuts's fuckup, and was fired right on the spot. They booted me on Yaara, and that was that. My resume was absolute poison, so I had no choice but to hitch a ride out to B-Sys and see what freelance work I could dredge up. Luckily, the temp agency I signed up with just so happened to place me with the Captain right away, and she hired me full-time halfway through my first run."

"Awww, well, I'm glad you found a home sooner rather than later!"

"You and me both, kiddo. That lady definitely knows how to pick 'em, that's for sure. Now, get back to work. Those bolts aren't going to loosen themselves."

"Heh. Ma'am, yes ma'am."

With each passing day, Phera found herself growing closer and closer with the acerbic little woman. She was fun (especially to annoy, provided one didn't go too far). And, as a happy bonus to their long work hours, she was able to avoid stirring up any reason for Straya or anyone else to properly spank her.

However, that didn't stop Kelt from landing the occasional swat to the back of her pants whenever she was being particularly obnoxious while they worked. It was a fun game for the two of them, though. And, as the days passed with her collecting only the odd token pop, Phera's thoroughly bruised seat gradually began to return to its original alabaster hue.

It wouldn't last.

—

The Mayhem's cargo hold was spacious and empty enough to be acrophobic and echoey, but the recent haul of Panorama semi-autonomous vac-mining and shipboard maintenance units filled up enough space to not make it too lonely.

The big, bull-sized ore crawlers had their tentacles halfway extended and magnetized to the deck, holding their barrel-shaped bodies unmoving about a meter and a half above the ground. The much smaller repair crawlers scuttled around them, climbing their larger bodies like ants over the corpses of giant insects, loosening panels and removing screws under the direction of the Blazar Bitches' tech crew. Humming in counterpoint to the small units' metallic *click-clack*ing, were a pair of trirotor support drones. Hovering around at eye level, ferrying lightweight tools (and the occasional snack) back and forth between the three humans in magboots as they worked.

Kelt and Phera, hair pulled back into matching buns, stood hunched over a tentacle-tip they'd had HVM-02 lift off the deck. The repair crawlers had just finished helping them remove the excavation laser and drill assemblies from its articulated length, and Kelt was now in the process of fitting a homemade wire interface and bracing ring inside the socket. Phera, meanwhile, was welding a gatecrasher kit securely into the newly removed module-holder. As the two of them worked, Obette climbed up among the scuttling crawlers on the barrel-shaped body overhead. Boots adhering to its dull, graphene-infused hull as his hands played over the control panel they'd exposed.

Truth be told, Phera was a bit distracted by those well-filled-out pants of his as he bent down over the interface with his hands and feet planted securely on the drone for balance.

"Ahem."

Kelt cleared her throat sharply, making Phera tear her eyes away from the overhead scenery and back to the gatecrasher.

"Nothing wrong with looking," she murmured to her fellow engineer in a low singsong, looking not the least bit repentant.

Kelt just shot her a stern glare over the bulk of the manipulator tentacle.

"Uh-huh."

Her annoyance only made Phera smile all the wider, though, and she blew the woman a kiss before sliding her welding goggles back down over her sweaty face and returning her attention to fusing the slightly too large module into its new home.

She and Kelt had gone back and forth quite a bit on how best to make it stay in place without snapping off under its own operational torque, and had eventually settled on a series of adaptive honeycomb support struts to bridge the gaps between the module and its housing. They'd fallen into a good rhythm by now, and said struts were coming together surprisingly well. With any luck, this tentacle's new head would be ready to go within the next half hour.

"Come on, Kelty, you can't blame me for looking," she added quiet enough for only the other woman's ears as she started working her way down her final passes on the module's seams, joining them together with a thick, bubbly line of molten tungsten alloy that rapidly cooled in the hold, raising the ambient temperature enough to plaster a couple more curls to her forehead. "He's got a great ass."

"Why, thank you."

Obette looked back over his shoulder at the two women as he spoke. His silver white hair was tied up above his head, but the ends flew freely in the wake of the trirotor hovering nearby, giving them an almost anemone like sway in the null-grav.

"I get even more compliments on my cochlear implants, though."

"Is that, um… Is that right?"

Phera felt the warmth in her cheeks rise by a few more degrees, and wished very much that she could blame it on her welding torch. Meanwhile, Kelt's smug grin gained a condescending edge to it as she watched her squirm.

"Infiltrators need situational awareness, you know."

Brushing past Phera's embarrassment, she took up the newly welded piece and turned it over in her hands appraisingly. Were it not for the lack of gravity in the hold, neither of them would have been able to lift it, but in the null-grav she maneuvered it easily.

"All right, let's try this out. Get one of your spiders over here."

Popping back up to a standing position, Phera nodded quickly. "Right!"

Cutting off the flow of fuel to her welding torch and leaving it to float freely in the air beside her (gods, working in null-grav was nice sometimes), she turned her wrist over and tapped out a quick sequence of commands into her comp to summon Number Seven over to her position. She'd been working on the crawler's object detection, analysis, and hazard avoidance routines in what little spare time she'd had these last few days. And, as it scuttled along the deck toward her from the other side of the hold, it only bumped into two out of four of the larger excavators.

"Not bad, huh?" she crooned, dipping her chin toward the crawler as it came to a stop half a meter away from her boots.

She could've just had it detach from the deck and send itself floating her way using its minimally-powered maneuvering jets, but this way was much more fun. And, eventually, more useful.

Kelt just rolled her eyes.

"Yes, yes, dear. I'm very impressed. Now, let's try and get at least *one* excavator done today so we can test it in the morning, all right?"

Stepping in closer, she delivered one of her sharp little swats that logically shouldn't hurt nearly as much as they did to the underside of Phera's left cheek.

SMACK!

"We don't have time to waste on pathfinding games."

Before moving on to the second multifarious tentacle-tip, where she began another disassembly. Leaving Phera to finish up her part in installing the new mod.

"You are going to be *so* jealous once I finally manage to get the adaptive learning net on these things sorted out and they can navigate their way to the mess for snacks," she pouted lazily at the other woman as she maneuvered the newly welded gatecrasher into position where the old drilling assembly had once been.

It took a bit of juggling (the new part was awkwardly shaped, and even in zero-g it was a pain to find a good spot to grip it), but she eventually managed to free her left hand enough to tap out more instructions for the spider-crawler to start the final connection process. With an acknowledging chirp, it released its mag-clamps and sprung from the deck plating, reorienting itself to clack into place along the tentacle and proceeding to manipulate Kelt's new wiring harness into position before beginning to make the many and varied connections required to operate the gatecrasher.

"Besides," Phera went on once she was sure the mating process was proceeding the way it was supposed to, sparing a look over toward where Kelt was quickly and expertly dismantling her tentacle tip. "The next unit should go *way* smoother than this one. We've basically got the process sorted out now, yeah?"

It was definitely a compliment. Kelt had managed their project spectacularly so far, and had kept them moving forward nearly non-stop. But, Phera couldn't help but make it sound just a *bit* sassy.

Her left cheek was still smarting, after all.

"Uh-huh. *Should.*"

Despite her clipped tone, Phera couldn't help but notice the tiny woman's hard line of a mouth curving up into a self-satisfied smile.

Overhead, Obette called out, "Ah, hell. Looks like the firmware rolled itself back again. I'm going to have to jailbreak that crasher's command system from the other side too."

He glared at the panel a bit, before loosing a melodramatic sigh and flopping back onto the raised arm behind him.

"Well, at least this means I won't be leaving the two of you so early."

He gave Phera an upside down, half-facetious eyelash flutter as he did so, still ribbing her about her open lechery.

"There's always something that needs tweaking, isn't there?"

Letting go of the gatecrasher now that it was safe to do so, Phera winked at the infiltrator and snatched up her slowly spinning welding torch.

"Try wiggling your hips a bit more while you work," she suggested just as facetiously as she floated past him and over to where Kelt and the next honeycomb assembly she needed to weld waited for her. "It helps the debugging."

Remagnetizing her boots, she settled down into a squat as Kelt freed the last of the old drill assembly and got to work fitting in another wiring harness. This next tentacle went as smoothly as the first, and the one after even more so. And, by the time the two of them were finished refitting the last of the excavator's manipulators, Obette had just about managed to catch up to them with the jailbreaking he'd needed to do.

They really did make a great team.

Phera tugged off her goggles and massaged the small imprints they'd left behind on her sweaty forehead. Sending the goggles and her torch sailing off in the general direction of the workbench they'd set aside for tool storage, she then turned to beam at her fellow engineer.

"See, now was that so bad?"

"Did I *say* it was bad?"

Kelt raised one thin, black eyebrow at her as she took off her greasy apron and stretched her lithe arms overhead.

Before Phera could come up with a sufficiently sassy remark, Obette's boots smacked onto the deck beside her as he launched himself "down" from atop the excavator.

"Phew! Talk about tedious. I'm really hoping I can just copy the new code over and reset the subsequent units."

Sighing in relief, he undid his hair. Letting it rise up around is head like a shifting silver cloud as he dragged a bare forearm across his forehead.

"But, I suspect we'll have some little bugs here and there. These octos have quite a few years on them, and well…"

He clapped Phera on the shoulder.

"I'm sure you know better than I do about 'resetting' a vac-computer that old."

"Hey, Phera." Kelt said then, cutting the younger engineer off before she could come up with a response, her usually stern lips quirking up into a thoughtful little smile. "I think that's yours?"

As she spoke, she pointed toward the welding torch Phera had left floating above the workbench. It had drifted down toward the deck, under the raised tentacle whose tip they'd just finished replacing.

"Huh? Oh!"

Eager to preserve the smile on the older woman's face (annoying her was fun, but it was nice to see her happy too), Phera pushed off from the deck and took a dive for her escaping torch.

"Get back here, you!" she exclaimed as she half-caught, half-slammed into the tool.

She'd been getting a lot of practice maneuvering in null-grav lately, and as her fingers wrapped themselves around the torch (double-checking that its valve was still closed since flammable gas leaking inside of a vac-sealed ship was a horrible combination), she tucked and rolled and stumbled to a stop just before the workbench (boots automatically resealing to the deck as she did so).

"Good catch, Kelt. Definitely wouldn't want this little guy running away."

"Yep. Now why don't you strap that thing in properly like you're supposed to before it wanders off again?"

"Right!"

Leaning forward onto her tiptoes, Phera tore open a velcro loop near the end of the workbench and secured her torch into place with a little pat of affection.

"There you go, buddy."

Kelt, meanwhile, still wearing her bemused smile, just shook her head and hit a button on her own wrist comp. The next moment, a massive tentacle manipulator arm began to lower itself down onto Phera's back. Pushing her belly further against the raised workbench they'd had it suspended over so that her sealed magboots forced her into a near perfect ninety-degree bent over position.

"What the?"

The arm came to a stop with only the faintest bit of pressure against the middle of her back just an instant before its safeties would've kicked in. And, where someone even a tiny bit slimmer than she was would've been able to wriggle free without much difficulty.

"Oops."

"Oops?" echoed Phera, wriggling and squirming, but staying right where she was.

She tried to look back over her shoulder. But, unfortunately for her, there was a thick, articulated metal arm blocking most of her view. She was pretty sure she could see the ends of a couple wisps of Obette's silver hair, though.

"Uh, Ob, buddy... You forget to disable something?"

She bobbed her hips behind her some more, the snugly stretched seat of her pants and the starkly visible panty lines beneath shifting back and forth with her movements.

"I think some proximity routine is still enabled."

"This one wasn't on me, I'm glad to say."

There came a subdued chuckle from the infiltrator then, and Phera heard him shift to address Kelt.

"Come on, Kelty, you can't blame me for looking. She's got a great ass," he cooed mockingly, throwing Phera's earlier leering justification right back at her.

"Hmmm... Now that you mention it, yeah. She does, doesn't she?"

"Hardy-har-har. You two are *hilarious*."

Heaving out a put-upon harrumph, Phera tugged and yanked one of her magboots free and stomped it back down into place. Sending a rather appealing wobble through her perfectly presented bottom in the process.

"I promise it looks even better walking away. So, would one of you be a sweetheart and give me a hand here?"

"Actually, I think I have a better idea," countered Kelt breezily. "Not to mention an idea to test out the finesse on these tri… Yep, there we go!"

One of the flyers hovered over behind Phera, and used its nimble grasper arm to pinch her waistband and drag her pants and underwear down to mid-thigh before zipping away again. To its credit, it didn't rip either garment. But, still!

"Hey!"

"Okay," interjected Obette with a gentle scoff. "That's sort of impressive, but also terrifying. I think I'm going to remove myself from the situation here before there are any more workplace accidents."

Before leaving, though, Phera heard his magboots advance, and then felt his strong, nimble fingers grasping a handful of her left buttock.

"Ouch. I guess I really did miss a show when I left the bar, didn't I?"

Apparently Phera's recovery wasn't quite as well along as she'd been trying to tell herself.

"It was definitely… memorable," she conceded, trying to shift her seat out of his grip in protest and only instead succeeding in partially exposing more of her anus. "Jerk."

Stomping again, working her pants another handful of centimeters further down and separating them from her panties, she blew out a breath and addressed Kelt directly.

"All right, all right, we're all very impressed with the manipulator packages on those trirotors."

She fully intended on tearing one down to study later, actually.

"But weren't *you* the one who was saying earlier that tools aren't toys, Miss Bossy Boots Head Engineer?"

Phera still had all too vivid memories of what had happened the last time she'd been bent over a workbench with her pants down in

Kelt's presence, and already her heartbeat was starting to accelerate. This was a very dangerous position to be in as Obette was so very clearly demonstrating.

"I thought you ought to have a demonstration as to *why* they shouldn't be used as toys." Kelt chuckled. "Well, I'm heading out now. I'll see you two later."

Then, still sounding thoroughly amused with herself, she added.

"Ob, you can come with. Or not. It's your call."

"Wait, you're *leaving*?!" demanded an incredulous Phera, fluttery panic starting to well its way up inside of her.

She wasn't sure if she should be upset about that or not, truth be told. It sure did seem like a waste for Kelt to trap her like this and then not take advantage. Aside from her demonstration of trirotor manipulator finesse, that is.

Kelt didn't answer her question, but the fading sound of her boots on the deck was answer enough.

Obette was still there, though.

"Ob, old buddy, old pal," she wheedled, rolling her hips for added encouragement against his palming grip. "Would you be a sweetie and pop open that control panel over there for me?"

She gave her hips another wiggle, this time to her right.

"And issue a rise sequence to manipulator appendage 8 for me? Also maybe fix my pants too while you're at it? Pretty please?"

"Hmmm..."

She heard rather than felt Obette's hands rise to his face.

"Contradictory impulses. Now, which shall win out?"

Phera smothered her smirk with a harrumph, foregoing the effort of stomping this time in favor of bobbing her cheeks up and down in protest.

"I know what I'd do if *I* were in your position," she pouted, deliberately choosing not to actually voice what she'd do.

Obette would look great bent over with those snug pants of his around his ankles, but letting him know that right now seemed like it would be counterproductive.

"Besides, didn't you tell me the other night that you like to do all of your sneaky tricks right in the open and proudly? How can your professional dignity stand such deceitful tactics like these? It's downright despicable!"

Again, her cheeks jiggled and bounced in protest as she shifted her hips the scant few centimeters the tentacle pinning her down allowed.

"It doesn't get much further out in the open than this, though, does it?"

Obette's magboots clicked a step closer again.

"Although... Now I'm curious. What *would* you do were our positions reversed?"

"I..."

Phera had never been a very good liar.

"I'd help you out, obviously."

"You hesitated nearly three seconds there."

She felt body heat against her exposed cheeks then.

"This leads me to suspect that I might be the intended victim of a deception."

Obette chuckled softly.

"Are you certain you don't want to revise that statement, Doctor Sinclair?"

"I... I... It wasn't *three* seconds!"

Obette's intimately close proximity made it possible for Phera to throw an accusatory glare over her shoulder at him.

"And, quite frankly, I'm offended you'd think I'd be anything other than honest with you."

She managed to maintain a straight face for most of that.

"Well."

SMACK!

A large, strong hand clapped down hard across her bare left buttock without warning then, leaving a long-fingered handprint in its wake and sending a meaty echo reverberating throughout the cavernous hold. Chased along by Obette's throaty chuckle as he squeezed her hard where he'd just swatted.

"You'll never be much of a pirate with that sort of attitude, now will you?"

SMACK!

Same cheek. Same spot. Just as hard.

"Huh- Oh! Rumph."

Phera tried to bump her hips back against the infiltrator in retaliation, but only succeeded in making them wobble again.

"I might not be a good liar, but I'll have you know the Captain asked me specifically to help reinforce her reputation back at Tortuga. And if that isn't a pirate stamp of approval, I don't know what is."

"I know, my dear. I saw the footage."

The infiltrator's low purr was velvety smooth as he glided both his palms along Phera's exposed seat.

"I'm not sure why you'd think that *helps* your case right now, though..."

SMACK!

He accompanied this observation with a lazy (but still hard enough to make her yelp) swat to her right cheek.

SMACK!

Followed by one to her left.

"My, that's a dramatic shake, isn't it?"

Drawing back half a step, he seized Phera's bottom cheeks and clapped them together.

And then *clapped* each one twice more with his palms.

SMACK-SMACK!

SMACK-SMACK!

"There's- Ah! FOOTAGE?!" yelped Phera, her jerk of surprise keeping the wobbling started by Obette's swats going long after the initial sting had subsided.

"Well, I didn't bother cracking the security footage, but there were enough uploads on Marcos's social pond that I didn't much need to. Cap had quite an audience."

SMACK-SMACK!

SMACK-SMACK!

"And you're well on your way to fully merited celebrity status, with an encore or two, I think."

SMACK-SMACK!

SMACK-SMACK!

"It's nice- Ow! To be popular," Phera attempted to deadpan.

Just then she was very grateful for the obstruction blocking her absolutely smoldering face from view.

"Send me a copy later, yeah?" she mumbled in the intervening silence that followed that final round of swats, before doing her best angry Straya growling impression. "And get me out of here while you're at it!"

"To the first, certainly, I'll do it right now."

Obette slipped his slate free from a pocket and tapped out a few commands. A moment later, Phera felt her wrist comp vibrate twice in quick succession.

"As to the second…"

Settling in along her left side, hip-to-hip facing away, he casually ran a fingertip up and down along the inside of her crack, and then lifted one buttock and let it bounce free.

"The gratitude of a fellow crew member, or my personal credo of not rejecting serendipity when it comes my way? Hmmm…"

He waited, as if expecting Phera to make an argument for one or the other.

"Isn't doing a good deed its own reward?" she teased in response, skin tingling from the infiltrator's casually authoritative touch. "I've been told I write *very* heartfelt thank you notes."

Just then, there came the sound of the grav acclimation tunnel's hatch swishing open along its tracks, followed by much heavier magboot footfalls than Kelt's.

"Hold that thought."

Swift as could be, Obette released his boots' lock on the floor and kicked himself up off the deck, grabbing hold of the manipulator tentacle and slipping with surprising grace across the excavator's body to hide himself from view. A moment later, an exasperated (and deep) female voice rumbled out, "Kelt, you TOLD me you'd be back in the shop to deal with-"

Lem's heavy, stomping footfalls stalked deeper into the cargo hold, only to come to a stop midsentence.

"What the?"

"Oh thank gods!"

Melting against the workbench beneath her in weak-kneed relief, Phera blew several burnt copper curls out of her face.

"Lem, Lem, over here!" she called, struggling to free one of her magboots to wave in an attempt to catch the first mate's attention just in case she'd somehow overlooked her. "This stupid manipulator has me pinned. Can you lift it for me?"

"What...?" came Lem's repeated question, followed a second later by a much more annoyed sounding. "Where the fuck is Kelt?"

"Now that is a *very* good question." Phera blew out a petulant huff. "Would you believe she just left me here like this?"

"Yes. Now where is she?"

"How the heck should I know?"

The first mate's notable lack of moving manipulator tentacles off of her was causing Phera's wry, good-natured tone to turn decidedly sassy.

"I'm pretty sure I heard her going that way."

She bobbed her faintly pinkened bare backside in the general direction of the hab cylinder.

"Did you check the workshop or the mess? It's not that big of a ship. She can't have gotten far."

"Yeah, I was just in the shop! Where the hell could she even-?"

Lem clenched a fist.

"That little..."

She clomped over behind Phera then and squatted down behind her, inspecting the pair of bare cheeks before her. Then, without another word, she began to tear into her with a vengeance.

SMACK! SMACK! SMACK! SMACK! SMACK!

"Ow! Ack! Fuck! Shit! Ack!"

The first mate's hand was far bigger than any that had struck Phera so far, nearly swallowing up an entire cheek with its breadth, and her muscular arm put Straya and Adryel's soldierly physiques to shame. It was as if she were being paddled by solid tungsten!

SMACK! SMACK! SMACK! SMACK! SMACK!

Amid a deluge of four letter words from the engineer, the big woman's big hand moved left and right, up and down, layering napalm atop Phera's already sensitive ass and making it ripple and dance more energetically than Obette and his little patty-cake claps could have ever dreamed.

"Oh my gods, Lem! Ah! Ah! Owie!"

With each sledgehammer blow, Phera's hips jerked forward in a reflexive attempt to escape the irate first mate who apparently had decided to take out her frustrations on her.

It didn't help.

"Oh! Ack! Come onnnn!" she whined, dancing on the balls of her feet inside her boots and inadvertently pushing her cheeks up higher for even more punishment. "This is- Owie! Kelt's fault- Urk! Not mine!"

Lem didn't respond, exactly. She spoke, but more to herself. Her warm breath tickling the undercurves of the roboticist's sit-spots.

"She fucking knew I was looking for her, didn't she?"

SMACK! SMACK! SMACK! SMACK! SMACK!

"Well, she's going to regret this when I get my hands on her lazy little ass, that's for damn sure!"

The meteor-like strikes continued unabated while Phera howled in increasingly frantic and worried protest.

"Spank *her*, not me, dammit!"

SMACK! SMACK! SMACK! SMACK! SMACK!

As if on cue, Lem's swatting came to a sudden stop with one final double *SMACK!* that pushed Phera's lips out into an agonized O. She rested a meaty palm on each of the engineer's now blazing hot cheeks then, giving them an appraising couple of squeezes. Her hands remained there for several blissfully long seconds, her cool palms absorbing some of the heat, before then drifting down to her thighs, where she proceeded to fondle those too.

"I swear. It's like herding a bunch of damned cats around here!"

The first mate absently tugged Phera's thighs a little further open as she spoke, before lifting aside one of her cheeks and poking gently at where she saw moisture.

"One of these days, I'm going to line all of you brats up and..."

Nibbling at her lower lip as Lem dragged a fingertip up and down along her exposed labia, Phera was definitely intrigued to hear what she had in mind for the crew, but was denied that knowledge when the bigger woman went back to spanking her suddenly.

SMACK! SMACK! SMACK! SMACK! SMACK!

Mostly lower down now, aiming for her vulnerable sit-spots and her equally vulnerable thighs.

Oh fuck, oh fuck, oh fuck!

If this was Lem venting her frustrations on a bystander, Phera's insides quavered to find out what she'd be like when she was pissed off at *her*. Though, at the moment, the distinction seemed largely academic.

Those thigh swats hurt!

"Oh my gods, oh my gods," she yelped, unable to hop around like she wanted to with her feet locked to the deck and the tentacle arm holding her in place. "Lem, please, I'm sorry!"

SMACK! SMACK! SMACK! SMACK! SMACK!

Her breath was coming faster and faster in the form of hissing gasps through clenched teeth as she was seized by a sizable surge of panic and excitement at just how quickly and easily the first mate had managed to accelerate her past her usual pain tolerance.

"Ack! Owie! Urk!"

Through gritted teeth, she started to plead, hoping to make a deal.

"Let me go and I'll help you find Kelt, I promise! I'll hold her down and everything too! Whatever you want!"

"Thanks for the apology, muffin, but you've got nothing to be sorry for. Or to help me with. At least, not right now."

She paused then to roughly cup a hand over Phera's glistening lips, and the engineer felt her heart soar in relief for an entire two and a half seconds. Before just as quickly crashing back down into the pit of her stomach as she watched Lem's heavily muscled forearm reach past her and pick up a loose piece of synth-rubber tubing that used to be part of a gatecrasher's safety insulation.

"Um, h-hold on just a second, let's not get too hasty!"

Phera's stuttering pleading went completely ignored, as Lem shifted back up to stand by her left side and *WOOSHED* the length of dense material through the air behind her. Causing the wetness between the younger woman's thighs to grow all the more intense as anticipatory goosebumps broke out all across her bare skin.

"I really can't believe her sometimes…"

WOOSH-THWACK!

"FUCK!"

Absolute, unadulterated agony exploded across the bouncy center of Phera's right cheek.

WOOSH-THWACK!

Followed by an equally intense eruption of pain lower down.

WOOSH-THWACK! WOOSH-THWACK!

And two more on her left cheek. Landing with the sort of precision born from years of practice.

Though not as heavy or as broad as Lem's palm, the synth-rubber was *extremely* dense and designed specifically for gripping onto smooth surfaces. Which it did exceptionally well as it exploded against Phera's wobbly seat again and again. Its rigid form contouring to match her natural curves and gripping tight, ensuring that every last joule of kinetic energy it was swung with was fully transferred into her soft and vulnerable bare bottom.

"Ah! Ah! Aieee!"

Each casual *THWACK!* Of the synth-rubber against her seat landed with a highly-concentrated miniature supernova that blazed white hot for several eye-popping seconds before collapsing in on itself to form a black hole of aching pain that sunk deep down into her rump where it continued throbbing well after the initial burning fury had dissipated.

It was honestly pretty impressive, and Phera was extremely glad that Lem wasn't swinging it as fast as she had her hand.

WOOSH-THWACK! WOOSH-THWACK! WOOSH-THWACK!

That was small comfort, though, when the first mate was absolutely annihilating her ass.

"Oh my gods, Lem, that thing is so *mean*!" she moaned in the same way she had the other night when Straya had stolen a bite of her dessert while she hadn't been paying attention, panting and bouncing on her toes in a futile attempt to shake off some of the monumental ache in her backside.

"Yes," Lem agreed.

WOOSH-THWACK! WOOSH-THWACK! WOOSH-THWACK!

"And it's all that smartass little engineer's fault."

WOOSH-THWACK! WOOSH-THWACK! WOOSH-THWACK!

Phera's bottom was already nearly as swollen as it had been after Kelt's mistreatment on their previous journey to Marcos Station, and completely repainted by dark crimson stripes that overlapped one another to cover just about every square centimeter of it.

"Oh well…"

Just as quickly as it had started, everything was suddenly over, and Lem was tying the infernal piece of rubber back around the rack on the side of the workbench she'd gotten it from. Then, squatting down nice and close behind Phera's absolutely livid buttocks, she returned to fondling, squeezing, and spreading them with no regard to the breathy, pained gasps and grunts her actions produced from the woman herself.

"Well, at least she knows how to decorate."

"Heh. Thanks…"

Panting in deep, exhausted breaths, Phera lay sagged across the workbench and pushed her hips as far back as she could to further encourage Lem. Steph had definitely been right when ve had said she'd enjoy finding out just how hard the first mate could swing, and she was also desperately hoping that the cute little doctor's stock of cooling gel would be refilled by the time she got around to visiting ver later.

"I… appreciate… the compliment," she groaned. "You big meanie."

Those last three words were muttered under her breath, and if they were overheard, Phera hoped they'd serve to further rile Lem up against the crew's senior engineer and not her.

She was half-right.

"Meanie, huh?" Lem asked, still groping Phera's blazing cheeks, fingers gripping the inside of her crack to expose the twitching rosebud above her by now positively sopping lower lips. "Totally fair, but also not very wise to say in your position."

SMACK-SMACK!

SMACK-SMACK!

Two brutal swats suddenly exploded across each of her sit-spots. (Which were *still* sore from the Captain the other night despite all the hot showers she'd taken!)

"Ack! Ah-!"

SMACK-SMACK!

Followed by a swat to the back of either thigh for good measure.

"Well, I'd love to stick around and play with you a little longer, cheeks, but I do need to talk to Kelt. And also *talk* to Kelt. I'll make sure she comes right back here as soon as I'm done to let you out, though."

Lem accompanied this casual dismissal with one final **SMACK!** Across the lower middle part of Phera's bare bottom, nailing the inner curves of both her sit-spots.

"For now, just sit tight and be very polite to anyone else who comes in, yeah?"

Phera felt a kiss being planted by large, full lips on her sizzling left cheek, and then a nibble and lick that would have been purely pleasant were her flesh not so sore and swollen. Then, Lem was back on her feet and clomping back out the way she'd come as if none of this had even happened.

"Whatever you say, *mom*," harrumphed the auburn-haired engineer with as much obnoxious sass as she could muster, endorphins and general horniness making her bolder than perhaps she should be.

"Okay, that is a tone you do *NOT* take with me! No matter how abusive and unfair I've been!"

Lem came clomping back to her then.

Fast.

In a flash, she was holding her improvised strap again, and it was whistling through the air faster than ever.

*WOOSH-**THWACK**! WOOSH-**THWACK**! WOOSH-**THWACK**!*

"Okay, okay, okaaaaaay!"

Howling, Phera's voice rose with each brutally punishing lash. Once again, the desire to voice whatever tidbit of sass that popped into her head had backfired on her in the most spectacular way possible. Which, she both loved and absolutely hated.

The consequences part of risking annoying a disciplinarian were always somehow much more painful than she'd thought they'd be.

"I'm sorry, ma'am, I'm *SORRY*!"

Her words were high-pitched and peppered with yelps and squeaks and squeals, but they were nothing if not sincere.

"You'd better be."

*WOOSH-**THWACK**! WOOSH-**THWACK**! WOOSH-**THWACK**!*

Lem stopped suddenly then, and as Phera sagged against the workbench beneath her in relief, she heard her rummaging in one of the drawers beside her. Followed by velcro unlatching from around one of the tools contained therein a second later.

"Let's see here…"

There came a short pause. Then, something extremely cold, extremely hard, and extremely wet and slimy pressed itself between her partially parted cheeks.

"Eep!"

"This ought to help you think about what you could have done differently while you wait," Lem chuckled to herself as she worked the freshly oiled handle of a tiny hand-wrench against Phera's anus.

"Oh my gods! Wha-? Oh-Ohhh my gods, oh fuck-!"

Ignoring the younger woman's increasingly inarticulate moaning, Lem worked the wrench in past its rounded tip and a good ten centimeters deep. Driving it in as far back as she had it greased, until only its angular head remained free to protrude between her carmine striped cheeks.

"Be good now, muffin."

Levering herself back to her feet using Phera's sizzling seat for support, Lem clomped back a step to assess her handiwork and then turned to leave once more.

"But… but…!"

Spluttering, but very specifically *not* sassing this time, Phera's bottom clenched and unclenched around the rigid wrench inside of her in sync with her breathing and the pulsing of her freshly reignited cheeks.

"This is so humiliating…" she groaned once she heard the acclimation hatch finish cycling, allowing her sweat-sheened forehead to flop forward onto the workbench with a melodramatic *thunk*.

Well, at least nobody else was around to see her just then.

Kelt was probably going to gloat like crazy, though.

"Humph."

And here she was with her hands trapped in front of her too.

"Talk about unfair."

A long, loud whistle came from up above her then, startling her out of her daydreams of the older engineer being shoved roughly against her bunk as Lem tore her pants off and had her way with her.

"Well, at least I didn't miss the *shipboard* reprise performance."

Swift as an arrow, Obette shot back down to the deck from his hiding place and magnetized his boots.

"Oh my gods!"

Squealing in terror, Phera's cheeks clenched extra tight, causing the wrench sticking out of her to bob up and down excitedly in greeting.

"Obette! What the-?"

She'd completely forgotten about the infiltrator.

"I thought you'd left!" she half-accused, half-laughed, face going scarlet all over again.

"Sorry, my dear. While I would have preferred to remove myself from the situation, the only ways out were through the first mate or through one of the airlocks."

He paused for a moment.

"Granted, I suppose I could have boarded your old shuttle, but... Well, I don't think Kelt wants anyone but you or her tampering with that for now."

There came a soft chuckle from him then.

"I must say, though, the engineering-themed fashion accessory suits you quite nicely."

Phera felt the man leaning over her again, and then a very attention-getting series of vibrations as he tapped his finger against the head of the wrench.

"I... That's... Ah-!"

All of that tapping was making stringing words together surprisingly difficult for her.

"Lem's not still in the hold is she?" she finally managed to ask, still panting.

"I certainly hope not with the kind of mood she seems to be in."

He gave the wrench a few more, lighter, taps.

"Also, the door did close behind her."

Before easing down to his heels behind the bench.

"On the topic of behinds, though, how is yours enduring?"

He took his hand off the wrench head and traced a slender fingertip down along one swollen, bruised curve.

"How do you think?" pouted Phera, relaxing slightly with the knowledge that Lem and her unnecessarily strong arms were well and truly out of earshot. "She was being *so* mean."

She gave her hips a little wiggle, indicating the wrench head sticking out from between her buns.

"I'll at least give her points for resourcefulness."

A fresh groan escaped Phera as her shifting caused Obette's fingertip to poke into a particularly sensitive welt.

"The extra swats seem like overkill if you ask me, though."

"No," Obette countered lazily. "She was only being moderately mean, at most. You have to make sure you're using the right scale for Lem and Kelt."

Another chuckle welled up from within him, and Phera felt his shoulders shrug.

"Although, I wouldn't recommend turning your back on Steph either."

That, at least, managed to draw out an amused snort from the engineer.

"You don't say?"

"I'm serious," insisted Obette. "After ver, I'd say the cruelest scoundrels aboard would be... Hmmm. I'd like to say either Straya, the Captain, or myself."

As he spoke, his finger dragged upward again.

"Though, I find myself wondering where our new roboticist ranks. Time alone will tell, I suppose."

Rising up from his crouch, he settled down onto the workbench beside Phera's pinned hips, draping an arm around her waist as though it were the shoulders of a movie date.

"Now then. Do I release you, or wait for Kelt to return and have the honor?"

Phera very nearly said, "You should follow your heart," but remembered at the last moment that telling pirates to do that wasn't the best call when it came to preserving her bottom or her dignity.

Blowing out a huff, her mind churned its way through some quick calculations.

"Well..." she ventured tentatively a moment later, drawing out the word and doing her best to keep her voice casual and not at all let on how desperate she was just then to escape. "Seeing as *you've* already gotten an eyeful."

She harrumphed good-naturedly.

"And a handful. My vote is for you. It would be an absolute delight to watch Kelt come limping back out here after Lem finishes tearing up her ass, only to have her find me already free and none the worse for wear."

Phera wasn't so sure she'd actually be able to pull such an act off without a trip to the head to scrub the tear tracks from her face, but her pants would at least hide the evidence of Lem's creative use of synth-rubber.

"Hmmm..."

Obette squeezed her waist a little tighter, and she felt his right hand cross over to pat her left cheek.

"And how much would that be worth to you, exactly?"

"I..."

Phera's pink lips pushed out once more into a pout.

"Negotiations have never been my strong suit. Just ask Panorama," she said with a self-deprecating smirk. "But, to answer your question, between all these..."

She waggled her hips from side to side, indicating the thick, dark welts left behind by the synth-rubber.

"And this..."

This time, she clenched her cheeks and her impromptu wrench-plug waved hello.

"I am in an *extremely* accommodating mood."

Lem had discovered that for herself, and left Phera frustrated beyond belief.

"So... I dunno... What do you want?"

The corners of the engineer's mouth quirked up into a sly grin.

"I'd offer to suck your cock, but that would require you to let me go. Which would kind of defeat the whole purpose of this little exchange, now wouldn't it?"

"I could always come around to the other side," the infiltrator mused with a lazy couple of pats. "But that wouldn't be very comfortable positioning for me either."

Slipping down off the workbench, he knelt on the floor again. A moment later, Phera felt a soft hand clutching each swollen sit-spot from below. Raising her cheeks, and then clapping them together again, this time around the wrench. Then a finger was stroking, just as Lem's had, down her labia to her clitoris, where it was joined by two others. Circling around the sides and gently pulling at glistening lips.

"How about this? I'm starting to feel a might peckish, and will retire to the mess hall soon for my afternoon repast. When I do, you'll accompany me. But, until then..."

He drew his fingers slightly further back, and slowly began to work them inside of her.

"I could... eat..." Phera managed to get out around a contented sigh. "Oh gods..."

The sensation of Obette's long, clever fingers inside of her caused her to reflexively tighten around the infiltrator as a hot shiver of delight cascaded through her body. Doing so also drew her attention back to the rigid length of wrench still lodged between her cheeks, making her stomach lurch with embarrassment and exhilaration.

It had been a long, long while since she'd last been penetrated in two places at once, and she'd forgotten just how much fun it could be.

"If... If you wanted a lunch buddy... All you... All you had to do was- Oh! Was ask, you know..."

She did her best to sound teasing and coy, but it was kind of difficult, distracted as she was.

"I'll take that as an invitation of your own."

Obette chuckled and continued working his fingers in and out, while also curling and uncurling them, for a minute more. Then, releasing his magboots while keeping one hand with its tips inside of Phera, he used the other to grasp the bench and maneuver himself. When at last he was floating with his back parallel to the floor, he grabbed Phera by the thighs to anchor himself and pulled himself up by them, bringing his lips to the engineer's glistening pussy for a peck. Then a proper kiss. Then a deep, probing one.

"Mmph..."

Growing up planetside, Phera was still surprised by how nimble people in null-grav could be when they put their minds to it. Obette didn't have Straya's or Steph's spacer hand-feet biomods, but that hadn't stopped him from positioning himself between her thighs with impressive ease and grace.

"I- Ah! Oh! Yeah, okay-"

For the second time that day, Phera's powers of speech failed her. That was fine, though. She was pretty sure the infiltrator was getting the message.

Obette's tongue penetrating her was absolute ecstasy, and the lingering, throbbing ache in her ass and thighs only made his efforts all the sweeter. The pain pulsing out from them in regular waves was traveling along her skin and in between her legs. Where it was fanned into an inferno by the pirate's velvety tongue and soft lips.

"You are the... the best kind of scoundrel. You know that?" she managed, eyes closed and vision pulsing white with pleasure.

Obette's mouth was too full to answer her, but he at least chuckled in appreciation.

"Oh fuck!"

Which sent another spasm ripping through the pinned engineer as her juices dribbled down his clean-shaven chin.

For the next two minutes, he continued to lick and suckle, with the occasional feather-light nibble here and there to make her squeak. And, when she at last came (making his name echo throughout the hold as she cried it out high and loud), he spun himself back around by her thighs again.

"Now then..."

Using one of Phera's thick thighs for support, he gripped the wrench with his free hand. First to spin it in place. Then to twitch it. Then, finally, to pull it out all at once.

"Ah! Oh my *fucking* gods!"

From there, he maneuvered himself back onto his knees behind her, floating in the null-grav. There came an unzipping and shuffling sound then, and Phera felt a much warmer, but only slightly softer, rod press itself against her sopping pussy.

"I see Lem gave you some ideas," she managed to tease, bumping back against Obette playfully. "Steph is going to be so jealous."

She was feeling *very* good just then, and also very bratty.

Perhaps unsurprisingly, she earned herself a much too hard swat across the center of both her cheeks for that last remark.

SMACK-SMACK!

"Mmph!"

Which served as a (semi) silent reminder of which one of them was in charge at that particular moment.

"Brat."

Then, still holding her thigh with one hand, Obette used the one that had just slapped her to guide his head in, before grabbing both of her hips and pulling himself forward up to the hilt in one smooth, powerful thrust.

"Ah!"

A fresh gasp not all that dissimilar to the one that had come from her with that surprise double-smack escaped from Phera's parted lips then as her head shot up and more of her red curls shook loose from the bun she had them piled in. Followed by breathy panting.

"Ah... Ah..."

And then a moan.

"Ohhh gods."

As of yet she hadn't actually seen Obette's cock, but judging by the way he'd just filled her up so thoroughly, the infiltrator was right to swagger as much as he did.

"Yep. I thought you might say that," he teased.

Phera knew that Obette wasn't all that strong for his height and build, and not being a born spacer he had to exercise constantly to keep what he had. However, the null-grav environment meant that he was weightless, and thus able to go for pretty much as long as he felt like.

"God damn," he grunted around an authoritative growl that made Phera's stomach lurch pleasantly as he began to roll his hips in an easy thrusting motion. "I've wanted to do this ever since that first night you got here."

He pulled his floating body back in and pushed it out faster and faster, letting his arms do more work than his hips. The weightlessness compensated somewhat for the tightness of Phera's slightly chubby body around him. Thus, as long as he stopped every minute or so to cruelly claw, slap, or squeeze her roasted, blazing hot buttocks while he caught his breath, there was really nothing to stop him from taking her for as long and as hard as he wanted.

Which he did.

"Oh gods, Obette! Oh gods!"

Over and over, and *over* again while the engineer gasped and moaned in chorus to the rhythmic slapping of his lean hips against her soft, crimson cheeks. Both of them urgent and chaotic, making the strapped down tools on the workbench rattle and bounce.

As five minutes passed into ten, though, Obette seemed to decide it was time to stop taking those bottom-abusing breaks and just pump away to completion.

"Fun as it is making you call my name, dear, I should probably wrap this up before Kelt gets back. Wouldn't want to make her jealous."

Suiting actions to words, he began to do just that. And, a good ninety seconds later, twitching hard inside of Phera, he emptied himself into her with a long, low grunt.

"Oh fuck… Oh gods…"

Remaining buried up to the hilt inside of her as he finished. Panting and squeezing her rump tightly as his cock twitched out the last of its hot load and slowly began to soften.

"You… You…"

Phera was floating along in her second or third post-orgasm haze, and feeling *thoroughly* satisfied with how things had turned out for her as she luxuriated in the fresh twinges of pain Obette's idle kneading of her battered bottom produced.

"Mmph. Okay, you definitely win," she giggled. "I don't think Kelt would've been nearly so nice in how she chose to let me up."

She teasingly squeezed herself around the infiltrator's semi-flaccid cock.

"I take it you're satisfied with our little bargain?"

"And how," Obette chuckled, pushing sweaty silver locks out of his face.

After a couple more minutes of slow withdrawal amid bottom-squeezing and fondling, he slid the last of himself out and dragged himself with lazy grace up the drone's pinning limb again while pulling up his pants; leaving Phera to dribble cum out between her spread thighs. He reached the necessary control panel soon enough, and a moment later its tentacle-inspired articulation arm raised itself up another fifty centimeters.

"Yourself?"

"No complaints here," Phera drawled, pushing languidly up off the table to properly stand for the first time in what felt like hours. "Well... Aside from having to sit down in the mess, that is."

Kneading her lower back, she threw a smirk over her shoulder at her swollen hips.

"That's definitely going to be a treat."

Pants and underwear still bunched up around her ankles, Phera shifted from massaging her back to tapping out commands on her wrist comp, and a moment later a trirotor swooped over and plucked up the wrench that had been inside of her not too long ago. She then keyed in instructions for the little flyer to retreat up, up, up to the top of the cargo hold and into a small bit of pooled shadow.

"I'll take care of cleaning that up later," she said, nodding toward the now out of sight tool and flyer with a wry grimace. "I'm sore enough as is. I sure as hell don't need Kelt deciding to take Lem's misuse of tools out on *me*."

She snorted then and reached back to rub her butt.

"At least, not today."

CHAPTER SIXTEEN

CHARGES ACCRUED

Fraud in the Third Degree, Indecent Exposure, Aiding and Abetting Unauthorized System Access, Accessory to Grand Theft

"Right this way, please. This shouldn't take more than a few minutes, I'm sure."

"Of course."

Fuck, fuck, fuck! Okay, okay. Hold it together, Phera. Hold. It. Together.

Fingering the embroidered Panorama logo sewn in over her left breast for what felt like the hundredth time that afternoon, Phera did her best to project an air of bland disinterest to match the bland pale chairs and the bland pale docking authority desk in front of her. The officious woman staring her and Straya down from between two bored looking members of station sec hadn't been something the nervous new pirate had seen coming, and it was taking all of Phera's self-control not to let her roiling stomach show on her face.

The plan had been simple.

Dock at Excaden, place an order for fuel, and (while the automated system handled the transfer) have Obette seed their modified ore crawlers onto the station's exterior. It had started off smoothly enough. They'd made it onto the station without incident and placed their order, and then Straya and Phera had decided to "stretch their legs" in the docking ring to head off anyone who might get too close while the infiltrator worked his magic.

Which, of course, was when the port authority inspector decided to show up.

Granted, it was a random surprise inspection, but still.

"Stall them," Obette's voice had hissed urgently into the tiny earpieces Phera and Straya both had on. "I can only keep the station sensors blind for so long. We're not going to get a second chance at this."

Fortunately, she and Straya had managed to intercept the woman and her escort before they could reach the berth connecting their flyer to the station, so all wasn't lost yet. And, even better, the inspection itself apparently was more of a formality than anything serious since nobody had cause to truly be interested in an empty relay shuttle. So, after brief introductions and an explanation of what was happening, they'd been ushered further into the station proper and over to a small customs kiosk situated just outside the docking ring.

For a few blissful minutes then, it seemed like maybe things were going to be fine, and Phera felt the leaden weight in the pit of her stomach starting to lighten just a bit (despite the pull of the station's artificial grav). They'd transferred copies of their falsified Panorama employee identification packets and the flight plan that the Captain had furnished them with along with their megacorp uniforms (pilot's coveralls for Straya and a smart pair of business casual slacks and cream colored blouse for Phera). The inspector had run their credentials through the system without any alarms blaring to life, but then it had all come crashing down with one simple request.

"Great. Now, I'll just need a copy of your cargo manifest and then we can get you two on your way."

"Uh… Cargo manifest?" repeated Phera, who'd taken the lead on dealing with the inspector since she actually had real-world experience as a Panorama employee. "We don't have any cargo, ma'am."

"That doesn't matter," the woman replied in the bored way of someone reciting from muscle memory, "Excaden Station enhanced docking inspection protocol requires that a cargo manifest be submitted in addition to a flight plan. Even if it's one that's devoid of any actual cargo."

"If you need the manifest," Straya replied, stepping in while Phera did her best not to sputter. "That's back on the hauler. We're not planning to dock or unload here. We're just here with the shuttle to load up on fuel."

She kept her voice even as she spoke, and affected a small amount of annoyance. Looking the very picture of a bored spacer on a long trip trying to deal with some local ordinance she'd never heard of.

"The cargo's half an AU out and moving at neg. You don't even have to look in its direction."

Straya sighed then and shook her head, the dark curls starting to grow out since Phera had first met her tickling at her neck. She looked tiredly back at the official across the desk from her, giving her eyes a meaningful roll that absolutely screamed "I don't get paid enough for this shit." The inspector's expression didn't change.

"They don't give us copies of everything on the shuttles," Straya continued, "they just tell me where to take the paper pushers and when."

"Yes," the inspector said. "But, be that as it may."

A note of annoyance crept its way into the official's voice as she flipped her slate around on her desk and slid it toward Phera. Tapping a long, manicured fingernail at a section near the bottom of its screen.

"You came in on a ship that has the capacity to carry excess fuel. Which, to Excaden, is classified as cargo. Therefore, you are required to complete Form 721Q for your inspection. And, you'll notice here, Miss Walters, that it says 'Cargo Manifest' clear as can be. I cannot mark your inspection as complete without one."

Despite their tenuous situation, Phera couldn't help but feel a giddy little thrill in the pit of her roiling stomach at hearing her fake name said so casually.

"Oh, you have got to be kidding me," she grumbled, not needing to affect annoyance at this latest bit of pointless corporate micromanagement.

In the nearly three weeks since she'd been swept up into her new life, she'd forgotten just how much she'd hated her old one.

Then, realizing that she was supposed to be the peppy company go-getter ruling over her tiny relay shuttle kingdom with an enthusiastically iron fist, she cleared her throat and said with a healthy splash of HR employee evaluation inspired charm. "Er... I am *so* sorry that our paperwork isn't complete. Would you mind waiting just a few minutes while I run this up the flagpole to confirm that I can prepare a copy for you?"

"I suppose so," the inspector said, drumming her fingers against the dull, minimalist plex worktop in front of her with a bored hum. "Or else I can perform an in-person evaluation of your hold to verify its contents, or lack thereof, myself. That would be faster, although there will be a fine for me to do so."

At this, she quoted a number that would've left Phera eating recycled nutrient paste for six months straight if she'd had to pay it out of pocket.

She hadn't brought any money with her for this part of the operation. Well, she didn't *have* any money. So, moot point. Which left her two partners in crime, and she doubted that Straya or Obette would be able to cover that fee themselves either. If they couldn't pay right away, the flyer would probably be impounded, and then they'd have to radio back to their supervisor (aka the Captain), and that had the potential to *really* start unraveling things.

"Do *not* let them on board the ship," Obette's hushed but insistent voice whispered into her and Straya's ears. "We're still nine minutes from being done."

Phera shifted her weight from foot to foot.

"Uh... That's, um..."

She sent a pleading look in Straya's direction. The inspector seemed ready to move on to the cargo inspection right there and then, and she had no idea how to tell her they'd rather make her wait while she cobbled together a manifest herself.

"Isn't this supposed to be *your* job?" Straya asked.

Shifting closer to Phera, the imposing pirate planted a hand on her hip and cocked her brows in exasperation.

"Cargo manifests and shit like that? Didn't you tell me you're the one who handles the Great God Pan's paperwork for him?"

Straya used Panorama's semi-ironic folk nickname. Phera got what Straya was surreptitiously asking her. *Phera, do you know how to fill out a manifest? Do you know how to give a proper Panorama signature that'll pass muster?*

Phera did indeed still remember how to fill out her ex-employer's flavor of paperwork. She'd been forced to submit enough budget reports and resource allocation requests during her time on The Bin that she was pretty sure she could do it in her sleep.

She was just about to open her mouth to say something to that effect, when the comp on her wrist buzzed and she heard Obette murmur, "I've pushed a timer out to both of you. Keep stalling."

Closing her mouth again and swallowing, Phera surreptitiously checked the display on the inside of her wrist, covering the movement by dragging some of her unbound curls behind an ear. The timer read four hundred and twenty-eight seconds, and Straya had just given her the perfect opening to do just as Obette had ordered. An opening that also just so happened to allow her to say some things she'd always wanted to to her old bosses.

Never mind that she was posing as the nominally higher-ranking crew member just then.

"Look," she huffed, rolling her eyes and casting a sidelong "can you believe this?" look toward their inspector. "I did *my* job, all right? I filed our flight plan and I made sure our credentials were all there. "

Straya had actually been the one to handle that initial transmission when she'd been bringing them into port, but Phera had at least given everything a once-over to confirm that it actually looked like it came from an official Panorama clerk.

Jabbing an accusatory finger at the taller woman, warming to her new persona as an aggrieved, newly-promoted middle manger looking for someone to pass the blame onto, Phera continued her berating tirade.

"Aren't *you* the one who's supposed to know if we need a manifest? You *are* the pilot, aren't you? I can't be expected to have prepared paperwork I didn't know we needed, now can I?"

Her tone wasn't quite belligerent, so much as the passively-aggressive kind of chipper sweetness that any good employee learned to use by the end of their first week on the job. She was pretty sure Straya's background was all military and mercenary work, so she didn't know if she'd pick up on what she was going for.

Straya stared back at her. Not just stared. Glared. "Pilot?!"

Oh thank gods, she got my drift. Never had Phera been so relieved to see her cabinmate looking so annoyed.

"Yeah, I drive the shuttle, but cargo manifests aren't in my pay grade. They're in the *freighter* pilot's. This isn't my area of responsibility."

Straya threw up her hands then, letting out a very long, very slow sigh. Unfortunately, she couldn't stretch it out beyond fifteen seconds.

There were still well over five minutes left to go.

"Look."

The raider's mannerisms were much too gruff to last long on a megacorp hauler. She was clearly trying, but she could only soften herself so much.

"The entire reason they gave us an extra person's worth of air is because we needed a clerk to fill out paperwork. You're the clerk. This lady has paperwork. I did my job by getting us here, now do yours."

"Excuse me, but the 'entire reason' the company tasked *me* with accompanying *you*," countered Phera complete with finger quotes, swelling up with all the pompous pride of a petty team lead finally getting her first real taste of power. "Is because I, unlike you, miss 'shuttle driver', happen to be *worth* the resource allocation."

Straya absolutely exploded at this.

So convincingly, in fact, that Phera was afraid she might've accidentally triggered some old trauma of hers or something.

"Worth the resource allocation?!"

Stalking forward until she was practically chest-to-chest with Phera, she banged her fist down on the desk beside her so hard that the inspector's slate bounced a full centimeter into the climate-controlled air, prompting the security officers to start moving in to intercept her. But, just as quickly she unclenched her fist and let her hands drop to her sides, which seemed to mollify them. However, the outrage on her face remained in place as she bore down on Phera, nostrils flaring.

"What? You think you can fly back to the rendezvous point all by yourself?"

"No, I just-" the startled not-clerk tried to reply, only to be cut off by Straya as she jabbed a forefinger into her left breast, just above the Panorama logo.

"By all means, go right ahead. Clearly, I'm just dead weight!"

She inhaled deeply then, puffing out her chest. The drab jumpsuit she was wearing wasn't exactly flattering, but Phera's attention was still nevertheless dragged to the breasts dominating most of her field of view just then. Only for a moment, though. Most of her attention was still stuck on the glowering, reddening face above the hot pirate rack she'd been ogling off and on since joining the crew.

"I- That's-!"

Phera's mouth opened and closed several times in a row without actually saying anything as she fidgeted fretfully with her embroidered top.

Under any other circumstances, she would've been apologizing as fast as she could. (Well, to be fair, she was pretty sure she never could have been that snide to Straya in the first place.) But, remembering at the last moment that they were supposed to be stalling, and also realizing that she'd probably never get another opportunity to be so brazenly bratty to the muscular pirate ever again, she forced herself to take in a deep breath and square her shoulders before jerking her chin up to meet Straya's smoldering, iron gray glare with coolly contempt indifference.

"Are you about finished with your little tantrum?"

Five long seconds passed in silence.

Then ten.

Unfortunately, there were still two hundred and thirty seven of them left to go.

Palpable tension hummed in the air between the two women, neither of them speaking, only glaring. The security guards looked about ready to step forward again before they could continue arguing. And the inspector, no longer spitefully amused, seemed like she was about to say something.

Straya beat them all to it, however.

"I," she said, her voice a low, slow, dangerous growl that sent a thrill of adrenaline shooting through the auburn-haired engineer as she took an involuntary step back. "Cannot believe you."

Then, to the surprise and confusion of all, one tan hand shot out and grabbed her by the ear. Phera yelped in shock and no small amount of pain as Straya's thumb and forefinger pinched down hard against the cartilage and twisted. The inspector opened her mouth, but immediately forgot whatever she'd been about to say. The two guards started to advance, but then stopped in confusion themselves when, rather than punching Phera or throwing her, Straya instead crumpled to a cross-legged position on the floor and dragged the yelping, supposed paper pusher down after her, hurling her face first across her strong lap.

So caught off guard was Phera by this sudden change in orientation, that it took her a full five seconds more before she was able to find her voice again.

"Wh-What the hell do you think you're doing?!" she demanded, clutching at her smarting ear.

Genuine worry was now very audible beneath the veneer of condescension she was still trying desperately to maintain.

"Yes, I'm rather curious about that myself," admitted the inspector, who Phera noted with no small amount of trepidation was beginning to look amused once again as she leaned over her desk for a better view.

"Getting fired, and probably charged with assault, but it's fucking worth it!"

Straya's hand whipped down in a vicious arc against Phera's upturned seat then, her arm a blur of hard muscle and gray fabric. Impacting just as hard as it had during their first meeting, when the engineer had nearly got them both killed.

SMACK!

Her bottom rippled awesomely even in the thick pants she was wearing, mesmerizing all.

"You condescending little *BITCH!*"

SMACK!

"Ow! OW!"

Phera was very much regretting not just opting to fill out the cargo manifest with exaggerated slowness right about then. Especially after jerking her arm in response to Straya's second swat and seeing how much time they still had left.

"You have-!"

SMACK!

"No right-!"

SMACK!

"To do this!"

She managed to yelp in between heavy-handed meteor strikes to the taut seat of her standard issue corporate work pants.

Which just made Straya swat her even harder.

SMACK!

"Ack!"

This time, Phera threw a desperate look toward the inspector and her two station sec officers through the frazzled halo of red hair half-obscuring her panic-stricken face. Surely they weren't going to just let Straya spank her in the middle of the station like this where everyone passing by could see?!

Judging by the way they were all grinning as they watched her ass jiggle and squirm across the taller woman's lap, though, they apparently were.

"Let me go you- Ack! You..."

Phera could think of a lot of things she could call Straya just then, but none of them were very nice. And, even if they were just vying for time, she really didn't feel comfortable yelling them at her friend. So, instead, she growled and tried to roll off her lap.

Which proved to be a *huge* mistake.

"YOU!" Straya roared, emphasizing each furious word with a full-body, open-palmed **SMACK!** that drove Phera's breath out of her in startled cries. "DO. NOT. ORDER. ME. AROUND!"

Phera, in counterpoint, gasped and yelped and beat the toes of her boots and her clenched fists against the cold deck beneath her.

"YOU. ARE. *NOT*. AN. EXEC!" continued her ostensibly furious coworker. "WE. ARE. ON. THE. SAME. FUCKING. PAY. GRADE."

Her hand kept descending, blindingly fast and ruinously hard.

SMACK! SMACK! SMACK! SMACK! SMACK!

"S- Ow! So?"

Muted as they were by the seat of her pants, Straya's palm exploding against her rear end was still far, far too loud for Phera's liking. And the way she was very vocally venting her frustrations with the "obnoxious, paper pushing, bitch of a brat" over her lap was even more so.

*Oh my gods, are spankings always this **loud**? I swear her smacks don't echo nearly this much on the Mayhem.*

On the bright side, though, the very were at least doing an excellent job of holding the inspection team's attention. Along with just about everyone else within a hundred meter radius.

"Fuck- Ow! Fuck you!" howled Phera. "I'm in the- Ack! In the admin- Oh! Department!"

This was *not* what she'd been imagining when the Captain had told her that she and Straya would be going undercover as Panorama employees for this part of their mission. But, like it or not (and the jury was still out on that, truth be told), she was committed now.

"You're just- Urk! A glorified autopilot!"

SMACK! SMACK! SMACK! SMACK! SMACK!

Straya's swats were seriously starting to add up now. The repeated impacts conspiring together to make the centers of her cheeks nice and tender as they grew warmer and warmer beneath the snug embrace of her panties.

Phera checked her wrist comp again. Still one hundred and fifty three seconds more to go.

Shit.

"Now, let me- Oh! Up- Ah! So I can fill out our- Owie! Paperwork!"

Straya looked up at the security officers and inspector. Both guards were barely suppressing smirks. The inspector herself had her mouth covered by one hand. But, going by the look in her eyes, she both took Straya's side in this dispute, and wasn't in that much of a hurry at that particular moment.

So, Straya redoubled her efforts and picked up the pace.

"YOU. LITTLE. STUCK. UP-"

SMACK! SMACK! SMACK! SMACK! SMACK!

Her hand was coming down so hard and so fast now that Phera was almost worried for her arm.

Along with her own furiously burning bottom.

"I'LL SHOW YOU WHO'S UNNECESSARY!"

With that maximum volume declaration, furious voice ringing off the hard surfaces of the hab around them, Straya grabbed Phera by the hair and hoisted her jarringly up off of her lap without warning. She pushed herself back to her feet then too, pulling her along with her, and then switched her grip to one of the belt loops on the engineer's pants, just as she started struggling away.

"Get your fucking ass back here, you little shit! I'm not even *close* to done with you!"

As she spoke (okay, yelled), one of Straya's hands roughly prized apart the clasp at Phera's waist, while the other seized a fistful of her back waistband and yanked down.

Hard.

These weren't the super flexible, formfitting pants the two of them had picked out for her back on Marcos Station. As a result, Straya only succeeded in bringing them about halfway down over the shorter pirate's expansive buttocks. Exposing just the top few centimeters of her crack and twin splashes of bright red skin.

"No, wait, please, you can't! I'm sorry-!"

"Shut up!"

Both hands darting in quick as lightning, Straya seized hold of Phera's waistband on either side of her hips. And, with one savage yank and an equally savage grunt, ripped them down to her knees. Splitting the material along its seams with a tearing sound that reverberated throughout the suddenly silent hab.

"Eep!"

For what felt like an incredibly long time after that, but in reality was only four seconds according to her wrist comp, Phera just stood there, mouth agape, not quite able to wrap her mind around what had just happened as cool air played across her suddenly naked curves.

That is, of course, until their inspector snorted out a laugh behind her hand and quipped, "Well, I guess we don't have to perform a strip search now."

"Feel free to anyway. Really." Straya growled, acknowledging the inspector while keeping her glower fixed on the disbelieving Phera. "Just give me another minute first."

"Oh, take your time."

Reality speeding back into being all at once for her then, Phera stiffened.

"Oh my gods, what are you doing?" she demanded with a panicked yelp, face flushing to match the hair spilling over her shoulders as she reflexively jerked forward to try and claw her ruined pants back up, only to remember at the last second that she still had a role to play (as humiliating as it might be) and continuing by snapping. "Stars and void! It's no wonder you got dumped into the shuttle pool."

She tried to half-step, half-shuffle away from Straya, glaring with all the professional venom she could muster while showing off her truly excellent ass to seemingly half of Excaden Station.

"I swear I'm going to make your life a living hell after this is over! When I get promoted I'll-"

Stall for time, just stall for time...

"Is that right?"

Straya's laugh was midnight dark and very nearly knocked the younger woman's knees out from under her.

"Y... Yeah!"

Phera's voice cracked with the word, and Straya made a show of blowing out a beleaguered breath through her nostrils as she shook her head.

"Just keep talking shit, kid, and see where it gets you."

Phera was in the process of opening her mouth to do just that, when her lips pulled back in a pained grimace as Straya's strong hand snatched up a fistful of her curls. The next thing she knew, she found herself being shoved roughly over the front of the dock inspector's desk to stare up at the still sneering woman.

She apparently favored a floral perfume.

It smelled kind of nice.

"Um, a little help?" she wheedled, pleading with her eyes as one functionary to another.

"Sorry, hon," the other woman crooned, eyes twinkling as she stared down the bridge of her nose at her. "It's station policy not to interfere with intra-corporate affairs."

"But-!"

"BE QUIET!" Straya snarled over whatever flimsy protest she'd been about to make, blistering the air with a torrent of invective as she blistered her ass with a volley of ruthless swats to the extra-sensitive undercurves of the faux-bureaucrat's bare bottom.

SMACK! SMACK! SMACK! SMACK! SMACK! SMACK!

With this new position, Straya was able to really put her back into it. Twisting her hips and following through with each devastatingly powerful *SMACK!* Making one cheek bounce for the benefit of all present, then the other, then the first again, and so on. Turning Phera's already red bare bottom rapidly raspberry, then strawberry, and finally cranberry colored as it splashed and jiggled under her relentless assault.

"NOW, YOU ARE GOING TO FILL OUT THAT *FUCKING* FORM!"

SMACK! SMACK! SMACK! SMACK! SMACK! SMACK!

"THEN YOU ARE GOING TO GET THAT FAT ASS BACK ABOARD THE SHUTTLE BEFORE I LEAVE YOU HERE!"

SMACK! SMACK! SMACK! SMACK! SMACK! SMACK!

"AND IF YOU GIVE ME ANY MORE GODDAMN LIP, I SWEAR I'LL TAKE OFF MY BELT AND SHOW YOU WHAT A *REAL* ASS WHIPPING LOOKS LIKE."

SMACK! SMACK! SMACK! SMACK! SMACK! SMACK!

"AM I *FUCKING* UNDERSTOOD?"

"Yes ma'am! Yes ma'am! Yes ma'am!" howled Phera, no longer needing to act as she squealed the two words over and over again until they became completely unintelligible, drowned out by her sobbing.

"Good."

SMACK!

With one final, full force swat to the center of the thoroughly-punished pirate recruit's cheeks, lifting her up onto the balls of her feet and nearly sending her toppling over the desk and into the inspector's lap, Straya stopped and grabbed Phera by the hair again; jerking her upright and thrusting a stylus into her trembling hand.

"Now, get to work."

"Any thoughts of going into management yourself?" the inspector asked with a wry chuckle.

Prompting Straya to snort out a laugh of her own, the scar on the right side of her face lending her smirk a dangerous edge that was decidedly not very corporate.

"Maybe. It sure seems like I have the skills, doesn't it?"

"And how."

"H-Hard disagree," sniffled Phera, sneaking a peek at the inside of her wrist while batting aside tears and further ruining the eyeliner she'd borrowed from Steph.

Thirteen Seconds. Thank all the gods and devils.

Groaning piteously, she snatched up one of the spare slates on the desk in front of her and started filling out a cargo manifest as fast as she could. She really would've preferred to do this after fixing her clothes, but the way her "coworker" had been yelling at her made it abundantly clear that this would not be an option. So, she tapped all the necessary checkboxes, and put in all of the pertinent identifiers and Panorama corporate codes as fast as she could. All while their inspector and her station sec associates continued to admire the glowing twin moons and visible glistening among the copper curls between her slightly parted thighs.

"You um… You *really* don't need to perform a strip search," she eventually said after double (and triple) checking the newly filled out manifest, queuing it up for transfer to the inspector's slate.

"Are you sure?" the woman snickered.

"Yes."

Phera threw a very petulant (and entirely genuine) glower in Straya's direction.

"She was just kidding, and… um… She doesn't have the authority to authorize that sort of thing. I think."

"I'd say go for it," Straya countered with an unconcerned shrug. "But this little brat has taken up enough of my time already as is, and I really don't want to miss our rendezvous."

She casually delivered another **SMACK!** to the underside of Phera's blazing buttocks that popped her up from her hunch over the desk with a high-pitched yelp.

"Gather up what's left of your pants, bitch. Unless you want to show that off to everyone we pass on the way back to the flyer."

With that, Straya gave the inspector and the station sec officers a curt nod, spun on her heel, and began stomping off back toward the docking ring.

Staring after the taller woman's retreating shoulders, Phera pushed her lips out into a pout.

"Her department is *so* going to cover getting these mended."

She'd been hoping that the tearing noises she'd heard earlier wouldn't be anything too important to maintaining her modesty. But, alas, it was not to be. Her panties had been torn in half along one side, and her slacks weren't doing too much better. She definitely was going to have to use both hands to keep from showing off to everyone she passed just how effective her cabinmate's management strategy had been.

"Hurry up! I swear if you're not with me when I hit the airlock, I *will* leave your ass behind."

"Right! I'm coming!"

Startling to attention, Phera threw a pleading look back over her shoulder toward the inspector while she tried (and failed) to find some way of holding her tattered waistline that didn't make it abundantly clear that she was keeping her pants from falling down.

"Is there, um, anything else, ma'am?"

"Nope. All of your paperwork is in order, and I am *extremely* satisfied with the results of this inspection."

"Oh, I can't wait to tell everyone about this," came Obette's laugh from her earpiece.

With the inspector's nod of approval to go, Phera went scurrying after Straya as fast as she could as she disappeared into the grav acclimation tunnel.

"Hey, come on! Wait up!"

Unaware the entire time that a large portion of her back right pocket was still dangling free behind her.

All in all, she supposed there were worse ways for a first mission to go.

Obette better have gotten all of those fucking drones into position, though.

CHAPTER SEVENTEEN

CHARGES ACCRUED

Fleeing the Scene of a Crime

Making her way back to the flyer with damp cheeks and an even damper crotch wound up taking far longer than Phera would have preferred. With her pants so thoroughly torn along the seams (and even around one back pocket somehow!) she was forced to take awkward, shuffling steps to keep her outfit together. Despite her best efforts, though, she couldn't quite manage to hold onto *all* of the ragged flaps that made up her ruined waistband. As a result, she wound up giving the various station workers and residents that she and Straya passed quite a show.

Things only grew worse for her when they hit the low-grav docking ring where their shuttle was berthed, and she had to use both her hands *and* her feet to navigate. Thankfully, there was hardly anyone in their particular slice of the ring just then. (Obette had made sure to pick one that wasn't busy when scheduling a landing.) But, the people that did manage to see her couldn't help but stare and catcall.

With good reason.

Her cheeks were absolutely livid and practically glowing neon as they peeked out from beneath the flimsy shreds of her tattered dignity.

"Damn girl, you sit on a sunsim panel?" choked out one of a pair of techs performing maintenance behind a detached wall panel.

"Awww, be nice, Jensen. Can't you see she's had a rough time?" their partner chided, all the while tracking the two pirates' progress down the corridor with the camera on the palm of her wrist comp. "Hey there, honey buns, I get off in thirty if you want a shoulder to cry on."

"She's busy," growled Straya, still in character as the pissed off shuttle pilot as she grabbed her teary-eyed "coworker" by the upper arm and yanked her along just a little bit faster.

Exposing most of Phera's right cheek in the process.

"Oh well..."

"Be horny on your own time, Watley. We've still got a job to do, and I'd like to get this done *today*."

"Yeah, yeah. Just let me send this off to Resh before I forget."

"Seriously? You're insatiable, you know that?"

"Hey! When the gods send you a gift like that, you make the best of it you can!"

"Uh-huh."

Heaving out a sigh as the two techs' bickering faded into the background, Phera cast her violet gaze up toward the ceiling in silent exasperation.

Looks like I'm about to make the rounds on yet another hab's social feeds. Great...

—

Obette was waiting for them inside the flyer's cargo hold when they finally arrived. He raised a curious eyebrow at Phera's state of partial undress as she and Straya dropped down from the flyer's ceiling to land with null-grav softness on the deck plates below, but otherwise made no comment.

"We good?" asked Straya straight away as she secured the hatch behind them and pushed off toward the cockpit.

"Good?" scoffed Obette, affronted. "Oh, we are far better than good. We are gods-damned fantastic."

Giving his silver white ponytail a self-satisfied toss, causing it to drift lazily behind him, the infiltrator grinned from ear to ear.

"All units are in position at the Class 3 docking cradle and awaiting our target's arrival. Once they sniff out its transponder ID, they'll fuzz the sensors again and transfer over."

"Great. Time to unlatch and disembark then."

"Good fucking riddance," harrumphed Phera, abandoning her attempts to hide her thoroughly toasted backside in favor of hooking a foot through a handhold in the starboard wall of the now empty hold so that she could continue to pout while floating sideways relative to the floor. "Why is it that every time I take a trip on this flyer with you, Straya, I end up bare assed and sore?"

"I think that might have more to do with *you* than the location, my dear," offered Obette with a bemused chuckle.

"Humph."

Arms still crossed in front of her, Phera threw a grimace in the direction of her ruined pants, and then cocked a hopeful brow at the infiltrator.

"Say… Do you think one of those vacsuit patch kits would work on polyweave fibers? I actually really liked these, and it would be a shame to have to throw them out, you know?"

"Lem can stitch your pants back together on the ship, you big baby."

Straya's voice was mirthful and teasing now as it echoed back to them from the cockpit.

"Nice performance, by the way."

"Heh."

Demurring as a splash of pink warmed her face, a modest smile curved the corners of Phera's lips while she brushed aside a few curls tickling her nose.

"Not to brag or anything, but I *did* take three years of drama in secondary school. So, you know…"

"Yes indeed, you were very convincing," agreed Obette with a teasing lilt to his speech, drifting in closer to peel back part of Phera's tattered pants for a better look at the angry red flesh beneath. "Why, if I didn't know any better, I'd say your bottom was actually sore!"

He accompanied this facetious declaration with an equally facetious gasp of surprise as he brushed his fingertips along the curves of first one cheek and then the other.

"What do you know? It's nice and hot back here too. Amazing!"

"Gee. Thanks. Really."

Phera tried to push her painted lips back out into a pout, but settled instead for a crooked grin as a pleasant shiver worked its way down her spine and between her legs at the infiltrator's touch. And, still keeping her arms folded (now more for the fun of floating in null-grav and looking cute than anything else), she shifted around to look toward the cockpit where her partner in crime was performing a pre-flight systems check.

"Seriously, though, you have *no* idea how good it felt to be just the most petty little corporate shit for once. I was never ranked high enough back on The Bin to get away with anything like that."

"What do you mean?" called back Straya, her voice only growing more teasing as she added. "You weren't acting any different from usual as far as I could tell."

Rather than dignify that blatant bit of bald-faced fibbery with a response, Phera instead just stuck out her tongue. There then came a series of loud clunking noises from outside the hull, followed by mechanical whirring as the airlock clamps disengaged and the landing arms began to retract.

"Put on your boots," Straya ordered, flipping Phera the bird with a snort before popping her neck and settling into her seat at the helm. "Or float. Whichever. We're not going to be pulling *that* much accel."

"Say, if you don't mind my prying," interjected Obette before Phera could reply, snapping what remained of her panties against the center of her swollen seat. "What exactly happened back there? I was busy handling my part of the operation, so I only caught the tail end of your little performance."

"Well, uh…"

The impact of Phera's waistband against her tender cheeks was enough to send her gently drifting toward the deck where she'd left her boots magnetized when she'd traded them out for her corporate-approved flats.

"Straya and I had to get creative to keep the inspection team away from the shuttle. And, apparently, my fellow Panorama employee didn't take too kindly to some snotty paper pusher from the admin pool looking down on her for not knowing that you needed to prep a cargo manifest even if you don't have any cargo."

Properly pouting now, she continued.

"And I'll have you know *Straya*."

She put a metric ton of sass onto the pirate's name as she said it, feeling safe in the knowledge that the other woman's hands were occupied at that particular moment.

"That I am a delight to work with."

Tucking her knees into her chest like the muscular raider had taught her, she executed a passably good tuck and roll to change direction and managed to (almost) gracefully snatch hold of a handhold near her boots.

'Just ask Ob," she added with a snicker as her knees rapped gently against the deck. "He and I had lots of fun prepping for the mission. Didn't we, Ob?"

"Hah. Well, we certainly had to accommodate a situation that we found forced upon us," agreed the infiltrator with a wink. "But, yes. Yes we did."

"How sweet."

Straya's voice was an even deadpan as it drifted back to them from the cockpit, but Phera could still hear the smirk that propelled it along. And, as soon as she heard her and Obette's boots magnetize to the deck, she began to ease the shuttle's throttle forward. Bringing the engines to life nice and slow as they departed Excaden Station, nine drones lighter than they had been coming in.

"All right, let's see now. Looks like clearing the perimeter is going to take a few minutes..." she drawled, thinking out loud as her hands moved with familiar ease over the flyer's controls, before looking back toward the hold and raising her voice. "Hey, Ob, you feel like making yourself useful?"

"Of course."

"Great. Take down whatever's left of Phera's pants then and teach her not to be so full of herself until we're ready to reach cruising speed, yeah?"

"Or, or!"

Clomping around to put herself between her two cabinmates while tugging up on her tattered pants just a little bit harder, Phera held up a desperate hand to stave off this suggestion.

"We could all congratulate Phera on how great of an actor she is, and how quick she was on her feet, and oh, I dunno, while we're at it, how about how nice her hair is looking today?"

Her comically fretful expression shifted to overtly smug then as she slid a smirk back in the direction of the cockpit.

"I suppose Straya should get some praise too."

Before blossoming into a genuine smile as she added with a relieved sag of her shoulders.

"I'm pretty sure we would've been royally fucked without her."

"Awww, thanks. You were great too, sweet cheeks," crooned the raider, saccharine as could be as her eyes flitted from status readout to status readout. "Ob, congratulate Phera on a job well done and thank her for helping us so much, and *then* spank her until we need main thrusters."

Stirring to attention, the infiltrator snapped off a crisp salute.

"Yes ma'am! Right away, ma'am!"

Before his hand drifted down from its salute to rest on Phera's shoulder, squeezing gently.

"I wasn't there in person, but whatever you and Straya pulled off gave me sufficient time to get the job done with change to spare. You've proven yourself to be a valuable member of the crew, adaptable and capable, and someone who I have no misgivings about entrusting my safety to under fire. Also, your hair is even lovelier than usual today. Especially with the way your bangs sway in the weightless air, they're reminiscent of the tall grasses of Typhon's twilight band when the red light of Proxima shines down on them from just over the horizon."

He eyed her swaying bangs with a faraway look in his sea green eyes as he spoke that Phera thought might actually be genuine, as opposed to just overly-flowery flirtation.

"Now then, orders *are* orders. So..."

Without the slightest bit of hesitation, Obette took hold of the engineer's torn pants at either hip and yanked them, along with her underwear, all the way down to the bottom of her thick, creamy thighs.

"Oh come on!"

Phera was seriously starting to hate magboots and how they made it all but impossible for her to quickly dart away in situations like these. Although, on the other hand, that was also very much a plus if she were being totally honest with herself.

"Sorry, Doctor," apologized the infiltrator, sounding anything but as he raised his hands palm out in a half-shrug. "I'm afraid my hands are tied in this matter."

"Oh yeah? Okay, fine."

Phera's breasts gave an appealing bounce in the null-grav as she folded her arms beneath them with a haughty sniff, face awash in a bright blush from both Obette's praise and the way he'd just oh-so-casually stripped her to reveal her still very wet labia.

"If you like following orders so much, then I order *you* to spank Straya for *her* ordering *you* to spank *me*."

She tipped her chin up to fix her fellow pirate with an extremely pleased "check and mate" sort of look then, just daring him to try and find a flaw in her logic.

"On the day you are promoted above me, I promise I will gladly obey," countered Obette with a sly smile that seemed to say otherwise, taking her by the wrist and leading her over to the very same bullet-hole ridden workbench Straya had spanked her over all those weeks ago. "Demagnetize, dear. If I have to pry you off the deck things will go much worse for you."

"Fiiiine."

With a mighty harrumph that was largely undercut by a wicked grin of her own, Phera did as she was told. But, before Obette could properly tug her into position, she sprang off the deck with a surprise jump. Using the infiltrator's own grip on her wrist to slingshot herself up and around to remagnetize her feet to the ceiling above his head.

"There you go," she said with an insuppressible giggle of satisfaction at her burst of malicious compliance. "I'm off the deck, just like you wanted."

"Oh, you simply had to, didn't you?"

"What can I say?"

Phera gave her shoulders an unconcerned shrug and winked down at the man.

"I'm a pirate."

"You're about to be a pirate who can't sit down!"

Quick as a flash, Obette released his boots and kicked up after her, using the hand he was still grabbing her with to twist her arm around behind her back and bend her "down" toward the ceiling. Discombobulating her sense of direction just long enough for him to snatch a handhold near her feet and bring a foot down after it, magnetizing it to the metallic surface there before doing the same on her other side.

"What the?"

It took Phera's planetside-raised brain several seconds to catch up with the null-grav aerial acrobatics that had just been performed on her, but it became all too clear soon enough that Obette was now sitting on top of her.

Well, sort of.

His taut buttocks straddled her upper back where her torso was neatly folded down toward her toes. His boots were locked against the ceiling on either side of her own, and he'd turned up his magnetic adhesion to the max. Sticking himself in place with her totally trapped beneath him.

Totally trapped with her exceedingly naked ass bent over and entirely vulnerable.

"Uh-oh."

"I did warn you, didn't I?"

"Yeah, but-"

SMACK-SMACK!

"Ack! Come on!"

"Oh, don't you worry," chuckled Obette darkly, squeezing either cheek nice and hard. "That comes later."

From his position, it was the easiest thing in the world for him to start bringing both his hands down in long, smooth arcs that impacted in simultaneous and very, very hard *SMACKS!* Each pair exploding against the thickest part of an already aching buttock, stirring the fading embers there back into a proper inferno all over again. One that burned even brighter than before!

SMACK-SMACK!

"Oh!"

SMACK-SMACK!

"Owie!"

SMACK-SMACK!

"Okay, okay, you win!" Phera yelped, still giggling even as her hips wriggled beneath Obette's full-body clench around her.

SMACK-SMACK!

"I said you win!"

Though he was aiming for the most heavily padded portion of her generally very well-padded posterior, centrifugal force was a hell of a thing, and him pinning her bent over as he was had the added benefit of pulling the flesh along her thighs and hips taut. Eliminating a fair amount of her natural shock absorption from the equation. It also didn't help that Straya had already done a pretty damn good job all on her own against those very same spots not too long ago either.

"You don't have to- Owie! Smack so- Oh! *Hard*, do you?"

"Afraid I do. Now, be a good girl and take it all without too much of a struggle. Oh, and be sure to work in more of those cute squeaks while you're at it."

SMACK-SMACK!

"Eep!"

SMACK-SMACK!

"Yes, exactly! Just like that."

SMACK-SMACK!

Obette, Phera quickly learned, was not one for scolding or teasing when it was time to give a spanking. Instead, for the next several minutes, he remained in place and just kept on doggedly dishing out a ruthless punishment. Making use of his well-toned physique to keep her ample bottom bouncing and jiggling in the null-grav for no other reason than because Straya had told him to and because he felt like it.

Although, he *did* pause every now and again to squeeze and fondle wherever his cabinmate was looking the most tender.

Which was just about everywhere by that point.

SMACK-SMACK!

SMACK-SMACK!

SMACK-SMACK!

Straya, meanwhile, put on some music in the cockpit and turned it up just high enough to hum along without drowning out the accompanying percussion and vocals.

"We'll be at the outer boundary of station space in five," she eventually called back toward the hold, sparing a quick glance over her shoulder and eying Phera's upside-down, rippling bottom and glistening pussy with a hungry grin. "Keep her pinned until we're done with our accel, yeah?"

"Can do."

Obette flashed her another salute, this one far more lazy, before seizing either sizzling cheek and pulling them apart to further expose their cabinmate's not insignificant charms.

"You want dibs on ass or pussy once we hit drift?"

Meeting Phera's watery eyes between her splayed thighs, Straya's smile turned absolutely feral and she gave her fingers a menacing wiggle that sent a knee-wobbling thrum straight into the engineer's clit.

"Both."

CHAPTER EIGHTEEN

CHARGES ACCRUED

Grand Theft, Piracy, Unauthorized Use of Company Property, Destruction of Property

"Coming up on the Altona now, Captain," came Shi's soft but confident voice from the Mayhem's shipboard comms.

"Very good." The Captain kept her eyes on the closest screen as she sat almost motionless in place. "Bring us into sensor range and match their V on a parallel course. I don't want them getting spooked before we're ready to go."

"You got it."

It was two days after their stopover at Excaden Station, and the Blazar Bitches (minus their pilot) were gathered around the "windows" in the mess hall, waiting eagerly to see the final phase of their plan in action.

"You sure you don't want some, Phera?" prompted Steph, angling a bowl of popcorn ve and Adryel had been munching on for the last ten minutes toward her.

"N..."

Phera, right then caught between wanting to throw up, wet her pants, or maybe jog laps around the hab cylinder, swallowed hard and gave her ashen face a minute shake.

"No thanks."

"Breathe," Straya ordered gently but firmly, squeezing her shoulder with her usual half-smile. "If you pass out, you're going to miss all the fun."

Not trusting herself to speak, Phera just nodded slightly and blew out a shaky breath.

"Yeah, don't sweat it," added Adryel around a mouthful of popcorn. "Everyone's nervous their first time."

"I guess you have a point there."

Despite her roiling nerves, Phera couldn't stop herself from snorting out a laugh. And, with it, came a loosening of some of the tension in her shoulders.

"My first big heist as a pirate really isn't *that* much scarier than hooking up with Miri Petirin during summer camp senior year," she teased somewhat brittly, although still managing a smile.

"Oooh!"

Steph's expression grew somehow even more slyly amused upon hearing that.

"Church camp?"

"Yep."

Snickering far more genuinely this time, Phera snatched up a handful of popcorn for no other reason than to give her faintly trembling hands something to do.

"We skipped out on the testimony meeting one morning and I ate her out by the lake instead."

"Why, Phera, you absolute *sinner*," drawled the Captain from her spot next to Lem, the sleepless pits of her amber eyes twinkling with wicked amusement as she gave her an approving leer. "I knew there was a reason I liked you."

Awash in a sea of jittery, nervous energy, Phera batted her eyelashes at the Captain where she sat behind the table.

"Hey, when you lose your vacation to your conservative parents trying to brute-force some piety into you, you've gotta make your own fun where you can."

"We're in position," Shi's voice cut in before the Captain could respond to that bit of shameless flirtation. "Signal whenever you're ready, Cap."

"Excellent."

With that totally calm, confident declaration, the Captain's demeanor shifted from teasing to serious, and an anticipatory silence fell over the mess as she straightened up from her lounging position against her first mate. Then, with a flick of her wrist, the projection of the Altona that everyone had been watching zoomed in so that the bulbous hauler now took up the entirety of the curving wall in front of them.

"All right, girls, it's showtime."

Phera wasn't sure exactly *how* the Captain triggered the signal. But, the next thing she knew, the modified ore excavators clinging to the cargo hauler's outer hull stirred to life. Following their preprogrammed instructions, each unit made its way over to a support strut or clamping arm and began attacking. All the while communicating with each of its fellows, making small adjustments to position, angle, and power output in a fluidly choreographed dance of algorithmic efficiency.

To Phera's wide eyes, it was absolutely beautiful.

Oh my gods, it's actually working!

Watching the individual excavators act as a single entity unified in purpose flushed away all of her lingering anxiety, replacing it with ecstatic awe. It was one thing to model simulations and verify calculations, but another thing entirely to actually *see* all of her hard work be successfully put to use in a real-world setting.

Come on, little guys, you can do it!

With each passing minute, the crew watched on in varying degrees of mesmerized awe. Eyes flitting between the scuttling ore excavators and the timer the Captain had overlaid on top of their feed. Phera had told the woman back on Marcos Station that with proper calibration and hardware, she could get the drones to execute her operation in ten minutes. In the end, it was done in nine and a half.

When at last it happened, it happened suddenly and without fanfare.

One moment there were nine flashing pinpoints of light on the exterior of the Altona as the modified gatecrashers pounded away at their targets, and then the next the entire pod was cleaved free all at once as if it'd never been joined to the ship to begin with.

"Holy shit..." breathed Shi into his mic.

"Yeah, no kidding," agreed Straya, reaching over to steal a handful of popcorn from the bowl Steph held in slack hands, eyes still locked on the pod.

The ship it had once been attached to continued to fly along, apparently having not yet realized that it was one cargo pod lighter than it should be. While the pod itself began to drift away in a diverging arc, borne along by small bursts of thrust from the excavators still clinging to it. They weren't capable of much output, but at the speed the pod was already traveling, any minor changes to its trajectory became major shifts soon enough.

"Bring us around to intercept," came the Captain's crisp order, eyes shining in the dimmed light of the mess and teeth bared in a triumphant, savage grin. "I want that pod in our clamps and us gone in the next four minutes."

"Already on it, Captain."

"Good boy."

Slipping in behind the still stunned engineer, the Captain beamed down at her.

"You beautiful, magnificent, devious little budding criminal, you. I am *so* proud! The original plan was to disable their engines with the drones and then board to force them to release their clamps, but this wound up being so much more elegant. Well done, Phera."

Looking up and over her shoulder toward her thoroughly pleased boss, Phera opened her mouth to say something, but never got the chance to. For, in that very same moment, the Captain seized a fistful of her hair and wrenched her in close enough to kiss her full on the mouth.

"Mmph!"

Phera's yelp of surprise was pushed back down her throat by the other woman's tongue as it shoved its way in past her teeth with her usual brusque authority. Rather than fight it, she instead found herself melting into the warmth of the Captain's lithe frame as her tongue danced with hers.

She tasted like coffee and icing from the cupcake she'd been eating while they'd closed in on the Altona.

It was wonderful.

When the Captain at last pulled back, leaving Phera breathless while she maintained her grip on her fistful of copper curls, her amber eyes danced with unabashed delight.

"Congratulations, honey. You're a proper pirate now."

"I…"

The realization that she no longer had to worry about proving herself lifted the corners of Phera's mouth into a wicked grin, and she offhandedly batted away a small bit of saliva trailing from her lips to the Captain's darkly painted ones.

"Hell yeah! Thank you, ma'am!"

Her enthusiasm was met with a rich, languid chuckle.

"No need to thank me, swabbie. You've more than earned it."

The Captain dragged her in closer then, pulling her voluptuous curves snug against the front of her lean body. Letting go of her hair, one hand held her close around her soft belly, while the other fondled her breasts with the sort of casual possessiveness that had had Phera dreaming of her the first few nights after she'd been brought aboard the Mayhem.

"We're eating like queens tonight, and it's all thanks to our favorite piece of ass," she crowed theatrically, pivoting her captured engineer around to face the rest of the crew. "Steaks for everyone!"

This was met by a round of rowdy cheers, and Steph threw the rest of ver bowl of popcorn into the air in celebration. Earning a death glare from Lem that went entirely ignored by ver in favor of dancing with Adryel around the mess as they both chanted.

"Steak! Steak! Steak!"

While they were busy celebrating, the Captain leaned in closer to Phera, bringing her lips right up to the younger woman's burning ear to murmur with a liquid warmth that had her lower abdomen quivering.

"And while the rest of them secure the booty, you, my dear, will be retiring with me to my quarters so that I can spoil my appetite."

She punctuated her order by slipping the hand not currently kneading her right breast inside the front of her stretchy pants to cup the damp patch soaking through her panties.

"Would you like to be my pre-dinner-time snack, Phera?"

Phera, hopelessly out of her depth and entirely too horny for her own good under the commanding woman's touch, made a strangled noise in the back of her throat that was partway between a moan and a panicked squeak.

"Come now," the Captain pressed, voice gaining just a touch of menace to it as she nipped at her earlobe perhaps a little harder than was strictly necessary. "I want to hear you say it."

"I- I- Um- I…"

"It's really a simple question."

The fingers cupping Phera's smoldering groin twitched then, the pads of the Captain's middle and ring fingers finding her clit through the thin material of her underwear.

"Do. You. Want. Me. To. Fuck. You?"

Each deliberately enunciated word was accompanied by an equally deliberate rub that drew out more half-suppressed noises from the engineer, as her knees all but gave out from under her.

"Ah!"

"Say it, girl."

Face molten and stomach roiling, barely managing to keep herself upright as the Captain found one of her nipples through her shirt and bra, Phera felt her lips pull back into a very piratical grin.

"Yes, Capt- Ack!"

"I thought we *nipped* this little habit of you not saying what I tell you to in the bud back on Marcos," the Captain chided with grim mirth, accentuating her double entendre by tightening her grip on Phera's nipple. "Or do you need a reminder of what happens when you sass me?"

Feeling the hard edges of the taller woman's belt buckle digging in against her lower back, Phera stiffened and squeaked out quick and loud.

"Please fuck me, ma'am!"

Prompting the rest of the crew to break out in uproarious cackles of delight.

"Now that's more like it!"

Quick as a flash, the Captain's hand was out of her pants and back in her hair, and she was dragging her latest recruit out of the mess while the rest of the crew watched on with no small amount of catcalling and wolf whistling.

"Take care of overseeing the unloading for me, will you, Lemmy cakes? I'll be in my quarters sitting on the cabin girl's face."

"Aye aye, Cap."

"Have fun, Phera," waved Obette.

"See you later, sweet cheeks," added Straya.

"Smooch her just below the bellybutton. That drives her wild!" Steph called as ve dodged out of range of Lem's snatching hand as it tried to grab the scruff of ver neck.

Face absolutely molten, Phera, managed a tiny wave to her friends. Yelping adorably as the Captain tugged her harder to stop her from dragging her feet.

"Th-Thanks for the tip!"

CHAPTER NINETEEN

CHARGES ACCRUED

Operating a Class 3 Spacecraft Without a License

Shi eased himself back into the adaptive memory foam of his pilot's seat under the Mayhem's bridge canopy, watching the projected stars spin around him overhead while his fingers danced atop the control pad in his armrest.

Based on the last updates we pulled, the furthest outlying asteroid of the Barrier Field should be just half a degree spin upward. So, disengaging the negative drive in...

He ran a quick set of mental calculations, and then double-checked them with the ship's nav comp.

Any time between twenty-five minutes and six seconds, and thirty-one minutes and eighteen seconds from now, and then hitting the thrusters when the photosensors start pinging off the rock should let us slingshot no problem.

Rolling his shoulders, the young pilot blew out a self-satisfied huff. He always loved this part.

"You never flee directly from the scene of the crime, my boy. Always slingshot," his predecessor had told him over drinks the night the Captain had hired him, and those words of wisdom had saved him and the crew from winding up in InterSec custody more times than he could count.

God, it felt so good to be coming away with a successful haul.

I'm going to buy so many books when we get back to Marcos. Oh! I should get Kelt something nice too as a surprise. She was eying that one jacket last time we went shopping together. Hopefully they'll still have it...

With a minor course correction and a radiometric sensor triangulation to confirm that they were still headed in the right direction, Shi closed his eyes and pushed his backrest further down.

Was it worth heading to the rec room to do a quarter hour or so of exercise? Kelt had been telling him he needed to fortify his muscles better. But, really? Getting up for just ten or fifteen minutes of exercise seemed like such a waste. Plus, with his luck, Straya would have finished making it up to the new girl for what she'd had to pull back on Excaden, and would be ready to take something he had nothing to do with out on him again.

Speaking of the new girl.

"Hey, Shi, you busy?"

Voice friendly but slightly tentative as if she wasn't sure she was allowed to be there, Phera Sinclair took a step onto the bridge of the Mayhem. Pausing at the threshold to run her pretty violet eyes along the various controls and readouts around him with a professional sort of wonder and curiosity, before swiveling her attention toward him.

Shi wasn't startled by her presence. The sound of the hatch cycling open was easy enough to hear amid the quiet thrum of their smooth cruising. He *was* a little surprised, however, that she'd come all this way to see him of all people, though.

"Not really," he answered, likewise somewhat hesitantly, thinking carefully over his reply as he spoke so as to not accidentally embarrass himself in front of the pretty hotshot who'd recently joined the crew. "Not for about the next twenty minutes or so, at least."

He reluctantly levered himself up out of the comfortable recline he'd been enjoying and looked over his shoulder at Phera. His olive skin and ebony hair contrasting with the cream whites and beiges of the helm around him, but blending in well with the black star field overhead.

"You need something?"

"Kinda, sorta."

Brightening at receiving confirmation that she wasn't interrupting anything important, Phera sashayed her way fully into the compartment while making a visible effort not to accidentally bump her broad hips into anything. Approaching Shi's side, she flashed him a guilty smile.

"I'm mostly just putting off hitting the treadmill and thought I'd come say hi and take a peek at the helm while I'm at it."

"What a coincidence."

Shi found himself barking out a laugh that he'd picked up after a couple months of being a member of the Blazar Bitches. Whenever Phera wasn't around, he resented her for all the extra spankings she'd earned him. But, whenever they came face-to-face, he was quickly reminded that it wasn't her fault.

Just Straya's.

Hmmm. Maybe I really should start lifting more? Might make it easier to get away.

"I was actually just trying to decide if I have enough time to hit the gym myself before the next thing I need to be here for happens."

Phera made a show of rolling her eyes good-naturedly.

"Lem been riding your ass too?"

"Nah, just Kelt."

"Oh really now?"

At her answering smirk to that unintentional double entendre, Shi straightened just a bit more in his seat and made himself look nice and busy.

"Um, yep."

Sensing that she'd made him uncomfortable, Phera quickly changed the subject.

"So… How's the flying going? We making good time?"

"Heh, well."

Glancing down toward his instruments, Shi's lips pursed together in thought.

"That's sort of complicated, actually."

Beckoning the redheaded recruit closer, he pointed out their course on one of the projected displays.

"We're not really on our way home quite yet. What we do after a job like this is head for a nearby gravity well and use it to swing around and take off in another direction at pretty much full speed without having to burn the thrusters after turning."

With a pinch of his fingers, he zoomed in on the asteroid he'd picked out for this maneuver.

"Even if InterSec is close enough to read our vector in close to real-time, they won't be able to tell exactly what direction we're flinging ourselves in from here. So, as long they don't catch us between the raid and the slingshot, they're also not going to between there and Marcos. See?"

Phera let out a long, low hum, brushing aside her bangs and bending down to squint at the dotted line of their trajectory.

"Now *that* is clever. I figured we'd maybe make a bunch of zigzags or something, or just accelerate really, really fast and hope for the best. But, well… Yeah."

Straightening, she gestured toward the zoomed in visual of the asteroid.

"That's awesome."

Shi smiled, eyes dipping toward the hem of the engineer's top in mild self-deprecation as his face warmed.

Was the enviro control acting up again?

"It's not my invention or anything," he demurred. "Pirates have been doing this sort of thing since long before either of us was born. So have regular haulers too, actually, especially if they're expecting pirate ambushes along the direct route."

Looking back up at Phera, his eyes lingered on the elegant line of her collar bones as she stared up at the canopy overhead. Now that she had her own clothes, he could appreciate her figure without any resentment or bitterness. And, from where she stood beside him, all of it was richly silhouetted by status displays and a crown of tiny stars.

Damn. No wonder Straya likes her so much.

"But, uh. Thanks anyway!" he continued, sliding his almond gaze back up to meet Phera's amethysts. "Really, though, you're the big shot innovator for this mission, not me. You actually managed to cut off that entire cargo compartment en route. That's just…"

Shi blew out his breath in a long "fwahhh" sound that made the engineer's lips twitch.

"That was like something out of an action vid, but it actually *worked*! It was wild!"

He gave her an admiring grin, slightly awed even.

"Kelt said she was sure you were bullshitting that your software could pull it off without losing a single crawler. But, well... I don't think I've ever seen her so happy to be proven wrong before."

"I know, right?"

Phera snorted out a laugh at that, right hand drifting up to twirl some of her loose curls around a finger.

"Watching her counting them after the raid was pretty fun, I'm not gonna lie. Though, I very nearly wound up counting swats instead. Hehe."

Her smile turned fond then.

"But, I really can't take all the credit. I'd have been totally screwed without her helping to get everything outfitted. My doctorate is in systems development rather than the actual mechanical engineering side of robotics. I definitely know my way around a wrench and a soldering iron, but Kelt's the one who double-checked all my math and welding joints, and made sure I wasn't missing anything."

As she spoke, her other hand drifted back to cup her prominent backside, and she grimaced slightly.

"I am still so getting her back for that stunt she pulled with the excavator arm, though."

Shi grimaced right along with her, though his held a conspiratorial edge of camaraderie to it.

"Oh, yeah, I heard about that. Well, um, if it makes you feel any better, Kelt had to sleep on her stomach for the next two nights after Lem caught up with her."

He wondered if he should go there. But, with his grimace turning embarrassed and his chin dipping toward the controls again, he found himself following it with.

"Which meant so did I."

"You don't say?"

The sound of Phera's snicker made his toes curl inside his boots and his stomach flutter.

"That must've been fun."

Shi wasn't sure at first if he should be offended by the teasing lilt to her tone. But, she was still smiling as she spoke, though, making it abundantly clear that she was being serious and not just teasing him. Confirming once again her reputation for being an absolute glutton for punishment.

"Pretty sure Straya would be on a similar trajectory if she were in her position."

"Yeah. You definitely know your rescuer."

Shi shifted awkwardly in his reclining pilot's seat then as memories of his last run in with the muscular former mercenary came rushing back to him.

"Speaking of… I heard you and Stray had to improvise some distractions for the customs office on Excaden that ended up hurting a little?"

Worrying at his lower lip, he gave her a shrug.

"Or a lot?"

He'd actually seen the vids Obette had pulled from the station's local social pond and knew for a fact that "a lot" was a major understatement. But, somehow he doubted telling Phera that would do him any favors.

"Definitely a lot," snorted the engineer, crossing her arms beneath the swell of her breasts in a way that had Shi licking his lips. "I'll tell you this much. If I'd had a supervisor like her back when I was with Panorama, I'm pretty sure I'd never have been late on any of my paperwork, like, ever."

She blew out an annoyed sigh through her nostrils then.

"Still, she didn't have to bare my butt like that right there in the middle of the damn hab. It was absolutely *freezing*, and I'm pretty sure the inspector would've been just as distracted with my pants *not* ripped to literal shreds. Humph."

Shi grimaced again, and this time rolled his eyes.

"Straya not baring your ass for no good reason?" he scoffed. "Maybe you still don't know her that well after all."

He pouted almost girlishly up at the canopy then.

"Everyone besides her would be a nudist if she had her way."

"Awww, I think you'd make a wonderful nudist," teased Phera, deliberately letting her eyes wander along the modest curves of his body in its partially reclined state before nodding at his hips. "I've seen you bending over to grab stuff in the mess. You've got a *very* cute butt."

She pressed a thoughtful finger to her cheek then.

"Actually, now that I think about it, everyone on this crew does."

Shi raised his thin, black eyebrows at her as she pontificated about the Captain's hiring standards. And, were his skin tone any fairer, the warmth he felt radiating through his face would've definitely given away how much he appreciated the compliment.

"That's, uh, kinda forward."

He chuckled nervously.

"But, um, thanks."

Looking away, he nibbled at his lip again.

When eventually he looked back, he said, "Though, to be fair, you've kinda been the talk of the town as far as aft shielding goes."

Deciding to launch a test satellite into the orbit of their conversation, he reached up and poked at the bulging underside of Phera's right buttock with a fingertip.

"Hah!"

The roboticist jumped in surprise at the unexpected poke, and her fair cheeks flushed an incredibly satisfying shade of hot pink. Even better, she didn't pull away.

"With how ready everyone around here is to bend said shielding over and test its impact tolerance, I'm definitely glad I've got a lot of it."

Her face lit up in a teasing grin once again, and she gave his prodding fingertip a friendly bump with her hips.

"And, as far as being forward goes, I'm pretty sure we're way past the awkward stage of our friendship given the position I was in when you walked in on me and Steph the other day."

Oh god, *yes*. The image of her face down and ass up had been seared into his memory all that afternoon, and had definitely featured prominently in his idle daydreams during the more boring stretches of time in the bridge as they'd made their final approach to Marcos.

"Well, I didn't want to make assumptions."

"I appreciate that, but you seriously don't have to worry about it. At this point, I think it's pretty clear that I'm down for whatever with this crew. The Captain definitely knows how to pick 'em."

"Noooo kidding."

Shi's chuckle was a lot more mischievous this time around as he felt his confidence start to bloom. Phera had a body that just would not quit, but she was also so easy to talk with to the point that he was honestly having a hard time remembering what things were like before she'd shown up a few weeks back.

"And, uh... Well, your shield geometry does seem to create targeting profile issues," he stammered, doing his best to channel his inner Obette and sound both suave and flirtatious. "Might be just a bit self-defeating at the end of the day."

As her hip shifted further in his direction, he decided to take another chance, and opened a soft-palmed hand to grab and squeeze.

"Not that I'm complaining at all, mind."

Phera giggled again.

"I like to think of it more as a feature than a bug."

"No arguments here."

Cheeks still flushed a bright pink, she favored him with a saucy wink as she let him palm her wonderfully warm and squishy seat to his heart's content. Though definitely a submissive himself, the feel of it was very much stirring up the desire in him to shove her over something and squeeze it with both hands as hard as he could before pulling them apart and-

"Oh, hey!"

Shi was yanked back from the precipice of imagining what color Phera's panties might be by her straightening up as an idea struck her.

"Do you think I could maybe try flying the ship for a bit?"

"Uh... What?"

"You said we're just headed toward somewhere to slingshot, yeah? It shouldn't be a problem so long as we stay on the same generalish trajectory, right?"

Snapping out of his callipygous reverie with a sharp upward jerk of his head (his hand staying right where it was), the young pilot did

his best to deepen his usual light, masculine tenor without drawing too much attention to the fact that he was doing so.

"You're a pilot too?"

"Well, I mean... Not as such, no," admitted Phera. "We had pilots back on The Bin who handled the flyers when we needed to go out."

She seemed to pour as much sunshine and sweetness into her smile as she could then.

"But, I *did* put a lot of hours into Interplanetary Long Haul Simulator Five back when I was with Pano. Plus, I was also watching pretty close while Straya was taking us into Excaden, and I think I more or less got the gist of how everything works. Sort of."

"That's, um... Not quite the same thing."

Smiling nervously, Shi withdrew his hand from Phera's ass and tried not to flex his fingers around the phantom memory of lace panty lines.

"I'm not sure I'd even let Ob take the helm while we're running negative. It's a whole different game than just flying around with normal physics."

He gave her what he hoped was a placating expression then.

"If you want flying lessons, though, I can probably get Cap to let me start you out with our next exit from Marcos. You can plot our acceleration vector once we've cleared the perimeter."

He thought for a moment, before adding.

"Actually, getting some practice on that flyer before you start on the Mayhem might be a good idea. I'd be happy to do that too!"

"Awww, come on, Shi," Phera whined, falling melodramatically into his lap with a petulant huff.

She paused in her pouting to say with a genuine smile, "That actually does sound like a lot of fun, thanks," before resuming her put-upon scowl. "But that's going to take *forever*. Can't you just let me make, like, one banking turn or zigzag or something?"

She gestured at the controls beside her with a glower that made Shi's palm itch despite himself. He could see now why she wound up bent over as much as she did. The majority of her mannerisms just seemed to scream "Go on, spank me!"

"All I've gotta do is drop the power going to one of the engines, let the other burn at full for a few seconds, flip-flop the power settings, and then bring them back up to full or whatever, right?" she pressed, swiveling around to face forward with him behind her.

"Well, yes... Basically."

The talk of the ship being pressed so snugly into his lap that it flattened out a little off of both sides occupied most of Shi's attention just then. But, with an effort of will, he somehow managed to stay on topic.

"As long as it's less than 0.5 degrees and you give the negdrive a second to realign the field before correcting, it should be fine. But, um, we really shouldn't be engaging thrusters at all unless we absolutely need to make course corrections or avoid stellar friction. It makes us stand out way too much, and we *are* hauling a hold full of stolen cargo, you know."

He adjusted himself with some difficulty in the reclining chair so that the soft depth of Phera's crack nestled around just the right spot, which began to stiffen against her in response. Then, resting a hand on each of her love handles ostensibly to steady her, he moved his head a little to the side so that he could speak without inhaling a mouthful of red curls.

"Then again, I mean, there's probably no InterSec on our tail right now. It was a clean getaway as far as I can tell. But, just in case, we should still keep thrusters to a bare minimum. Like, really."

"Bare minimum, gotcha."

Leaning forward, Phera shifted her hips further back against his stirring cock as she laid a hand atop both the port and starboard engine control yolks. She made no move to push them or any buttons just yet, though. Apparently having learned her lesson about messing with active engines mid-flight after having it drilled into her ass three or four different times.

"So, like this?"

She looked back over her shoulder and batted her eyelashes at him with shameless, flirtatious excitement.

Oh god... Why is she so hot?, Shi found himself moaning internally, eyes tracing over the faintly visible valley of the spine in front of him.

"I disengage the fields, wait a few seconds, and then just give the engines a tiny tap, yeah?"

"God no! Disengaging the negdrive is a whole production. You only do that when you need to change vectors. And, uh, you need to let engineering know before you do it too. Then again... As long as you don't change more than a degree per second, you're *probably* not going to cause any serious wear and tear. Though, you really should keep it to less than half that just to be sure."

He gripped her stomach a little more tightly, partly to steady his nerves, and partly as a silent warning for her not to rush ahead.

"But, yeah, um, like I said. Engines burn as little as possible once we've reached our target velocity during an escape. So, I guess just remember everything I said for next time?"

Then, with a little sigh, he added.

"How much of this should I be taking as actual interest, as opposed to trying to seduce me into letting you fly? I'm guessing somewhere around forty-sixty? No worries either way. I just want to know so it won't be awkward later."

"Oh, come now, Shi. It's easily sixty-forty," crooned Phera with a fond smile that held only a slight edge of impishness to it. "Believe it or not, I actually wanted to be a fighter pilot back when I was younger."

"Wait, a *fighter* pilot? Seriously?"

Shi wasn't sure if he should be impressed, disbelieving, or laughing. So, he decided to go for all three.

"I'm serious!" insisted Phera, joining him in his laughter before letting out a wistful sigh. "Turns out, that chronic anxiety and being easily overwhelmed in stressful situations isn't the best combo for an aspiring pilot, fighter or otherwise."

"Sorry, just... You didn't really seem like the type."

Shi paused for a moment, feeling slightly awkward.

"And, well, I guess you weren't in the end."

"Not even a little bit," agreed Phera brightly. "But, learning to maneuver a little flyer like that Pano one we stole would be pretty fun if you're up for it."

She put some deliberate emphasis on the word "up" and gave her hips a wiggle that had him swelling even harder between her cheeks.

Would fucking her count as a workout? I'd be using a lot of core muscles to do it, wouldn't I?

"I... Heh. I actually didn't think about flying at all until I was twelve or thirteen," Shi said somewhat shakily in an attempt to distract himself, breath quickening as he pushed her hair over one shoulder so that it wasn't in his face as much. "I wanted to be an archaeologist before that. But, um, y-yeah. If you want to play around in that shuttle, I'll bet we can."

He worried that the ambiguity in his choice of phrasing would maybe go over the slightly older woman's head. But, judging by the giggle that bubbled up from her as she flexed her cheeks around his cock, she'd gotten the message loud and clear.

"I'd like that," she purred. "Oh!"

Before straightening up into a proper seated position atop his lap without warning, and proceeding to tap out something on her wrist comp.

"That reminds me. I saw a whitepaper a few months back about how the University of Cilara's archaeology department was experimenting with distributed ultrasound imaging using semi-autonomous drones to map potential Precursor ruins. I don't know if you're still into that stuff, but I'll snag you a copy when we get back to Marcos if you'd like."

"Really? That sounds awesome, I'll absolutely take a copy."

"Great!"

Just as quickly as she'd sat up, Phera was once again hunched forward with her hands on the control yolks.

"Okay. You ready to take this girl out for a very controlled and deliberate spin... or yaw? I think it'd be yaw if we're just doing fun zigzags, right?"

"Um, yeah, it's yaw," answered Shi automatically, both heads spinning from the engineer's ability to shift discussion topics in the blink of an eye. "Just let me... Uh, excuse me."

He maneuvered the eager new pirate forward just a bit more with a gentle hand between her shoulder blades that made him sorely wish they were back in his cabin instead just then as he pulled up a smaller display on his seat's left arm. The screen showed a roiling mass of red, orange, and yellow blobs against a beige background.

"Well, I'm not seeing anything that looks like company, and we'll have to make at least two or three more corrections at some point anyway, so…"

"So…?"

"Okay, fine, you win. Just don't tell anyone I let you do this, all right?"

"My lips are sealed."

I can think of something to occupy them, for sure.

With a private smirk, Shi dismissed the sensor display and the mental image of Phera on her knees, and adjusted his backrest a little upward so that he could better see the controls over her shoulder. Which had the unintended (but very welcome) side effect of concentrating her chubby ass even more heavily over just the right spot to make him shiver.

"First, um…"

Swallowing his nerves, he forced some moisture back into his dry mouth.

"First, you're going to need to unlock the helm controls by entering the sequence here. It's red, blue, hold down red and press green."

"Red… Blue… Hold down red, and press… green!"

Repeating the instructions aloud as she carried them out, Phera let out a triumphant noise and bounced up and down excitedly as the helm display's status shifted from "standby" to "active". With each bounce, it felt more and more like she was falling back down onto a raised rod and Shi was starting to seriously worry that he might have to go change before too long.

"Oh my gods! Yes! Okay, cool, all right…"

Heedless of his struggles, the engineer forced herself to calm down and took in a deep breath. Letting it out slowly through pursed lips.

"Now I take the yolks, yeah?"

"Y-Yep."

Swallowing again, Shi reluctantly lifted one hand from her love handles to gesture toward the controls.

"You're going to want to hit the button on the right that says 'trajectory,' *not* the one below it that says 'reset trajectory.' And, um, once you do that, you look at what it says about the environment when the extra display comes up."

As Phera pressed it, the star field of the canopy compressed into just half of the overhead half-dome. The other half showed a blue dot surrounded by expanding and contracting red blotches, with areas around it being highlighted for a few seconds at a time by softer mauve fields.

"So, blue is us. Red is what little we can see of stellar wind and stuff outside of the negwell. Those fainter blotches are where the computer thinks there's more likely to be stuff, whether we can see it or not, based on where we are in the system and what's around us according to the latest forecasts we pulled. You can see *most* of the red dots are inside of them, but not all. So…"

Reaching forward, he tentatively laid his hand on top of Phera's own and guided it into position on the starboard engine yolk.

"Hold down the button on the front."

He pressed her thumb down onto it.

"And turn the dial to… Oh, let's call it 0.3 degrees."

He guided her fingers on the wheel as well. Her hands were so soft.

"Okay, now, adjust the yolk in a direction that's not going to send us into one of those big clouds."

"R-Right!"

Phera's fragile calm had evaporated with his instructions, and she spent a three count staring hard at the canopy above, tongue caught between her lips as she picked a relatively clear looking spot that seemed stable. Then, with another deep breath and a partially-forced smile to hide her nervousness, she began tugging the yolk in her right hand *very* slowly toward her.

"Is… Is it working?" she asked, eyes tracking their blue avatar on the canopy above adjusting itself to match her change in trajectory. "It doesn't really feel like anything is happening, you know? Is that good?"

"You wouldn't feel any serious shifts, no. Which is kind of the whole point. We're trying to be gentle on the ship. Now, take your thumb off the button, but be ready to press it down again when I tell you to."

"Got it!"

Phera released her hold on the button with a broad grin, clearly doing her best to transmute her anxiety into excitement. Hearing confirmation that she hadn't accidentally blown out an engine seemed to restore a great deal of her earlier confidence.

"Now, let's just give this a shot in the other direction, shall we?"

Depressing the button on the yolk in her other hand without waiting for his go ahead, she gave it a twist like she'd just been shown and drew it in toward herself with an excited tug.

"Whoa, whoa! Hold on!"

Heart leaping into his throat, Shi's other hand shot out to wrap itself around hers, palm smacking into the smooth back of her hand with a sharp *THWAP!* before pressing her thumb down almost painfully hard to make sure that she couldn't release it.

"That one's more sensitive. You went all the way up to 0.7 degrees!"

"Sorry, sorry, sorry!"

Shi let out the big gasp he'd sucked in, making his student's hair blow around in front of him as the tension in his shoulders slowly started to ebb away.

"It's okay. Just. Turn it back down, *slowly*."

"Turn what down? The right one or the left one?"

"The portside one."

"Is that right or left?!"

"It's-"

Shi let out a slightly exasperated breath.

"Here, let me do it."

Rotating the yolk wheel back into position with her thumb still on it, he corrected their course.

"Finger off," he instructed then.

"Sorry," Phera repeated, starting now to sound more chagrinned than panicked as she eased her assisted death grip on the yolk. "I thought you said it was fine if we kept it under one degree, though?"

"I said that under one degree you're *probably* not going to cause any pylon stress," corrected Shi. "And, really, you should keep it under half that to make sure. Plus, there's the fuel consumption to consider. Turning a degree per second is pushing it. 0.7 is something I'd rather not do unless we absolutely have to, understand?"

Shi busied the hand that had just been gripping the engineer's own with sorting out the hair he'd displaced.

"Anyway, you didn't take your finger off, so no harm done. Just, if we do this again, you need to wait for me to walk you through it."

He hit the colored buttons in order from left to right to lock the controls again and leaned back against his headrest. Hands drifting back to the engineer's sides a bit more hesitantly now, worried the mood might've passed. But, Phera let out a breath of her own as soon as she saw the controls switch back to standby, and flopped against him, hand to her heaving chest.

"Yeah, I think I'm probably tapped out on hauler flying for the rest of my life. I'm not sure my heart can handle any more of that kind of stress."

With a sassy snicker, she gave her loose curls a teasing toss right in his face, ostensibly shaking them out of her eyes as she wriggled around on top of his lap for a more comfortable position.

"Thanks for letting me try anyway. We should definitely do this again with something not quite as expensive or complicated next time, though. The Captain doesn't pay quite *that* well."

"Heh. No problem. And, yeah, if you ever want to take that shuttle out for a spin, I'd love that."

Deciding to take a calculated risk now that they were no longer in imminent danger of snapping one of their engine pylons, Shi brought his left hand up from where it rested along the curve of Phera's waist and gave one of her breasts a gentle squeeze through the material of her shirt. When she pressed her chest further out and giggled happily, he added.

"God... You're the hottest thing in the system, you know that?"

To which, another voice from behind them replied, "Oh, I think you're *both* going to be once Cap and Lem find out about what happened here."

Phera and Shi let out simultaneous high-pitched yelps of surprise.

"Steph!" they said in unison, each with a rising note of panic in their voice.

Shi spared a split-second glance at the sensors to make sure they were still reporting clear flying and that they were far enough off from their approach to the asteroid that it would be safe for him to turn away, before thumbing the swivel-lock on his seat and turning so that he and the equally red-faced engineer on his lap could look at the doctor.

"When did you get here? I didn't hear you come in," he demanded, hating how guilty he sounded, while Phera dove straight into damage control.

"We weren't doing anything! Shi was just... showing me the helm!"

"Oh, I know," Steph said, face alight with a crocodile smile. "I was recording."

Putting ver hands on ver hips, ve took a step forward.

"Anyway, I just came to ask if you'd finished that book I lent you, Shi. Buuuut, since you're busy, I think I'll just go watch a movie with Cap or something instead. Later."

"Wait, hold on!" pleaded Shi, inadvertently launching Phera off his lap and two or three stumbling steps ahead of him as they both scrambled to get back to their feet.

He hadn't been joking about Kelt making sure he slept on his stomach every night that she'd had to, and it hadn't been so long since he'd last had some one-on-one time with one of his commanding officers that he couldn't remember just how vicious both women could be when they were upset with you.

"Yeah, what's the rush?" added Phera, using her sudden acceleration to overtake the slender doctor and cut off ver path to the hatch. "Besides, I don't see why the Captain would be interested in some boring old vid of two crewmates getting to know one another better by expanding their professional horizons during some downtime."

She gave her head a firm nod, crossing her arms beneath her breasts once more. Very obviously doing her best to look like she was actually doing Steph a favor.

"I really wouldn't bother her if I were you. I'm sure she's got lots of important Captain things to do."

"Oh, there's no rush."

Steph shrugged ver slender shoulders and fixed the interdicting engineer with a malevolent grin.

"I can tell her later. When I do, though, ooooh *wow*."

Ver head tipped back in revelry, mother of pearl eyes sparkling and mouth grinning so wide it had to be hurting ver cheeks.

"You two aren't going to need thrusters to fly. You're going to be bouncing all around the ship and screaming yourselves hoarse. There's gonna be smoke trailing after those tails!"

Crossing ver arms in a mocking imitation of Phera, ve bounced in place with glee.

"Ooooh! I hope I get to see it happen in person. Even if I don't, just the aftereffects alone are going to be a great show."

As ve continued to taunt them, Shi's olive skin paled, and Phera's fair cheeks flushed hot pink as her brittle facade of calm disintegrated into full on panic.

"Oh come on, Steph!"

If the pilot had been able to see inside of her head just then, he might've been surprised to find that the doctor's ominous predictions were producing a surprising amount of excitement along with the more obvious spikes of frantic worry scrunching her brows together.

Phera's boot stomped against the deck as her hands balled themselves into frustrated fists at her sides.

"You saw how sore my ass was after Lem got at it the other day. I'm, like, *barely* back to normal from that. Can't you cut us some slack?"

"Please?" echoed Shi from behind ver, hands fidgeting with his top as he fought to slow down his racing heart.

Unlike Phera, he knew exactly what a disciplinary punishment from Lem was like. And it was a *lot* worse than those quick couple dozen swats he'd seen her get in that vid Obette had sent him.

"We already agreed she'd never touch the Mayhem's controls again."

That wasn't exactly true, but it was close enough.

"Besides, she didn't actually make any serious mistakes or hurt anything. So, it's fine, right?"

Steph just shrugged.

"Oh, it's totally fine with me, sweet thing. I just want to watch you two dance around the ship for an inordinately long time while clutching your butts in agony, because that would be hot."

Ver smile somehow managed to gain another couple of teeth as ve continued to talk with ver hands.

"So, since I have a way of doing that now, I will."

"Oh my gods, you are such... such..."

Phera's round, pretty face was twisted into a mask of honestly adorable outrage as she glared daggers at the wickedly smiling crew doc. She never actually finished that sentence, though. Instead her tense posture melted back into something approaching her earlier attempt at a confident swagger, and her balled fists shifted up onto her hips.

"Okay, fine. Let's make a deal, you sadistic jerkface."

Shi winced as she said that last bit, expecting it to be the final straw that sent Steph streaking past her. But, she'd said it with enough wry amusement to make it clear that she was just teasing.

Not that *he* would've called the person with such damming blackmail evidence on them anything like that.

"I am fully prepared to make whatever offer I need to to ensure that video stays between the three of us."

She leaned around to her right then, locking eyes with him.

"And I'm sure my fellow co-conspirator is as well. Aren't you, Shi?"

Shi wasn't quite sure he and Phera had anything that the doc could possibly want, but if she was willing to take the chance that they might make it out of this without the Captain and Lem tearing their asses apart, he was willing to try.

"Sure! I've got a dozen cupcakes I've been holding onto. How about that?"

Steph snorted out a laugh and rolled ver eyes.

"Who do I look like? Adri?"

Before shaking ver cropped blonde head in bemusement.

"No. Nope. Uh-uh. You're going to have to do waaaay better than that."

Reaching up, ve gave Phera's head a couple of condescending pats.

"The two best butts on the ship getting it *that* hard? Come on. Don't insult me."

Technically, Lem might have been the contender for that particular claim, Shi found himself musing on reflex. But, as hers was off-limits to the non-suicidal, it didn't bear mentioning.

"And if you do have a better offer, you should make it fast, because pretty soon I'm going to get…"

Steph licked ver glossy lips.

"Bored."

"I-"

Judging by the look on Phera's face, she was about to say something that would no doubt make their situation a whole lot worse, so Shi spoke up before she could. The words leaving his mouth before he'd even had a chance to think them through.

"You could spank us!"

A dusky maroon rushed in to color his face then, and his stomach dropped to his boots.

"Yeah!"

Phera sounded far less embarrassed by this proposition, though the pink hadn't yet left her face as she seized upon the opening Shi had just given her.

"Why be a witness when you could have all the fun to yourself?"

Her lips quirked up with that, and Shi was pretty sure he could see the gears turning in her head as she came to the conclusion that a spanking from the slender crew doc would be far more bearable than one from Cap or Lem.

Or, god forbid, both of them.

She even went so far as to give her hips a little wiggle to drive her point home as she moved to stand beside Shi.

"Come on, Steph. Not one, but *two* cute butts all to yourself? If that's not a bargain, I don't know what is."

"Hmmm… That is pretty tempting."

Cupping ver delicately pointed chin with one hand, Steph cocked ver head to the side in exaggerated thought.

"Then again, I'd have to get extra creative to do anywhere near as much damage…"

Ve started walking in slow circles around the bridge then, openly ogling the goods on both potential victims as ve spoke.

"But, on the other hand, I'd get to be creative and you'd still be better off than you would if I told. Plus, you're definitely right about the benefits of the in-person experience. Well… All right."

Ver face split into a wicked grin that Shi knew all too well.

They were absolutely, undoubtedly, unavoidably screwed.

"I'll be waiting for you in the medbay in thirty minutes. *Both* of you."

Slipping between the two of them, Steph grabbed one plump rear end in either hand and squeezed hard enough to get them both up onto their tiptoes as they each squeaked.

"Show up and take whatever I decide to give you, and no one else has to see the video. Deal?"

"Deal!" they said in unison, not needing more than a split-second's shared look over the doctor's platinum head to agree that they weren't going to get a better offer than that.

Looking back over his shoulder at the helm's status displays, Shi saw with a sinking feeling in the pit of his stomach that that would give him ample time to perform their slingshot maneuver and get them on course for the journey back to Marcos. Which, unfortunately, because he was a skilled navigator and a careful planner, was projected to be free of any major hazards for at least four hours.

Dammit.

Phera, meanwhile, opted for false bravado once again, as she waved goodbye to the departing doctor.

"See you later, cutie."

But, judging by the way her free hand had drifted back to clutch protectively at one bouncy bun, she knew just as well as he did that they were both going to be sleeping on their stomachs that night. And probably the night after that too.

Shi could already tell that it was going to be a long, *long* afternoon.

CHAPTER TWENTY

While Shi busied himself with coordinating the approach for the Mayhem's upcoming slingshot maneuver, Phera flitted around engineering, the cargo bay, and the workshop double and triple checking that she hadn't left out any tools and finishing her recalibration of the water recycler's secondary purifier module. The absolute last thing she needed just then was for Kelt to find some excuse to be annoyed with her. Steph had seemed very determined to absolutely roast her ass one way or another, and she wasn't about to take any chances of tacking on extra nights of sleeping on her stomach to the ones she knew she already had coming.

Then again, she might be able to parlay that into cuddling with Straya...

No. No, better not to risk it.

As their deadline crept inexorably closer, Phera braided back her curls since she wasn't in the mood to constantly be spitting out hair while she howled across the doctor's knee and then met up with Shi in the corridor just outside of medbay. Each of them were looking more than a little nervous, and maybe just a *bit* more excited than they thought the other would be. Apparently, she wasn't the only one among the crew who enjoyed the tension that preceded what was sure to be a very hard spanking.

"You ready?" she asked, smirking in spite of herself as she ran one hand down the front of her top, smoothing it out and pulling the dark gray material taut across her breasts.

If she was going to get punished, she might as well look her best for it, she'd decided. Which was why she'd borrowed some of

Lem's lipstick. Though, she'd decided to forego the eyeliner this time around after the disaster it had made of her face back on Excaden.

"I guess so," mumbled Shi, face coloring to match her lips as his eyes lingered on her chest.

"It'll be fine."

Phera's smile pushed her flushed cheeks up into dimples as she patted him on the shoulder.

"Well, probably."

Switching to a pout, she thumbed the hatch control to medbay, calling into the intercom.

"All right, Steph, we're here."

Before releasing the talk button and adding.

"You sadistic jerkface."

Which made Shi snicker, just a little.

"Door's open, kiddos, come on in."

Uh-oh.

Steph's melodic cadence was even cheerier and more singsong than usual.

Yep. That's definitely not a good sign.

While she fretted, it was Shi's turn to favor her with a dim smile.

"Might as well get this over with."

"I suppose so…"

Phera was left nibbling at the red on her lower lip while Shi pushed the button that cycled the hatch open. It swished aside to reveal Steph ready and waiting for them, standing between the lab's two examination cots wearing both ver lab coat and a wicked grin.

Easy, Phera. Easy. Ver arms are tiny. It can't possibly be all that bad, can it?

"Close the door behind you. I think it would be best for all of us if we kept this as secret as possible, yeah?"

"You can say that again," agreed the flustered engineer with a sheepish grin that mostly managed to beat back her bubbling anxiety, slipping into the room with Shi hot on her heels, eyes fixed squarely on the back of her formfitting pants to avoid having to look at anything else.

After the pilot had made sure that the hatch had fully actuated back into its closed position, he let go of a shaky breath he'd been holding and did his best to meet Steph's grin with a brave attempt at casual nonchalance.

"Thanks for covering for us," he mumbled, gaze drifting back down toward the doctor's knees while his cheeks flushed a dull red under his smooth brown skin.

Phera just rolled her eyes, sighing explosively as she folded her arms and opted to stare at a spot just above and to the left of Steph's light hair.

"Yeah, *thanks*. Really."

"Thank me afterward."

Completely unfazed by her pouting sarcasm, Steph crossed over to them and reached up to ruffle Shi's mop of messy hair.

"Don't worry, I'll force you to."

Phera just barely managed to stifle a snort at that, but still caught a wink from the petite enby as ve sashayed over to one of the cots where an adjustable tool table stood patiently waiting with two bottles of a familiar looking gel and something else Phera wasn't at all happy to see.

"So," ve declared with a chipper clap of ver slender hands, getting straight to business. "Both of you are going to strip from the waist down, including shoes. The last one to finish gets the slowpoke penalty. Ready set go!"

"Um..."

"I..."

It took a full second and a half for the petite doctor's words to penetrate through Phera and Shi's embarrassment and nerves, but when ver words finally registered, they each sprang into action with an alacrity that would've made Lem and her morning calls for the crew to get their asses out of bed proud.

Shi hurriedly slipped his feet out of his boots without bothering to unfasten their latches and yanked off his socks before losing a couple precious seconds to indecision as his hands hovered around his waist, clearly unsure if he should fumble their catch open or not. In the end, he opted to just shove them and his underwear down together, taking advantage of the fact that they were designed to be both flexible and comfortable for long journeys aboard ship, and probably also because that was what Phera had just done with her own clothing. He'd had his eyes downcast at the time, and so was in the perfect position to watch as her round, full, and still faintly bruised chubs bounced free when she brute forced both her pants and panties down to her knees.

Unfortunately for Phera, though, she'd neglected to take off her boots first, and lost much more time bending over to try and wrestle the crumpled legs of her pants out of the way to get at the latch releases on them. Which gave Shi the edge he needed to slip free of his own clothes. Leaving him standing in front of the broadly beaming Steph with his balled up pants and underwear strategically held in front of his stirring groin while he and the doctor watched Phera at last manage to yank her feet free from her boots and nearly send herself toppling as she kicked off the clothes trapped around her ankles.

"Done!" she declared triumphantly, panting slightly as she straightened back up with her hands on her hips in a victory pose that left her modest thatch of neatly trimmed copper curls fully exposed.

"Yep, done!" agreed Steph, making a swirling gesture with ver right forefinger. "Now bend over the end of the cot, loser."

"Wha-? But…"

Face falling, Phera threw a disbelieving look in Shi's direction. She'd been sure that she was going to easily outpace the shy pilot if for no other reason than that she was pretty sure she'd had a lot more practice having her bottom bared in the last few weeks than he had.

Though, to be fair, she hadn't actually been doing most of that baring herself.

Steph wasn't about to budge, however, and instead just held her gaze with an implacably smug look framed by ver usual pair of shiny silver hoops.

"All right, *fine*," she groused, before adding under her breath. "You're lucky you're pretty."

With an exasperated harrumph and an accompanying toss of her braided hair that whipped with a satisfying *thwop* against her shoulders, she half-stomped and half-walked forward the three steps to the cot in front of her and fell onto her forearms with all the performative melodrama of someone well used to being bossed around and loving it.

"Happy?"

"I mean, I was happy before, but yep! This is good!"

Moving to stand to her left, Steph dragged ver fingertips along Phera's exposed and thrust back seat, raising goosebumps across the engineer's alabaster cheeks.

"Shi, put those clothes down on the other cot and stand riiiight here."

Ve pointed to the empty space near the entrance to the lab where he'd have a perfect head-on view of Phera's naked ass, legs, and crotch.

"And keep your hands on top of your head if you don't want a penalty of your own."

"R-Right!"

Scurrying into position where the crew doc had indicated, Shi let out a tiny sigh and then reached up to thread his fingers together through his dark locks. Doing so caused the hem of his lightweight top to rise up several centimeters, spacing any hopes he might've had of at least partially covering his smoothly shaven groin.

"*Much* better."

Nodding in approval at the slender pilot and his stirring erection, Steph resumed letting ver right hand explore the bare undercurves and ripe, taut centers of Phera's exposed cheeks. Paying particular attention to the fading browns and yellows of the old bruises mottling her perfectly pinchable sit-spots.

"I see Cap decided to eat you out in more ways than one," ve observed with an approving chuckle, fingering the faint traces of bite marks still visible on Phera's right cheek.

"Um... A couple of those are Straya's."

"Hehe. Sweet cheeks indeed."

Looking over her shoulder to distract herself from Steph's nimble, wandering fingers, Phera felt her lips twist back up into a smirk.

Damn, Shi.

Wearing only a thin t-shirt served to further underscore the darkly blushing pilot's nudity. Even more so than if he'd actually been completely naked. And, the unimpeded view he had of one of the crew's cutest butts and all that lay hidden between its owner's thighs was doing him absolutely no favors in his attempts to not draw any attention to himself.

He could definitely give Adri a run for their money.

Her mental filing of the pilot's size compared to the rest of her fellow crew members' anatomy was cut short, as Steph spread her cheeks without warning. Exposing the deep crevice and tiny pucker within for several humiliating seconds before allowing them to bounce back into place with an extremely satisfying residual wobble.

"This kinda messed with your judgment, didn't it Shi?" ve taunted, repeating the motion and resetting the jiggle show. "You let *this*-!"

Ve let go and sharply slapped Phera's left cheek from a low angle.

SMACK!

"Owie!"

Catching her right over a still tender bruise and making the buttock bounce upward this time.

"Do the piloting instead of that trained and certified brain of yours."

SMACK!

"Isn't-"

SMACK!

"That-"

SMACK!

"Right?"

SMACK!

Four more upward slaps ricocheted against the undersides of the engineer's curvaceous cheeks, producing four more half-suppressed grunts of discomfort. Then, Steph paused, waiting for an answer with ver palm circling over the "this" that had gotten the two of them into their current predicament.

"I... I mean..."

Shi hesitated, face darkening further as he shifted his weight from one foot to the other and back again.

"Maybe?"

Though his answer might have been evasive, the gently bobbing tip of his cock in front of him more or less answered Steph's question for him.

Which made Phera snort out another harrumph.

"I don't know why you're smacking *my* ass, when it was *his* cock that's the one to blame here," she pouted, tossing her hair and blowing a kiss in the pilot's direction. "I can't help that I've got a cute butt."

"Oh, honey, you're not being spanked for what happened in the cockpit," cooed Steph mock-consolingly, not contesting Phera's claims of irresistible curvaceousness in the slightest as ve gave one of them a squeeze. "Right now you're getting spanked because Shi got his clothes off faster than you did."

SMACK! SMACK! SMACK!

"Ah! Oh! Urk!"

"The cockpit thing comes after."

High, full-armed swats started pummeling against her sit-spots then. Sharp, small hands (not as hard or calloused as Straya's, but still stingy and shocking now that the doctor was giving it ver all) sending shockwaves of rippling flesh out across either cheek.

"You should-"

SMACK!

"Really-"

SMACK!

"Pay-"

SMACK!

"More-"

SMACK!

"Attention-"

SMACK!

"Phera."

SMACK! SMACK! SMACK!

Steph looked back to Shi then, glossy lips curling up in amusement.

"Well, at least someone seems to be."

"Hehe, yeah…"

Phera managed to push a giggle past her carefully controlled mask of kinda sorta stoicism. She knew things were going to get a whole lot worse before they got better, and she wanted to put up a good front for Shi before she eventually broke down and started properly crying and whining.

"Now I'm kinda wishing I'd asked you to send him in to finish up after we got interrupted back on our way to Marcos."

She winked at the pilot. Which in turn cranked up his awkward fidgeting by a factor of five.

"I- Um, I…"

"Did I *say* you could talk?"

With a slight screwing up of ver mouth, Steph grabbed the still smirking engineer's left buttock and pulled it outward so that ve could deliver the next volley of crisp swats directly to the inside of it. Along the interior of her exposed crack.

SMACK! SMACK! SMACK! SMACK! SMACK!

"Oh my gods, oh my gods! Ow! Ow! Ack!"

Slapping her palms against the padded exam cot beneath her, Phera's left foot stomped out a protesting rhythm in time with the doctor's swatting as the inside curve of her cheek all but burst into flames. Ve couldn't properly swing ver arm and still hit at this angle, so had to make do with whipping ver wrist and elbow down from closer in. But, the insides of Phera's cheeks were still more than sensitive enough that this still worked out quite significantly in ver favor.

SMACK! SMACK! SMACK! SMACK! SMACK!

Up and down the interior ve went, making sure to paint every square centimeter of pale, sloping skin a bright shade of pink.

"Please- Owie! Steph! I'm- Ah! Sorry!"

Ignoring her, Steph let go of the inside of her cheek and instead hefted it up so that ve could slap much harder and with ver full arm against the back of Phera's upper thigh and the inner curve of sit-spot that would rub against its twin whenever she had to walk somewhere after her punishment.

SMACK!

"Urk!"

SMACK!

"Owie!"

SMACK!

"Please!"

And didn't stop.

SMACK! SMACK! SMACK! SMACK!

Spanking the yelping engineer's thigh for well over thirty seconds before crossing over to her other side and starting all over again from the interior of her right cheek this time, before moving down to that thigh as well.

Whatever resolve Phera might've had to maintain her composure in front of Shi had started to crumble as soon as Steph had begun attacking her delicate inner cheeks, and had then been completely obliterated by the time ve turned ver attention to her thighs. Though ve was nowhere near as strong as Straya and ver hands were delightfully soft when not moving at high velocity, ve was putting ver entire back and shoulder into ver swings now and they were absolutely taking the auburn-haired engineer's breath away.

She hadn't been expecting Steph to be so cruel so soon, but she'd apparently struck a nerve. And, as the insides of her cheeks sizzled and burned, she started babbling out apologies as fast as she could.

"Okay, okay, I'm sorry, I'm sorry, I'm sorry! It was just a joke- Ack! I'm sorryyyy!"

"Yes. Good to know. I believe you. Uh-huh. Again, good to know."

Steph answered each exclaimed squeal with a serene and unperturbed chipperness that only served to further ratchet up Phera's burgeoning panic as ve finished up on her right thigh.

SMACK! SMACK! SMACK!

And then went back to her left.

SMACK! SMACK! SMACK!

Before switching things up again, and delivering quick bursts of two swats to the back of each plump, rapidly pinkening upper thigh. Back and forth, heedless of their owner's increasingly frantic whining as she was rocketed past her pain tolerance threshold.

SMACK-SMACK!

SMACK-SMACK!

SMACK-SMACK!

"Alrighty then! That's the penalty," ve eventually declared one or two eternities later, gliding a palm up and down along each thigh, squeezing possessively. "I'll bet you're glad you took me more seriously than *some* people did. Aren't you, Shi?"

Hands still planted firmly atop his head, Shi nodded very quickly while his own as yet unmarked cheeks clenched and unclenched in sympathetic response to Phera's pained shifting. Each new adjustment to what foot she was resting her weight on produced a fresh wobble of her pink-on-the-inside cheeks and drew his eyes inexorably back toward the vivid splotches of red all along the backs of her legs

"Yes doctor!"

"Ooookay then."

Steph gave Phera's bottom one final pat, and then dusted off ver hands.

"Get up."

"Oh thank gods!"

Not needing to be told twice, Phera popped back up to a standing position and immediately went to work kneading her penalized posterior.

"Might want to hold off on the exhortations to the deities until *after* we're finished here, sweet thing."

Chuckling to verself, Steph glided around to the middle of the cot Phera had just abandoned and settled down with a laconic flop. Then, grabbing something off of the adjustable table beside ver, ve pulled up ver right sleeve to reveal the circular, plex-covered port embedded in ver bicep just below ver shoulder.

"Now then, let's just get these muscles up to the task."

"Uh…"

Phera's lips pursed in confusion as her stomach began to flip-flop, while Shi just sighed in forlorn acceptance.

"That's right," crooned the doctor, winking one mother of pearl eye at the pouting pilot before turning ver attention back to the implant ve'd just exposed.

Flipping open its clear lid, ve inserted what Phera only belatedly recognized with a knee-wobbling wave of dread as a MitoStim tablet, before pressing a couple of buttons near the exposed socket and closing it again.

Biochemistry was nowhere near Phera's strong suit. In fact, she'd barely passed her required class on it in college. But, she knew enough to understand what popping a MitoStim tablet directly into an artery-mounted mod port in someone's arm was likely to do. And, judging by the blatantly horrified look on Shi's cute face, so did he. Anyone who'd ever watched an action vid would know all about the benefits of the stim Steph had just inserted, and concentrating it all into one arm, well…

"One of the best things about this little baby?" Steph spoke with ominous casualness as ve pulled back down the sleeve of ver lab coat. "It doesn't just let me power *other* things."

"You don't say?" Phera tried to drawl, not quite managing to hit the balance of nonchalance and disinterest she was aiming for.

"Yep!" confirmed Steph, as if ve hadn't just been sassed. "Granted, using it this way comes with one hell of a lactic acid hangover for the next day or so, but it's totally worth it for special occasions like this."

Arm trembling ever so slightly as the muscle fibers therein began to thrum with a sudden burst of biomodded energy, ve picked up the item Phera had been doing her best to ignore that entire time from the table.

A stout, rubber-coated table tennis racket from the rec room. *Shit.*

"Right then."

Tapping ver repurposed implement against ver left palm, Steph pushed aside the rolling table of tools with a foot, clearing enough room for someone to lie across ver lap.

"I want you each to pick a number between one and one hundred."

"Seventy-three!" Phera squeaked.

While Shi opted for a much lower, "Fifteen!"

"Funny coincidence, Phera, you were closer."

Steph scooted further back so that the hollows of ver knees were supported by the edge of the cot.

"So, you get to be the first one over my lap."

Ve patted the lap in question with ver left hand, the right still holding the paddle in a white-knuckled death grip.

"Lucky me…" deadpanned the engineer while Shi breathed out an audible sigh of relief and relaxed, hands still threaded together atop his head.

Though her thighs still smarted, the small break she'd been given between her penalty swats and now had allowed a decent amount of her innate sass to recharge itself.

Still, she'd definitely learned her lesson about testing Steph (well, mostly), and wasted very little time in shuffling around to the doctor's right side. And, after eying ver tiny lap and thinking for a moment, opted to rather than bend directly over ver knees like she would with the Captain or Straya, to instead climb up onto the cot beside ver and lay across ver lap so that her weight would be supported on either side and she wouldn't be half-sliding off of ver thighs the entire time she was being paddled.

"Mmmm… Yes. *very* nice."

Steph wasted only a little more time on groping and fondling before draping ver left arm over Phera's waist and raising ver trembling right hand up high, paddle gripped tight within ver slender fist.

CRACK-CRACK-CRACK-CRACK-CRACK!

"Aieee!"

Right from the outset it was full shoulder, full arm, and full speed all over Phera's cheeks. With two out of every three swats finding their way to her sit-spots as ve worked them in an explosive circle around each bun.

Unlike her previous penalty swats, Steph was leaving her no room for her usual litany of pained yelps and apologies. Instead, she was reduced to a howling mess of flailing arms and legs as her bottom was flambéed with a ruthless efficiency that would've made even the thoroughly muscular and equally cruel first mate wince.

Well, wince and then beam with pride from ear to ear.

Phera's ass was at maximum jiggle as she cried, aptly showing off just why she was so popular among the crew.

CRACK-CRACK-CRACK-CRACK-CRACK!

"Shit, shit, fuck, shit, FUCK!"

The sound of hard plastic and way too dense, unforgiving rubber exploding against naked cheeks echoed violently around the somewhat cramped confines of the medbay, accompanied by a chorus of four letter words from the howling roboticist. In the glass tank in the back of the room next to the temperature-controlled storage cabinet, a many-legged creature raised its tail and swished it around in alarm, three beady eyes likewise staring out at the source of the noise.

CRACK-CRACK-CRACK-CRACK-CRACK!

Phera kicked and wriggled, yelling herself hoarse, but the doctor didn't care. And ver paddle must have descended well over a hundred times in under two minutes before ve finally released ver hold around her waist and gasped as if having just finished running a sprint.

Which, in a very real way, ve totally had as far as Phera was concerned.

"You! Go stand where Shi is."

CRACK!

"Ah! Yes, okay, yes!"

"Shi, you get that ass right where hers was!"

Steph gave Phera's positively steaming backside one more hard swat for good measure.

CRACK!

"Now!"

"I'm going, I'm going!" a teary-eyed Phera yelped, tumbling off the doctor's lap and onto the deck before popping back up and scrambling to where Shi stood with her hands clamped over her space debris marker red ass.

"Shi, I'm not going to tell you again."

"Coming!"

Shivering, hands still mag-sealed to his head making maintaining his balance while navigating around the sniffling engineer slightly more difficult, Shi scurried over to Steph's side. Unlike Phera, his hips were much more narrow and fit across the doctor's lap without a problem, so he didn't bother with climbing up onto the cot first like she had and instead just tipped himself forward across ver waiting thighs.

Feeling that it was probably safe to move his hands away from his head then, Shi let go of his hair and instead shifted his arms underneath his chest and clenched his hands into worried fists as his pale brown buns flexed behind him.

"R-Ready..."

"No you aren't," taunted Steph with a malevolent chuckle that reverberated right between Phera's legs as she watched from the sidelines. "And you'd better stop lying, or else I might just have to take a page out of Kelt's book and find some soap for you to suck on."

"No, please! I'm sorry!"

"Mmhmm…."

The doctor's left hand cupped itself around Shi's right buttock, lifting it and fondling its generous curve. He might not have had hips like his partner in crime's, but his body still managed to fit as much padding onto them as it realistically could (especially with the crew's penchant for confectionary treats). After another couple of squeezes, Steph's hand moved over to fondle his left buttock next, fingers sliding up and down along the crevice between with a wicked leer that made Phera's mouth water and her pussy clench.

"Anyway!" ve eventually continued. "*I'm* ready, and that's all that really matters here. Oh, and Phera, you'd better get those hands on your head right now. If I see you rubbing again, front *or* back, you're going right back across my lap after Shi."

"Eep!"

There was a muted slapping sound as Phera's palms snapped to the top of her sweaty curls, followed by a myriad of far louder slapping sounds as Steph set to work on Shi's as yet unspanked seat.

CRACK-CRACK-CRACK-CRACK-CRACK!

Just as hard and just as fast as ve had with Phera.

CRACK-CRACK-CRACK-CRACK-CRACK!

Circling at high speed around the pilot's equally bouncy but less expansive target area with the same amount of force. Concentrating the same amount of pain atop a smaller number of nerve endings with unadulterated glee.

CRACK-CRACK-CRACK-CRACK-CRACK!

Similarly high-pitched and desperate cries and yelps like those the still sniffling engineer had made immediately started escaping Shi as Steph set his ass to bouncing and burning. The MitoStims weren't only making the doctor's arm swing *much* harder than ve was usually capable of, but also granting ver a significant speed boost as well. Phera had understood this on a more visceral level when she'd been the one on the receiving end. But, watching now, it was truly a sight to behold.

Never have I been happier for all of my aft shielding.

"Ah! Ah! Steph-! Please-! Ack! I'm sorry! I'm sorryyyy!"

Each merciless *CRACK!* of the paddle was coming so fast now so as to almost be one continuous, never-ending swat. One that landed with an almost wet impact thanks to the rubber on its surface that sent a seismic wave rippling out from where he'd just been swatted. Compressing Shi's curvaceous bubble buns for a split-second, before pulling back to allow them to spring once more into place with another equally hypnotic ripple.

As the adorable young man began to sob in earnest, Phera had to admit that it was actually a *lot* of fun to watch him squirm and suffer. His kicking was absolutely delicious, and occasionally afforded her a brief peek between his legs that made her smirk in spite of herself. It was just too bad that she'd been ordered to keep her hands on top of her head. Because the broiling heat in her bottom and the jiggling of Shi's own was really making her wish that she could put them to work in a couple more expedient places just then.

"Shi. No. Yes, I believe that you are."

Steph answered each of Shi's stammers and pleas in the same mocking way ve had with Phera's. And, once he'd taken approximately the same number of swats as she had, leaving his round globes a dark, ruddy brown that hurt just to look at, ve released ver grip on his slender waist paddle.

"Up!" Right next to your girlfriend!"

SMACK!

"Go!"

Phera couldn't help but snort a little at that last remark, but Shi was far too busy fighting back his free-flowing tears to really appreciate the jab. Still, he flew obediently across the medbay to stand directly to her left and immediately put his hands back on top of his head without needing to be told to.

All in all, Phera had to admit that as far as horribly mean and hard spankings went, she and the pilot were definitely getting off pretty light all things considered. Especially compared to what the Captain or Lem would've likely done to them. Her ass was still on fire, true, and would likely still be come bedtime later. But, thankfully, that stupidly sturdy table tennis racket hadn't had a lot of weight behind it, so all of the throbbing she was experiencing just then was largely surface sting that would be gone by the time she woke up for breakfast tomorrow morning.

"Is your arm okay?" she asked over Shi's sniffling as he worked to regain his composure, shifting over just enough so that her warm hip came into reassuring contact with his sizzling right one as she nodded toward Steph's trembling arm. "You definitely put it through a workout... or ten."

She said this last bit with just the hint of a wry smirk. She still remembered what had happened the last time she'd gotten a bit too mouthy with Steph, so she made sure to at least keep her tone respectful.

"Ask me again when we're closer to being done," ve answered her with a sinister grin, pushing verself up off the cot and rolling ver right shoulder, making the joint pop in its socket.

Ve then picked something up off of the adjustable table. An unlabeled plastic squeeze bottle.

"Time for the next contest," ve announced with an accompanying set of jazz hands. "You each have five minutes to rub this as thoroughly as you can into each other's asses."

Ve tossed the bottle to Shi who just barely managed to catch it.

"You're up first, flyboy. Make it count."

"Right!"

The bottle in Shi's hands looked to be reassuringly ice cold. And, upon squeezing it, a familiar smelling gel began to ooze out the top.

"Um, uh..."

Once again, the pilot's olive features developed a dusky hue to them, almost matching his brightly burning backside.

While it was obvious that he'd been hoping to get his hands on her ass before they'd been interrupted in the cockpit, Phera felt that it was pretty safe to assume that this hadn't quite been how he'd imagined it going down. Still, Steph had literally just handed him everything he could've hoped for, and he wasn't about to let this opportunity go to waste.

"All right, Phera," he said, summoning some bass back into his voice and clearly doing his best to channel Kelt's intense, commanding energy as he puffed out his chest and stared at a spot just past the roboticist's right shoulder. "You, uh..."

He gestured toward the cot Steph had just been sitting on.

"Bend..."

Before swallowing hard.

"Bend over."

"Sir., yes sir," crooned the auburn-haired engineer, sashaying her way past him with an extra sway to her step as she moved to take up her earlier position from when she'd received her penalty swats.

"Good."

Her condescension seemed to have solidified Shi's resolve somewhat.

"This is entirely your fault, you know," he hissed soft enough for just her to hear as he took up a stance behind her.

"It takes two to tango, you know, cutie."

Phera accompanied her retort with another saucy hip wiggle.

"Ahem."

Prompting Steph to clear ver throat impatiently.

"Tick-tock, Shi."

"Oh! Uh, right. Let me just..."

Squaring his shoulders, Shi stepped in close enough that Phera could practically feel his body heat radiating against the back of her hips (or maybe that was just the lingering heat from her earlier paddling?) and held the bottle of cooling gel upside-down directly over the top of the divide between her cheeks. And, giving it a firm squeeze, sent a generous dollop of the soothing stuff cascading down along it and in between her cheeks. Making her gasp and start to squirm involuntarily, before repeating the action with either cheek to similar results.

"She is an antsy one, isn't she?" taunted Steph.

"Sure is," nodded Shi, grinning with abundant self-satisfaction as he set aside the bottle and gave each sizable bare cheek in front of him a firm pat.

"Even more so than you are when Kelt gets her hands on that cute bubble butt of yours."

Flushing once again, Shi's reply this time was slightly less smug.

"Um, yeah."

Deliberately keeping his back to the smirking doctor, the young pilot grabbed hold of a handful of cheek in either hand and started kneading the gel into Phera's battered skin as hard as he could. Which produced some *very* satisfying yelps and whining from the engineer, encouraging him to continue being nice and rough as he worked his long-fingered hands between her cheeks before turning his attention to the backs of her thighs.

"That's right, make sure you get it in *everywhere*," encouraged Steph, hands stuffed into the pockets of ver lab coat as ve stood off to the side tapping the toe of one of ver flats against the deck plating.

Phera, thoroughly enjoying this impromptu massage and the cooling effects of the gel, groaned her agreement.

"Yeah, Shi... Sh-Show the doctor how good of a job you can do."

After a minute or two more, however, she started to feel the cool tingle all over her cheeks, inside her crack, and along the backs of her thighs begin to grow more intense.

"Um..."

A minute after that, it became an all-over warming sensation, and seemed to be working its way deeper into her muscles as it gradually began to grow hotter and hotter.

"Uh..."

Not long after that, it flared into a full on *burning* sensation. Broiling her already thoroughly tender skin, especially where Shi's fingers had pressed against her more sensitive bits.

"Oooh... Ah! Ah!"

Gasping, toes curling and uncurling in time with the clenching and unclenching of her vermillion cheeks, Phera lay bent over the exam cot breathing in and out through clenched teeth like she had several nights back when Adryel had goaded her into eating an entire nova pepper all at once.

"Ooooh crap- That's- Urk! That's not-"

She'd been wondering why Steph was being so nice and letting Shi and her cool off their cheeks so soon. She'd assumed that it was so they'd be as "fresh" as possible for round two of paddling or something. But, as her cheeks and everything in between continued to flare hotter and hotter, and a sheen of sweat broke out across her forehead and down her back, she was starting to realize that the doctor might actually be a *lot* more mean than she'd ever suspected.

"That's not... C-Cooling gel- Oh! Is it?"

It seemed like a silly question to ask given the fact that she was now actively dancing in Shi's firm grasp while he continued to hurriedly rub his hands up and down her thighs and cheeks as if that could somehow stop the burning from getting worse, but it was really all she could think to do just then.

"Oh, it's cooling gel all right," confirmed the doctor. "I just mixed some *other* stuff into it is all."

Steph's giggle as ve said that was laced with a truly inappropriate amount of innocent mischief, and Phera felt herself snorting out a laugh despite everything.

It was either that, or start begging.

"Time's up, by the way. Shi, it's your turn to let Phera frost those cakes!"

Shi's buttocks were swollen enough that they resembled cakes far more than usual, at this point. While Phera's bottom, thighs, and everything he thought he'd been soothing before were reaching an eye-watering level of burn.

"You are such... such... Ugh!"

There were several things that Phera could think of to call Steph just then, but she didn't want to hurt ver feelings. So, instead she let out a spectacular growl that would've made Straya proud and pushed herself up onto a pair of shaky arms. Breathing heavily and trying (and failing) to master the fury roiling all over her where she'd been enjoying Shi's handling of only a few minutes earlier.

Rounding on the extremely worried looking pilot, she snatched up the spiked gel bottle from where it had been resting atop the cot and stepped aside, jabbing a finger at the spot she'd just vacated.

"Right. You heard the doc. Bend the fuck over, you little brat!"

Just like Shi, Phera tried to pour as much commanding control into her voice as she could, but the way she kept hopping from foot to foot and quietly hissing largely robbed her words of any of the authoritative weight she'd been aiming for.

Still, they were enough for Shi to spring into action, albeit with an adorably worried pout.

"Yes ma'am!"

"Hah! 'Ma'am', huh?"

Phera's flash of vehemence dissipated into a giggle then as she settled in along the pilot's left side and likewise squeezed out an initial soothing cascade of gel between his partially parted cheeks.

"I think you might be the first person on this ship who's actually called me that."

She gave Shi's firmly swollen, slightly leathery feeling right cheek a friendly pat and then started working the soothing gel in just as hard as he had, spurred on by Steph's highly-amused snickering and her own thoroughly burning bottom.

"That doesn't mean I'm not going to win this little competition, though!"

Drawing in closer, Steph watched Phera work with genuine interest. Appraising. Taking note of where and how far her fingers ventured as she explored every soft centimeter of the panicking pilot.

She hadn't been exaggerating about making sure she did a good job, and was doing her best to ensure that the entirety of Shi's full yet compact caboose got a healthy amount of gel worked into it. Although Steph hadn't actually swatted them, she also made sure to give his thighs a thorough going over as well if only for completeness's sake. She did hesitate for a brief moment, however, before managing to work up the nerve to slip her fingers between his cheeks. But, when his complaining didn't intensify as she brushed the tips of one hand over his twitching aft airlock, she used her left hand to spread them as wide as they would go. Giving both her and the doctor a clear, unobstructed view of where she'd just been teasing. Then, before her resolve could fail her, she gave the gel bottle another squeeze near where his tailbone poked up from under his skin. Setting the bottle aside and using her free hand to work the gel up and down in between his buns.

After all, if she had to put up with it, then so did he! Though, she was nice enough not to probe at Shi's twitching anus like he'd done with hers.

"Oh come on, Phera!" the pilot whined as her fingertips rubbed firmly over his perineum and down to the base of his scrotum, giving it a friendly squeeze.

"Sorry," replied the engineer, only partially meaning it, her hands were developing a warm tingle to them now and she had a pretty good idea how Shi must be feeling given all the squirming he was doing. "Fair's fair, though, yeah?"

While the younger man just groaned, Steph looked at ver slate.

"Time's up!" ve declared with a little clap before stepping in just a bit closer and assessing both asses before ver critically. "And the winner is…"

Ve waited for both Phera and Shi to look at ver anxiously. Shi from his place over the cot, and Phera from where she stood half bent over beside him.

"Phera!"

"Yay!"

Steph favored her with a coy smile as she clapped her sticky hands and performed a victory dance fueled by the non-stop boiling in her backside.

"Okay, now I want both of you naughty little co-pilots to bend over the cot. Side-by-side, and make sure you stick those butts out nice and far for me!"

"Wait-!" came Phera's high-pitched squeak, celebration arrested mid hip-waggle. "Are you serious?"

"As a heart attack, love."

Steph picked back up ver paddle.

"And this time Shi's the one to win some extra medical attention from Doctor Steph."

"Oh thank gods!" exclaimed Phera, content in the knowledge that she wouldn't have to suffer another penalty this time at least, while Shi just whimpered cutely.

As the pilot pushed himself up from where he'd been laying on his chest against the cot, panting and gasping, Phera helped him the rest of the way up and they each took up a spot along its longer side, spacing themselves far enough apart so that their hips just barely were touching. They could still feel the heat radiating off of them, though, and let out matching watery sighs as they flopped onto their forearms together.

Both of their bottoms were already smoldering worse than they had at the height of their time across Steph's lap earlier. And, while the redness and swelling had diminished noticeably, the overlapping, rounded welts left behind by the hard edges of the racket were acting as an excellent catalyst that spurred the gel their skin had absorbed to burn just as bright as any swat (without any of the accompanying fading sting to go with it).

Closing the distance behind them, Steph took a moment to drink in the mouthwatering scenery and palm the heat emanating in waves from the four swollen, dark red cheeks arrayed oh-so-obediently before ver. Then, without warning, ve delivered ver first long-armed paddle swat to Shi's left sit-spot. Making it splash and bounce just as before, blowing concentrated oxygen onto the fire that was already burning there.

CRACK!

"Ah!"

Before repeating the process on his other cheek.

CRACK!

"Oh god!"

CRACK-CRACK!

CRACK-CRACK!

Back and forth, again and again.

CRACK-CRACK!

CRACK-CRACK!

Swatting twice per cheek, before switching to its fellow as Shi's short-cropped head of hair tossed back with his howling.

Then, just as quickly as ve'd started, ve turned ver sights on Phera.

CRACK-CRACK!

CRACK-CRACK!

"Oh! Fuck! Owie!"

Assaulting those big, burning buns a little harder since ve had more ground to cover. She was fortunate, though, as she only had *two* buckets of gasoline thrown onto each cheek, whereas Shi's had gotten three.

Then, Steph was back to swatting Shi.

CRACK-CRACK!

CRACK-CRACK!

CRACK-CRACK!

Dishing out six more licks of the paddle to the pilot's magma-doused buttocks.

CRACK-CRACK!

CRACK-CRACK!

Followed by four more to Phera's.

"Owie! Please!"

Then six for Shi.

"I'm sorry, I'm sorry!"

And four for Phera.

"Oh my gods- Oh! Me too- Fuck! Me too!"

Repeating ver full-armed, full force salvos over and over again with a ruthless efficiency augmented by the MitoStims still coursing through the muscles in ver right arm.

At first Phera was more than a little miffed that Steph was still swatting her, even if she was collecting less swats than Shi was overall. But, her indignation was quickly replaced by enthusiastic squealing and dancing as the surface temperature of her already sizzling bottom approached supernova levels.

CRACK-CRACK!

"Owie! Ack!"

CRACK-CRACK!

"Oh my gods! Fuck!"

As ve worked them over, Phera and Shi's cries grew sharper and more desperate, intermingling and forming a chorus of extreme remorse that was absolute music to the small doctor's ears. And, as they continued to gasp, pant, and cry out, their hands found each other and squeezed tight. It didn't really help with the actual fury being stoked in their backsides, but it was still better than nothing.

Now, it was just a race to see who would break down into tears first.

CRACK-CRACK!

CRACK-CRACK!

CRACK-CRACK!

Six for Shi, wringing out proper sobs from him this time.

CRACK-CRACK!

CRACK-CRACK!

Followed by four for Phera, who likewise began to dribble tears onto the padded table beneath her. After all, now that Shi was crying, what was the point of holding back?

CRACK-CRACK!

CRACK-CRACK!

CRACK-CRACK!

Six for Shi.

CRACK-CRACK!

CRACK-CRACK!

Four for Phera.

Then, finally, mercifully, miracle of miracles, Steph stopped.

"Mmmkay!"

Giggling while ver fellow crewmates continued to sniffle and sob, arms and legs trembling with the effort of resisting rubbing and dancing around the medbay, ve set ver paddle aside and rested a petite palm on each smoldering rump.

"How are my patients doing?"

"H-How do you think?" Phera managed to grumble through her tears, while Shi took deep, measured breaths and worked to get his own crying back under some semblance of control without actually touching his eyes.

Phera's bottom was a vivid shade of bright red bordering on carmine, while Shi's was a dark and dusky maroon with splashes of dusty, whitish bruising that looked equally as painful.

"We're *very* sorry, Steph," the pilot panted, attempting to smooth over Phera's reflexive sass.

"Mmhmm!" agreed the redhead immediately, still pouting.

Prompting Steph to pinch the bridge of ver nose in mock-exasperation.

"Seriously? When are you two going to start paying attention? I keep telling you *I'm not mad at you.* You've got nothing to apologize to me for."

"But-!"

"Exactly. I'm just taking advantage of your misconduct for my own sadistic pleasure."

Ve squeezed Shi's right buttock and Phera's left then, fingers probing inside each of their broiling cracks.

"Speaking of..."

Ver grip tightened then, fingers just a scant few millimeters from pushing inside of two extremely sensitive bottom holes.

"Back those asses up a little more for me."

It took every ounce of self-control Phera possessed not to repeat that last order in a mocking cadence. Instead, she contented herself with a powerful harrumph that Shi echoed somewhat less enthusiastically. Nevertheless, both pilot and engineer obediently shuffled backwards. Arching their backs and thrusting their cheeks further behind them and slightly apart as Steph knelt down to inspect the two sets of genitals as they came into view.

Shi wasn't completely soft, but was significantly less erect than he had been while he'd been groping and fondling Phera's recently paddled butt. There was, however, a visible bead of precum glistening along the underside of his head that made it abundantly clear that, despite his tears, he wasn't having a bad time. Likewise, Phera was also showing off just how much of a masochist she truly was. Her labia were swollen and thin dribbles of arousal coated the insides of her thighs where they'd been rubbing together. And, if Steph had been able to see them just then, ve would've also found that her nipples were standing painfully erect beneath the taut material of her shirt as her breasts swayed above the exam cot.

"Okay now..."

Gliding a bare fingertip up along the inside of Phera's left thigh, Steph sampled what ve found there while reaching out and casually starting to stroke Shi's manhood.

"For this next part, hmmm... Oh! I know. Hehe."

Popping back up with purpose, ve flew over to one of ver cabinets and began rummaging around inside.

"Hey, no peeking! You two look ahead!"

"Yes doctor!" came simultaneous squeaks of obedience, wringing out another cackling giggle from the petite enby.

A few moments later, both bending brats heard Steph's eager footsteps returning. Then, ver hands were on Shi's bottom, spreading his white hot, brutally swollen cheeks apart before pressing a thickly lubricated test tube plug against what ve'd just exposed.

"Ah! S-Steph, what-?!"

"Shhh… Just relax," the doctor cooed, ignoring his half-formed protests as ve gave the slick length of girthy synthrubber a taunting couple of twists. "That's right, good boy. And… in… we… go!"

As the improvised plug slid home with an ease that belied Shi's protesting, Steph gave his bottom a fond pat.

"Your turn, sweet thing."

Before turning ver attention to Phera, producing a similar set of yelps and moans from the thoroughly horny engineer as her bottom too was plugged with only slightly more resistance than the pilot's.

With that taken care of, Steph then knelt back down again and resumed gently stroking Shi's cock.

"Oh god, S-Steph…"

Gliding ver fingers up and down along the length of his shaft and occasionally rolling ver palm around the head, bringing it back to life so that it stood fully erect and engine-strut hard in the doctor's grip.

Phera, meanwhile, was doing her best not to feel left out of the fondling fun. However, that quickly became the least of her worries. For, just as she'd resolved to pick up a new vibrator and maybe a proper plug for herself if she could find them on Marcos after she got paid, the pleasantly cool lube on the improvised plugs Steph had stuffed them with started to tingle in a familiar and *extremely* distressing way.

"Oh fuck."

Shi, distracted as he was, took a little longer to catch on to what was happening. But, soon enough, he too was panting right along with her. Squirming in Steph's clutches as the inside of his bottom began to boil just as much as his cheeks and thighs.

"Steph, you are so meannnn!"

Whining and whimpering, Phera pushed herself halfway up onto a wobbly pair of arms and shook her sizzling backside from side to side, stomping one bare foot in rising panic while Shi just moaned pitifully.

"I know."

Abruptly stopping ver stroking, Steph used ver grip on the pilot's cock to pull verself back up to ver feet and immediately began dishing out a fresh volley of slaps with ver right hand. Aiming exclusively for the sit-spots of both panting pirates.

SMACK-SMACK! SMACK-SMACK! SMACK-SMACK! SMACK-SMACK!

"Now then," ve eventually continued, voice nice and bubbly as if they were discussing their plans for shore leave. "Who wants theirs out first?"

Sufficiently motivated, ver question was answered by a rousing, overlapping chorus of, "Me! Me! Oh gods, me!" and "Please, Steph! I'll do whatever you say!"

Accompanied by some downright lewd bottom shaking as both pilot and engineer thrust their hips further back at the crew doc.

"*Anything* I say?"

Steph giggling turned decidedly dangerous as ve slid in behind Shi.

"Can I hold you to that?"

"Uh-huh!" he nodded, while Phera let out a frustrated growl and snapped. "Whatever he's paying, I'll double it!"

Never mind that she didn't actually have anything to pay the wickedly grinning blonde with. She could dock at that station when she reached it.

"Double it, eh? Hmmm…"

The grin that lit up Steph's face then was positively luminous and Phera had a sudden suspicion that she'd just wandered assbackwards into another trap.

"You really are a genius, Phera, you know that?"

Releasing Shi's cheeks without warning, Steph sidestepped over to the roboticist. And, with a jarring *POP!* that had her toes curling against the cold deck while she squealed in alarm, yanked out her plug in one sharp motion.

"Thank- Fuck!"

"You're welcome."

Pocketing her plug, Steph gave the center of her cheeks a firm pat before snapping ver gaze back over to her partner in crime.

"And, Shi, don't you dare move from that spot. You hear me?"

"Humph! I was just adjusting my stance."

"Suuuure you were."

While the pilot busied himself with glaring daggers at the heavily panting Phera, Steph sashayed ver way back over to ver cupboard and began rummaging around inside for something else. The reprieve was a welcome one for the redheaded recruit as her ass continued to smolder behind her, forcing her to take in long, deep breaths in a futile attempt to will her cheeks to cool back down. Then, just as she was starting to worry that she was going to be stuck bending over like that until dinner time, Phera suddenly felt the unmistakable sensation of the head of a thoroughly lubed up cock pressing against her still gaped and sizzling anus.

"Um... Um...!"

"Get ready, sweet thing."

As ve spoke, Steph spread her cheeks wide again and began applying steady, insistent pressure to the opening ve'd just exposed.

"Oh gods, oh crap!"

Going red in the face all over again, Phera tried not to let her leaping heart escape through the disbelieving O her mouth had just become. It had been a very long time since she'd been properly fucked in the ass, using a genuine cock or otherwise. And, given the still warmly burning state of her puckered rear entrance just then, she had a feeling it wasn't going to be the most pleasant of experiences.

Which, honestly, just made it all the hotter. Even if (or especially because, depending on your point of view on the situation) it was totally unfair!

"H-How does you pounding me in the ass- Ah! M-Make me a genius?" she tried to demand, breath coming in ragged gasps as she did her best to relax and let Steph inside of her.

"You'll see..."

Steph's tone was an ominous singsong as ve pushed past her initial resistance and slid all the way up to ver hilt in one hard, smooth thrust.

"Ohhh gods, oh fuck."

While Phera went cross-eyed at the sensation of a fully erect cock shoved all the way inside of her, Steph reached forward and snatched up the tail end of her braid. Yanking her up in a cruel arch while ver other hand took a firm grip on one crimson hip.

"That's right, you little engine slut. I'm about to pound your sweet ass raw, and you're going to take it all, aren't you?"

SMACK!

"AREN'T YOU?"

"Ah! Yes vir!"

"Good girl."

Despite ver aggressively arousing tone, Steph started out by taking her nice and slow. Moving ver hips back and then forward while also rolling them around so that ver cock pushed against Phera's insides from seemingly every direction.

"Stars and void, I am *so* glad I had an inoculation for this stuff still in storage."

"Um- Ah!" gasped Phera. "Wh-What now?"

Which just made Steph giggle all the more.

"For the synthetic capsaicin-analogue, silly."

"Oh..."

As Steph's cock continued to rhythmically work its way in and out of her with ever increasingly forceful thrusts, making her tender bottom ripple and bounce as ver lean pelvis smacked against it, Phera began to feel a telltale tingling that sent her heart leaping right back up into her throat.

"Oh shit!"

Soon, the by now familiar sensation of chemically-fueled fire started to take hold deep inside of her. And, as it did, she instinctively tightened around Steph's length, which only served to further increase the burning ver cock was producing as she jerked forward against the exam cot with a particularly powerful thrust.

"Feeling it now, I take it?"

Steph sounded inordinately pleased with verself as ver fingernails dug in hard against a handful of crimson cheek.

"Y-Yes!"

"Hehe. Yay!"

With the doctor maintaining ver grip on a twisted fistful of her hair, Phera had nowhere to go and instead could only angle her head further back to whimper and moan as Steph's hips continued to bounce roughly against her thoroughly tender backside. Taking her hard, fast, and with the sadistic skill of someone who knew exactly what they were doing and didn't feel even the slightest shred of remorse about it.

Which, had Phera not been in the middle of yelping, whining, and babbling out half-curses that weren't actually very mean, she would have found *extremely* hot.

Oh, who was she kidding?

This was hot as hell.

"You little- Ah! You are *such* a- Urk! Jerk!"

Rather than retort, Steph just wrapped one hand around her babbling mouth, wrenching her up off the exam cot while ver other hand snaked beneath her top to give one of her nipples a merciless pinch.

"Mmph!"

As she yelped into ver cupped palm, ve picked up the tempo with ver hips. Fucking her ass like ve meant it now. Every stroke shoving the fronts of her dancing thighs against the edge of the exam cot in front of her while burning her hotter and hotter deep inside; swelling her tighter and tighter.

It didn't take too long after that for Steph to shudder to a gasping, jerky half-stop, releasing Phera's mouth and chest so that ve could grab both hips to steady ver final, mid-orgasmic thrusts.

"Oh my gods, oh my gods!"

The tingly and mild, pleasant chilly burn around ver tightly constricted shaft was pure heaven for the engineer, and ve kept on thrusting as ve came. Cock jerking and twitching as it moved in and out with gradually diminishing intensity. Then, next thing she knew, ve was gently pressing her chest with it's rucked-up top around her armpits and her sweaty head back down over the cot. Taking a moment to catch ver breath, still inside of her, while Shi remained obediently bent over right beside them.

Phera was only too willing to lay flopped out against the cot, floating along in a haze of humiliated, pained ecstasy as she too caught her breath. She'd had no idea that the petite crew doc could be so... so... *forceful.*

Yep. Definitely need to pick up that vibe next time we're in port.

Her ass was still burning. But, the heat had dimmed to something just a hair's breadth over the line of being manageable, and the sensation of Steph's extremely hot feeling cum inside of her was...

Well, not to be redundant, but it was pretty hot.

"I... I..."

Though her mouth was no longer being covered, Phera was having a difficult time stringing words together, so she just let out a contented sigh, winced as Steph shifted against her throbbing ass in a way that reignited a fresh flare of pain, and mumbled.

"Okay. I think I see what you mean. That really was a pretty great idea."

"Told you so."

Steph, recovered now, gave her right cheek a fond squeeze and then slowly began pulling out of her.

"Shi," ve ordered as soon as only ver head remained, nestled snug around the engineer's twitching anus. "Get over here."

"Um, okay."

When the pilot nervously obeyed, Steph pulled verself out of Phera all the way (forcing her to raise up onto her tiptoes to avoid an extremely embarrassing dribble) and then grabbed the tube of almost empty not quite cooling gel again and used the last of ver right arm's superlative energy to rub fresh spice all over the young man's rigid cock.

"Your turn!"

"Wha-?"

Shi's face went a truly fascinating mixture of ashen and giddy as he looked to where Phera lay sprawled, the side of her face pressed against the cot, legs spread wide and her back arched to angle her hips in a way that helped preserve her dignity (in exchange for showing off a ridiculous amount of her absolutely sopping pussy).

"You um…"

Shi licked his lips, eyes never leaving Phera's spread thighs.

"You don't mean-?"

"This."

Rolling ver eyes, Steph grabbed Shi's cock and dragged him by it until he was pushing right up against Phera's still gaped, slightly oozing asshole.

"Here. Now."

Ve snatched up ver table tennis racket then.

"Or else."

"R-Right!"

Now *that* managed to galvanize the young pilot (who, truth be told, hadn't really needed all that much convincing judging by how his hands immediately went to work spreading her cheeks).

Phera, meanwhile, threw an exasperated look over her shoulder at Steph and him.

"You have got to be kidding me."

She didn't actually sound upset about what was about to happen, though. And, again, truth be told, she wasn't.

However, as the head of Shi's slightly narrower penis (like with everyone's various spanking idiosyncrasies, Phera was rapidly developing a surprisingly detailed personal database of her fellow crewmates' genitalia) began to push inside of her, she finally noticed the tingle of the deceptively cool gel that the doctor had lubricated his length with.

"Oh fuck. Not again."

"Yeah, uh, sorry," the pilot winced, obviously feeling the effects as well.

Before apparently deciding to make the most of the opportunity he'd just been given and tightening his grip on either cheek as he thrust himself all the way inside of her in a similarly smooth, well-practiced motion to that of Steph's first stroke.

Which prompted Phera to toss her head back again with a cry of mingled delight and panic.

"Oh *fuck*!"

"You heard the little slut. Fuck!"

SMACK!

Steph accompanied this order with a hard slap to the center of Shi's still plugged ass with ver left hand. Making the test tube topper tremble inside of him, and making him tremble inside of Phera.

The message was all too clear. Either get going, or else it would be the paddle's turn next.

"Understood!"

Falling back on training drilled into him over several years, Shi stopped thinking and immediately fell into action. Still maintaining his hold on Phera's carmine cheeks, he rolled his hips back and then forward again with a surprisingly powerful thrust that bucked the engineer against the cot in front of her with each pistoning push.

"Oh gods, oh gods!"

In and out, in and out, Shi pounded Phera's ruby red rump. Pouring all of his strength into the movements and fanning the lingering heat of her paddle welts nova bright once again as his pelvis relentlessly drove into them over and over. Still, he wasn't nearly as cruel as Steph was. And, while maintaining his rhythm, he leaned forward and tugged her up by the collar of her bunched up top. Lifting her away from the cot until he was able to slip his hands around her front to fondle her bouncing bare breasts while he made good on the sexual tension that had been mounting between the two of them ever since she'd popped into the Mayhem's bridge earlier that afternoon.

"Oh god, Phera, I'm coming!" he eventually gasped some inexorable amount of time later after the hellish burning from his cock had simmered down to only a gentle smolder.

Phera, for her part, just moaned, too spent to articulate herself any further than that.

Not that it really mattered.

She wasn't the one in charge just then.

She was at the bottom of the ladder as far as the Blazar Bitches went, and was being treated as such.

And she loved it.

Hot semen shot into her where Shi had just been thrusting then, filling her up just like Steph had. And, as he spasmed and groaned his way through the final, blissful twitches of what sounded like an absolutely outstanding orgasm, he released his hold on her breasts and pushed her back down onto the cot so that he could properly rest his hands once more atop her hips.

As far as punishments went, this was honestly in Phera's top ten.

"Great show, you two!"

Steph was nice enough to wait until Shi had more or less caught his breath before clapping ver hands.

"Now then..."

While the pilot remained stuffed inside of Phera, ve spread his dusky cheeks and yanked out his plug without any fanfare.

"Oh!"

Causing his spine to go ramrod straight.

"Ah!"

And his hips to involuntarily thrust forward into Phera.

"Well, kiddos, you kept your end of the bargain, so I suppose I'll do the same. Let me just wipe that video and we'll be even."

Slipping ver slate out of one of ver lab coat pockets, Steph tapped on its screen several times, while humming happily to verself. Though, had either Phera or Shi been in a proper headspace to actually watch, they would've been shocked to discover that the last video the doctor had actually recorded was of ver bone wasp larva from three days earlier.

"Done and done!" ve declared a moment later before stepping in beside Phera's left side, the warmth of ver pelvis pressing in against the side of her hip. "Now, Shi, how about you go ahead and pull *that* thing…"

Ve poked ver finger down between Phera's spread cheeks where they were smooshed up against Shi, rapping a fingertip against the top of his half-deflated cock.

"Out of *this* thing."

Ve then gave Phera's bottom a hearty *SMACK!*

"Owie!"

"And we can wrap this up."

"Yes doctor!"

Not one to disobey orders, Shi pulled out of Phera just as quickly and smoothly as he had entered her.

"Shit, shit, shit!"

Which immediately had the engineer yelping in sudden panic as she clenched her sore buns tight and shot up to her feet with both hands clamped tight over her swollen rump for added protection. (Leaving her bare breasts to sway free before both the crew doc and pilot.)

"I hope you know that you are just the most meaniest of meanies," she grumbled at Steph, smiling from ear to ear all the while as she did so. "Thanks for keeping this between the three of us."

"Yeah, seriously," nodded Shi.

"Oh, don't mention it."

Waving away their thanks, Steph dropped down onto one knee and unhurriedly pulled Shi's softened cock into ver mouth. Holding the younger man transfixed with another squeak as ve started sucking and licking firmly on his head before taking his length in deeper. Scouring away the fluids coating it, replacing them with mere, blessedly pH neutral, saliva. Taking absolutely no care at all for the highly sensitive state the organ was in as its owner trembled and jerked.

"I- Um- Oh- Ah!"

About a minute or so later, ve drew ver head back, and started sucking and licking all around the base of the pilot's shaft, making sure ve got absolutely everything. With the pill ve'd taken earlier, it was only mildly spicy. The gel, of course, was nontoxic and ingestible by design, being meant for laryngeal pain among many other things.

Phera couldn't help but giggle a little as she watched Shi writhe under Steph's ministrations. She'd never seen someone make sucking a cock a powerfully dominant move before. But, as the pilot gasped and squirmed, clearly doing everything within his power not to pull away, she had to admit it definitely worked.

Then, she remembered her shirt was still rucked up around her chin, and hurriedly yanked it back down into place with one hand.

"I uh… I don't suppose you might be willing to part with some cooling gel later this evening by any chance, would you?" she wheedled with a flirtatious grin, before making a face. "The real stuff, I mean. Not your super mean spiked variety."

It seemed audacious to ask, especially given how tender her bottom still was (both inside and out), but she just couldn't help herself.

That paddle had *hurt*!

"Hmmm… Maybe," answered Steph, ver mouth half-full of Shi shaft. "Try asking me again this evening and we'll see how I feel."

As ve finished ver work on the pilot, ve immediately turned and began to knee-walk over toward where Phera stood watching. And, grabbing her by the hips, spun her around.

"Can't have you dribbling all over the medbay, now can I?"

It was a rhetorical question, and as Phera struggled to master her new blush, ve pulled her thighs further apart and put ver tongue to the bottom of the rivulet in question. Licking and scouring up toward its source. Then, Phera found herself being shoved back over the cot with an undignified grunt. Only, she wasn't given time to complain as Steph went to work doing ver very best to clear the remnants of spicy gel and semen that had mixed together inside of her. Tongue twirling around her gaped anus, and then swiping inside as ve sucked hard while still squeezing a swollen red cheek hard in each hand.

"You… Ah! That's-! I mean… Oh gods…"

Again, Phera was surprised by just how dominant and in control Steph was. Even as ve was eating her out like this, there was no doubt that she was completely at ver mercy. And so, she abandoned herself to the moment and opted not to fight, but instead to drift along enjoying the sensations of ver tongue probing at her thoroughly tender and ravaged back door while her cheeks were cruelly kneaded.

Meanie? Yes. Absolutely.

But, she couldn't have asked for a better crew doc, or friend.

Steph kept ver face between Phera's cheeks and ver tongue working up toward the inside of her belly until it seemed ve was reasonably sure ve'd swallowed as much of ver and Shi's seed as ve was likely to get out this way. Then, ve slowly pulled ver head back and tickled Phera's pussy with one finger.

"Mmmkay. I don't know about you two lovelies, but I need a nap after all that. You can go now. I'll be in my bunk if you want anything."

"Ugh, that sounds like an *outstanding* idea," agreed Phera, stretching her back on the cot before standing up and turning to face the doctor and the pilot.

Now that Steph mentioned it, she too was totally beat (in more ways than one).

That drone maintenance she'd told Kelt she'd finish for her could keep for another hour or two (or three). She'd get them sorted out before dinner.

Or maybe bedtime.

Or breakfast…

"How about you, Shi?" she asked, rolling her shoulders and smiling drowsily at the younger man. "You gonna take a nap?"

"I wish."

Sighing, the pilot ran a hand through his disheveled locks and shook his head.

"I've got to get back to the helm and make sure we don't run into any surprises on our way back home."

"Bummer," Phera and Steph said in unison.

"Well, have fun," the roboticist chirped, hugging both pirates before snatching up her discarded pants, underwear, and boots, and sashaying her way out through the medbay hatch, still bare assed and carmine hipped.

"Yeah, uh… you too," smirked Shi as he watched her go. "God, I love this job."

"Me too, kiddo."

Steph gave his swollen seat a friendly pat as ve trailed after Phera, sans pants and stretching ver trembling arm over ver head while yawning.

"Me too."

CHAPTER TWENTY-ONE

The crew's homecoming to Marcos Station this time around was far less humiliating for Phera since she had actual clothes to wear for a change. She still caught a leer from the food vendor outside the docking ring who'd offered to let her sample his meat the last time they'd been in port. Though, this time, he'd wisely chosen to keep it to *just* a leer since Lem was walking right beside her. But, beyond that, nobody paid her any more special attention than any of the other Blazar Bitches.

Even better, the station itself was starting to feel more and more familiar. Like actual stomping grounds that Phera could enjoy herself in, as opposed to a scary Proxward port she'd disappear into forever if she wasn't careful. Granted, it was definitely still that too, but she did her best to ignore that nagging sense of worry whenever she was walking around with the crew. Scary port or no, it was still nice to feel like she was starting to get the hang of this whole being a pirate thing.

—

A few days after docking, Phera was feeling exceptionally bouncy as she walked alongside Straya through the cramped, mostly well-lit corridors of the station's entertainment mod. The Captain had sold off their haul that morning (along with the Panorama flyer since it was likely to be tied to the crime eventually), and the entire crew had gotten paid.

Had she been in null-grav at the time, Phera would've literally been bouncing off the walls when she'd seen the balance in the anonymous bank account Obette had furnished her with. She was by no means rich, but the crew shares from a literal cargo hold's worth of premium stolen commodities were still extremely substantial. The bank balance projecting from the back of her comp glove had an actual comma in it and zeroes at the *end* for a change! And, best of all, there was no megacorp "just pay it back when you feel like it" loan hanging over her head or company store to buy things from to drain away her funds.

It was all hers!

So, when Straya had tracked her down in the workshop, slapped her on the ass to pull her attention away from the slate she'd been bent over, and invited her to go drinking to celebrate their payday, she hadn't even had to think about it.

"Do you think the Captain will be at Tortuga tonight?" pressed Phera as she attempted to pick her way around some people walking the other way in a particularly narrow stretch of station corridor, while Straya just shouldered through them. "I promised to get her absolutely plastered the next time I got paid, and it'd be nice to be able to make good on that."

"Oh yeah?"

Straya favored her with a knowing smirk as she absently threw a middle finger over her shoulder toward the grumbling stationers they'd just passed.

"She told me you already paid up."

Stepping over a discarded pile of boxes, she pulled the younger woman in closer with an arm around her waist, cocking a brow as Phera's face flushed.

"Tortuga, though? Hmmm, that's not a bad idea. Haven't actually been back there since we docked."

Straya's fingers idly traced circles around the engineer's hip, making her smile as she settled in more comfortably against her reassuring sturdiness.

"As far as Cap goes…"

She gave a little shrug then that bumped the shorter woman against the warmth of one breast.

"She *might* be there. It's hard to say. She tends to keep to her own schedule, especially when we're in port. We're lucky if she tells us anything besides 'be on board and ready to push off in the morning'. So, who knows?"

Rounding a corner, the familiar bright neon turtle with an eyepatch and cutlass in hand blinked merrily down at the two of them along with the words "Tortuga Cafe and BARRRR".

"Huh. Weird."

Pausing outside the entrance to the building, Straya's scarred mouth dipped down into a frown.

"Awfully quiet tonight."

"Seriously."

Cocking her head to one side, which had the added benefit of letting her rest her cheek against Straya's collarbone and get a better whiff of her heady musk of sweat, oil, and some spice she still couldn't put her finger on, Phera listened. And, yep, there wasn't the usual din of half-shouted conversations being carried out over energetic dance music and bone rattling bass.

"Weird," she echoed. "Maybe there's some big event going on somewhere else that everyone's at?"

Either way, she was more than okay with there being less people in the bar that evening. She'd pulled a copy of the local social feeds as soon as they'd docked a couple days ago, and she *still* had to fight down a blush every time she thought about them. Obette definitely hadn't been exaggerating about her ass being all over the place that fateful evening when the Captain had picked up the tab for her.

"Whatever. Works for me."

Slithering out from under Straya's arm, she took her hand and started pulling her along after her.

"Come on. Let's get wild!"

"Heh."

Straya, still smirking, allowed herself to be dragged.

"We'll try, at least."

As the door before them cycled open, though, Phera's exuberance fizzled out into confusion.

"Whoa."

Stumbling to a halt, she was stunned into silence for a long moment upon seeing that the bar wasn't just low-key that evening, but completely empty. Every table clean and pristine. Every seat in its place and unoccupied. The lights were all on, and the drinks and decorative, luminous bottles arranged as per usual behind the bar, but there was no one attending it.

Or anywhere else for that matter.

"Um... Are they not open yet?"

It was only after she took another, considerably less enthusiastic pair of steps into the oddly silent bar and started to turn around to ask her drinking buddy if they should maybe go that she saw them. Straya, standing just in front of the door, formed the center of the line. All of them wearing stupidly big grins on their faces, while above them hung a large banner with the words "Welcome Aboard Phera" printed in a gigantic, color-strobing font.

"SURPRIIIISE!"

Heart leaping, stomach lurching, and face going bright pink, Phera's mouth fell open in absolute shock and delight.

"Wha-?"

The question remained half-formed on her lips for a full five count as she stared with disbelief from the banner, to her beaming crewmates, and back again. Before being swallowed and replaced with a smile so big it made her cheeks hurt. There were the beginnings of tears starting to form in the corners of her eyes now too, and she quickly batted them away before they could take root.

"Oh my gods, you all are just... just the sweetest ever!"

It was perhaps an odd thing to say to a bunch of scoundrels, several of whom had personally reduced her to a quivering pile of tears on more than one occasion. But, she absolutely meant it and made a point of making eye contact with each and every one of them in an effort to convey just how much this meant to her.

"Nobody's ever thrown me a party before."

Oh, a girlfriend in college had sprung a cupcake on her for her birthday one year, but her parents had never really been the "let's throw our kid that we're supposed to like a party" types of people. Even if the Church of Harmony hadn't discouraged birthday and holiday celebrations as being frivolous, the closest thing she'd ever gotten from her parents was a slightly fancier Worship Day when she'd come of age.

But, as she'd told herself over and over again since her sophomore year of college, *fuck* her parents.

"Seriously."

Swallowing hard, she dragged a forearm across her traitorously moist eyes with a shaky, sheepish laugh.

"I just…"

In the weeks since she'd been roped into traveling with them, she'd really come to love her crew as the sort of family she'd always wanted (casual sex and hard-handed disciplinary dynamics and all), and the fact that they cared enough to make an effort like this for her was enough to have her practically levitating off the floor with happiness.

"Don't take it too personally, swabbie," the Captain said with her typical lopsided half-grin while the others snickered. "Everyone gets this treatment once they've proved themselves."

As she spoke, she swaggered away from the wall, drawing the crew along after her in her wake.

"Drinks are free for the new recruit tonight!"

"Here, here!"

She favored Phera with a knowing wink the n, prompting the engineer to blush just a bit brighter, but look no less ecstatic.

"Awww, do I really not get a finder's fee?" Straya complained, slipping in beside her again and draping one muscular arm around her slightly trembling shoulders.

The Captain just sighed in mock-disgust.

"The last thing *you* need is free drinks."

She put a hand of her own on the top of Phera's head then.

"However, I suppose the special girl can give you *one* of hers if she wants."

As the lean woman removed her hand, Steph snuck up behind Phera, rose up onto ver tiptoes, and slipped a pointy party hat onto her head.

"Special hat for the special girl!"

Still beaming, Phera felt her throat go tight all over again, and had to swallow a couple more times to loosen it before she could speak.

"Thank you so much, Captain! You have no idea how happy this makes me."

It was perhaps a bit on the painfully honest and soft side for something a pirate should be saying.

But, well, it was the truth. Pure and simple.

Above all else. Above getting paid. Above pulling off a daring raid that she was a major participant in, or even living aboard the Mayhem for over a month now. This sweet, little party and the silly hat Steph had just sat atop her curls were what finally made her feel like she was actually, officially, for sure part of the crew and not just a hanger-on who'd been getting by on her sparkling wit, cute ass, and doctorate in robotics.

And it felt good.

It felt *really* good.

Leaning into Straya's sturdy warmth, she blew Steph a kiss before tipping her chin up to regard her cabinmate with a lopsided grin of her own meant just for her.

"Don't worry, Stray. We'll find you something that comes in one of those really long, goofy glasses to drink."

"Don't go pushing your luck, sweet cheeks."

Straya accompanied her warning with a not very serious glare, and then ruffled her hair, knocking off the party hat in the process. An outraged gasp from Steph ensued, who Phera saw was now glaring at the taller woman with significantly greater seriousness. However, Adryel swooped in before either of them could say anything, slapping her lovingly on the back.

"Lem and I saved most of a sheep from the haul just for tonight. Figured something pirates used to eat back on the home planet would be appropriate. So, it's mutton chops and steaks for all, me hearty!"

They looked back toward the kitchen then.

"Speaking of, I'd better go warm those up before Lem has to do it and decides to warm *me* up."

They gave her back another pat.

"Meanwhile, you'd better start on those drinks. They're only free for tonight, you know."

The Captain's half-grin remained firmly in place as she watched Adryel depart with a shake of her head.

"Not having second thoughts about tossing your lot in with us, are you, Phera?"

"Are you kidding me?"

Laughing, the auburn-haired engineer turned and used the action of ducking down to snatch up her party hat to admire the crew cook's ass as they walked away, before popping back up and reaffixing the pointy, sparkly monstrosity into place atop her head.

"I finally get to use my degree for something interesting, stick it to megacorps, and have fun doing it with a bunch of lovely and talented people who I really, really like. It's like a dream come true!"

"Plus, the sex isn't too bad either, now is it?"

This managed to darken Phera's face nearly to the same shade of red as her hair, but her smile never faltered.

"Oh gods, tell me about it."

She knew it was probably bad spacer manners, but her planetside upbringing and overabundance of excitement had her moving before she could stop to think about it. Closing the distance between her and the Captain in two quick strides, she all but tackled the woman, wrapping her arms around her middle in the tightest hug she could manage.

"I couldn't be happier, Captain. Thank you again for taking me on. You are *seriously* the best!"

The Captain, for her part, went stock-still as her face fell for a full second and a half while the exuberant engineer squeezed her narrow midsection.

"Um… Uh… Ahem. You're welcome."

Face rearranging itself back into a warm smile then, she returned the embrace just as firmly. Lifting Phera's boots clear off the floor before lowering her back down with an easy chuckle.

"If it helps, I have it on good authority that you're rather well-liked yourself, hon."

Her nervous freezing-up had passed as if it had never happened. Leaving Phera to wonder if she'd just imagined it.

"So," Straya broke in then, stepping closer. "About that ugly, girly drink you promised- FUCK!"

However, she was interrupted with a decidedly un-Straya-like yelp as both her hands flew back to her muscular ass, hissing in pain and surprise as a minimum-force coilgun round bounced to the floor behind her and rolled away. Immediately, her head snapped around toward the bar where Obette, Kelt, and Shi were chatting, and where Steph was leaning against the wall behind them with a serenely innocent expression on ver face and ver hands in ver pockets.

"I'll be back in just a second."

With that ominous pronouncement and an equally ominous glare, Straya stomped off in the direction of her fellow crewmates.

"Have fun!"

Phera waved after her retreating (well, stalking) form before turning back to the Captain.

"Geez. I had no idea Steph was such a good shot," she chuckled, one hand drifting back to cup her own seat in sympathy. "Hope ve's fast too."

That was very much a lie. She was still tender from her and Shi's private session with the crew doc, and she was very much looking forward to seeing that cute bubble butt of vers on the receiving end for a change.

The Captain, meanwhile, just rolled her eyes.

"Stationary target at less than ten meters? My grandma could've made that shot, and she's been dead twenty years."

SMACK!

Her hand clapped hard against the seat of Phera's shorts then, making her jump, just as Straya grabbed Steph by the hair and began dragging ver toward the nearest restroom.

"Sheep's coming out soon. Better have some, or you're gonna have a target of your own to cover when Lem gets offended."

"Heh. Aye aye, ma'am."

—

As tempting as it might've been for Phera to paint a target for Lem, she and Adryel had done an absolutely outstanding job with the sheep they'd stolen. The tender meat bloomed on her tongue with juices and a mixture of spices that had her reaching for another bite before she'd even finished swallowing the first. She would have absolutely gone in for thirds if she thought her stomach had room for it, but there were drinks to be drunk, and she wasn't about to squander the gift her Captain had given her.

And so, she ate and she drank along with her crewmates. Sharing stories of past adventures, laughing about the raid they'd just pulled off, and singing loudly and mostly in key to the music Shi picked for them. It was an absolute delight of a time, and as the last of the mutton chops were finished off by Steph and Lem, Phera rose from the tables they'd pushed together and made her way back behind the bar to fire up the blender for another ugly, girly drink that Straya would've absolutely hated.

"Anybody want anything while I'm back here?" she called back, voice muffled somewhat as she bent down to dig out ice from the box below the counter, hips bobbing in time with the music thrumming overhead.

"You might want to hold off on that, actually."

Lem's voice was decidedly gloating as it floated back to her.

"Yeah, it's time for your main event!"

There were whistles and cheers at this pronouncement. Some of them rather ominous sounding.

"Main event?" repeated Phera, a fresh bubble of unnamed, vaguely worried excitement buoying her back up over the bar. "Don't tell me I have to arm wrestle all of you or something?"

She snickered then.

"I'll do it if you really want me to, but Steph has to promise not to cheat."

"I won't-" the doctor started to reply indignantly before a sharp slap turned her sassing into a pained "Ow!" as Straya grinned at ver smugly before turning her attention back to Phera.

Come to think of it, the entire crew was grinning at her now.

"Um…"

While she'd been busy fishing for ice beneath the bar, Adryel had pushed a pair of chairs together back-to-back on the edge of the empty dance floor. Beside them stood the Captain, holding an odd, half meter long, board-shaped object. It was made out of some sort of clear plex and terminated in a long, comfortable looking handle on one end, while a matrix of tightly packed LEDs blinked garishly through a rainbow cycle beneath the thick surface of its business end.

"Being a Blazar Bitch is fun, but it's also rough," the tall pirate crooned, amber eyes glowing nearly as bright as the LEDs she was menacingly tapping against her open palm. "As such, our initiation parties reflect that."

The word "initiation" coupled with seeing the Captain holding what appeared to be the kind of paddle Tortuga's usual bartender would've immediately fallen in love with had the suddenly dry-mouthed engineer flashing back to daydreams from when she'd first entered college and debated joining a sorority. And, stomach lurching with its own blend of mischief and bashfulness, Phera slipped out from around the bar and approached where the woman stood on a pair of much shakier legs than all of her drinking up until that point could possibly account for. Still, she wasn't about to give in that easily. After all, half the fun of being on this crew was getting to fully exercise her bratting muscles.

"Oh, okay. *Now* I see what's going on here," she said with an exaggerated nod of understanding, locking eyes with the Captain for the briefest of moments before half-jerking back toward her gathering audience when her self-preservation instincts kicked in. "Okay then, which one of you am I giving it to first? Adri? Straya? Oh, oh! How about Kelt?"

Lem snickered, albeit the word sounded somewhat wrong in relation to her broad features and broader build.

"That's not a bad idea. How about whoever loses gets it from Phera at the end?"

Shi and Steph both squawked out a startled "No thanks!" in one voice to this proposal, the latter of whom clutching ver still sore seat protectively.

"Hmmm... Now there's an idea."

Still tapping the paddle against her open palm, the Captain sauntered her way toward Phera at a lazy pace, hips swaying far more dramatically than usual as she did so. Her dark skin seemed to almost shimmer where it emerged from her short pants and sleeveless shirt, and whenever the paddle bounced off her palm it lit up even more brightly as a collection of digits flashed across its back side.

"Everyone has to run a little test when they join up, honey," she explained with a languid ease that did absolutely nothing to ease the wobbling in the new recruit's knees. "We were all brainstorming what yours should be the other day, and, well..."

"I voted for blow job contest, but this won out," chimed in Adryel.

"That's because there's no good way of measuring how well someone can *receive* oral," countered the Captain with faux-exasperation.

"Still would've been fun, though."

"Tell me about it," grumbled Steph.

"Face fuck the cabin girl on your own time, you insatiable whores."

The Captain's grin rose to potentially face-damaging proportions then.

"But, yes, Phera. We decided that since every member of the crew seems to be relating to you more or less in the same way."

Phera jumped as the paddle impacted with a particularly loud SPLAT! against the Captain's palm.

"That this would be a fitting trial for our new roboticist."

"More like Robutticist," countered Adryel from the sidelines without missing a beat.

There were a few chuckles at this, which transformed into full on cackling when Lem casually shoved them off the table they were sitting on. Sending them crashing to the floor, gasping.

"And," the Captain continued just as lazily as before once her crew had settled. "With this marvelous invention courtesy of our beloved Kelt."

At this, the Mayhem's senior engineer gave a little wave to a round of applause.

"We can see exactly who relates to our new shipboard sweetheart the best."

She gave her palm another menacing tap then, and Phera finally noticed that when she did so the numbers on her paddle's embedded display updated with a fresh rainbow starburst.

"Huh."

She had to admit that that was actually kind of cool. Even if it didn't bode well in the slightest for her backside.

"Well…"

Drawing in a shaky breath through her nostrils, she thought about arguing that this was rank abuse of her privateering posterior just long enough to say that she had before clearing her throat.

"Ahem. That could… That could be fun," she conceded, doing a very poor job of hiding her rising excitement, before throwing the sauciest look she could muster back over her shoulder, aiming it mostly at Shi and Steph as she added. "And, I for one think that it's only fair that whoever among you isn't pulling your weight in regards to our team-building should definitely be getting some extra time with me."

Everyone who wasn't named Shi or Steph cheered their agreement to this, spurred on as much by Phera's enthusiasm as anything else. Steph, in addition to not cheering, started doing something with the port on ver right arm. While Shi somehow looked even more unhappy about the mess he'd suddenly found himself thrust into.

"Looks like we're all in agreement then. Excellent."

The Captain threw a particularly malevolent look in the pilot's direction with that. Then, returning her full attention to Phera, she pointed at the improvised spanking bench beside her with her paddle.

"Get into the position you know you belong in, girl."

With that crisp command, the big monitor overlooking the dance floor flickered to life, displaying a line of zeros and eight empty fields on the right-hand side with a crew member's name above each. Resembling nothing so much as a bowling alley scoreboard.

Phera let out a low whistle.

"Heh. Nice touch."

Instead of moving forward right away, she instead took a moment to prepare herself both mentally and physically for what was about to happen. Totally buzzing with adrenaline and anticipation (and a respectable amount of alcohol), she drew down the zipper on the front of the functional and many pocketed, half-sleeved jacket she was wearing and shrugged it off so that she stood only in a pair of stylish station boots, some flattering (and snug) nylon shorts, and a teal undershirt. Then, tossing her discarded top in the general direction of the bar (very much hoping that the maneuver looked cool), she approached the foot of the back-to-back chairs.

Standing before them made the reality of what was in store for her suddenly come into sharp relief. And, in order not to draw any attention to the heat rapidly climbing its way up her neck to suffuse her cheeks, she climbed up onto one and positioned herself so that she was on her hands and knees with the cool, rounded over tops of the chairs supporting her middle while the material of her shorts strained taut over the thoroughly well-rounded backside pointed squarely toward her crewmate audience.

Prompting many fresh catcalls and appreciative whistles that wrung several embarrassed wriggles out of the roboticist's hips as she strove to get more comfortable.

"Um... Ready."

"No."

The corners of the Captain's mouth pulled down into a scowl as she descended upon Phera's upturned seat like a hurricane.

"You're not."

SMACK! SMACK! SMACK! SMACK! SMACK!

Immediately, her hand began cracking down in a barrage of mercilessly swift, arcing swats all over the younger woman's lower cheeks. Biting into the soft flesh there as their owner yelped in both surprise and no small amount of pain as two extremely precise, palm-sized circles of fire burst into life along the crease where her bottom met her thighs.

"What-? But-! Come on!"

Yelping in time with the taller woman's hand exploding against her seat, Phera's wriggling increased tenfold as she tried to find some angle of presenting her bottom that could mitigate how hard the Captain was capable of spanking her.

It didn't help.

SMACK! SMACK! SMACK! SMACK! SMACK!

"I don't paddle shorts," she eventually deigned to explain.

All the while still spanking.

SMACK! SMACK! SMACK!

"So, get them off."

SMACK! SMACK! SMACK!

"Now!"

SMACK!

"Okay, okay, okay!"

As soon as the pressure on her lower back had lifted, Phera was up off her chair-bench and rubbing furiously at her backside.

"You could've mentioned that *before* I got into position, you know," she pointed out with all the devils-may-care peevishness of someone already in for a paddling from some very motivated individuals as she slipped her hands beneath the stretchy waistband of her shorts.

Peeling them down to her ankles required her to bend over again. Pushing her robust hips and the orange thong running between them out behind her in a way that made her smile beneath the veil of hair that fell around her face while she worked to slip the snug yet stretchy material over and off of her boots.

"And *you* could have waited," countered the Captain, completely unfazed by her sass as she and the rest of her crew admired the pair of lightly pinkened hams swaying from side to side in front of them with their owner's hopping.

She waited just long enough for the bratty engineer to bend back over and for everyone to finish laughing at her reaction to that surprise attack before finally lining up the paddle for its first salvo.

Oh dear...

Phera could feel seven pairs of eyes glued to her seat, but they all blurred into the background at the cool press of plex against her basically bare skin. The paddle itself was a long-handled affair that could be comfortably gripped in either one or two hands (the Captain had opted for the two-handed approach, she noted with some small degree of trepidation), and was substantial enough to run fully from hip to hip, covering a good third of her vulnerable and bouncy backside vertically.

"Always save the best for first," quipped the Captain.

Phera was briefly aware of the paddle being drawn back, followed immediately by a burning hot *WHOOSH-CRACK!* that exploded across both cheeks at once, the thong she was wearing doing absolutely nothing to stop it.

"Gods above! That fucking *stings*!"

A low chuckle reverberated from the Captain.

"Doesn't it, though?"

She followed this rhetorical question with a friendly pat that made the panting girl's left cheek wobble.

"Breathe, honey. You've got a long, *loooong* way to go yet."

"Y... Yes ma'am."

Sucking her teeth in painful glee, Phera did her best to hiss her way through the flash of nova-bright heat that had just erupted across both her buns, painting a crisp white rectangle there that had flooded in with dark pink a second later. The paddle's surface was glossy and mirror smooth, which meant that when it had impacted, it had gripped her skin tight and hadn't let go, ensuring that all of its kinetic energy was transferred as efficiently as possible.

And that her curvaceous cheeks felt like they'd just been bombarded from orbit!

Even after spending the last handful of weeks building up her pain tolerance, paddle swats right on the bare without any sort of warm up were no joke. Especially with this particular paddle. The plex that encapsulated its electronics was very clearly meant for high-impact industrial applications, judging by how dense it had felt. Not only was the paddle big, but it was also *heavy* too. Which meant that when it had found its mark, it had hit like a runaway cargo freighter.

It. Was. Awesome.

Phera hadn't been able to see the rainbow starburst of color that exploded across the length of the paddle with its impact, but the scoreboard to her left had helpfully updated itself with the results of the Captain's first swing. Which produced a general chorus of good-natured heckling from her crewmates.

"Six-fifty-eight, seriously?"

"Boo!"

"Come on, Cap, don't go easy on her!"

"Just giving honey buns here a warm up."

The older woman gave the honey buns in question another pat.

"And giving the rest of you rats a fighting chance."

Sure enough, the Captain had been telling the truth.

WHOOSH-CRACK!!

"Holy- Ack! Shit!"

For, half a heartbeat later, blinding, white hot pain had once again blossomed across Phera's upturned seat. Searing her tender skin like the brand of an angry god.

"Seven ninety-five!" someone called out.

"Mmhmm," murmured the Captain as she lined up the paddle a third time. "And, last but not least..."

WHOOSH-CRACK!!

As Phera's backside lit up once again, the number 797 flashed onto the scoreboard. Finishing out the woman's designated section of the display, showing her highest, lowest, and mean force scores below her name.

"You're up next, Kelty."

Panting and hissing, bottom throbbing and pulsing with a mind all its own, Phera's tightly coiled muscles slowly began to relax. And, seeing the paddle being passed off to the tiny engineer, she heaved out a sigh of relief.

"Oh thank gods," she breathed, hopefully low enough to avoid being overheard above her crewmates' mingled golf-clapping and combination teasing-encouragement of Kelt.

"You can do it!" cheered Shi.

"Try to at least crack four hundred if you can, noodle arms," added Adryel, once again back on their table perch and grinning wickedly.

"Yeah, Kelt."

Unable to stop herself, Phera shuffled her bright red and extremely precisely marked buttocks (she couldn't see it just then, but the Captain had managed to layer all three of her swats directly atop one another) further back, pushing her hips tauntingly toward the older woman.

"Big act to follow," she teased, the raggedness of her breathing undercutting her smugness ever so slightly. "Better not choke. It'd be a real shame if I got to put *you* over a workbench when we're done here."

Kelt didn't even credit that with a response.

Instead, she grabbed the waistband of Phera's thong and yanked it up high and hard so that it cut painfully into her crack and pussy.

"Ack!"

Refusing to give her enough time to properly react to this new clothing arrangement, she landed her first attack; still holding the thong high and painfully tight with her left hand.

WHOOSH-CRACK!

Right on the smart-mouthed sailor's sit-spots.

WHOOSH-CRACK!

And then her thighs.

*WHOOSH-**CRACK!***

Before returning to her sit-spots one last time.

"Ack! Okay, okay! You're great, all right?"

"Uh-huh."

The whole thing had taken less than ten seconds, and hadn't even given Phera a chance to properly howl or reorient herself between swats.

"I think you and I will be having another meeting in the workshop sometime soon, young lady."

"But- Urk!"

Phera squeaked out another yelp as Kelt yanked up on her captured panties one last time, hauling her a full three centimeters up off her makeshift bench before letting her go with an extremely self-satisfied snort. She spared a moment to appreciate the wobbling said actions produced, before spinning on her heel and striding confidently back toward her cheering crewmates.

"Add fifty for style," instructed the Captain, grinning from ear to ear.

"With pleasure."

Chuckling, Obette tapped out a quick sequence on his slate that updated the scoreboard.

"Think you can beat six-fifty-three, Shi?" came the Captain's challenge as the pilot's name lit up on the screen above the dance floor.

"Gods, I hope not," groaned Phera, producing still more chuckling among her audience as she reached back to try and fix her underwear.

"I'll do my best," came the young man's nervous sounding confirmation.

He swept back his bangs and started forward then.

SMACK!

Barely making it halfway to Phera before catching a motivational swat from Obette.

"Good luck, boyo!"

This bit of kinetic encouragement was met with laughing from all around, and a bone-chilling glare from Kelt.

"Just helping him shake off his performance anxiety," the infiltrator soothed the shorter woman, both hands held palm out in front of him in surrender. "Wouldn't want him to come in last, now would we?"

Shi just huffed at the flirtatious man a little before putting his seat of encouragement well out of range of the rest of the crew and accepting the paddle from Kelt as she crossed back to the watchers; stepping hard on Obette's toes as she did so.

As Shi took up his position behind Phera, she heard him whisper sotto voce, "This is totally payback, I hope you know."

"For *what*?" demanded the auburn-haired engineer in an indignant hiss, emphasizing her exaggerated aggrievement with an admonishing bounce of her hips while deliberately not looking back at Steph. "Pretty sure you came out more than ahead from that little afternoon adventure, flyboy."

"That whole thing was your fault!"

Shi sounded just a touch defensive, as if he wasn't sure how much to regret everything. But, rather than prolong anymore, or (worse) give anyone a chance to get curious over what they were whispering about, he bent his knees, squared his shoulders, and...

WHOOSH-CRACK!

"Ack!"

Shi was slim and not particularly muscular. But, he *was* still a man who'd finished puberty, and also a member of a crew whose first mate was borderline militant about making sure everyone got in regular exercise.

"Six-forty-eight. Not bad, kiddo!" cheered Kelt.

Cheeks warming ever so slightly, Shi waited just long enough to get his arms straight again, and then...

WHOOSH-CRACK!

"Oof!"

This one, while definitely enthusiastic, was slightly off-center. Catching Phera's left cheek heavily while only making the right bounce a bit with spare momentum.

"Oops, sorry!"

Realizing what he'd done, he shifted his feet further apart and made his last swing a wide one.

WHOOSH-CRACK!

And ended up overcorrecting as more or less the entire paddle struck across Phera's right cheek instead.

"Damn. Seven-oh-seven on that last one, nice."

"Off-center, though. I say minus fifteen points."

"Cap?"

"No, no. Leave him be. I won't penalize the boy for enthusiasm."

"Thanks, boss."

Shi was looking a fair bit more confident than when he'd started as he sauntered away from Phera's steaming seat and passed the paddle on to the next contestant to come swaggering up.

As annoyingly frustrating as the pilot's lack of symmetry with his swats might've been, Phera took a profound glee in noting that he'd still managed to outdo Kelt. So pleased was she, that she actually spared a moment to look back at the petite senior engineer and wink. Her smile dented out of shape just a bit, however, when she adjusted her glance back over her other shoulder and saw Steph closing in on her, looking both eager and determined.

"Uh, hey there, doc," she hesitated, shuffling her knees a little further forward in an unconscious attempt to put some minute distance between her seat and Steph (which mostly just angled her cheeks further out and granted her audience a slightly better view of the thong running between them). "You, uh…"

She wanted to say "You promised not to cheat, right?", but didn't want to risk having to explain what that meant to the rest of her crewmates, so instead settled for a lame, "You're not going to let Shi show you up, are you?"

It was perhaps not the wisest idea to taunt someone who she still had faint traces of marks from the last paddling she'd taken from, but she felt that she had to at least to say something.

This *was* ostensibly a test of toughness, after all, wasn't it?

"Probably not. No."

Grinning, Steph favored her with a mysterious wink.

Then, ve did exactly the same thing as Kelt had, albeit not as harshly. Yanking her thong up just enough to be uncomfortable as ve brought the heavy paddle down in a casual swing.

WHOOSH-CRACK!

It made Phera wince and squeak, but not nearly as badly as Shi's first stroke had.

WHOOSH-CRACK!

"Oh!"

Again the paddle struck. Lower down this time, catching some thigh.

WHOOSH-CRACK!

"Phew!"

Before finding its home one final time higher up along the crowns of the engineer's bouncy bottom. All in all, it had taken less than ten seconds, and had been surprisingly mundane and underwhelming compared to the last time Phera had been on the receiving end of the small doctor's attention.

Almost suspiciously so.

"That's it for now."

Giggling, Steph patted her bare sit-spots with ver free hand, before handing the paddle off to Lem, who approached amid heavy footsteps.

While Steph's swats might've been (comparatively) light, they and the tauntingly enjoyable thong tugging had still been more than enough to help contribute to the damp spot between Phera's splayed thighs that had been growing ever since the start of her initiation. The pacing of this paddling was such that she had ample opportunity to savor the heat radiating from her gradually darkening bottom and thighs. And, between that and the delicious meal and pleasant buzz she was still riding from the alcoholic fruit smoothies she'd been enjoying with it, she was feeling loose and sassy.

"Hey, hey *Lem*onade," she singsonged (wringing an appreciative snort from Adryel), tossing her hair to hide the sudden thrill of horny panic being so flippant produced within her as the altogether distressingly buff first mate advanced on her like a looming asteroid. "Is your aim going to be okay without me being pinned down?"

SMACK! SMACK! SMACK! SMACK! SMACK!

Without so much as a warning, Phera's nearly bare, bright red caboose was assaulted with some of the hardest, fastest, most breath-haltingly agonizing hand swats it had ever experienced.

SMACK! SMACK! SMACK! SMACK! SMACK!

Followed by even more for good measure.

"Ack! Oh! Owie!"

Each meteor strike lifting a cheek so hard her hips were raised after it. All right on her extra-abused undercurves.

"Can I take my turn now, or do you have more to say?" Lem eventually asked, pausing to crack her knuckles, sending the muscles along her chest and arms rippling.

"Yes ma'am!" gasped Phera around a pained, panicky giggle, before realizing what she was saying and quickly amending. "I mean, no ma'am!"

That also didn't sound quite right either, she realized with a sudden burst of fretful accel-shift in her stomach. Was she saying no to her not taking her turn, or no to her not having anything else to say?

Shit!

"Er, uh, go right ahead," she hurriedly added as she relaxed back over the backs of the chairs propping up her hips.

The initial sting from Lem's rapid fire assault on her ass was starting to fade now, and with its departure came a fresh influx of reckless sass.

"I'm all yours," she managed to croon with a crooked grin, going so far to angle her seat just a bit higher toward the bigger woman.

SMACK!

This last bit of spirit earned her one final swat across the center of both cheeks. Then, amid the preemptive cheers and ominous chuckles of the others, Lem lined up the paddle.

The *WHOOSH!* preceding the impact this time was almost too fast to pick up. However, the resulting **CRACK!!!** was far less so, as the impact managed to push Phera a couple of centimeters forward across the chairs before she bounced back down onto her knees again.

Holy shit, that woman could *swing*!

"Okay... Ow," she eventually managed to grate after hissing in for several long seconds through clenched teeth; laughing into a deep groan as the heat from that first swat reached its crescendo and began to dissipate.

Though, worryingly, not entirely.

Heaving out an explosive sigh as her hands latched onto either side of the chair beneath her to avoid reaching back to verify that her butt was still attached to her body, she pushed herself back up into a proper all-fours position and continued with a shaky.

"Yep. Definitely... Ugh. Definitely felt that."

It was only two more. She was practically halfway there. She could do this.

Probably.

WHOOSH-CRACK!!!

"Fuck! Shit! Ow!"

Scratch that. She definitely couldn't.

The second swat had been exactly as powerful as the first had been. Bouncing her up off the padded seat of the chair she was kneeling on with the force of its impact.

"Oh my gods, Lem. Save... Save some for the others, would you?"

"There's plenty to go around, don't you worry, muffin."

As if to prove her point, the first mate gave one of the muffins in question a firm squeeze and a firmer jiggle.

"F-Fair enough..."

Despite her teasing, Lem still allowed Phera a few moments to (mostly) master the fury in her seat before lining up her final swat.

Tap... Tap... Tap...

The third, when it eventually came, was clearly delivered with the thoroughly yolked woman's full strength, as opposed to just most of it like the two previous swats had apparently been.

WHOOSH-CRACK!!!!

"Ohmygods, ohmygods, ohmygods!"

Phera's knees had definitely left their minimally padded perch with that final swat, and she continued to wriggle, whine, and babble out jumbled exclamations and expletives for half a minute after. Taunting the first mate as much as she had had perhaps been a *bit* of a mistake.

Then again...

Mmph. Okay. That was hot.

The redheaded roboticist wouldn't be forgetting the way her cheeks had rippled and bounced with the clear paddle's bone-jarring impact for a long, long time to come.

"Oooh, eight-eighty-five," announced the Captain in unabashed delight once everyone had gotten their fill of Phera's bobbing and weaving. "Well done, first mate. Well done."

"Yeah, no kidding," agreed Phera with a faux-pout. "You know, Cap, there *is* such a thing as a shutout. Maybe we should just, uh… say she won and see who can make the best ice pack instead?"

"Hmmm… I don't know how fair that would be to the remaining contestants, honey. Stray, Adri, Ob?"

The Captain's question was met with three simultaneous boos, and Phera felt several kernels of popcorn bounce off her sizzling seat.

"Oh, well, will you listen to that? Our new roboticist is outvoted. Such a shame."

"Damn right."

Snatching up the paddle from Lem, Straya gave the rest of the room a half-sarcastic bow.

"I was the one who brought this little critter home, so I guess it's time I started taking responsibility, huh?"

As she spoke, she put a hand on Phera's left cheek, petting and fondling it much more gently than any of the others had.

"Say, Cap, do I get any extra points for that?"

A resounding chorus of "No!"s and "Go fuck yourself!"s answered her question for her, prompting Straya to roll her eyes.

"Humph. See if I bring home any more cuties if that's how you ungrateful cunts are going to be."

She squeezed Phera much more possessively as she groused, before taking up a stance similar to Shi's, winding up with the glowing paddle in both hands.

WHOOSH-CRACK!

"Ack!"

Straya held back a little more than Lem, and wasn't quite as strong as she was in the first place, but her swat still landed as hard as any of the others had. Squarely across the centers of both of Phera's cheeks.

WHOOSH-CRACK!

"Oh my gods!"

Again.

WHOOSH-CRACK!!

"Eek!"

And again one final time, lower down on the howling engineer's sit-spots, overlapping with her upper thighs.

"Eight hundred!" Adryel cheered.

"Seven hundred and fifty," the Captain corrected with a smirk. "Minus fifty for the entitled whiner penalty."

"Whomp-whomp," taunted Phera in the brattiest deadpan she could manage, breath ragged as she clenched and unclenched her way through the lingering pain left behind by those three perfectly-executed paddle swats.

They would've been bad enough as is on a fresh pair of buns, but as thoroughly sore as she was already, they each had had her yelping; half-rising from her bent over position and cursing up a streak foul enough to make all of her crewmates applaud in approval.

"Better luck next time," she continued with an utterly unrepentant chuckle before melting back into position with the sort of long, contented sigh someone might give upon slipping into a hot bath after a long day's work.

"Gee, thanks."

SMACK!

Perhaps inspired by Lem's earlier display, Straya gave Phera an annoyed slap across her right cheek before stomping off and shoving the paddle into Adryel's muscular chest.

"All right, chica," they crooned as they slid in beside her, openly assessing her already starting to swell ass. "I just know we can beat Lem if we work together and believe in ourselves. Are you with me?"

"Isn't true strength showing that you don't *need* to be strong?" countered Phera, her internal pendulum of sass and anticipatory dread swinging rapidly toward the latter as she adjusted her position on the chairs, parting her thighs ever so slightly as she arched her back in an attempt to stretch her spine.

Then, sensing that her appeal to the pirate's nobility might not be enough, she decided to sweeten the deal.

"If you throw your swats, I'll totally take it easy on you when it's my turn."

That was an absolute lie, but Adryel didn't have to know that.

"Good try, but that ain't gonna help me tonight. Or you."

"But-"

*WHOOSH-**CRACK**!!*

"Ack!"

Adryel swung shockingly hard. Enough to take Phera's breath (and her supposedly nonchalant posture) away as the display above the two of them recorded eight hundred and seven.

*WHOOSH-**CRACK**!!*

"Holy shit!"

Their second swat was even harder. Pushing her forward roughly against the chair back in front of her.

There came a short pause then as Phera hissed and groaned, followed by a final *WHOOSH-**CRACK**!!* that had her very nearly bolting upright. She probably would have too, had the last couple of weeks not drilled the futility of trying to escape a spanking from her crewmates into her.

"Eight hundred and seventeen! Better watch your back, Lem. You're starting to lose your lead."

"I'm quivering in my boots. Really."

The first mate's deadpan was belied by the grin on her chiseled face.

"You… You…" gasped Phera, eyes still wide and face still stuck in an expression of disbelieving pain from that final swat.

She was exceedingly tempted to just lay there and let her ass sizzle and steam for the next thousand hours, but her pride as a pirate and her rapidly returning reckless excitement to see just how hard of a swat she could take without calling uncle had her pushing her ass back up in defiance.

"Fucking showoff," she grumbled petulantly, though with a broad grin over her shoulder to make sure that Adryel understood there were no actual hard feelings.

If anything, she was sorely tempted to offer to suck their cock right there and then. There was something about being physically carried along by a powerful swat like the buff chef had managed to deliver (twice!) that just spoke to her on a deep, emotional level.

"Told you. You just needed to believe in yourself."

Chuckles and groans accompanied this bit of saccharine wisdom. Followed by the soft, padding footsteps of Obette drawing closer.

"I'll not lie," he said as he swapped places with Adryel beside Phera's ever-swelling rear end. "I'm not going to win this, but I'm also not going to lose."

WHOOSH-CRACK!

True to the infiltrator's word, his first swat was harsh and hard. But, after Lem and Adryel's showings, was almost merciful by comparison. He even granted her a moment to catch her breath, twirling the paddle by the tip of its handle atop his open palm with casual ease as he waited for her to recover.

"And here I thought Adri was the showoff!" came a jeer from the sidelines.

"It's called *showmanship*."

Snatching the paddle out of the air just as it was starting to lose its balance, Obette gave a twirl on one foot, bringing the flashing implement around in a ballet-like movement and landing it against Phera's ass with the full force of the pirouette.

WHOOSH-CRACK!!

His aim was perhaps a little lopsided, but the overall strength of the impact was something to be reckoned with.

"Oh my gods!"

As Phera twitched and yelped and gasped her way through that supernova of a swat, she felt the infiltrator draw in closer and deftly slip his nimble fingers inside her panties.

"Now then..."

"Wait! Wait-!"

In a flash, her thong was down in the hollows of her knees, and her crack and thoroughly soaked pussy tasted open air.

"Hey! That's not allowed!" Lem snapped irritably

The Captain just shushed her, though.

"I know we wanted to save that for the final round. But, I also didn't tell anyone not to. So, it's fair."

"Humph."

Phera was just in the process of mirroring the first mate's harrumph, when her pouting was unceremoniously trampled on by Obette's singsonged, "Begging your pardon for the exposure, my dear."

*WHOOSH-**CRACK**!!*

Before wringing another frantic, high-pitched squeal out of her with the paddle's third and final impact.

"Ow, ow, owie!"

"Seven-thirty-five," the infiltrator announced cheerily. "See? What'd I tell you? A nice, respectable showing."

"That's one way of putting it."

Grumbling, Phera returned to her pouting as an unseen waft of station-cooled air glided along her glistening lips, making her shiver. Though literally every single one of her crewmates had seen her pussy before (and just about all of them had been inside of it in one way or another by now), that still didn't make the embarrassment of being so casually bared in front of all of them any less substantial.

"Way to not half-ass it, Ob."

"Yep, he definitely got your whole ass there," agreed Adryel to another round of groans and a snicker from Phera and the Captain.

That twirl *had* been pretty stylish, the engineer had to admit. But, she wasn't about to let that stop her from being petty.

"Shouldn't he still be given some sort of penalty for his blatant headspace tampering?" she whined, emphasizing her point by waving her totally naked hips toward where the Captain sat grinning on one of the tables behind her. "I mean, baring me without warning like that is pretty shocking."

Throwing a look toward the scoreboard to her left, she did some quick mental math.

"Surely a, oh… four hundred point deduction is called for?"

That would put the infiltrator a handful of points below Steph, and Phera was very much okay with that just then.

"Fortune favors the bold," was the Captain's sneering reply. "Fifteen bonus points for Ob."

Prompting Kelt to scoff.

"Is this whole thing just going to be determined by fiat in the end?"

This was met with no response. Instead, the Captain rolled her head around on her shoulders, popping her neck and splashing her neon white undercut onto one shoulder, before hopping down from her table and striding forward once again.

"Final round, swabbie," she declared. "Now, this *was* going to be the bare round. But, since our delightful field agent went ahead and ruined that. Hmmm…"

At an unseen cue from behind her, Phera heard the Captain's cadence rise excitedly.

"Ooooh! Great idea, Doctor."

This acknowledgement was accompanied by a round of snorts and half-suppressed cackles from the rest of the crew.

Uh-oh.

Phera was just about to demand to know what was so damn funny, when she felt the Captain's hands seizing hold of either of her burning, swollen, and extremely naked cheeks. With a firm squeeze that carried with it an unseen smirk, she spread them as wide as they would go, exposing all of her charms to their audience. Then Steph (who'd apparently come up with the Captain while she hadn't been paying attention) was there and pressing the tip of something smooth and rounded against her reflexively twitching anus.

Something whose surface was both cold and wet in an all-too-familiar way.

"Say 'ahhhh', sweet thing."

"Wha-?! Um, Captain, Steph? What's, uh… What's that?" she managed to choke, failing spectacularly to sound even remotely close to unconcerned.

With the heat from her cheeks still cranked high (radiating all throughout her body, and coalescing in an absolutely unbearable ache where she was all but dripping between her legs) the coldness of whatever was lubing the thing pressing against her aft airlock was magnified tenfold, making her tremble with need and trepidation.

"Don't worry."

Giggling, the slender crew doc reached over and tousled her artfully brushed out and loosely styled hair affectionately.

"No chemical warfare this time, I promise."

"Oh. I, um... Okay."

This revelation helped Phera relax enough to accept the entrance of the doctor's plug inside of her. Granted, that didn't exactly make it easy to take. Even absent any burning or tingling or the like, the object itself flared dramatically as Steph insistently pushed it deeper and deeper into her. Stretching her poor anus to the point where she was starting to feel some genuine pain despite her best efforts at staying fully at ease. Then, just when she was about to start pleading, it was suddenly past its widest point and the rest of it was sliding home without a problem as she instinctively cinched down around the narrow, fluted neck at its base.

"Phew!"

"First part's done," cooed Steph. "Now, hold on juuuust a sec while I-"

Phera felt ver tapping against the base of the plug ve'd just inserted, making her squirm and grit her teeth to keep from gasping before there came the faint *click* (felt more than heard) of a button at its base.

"Done!"

Ve moved back over to her head then and whispered into her ear.

"You're welcome."

Before kissing her blushing cheek.

"You... That's, uh..."

The sensation of the doctor's melodic voice murmuring so close to her ear, to say nothing of ver soft lips against her skin, sent cascades of tingles directly into Phera's aching clit. Which, combined with the very sizable plug she now had shoved inside of her for all to see, was doing little to diminish the dampness between her splayed thighs.

"Out of the way, brat!"

Phera heard a loud **CRACK!** and an accompanying howl of pain right in her ear as Steph stumbled back and danced away. The Captain having just applied the back of the paddle to ver while ve'd been hunched over, seemingly quite hard. With the sensors on the front surface of the business end, however, it hadn't affected her score.

Lucky me...

A moment later, she flipped the paddle around in her hand again, giving Phera barely enough time to brace herself before the next *WHOOSH-CRACK!!* exploded against her completely bare skin.

"Cyan!" Someone shouted from across the bar over the engineer's strangled yelp. "Seven hundred and fifty-eight, cyan!"

"Captainnnn!"

Phera cut loose with a truly spectacular whine then, dragging the taller woman's name out with all the disbelief and indignation she could summon as her freshly reignited cheeks wobbled and bounced behind her with her attempts to shake off the roiling plasma ravaging her already scalded seat. The thick plug lodged inside of her had prevented her from being able to even possibly mitigate some of the fury by clenching like she'd wanted to. Instead, it had just served as a silent reminder of how stuffed and on display she was as her bottom rippled freely beneath the force of her boss's devastatingly precise paddle swat.

"Yes?"

"You already had your turn!"

Hissing out a breath to recenter herself, Phera threw a glare to her left to confirm that the Captain's scores hadn't disappeared. They hadn't, but there was now a new line beneath the first set of three results displaying her latest score.

"Buck up, swabbie."

Sighing dramatically as she twirled the paddle through the air beside her, the Captain rolled her eyes for the benefit of their audience before fixing Phera with the biggest grin she'd seen on the woman yet.

"We're more than halfway there."

Her smile gained an edge of menace to it then that made Phera once again extremely grateful that she was on her side. Even if all of that menace was currently being directed between where her cheeks were parted just then.

"Granted, that's only by one lick. But, still."

WHOOSH-CRACK!!

"Aieee!"

"I think you get my point."

"Close," Phera just barely heard Lem remark over her own cry of pain, "*Really* close."

"Next color is..." Straya mused aloud in a thoughtful slur, before Adryel interjected. "Blue, dumbass!"

Whatever the other raider's response was, it was drowned out by the Captain's third and final *WHOOSH-CRACK!!!*

And the resulting chants of "BLUE! BLUE! EIGHT-OH-ONE, BLUE!" as the entire bar of pirates erupted into stomps and cheers.

"Shit fucking gods damn, *owie*."

Phera wasn't totally yet sure what all this color business was about, but she sure as hell understood eight-oh-one. Once again, the Captain's swats had been absurdly precise in their placement to the point where the swollen-cheeked engineer was pretty sure she could actually feel the outlines of the glowing paddle's business end still throbbing along the raised welts it had dug into her carmine skin.

Shifting on her knees, which had the embarrassing side-effect of sending some of her arousal dripping down along the inside of her left thigh, Phera huffed and threw a good-natured glower back over her shoulder at her leering crewmates.

"Why do you people keep calling out colors?" she demanded, doing her best to scowl through the smile she had on her face.

That last swat had been... a lot.

Maybe she'd offer to eat the taller woman out instead of bothering Adryel.

Or maybe she could do both?

Definitely going to be busy tonight.

By way of response, Kelt, who had just trotted up, held a slate in front of Phera's flushed, teary-eyed face. The sight of her own wine colored buttocks, puffed and swollen out around the head of a plug that slowly blinked a golden white greeted her. Followed by a slow motion recording of the paddle descending, her cheeks splashing out like water under a meteor strike, and then the head of the plug lighting up in a bright, cold cyan.

"You're an engineer. You should know the EM spectrum," she admonished with a maternal cluck of her tongue that didn't quite manage to smother her amusement.

Not bothering to wait for a response, she moved back behind her and began adjusting the plug with the brusque authority she always carried herself with around the ship. Straightening the oversized device gaping her back door wide while also twisting it around inside of her. Then, while Phera's eyes were still lodged where they'd rolled up into the back of her head, she brought the paddle down in three lightning-fast swats all against where red thigh met even redder sit-spot.

WHOOSH-CRACK!

WHOOSH-CRACK!

WHOOSH-CRACK!

"That's- Ah! Aieee!"

Between the shivers that the plug shifting around inside of her had produced, and Kelt's extremely efficient approach to dishing out no-nonsense discipline, Phera's initial response was lost amid a high-pitched, sustained howl and a whole lot of hip thrashing and boot flailing that earned her plenty of wolf whistles and catcalls from her fellow crewmates.

Kelt's swats hadn't been as hard as the Captain's, but with how thoroughly abused her sit-spots already were, they didn't have to be. They'd already been throbbing with the kind of ache that she knew meant sitting down was going to be a near impossibility for at least the next two days, and now they were blazing infernos once again.

Better make that a full week just to be sure...

"Green, cyan, and even more cyan, nice!" cheered Shi while Phera's head dropped so that she could use her brief respite to bat away the tears the tiny engineer had managed to knock loose from her.

"I... I..." she panted a moment later, craning her head back to try and see if there was any light being reflected off anything behind her. "Okay, fine. That's pretty cool."

She gave her bottom an exploratory clench then, and felt the thick mass inside of her continue to remain unyielding and undeniably thick in a way that made her pussy all but gush.

"Guess that explains the size. A battery, control board, and all the necessary input and output components would definitely make for a snug fit."

Phera couldn't help but burst into an endorphin and alcohol-fueled fit of giggles at her unintentional double entendre, shaking her hips to make it clear what she meant.

"Yep!" Steph chirped from somewhere in the back. "I got it on Polyphemus-3 if you want one for yourself!"

"You sure you aren't just gonna let her keep yours?"

"Hmmm... Maybe if she asks me *really* nicely."

"She does wear it pretty well."

"No kidding."

From amid that conversation, Phera heard Shi walk up behind her, along with another sharp *SMACK!* as Kelt gave her boy toy a nice hard swat along with the paddle she handed him.

"So..."

Letting out a much more confident sounding laugh compared to his last time up to bat, Shi took up his position behind Phera.

"Try for violet and see where we end up?"

"Isn't red a more traditional color to aim for when spanking someone?"

Ignoring the resurgence of nervous excitement fluttering around inside her stomach, Phera steadied her position on her makeshift spanking bench and locked eyes with the pilot, favoring him with her sauciest wink.

"Surely a big, tough, cutie pie like yourself can make a girl's bottom nice and red. I bet Kelt's shown you how that's supposed to look enough times by now, yeah?"

"Okay. You just lost yourself all of the sympathy I might've had for you. All of it."

Shaking his head in wry bemusement, Shi spread his legs into a steadying position about a shoulder's width apart and raised the paddle two-handed. He'd never seemed quite so traditionally masculine to Phera as he did at that moment with his pose upright and muscles coiled tight and ready for action.

This was worrisome.

And, honestly, kind of hot.

"Oooh, two-handed, eh? Nice!"

"Careful, Phera," someone else called with a laugh. "Looks like he's gonna try and send your ass into orbit."

"Damn right I am."

WHOOSH-CRACK!

Spurred on by the cheers of the others and the engineer's blatant sass, Shi brought the paddle crashing down with all his might across the middle of both her cheeks. Even going so far as to twist his hips into the follow through of the blow as he did so.

"Green!"

WHOOSH-CRACK!

His aim was slightly higher up this time.

"Green again!"

"Fuck! Shi, I-"

The pilot ignored her as he breathed in deeply, taking several seconds to collect himself, before winding up and bringing the paddle down one last time with a cheek-exploding *WHOOSH-CRACK!!*

"Cyan!" cheered Kelt. "That's my boy!"

Each **CRACK!** of the paddle had been accompanied by a simultaneous howl from Phera, and by the time this last one had found its mark, she was thoroughly grateful that each turn was limited to only three swats.

"Totally…" she panted, dragging in deep breaths through her mouth while her toes curled and uncurled behind her and a fresh rivulet of arousal slithered its way down the inside of her right thigh this time. "Totally worth it."

She winked again and blew Shi a kiss.

Now that he was passing the paddle off to Steph, he was totally fair game for teasing as far as she was concerned. He just smiled and blew a kiss of his own right back at her, before surprising her yet again by putting a hand on her now rough and ridged left cheek and giving it a possessive squeeze.

"Just remember this the next time you think of sassing me," he managed to say with a passably menacing timbre, helped significantly by his neatly trimmed fingernails digging in against her welts. "I don't need to cheat like Steph to paddle your pretty ass raw, you know."

Face going slightly pink, he leaned in nice and close so that only she'd be able to hear him, and added.

"Or fuck it."

"Heh. That's some pretty big talk, flyboy."

Snickering, Steph strode up beside the smirking pilot and made him jump as ve pinched his unsuspecting seat.

"Say, Cap, do I get a bonus for coming up with the new round two addition?" ve asked over ver shoulder, before reaching forward and tapping the glowing head of the plug a few times, making it shift inside of Phera as she hissed and gasped.

"Yep. Fifty points to this round. You did save the day and all."

"Yay!"

Steph bounced happily on ver heels.

"Now, let's see..."

WHOOSH-CRACK!

Ve seemed to have not given verself as much stimulant as Phera had at first feared, as the yellow light that apparently flashed between her cheeks had the audience all disappointed.

"Damn..."

Ver next two swats were each delivered sharply to one sit-spot and then the other.

WHOOSH-CRACK!

WHOOSH-CRACK!

And both were a mere green.

"Too much to drink?" someone taunted.

"Maybe..."

Steph's voice sounded oddly flat to Phera, as if ve was holding something back.

"Awww, leave ver alone," she sneered not unkindly instead of dwelling on that further, having already bounced back from the slender doctor's patty-cake session. "It's not ver fault ve can't handle ver booze."

She let loose with a snort that bordered on the slightly hysterical then as Lem advanced toward her. Her mini reprieve was well and truly over and her heart rate was already surging into overdrive.

"Don't worry, Steph. I'm sure Lem will be more than happy to pick up your slack. Though *some* people might argue that she really, really doesn't have to."

"Who's 'some', and does their name rhyme with bare-uh?" taunted the first mate with a deep rumble of laughter.

Phera felt Lem's large hand resting itself on a swollen undercurve then.

"As you said, though, I'm more than happy to make up for the doctor's piss poor showing. And, yes, Phera, I know I don't *have* to."

This pronouncement was accompanied by a squeeze hard enough to have her arms going rigid as if she'd just been electrified.

"I will, but I don't have to."

Her squeezing evolved into firm pats. Then, lifting the paddle, she gave her a moment to brace herself, before…

WHOOSH-CRACK!!!

"FUCK!"

Both cheeks blazed nova bright. The plug jarred painfully inside of her. And, the gasps from around the room rose up into a crescendo of cheers and whistles as the first mate's score came ever so close to meeting the violet threshold.

"Oh… my… g-gods…"

A few moments later, the second swat landed entirely against her left cheek, covering the whole of it and jerking Phera forward and to the right against her chair.

WHOOSH-CRACK!!!

Followed by another that was equally as vicious immediately thereafter, this time to her right cheek.

WHOOSH-CRACK!!!

Lem had given it her best shot with that first one, and the two that followed were slightly less brutal. Though, being focused on just one cushion each more than made up for it.

Phera doubted she'd be forgetting any of those swats for the rest of her life.

"Lem, honey, you always do such wonderful work," cooed the Captain, her face alight in unabashed mirth.

"That's one fucking way of putting it," agreed the trembling engineer without any heat, just barely managing to keep a lid on her tears as her bruised bottom continued to throb behind her with a deep and altogether intoxicating ache. "Sh… Showoff."

Her white undershirt clung to her like a second skin now, plastered to her spine and the curves of her breasts with sweat, silhouetting her firmly erect nipples for all to see should they just angle their heads a bit to their right.

One down. Just three more to go. You can do this, Phera.

"All right, all right, all right," came Straya's familiar drawl, her words sounding fairly slurred by now as she stumbled forward on graceless legs.

Apparently, she'd been making use of Phera's free drinks pass while the others had been pummeling her shapely ass.

"I... I'm gonna..."

A hand clutched each of Phera's cheeks and squeezed them together around the plug.

"Mmmm... Hot. *Engine* hot."

Phera felt the woman's scarred face nuzzling against her bruised, battered, and white hot bottom.

"And soft..."

There came a good deal more fondling then.

"Wait... Am I supposed to-? Oh, right."

The muscular raider's hands didn't leave Phera's seat, but her face did.

"Um, where'd Lem put the, um, you know, the thing?"

At this, the Captain loosed a long, low sigh.

"Someone please put the town drunk to bed. I'll deal with her tomorrow."

Jeers and chuckles from all around answered this exasperated order.

"Wha-? Wait... No... Cap, I can totally..."

Lem and Adryel stepped up and pulled Straya away then, the latter of whom continued to cling resiliently onto Phera's ass for a moment or two more before finally giving in.

"I love you, though!" she called out as they dragged her away. "Leggo! I can walk, seriously..."

As Straya was escorted back to the ship, Phera was left to stew bare assed and plugged for the viewing pleasure of the rest of her crewmates as they went back to singing karaoke and raiding the bar. At one point, she tried to push herself up from her perch to join them, but that was swiftly shut down by the Captain.

"Oh no you don't."

"But-!"

SMACK!

"We aren't finished with your initiation yet, swabbie," she replied, lounging with one elbow against the small of her back while her other hand idly toyed with her glistening lips. "Besides, it's fun making you edge."

Suiting actions to words, the Captain slid a pair of fingers inside of her, twitching and curling them as Phera's breathing hitched and her muscles tensed. However, just as she was about to come, she withdrew her thrusting digits and treated her to a pair of cruel, and truly unnecessarily hard swats to either cheek.

SMACK-SMACK!

SMACK-SMACK!

Adding insult to injury as Phera opened her mouth to complain, she found the tall pirate's soaked fingers pushed between her lips with strict orders to clean up her mess.

Which she did.

Albeit with a face hot enough to melt tungsten.

"There's a good girl," she cooed once her fingers had been sufficiently cleansed of the engineer's arousal, patting her on the side of the face with a wicked grin. "Behave yourself and I might just reward you later."

"Yes ma'am…"

While the Captain delighted in torturing her, Kelt at least took enough pity on Phera to bring her a drink to help pass the time once their commanding officer had finished having her fun. Even if she had to drink it while still bent over, she wasn't one to look a gift horse in the mouth and accepted the tumbler with a grateful smile.

"Oh, wow, that's *really* good!" she marveled after the first sip, smacking her lips and wiggling her hips as the smooth whiskey slid down her throat to warm her stomach.

"It damn well better be," the older woman chuckled, her tone curt with affection as she sauntered back toward Shi, swatting her as she went. "That booze is old enough to be your grandfather."

—

Some twenty or so minutes later, Lem and Adryel finally returned to the bar and the crew cook took up their rightful place at Phera's now slightly cooled off backside.

"Sorry for the delay, ma'am. I'll be your new attendant."

Phera, who'd endured the awkwardness of remaining in position with her legs spread all that time while Straya was being sorted out was more than ready for them as they hefted the paddle in their hands behind her.

"Are you *sure* you're not thirsty, Adri?" she wheedled with an accompanying hip waggle. "I wouldn't hold it against you if you opted to hydrate this round, you know. Eight-seventeen isn't anything to be ashamed of. Why not show some cabinmate solidarity and bow out gracefully like Straya did?"

"You're shaking that thing like that while calling *me* the thirsty one?" they chuckled, giving her much-abused rump a crisp swat.

SMACK!

"Nah, you've already played your get out of jail free card. Time to serve the rest of your sentence, chica."

"Fiiiine. Humph."

"That's the spirit!"

WHOOSH-SMACK!!

Adryel's paddle swats were…

Well, they were three more paddle swats.

Like all the ones before, discounting Lem's asteroid pulverizers, Kelt's stingers, and Steph's relative respite. They were three hard, loud, even cracks that left Phera howling and her cheeks turning even redder. All three were cyan, and all three were thoroughly painful. Then, without any further ceremony, they were passing the paddle off to Obette.

"Oh thank every fucking god and devil there is, it's another tech!"

Even with the infiltrator's penchant for flare and respectable paddle swats, the prospect of reaching the end of what she very much hoped was the final round of her initiation had Phera flushing with fresh bravado and daring as she caught her eleventh or twelfth wind of the evening.

She could totally do this!

"No more panties to pull down this time, Ob."

Grinning back at him, she thrust her hips up in defiant challenge.

"Do your best to at least hit yellow, yeah? If you hit blue, I'll even buy you a drink."

Phera giggled with this last bit of (to her, at least) very clever sass. She knew that she was absolutely courting danger by being so obnoxious, but she was way too tipsy, horny, and brimming with endorphins to care. The end was in sight, and she'd made it.

She was feeling inordinately proud of herself for doing so, actually. Even if she'd done it with more complaining, tears, and yelps than she'd maybe perhaps have hoped to, she'd still proven to everyone that she was tough enough to be a Blazar Bitch.

"Blue? Well, I suspect you'll be by the end of this evening, among other shades. As for myself... Let's find out together, shall we?"

Obette was starting to sound pretty drunk himself, and his swats were slightly off this time.

WHOOSH-CRACK!

"Ah!"

Not that it mattered much when that absurdly heavy paddle was exploding against the backs of her thighs.

WHOOSH-CRACK!

"Geez!"

And then mostly on point, angled across both cheeks.

Finally, after a much longer pause there came the last *WHOOSH-CRACK!* Of the evening.

"Oh! Oh! Yeesh!"

Impressively enough given his obviously inebriated state, the infiltrator still managed to reach the lower cyan threshold with that final swat. His previous ones only being a mostly respectable green.

"Well, at least we didn't lose. Did we, dearest?"

"If you- Ah! Say so.."

Phera jerked a little as he set the paddle aside and gripped one of her thighs with a hunger she immediately recognized. It was just too bad they weren't back in their cabin just then.

Then again... Given this crew and where Obette's other hand was starting to wander, that might not matter.

"Yes, yes!" agreed the Captain, hands clapping as she grinned a very wide half-grin. "Excellent work, all of you. It's so reassuring to know that I run a crew of spectacular muscle babes."

"Fuck yeah you do, Cap!"

"Even so," the lanky pirate continued with a chuckle. "I'd say it's pretty obvious that we've got ourselves a clear winner, *and* a clear loser."

"Hell yes we do!" agreed Phera with a laugh of her own, pushing herself up into a kneeling position on the chair for what felt like the first time in hours as she reached back and tentatively massaged her still sizzling seat.

She spared a moment to take in a breath, compose herself, and wipe away as much of the moisture still clinging to her face with the backs of her hands as she could, before throwing a neon bright smile over her shoulder at her crewmates.

"Congratulations, first mate," she beamed, before her smile turned sinister. "And to you too, *Doctor*."

She was going to enjoy making Steph howl.

"Thank you, thank, you."

Grinning from ear to ear, Steph gave the gathered pirates a banal, awards ceremony wave.

"Really. I do appreciate it."

Then, turning to Lem, ver grin grew absolutely luminous.

"I'm calling it in."

All those assembled looked at ver, and then at Lem, confused.

Lem just looked blank.

"You what now?"

Steph folded ver arms under ver modest breasts and swiveled one shoe against the floor.

"Do you *really* want me to remind you in front of everyone?"

At that, comprehension struck, and Lem's eyes went wide.

"Ooooh!"

Phera's violet eyes went wide and giddy right along with hers as she leaned into Obette's chest to get a better look at the crew doc and first mate.

"Don't tell me the oh-so-responsible Lem let Steph take the blame for something she did?"

Both pirates gave Phera a very sharp glare at her taunting singsong. Though, Steph's was far more playful than Lem's.

"YOU STAY OUT OF THIS!" came the first mate's heated reply, one tinged with more than a hint of embarrassment that was all the cuter on her for it's out of placeness.

Locking eyes with Steph once again, Lem seemed about to say something more, but at a quirk of one platinum brow, decided it was a bad idea. Steph, in turn, brought ver hands down to ver hips in a remarkable imitation of one of Kelt's favorite stances while lecturing.

"So," ve said, all business even as ver grin took on a decidedly shit-eating edge to it. "If you don't mind, shall we ask the Captain to switch our names on the scoreboard?"

All eyes turned to Lem, and then to the Captain. Who, standing near the back of the room where she'd just poured herself another lemony-looking drink in a thin, spiraling glass, gave one of her widest half-grins yet. Lem returned the taller woman's smile with an outraged, disbelieving glare. But, her ire just rolled off the pirate leader's shoulders as she bounced her bemused gaze from her first mate, to Steph, and then to Phera.

"Mister Obette, if you would be so kind."

She flicked a pair of fingers toward the scoreboard.

"Aye aye!"

Phera lost her support as the infiltrator busied himself with carrying out the Captain's orders, but she didn't mind in the slightest. Not when she saw Lem and Steph trade scores. Instead, she began to giggle.

Well, more like cackle.

She was drunk, and horny, and high on endorphins and her newfound status as a full-fledged pirate.

Slipping off her makeshift bench, she opted to kick off the thong that had dropped down to her ankles. It wasn't like she wasn't used to her crewmates seeing her in just a shirt and a ruby red ass anyway. Plus, there was no way in hell she was going to try and put her shorts back on until she'd had at least two or three more drinks and the swelling in her seat had started to go down.

Maybe she'd make herself an ice pack to go along with her next slushy!

"You and I are going to have soooo much fun together, Lem," she managed to get out with a straight face, before dissolving into another fit of giggles and having to cover her mouth with both hands to stop herself from devolving into even further hysterics.

"Yes. We will."

Lem's tone was absolutely murderous as she locked eyes with Phera and then Steph, before returning her full attention to the engineer.

Rolling her eyes, she took a heavy step toward the bench.

"All right then, let's do this."

The implications of her wording took a moment to penetrate Phera's drunkenness, but only a moment. Lem was still going to be the first mate after tonight. Which meant she'd still be in charge of shipboard discipline. That, and she was most definitely not above playing favorites.

Or disfavorites.

This realization was the only thing that stopped Phera from repeating the Captain's earlier line about getting into the position she knew she belonged in. Instead, she busied herself with collecting up the paddle from where Obette had set it down, before rounding on the first mate and taking a moment or two to appreciate how well she filled out the seat of her dark cargo pants.

"Honestly, it's probably better this way," she said, dragging her eyes up from the muscular woman's iron cheeks to grin at her sheepishly. "At least with you I can swing as hard as I want without worrying I'm going to hurt you."

Some people could be such whiny babies about getting spanked, but she figured it was best to assume that Lem could take it at least half as well as she could dish it out. Still, she found herself adding, "Um, right?"

"It'll take more than one half-drunk gearhead to break my ass."

"I volunteer!" piped up Adryel then, pitching their voice to sound like Obette's as they crouched behind him.

This produced a proper round of laughter from the crew, easing much of the tension Phera had been trying to hold at bay. And, as the mirth dissipated, she gestured with her paddle toward the chairs of her makeshift spanking bench.

"You can go ahead and drop those pants right now before you get into position if you want. I know I technically got all of my swats on the bare, but I won't make you pull your panties down if you don't want to, *Lem*on cake."

A full armada of butterflies stirred to life inside her stomach as she spoke, but she did her best to mimic the Captain's swaggering half-grin instead of blanching at her own boldness.

"Pull 'em down if you want, muffin. It's all the same to me."

Lem stepped up to the chair, and let out a long sigh as she bent her tall, thick frame over it, resting her palms against the slightly damp seat Phera had recently vacated.

"Um… R-Right."

Juggling the oversized paddle, Phera peeled down the first mate's trousers. Two extremely round cheeks bounced free as she did so. Still high and muscular as hell, but quite a bit softer and jigglier looking than they had clothed. She wore a set of lacy black panties that covered her crack and crotch with room to spare, but left most of the undercurves of her impressive cheeks bare and bulging.

Every eye was on Phera now, and not a breath could be heard.

I… Might've made a mistake.

Swallowing to remoisten her suddenly dry mouth, she shook herself out of her stupor as she scrambled to recenter herself.

Oh well, no turning back now.

"Muffin, huh?" she pressed with a shaky snicker as she tucked the paddle under one arm and seized hold of the delicate waistband of Lem's panties, deciding that if she was going to die, she might as well go out in style. "Then I suppose that'd make you burnt buns."

"Nope, that's still definitely you," quipped Adryel, receiving nods of agreement all around.

"Definitely."

"Not even close."

"Humph. Whatever."

Pouting, Phera jerked the brief pair of panties down past their owner's surprisingly soft cheeks and to the first mate's ankles. Squatting down as she did so and shamelessly sneaking a peek between her legs.

"We can have two sets of burnt buns."

As she straightened up and retrieved the paddle from between her bicep and left breast, Phera threw a smug look back over her shoulder toward Steph.

"Well, I guess technically it would be *three* sets of buns, now wouldn't it?"

Steph gave Phera a malevolent expression that clearly said "don't push your luck."

"If we're using stupid food metaphors," Lem said meanwhile. "Then neither of you scrawny little bitches could warm up a sandwich with all day and a toaster oven."

Before huffing in exasperation.

"Are we going to do this, or should I go get another drink?"

"I tried doing that once with a girlfriend back in college," Phera quipped, keeping her tone breezy and conversational despite the flash of annoyance the other woman's challenge to her temporary authority produced within her. "Definitely wouldn't recommend it. You'll end up with a bunch of rum and cola going up your nose and then get extras for breaking position."

Shifting over to Lem's left side, Phera adopted her best power stance, planting either foot a shoulder's width apart and giving her gathered crewmates another unobstructed view between her legs. She was far too busy adjusting her sweaty grip on the smooth, angled handle of the paddle to care just then, however. Instead, focusing entirely on adopting a two-handed grip just like she'd seen Shi using earlier, she raked her eyes over her target in search of the best spot to swat.

"So… I get six of these, yeah?" she asked the Captain while bringing the paddle up and down in slow, smooth movements to perfect her aim. "Three for each round?"

She very much doubted she'd get a chance like this ever again, and she was determined to make sitting down for Lem at least a *little* difficult for the next hour or two if she could.

"Three is plenty. But since it's your special day, I'll let you have one to grow on," countered the Captain. Before turning a teasing grin on Lem. "It's your initiation. That's basically the same thing as a birthday."

She took a deep sip from her ridiculously helical glass and leaned back against the bar.

"Hop to it, swabbie. Lem's not the only one starting to get impatient, you know."

"Oh! Um, right!"

Blowing out a breath and taking in another in quick succession, Phera squared her shoulders and drew the paddle up parallel with her head.

"Hold on tight. This one's going straight to cyan, so hang on!"

—

In the end, Phera never did manage to crack the cyan threshold, but she didn't mind. Paddling the first mate had been an absolute blast! Still, she did her best to make sure that Lem was all right after she'd received the last of her swats. Helping her up and hugging her tight while quietly confirming that there were no hard feelings between the two of them as she did so.

"You know that was just for fun, right? I'd never try and boss you around for real, I promise."

Lem just patted her back and rumbled out another low chuckle.

"No. No hard feelings," she said with the frostiest, most threatening smile the engineer had ever seen, before reaching down to grab her by both cheeks. Hoisting Phera up so that she straddled her broad waist as she held her in the air by her seat, squeezing hard. "But this is *far* from over."

"Heh. Fair enough."

Matching her smirk, Lem leaned forward so that their foreheads touched, eyes dancing with fondness and more than a hint of kind irritability.

"Welcome aboard, muffin."

CHAPTER TWENTY-TWO

CHARGES ACCRUED

Operating a Class 2 Firearm Without a License

The morning after her initiation party (well, afternoon, since nobody was getting up even close to early after that much drinking), Phera awoke to her tongue feeling like sandpaper and her face nestled between the Captain's breasts beneath her absurdly high thread count bed sheets; sore as hell, but profoundly satisfied.

She'd really done it.

She was officially a pirate!

"Uggggh..."

She was also officially hung the fuck over.

"*Ow.*"

Most details after that second glass of whiskey Kelt had given her blurred together around the edges, but Phera vaguely recalled being dragged by the scruff of her neck into the Captain's cabin once she and the rest of the crew had stumbled back to the Mayhem sometime after the station's sunsim started kicking back to life. The beatific smile on the snoozing pirate's face now seemed to suggest that she'd done an excellent job showing off just how happy she was to be a member of the crew, but Phera couldn't help but notice with a tiny thrill of submissive pride and bratty indignation that she'd neglected to allow her to take out her plug.

What had she said again?

Organizing her thoughts was an uphill battle just then, but after another groan and a couple attempts to remoisten her arid mouth, something along the lines of liking her cabin girls with "luminous personalities" drifted back to her.

And here I thought Adri was the crew's resident smartass.

Rolling over onto her back and taking a moment to revel in the undeniable bulk lodged firmly between her still tender cheeks, Phera smiled up at the curving ceiling and sighed.

"There are definitely worse places to wake up after a heavy night of drinking, I suppose."

"Mmmm… That's the spirit."

The Captain, a lot more awake than Phera had realized or else just way better at shaking off sleep than she was, tossed back her sheets without warning then and rolled over to straddle her newly-minted privateer; pinning her wrists above her head with one hand while the other went straight between her thick thighs.

"And how is my favorite cabin girl feeling this fine afternoon? Piratical? Marauderous? Buccanneery?"

With each increasingly comical adjective, the Captain's long, nimble fingers twitched inside of Phera, wringing out a gasp from the younger woman as her amber eyes bored into her with an intensity that further heightened the toe-curling ecstasy the heel of her palm was producing as it ground against her clit with just the right amount of pressure.

"M-Maybe a little- Oh gods! A little plunderous…"

"Plunderous, eh?"

The Captain's hand grew frustratingly still against Phera's smoldering mound as she chuckled languorously, her fingers still knuckle-deep inside of her.

"You're going to have to do better than that."

"Raiderific?"

"Oh, come now, that's not even a word."

Whimpering at being denied when she was so close, Phera's hips rolled with shameless abandon beneath the older woman's touch in an attempt to finish the job herself.

"Uh-uh-uh."

Causing the Captain's grin to widen into something stomach-flutteringly carnivorous as she shoved her roughly back down against the mattress with an authority that would not be denied.

"We've talked about this," she tutted, drawing in close enough for her breath to tickle Phera's pouting lips. "You get to come when *I* say so."

"Y-Yes ma'am!"

"Good girl."

Her fingers twitched inside the desperate pirate again then, causing her hips to buck on reflex as she closed the distance to her captain, capturing her lips in a desperate, wordless plea. A plea that was answered with a tongue pushing its way inside her mouth and another taunting twitch that very nearly sent her careening over the edge before the Captain drew back enough to nip at her lower lip.

"Awww, look at you," she cooed, withdrawing her hand from between the plaintive younger woman's legs and cutting off her protests by shoving her glistening fingers inside her mouth. "This is your own fault, you know. If you didn't look so cute when you're desperate, I wouldn't have to be so mean."

Phera very much doubted this, but was way too busy trying to wring an orgasm out of herself through creative clenching of her pelvic muscles to do much more than huff out an exasperated breath through her nostrils.

"Yes! That's the look!"

Loosening her grip on Phera's wrists and retrieving her thoroughly cleansed fingers from her mouth, the Captain eased her lithe frame up along the engineer's torso until her clean-shaven pussy nestled firmly against her petulant pout.

"Now then, why don't you show me just how much you feel like coming, and *maybe* I'll be nice."

———

After the greasiest breakfast-lunch on station she and her crewmates could find, along with a cocktail of painkillers and saline patches from a benevolent (and equally hungover) Doctor Steph, the latest member of the Blazar Bitches had been informed that with her newfound official crewmember status came the requirement that she travel armed while not aboard ship. Upon hearing this, Phera had immediately declared that she wanted to carry a big, fuck off coilgun. Much to the amusement of Lem, who'd countered that she could carry a weapon that wouldn't tip her over, so long as she could prove that she was capable of actually using it without blowing off her toes.

"I'm not about to catch a second asshole just because you don't know what you're doing in a firefight," she'd grumbled good-naturedly over a mountain of scrambled eggs and entirely too much ketchup.

Which, Phera had to concede, was a pretty good point. Luckily, she knew just the former soldier to talk to about getting herself nice and deadly.

—

"So, this place we're headed to…"

"Anne's."

"Yeah, Anne's."

Stepping off a motorized pedestrian pathway, Phera tucked some of the curls that had escaped the ponytail she'd pulled the rest of her hair into behind an ear in an attempt to keep her hand from hovering near the grip of the coilgun holstered against her right thigh. Even with the livid marks from her initiation a couple nights ago on full display along the backs of her thighs and the handful of centimeters of cheek peeking out from beneath the scandalous pair of short-shorts she had on that afternoon, the cold weight of the weapon shifting against her bare skin with every swaggering step she took had her feeling like a total badass Blazar Bitch.

"I'm not going to have to, like, prove myself to a bunch of crack shot regulars or anything, am I?"

"Maybe, maybe not."

Straya shrugged and favored her with one of her more pointed sardonic half-grins.

"Business at Anne's tends to pick up toward the evening. So, if you want to impress people, you'd better spend the next ninety minutes paying close attention."

Cutting loose with a nervous giggle, Phera flashed the taller woman a sloppy salute.

"Ma'am, yes ma'am!"

SMACK!

Earning herself an offhanded swat to the seat of her shorts for her troubles.

"Brat."

"Hehe. You love it."

"Sure do."

SMACK!

"Now, come on. We're almost there."

Straya took Phera down one last lift (a cramped conglomeration of exposed iron scaffolding and an unfinished, rough metal platform inside a round stone shaft), and then out onto another steel-lined corridor in the darker, lower-ceilinged cavern below. The air was damper here closer to the asteroid's center of gravity. Not to mention a good deal colder too, causing the engineer to slightly regret her tastefully slutty choice of outfit as her nipples pebbled visibly beneath her top.

Only just slightly, though.

Straya seemed to like it, which made the series of goosebumps on her exposed arms, legs, and midriff totally worth it.

"Up here."

Palming a handful of Phera's right cheek where it spilled out of her shorts, Straya guided her toward one of the doors excavated into the exposed stone wall of the corridor. Overhead, a neon sign with writing in three different languages Phera recognized but couldn't read, along with a stylized depiction of an ancient revolver, blinked merrily down at the two of them. The well-oiled hatch slid aside at their approach, and she used the motion of turning to fit her hips through the narrow front entrance of the shop as an excuse to slip out of Straya's grasp before she could give her still tender cheeks a proper squeeze. Only to stop short a meter past the threshold when she got her first proper look at where she'd just wandered into.

While the iconography above the door might've been ancient, the rifles and small arms (and was that a sword?) lining three of the four walls in the little shop were anything but.

"Oh... Shit," she breathed, heart rate accelerating as her face split into a broad grin at the sight of all the neatly tagged (and *very* illegal back where she was from) weapons.

She'd been wondering where all the cool armaments had been hiding whenever she'd gone shopping in the local markets around the station's entertainment mod. All the action vids she'd ever seen had led her to believe that an out of the way Proxward port like Marcos would be absolutely wall-to-wall with contraband and illegal arms. But, up until then, she hadn't seen any that weren't already strapped to someone's hip or the small of their back.

"Well, hey there, Straya. Long time no see," came the lazy drawl of the woman standing behind the counter at the back of the store, looking up from a piece of coilgun she'd been cleaning with an oily rag.

"Been busy, Anne. Legitimate businesswoman work is a real pain in the ass it turns out. No time off."

"That so?"

The woman, Anne, rolled her eyes and went back to her project. A riot of color and lines undulated their way down arms corded with muscle and peeked out over her collarbones as she worked, intricate tattoos that captured the eye and complimented the tight black curls and blue highlights atop her head. Her face had a lean, powerful symmetry to it, with dark eyes that somehow looked both sleepy and alert all at the same time.

Noting Phera's continued, open-mouthed staring at her wares, an evil grin spread across her metallic blue painted lips.

"So, who's your friend with the big eyes and cute rack?"

This time it was Straya's turn to roll her eyes, laying a hand on Phera's shoulder and pulling her in slightly closer.

"My big-eyed, cute-racked friend can handle her own introduction."

"Oh! Uh, hi, I'm Phera," supplied the engineer brightly, raising a hand to wave before remembering that she was on a station and bowing her head slightly instead. "I'm a, uh… *coworker* of Straya's."

She covered her embarrassment at her ham-fisted attempt at subterfuge by giving a self-deprecating shrug as she allowed herself to be led toward the counter where Anne stood.

"And, uh, yeah. Can definitely confirm that work's been a pain in the ass a few times these last couple weeks."

Which at least made the other woman snort.

"I noticed. Your handiwork, Stray?"

"Some of it. Sweet cheeks here tends to get around among the crew."

"Lucky gals," answered Anne with a smirk. "Well, hope you last longer than the last one did."

"Last one?" squeaked Phera, going rigid as the heat that had been rushing into her face drained away all at once. "Um… *What* last one?"

"Kidding, hon. Kidding."

"Ah! Oh, I see. Okay, phew!"

Phera felt her chest flutter as Anne winked at her, before turning her attention back to Straya.

"So, here to stock or shoot?"

"Shoot," she replied, sweeping back her dark hair from her forehead with her free hand.

It was starting to get longer, Phera noticed. She could comb her fingers through it pretty easily now. Not to mention grab a good fistful if she was feeling saucy, though that hadn't gone quite so well for her the last time she'd tried.

"Five milis, variable. Just give us a box."

"Oh ho, getting the new legitimate businesswoman acquainted with your totally unrelated hobby?"

Anne batted her eyelashes a few times before bending down and retrieving a compact box of ammunition from under the counter and sliding it toward them.

"How about you just shut the fuck up and let us shoot, yeah?"

Anne sighed.

"Charming as ever."

Straya, in turn, made a rude gesture at the other woman as she snatched up the ammunition, but they both just laughed.

"Have fun, you two."

—

The shooting range Straya led her into looked a lot like it might have once been on its way toward becoming some sort of equipment storeroom or vehicle hangar to Phera. There was a cargo lift sized rectangular outline etched into the ceiling, and only about two thirds of the floor had been leveled out. Lights were set up along the walls to illuminate the cavernous space, along with four torsos made of some sort of translucent ballistics gel near the back wall's left side. While on the other stood an empty space with some sort of motorized-looking equipment folded up against the floor. (Moving targets maybe?) Needless to say, the stone wall behind the targets was riddled with pits, cracks, and an assortment of different sized holes.

"You've never shot anything before, right?"

Straya's question drew Phera out of her attempts to join the disparate bullet holes into some sort of design in her head.

"Only in sims," she confirmed with a sheepish grin, thumb fiddling with the snap on her holster as the lingering scent of ozone from countless coilgun discharges made her nose wrinkle. "I think I get the gist, though. You point, you shoot, and if you do it right, you hit what you're aiming at, yeah?"

She was perhaps being a bit blasé, but it was either that or be a total nervous wreck, and she was already bouncing on her heels enough as is. On the bright side, though, the chill air of the range felt nice on her semi-exposed cheeks as they jiggled with her anxious movements. The slight ache each wobble produced helping to center her just a bit.

Straya snorted as she ushered her up to the white line painted across the cavern floor, positioning the two of them in front of a pair of low tables facing stationary targets.

"Well, you're not exactly wrong. Though, if you didn't know that much already, I don't think I'd let you outside, much less handle a firearm."

"Charmer," teased Phera in response, making the corners of her fellow pirate's iron gray eyes crinkle in amusement.

"Okay, so. First issue we need to sort out is hand-eye coordination. Second is recoil. That second one's where you'll probably have the most trouble, assuming you've got an ocular to deal with the first. Steph said you've got a visual AR?"

Straya gave her a curious look then, clearly searching for the telltale scars from implant surgery.

"Mmhmm!"

Angling her head up and to the side, Phera brushed the backs of her fingertips across the discreet, gold-plated connection port embedded into her skin just below her right ear.

"Great. Manual feedback, or just ocular?"

"Uh… I think just ocular?" she replied, answering the taller woman's second question with far less confidence than she had her first. "I got it for hallucinographic interfacing with systems when I was twelve. Is that going to work?"

"If it can layer AR feedback on top of your vision in real time, then yeah, that'll work. You can interface with the targeting and orientation packages to dial in your aim."

That had Phera grinning.

"I mean, I've got the implant, so I might as well use it, right?"

Rather than smile, the corners of Straya's mouth tightened, drawing the scar there into stark relief.

"It's still going to take weeks to get you up to snuff," she countered in a surprisingly stern tone. "The interfacing mod helps, but you still need training and muscle memory."

"Yes, yes, I'm sure I won't be drilling headshots immediately, Stray. That's obviously day two stuff."

Undeterred by the other woman's dour countenance, Phera snickered a little as a memory from a couple nights ago bubbled back up.

"Then again, if Steph could nail you from across the room all on ver own, maybe syncing up my implant is overkill? The Cap said her dead grandma could've made that shot, and I figure that's probably about as hard of one as I'm ever likely to need to make, yeah?"

Straya just shrugged at that, still not smiling.

"Depends on if we get boarded by InterSec or not."

Which managed to finally wipe the smirk off of Phera's face.

"They… They wouldn't really do that, would they?"

Straya remained deadly serious.

"Hasn't happened yet, but that doesn't mean it won't."

She shook her head then, countenance growing cloudy as she continued to regard the shorter woman who was currently nibbling fretfully at her lower lip in front of her.

"Look, Phera. You said you thought you needed self-defense lessons. Cap agreed. I agreed. But, if you just want to learn how to shoot at targets, let me know now and we'll do that."

Drawing her own coilgun, she set it onto the low table beside her almost as a challenge.

"So, let's clear this up right now. Do you want to learn how to *shoot*, or do you want to learn how to *fight*?"

"I… Sort of assumed they were the same thing?"

"Not even close. Actual combat is…"

At this, Straya let out a long, slow breath, eyes going distant.

"It's dirty. You don't get time to think. You hesitate, you die. You try and deescalate, you die. If you're not ready to immediately do whatever it takes to hurt whoever's on the other side of that line, and *keep* hurting them until they're fucking dead, you die. No second chances. No miracle rescues. Just you bleeding out in some god forsaken hab while the other guy gets to go home."

Shrinking away from her cabinmate, Phera kicked at a loose shell casing on the floor while she attempted to gather her thoughts. Suddenly, memories of Sergeant Ember's body jerking back under a hail of his own reflected gunfire rose up unbidden in her mind's eye, and she blanched as a cold, nauseous dread she hadn't felt since that fateful hijacking half a lifetime ago twisted at her insides.

"I'm… Um… If I'm being totally honest with you, Straya," she forced herself to say when it became clear that the other woman wasn't going to let her get away without answering her question, pushing out a deep breath and looking up again with what she hoped was the level of seriousness her friend was expecting of her. "I don't think I have it in me to kill someone."

Her cheeks colored then, and she inexplicably felt silly for admitting that for some reason.

"I mean, I feel bad just yelling at people when I'm really mad at them, and I was a total mess that one time I accidentally gave someone a black eye in gym. So, uh… Yeah. I'm sorry if I misled you, but I really would rather just learn how to shoot at targets and know that if I absolutely had to, I could probably hit someone rushing at me or you, or whatever. I, um… Maybe something like that stun gun Shi has might be more my speed?"

Straya's expression upon hearing this was surprisingly complicated. Disappointed? Relieved? Ashamed? It seemed like a weird mix of all three, and it was several long, interminable seconds more before she finally replied.

"Sure."

Her smile as she spoke was even weaker than usual, but seemed to somehow run far deeper as well.

"Well, they're both point-at-the-shithead-and-pull-the-trigger weapons, so this should still work for practice. We'll just keep things on the lower settings. Don't want to teach you to compensate for more recoil than you'll ever have to deal with, you know?"

"I think I'd like that."

"Great."

Straya patted her again, and her smile made an attempt to pull itself up from bleak to just weary.

"So, want to learn how to load a Darner Mark Two, or should I do it for you?"

"Oh, I absolutely want to learn!" declared Phera, relief flooding into her like a punch to the gut with the taller woman's smile. "Is *that* what this thing is called?"

She hadn't thought to ask any more questions about her coilgun after she'd confirmed with Straya that it wasn't going to go off by accident while she was walking around. Ever the gearhead, though, she thumbed open the clasp on her holster and drew the surprisingly heavy firearm. Sure enough, there on the side of the barrel in embossed metallic lettering were the words "BHR Combine DARNER MK.2"

"Well. It's what *they* call it," corrected Straya. "Look at the edges on that print."

Adjusting her grip on the gun so that its business end was pointed safely away from the both of them, the raider held a fingertip to the raised text. And, upon closer inspection, Phera saw that the edges of some of the letters looked odd. Eroded away, but in a much more geometric fashion than you'd expect from regular wear and tear. She'd done enough printing to know what the products of a bad template looked like.

"The Combine's struggling just to get by these days. Couldn't afford to defend their IP, and it snowballed from there. This one could've come from pretty much anywhere."

Straya's smile turned sardonic, and Phera felt her own lips begin to mirror it.

"Most of those generics work as well as the real deal, but they take a lot more maintenance if you plan on using them long term."

"I see…"

Gliding the pad of her thumb across the material (some sort of ceramic-infused polymer by the feel of things), Phera gave the gun an appraising heft. As far as she could tell, apart from the templating imperfections, it felt like a coilgun should.

Granted, she'd never actually held one before today. But, still.

"Oh well, guess that just means I'll have to tear this down after we're done for cleaning and lubrication and whatever else you're supposed to do to keep these things from falling apart."

Phera didn't actually sound upset about this, but a moment after she spoke, a stray thought hit her and she grimaced.

"Come to think of it, though, I don't really know what *could* go wrong with one of these. All the vids make it seem like the worst case scenario is that it jams up right as the bad guy kidnaps the hot sidekick, or when the heroine is about to be executed."

At that, the weighty coilgun shifted from an interesting engineering project to an unpredictable, dangerous weapon, and Phera's hands tightened around it as she looked to Straya for support.

"This one being a generic isn't going to mean that it… I don't know, explodes when I try shooting it without having given it an oil dip or whatever, yeah?"

"Not that kind of generic, no. You can usually tell those just by looking inside the barrel. Cap doesn't skimp on crew armament, though, but the next time I find a bad one I'll show you the difference."

Straya shook her head and heaved out a sigh then.

"Worst case scenario? If the coil is misaligned, the barrel could tear itself in half."

"Uh… Tear? Like in one of those old cartoons?"

"Basically. Don't think you'd lose a finger, but the shrapnel would definitely give Steph a workout."

Phera felt herself wince as her fingers gave a fretful wiggle around the barrel she was gripping.

"Well, at least scars are sexy."

That managed to make Straya snort.

"Pft. You're sexy enough as is, sweet cheeks."

Before growing serious once again.

"If your weapon's malfunctioning, most likely it just won't fire. That, or the conductor pathways will be worn down to the point it'll only give you something like ten percent of the voltage it should, and your bullet will drop two meters ahead of you."

"That, uh... wouldn't be ideal."

"No kidding," agreed the taller woman. "Dud rounds are likelier than any of that, though. Which is why you need to look for chips in the capacitors when you load."

Thumbing open the box of ammunition they'd gotten from Anne, Straya removed a tiny, rounded-over metal cone.

"See here?"

Phera had to look very closely to see what Straya was indicating with her fingernail. A small, plastic-coated, ceramic disc with two exposed metal terminals was affixed to the flat end of the projectile cone in a bright yellow that contrasted the dark gray of the rest of the round.

"If it's cracked, throw it away."

The auburn-haired engineer gave a firm nod.

"That seems easy enough. What about swelling?"

"Munitions grade charging caps are always ceramic, so no worries there."

"Ah, yeah, I guess that makes sense."

Setting her coilgun onto one of the waist-high tables between them and the targets at the far end of the range, Phera accepted the round as Straya passed it to her and rolled it between her thumb and forefinger.

"So, we just stick a bunch of these into the well in the grip and slap it in on the bottom?"

"I'd like to stick a bunch of things in you and slap you on the bottom."

Grinning, Straya cupped a calloused palm against the bottom in question.

"Awww, you say the sweetest things."

"But, yeah, you can just insert the whole clip and let it shuck the casings off when you flip the chamber shut, but I wouldn't recommend it. Like I said, you're better off checking each round and putting them in one by one yourself. It takes longer, but that's the kind of thing that keeps you from catching a spare hole you don't want."

Setting the box of ammunition down in front of Phera, she guided her fingers to each bullet, taking her through the process of checking every individual round for faults before rolling them into the empty well at the base of her pistol's grip until it was fully loaded.

"Click this shut, lock it in place, and now you can take off the safety."

Straya indicated the little slider that ran the length of the barrel with a nub that was currently locked in place. She turned it ninety degrees while keeping herself well clear of the muzzle.

"So. Safety is way up near the mouth of the barrel. That means that when you flick it off, you're going to be on the lowest setting by default. That's just an extra safety precaution."

"Oooh, clever!"

Phera, face still warm from Straya's declaration regarding her bottom and the various things she'd like to do to it, busied herself with dragging the little slider a few centimeters back and forth along the length of her coilgun to gauge its feel. It took a lot more muscle power than she would've expected to move it, but she supposed that was probably a good thing. She wouldn't accidentally shift it into "let's put a hole in an engine block" mode by accident that way.

"All right," she declared, shifting her right foot back behind her and raising the gun in both hands to point downrange with one eye shut just as she'd seen in literally every action vid ever. "Now comes the fun part!"

With her weapon fully loaded and feeling very real and heavy in her hands, her anxiety was washed away in a tidal wave of anticipation. This was going to be loud and exciting, and she was suddenly very eager to see just how good of a shot she was in real life compared to the games she played.

"Head, chest, or junk, boss lady?" she asked, gesturing with the coilgun's muzzle to indicate the various spots on the target some fifteen meters ahead of her.

"Well, first off, you should keep both your eyes open. Closing one of them might make you feel like you can see better, but not actually."

She put a finger above and below Phera's closed eye and gently pried it open.

"See?"

"Oh hey, what do you know? Depth perception!"

"Mmhmm."

Straya's low chuckle against her ear made Phera blush, especially when she felt her strong hands move to grip her on either side of her hips.

"As far as stance goes, that mostly depends on if you're wearing armor or not. If you've got something on that can absorb fire, you want to stand with your legs spread and your knees bent for better stability. But, since you're not, it's better to stand side-on from whatever you're aiming at to present a smaller target."

Another half-rumble of laughter bubbled up from Straya.

"Well, as much as you can at any rate."

Her hands slipped slightly lower to give Phera's partially-exposed seat a firm squeeze through her short-shorts as she shifted her back foot over with her own.

"There we go, much better."

"If you say so."

"Does it not feel better?"

"Not really..."

"Okay, here."

Shifting to stand directly behind her, Phera felt Straya's hands pushing down on her shoulders.

"Stick your butt out more."

Doing so caused the engineer's cheeks to press up against the front of her friend's thighs.

"Your center of gravity is in your hips, so you want to keep that nice and stable, and you do that by keeping it low," she explained. "Better?"

"Uh..."

Still blushing, Phera did her best to assess how she felt as she aimed her coilgun at the torso downrange.

"Yeah, actually. Huh."

"Great."

Straya spared a moment to squeeze her seat one more time, and then resumed her businesslike tone as she stepped away.

"Next, pull that slider on the barrel down about two centimeters. These targets are kind of hard, and you're not going to leave a mark on minimum power."

"Oh, I dunno," teased Phera as she adjusted her coil's power slider as instructed. "I've felt your butt before. It's pretty hard, and Steph still managed to put quite the mark on it on low power the other night."

She snickered at her own dumb joke as she tried to line up her front and rear sights, hoping she looked cool and in control and not at all like her shoulders were already starting to get sore.

Straya, in turn, cocked one dark brow at her.

"Do I need to give Anne a reprise of your little performance with Cap from before the last mission?"

"That's not a bad idea now that you mention it. You *were* being kind of mean to her earlier. I'd be more than happy to bend you over once we're done with this if you'd like."

Phera did her best to maintain a straight face as she spoke, honestly impressed with her own audacity as she let the muzzle of the coilgun drift down a few degrees to ease some of the load on her poor shoulders.

Seeing Straya starting to unbuckle her belt out of the corner of her eye, though, she quickly added.

"Kidding, kidding!"

"Uh-huh."

Straya's tone hadn't changed, but the temperature in the cavernous room felt like it had just dropped ten degrees all at once, leaving Phera all too aware of just how little her shorts actually covered.

"Seriously. That, uh… That was just a joke, you know."

"That's still not going to save your ass."

Shrugging her broad shoulders beneath her tank top, Straya made no move to refasten her belt as her eyes narrowed with the sort of intent that threatened to knock Phera's legs out from under her.

"Put that down and bend over."

"But... but..."

"*Now.*"

Gods! When Straya got that "I'm going to do whatever I want to you" look in her eyes she could just...

While the younger woman continued to stew in her nerves and excitement, Straya looked back over her shoulder and waved.

"Oh, hey, Anne."

"Anne?" echoed Phera with a startled yelp, jerking out of the tattered remnants of her carefully adjusted stance and slapping her coilgun down onto the counter in front of her lest she accidentally pull the trigger. "Um, uh... Hi! Wh-What's up?"

"Obviously not as much as there is out here with you."

The tattooed woman gave Straya and her open belt a weary grimace, before turning back to Phera and stepping closer.

"How's your first time *shooting* going, sweetness?"

It seemed that she could barely keep herself from giggling as she enunciated the word "shooting" with sarcastic emphasis.

"Oh... You know..."

Fixing a bland smile in place, Phera willed the blush cascading its way up her neck to go away as she twirled a couple of loose curls tickling the side of her face around a finger.

"So far, so good."

She gestured awkwardly at where she'd left her coilgun while Anne gave her an unapologetic once-over.

"Lots of things to learn about, uh... Proper ammunition inspection and what have you."

Clearing her throat, she *almost* managed to meet the other woman's eye.

"I hope we weren't being too loud."

"It's a shooting range, hon. It kinda comes with the territory."

Snickering, Anne turned her attention back to Straya.

"I swear. Why Crunchy lets you out of the docking ring without a handler, I will never fucking understand."

Straya, in turn, breathed out long and ruefully, but looked more chagrinned than actually outraged as she refastened her belt buckle.

"I still want to see what would happen if you called her that to her face."

Anne's heavily-inked shoulders gave an unconcerned shrug.

"I'd win another fight. Yawn."

Which made Phera giggle despite herself.

"I'd pay good money to see that."

Anne looked like she was perhaps a bit tougher than most of the people who made Marcos Station their home, especially with the very clearly heavily-modded sidearm she had strapped to her thigh, but not so much so that she'd be able to trounce the Captain. That woman was wickedly quick when she wanted to be, and had already demonstrated for Phera multiple times over that she had no qualms about playing dirty.

"I can shoot you a message the next time we're all out drinking if you'd like," she offered with an impudent grin now that the initial awkwardness of her walking in on her and Straya had passed.

"Just shoot Straya instead. You'll probably be saving me trouble down the line."

"I'm trying to remember why I keep coming back here," grumbled Straya as she glared at the other woman.

"It's because you're in love with me. Obviously."

"You are such a cunt."

"How would you even know the difference?"

Just as Phera was starting to worry that the two of them might actually come to blows, they instead hugged each other, both grinning.

"Really, though. Take that ass and the girl attached to it somewhere private if you want to start beating on it, yeah? I'm trying to run a business here."

"All right, all right, you've made your point. I'll deal with her later. Now, would you mind getting the fuck out? Some of us still have shit to do."

"Whatever you say, sugar lips."

Chortling, Anne turned and minced her way out of the shooting range, shaking her hips perhaps a little more than she'd done before as she went. Straya stared after her for a moment or two more once she'd gone, before making a disgusted noise in the back of her throat and returning her full attention to Phera.

"Your gun's still loaded. Get back in your shooting stance. Two eyes."

"Ma'am, yes ma'am!"

Phera's mouth quirked up into a wry, fractional smirk as she did as she was told. The weight of the coilgun in her hands felt less awkward this time as she shifted one foot behind her and bent her knees, pushing her hips slightly further back than she would've preferred. Secure in the knowledge that her seat was safe from Straya for the time being.

"Like this?"

"Like that."

Straya pulled her arms a little bit back toward her chest so that they had some bend at the elbows.

"Leave the slider near the end for now," she ordered, reaching over and adjusting it so that the power control nub was just barely past the "safe" position. "You need to practice aiming with less-lethal before you have to deal with any real recoil. At this setting, gravity is going to be acting on the bullet pretty much as soon as it comes out of the barrel, so when you're aiming you should err a little on the high side."

Licking her lips, Phera adjusted her front sight another centimeter or two above the center of the silhouette she was staring at downrange.

"Good."

Straya's lips were back near her ear again as she molded her body to hers, reaching around to help steady her hands for her first shot.

"Now, aim, breathe out, and *squeeze* the trigger nice and slow."

Exhaling, Phera did just that. And, four seconds later, she jerked in surprise as the gun in her hand gave a small *pop*.

"Holy shit!"

So surprised was she that she'd actually done it, she accidentally pulled the trigger again.

Pop.

Sending a second magnetically-charged projectile ricocheting off the side of the stone wall some five meters ahead of her.

"Oops!"

Firing as it was at such low velocity, the projectile made hardly any noise as it discharged from the end of her barrel and the kick was all but nonexistent. No, what had startled her was just how fast it had all happened. One moment she'd been adding pressure to the pad of her index finger, and the next there was a muted report, a puff of ozone, and a spent charge casing ejected from the side of her weapon and bounced to the floor.

"Louder than you expected?" Straya asked. "You kept your grip solid. Maybe overcompensated just a little for that level of recoil, but that was pretty good wristwork."

"I've been told I have *excellent* wristwork."

"I know. I've seen it." Straya cast a rueful look at the new chip in the cavern wall as she added, "You should give yourself more time to correct between shots, though."

Before favoring Phera with her usual faint semi-grin.

"The target's not going anywhere."

"Good point. Okay, let's try this again."

Rolling her shoulders to shake loose some of the tension there, the engineer brought the muzzle of her firearm back up and positioned its front sight two centimeters above the center of the target downrange.

"Squeeze, and…"

Pop.

"Got 'em!"

This time, knowing what to expect, she didn't accidentally pull the trigger again. And, as she slowly brought her weapon back down to point at the floor in front of her, she was pleased to see that she had indeed managed to punch a fingertip sized hole in the right shoulder of her silhouette.

"I don't think he'll be causing any more trouble."

"At that setting? He'll be bruised for a week or two. Tops."

Straya almost chuckled, but not quite.

"Try a few more times, and then we'll see how you handle anti-personnel."

"With pleasure."

Over the course of the next minute and a half, Phera's coilgun barked out six more muted *pops*, and four more holes appeared in the general vicinity of her target.

"Oh yeah! That's what I'm talking about!" she cheered as her final shot managed to punch through the centermost ring on the chest of the silhouette.

"First bullseye! Nice."

"Hehe. Thanks."

Setting the coilgun down on the table in front of her with slightly shaky hands, Phera began kneading her right forearm as she turned to Straya with a broad grin.

"It might've taken a few tries, but I managed to get 'em eventually."

"You sure did, deadeye."

Straya smiled a little more as she gently cupped her beaming face.

"Think you're ready for higher-powered shots now? You'll have a lot more recoil to deal with, but it's also easier to aim."

"Yes, totally! Let's do it!"

Absolutely incandescent with excitement now, Phera gave her fingers an animated wiggle and then snatched back up her coilgun, dragging its power slider all the way toward her at the other end of the barrel as she turned back to face her target downrange.

"All right, buddy, get ready to get fucked. No more warning shots this time…"

"*NO!*"

Straya barely raised her voice, but her tone was so commanding that it had Phera freezing in place.

"Slide that back two thirds of the way. If you set for anti-material without doing a whole bunch of exercises and getting the necessary biomods, you are going to dislocate your wrists. Not might. *Will.*"

"What?! Oh no, oh fuck, oh shit-!"

"Look, it's fine. You haven't fired yet. Just do exactly as I say, all right?"

Straya kept herself half a meter back and spoke slowly, eyes hard but voice steady.

"All right. Just, um… Walk me through it?"

"Sure. So, keeping your finger *off* the trigger, point that at the ground in front of you at a forty-five degree angle and slide the power adjuster up to the little yellow stripe."

"O... kay."

Hammering heart lodged in her throat, Phera very slowly and very carefully shifted the muzzle of her coilgun down to point at the ground, making sure to keep her forefinger well away from the trigger the entire time as she did so. To her credit, her hand barely trembled as she pushed the power slider back down to where she'd been instructed.

"Better?"

"It would've been hard to do worse."

Straya's sardonic semi-smile was in full effect now.

"No offense."

"I mean... Fair."

Slipping in behind her once again, Straya helped bring her hands back up into position.

"So, don't aim for above the target anymore. This is low-powered anti-personnel, but the target's not too far away, so you're only going to have a millimeter of drop in this grav. Elbows bent, arms tensed. Yeah, just like that. The recoil is probably going to take you by surprise your first time, so do your best to prepare for that and try not to jerk in anticipation when you pull the trigger."

"R-Right!"

"If you want to keep shooting on minimum, you can, you know. We don't *have* to escalate."

"No, no, I want to get the full Straya boot camp experience," Phera reassured her, channeling some of her lingering anxiety into a friendly hip bump. "Just don't tell me to drop and give you twenty."

"Straya boot camp isn't compatible with shooting for fun. Sorry."

"Humph. I thought you might say that."

Phera found herself suddenly wishing very much that she'd gotten around to curling those free weights during her regular crew-mandated exercise time like she'd been meaning to as she once again drew a bead on her target, but she wasn't about to let that slow her down. Instead, she squeezed the trigger before she could think about it anymore. And, this time, there was an accompanying whip **CRACK!** of a sonic boom as her coilgun jerked up in her hands, very nearly torquing itself right out of her hands.

"Whoa!"

Gasping, she gradually eased into a brittle laugh as she readjusted her slightly sweaty grip on her gun.

"Okay. Maybe we should move the power setting just a *bit* further down."

Watching the younger woman struggling with her Darner, Straya winced in sympathy.

"Yeah, push it back toward the muzzle by about a centimeter. Too much too fast. That's my bad, sorry."

Then, after a moment's thought, she added.

"By the way, do you need ear protection?"

"That… Hmm… Yeah, probably."

Now that she mentioned it, Phera's ears were still ringing from that last shot.

Maybe it was their cramped confines and the hard walls around them, or the fact that she wasn't wearing a full vacsuit, but her weapon's discharge had been a *lot* louder than she remembered Ember's being.

"I didn't even think to bring some," she admitted as she dialed down the coilgun's power even further. "Do you have any I can borrow, or should I just stick to low power? I don't have any hearing mods I can use to compensate, and something tells me Steph wouldn't appreciate me coming back tonight with a busted eardrum."

"I'll get some from Anne. Don't worry."

Straya's hand affectionately patted her hair before gliding down to cup her jaw.

"I forget that not everyone is spec'd for combat like I am. I've got the hearing mods, and so did everyone I trained with."

She hesitated for just a moment then, before leaning in and pecking her on the lips.

"Sit tight. I'll be right back."

She started striding her long legs back toward the office then, leaving Phera to watch her go with a lopsided grin and pleasantly warm cheeks.

"Take your time," she called after her, waving dreamily. " I'll just be here working on my one-liners."

"Oooh, fancy," marveled Phera when Straya returned a few minutes later with a pair of oversized plastic earmuffs with a knob and a pair of switches on one side. "My university's machine lab had pairs like these."

Accepting the adaptive ear protection from the taller woman with a nod of thanks, she slipped them on and flicked their power switch. Filling her hearing with machine-augmented, crystal clear audio.

"Must be nice having actual mods, though. I bet those have come in handy a time or two."

Then, on a whim, wanting to test just how sensitive her friend's hearing assistance tech really was, Phera leveled a wicked grin at Straya and mouthed.

"You look stupid hot in that top, by the way."

"Thanks."

Straya rolled her eyes in only somewhat false modesty.

"The ear mods were required for all new recruits. For a while, at least. They wound up relaxing restrictions pretty quick when… Well, I was already pushing sergeant by then."

Phera didn't need any sort of hearing augmentation to pick up on the tired note the other woman's voice carried with those last couple of sentences.

"You, uh…"

Not quite sure how best to broach the subject, but wanting to understand where Straya was coming from and maybe help her feel better, she reached out and gave her elbow a tentative squeeze.

"Sergeant, huh? That's pretty high up, yeah? Why didn't you stay in the… Army? Fleet? It has to be easier than being a pirate, doesn't it?"

Phera felt her lips twitch as her tender and totally bare thighs gave a pleasant throb.

"Then again, there are a few perks I can think of on this crew that you probably couldn't get away with in the military outside of some very specific adult magazines."

Rather than rise to her blatant bit of flirting, Straya remained silent for several long, increasingly awkward moments. Then, drawing her own coilgun from the holster at her hip, she took up a shooting stance facing the target next to Phera's.

"You ready to keep going?"

"Um, sure."

Straya's expression grew closed and bitter as she drew a bead on the silhouette menacing her from downrange, drawing the power slider on her weapon about halfway back.

"I guess you could say it's not so much that I left the army, as it left me."

CRACK! CRACK! CRACK!

Her coilgun coughed out three crisp shots, the reports of which were filtered out by Phera's newfound hearing protection to only a mild *pop* while leaving the muscular pirate's voice crystal clear.

"And, well, guess there's not really much army left now either."

CRACK!

The weapon in Straya's hand jerked again, while at the same time her target developed another puncture. This time directly between its eyes.

"Oh."

Phera's reply was low and long, half-impressed exhale and half-acknowledgement as a couple things clicked into place for her.

"I, uh… I take it the war didn't go so well for your side then?"

She felt like a jackass as she was saying it, but she couldn't think of anything else to say just then to keep the other woman talking. It wasn't like she hadn't heard of territories and micronations scrabbling for control out in the Proxima sector. But, up until then, the idea had always been more academic than reality.

Perks of growing up on a stable planet, I guess, she added silently to herself, grateful once again that she'd opted not to pursue military service when her scholarship had run out.

She very well could've found herself on the wrong side of a battle with Straya and never even known it. And, given how she kept precisely drilling holes into her target at the far end of the range, that would've most likely gone very, very poorly for her.

"No."

Straya's next bullet hit a few centimeters off to the side of the target's head. And, swearing under her breath, she adjusted her aim further down and to the right.

"Well, actually. I guess that would mostly depend on which war you're talking about, or what even counts as one."

She opened another empty circle in the target, this time near the middle of its right pectoral. Phera saw her adjust the muzzle just a tiny bit to the left.

"We did pretty well up until Cilara."

CRACK!

The next bullet hit right where a human's heart would be.

Phera, her own coilgun completely forgotten about for the time being, felt her stomach give an extremely unpleasant lurch at the same time as Straya sent a second bullet through the hole she'd just made in her target's non-existent heart.

"You, um... Cilara?" she managed, licking her lips.

She knew that there was no reason for her to feel like she'd suddenly been caught in a lie, but the unexpected mention of her home planet had her feeling like they'd just lost grav.

"You fought on Cilara? When?"

While it was true that history had never been her strong suit, she couldn't recall any sort of major military action on planet being mentioned during the global history courses she'd taken during grade school. The last time she could even think of that the planetary defense force had been deployed for anything other than suppressing protests had been back when the old regime had been toppled when her grandparents were still kids.

"Not on. Against."

Straya spoke through a thin rime of ice as she adjusted her coilgun's power, bringing it down to light anti-personnel.

"You remember the Midway Cluster wars?"

Phera tilted her hand back and forth in front of her.

"Kind of."

"You were probably pretty young, but... Well, I guess I don't even know how much of it was covered on Cilara."

"I was barely into secondary school when that was all going on and mostly just remember the newsfeeds my parents watched talking a lot about how some radical insurgent group had taken over a cluster of stations and how it was Cilara's duty to help liberate the people they were holding hostage or something."

As she spoke, a fresh wave of nausea overtook her, and she winced. She'd never really given the matter more than a passing thought back then. But, now that she did, it sounded a lot more like corporate propaganda to justify a bunch of resource grabbing than she'd have liked to admit.

"I take it you were one of those 'insurgents'?"

"No. The big cluster with the radical ideas was the Dornu Republic. Which, ironically enough, wasn't really all that republican."

Straya took another shot, this one punching through her target a bit lower, toward the stomach, making her scowl.

"That's who we were fighting most of the time after we kicked the previous corps out. There were three other factions that could've lasted. We were one of them."

CRACK! CRACK! CRACK!

"Did they ever mention Gilgamesh in those reports?"

"I thiiiink I remember hearing that name being thrown around once or twice," answered Phera slowly, trying to remember all she could of that time in her life, most of which she'd spent away from home whenever she could. "I was a lot more focused on drama club and this one girl in my trig class if I'm being totally honest."

Her lips twitched up into a brittle half-smirk as she said this last bit, hoping that it might lighten the mood just a bit and again immediately feeling like a jackass.

"Was that who you were fighting for when Cilara was brought in?"

She might not have known much about the various factions involved in the Midway Cluster war, but she'd seen more than enough mission accomplished celebrations to know how it must've ended for Straya and her side.

"Mostly. We joined up with them to fight the coalition forces from Alpha when they showed up. Not for very long, though."

Blowing out a heavy breath through her nostrils as she absently reloaded her weapon, Straya stared at the pitted and pockmarked back wall downrange. Though, Phera doubted very much she was actually seeing it.

"That lasted for a while, and then we started coordinating our own strikes on Dornu and their pole-polishers in the Aphrodite subcluster with the Alpha coalition. They said we'd get recognition if we cooperated. But, whatever it was they'd asked for from our representatives, it was more than we could give."

Slapping the loading well on the butt of her pistol's grip closed harder than she strictly needed to, Straya drew a bead on her target and squeezed off four shots in quick succession.

CRACK! CRACK! CRACK! CRACK!

"The fucking criminals running Dornu could, though. They just had to change their name and shuffle their government's organizations a little so that Cilara and the others could call it a regime change."

"Shit. That's…"

Phera's face twisted with disgust, both at the situation as a whole and at how as a kid she'd let all the fawning, positive takes from the newsfeeds about the "systemic overhaul" of the region wash over her without a second thought. She could feel herself getting angry now on Straya's behalf. Not knowing enough about the intricacies of the far-off conflict from her youth, but understanding enough to know how absolutely horrifying and stupid it all was.

"That's some absolute bullshit," she eventually settled on, her usually plump and pouty lips pinching together in a tight scowl as she turned back to her own coilgun and snatched it up again.

Adopting her previous shooting stance, forgetting how she'd been told to keep her arms, she squeezed off three quick shots.

CRACK! CRACK! CRACK!

Two of which sailed past either side of her silhouette, while one managed to hit somewhere in the general upper vicinity of its torso.

"I'm sorry, Straya," she said after forcing herself to exhale a shaky breath, lowering her gun. "I just… Shit."

A heavy silence fell over the pair of them then, marked only by the steady *CRACK! CRACK! CRACK!* of her and Straya's coilguns as they continued to drill holes through the memories of enemies past. All the while, thoughts of hugging her friend ran through Phera's mind, but acting on them seemed somehow inappropriate. Like she wasn't allowed to help shoulder some of the grief she was feeling. So, instead, she opted to just keep firing.

"That's just awful," she eventually said when the silence between the two of them became too much for her to handle, the anger having drained from her voice in a worn, tired trickle.

Shrugging, Straya took another shot.

CRACK!

Blasting yet another neat hole through her target's forehead.

"It was easily the second worst thing that's ever happened to me, but I at least got to vaporize a few of the motherfuckers on my way out of the cluster. So, there's that."

Her smile ghosted back into place then, and her eyes lost just a bit of their jagged edge.

"Like I said, I've killed a lot fewer people after turning pirate. Cap runs a clean operation."

As she spoke, she cut a glance toward Phera's comparatively less perforated but still fatally wounded many times over target.

"That's pretty good. Try and let your arms flex a little more vertically if you can, though. Shoot a little too high or low, and you'll probably still hit him somewhere. Left or right, not so much."

"Ah, yeah, okay. That makes sense."

A fair amount of her earlier fire having cooled at the thought of her friend literally vaporizing people (even if they deserved it), Phera suppressed a wince as she gave her shoulders a quick roll and drew her weapon back up. This time, she pulled her hands in closer toward her ample bosom and bent her elbows to give her arms more flexibility, pushing her wide hips slightly further back to compensate for the shift in balance. Doing so made her feel much less striking and cool, but the next three shots she loosed all managed to find their marks somewhere within the outermost ring marking center mass on her target. Best of all, her wrists didn't feel like they'd been smacked with a hammer this time around.

"Heck yes!"

Letting go of her gun with her non-trigger hand, she gave her fist a triumphant pump and turned to regard her fellow pirate.

"So, what recruitment office did the Captain wind up plucking you out of?" she asked with the faintest trace of a teasing grin. "No offense, but I'm a little surprised you went pirate. I would've expected you to find some nice mercenary group to settle down with. It kinda seems like your thing, you know?"

As she said this last bit, Phera once again felt like an asshole. Maybe Straya hadn't *wanted* to keep fighting? Maybe she'd just wanted to find somewhere quiet to recover in?

"Er... Sorry if that came off as insensitive," she added, marveling at how she'd just managed to deepthroat her own foot.

"Just a little."

Straya rolled her eyes, but didn't get visibly angry.

"The problem with being a mercenary is that you fight for whoever can pay. And, well, most people who need fighters and can afford them... "

She didn't finish that sentence. Just nailed her target through one of its eyes.

"I stuck with some other Gilgamesh remnants till our ship was only good for parts. We scrapped it right here on this station, actually. Then, an interplanetary woman of mystery picked me up at Tortuga."

"Heh. You don't say?"

The weight on the corners of Phera's mouth started to lighten as they drew once more into the orbit of less emotionally scarring topics.

"That must've been fun. I'm sad I missed it."

Leaning back, she snuck an unsubtle peek at the older woman's fit and well-rounded bottom through her dark pants as memories of her own time with the Captain at that particular bar came rushing back to her.

"Did you beat her in an arm wrestling contest or something, or does she just dig scars?"

She made sure to give her voice an exaggerated lilt as she spoke, hoping to draw out one of her cabinmate's trademark strained but begrudgingly amused smiles. She might not know how to help her through black hole heavy emotional trauma and PTSD, but she could at least make her smirk, couldn't she?

"If she does, she's never told me."

Straya rewarded Phera with just such a reluctant semi-smile, and she felt her heart leap.

"She wanted to buy some of our shield capacitors, and I was the only one she could get a hold of that night. She warned me I was drinking too much. I told her to fuck off before I cut her."

She stopped and reloaded her coilgun again.

"We got into a fight with someone later that night, don't remember why. The next morning she commed me and said I had a job. Don't remember giving her my contact info, but everything after I broke that bottle over that one guy's head is kinda foggy, so I guess I must have."

Phera let out a long, low whistle at that.

"That is… Very you," she said with an impressed (if slightly incredulous) shake of her copper curls. "I can't believe you actually threatened to *cut* her. I'd have to be pretty tanked to so much as think about talking to her like that."

"Well, I'm bigger than Cap. You're smaller. Kinda makes it easier to be brave."

Snorting, Phera turned back to her target, taking aim at its formless face to see if she couldn't shoot out its eye like Straya had as she made a mental note to pick up some platform boots the next chance she could.

"I'm glad it all worked out, though."

CRACK!

Miss.

CRACK!

Hairline graze.

Phera shivered as her mind started running through the ramifications of Straya joining the Blazar Bitches.

"And not just because you going pirate happened to eventually put me in the Captain's sights."

CRACK!

Another miss, but at least her target was going to need a nose job now.

"I, for one, absolutely *adore* being gay and doing crimes with you, Straya."

"Me too, Phera."

That actually managed to get a chuckle out of the older woman as she leaned over to give her pushed back backside a fond pat.

"Me too."

Followed by a pinch.

"Now, I want to see ten headshots in the next two minutes, or else I might just bend you over after all."

CHAPTER TWENTY-THREE

"Bull-fucking-shit! No way you could kill someone with a handful of diced onions!" exploded Phera with friendly belligerence as she scooped up a mouthful of the vegetable in question with some of her noodles.

"I could if they were allergic," countered Straya with a malevolent smirk, causing her to choke on a laugh and very nearly do a spit take with her soup. "See? Told you so."

Phera continued to both cough and laugh for nearly half a minute while Straya slapped her on the back.

"Okay, okay. You win," she eventually managed to wheeze after downing half the beer she'd ordered with her dinner.

"What else is new?"

"Humph."

After she and Straya had ensured that no stationary target would ever menace Anne's shooting gallery ever again, the two of them had wound up wandering around the station's entertainment mod; window shopping and enjoying each other's company before stopping off at an "outdoor" (aka one with stools arranged in front of an open bar facing the corridor it was in) noodle stall that caught Phera's attention. Over bowls of spiced ramen and some surprisingly good locally brewed beer, Phera shared stories of stupid pranks and other dumb shenanigans she and her dormmates had gotten up to back in college, while Straya told her about some of the happier times she'd had back when she was a soldier. Neither of them was in the mood for anything somber or sad just then, so they kept their banter light and easy. Phera laying on the sass and Straya batting it right back at her in a casual game of verbal tennis that felt warm and comfortable.

"So…"

Bringing her bowl up to her lips, Phera drained the last of her broth while she cut a sidelong glance toward Straya.

"You, uh… wanna catch a vid or something?" she asked, suddenly feeling like an awkward freshman who didn't want the evening to end. "Or, I don't know, go dancing, maybe?"

"Hmmm, that could be fun."

Straya's voice was low and contented as she hooked a calf around her stool and dragged her closer until they were sitting hip-to-hip.

"I've got a better idea, though."

"Oh yeah?"

Stomach fluttering at the sudden press of warm muscles against her side, Phera leaned in to rest her head on her cabinmate's bare shoulder.

"What's that?"

"Well…" Draping an arm around her waist as she spoke, Straya murmured just loud enough to be heard over the din of people milling about the mod behind them. "I've been wanting to get you naked ever since we left the ship."

"Y-You don't say," came Phera's half-laugh, half-squeak of a reply as the bigger woman's hand slipped inside her shorts to cup one cheek there in the middle of public.

"Mmhmm… And I know just the place to make that happen. You in?"

Face molten and thighs pressed firmly together as Straya's grip on her tightened, Phera nodded into her chest.

"Let's do it."

Prompting Straya to kiss her cheek.

"That's the plan, sweet cheeks."

—

As it turned out, the place Straya had in mind was a bathhouse tucked into an out of the way corner of the station's entertainment mod.

"Holy shit!"

Voice rising and hands gesturing excitedly, Phera rushed ahead when she saw the sign above the door.

"Are you serious?"

"Awesome, right?"

"You have *no* idea."

She hadn't had an actual bath since she'd lived at home with her parents. Her dorms and The Bin had both had communal showers, and the head on the Mayhem wasn't much better. Which, she couldn't really hold against the ship. Space was at a premium on board the habitation cylinder, and you could only purify so much gray water at a time. Still, the prospect of being able to just sit in a pool of hot water and soak away her cares without having to fret about resource usage or allocation schedules nearly had her in tears.

"Come on, stop staring," chided Straya with a chuckle, ushering her ahead with a hand on the small of her back. "All the fun stuff is inside."

"Hehehe, yay!"

Phera, for the life of her, couldn't even begin to guess what this refitted space had once been used for before Marcos's original owners had abandoned the station. But, honestly, she couldn't bring herself to care all that much either. She was way too excited for professional speculation, especially when Straya told the attendant at the reception area that they wanted a private room. The cost the woman quoted them was over half of what she'd used to make in a month back with Panorama. But, piracy paid far better than her old corporate job did, and she was more than okay with parting with a sizable chunk of her cut of the crew's last heist if it meant actually getting to take a genuine bath. So, she didn't bat an eyelash as she and Straya both pressed their thumbs to the till's scanner so it could read their fingerprints and capillary configurations and split the fee for a *private* room all to themselves.

The room they were ushered into then smelled of floral soap and was thick with steam from the oversized pool of water that dominated one half of the space. It was lit by discreet sunsim panels set perpetually for mid-afternoon whose bright white light was softened by smooth floor to ceiling tiles (gray for the floor and a cool blue for the pool and walls), with only the natural stone ceiling overhead to remind Phera that she wasn't back on Cilara.

"Enjoy your soak, ladies."

"Sure will."

"Thank you!"

As soon as they were alone, she and Straya made quick work of stripping naked and sealing their clothes inside the plex containers they'd been provided with, before rinsing off in a shower stall set into one corner of the room.

"Oh gods, that feels *so* nice," the auburn-haired engineer sighed as she eased slowly into the delightfully hot water a couple minutes later, settling down onto a submerged stone bench next to Straya.

"Noooo kidding," came the other woman's thoroughly relaxed reply as she scooted just a bit closer. "Kelt told me about this place a few months back. Apparently, she likes to take Shi out for bath time when we're in port."

"Awww, that's adorable."

"She's got rubber duckies and everything."

"Shut up, no she doesn't!"

"I'm serious. I'll send you the pics later. He's got a full on bubble beard in one of them. It's great."

That sent Phera into a fit of giggles.

"Bubble beard to go with his bubble butt!"

"Pretty much. Though, better not let her hear you saying that, or else it's gonna be your bubble butt boiling."

"Threaten me with a good time, why don't you."

"Good point. You and Shi both looked pretty fuckin' hot side by side in medbay."

"Y-You saw those?!"

Spluttering, Phera sank a few centimeters deeper into the water to hide her sudden blush.

"Well, *duh*."

Straya opened her eyes just long enough to roll them at the ceiling.

"Steph sent them out to everyone that same afternoon. No idea what you two did to wind up alone in medbay with ver and a MitoStim, but it sure looked like ve gave it to you good."

"You have noooo idea."

Sinking lower, Phera blew out a stream of bubbles with her snicker.

"They both did, actually."

"Saw that too, sweet cheeks."

"Urk!"

"Well, just a couple pics," amended Straya, dragging her head back above the surface by her hair before she could drown her embarrassment. "Steph and Shi back-to-back like that, though? I knew you could take it like a champ, but, damn…"

"That was something, all right. I slept like a rock that night."

"I bet."

Phera was just grateful that Steph hadn't shared any details about what ve'd spiked ver lube with. The absolute last thing she needed was for ver to be giving Straya (or, gods forbid, Lem or the Captain) any ideas.

The two of them lapsed into a comfortable silence then, simply letting their muscles unwind in the soothing warmth of the water, before Straya finally broke it.

"So, drama club, huh?" she ventured, surprising Phera just a little by remembering that offhanded mention of her past from earlier that afternoon.

"Yep, that's right. Took the classes and was part of the club all through secondary school."

"You do any shows?"

"A couple musicals. I was usually chorus, though, so don't go asking me to belt anything out for you."

"No worries, I prefer to do my own belting anyway."

"I've noticed."

The mention of Straya's belt brought back a whole host of thigh-squirming memories of her telling her to bend over back at Anne's, and Phera quickly veered back into safer topics for her backside.

"Never got any solos in our musicals, but I *did* manage to snag the lead in a couple of the one-act dramas we did for competitions."

"Nice! Did you win?"

"Did we *win*?" she repeated with smug incredulity. "Not to brag, but you're looking at the Palm Valley regional acting championship's sixth place runner-up."

"Wow."

Straya's answering deadpan did nothing to deflate Phera's puffed out chest and they both dissolved into a fit of laughter.

"I liked drama club, even if I wasn't ever particularly good at it," the younger woman eventually continued as she settled back against the smooth wall behind her. "It was a good excuse to stay out of our apartment, and I made a lot of friends through it. Even had my first kiss there."

"No shit? Were you Romeo or Juliet?"

"Stop it!"

Snickering, Phera batted Straya's shoulder playfully.

"I forget her name. She was a senior and I was a sophomore, and we made out behind the set of whatever musical we were doing at the time during rehearsals one day."

"Secret make outs, huh? That's pretty risqué for a Harmony girl, isn't it?"

"Absolutely scandalous," confirmed Phera. "My parents would've shit a brick if they'd found out."

"So, what? You two run off to get married or something? Make it nice and legal?"

"Pft. Not even close. We 'broke up' a week later and I cried in my room for, like, a month."

"Awww, that's actually really cute."

"Secondary school Phera was an absolute baby."

"I dunno, seems like pirate Phera does her fair share of whining and sobbing too."

"That's because all of you hit *way* too hard. Humph!"

"Your fault for having such a spankable ass, sweet cheeks."

"I mean... Fair."

Phera pushed her cheeks out into a performative pout before succumbing to another laugh when Straya flicked some water at her.

"Seriously, though, I think you've changed a lot these last few weeks," she added. "For the better, I mean."

"Have I?"

Phera gave her left breast an appraising squeeze.

"I don't *feel* any different."

Straya splashed her again, using her whole arm this time.

"Blech! Hey!"

"That's not what I mean and you know it, smartass."

"Yeah, yeah…"

Slicking back the sopping locks plastered to her forehead, Phera's mischievous smirk softened into something gentle and genuine.

"So, what did you mean?"

"God, uh… I don't know…"

Straya scrubbed a hand over her face and studied the stone ceiling above her for a what felt like a very long time before she finally spoke again.

"When we first met, you were way more… I don't know, timid? Like, you were still energetic and curious, I guess, but it always seemed like you were expecting someone to start yelling at you or threatening to kick you out any minute or something. I just… I don't know. You seem way more happy and confident now, is all. I like it. It's nice."

"Awww, Straya, that's really sweet."

"Whatever. I just thought I'd mention it is all."

The bigger pirate attempted to cover the visible flush darkening her tan cheeks by dipping her head below the water for several seconds, before popping back up again and tipping her soaked curls back against the edge of the pool behind her. While Phera, incredibly touched, nestled more fully into the crook of her arm.

"I *am* happy," she murmured, face no less warm than Straya's as she snuggled more fully into her. "And not just because Steph put me on some actual meds for my anxiety. Though, those have definitely helped a ton."

"I was wondering what all those pills you were taking with breakfast were."

"Yep. I've got an SSRI, some anti-anxiety stuff I can't remember the name of, and a vitamin D supplement since Pano totally screwed me over while I was working for them."

That made Straya grimace, though no less affectionately.

"Shitheels."

"Tell me about it."

"Your bones going to be all right? Low grav plays hell on density, and that's *with* good sunsim."

"Steph says my levels are rising like ve was hoping. So, give it a couple more months, and I'll be good as new."

"I'm glad."

"Me too…"

Phera found herself breathing out a half-nervous, half-contented sigh then. And, on a whim, decided to share something she hadn't told anyone up until then.

"I actually made a decision that very first day while I was waiting for you outside the Captain's office. You remember that?"

"Wasn't that right before I beat your ass for nailing Adri with those noodles?"

"Mmhmm, that's right. Though, I still maintain they could've dodged that had they not been staring at my ass like they were."

"Awww, but that was such a good bonding exercise," crooned Straya. "If it makes you feel any better, they told me they thought you were a total hottie while they were massaging me afterward."

This time it was Phera's turn to awww. The memory of her very nearly wetting herself when she'd seen the fire in the crew cook's eyes while they bled from their forehead had lost its edge with time so that it was more funny than terrifying now.

"Oh, they're a total sweetie for sure too."

"Sweetie, huh?"

Straya snorted.

"That's the first time I think anyone has ever called Adri that."

"I mean it!" insisted Phera with exaggerated petulance. "That's actually part of the reason why I was okay with sucking their cock that next night."

"*Part* of?"

"Well, that and it sounded like fun."

"Heh. Slut."

This was said with a surprising amount of tenderness, and Phera felt herself smile.

Demurring for a moment, she occupied herself with pulling her hair back behind her in a loose pile.

"But, yeah. That's basically what I mean by that whole decision thing."

Part of her expected Straya to say something teasing about resolving to give lots of good head, but when she instead remained quiet and attentive, Phera felt her confidence solidify.

"I spent nearly three years out in the middle of nowhere with no friends, no prospects, and a mandate to squeeze out a tenth of a tenth of a percent yield increase from that shitty asteroid. So, when the Captain told me she was going to let me stay on as part of the crew, I decided that I was going to embrace whatever came next with open arms. No limits. No second guessing myself. I was lucky enough to get a fresh start, and I wasn't going to let it go to waste."

"I think I know what you mean."

"Yeah, I kinda thought you might."

She and Straya lapsed into another comfortable, contemplative silence then. Neither of them saying anything as they listened to the steady rhythm of an unseen waterfall drifting to them amid the steam.

Gods, this is nice...

Eventually, though, Straya stirred, and with a grunt and a heave, dragged the engineer onto her lap.

"Oh! Um, hello."

"Hey."

Straya's usual sardonic smirk twisted into something a bit more dangerous as she regarded Phera while fondling her thighs and cheeks beneath the water.

"So, what's it gonna be, sweet cheeks?" she pressed, her brassy alto making Phera's toes curl. "Get spanked and *then* fucked, or the other way around?"

Phera, in turn, fixed her friend with the poutiest pout she could muster.

"Can't we just fuck twice?"

"Nope. I still owe you for all that shit-talking you were doing back at Anne's."

As she spoke, Straya cupped her chin in one calloused hand. Dark eyes met violet, and Phera smirked.

"Oh, right... That."

"Mmhmm. *That.*"

"I suppose-"

Phera's hesitation was cut short as Straya, still cupping her chin, leaned in and kissed her.

Hard.

"Besides, do you *really* think you can stop me?" she added in a husky murmur against the side of her mouth.

"No, but I bet I'd have a lot of fun trying."

Phera's glare was so adorably irate that it managed to wring a genuine smile out of Straya.

"How about I save us both the trouble and show you where you'll end up either way?"

"I-"

Again, Phera was silenced by Straya. This time by her gently running her thumb along the bow of her lower lip.

"Shhh…"

They kissed again then, long and lingering, and the next thing she knew, Phera was being dragged by her hair up and over the edge of the pool. Leaving her to stand with her legs half-submerged beneath the water atop the bench they'd just been sitting on while her bare breasts flattened against the smooth, slick tiles beneath her.

SMACK!

"Ah!"

"See?"

SMACK!

"You're right where you should be."

SMACK!

"And so am I."

"I-!"

SMACK!

"Ack! Suppose."

Squirming against the tiles, Phera found that she was totally immobilized by Straya's hand on the small of her back.

SMACK!

"Ow! Geez! Those really sting on a wet bottom, you know!"

"Oh, do they?"

SMACK-SMACK!

SMACK-SMACK!

Straya punctuated her facetious reply with a pair of hard swats to either of Phera's sit-spots. Making her kick and squeal, sending torrents of water exploding into the air behind her.

"Yes, gods damn it!"

SMACK!

"Owie! They do!"

"Awww, poor baby."

Pausing in her swatting, Straya glided her palm over each upturned chub, her hand's passage made all the smoother thanks to the water clinging to them. Phera's bottom and thighs were still mottled with fading brown and yellow bruises from her initiation paddling, but that wasn't about to earn her any sympathy from Straya, she knew.

'Okay, fine, I won't spank you," the older woman suddenly declared with false cheeriness, capping off her sentence with an extra-hard swat to the center of her seat.

SMACK!

"Urk! Um... Thanks?"

Though dubious, Phera felt herself start to relax nevertheless.

Tap. Tap. Tap.

That is, until she felt something hard, plastic, and distressingly bumpy rapping gently against her cheeks.

"Wh-What the fuck is that?"

"Oh, this?"

THWAP! THWAP! THWAP!

"Ack! Owie! Oh!"

Three hard (though, not as hard as they could've been, she noted) swats impacted against her bouncy bare bottom with Straya's far too innocent sounding question.

Followed by three more.

THWAP! THWAP! THWAP!

"You mean *this*, right?"

And three more after that for good measure.

THWAP! THWAP! THWAP!

"Yes- Ah! Yes, dammit!"

Phera felt Straya's shrug through where her bare hip was pressing up against the front of her thighs.

"It's just a bath brush."

THWAP! THWAP! THWAP!

"I- Owie! I know *that*!"

THWAP! THWAP! THWAP!

"I meant why do you have it?!"

This whining demand was met with yet another unconcerned shrug.

"Seemed like a fun idea."

THWAP!

Phera briefly considered complaining that she'd been lied to, but knew that Straya would've just countered that she said she wouldn't *spank* her. That, or play her usual card of, "Sorry. Pirate."

THWAP! THWAP! THWAP!

"Ack! Fuck, that stings!"

Still, though, even for as lazily as the older woman was whaling on her with it, that bath brush packed quite the punch. Stinging like the fury of a thousand supernovas as it set her cheeks to rippling and her feet to shuffling through the shallows. Squirming around against the tiles, Phera threw a dirty look over her shoulder that made Straya laugh as she caught her first real good glimpse at what she had in hand. Sure enough, it was one of the long-handled scrub brushes she'd seen hanging on the wall when they'd first walked in. When Straya had snagged one, she had no idea.

THWAP! THWAP! THWAP!

"Oh! Geez! Owie!"

But, figuring out that particular timeline seemed like a waste of valuable yelping energy just then. Especially when she turned her attention to her sit-spots.

THWAP!

"Eep!"

"Mmmm... I love the way you whine. Did you know that?"

"I had-"

THWAP!

"Ah! A suspicion."

THWAP!

"Jerk!"

"Watch it…" warned Straya, laying on three extra-explosive swats in a row in a not so subtle reminder that she was going easy on her.

THWAP! THWAP! THWAP!

"Yes ma'am! Yes ma'am! Yes ma'am!"

"Yep."

THWAP!

"Just like that."

THWAP!

"Humph!"

Straya paused then to glide the rounded-over bumps dotted across the oval head of the bath brush against where Phera's bottom was developing a vivid red hue. Dipping it into the pool and using it to splash more water onto where her cheeks and legs had started to dry off.

"Gotta keep up the sting," she singsonged with so much menace that Phera very nearly came right there and then.

THWAP!

"Now, let's just see how red we can get you before I get bored."

—

As it turned out, Straya was capable of keeping herself occupied roasting Phera's voluptuous bare bottom for a very, *very* long time. There were no clocks on the walls of their private bath, and her comp glove was securely stored with the rest of her clothes, but it sure as hell felt like she continued to alternate between paddling, rewetting, and then paddling her ass again for at least one or two myriads.

Maybe three.

While not as bad as it could've been, the spanking itself still definitely hurt, especially coming as it was on a wet bottom. But, Straya clearly wasn't aiming to leave her sore for multiple days. Just sore enough that she'd be sleeping on her stomach that evening (hopefully next to her). She took her time layering her swats in slow, lazy circles around each cheek, making them ripple and jiggle hypnotically before giving her thighs a taste as well. By the time she was finally through, Phera's entire rear end and the thighs attached to it were a swollen, angry shade of emergency alert red made all the more attractive by their slick sheen of bath water.

"God, you look so fucking good like that."

Groaning, Phera flashed her cabinmate a thumbs up.

"Heh. Thanks…"

She was pretty sure she'd collected a whole bunch of new bruises from those stupid, fucking bumps on the back of the brush's head. But, just then, she couldn't say she wasn't content.

Sore, yes.

But also content.

And *extremely* horny.

Straya had stuck to her promise not to use her hands to spank her, but that wasn't to say they hadn't been put to good use between her legs. Apparently, she wasn't the only one ready and eager to get on to the next half of their activities either, because the next thing she knew, Straya was molding her strong, muscular frame to hers in a way that made Phera feel as though they'd been crafted just for each other.

"Mmmm… Engine hot. Just the way I like it."

Draping her torso forward over Phera's bare back, Straya glided her palms up along the valley of the younger woman's spine, slipping her hands around to cup her breasts in strong, lightly calloused palms as she reached her shoulder blades.

"Oh gods, Straya…"

"Uh-huh?"

Straya's touch was feather light as her fingers found her nipples and began to play. Pinching them gently in between massaging, as she pulled her up from the tiled floor right as her knees gave out beneath her.

"You… You…" she panted breathlessly while jolts of pleasure arced directly from her nipples to her aching clit, before eventually giving up on anything more articulate and simply huffing out. "That was nice."

Straya's laugh against her ear sent goosebumps across Phera's skin even in the warmth of their private room.

"It sure was."

With those murmured words, a thrilling stab of terror struck the engineer deep in her gut. And, just like that, a switch was flipped inside her head.

Oh. Shit. Do I love her?

She'd slept with just about every member of the crew (aside from Kelt, who she was sure she'd sway sooner or later), but only when she was with the raider currently grinding her groin against her burning backside as she pinned her against the edge of their pool did it feel like something more than just casual fun between friends.

With Straya, it felt... *Right.*

Though she still harbored a fondness for Daziqir, and in some of her lower moments had even made small offerings for guidance from the precursor goddess of wisdom, Phera had long since left organized religion behind with her parents. She didn't believe that people were guided to each other in some sort of cosmic pre-ordination or anything like that. Soulmates were just something corporations used to sell overpriced jewelry and romantic getaway vacations.

But...

Damn it all!

Straya was just so lovely, and made her feel safe, and made her smile, and-

Yep. You've caught feelings big time, girl.

She hadn't quite reached the "I cannot live in this cruel world without you!" stage of things, but the idea of spending the rest of her life sailing the stars with Straya by her side, robbing megacorps and bratting her beyond belief, sounded like pure heaven to Phera.

Plus, the sex was really good too.

Like, *really* good.

Of course, actually acknowledging this to herself didn't exactly do anything for her from a practical perspective. Did Straya feel the same way about her? And, even if she did, did she want to do something about it? Hell, what did being girlfriends on a pirate ship even look like anyway? Clearly, neither of them were interested in something strictly monogamous. Half the fun of being on a crew of certified hotties like the Blazar Bitches was being able to fuck and be fucked by them on the reg, after all. But, the thought of continuing on as just work friends and occasional fuck buddies with Straya dug at Phera's heart in a way that made her want to cry.

Ah, screw it.

She'd figure out what to do with her feelings later. For now, it was enough that they were together like this. And, with a slight shake of her head, she resolved not to let her anxieties about what might come next for their relationship get in the way of their time together now.

"Okay, seriously. If you don't fuck me, like, now, I'm going to lose my gods damn mind."

Phera felt a little silly being so direct, but the two of them were well past the point of worrying about preserving any sort of virginal pretense. They were both adults who knew what they wanted, and what they wanted was each other.

"Can do."

Straya's laugh was rich as honey as it tickled Phera's ear, making her heart swell with joy and her clit ache with need.

"Up!"

SMACK!

With another sharp slap, she was sent scrambling out of the pool while Straya followed after at a leisurely pace. Watching her thoroughly reddened cheeks roll and wobble with an extremely self-satisfied look on her scarred face.

"Come here, you!"

Phera's back hit the wall with Straya's shove. And, half a heartbeat later, her hands joined it. Framing her face on either side and trapping her in place.

"The sign outside said 'no pushing', you know."

"I know…"

Straya's teeth shined white as her mouth split into a crocodile smile.

"Don't care. Pirate."

"Oh, um, yeah."

Face flushed tomato red as she shifted from foot to foot with the fresh twinge of pain her cheeks' impact with the tiles behind her had produced, Phera licked her lips and turned her violet eyes up to meet the iron gray gaze of the devastatingly sexy pirate looming over her.

Gods. How is she so pretty?

Straya's scars only made her that much more striking, and she could trace the curves of her proud cheekbones and full lips for forever if she wasn't careful. Fortunately, the bigger woman knew just how to distract her. Clawing at her hair and pulling her up onto her tiptoes for a kiss with a low growl as she captured her lips in a hungry, passionate embrace, tongues dancing and probing at one another, before working her way down to her neck.

"Ah!"

Phera's yelp as she bit down hard enough to leave a mark was high and breathy. And, writhing in her clutches, utterly incapable of escape and loving every second of it, pleasure ripped through her chest, causing her heart to pump all the harder. Then, just as she began to whimper in genuine pain, the pressure on her skin was gone, replaced by a tender kiss and then the warmth of Straya's tongue running along her collar bone and down to her breasts. There, she buried her face between them, kissing her way over first one and then the other as her hands massaged them fondly.

Even with hands roughened by years of hard combat, Straya knew just how to make her melt with the simplest of touches.

"Oh gods…"

At Phera's exaltation and its accompanying shiver, Straya laughed around the nipple in her mouth, making her spasm all the more. For seemingly countless, blissful eternities, she suckled and nipped, pinched and rubbed at the two hard pink pebbles while their owner altered between gnawing at her lower lip and raking her fingernails over the pirate's broad shoulders and well-defined back. Eventually, though, Straya started trailing kisses down her ribs and to her hip bone. Dropping to her knees in front of her and hooking one thick thigh over her shoulder as she buried her face between her absolutely drenched auburn curls.

"Mmph!"

At the sensation of Straya's velvety tongue against her labia, dragging its way up to tease at her swollen bud, Phera's hands threaded through the bigger woman's hair. Holding her in place as her eyes drifted up inside her skull in a silent prayer of thanks. Then, when Straya pushed two fingers inside of her, stars exploded behind her eyes and one of her hands found its way back up to her breasts.

Resuming the work the other woman had started as she pinched and rolled one of her nipples between her thumb and forefinger.

By now, the ability to actually speak had completely abandoned the engineer. Instead, she gasped and moaned, legs tensing and thighs trembling as Straya brought her higher and higher with her mouth and hands. She'd already been building toward an orgasm all the while as she'd been spanking her. And now, as she lashed her clit with her tongue and pumped her fingers in and out of her sopping slit, she was all but shoved bodily over the edge into absolute bliss.

"Strayaaaa!"

Crying out her lover's name as she tensed around the fingers curling and twitching inside of her, heedless of who might hear, Phera came, and came *hard*. Her breath ragged and eyes screwed shut tight as wave after wave of muscle-trembling, brain-blanking, breath-stealing ecstasy ripped through her. Turning her limbs to jelly as her cabinmate snickered into her folds and continued to lick and tease.

"Heh."

Once she'd ridden out the last, lingering tremors of her orgasm, Straya gave her enough time to get a grip on her breathing before drawing back and swiping the back of her hand across her mouth and chin where her arousal still clung like dew.

"How you feeling, sweet cheeks?"

"E-Eleven out of ten," the newly-minted pirate panted while sagging against the wall behind her, keeping herself upright as much by willpower as the leg she still had hooked over Straya's shoulder. "All the stars. Best orgasm ever."

"No shit?"

Straya sounded inordinately pleased with herself as she carefully shifted her leg off of her and straightened back up, kneading the Gilgamesh tattoo on her lower back as she regarded the quivering engineer with an evil, leering grin.

"Hope I can keep that up for round two then."

"Round... Round two?"

Phera's question was very nearly lost to her panting, but the note of combined worry and interest in her voice had the corners of Straya's lips twitching up just a bit higher.

"Mmhmm..."

Rolling her well-defined hips and perky cheeks as she sauntered over to the hermetically-sealed container with her clothes and the small sling bag she'd brought with her, Straya popped the seals and started digging around inside. A moment later, she turned back with a bright purple length of silicone attached to a bundle of straps and a small triangle of synthleather.

"Well, hello there. Where has *that* been this entire time?" giggled Phera, starting to catch her second wind.

"Picked it up yesterday."

Straya's shrug didn't quite manage to hide her relief at the pleased look on the younger woman's face as she stepped into the strap-on's harness.

"Figured it wasn't fair that I was the only one in our cabin who hadn't taken you to pound town."

"Huh. Well when you put it like that..."

Phera's grin went lopsided.

"You really don't have much of a choice at all, do you?"

"Afraid not."

Easing up into a more stable position on a pair of still wobbly legs, she watched with wide-eyed, eager anticipation as her cabinmate worked her end of the double-sided dildo inside of her with a half-suppressed gasp that made her breasts sway delightfully, before pulling the straps around her hips nice and snug.

"Oh. Um, wow."

Leaving her with easily twenty-five centimeters of bouncing psuedocock that was made all the more intimidating by the positively ravenous look shining in Straya's iron gray eyes.

"So, uh... Where do you want me?"

Licking her lips, Phera cast about for a padded lounger or towel she could lay on the floor.

"Right there is just fine."

Straya closed the distance to her with the smooth, confident gait of a predator cornering its prey.

"It's time I showed you just what I've been dreaming of doing ever since that first day, sweet cheeks."

Her hands were all over her then, clawing at her damp hair and pulling her in for another hungry, almost desperate kiss. As they

drew apart, the olive-skinned pirate's teeth captured her lower lip, pulling it back before letting it go with a wicked chuckle.

Then, Phera was being pushed harder against the wall and Straya was clawing at her hips.

"Wha-!"

"Shhh…"

Pressing a finger to her lips, Straya winked.

"Just relax and enjoy the ride, yeah?"

She didn't actually give her a chance to answer that, and the next thing she knew, Phera was being hoisted up off the floor and against the wall. Straya's strong hands gripping her cruelly by the sit-spots while she used her hips to push her thighs apart so that she was straddling her waist. No sooner had she spread legs around the other woman, than she was being half-lowered onto and half-impaled by her strap-on.

"Mmph! F-Fuck!"

With her own bodyweight pulling her down, Straya easily thrust all the way up to the hilt inside of her. Filling Phera far more than either Adryel, Steph, or Obette ever had.

"You good?"

"Y-Yeah… It's just a lot to take all at once."

"I believe in you."

Straya sealed her support with another kiss, one that Phera accepted eagerly.

They stayed like that for an indeterminate, yet blissful, amount of time. Phera panting and using Straya's broad shoulders for support, while she in turn drank in the expressions on her face with a mixture of fondness and unabashed amusement.

"Ready?"

Breathing shallowly as she writhed atop the cock inside of her, Phera steadied herself by wrapping her arms around the taller woman's neck and leaned in for another clawing, greedy kiss.

"I want you to fucking wreck me," she gasped, voice thick with lust.

"Hah! Now that I can do."

Kissing and biting, Phera's hands tightened in Straya's curls as she started to bounce her up and down on her cock. Using her superior strength and ruthless grip on her aching thighs to take her right there against the wall with a passion that made her dizzy.

"Oh gods, oh fuck, oh gods, oh fuck!" she gasped in time with the bigger woman's grunts of exertion and groans of pleasure, clawing at her back as they lost themselves in each other.

"Mmph! You are so fucking great, Phera. I… I…"

Straya's steady rhythm briefly lost its measured pace as her breath hitched. Then, mouth buried against the younger woman's auburn hair, she resumed thrusting just a bit harder and breathed.

"I love you."

Those three simple words, barely audible over their grunts and moans touched off an explosion of happiness inside Phera's heaving chest.

"Oh gods, I… I love you too!"

With that, nothing more needed to be said between the two of them. Instead, they lost themselves in a universe all their own.

No ship, no crew.

No shitty pasts, no megacorps.

Just Straya and Phera. Together in this warm, safe, private heaven made just for them. Bringing each other higher and higher as their bodies melted into one and their hearts intertwined.

"Oh fuck, Pheraaaa!"

Hearing her name being groaned with such genuine sincerity and affection sent Phera tipping headfirst into another orgasm. Straya right behind her. Tossing her head back, she cried out in absolute ecstasy, back arched and breasts swaying as Straya's fingers dug into her tender flesh while she trembled and twitched inside of her with the force of her own orgasm.

Some fathomless eternity later, Phera let her body go slack and her head lulled against Straya's shoulder as she carefully eased the two of them down to floor. There, they sat on the slick tiles, sweating, out of breath, Straya still inside of her, and utterly content.

"O… Okay, now *that* was twenty out of ten," Phera eventually managed to snicker into the crook of the bigger woman's neck.

Who, still panting, laughed right along with her, soft and low.

"I'd say that was more like thirty," she countered, and the two of them giggled.

"Works for me."

"So," Straya eventually managed with something approaching her usual sardonic cadence once the two of them had had a chance to catch their breath and come up from the post-climax lethargy that had claimed them. "You up for another soak?"

Looking down at herself, taking in the thick sheen of sweat and other bodily fluids she was covered in, Phera snorted out a laugh and very carefully extricated herself off of Straya with another gasp and shiver as her strap-on at last slipped free.

"I would *love* a bath."

Before leaning in for another kiss, pulling the taller woman up after her.

"Especially if it's with you."

CHAPTER TWENTY-FOUR

CHARGES ACCRUED

Conspiracy to Commit Grand Theft, Conspiracy to Aid and Abet Unauthorized System Access

"So, um, basically, Captain, what we'd like to do is hit Iotech."

Standing before the gathered crew in the Mayhem's rec room, Phera swallowed a sudden burst of nervous energy. When no one said anything, she sucked in another breath and tapped at her wrist comp to advance the projection beside her and Steph to the next slide she'd prepared.

For the last two weeks, the Blazar Bitches had been running a load of surplus hydrocarbons they'd (legitimately!) acquired from an independent B-Sys asteroid mining operation over to an out of the way hab just on the border of Alpha space. Everyone needed solar cells, after all. And, as Straya had explained to her on her very first day, doing non-piracy work between bigger jobs was an excellent way to keep the crew from gathering too much unwanted attention. Plus, legitimate work actually paid pretty well when you didn't have a bunch of executives hoarding all the profits at the top. Nowhere near as much as a proper heist would, but Phera was still looking forward to spending some quality time shopping in Marcos Station's entertainment mod the next time they were in port.

That, and dragging Straya out to go dancing.

The nice thing about above board work too, Phera had discovered, was that it gave her and Steph ample opportunity to put their heads together on a potential raid idea to bring to the Captain. Ever since leaving port, the two of them had been pouring over whitepapers and compiling lists of potential bits of tech and research data that would be worth the effort of absconding with but also not so well-guarded that they'd be likely to wind up in an InterSec cell if something went awry. That last detail in particular was still very much a concern for Phera, whose recurring stress nightmares centered around either having to go back to The Bin or getting arrested. But, after refining their developing plan with Obette and Straya, relying on them to fill in the gaps regarding systems infiltration and the more practical aspects of getting in and out of a secure facility, she was feeling pretty confident that she and Steph had something solid to bring to the table.

Still, that didn't make standing before the Captain as she lounged on a couch with her arms draped around Lem and Kelt any less daunting.

"Iotech, huh? Can't say I'm familiar with the name."

The Captain cocked one dark, perfectly manicured brow at her, and Phera hurriedly cleared her throat.

"You probably wouldn't have, um, ma'am. They're not exactly a big player. At least, not yet."

"They've been working on some bleeding edge gene therapy tech," interjected Steph, practically salivating at the prospect of getting ver hands on said tech. "Based on the whitepapers they've put out, and the chatter we've picked up on a few different medtech social feeds, they're probably going to get bought out by one of the big three Alpha companies sometime in the next few months."

"Which is why if we want to get away with their research and as many of their bio samples as we can, we need to hit them sooner rather than later."

Phera added this last bit with her best approximation of one of Straya's sardonic half-grins.

"From what Steph and I have managed to dig up, this research could potentially revolutionize the way we do neural mesh implants, and probably a whole bunch of other micro surgical procedures too."

"In a few more years," added the doctor with a cautioning finger. "They aren't ready to go to market yet, and only started preliminary animal trials a couple months ago. But, so far it all looks *extremely* promising."

"Is that right?" The Captain's eyes seemed to glow just a bit above their dark circles of sleeplessness. "It would be such a shame then if they were to lose their edge to one or more Proxward medtech concerns I can think of off the top of my head, now wouldn't it?"

Clearly liking what she was hearing, she draped one leg over the other as a serenely malicious look of contemplation settled onto her sharp features.

"How would you get in?"

"Oh! I'm glad you asked."

Grateful to be able to answer this particular question with confidence, Phera issued another command to her wrist comp that skipped past the stock projections and market share graphs she'd prepared, moving straight to a three-dimensional rendering of the Iotech research station she and Steph had picked out for their raid.

"Ob did some digging for us and discovered that Iotech routinely rotates low to mid-level staff between their research station off the primary Excaden route, and their corporate campus on Konnara."

"Konnara?"

Looking up from where he'd been reclining on the deck between Kelt's legs, Shi's soft face took on a professional grimace.

"That's pretty remote for a corporate headquarters, isn't it?"

"It is," agreed Phera. "Though, 'headquarters' is a bit of a stretch. It's not much more than an outpost, really. Staff barracks, admin offices, and some local labs for prepping samples to be sent up to their *actual* research station. They're absolutely hemorrhaging money to some third-party investor we haven't been able to pin down quite yet with all of their staff rotations, but they're pretty confident it'll be worth it in the long run."

She brought up a slide detailing several biological specimens from the planet then. Though they were all clearly derived from known Precursor-seeded species, they'd evolved some unique characteristics of their own in the twenty million years since then.

"For the longest time Konnara was largely ignored by most megacorp interests due to it being so far off major shipping routes to the point of making the fuel expenditure not worth the trip. As a result, Iotech was able to stake a claim to a huge swath of surface that apparently is home to some rather unique organics."

"Not to mention that keeping their staff constantly shuffling between a research station and a remote planetside base has the not insubstantial side benefit of keeping information leaks about ongoing projects to a minimum," added Obette, taking a pull from the coffee thermos he'd been nursing in favor of eating breakfast that morning. He still had bags under his eyes from the all-nighters he'd been pulling for them, and Phera flashed him a thankful smile. "Would you believe they actually market their middle of nowhere campus as a feature in their recruitment materials?"

"Yes," intoned Kelt with a bitter stare, looking up from where she'd been fussing with combing out the tangles in Shi's hair. "'See a wild frontier!' 'Relax on a private beach!' Shit like that, yeah?"

"Wow! How'd you guess?"

"I wonder."

"Either way," interjected Phera before they could get any further off topic. "Those staff rotations are our best way in. All we need is an Iotech shuttle pilot that can be bribed or blackmailed into flying us to the station as new employee transfers."

At this, Obette piped up again.

"Shouldn't be too hard to forge some staff records that'll pass basic scrutiny, Cap. We'll definitely start to raise questions after a couple weeks on-station, but we should be long gone by then, so it won't matter."

"Exactly!"

Phera gave her loosely tied up copper curls a firm nod in agreement, making the amethyst studs in her ears she'd picked up during their last shore leave sparkle in the sunsim. Obette's unshakable confidence was definitely an asset in selling this operation to the Captain as far as she was concerned, and was well worth the blow jobs she'd promised him in return for sacrificing his free time to do mission research for them.

"So, Steph would be posing as a doctor, which shouldn't be too hard since that's what ve actually is. I'll be ver research assistant. Which, again, won't be too hard since I actually was one through most of grad school. Ob, meanwhile, will transfer in a couple weeks ahead of us as a member of station sec."

"Love a bit of muscle on the inside," quipped the doctor.

At this, Obette made a show of flexing one respectably toned bicep for the crew's benefit, sending nearly half a dozen pairs of eyes rolling up toward the curving ceiling.

"Steph and I can handle locating and packing the samples we want when it's time to evac," continued Phera, feeling more and more excited by the moment now that she'd hit her stride. "In the meantime, Obette will sort out the systems side of everything."

"Basic copy and compress, along with a delayed wipe if I can swing it," he clarified at the Captain's questioning look. "I'll make sure to cook up a work history that'll grant me access to secure systems areas, which will make things nice and easy. From what I can tell, their station's running a pretty similar management suite to what Excaden had, so it ought to be a cakewalk."

"And how will we be getting you out, exactly?" prompted Lem, who up until then had just been listening quietly.

"Oh, that's easy."

Steph's answering grin had an edge to it that made Phera's stomach flutter given how many cruel and creative things she'd seen it precede.

"We trigger a medical containment breach near the shuttle bay. It's a research station, so they'll have plenty of not *really* toxic, but still dangerous enough to be worried about, samples on-site. We grab one of them along with the stuff we want, spill it all over the floor on our way out, the station triggers a quarantine, and while everyone's shitting their pants and scrambling for haz suits, Shi swoops in and picks us up."

"We'll want to get our hands on a shuttle for the extraction," corrected Straya, while Adryel nodded in agreement. "The Mayhem is way too cumbersome for a fast exit, and there's no guarantee that you won't have station sec on your ass even with the spill."

"Plus, I'd rather not have our ship on record when they start investigating what happened," added the Captain.

"It'd be best if we could use an Iotech shuttle," put in Lem, mouth pursed in thought as she idly drummed her fingertips against one of her support-strut-thick thighs. "That wouldn't be out of place near their station space. We can keep it back until it's time to pull them out and have the pilot report engine trouble if they ask why they aren't coming into dock."

"So, we'd need to bribe someone for both a drop off *and* a pick up," summarized the Captain.

She didn't sound like this was a deal-breaker, and Phera felt her heart leap.

Lem nodded. "Shouldn't be too hard."

"Adri and I will be there for the extraction too." Straya said this last bit with the sort of steely tone she usually reserved for ordering people (mostly Phera) around. "I don't trust some company puke not to cut and run, and I want to be there in case shit hits the fan and we've got to pull you three out under fire."

"Awww, Stray, that's so sweet," beamed Phera, while Steph just blew her a kiss.

"You're too pretty for prison, sweet cheeks," winked the raider in response.

"Hmmm..."

The Captain's face went blank for half a second then, eyes slipping out of focus in what Phera had come to understand as her "I'm giving this some serious consideration" look, before her painted lips split into a grin with just a bit too many teeth for the engineer's liking.

"All right, let's do it," she declared, making her decision with such suddenness that it took Phera a couple seconds to realize she'd just given them the green light.

While she continued to stare, open-mouthed, the Captain flicked a toe toward the crew's systems infiltrator.

"Put together a roster of Iotech pilots for me and I'll pick one out."

"Already on it, boss."

"I knew there was a reason why I kept you around."

"Besides my dashing good looks?"

"Yes, yes, you're entirely fuckable," dismissed the Captain with a roll of her eyes that didn't budge her smile in the slightest. "Have that list to me by tomorrow morning. I want to get going on this as soon as possible."

"You got it."

"Good boy."

"Um, wouldn't it be easier to just have Ob handle picking the pilot?"

The question was out of Phera's mouth before she'd taken the time to consider it. But, thankfully, it seemed she hadn't just offended her boss.

"Cap is *way* better at this sort of thing," explained the infiltrator with an easy shrug.

"We all have our talents."

Rising to her feet along with the rest of her crew, the Captain straightened out her only partially buttoned up button-up shirt and dragged one talon-tipped hand through her undercut as she regarded Phera and Steph with her still slightly unsettling amber eyes.

"As for you two… You'd better start preparing for your roles as model employees. I expect you both to be positively bubbling with corporate buzzwords and naked ambition by the time we're ready to insert you."

"Aye aye, Captain!" came Phera's eager confirmation, very nearly saluting and just barely managing to stop herself by squeezing her sweaty palms against the sides of her hips.

"No worries there."

Snickering, Steph gave ver platinum pixie cut a dismissive toss.

"Naked ambition is my specialty."

"I couldn't have put it better myself," came Lem's rumbling voice from behind them then as a hand seized each of them by the scruff of their shirt and drew them up onto their tiptoes.

This seemed to be a signal for something Phera had been unaware of, because immediately the rest of the crew sprang into action, though not to help her or Steph. Instead, Obette and Kelt went for a pair of bar stools while the Captain retrieved a storage container from underneath where Lem had been sitting. Straya and Adryel, meanwhile, advanced on the two of them. The latter of whom was making exaggerated grabby-hands gestures as they licked their lips.

"H-Hey! What the hell?" protested Phera, squirming uselessly in Lem's steel vise of a grip, knowing better than to actually kick at Straya as she seized hold of the stretchy waistband of her pants and roughly dragged them down to her ankles along with her panties.

"Official ship-board discipline," sighed the doctor with only somewhat affected exasperation from beside her as ver pants and underwear likewise dropped to ver slender ankles with Adryel's help. As the crew cook wriggled them off along with the boots ve'd been wearing, Steph just huffed. "Geez, Lemmie. I was wondering what was taking you so long."

"Had to wait for just the right moment," supplied the first mate with an answering full-throated chuckle that made Phera's suddenly bare toes curl on reflex. "Bet you bitches thought you were soooo clever with that shit you pulled back at muffin here's…"

At this, she gave Phera a rough shake.

"Initiation."

"Hey, it *was* clever," countered Steph with affronted dignity.

"Yeah it was," agreed Phera as a slightly hysterical giggle bubbled up from inside her.

Her stomach now an icy ball of mixed fear and growing excitement, she exchanged a look with the adorably indignant crew doc, and giggled again.

"Besides, I don't know why you're dragging *me* into this. I was just taking advantage of the opportunities afforded to me."

"What a coincidence," answered Lem, voice positively dripping with grim promises of retribution to come as Straya pulled Phera's top and bra up to her armpits, allowing her breasts to bounce free. "So am I."

"Eep!"

At the caress of recycled air around her rapidly firming nipples, whatever sassy retort Phera had been about to fire back with died on her lips.

"Oooh, nice touch, Stray!"

Seeing her nakedness, Adryel immediately copied the maneuver, baring Steph's smaller breasts to the crew.

"You know, if you wanted me naked, Adri, all you had to do was ask."

"And where's the fun in that?" countered the cook just as easily, giving one peach colored nipple a friendly pinch that wrung out a slightly higher-pitched version of Phera's earlier yelp from the doctor.

"Hey! Wait your fucking turn!" growled Lem, yanking away her two captured crewmates from their disrobers' wandering hands.

Adryel and Straya both, in a single motion, flipped her off.

"Spoil sport."

"Greedy bitch."

Which, in turn, made the mountain of a woman snort out another laugh as she hefted the doctor and engineer a bit higher so that their toes no longer touched the deck at all. And, with the sort of effortless ease that had the ball of ice in Phera's stomach tripling in density, she carried them over to the bar stools Kelt and Obette had prepared for them. Draping them across their padded seats, while Straya and Adryel moved to secure their wrists, ankles, elbows, and knees with synthleather cuffs and metallic clips from the container the Captain held open between them. Locking them in place around the support rungs and legs of their stools in short order.

Of course, *now* was when Phera's nose started to itch.

"This really seems like overkill if you ask me-" she started to huff, wrinkling her nose in a futile attempt to sort out her itch.

"Nobody did."

Before jerking with a very un-pirate-like yelp when Lem pinched her inner thigh way harder than was strictly necessary.

"Urk! Hey!"

The whole process had taken less than a minute, and had been carried out with the sort of well-oiled efficiency that made Phera guess that this probably wasn't the first time that one or more of the crew had been (un)lucky enough to be singled out for discipline by Lem.

Truth be told, it was actually pretty hot.

Still, that wasn't going to stop her from whining about it.

"But... but...! Come on!"

Protesting more for the sake of protesting and so as to not have to dwell too much on what was to come next, Phera attempted to simultaneously close her lewdly splayed thighs and wriggle free from her restraints. Succeeding only in producing a chorus of helpless, metal-on-metal rattling sounds as she flailed her wrists and ankles the handful of centimeters she had available to her.

"I can understand why you'd be mad at Steph, lemon cakes, but why me too? You agreed to that competition before we even started!"

"Phera, Phera, Phera…"

Heaving out a long-suffering sigh, Lem pushed back her long swoop of cobalt hair with the sort of smile that, had she actually been able to see it just then, would've had Phera scrambling for the cargo bay and a vacsuit as fast as she could, stool and all.

"Yes, Lem, Lem, Lem?"

"I thought you were supposed to be smart."

"Humph. I *am* smar-"

SMACK!

Lem surprised her then by cutting her off with a swat that was far lighter than her usual missile impact.

"Aieee!"

But, landing as it was against her already starting to glisten vulva, that didn't really make that much of a difference.

"I'm doing this because I can," the first mate continued conversationally, rubbing her surprisingly soft fingers in slow circles along where she'd just swatted while she did much the same between Steph's legs. "Well, that, and because I haven't had a chance to introduce you to my tawse yet."

"Oh… Oh my gods! H-How is this even remotely fair?"

Phera's grumbling was largely robbed of its impact by her rolling hips and shortened breath as Lem parted her lower lips and teased at her opening.

"Privileges of rank, my dear," chimed in Obette from in front of her.

Who, she noticed with some confused trepidation, was currently in the process of extricating Steph's rather lacy briefs from ver crumpled slacks. Looking to her left, she saw that Straya was doing much the same with her own pants. She was just about to ask what was going on, when her newfound maybe-probably-girlfriend balled up her pastel purple panties and advanced on her with a smile so broad it surely had to be making her face hurt.

"Open up, sweet cheeks," she ordered.

"Wh-?"

Phera's question was answered for her when Straya shoved her balled up panties into her half-open mouth.

"Umph!"

Face going molten and her hip wiggling against Lem's probing fingers increasing tenfold, all of her protests were stifled by her makeshift gag as Straya poked it further into her mouth.

"It's going to be *soooo* much fun watching Lem destroy your ass," she murmured, her tough, sweet laughter making Phera's heart soar and clit ache as she pushed back her bangs to kiss her forehead. "Take your licks like a proper pirate and I might just kiss them better for you later tonight, yeah?"

As enticing as that offer was, Phera was extremely grateful that her reply was stymied by her panty-gag, as she was pretty sure Straya would've had her paying for it in spades.

"I'm a little curious too as to why you took so long to exact your well-earned Revenge, Lem, honey," put in the Captain then as she sauntered over with a wicked looking length of what appeared to be genuine leather gripped between her hands.

It was long enough to cover both of Phera's cheeks in a single swing, split into two tails down the middle, and looked *way* too thick as far as the auburn-haired engineer was concerned.

"Wanted to wait for muffin's muffins to cool off first," explained the first mate with a shrug, drawing back her hand and gliding an arousal-slicked pair of fingertips along the pressure lines left behind on Phera's ample cheeks by her panties.

That managed to get a snort from Straya and just about everyone else in the room.

"Yeah. Good luck with that."

"Pretty sure only a *little* bruised is about as good as you're likely to get."

"No kidding."

"Well, I applaud your self-control. I would've had these two teases over my knee the very next day," crooned the Captain, sneering at the pair of upturned seats before her as she passed along her implement. "Put on a good show, would you?"

"Abso-fucking-lutely," intoned Lem, her deep voice going dark as the void as she lightly rapped the tawse against first Phera's seat and then Steph's. "They aren't going to be sitting for a month by the time I'm through with them."

This pronouncement was met by simultaneous muffled squeaks from the two trapped teases in question.

With arms like Lem's, Phera very much believed her threat.

Well, at least never sitting down will make me look like a real go-getter when we hit Iotech...

"Right then, girls!"

Clapping her hands with one of her trademark bursts of sudden energy, the Captain hurried back to the rec room's couch and flopped down onto her spot from earlier.

"Place your bets. Who's breaking first?"

"Phera."

"Phera."

"Phera."

All around the room the crew piped up with the name of their latest recruit as they moved to join the Captain on the couch, with only Obette and Shi arguing for Steph.

"Oh come on, she's got *way* more padding back there!" insisted the silver-haired infiltrator, while Shi just nodded, blushing as he assessed said padding and licked his lips. "She'll outlast ver on pure physics alone."

"As if," scoffed Straya, smirking fondly at the engineer's fully ripened peach of an ass, no doubt imagining what she'd be getting up to with it later. "Phera's a total pushover compared to Steph. Trust me, I have plenty of experience."

"We all do, Stray," countered the Captain, likewise leering at the well-rounded curves and compact yet jiggly cheeks awaiting their first taste of the tawse. "My money is still on our good doctor's pain tolerance outlasting the cabin girl's, though."

"See? Cap gets it."

Cutting loose with an annoyed growl, Straya shoved Obette good-naturedly, but still hard enough to send him toppling off his perch on the arm of the couch.

While everyone else (including Steph and Obette) laughed at this exchange, Phera threw as pointed a glare as she could back at the gathered audience behind her. However, she didn't have much time to glower before the first of what was sure to be way too many lashes found its mark.

SWISH-CRACK!

Lem, clearly trying to secure her wager brought her twin-tailed leather strap exploding down against the thoroughly restrained roboticist's raised rump. Each tail seeming to land as its own separate, vengeful entity before blending together with its fellow to carve out a six centimeter wide band of plasma exhaust across both of Phera's cheeks at once that terminated in hard, right-angled welts along the outer curve of her right hip where the tips of the tawse had dug in with particular menace.

Straya and Adryel whistled in unison.

"Damn."

While Phera cried out for all she was worth.

"Aieeth!"

Muffled as her protests were by her saliva-soaked panties, her howl of pain was still audible. Accompanied by a chorus of metallic clinking from the clips holding her frantically bobbing arms and legs in place against the stool.

She'd barely had time to even register that first swat, though, before...

SWISH-CRACK!

SWISH-CRACK!

Two more fell in rapid-fire succession against first her sit-spots and then her upper thighs.

Stars and void! Is there a fucking steel core hiding in that thing?

Vision already starting to blur with the first stirrings of hot, salty tears, Phera threw an accusatory look at Lem, but only saw her hefting regular leather with a broad smile, looking pleased as could be.

Biceps that big should be illegal. Humph.

SWISH-CRACK!

Then again...

Hearing Steph's equally-muffled yelp and accompanying restraint rattling had Phera thinking that perhaps she might've been premature in her rush to judgment. She was starting to see now why the first mate seemed to like her tawse so much.

SWISH-CRACK!

SWISH-CRACK!

Especially when the squirming, platinum-haired crew doc caught two more absolutely ruthless lashes across ver far more compact sit-spots and thighs. However, Phera couldn't help but notice too that other than faster breathing through ver nostrils, Steph seemed to be handling ver lashes far better than she was.

Uh-oh.

*SWISH-**CRACK!***

As if to drive that point home for her, Lem whipped her tawse down against the centers of Phera's unprotected, wobbly cheeks with a truly astounding amount of force then. Putting her entire, absolutely jacked body into the swing and pivoting her hips in a picture-perfect follow through as she did so. So powerful was her swat, in fact, that Phera was pretty sure she'd actually managed to push her stool forward by a centimeter or two.

Lem wasn't about to give her even a cursory moment to catch her breath this time, though, and instead brought the tawse whipping back down three more times in merciless succession.

*SWISH-**CRACK!***

*SWISH-**CRACK!***

*SWISH-**CRACK!***

All atop her sit-spots with the sort of eye-popping precision that can only come from years of practice coupled with natural talent.

Fuck, fuck, shit, fuck, OW! she howled internally, while aloud her wailing came out as unique and varied permutations of "oomph!" and "ackth!"

*SWISH-**CRACK!***

*SWISH-**CRACK!***

*SWISH-**CRACK!***

*SWISH-**CRACK!***

Steph, by comparison, seemed to favor high-pitched squeaks and the occasional low guttural growl as Lem turned her attention back to ver. Which, had she not been in the middle of trying to will the nerves in her bottom to stop screaming at her, Phera would've found pretty damn cute.

Ah, hell, ve's still cute, she admitted to herself, toes curling and uncurling with her labored breathing as Lem shuffled back over to stand beside her. *Oh fuck, here we go again...*

—

As was so often the case, Phera's overexcited horniness helped to elevate her pain tolerance well past its usual norm. Not that that stopped her from howling and thrashing with every cruel, full-bodied cut of the lash across her unprotected flanks and thighs. Still, about two dozen whip cracks of the tawse later, she indeed was the first to break. And, two dozen more after that, Lem finally decided that she and Steph had had enough.

Which was good, because by the feel of her absolutely molten, throbbing backside and thighs, Phera was pretty sure there wasn't a square centimeter of unwelted skin to be found from the crowns of her now extremely swollen cheeks down to just above the backs of her knees. Lem hadn't been kidding about keeping them from sitting for a month, it seemed. Though, she suspected she'd probably be back to sitting somewhat comfortably (on a pile of pillows) in only a few days. Being as voluptuous as she was definitely had its advantages, and Lem's tawse wasn't quite as heavy as she'd at first feared. Either way, the first mate had still managed to deliver a truly universal-class spanking, and she knew she'd be remembering it long, long after all of her welts and bruises eventually disappeared.

Sometime in the next decade or so, she guessed. Judging by the exhaust she could practically *feel* radiating off of her aft thruster of an ass just then.

"Well, well, congratulations to everyone not named Obette or Shi," crowed the Captain, slow-clapping from her position lounging against Straya while resting her knee-high booted feet atop Adryel's lap. "You two get last dibs on the prizes."

"Ah, dammit!"

"Oh well…"

Phera, meanwhile, had not at all liked the emphasis the older woman had just put on the word "prizes", and her look of mingled confusion and worry must've shown on her face, because the Captain favored her with one of her more piratical grins.

"It's tradition, swabbie," she explained with a casual flick of her fingers. "Whoever Lem snatches up for these 'official' discipline sessions stays locked in place until dinner time for… Well, let's just call it community service."

"That's right!"

Extricating themself out from under the Captain's legs and moving to join Lem behind the two sore-seated sailors strapped to their stools, Adryel rubbed their hands together with eager anticipation.

"Which one you want first, Lem?"

"Hmmm…"

Phera felt herself shiver and her ankles flutter on reflex as the muscular first mate dragged her length of leather up and down between her legs. Blushing all over again as she felt her arousal slicking its passage.

"New girl here's basically begging for it," she mused with her typical rough affection. "And far be it from me to turn away such willing tail."

Rapping the now thoroughly oiled tawse against Phera's glistening lips, Lem coaxed an encore performance of restraint rattling out of the panting pirate.

"Yep. She's first."

"I call seconds," piped up Kelt then, pulling her salt and pepper hair up off the nape of her neck and twisting it into a slightly messier bun than usual as she rose from the couch and made her way toward the hatch leading out to the rest of the hab cylinder. "Just need to grab my equipment first. You want me to get yours while I'm at it, Cap?"

"Would you?"

Nestling more fully against Straya's full chest, hands pillowed behind her head as she settled in to watch the upcoming show, the Captain flashed her senior engineer an approving smile.

"It's been far too long since I had such ready access to our good doctor and ver innumerable charms."

With this, she winked at Steph, who still somehow managed to look shamelessly flirtatious despite being gagged and drooling slightly as ve waggled ver eyebrows at her.

"Grab mine too, yeah?" put in Straya as Kelt turned to leave. "It's under my bunk."

She received a wave in acknowledgment, just as Adryel's pants came down and their cock bounced free.

"I do so love a well-disciplined crew."

Grinning, the Captain punctuated her content sigh by reaching up and dragging Straya's head closer by her newly grown out curls for the sort of casually possessive kiss that was so typical of her.

"You and me both, boss."

Returning the kiss, Straya looked up and fixed Phera with a decidedly hungry grin.

"Give her a fun ride, Lem," she called, just as the woman in question was finishing securing a harness around her hips that she'd procured from the restraint container at her feet. "I'm coming for that ass as soon as Kelt's had her fill, and I'm not going to be nice."

This news very nearly made Phera's eyes pop out of her head, especially when she felt the tip of Lem's strap-on rubbing up and down between her absolutely drenched lips.

"What a coincidence."

The first mate's answering chuckle was smooth velvet over unyielding tungsten, and sent shivers up Phera's spine.

"Neither am I."

Gods. I love my job.

CHAPTER TWENTY-FIVE

CHARGES ACCRUED

Lewd Conduct, Indecent Exposure, Solicitation

Now that the Captain had given her approval for the Iotech raid, things began to move, and move fast. Within a month, a promising shuttle pilot had been identified and reached out to with an offer for some extra-curricular flying. And, after a handful of heavily-encrypted messages back and forth, had been convinced to ferry the insertion team to and from the research station. Just *how* the Captain had managed to do that so quickly, Phera had no idea. But, hey, it was hard to argue with results.

With their transportation secured, Obette turned his attention to forging employment records for the three of them, while Lem acquired Iotech uniforms from a small textiles printer on Marcos Station the crew had done business with in the past. From what Phera could tell based on the mannequins and projection displays she'd seen when they went in to collect their order, they mostly specialized in producing cute outfits for dancers and people looking to hook up at one of the station's many clubs. Still, they'd managed to knock out a flawless recreation of Iotech's navy blue and silver uniforms.

When Phera had tried hers on, she'd had to fight down a fit of ecstatic giggling. She hadn't even given the first mate her measurements, but either the woman had an exceptional eye for sizing people up or Straya had checked for her, because when she saw herself in the three-sided mirror in the back of the little shop dug into the asteroid, she looked the very picture of an Alpha-side corporate functionary.

It. Was. *Perfect.*

———

Well, almost.

Sitting between Steph and Obette at a corner table in a noisy Alpha-side station bar a few days later, it seemed that things were starting to come apart at the seams before they even started. They'd met up with their Iotech pilot. And, after a round of awkward introductions with false names and drink ordering, he'd said that there was a problem they had to discuss right then and there. Only, when they tried to press him on what said problem actually was, he began to dither instead.

"I mean... It's just..."

"You received your fee, yes?" prompted Obette, posture relaxed as he regarded the man who'd introduced himself to them as Vernie with a piercing stare Phera had never seen him use before.

"Half of it, yeah," confirmed the forty-something pilot, starting to get defensive. "It's just-"

"Right."

Obette cut him off with one imperiously cocked silver eyebrow. Swirling his liquor in its fluted glass, looking completely at ease and not at all like he was worried the linchpin to their entire operation was about to bolt.

"And, you *also* understand that you'll receive the second half once we've concluded our business?"

"Yes, yes. Your 'associate' made the terms of our arrangement very clear in their message."

"Then what's the problem here, exactly?"

Mopping at his brow with a napkin, the Iotech pilot cast a wary glance around the packed bar and then lowered his voice to just above a stage whisper as he leaned in across the table.

"Look. They're going to figure out that I was the one who brought you three in after you do... whatever it is you're going to do, aren't they?"

"Of course," agreed Obette with his usual impenetrable affability, finding Phera's bouncing leg beneath the table and giving her thigh a reassuring, but nevertheless commanding, squeeze. "What's your point? As far as the company will know, you were just doing your job. You received orders to shuttle three transfers, you shuttled those three transfers. Easy as could be."

"I suppose so..."

Staring intently at what Phera had to guess was his second or third drink of the evening going off of the flush in his face and the sweat shine on top of his balding head, Vernie gave the dark liquid a stir with his straw, making ice clink against the sides of his glass as he did so.

"But, what if they check with security here? They'll know that I stopped off for fuel, and they're going to see that you didn't disembark with me, aren't they?"

Wincing into her own glass of fruity alcohol, Phera had to admit he raised a good point.

Obette just scoffed.

"Oh, please. Who do you think you're dealing with here, friend? Corrupting cam feeds for a minute or two is child's play. When Iotech eventually checks with station sec here, all they'll see is you departing to stretch your legs upon landing, and a scrambled feed when you take off tomorrow morning."

"Such a shame," piped up Steph then, sucking condensation off the tip of one slender, pink-painted fingertip. "Someone in maintenance really ought to double-check their repair schedules." Ver shoulders rose and fell in an unconcerned shrug then as ve winked one mother of pearl eye at the grimacing man. "Oh well."

"Okay, okay, *fine*. You've got that covered, I guess. But, still." Draining half his glass with obviously mounting frustration, Vernie gave an irritable huff. "What about your pickup then, huh?"

"Did our mutual friend not explain all of this to you already?"

Although his tone hadn't changed, Phera could still tell that Obette was starting to lose his patience by the set of his shoulders and the tightening of his jaw.

"They did," the pilot allowed, gaining some measure of courage from shotgunning the rest of his drink before letting out a hiss from the burn in his throat and croaking. "I still don't see how I'm not going to catch hell for pulling you three out of there, though."

"Oh, you definitely will," agreed Obette, waving a hand in a dismissive gesture. "That's why we're paying you so much. Even so, as far as the company will be able to tell, you'll just have been following your schedule. After all, how were *you* supposed to know that some nefarious ne'er-do-wells had hijacked their staff transfer system? If anything, the IT department are the ones who will be under the most scrutiny."

"Still…"

Blowing out his breath with exaggerated weariness, Vernie shook his head.

"Look. Bottom line here is I'm taking on an awful lot of risk for you people."

"Yes," agreed Obette once again, voice totally even. "Which is why we're *paying* you."

"See, that's the thing, though. The way things stand right now, I'm not so sure it's really worth risking my neck. Especially since chances are pretty high that you'll wind up getting caught anyway."

Eyes narrowing, it finally dawned on Phera then what was happening. Vernie was trying to angle for a better deal!

Oh, you have got to be kidding me! she fumed silently, any sympathy she might've held for the man evaporating with the wave of exasperation that rushed through her. *We're already paying you out the ass to just do your regular job and now you want more?*

Obette didn't seem to be all that concerned, however, which she took as a good sign.

"Oh? Caught you say? And why would that be?"

"I mean, come *on*!" exploded Vernie, drawing curious glances from their nearer neighbors before remembering that this was supposed to be a confidential meeting and lowering his voice. "It's a corporate research station. You really think they're just going to let you waltz out the door?"

"The plan was to jog or maybe sprint, but that is the gist, yes," nodded Obette, eyes hardening. "Again, I have to ask. What's your point here, friend?"

"Well, I mean… Who's to say you're not going to rat me out if you get caught? I don't exactly know you, now do I?"

Rubbing one hand over the back of his neck, Vernie dropped the scared shuttle pilot routine altogether in favor of a smug half-grin.

"Sure, your money's good. But, like I said, this is a *corporate* station we're talking about here. There's a reason why they hire all that extra security, you know."

"Again," came Obette's now frosty reply for the third time. "What's your point?"

"Well, not a *point*, exactly, but…"

Face splitting into a full on shit-eating grin, the pilot lifted a slate out from under the table and gave it a waggle.

"It just seems to me that I could save myself all sorts of headaches by taking this here recording of our conversation to Iotech *and* keep my half of the fee your boss already sent. Pretty sure they'd be willing to fill in that second half too in return for scooping up three corporate spies. I'd be a damn hero."

"Um! You definitely shouldn't do that," Phera found herself blurting out in a rush while Steph just snorted. "Our Cap- I mean, our boss… She's someone who you *really* don't want holding a grudge against you."

"And, yet…"

Vernie made a show of buffing his fingernails against the front of his shirt.

"I think I may just have to take my chances, little lady."

With that, Vernie began to push himself up from his seat.

"I'll just be on my way then."

"But-!"

However, before Phera could say anything more, Steph cut her off with an exhausted sigh.

"Okay, fine," ve huffed, rolling ver eyes. "We'll throw in Astrid as a bonus if it'll shut you up."

"What?"

This reply was delivered in stereo by both Phera and the shuttle pilot.

"*Clearly*, you're stressed out about all this," Steph surmised with the sort of semi-exasperated contempt of someone having to explain something extremely obvious. "So, take her out back and have her suck your cock or whatever until you're ready to calm down, yeah?"

"Huh. Now there's an idea."

The casual way the platinum-haired enby had just offered up ver friend for service to the pilot had the desired effect of completely short-circuiting his attempts to leave.

"She gives some truly excellent head, I can promise you that," continued Steph with a smirk.

"I can attest to this as well," agreed Obette, all cordiality once again as he took a sip from his drink. "She's a bit of a staff favorite, actually."

"Hmmm..."

Easing back into his seat, Vernie gave his scraggly chin a thoughtful rub while his watery eyes swept up and down over Phera's soft features and plump lips.

"It *has* been a while."

"I- I- I-!"

Face flushing to match her hair, Phera continued to splutter in indignation while Steph leaned in and whispered in her ear; kissing her cheek to cover the movement.

"This guy's been staring at your tits ever since we got here. Just roll with it, yeah?"

Swallowing whatever she'd been about to say next, Phera's cheeks pushed out in a mildly annoyed pout. But, between the doctor's quick peck and reassuring pat beneath the table, she was quickly mastering her initial flustered outrage. And, well, while the pilot wasn't *exactly* her type, he was attractive enough in a sort of intentionally unkempt way that she was pretty sure she could make it work.

Especially if it meant keeping their mission on track.

Plus, well... She'd be lying if she said she hadn't just discovered a brand new kink in being whored out like this.

"Ahem."

Clearing her throat, Phera turned to more fully face the pilot, inviting his scrutiny now as she unconsciously began twirling a lock of unbound hair around a finger.

"I'm game if you are, Vernie."

Her new burst of confidence managed to knock some of the smirk off his face.

"That's... Ahem."

Smiling internally at having managed to throw the man so off-balance *and* cut short his attempts to wrangle more money out of the Captain, Phera gave him a flirtatious wink while Steph slipped an arm around her shoulders; pulling her in nice and close in a way that pushed her round breasts up and together in front of her.

"She swallows," ve singsonged, fingers wiggling enticingly.

"I, um... R-Really?"

"*Every. Last. Drop.*"

Beaming now, Steph gave Phera's upper arm a little rub.

"Isn't that right, Astrid?"

Fully leaning into her slutty persona now, Phera lasciviously licked her lips while maintaining unwavering eye contact with the pilot.

"My parents always taught me to clean up after myself."

Clearing his throat again, the color in his cheeks only partially due to the alcohol he'd been consuming, it finally seemed to dawn on Vernie just what all was being offered here.

The profile the Captain had pulled together on the man had made it abundantly clear that he very rarely managed to find much success in his romantic life. Despite the number of profiles he maintained on different dating websites, Vernie was someone who mostly kept to himself and thought that being "nice" and "into music" were somehow personality traits. Casual sex, likewise, was harder to come by on Alpha-side habitats, as Phera had spent years miserably learning. And, well, she was hot.

"You're, um. You're sure?" he pressed, mopping at his forehead once again as he tried to surreptitiously adjust himself beneath the table.

"Of course she is!" insisted Steph before Phera could respond.

"If it'll put your mind at ease, I'll be happy to blow you, yeah," she added a moment later when it became clear that the pilot was going to need a little more prodding, her head swimming with an odd mixture of humiliation at being offered up like this in the first place and exhilaration at being able to use the man's own libido against him.

"I, uh... I was kind of hoping maybe we could do more than that actually..."

Failing to meet her violet eyes, Vernie gave his ice cubes another stir.

"Fuck her too if you want. There's a reason why she's a staff favorite," interjected Obette as smoothly as ever before Steph could offer up any other sexual favors on ver crew's behalf. "Just make it quick, yes? We've got an early push off tomorrow, and I'd like to be well-rested for my first day on the job."

"Don't you worry, Obble."

Pushing her chair back from the table, Phera summoned up every ounce of piratical swagger she'd been developing over the last couple months.

"I'm sure we can find a happy medium in terms of time," she cooed, sashaying her way around to the other side of the table with as much hip swaying as she felt she could safely get away with. "What do you say, big guy? We have a deal?"

Apparently deciding to surrender himself to his good fortune, Vernie put up absolutely no fight as Phera drew him up out of his seat and threaded her arm around his.

"N-Now?"

"No time like the present, yeah?"

"Ahem."

Straightening to his full height with yet more exaggerated throat-clearing, the pilot slipped his arm free of Phera's and seized a handful of her ass instead. Making her jump as he squeezed as hard as he could.

"Never had a spy girl before," he chuckled. "This ought to be fun."

His bravado was back in full swing now, and it took all of Phera's self-control not to roll her eyes or stomp a heel down on top of his foot.

"Flatterer," she simpered instead.

As she allowed herself to be led away by the pilot's hand inexpertly groping at her ass, she felt her wrist vibrate. And, turning her hand over to peek at the display of her wrist comp, saw that she'd received a pair of messages. One from Steph and the other from Obette.

[Tell him anal costs extra. <3]

[Ping us if you need help and we'll come get you.]

Rolling her eyes, Phera cast a petulant pout back over her shoulder at her fellows. Who, in turn, raised their glasses to her in salute, Steph blowing her a kiss. And, still smiling for Vernie's benefit, she quickly tapped out a response to the both of them.

[BOTH of you are making this up to me later tonight. >:|]

———

Forty-eight minutes, one awkward blow job, and an entirely below average (though to be fair, Phera's standards had risen dramatically in recent times) fuck that left her with a stain on the back of her top that she'd have to hide with her jacket for the rest of the night later, Phera and Vernie returned to where Steph and Obette waited for them inside the bar. They'd since ordered snacks while she was away, she saw. And, with an exaggerated harrumph, she snatched up the bowl of fried peppers the infiltrator favored and began popping them into her mouth two at a time in retaliation as she plopped back down onto her seat.

"We got you a drink too."

Patting her shoulder, Obette slid a tall glass of pastel pink slush topped with sliced fruit and a healthy dollop of whipped cream over to her.

"Awww, thanks!"

Any lingering annoyance Phera might have still been harboring over having to put up with Vernie's half-assed pumping immediately evaporated as she accepted the beverage. And, after taking a long pull and smacking her slightly swollen and no longer painted lips in satisfaction, she made a cursory attempt to straighten out her rumpled top as she flashed her fellow pirates a conspiratorial smirk.

"We good to go?" prompted Steph, turning ver attention to the swaggering pilot, as ver usually playful mother of pearl gaze hardened. "No worries about the company finding rogue hair follicles on the passenger couches or anything like that?"

Vernie, still grinning like an idiot, just nodded as he settled into his seat with a satisfied sigh.

"I am completely confident in your competence, yes."

Drawing his slate out of his pocket, he showed Steph and Obette its screen, letting them watch as he deleted the recording he'd made.

"Great!"

Glossy lips tipping up at the corners, the doctor tugged the bowl of peppers Phera had stolen to a spot between the two of them and popped one into ver mouth, taking ver time chewing as ve continued to stare the pilot down.

"You live up to your end of the deal and pick us up on time, and I'll be sure to give you the antidote to that bioweapon I infected Phera with once we're done."

For the second time that evening, a verbal grenade the doctor oh-so-casually lobbed into the middle of the conversation was met with a pair of simultaneous "What?!"s.

Phera, about to jump to her feet, managed to spot the familiar gleam of mischief in Steph's eye just in time, though. And, rather than start shaking the doctor, demanding ve fix whatever ve'd done to her, she instead pivoted her outrage into bemusement.

"Oh for fuck's sake...I was *wondering* what that injection was for!" she laughed, slapping her forehead as if she'd just remembered she'd forgotten to water her plants. "You're the worst, Doc."

"Just a little insurance policy, sweet thing," Steph crooned, offhandedly petting her sweat-matted copper curls while continuing to pin the pilot in place with ver stare. "I take it we have an understanding, Vernie?"

"I-! That's-! You can't be-!"

"Yessss?"

Steph remained completely unflappable in the face of Vernie's incoherent, accusatory half-starts at an exclamation. And, soon enough, the storm of indignation that had been brewing in the man's expression gave way to horror as it finally dawned on him just how much he'd fucked up.

Both literally and figuratively.

"Um, yes!" he all but squeaked, posture tightening in his seat as a fresh sheen of perspiration broke out across his forehead and receding hairline. "I... I'll do whatever you say! I'll-!"

"It'll be fine, friend. This sort of thing happens surprisingly often with our good doctor here."

Obette, draping a soothing arm around the man's shoulders, drew him back to his feet before he could really start to panic.

"Besides, it usually takes at least a month before you start seeing symptoms anyway. You'll be fine."

"I… Really?"

Clinging to the lifeline the suave infiltrator was dangling before him, the pilot's ashen face lit up with cautious hope.

"You definitely don't want to let it go more than six weeks if you like having your cock not necrotize," confirmed Steph with the sort of malicious smile that would've made the Captain proud. "But, yeah, you'll be fine."

"NECROTIZE?!"

"I know, right? Scary stuff for sure," agreed Obette with grim solidarity, steering Vernie toward the bar while doing his best to continue sounding reassuring. "Like I said, though, you'll be fine. As soon as you pick us up, ve can stick you with the antidote and that'll be the end of it. In the meantime, how about I buy you another drink? No necrotoxic prions in this one, I promise."

"I…"

Shaking his head to clear it and summoning a hollow shell of the earlier bravado he'd had while he'd been taking her from behind some ten minutes earlier, Phera watched the pilot straighten back up.

"I think I could use about six."

"You and me both, friend," sighed Obette, throwing a "we are so going to talk about this later" look back at Steph who just wiggled ver fingers in a flirtatious wave. "You and me both."

CHAPTER TWENTY-SIX

CHARGES ACCRUED

Identity Fraud

The next two weeks wound up being some of the slowest of Phera's life as she and Steph sat around waiting for their turn to infiltrate the Iotech station. Oh, she understood *why* they needed to stagger out their insertions, Obette being able to pull off his end of the operation as their infiltrator on the inside hinged largely on him not being associated with the two of them in the slightest. Which, unfortunately, meant that she and Steph were left with no other choice but to wait for Vernie to make another trip back to Konnara to "retrieve" the two of them before they could join their fellow pirate and start snatching up megacorp goodies.

It all made sense, sure. But, still, understanding *why* something had to be done a certain way didn't make it any easier to deal with in the moment.

Still, it wasn't all bad. She spent the next two weeks laying low with Steph in a hotel room on the station they'd met Vernie on. Watching vids on the cramped room's holodisplay, ordering takeout, performing degenerate acts that would've given Phera's parents a heart attack to learn about, and putting the finishing touches on their cover identities and disguises. Which was actually a lot of fun!

One evening, they dyed Steph's platinum pixie cut a deep black, and Phera managed to give ver bangs a slight trim that lent ver a stern air of authority. Hard though that was to reconcile with ver borderline mad scientist personality, ve worked it surprisingly well to the point that she had no doubt that "Doctor Iris" would fit right in as a no-nonsense corporate scientist once they were among Iotech's research staff.

Phera's own dye job, on the other hand, turned her copper curls a cascading gradient of purple and teal that she thought offset her violet eyes rather nicely. After a mortifyingly short amount of back and forth among the crew, it had been unanimously decided that she'd pass much easier as a ditzy research assistant fresh out of college than as a stuffy academic like Steph. Which, Phera had to admit as she took in her brand new look in the full-length mirror in their hotel room, fit her like a glove. With her crisply pressed Iotech uniform and its flattering embroidery of silver accent lines tracing over her curves in all the right places, she could've been straight out of a corporate recruiting pamphlet.

This particular revelation managed to put a rather petulant frown on the newly-minted pirate's pretty face, but her annoyance quickly transmuted into a pleasant thrumming low in her abdomen when she eventually received Straya's reply to the pictures she'd sent her.

[Looks hot. Bet it'd look even better between my legs.]

Steph had noticed her flush as she'd stared at the inside of her wrist. And, after spying at her comp glove's projected display over her shoulder, had immediately snapped a second picture of ver groping her chest while grinning into the mirror in front of them. Sending it along with a message of ver own.

[Don't worry, I'll be happy to test that hypothesis for you.]

"Oh my gods! I can't believe you just did that!"

Phera had to press a fist to her mouth to contain her giggles as Steph's slate pinged in acknowledgment that ver message had been sent successfully.

"She is *so* going to get you back for that later. You know that, right?"

"Oh please."

Steph didn't quite cackle in response, but it was close enough to shake loose Phera's own laughter.

"What's life without a little bit of danger?"

"You know… Can't say I disagree with you there, doc."

It would take at least an hour for Steph's message to work its way through the patchwork network of data buoys between them and wherever the Mayhem had withdrawn to in B-Sys, but Phera had no doubt that her cabinmate and recently outed paramour (it was near impossible to keep secrets on a ship that small, and Straya had taken a liking to having her sit on her lap during meals) would absolutely take the impish doctor's reply for the challenge that it was.

"Anyway…"

Completely unfazed by the prospect of impending retribution from the owner of the Blazar Bitches' third largest pair of biceps, Steph found one of Phera's rapidly hardening nipples beneath her top and gave it a playful pinch while ver other hand slipped down the front of her pants in a caress that melted her completely.

"Come along now, sweet thing," ve purred, dragging her toward the bed they'd been sharing for the last few days. "Let's give your girlfriend something to *really* be annoyed about."

"Why, Steph!"

Phera let loose with a haughty, affected gasp that quickly devolved into a fit of giggles as she was shoved down onto the mattress.

"You're not trying to get *me* in trouble too, are you?"

"Of course I am."

Reaching for the front clasp of ver shorts, Steph's smile continued to twist up and up as ve raked ver gaze across Phera's curves.

"Now, lose the outfit, *Astrid*."

Again, Phera gasped, one hand pressed to her breasts.

"I do believe this is workplace harassment."

"It sure is," agreed Steph with a wicked grin. "So you'd better start taking off those pants before I decided to show you how we handle poor performance reviews around here."

"Oooh, is it with a paddle?"

"And a belt."

"I knew there was a reason I liked it here."

"Hehe. Good answer. Now…?"

"Yes, yes, I'm going, I'm going."

"Good girl."

All right, fine.

Perhaps it wasn't the *most* boring two weeks of Phera's life. Tugging down the zipper on her uniform top, she had to admit that there were certainly worse ways to kill time.

She'd just have to make sure she made it up to Straya later.

—

"Bye-bye, Vernie," Phera called, anchoring herself in place with a twist of one boot against a handhold as she turned back to blow a kiss toward the shuttle pilot while Steph drifted through the open airlock passthrough behind her. "See you in a week."

Of course, it was only *after* she'd said this last bit out loud that it occurred to her that there were probably several microphones recording her every word now that they'd reached their destination. So, in an effort to cover her potential blunder, she added in a much less confidently flirtatious rush.

"Or, um, you know, whenever! Shoot me a message next time you're inbound, yeah? We can grab drinks or something."

Vernie's earlier smug swagger had given way to a pretty pronounced pair of bags beneath his eyes since that night he'd attempted to renegotiate the terms of their arrangement. Apparently, fretting over his cock falling off wasn't doing much to help his quality of sleep. Even so, Phera was still gratified to see that her invitation managed to elicit a pair of ruddy spots in the older man's sallow cheeks.

"Uh, yeah, sure. See you later, Astrid," he called back with a weak wave. "Make sure to bring your *friend* along next time, yeah?"

"Oooh, three way, huh? Now that could be fun."

Winking, Phera righted her orientation with a brief tap of her fingertips to the "ceiling" of the airlock above her before launching herself ahead to catch up with Steph.

Or at least she tried to.

"Crap, crap! Incoming!" she yelped when her miscalculated use of force sent her hurtling far faster than she'd intended to toward her supposed supervisor. "Heads up, Doctor!"

"Oh, Astrid…"

Boots anchored securely to the deck, Steph heaved out an exasperated sigh and held out a friendly hand to arrest ver assistant's overexcited null-grav approach. As Phera was about to impact with ver palm, however, ve stuck out ver pointer finger instead. Impaling the engineer right in the softest part of her stomach with her own momentum.

"Oof!"

The movement was subtle enough that any cams trained on them would've only captured a responsible superior catching a reckless employee, save for Phera's reaction.

"Do try and conduct yourself with at least a little dignity, would you?"

Steph kept ver usually mellifluous voice cool and disinterested, as was only fitting for a highly-focused corporate scientist.

"I swear. Who I pissed off in admin to have them foist you off onto me, I'll never know."

Rolling ver eyes, "Doctor Iris" returned ver attention to the hatch whose edge ve was still gripping. And, with a graceful (and far gentler than Phera's earlier attempt) pull, sent verself drifting into the station's docking ring.

"Oh, I'm sure we'll be the best of friends by the end of this rota," dismissed Phera, making a point of not rubbing at where Steph's blunt fingernail had just dug into her.

Instead, she floated along after ver toward the grav acclimation tunnel at the far end of the curving room, where their station liaison was already waiting for them.

"Hello there," she started to call as they reached her, before just as quickly remembering that she was supposed to be an underling and attempting to cover her awkward bit of line overstepping by clearing her throat. "Ahem! Er, I believe this is the person the pilot told us to expect, Doctor."

"You don't say?"

Steph's sarcastic drawl was easily as acerbic as Kelt's on her most grumpy of days, and Phera couldn't help but grin just a little. Annoying ver as "Astrid" was proving to be far too much fun. Plus, doing so helped to cement her cover identity, which was a nice bonus.

"Shaela Roberts, Director of R&D Subgroup H," the woman droned in a bored tone that somewhat deflated Phera's good cheer.

She wore a slightly less well-pressed version of Phera and Steph's own Iotech uniform (though, with a pencil skirt instead of the more low-grav friendly slacks she and her fellow pirate were sporting), that clashed exquisitely with her bright blue hair. Tall, but thin and lanky, she honestly looked a little like the Captain with her dusky complexion and high cheekbones. Albeit a version of her that was about a decade older with far worse color sense and an infinitely more gloomy expression.

"This way."

Turning on her heel, she started advancing through the hatch behind her without pausing to see if she was actually being followed.

"Oh! Um, right!"

"Of course."

As the three of them descended into the pseudograv of the station's hab cylinder with a trio of successive clangs of magnetic soles on metallic deck plates, Phera saw that their new colleague was now separated from her and Steph by a transparent wall with its own exit behind it.

"The terminal is there," her dour voice explained via a speaker somewhere in the ceiling above their heads while she gestured toward a console mounted on the far wall displaying a cheery blue and white Iotech logo. "Confirm your identities and then move through decon. One at a time."

She indicated the door on their side of the partition with a jerk of her chin.

"Someone from HR will meet you on the other side to show you around."

Phera was just in the process of nodding in acknowledgment, when the woman's entire body gave a hard couple of jerks and she suddenly perked up. And perked up *hard*. Her painfully white smile stretching to a borderline manic width on her lean face.

Yikes. Looks like someone's stims decided to kick in all at once.

"Welcome to Epiphany Station!" the woman chirped, pupils blown wide enough to all but swallow the green of her irises. "We look forward to integrating your unique stories into our corporate journey as we advance the state of medical science!"

"Uh, thanks. Us too!"

Phera took it upon herself to reply to the suddenly extremely peppy woman's monologue while Steph grunted something noncommittal and pressed ver palm to the waiting terminal.

Oh gods, here we go...

She felt her stomach clench tight as the display whirred to life and began to scan the doctor's petite palm. Comparing ver handprint and unique capillary configuration to the records Obette had seeded into the station's employee database a few weeks back. If something was going to go wrong, now was when it would, she knew. But, a moment later, the terminal pinged out a happy *beep-beep!* and the door to the decontamination chamber slid open.

"No dawdling now, Astrid," Steph chided as ve advanced into the room, only the pinched corners of ver mother of pearl eyes giving away ver amusement as ve turned back to waggle an admonishing forefinger at her. "We've got a lot of work to do, and I want to get to it as soon as possible. Am I understood?"

"Yes Doctor!"

The heavy decontamination chamber door sliding shut cut off most of Phera's knee-jerk corporate go-getter response, but their still beaming escort seemed to approve nevertheless. A moment later, the terminal in front of her gave another beep as it returned to its ready screen.

"Right then. Guess I'm up..."

"First time doing decon?" the woman behind the plex wall asked, face twisting into an exaggerated caricature of concern as she eyed Phera nibbling at her lower lip.

"Never really needed to back on Konnara since I wasn't in the labs," the currently purple and teal haired pirate found herself replying before her stomach flip-flopped hard enough to make her stumble.

Shit! What if they have mandatory decons planetside?!

Her spur-of-the-moment fib seemed to pass muster, though, because her escort's face maintained its aggressively reassuring cast as she watched her self-consciously tug at her uniform top.

"You'll be fine, hon. Just hold still and don't try to close your eyes during the UV flash."

"Heh. I think I can handle that. Thank you, ma'am."

"Oh please, we're family now," the woman dismissed, pouring even more sugar-free sweetness into her tone as she splayed a hand over the front of her rumpled uniform. "You can just call me Shaela."

Ah, a "cool" boss then. At least while the drugs are working.

"Sure thing, Director."

Phera had actually been through more decontamination cycles than she could count back when she'd been a research assistant in grad school, but the other woman's chemically-fueled encouragement was a welcome distraction from her own painfully hard heartbeats just then.

Okay, okay. It worked for Steph. There's no reason why it won't work for you. Just do what ve did and act like you're supposed to be here and you'll be fine.

Squaring her shoulders and doing her best to channel her past life as a corporate functionary, Phera stepped up to the panel and pressed her slightly clammy palm to it. A warm wave of tingling static radiated down her hand from the tips of her fingers to the base of her wrist. Then, a moment later, the machine gave another *beep-beep!* as the decontamination door slid open for her.

"I'll see you later, Astrid. Have a happy and productive work cycle!"

"Thanks, you too!"

Phera endured several puffs of pressurized air that stank of aerosolized disinfectant, and a way too bright flash of UV light that left her blinking away phantom spots of color from her vision. Nothing new, but that didn't make it any more pleasant. Finally, the door ahead of her slid aside to reveal a performatively scowling Steph waiting for her as who she supposed must be their new escort jogged up to meet them.

"Hello, hello! That'll be Doctor Kris Iris, and…"

He consulted a small slate he produced from his front pocket.

"Associate Technician Astrid Clary?"

"That would indeed be us," nodded Steph, formal as ever. "And you are?"

The clean-shaven young man, about as tall as Obette and with a similar trim figure, smiled cordially (albeit a bit stiffly) at each of them in turn before turning to lead the way into a well-lit and lightly furnished lounge area.

"Superintendent Maxim Fraec. Feel free to call me Supermax if you want. Lots of people do."

He laughed self-deprecatingly at his deliberately awful joke.

"Happy to be here!" Phera squeaked dutifully, going ramrod straight with her palms glued to her sides. "Um, Superintendent, sir!"

Rather than be disappointed by her totally chickening out on potentially humiliating herself by using his stupid nickname, Maxim seemed amused. At least, judging by the brief twitch of one clean-shaven cheek. Going so far as to wink at her over Steph's void black bob while ve wasn't looking.

"Likewise, Technician Clary. We're all excited to have you two after our last rotation," he continued smoothly, stepping toward a sideboard table and pouring the three of them each a tall cup of coffee. "I had some free time before my next meeting, so I thought I'd show you two around the station myself. Milk? Sugar?"

He held up a clear container in either hand and gave them both a brief waggle.

"Yes and yes. Too much of both please," answered Phera without missing a beat, still at attention and feeling slightly startled at how easy this all was now that they were past the major hurdle of actually getting onto the station.

"Certainly, young lady."

Favoring her with another small smile, Maxim or Supermax or whatever Phera was supposed to call him proceeded to turn her black coffee a pale shade of tan.

"Doctor?" he prompted a moment later after passing along her beverage.

"Same as hers, if you would."

Steph's stern persona was still firmly in place, but ve somehow managed to sound friendly through ver formality as ve addressed the man.

"Can do," he replied just as cheerily as before, likewise cementing himself as yet another upbeat, "cool" corporate overseer.

Phera had been exposed to enough of his type back when she'd been on The Bin to be able to spot the signs, and knew that she definitely couldn't let her guard down around him. His manner might seem easygoing on the surface, but gods help you if you were ever late with a report or failed to meet your performance goals. Hopefully, though, he would be too busy doing whatever a station superintendent did all day to pay her or Steph too much attention after their initial orientation tour was over. She was pretty sure Director Roberts was their section supervisor anyway. (Her name sounded like one of the ones she'd seen on the information dump Obette had managed to pull on the station, at any rate.) So long as she and Steph kept up the appearance of being busy, she'd be way too busy floating along in a haze of chems to give either of them much more than a passing glance.

Hopefully.

"Ready to get going?" prompted the superintendent, drawing her out of her reverie with a start as he handed off Steph's disposable cup to ver.

"Of course," the doctor answered for both of them, earning an approving nod from the man in the process.

"Wonderful! In that case…"

He turned and gestured down the corridor, drawing their attention to the colored lines painted on the floor that split off with each branching turn as he began walking.

"If you'll follow me, I'll show you to the labs and employee barracks."

And, just like that, they were in.

Oh my gods! I've always wanted to say that!

—

"The… *fuck?*"

The medical researcher currently going by Kris Iris banished the wraparound display of holographic projections surrounding ver, sliding ver hand free of the interface pad ve'd been using for the last half hour and rubbing at ver tired eyes with sudden, renew energy.

"That… But if that's…"

Phera's earpiece just barely managed to catch the doctor's disbelieving subvocalizations as ve shook ver head and flopped back with a heavy sigh into ver ergonomic seat.

"That ex of yours is going to freak out when this finally goes public, Astrid."

"Who, Alecto? Or that pretty botanist with the nice collarbones? You're going to have to be a lot more specific here, Doctor."

The two of them were alone, nestled deep in the analytics stack at the heart of Epiphany Station. Steph inside the sealed, secured data room while Phera sat at a desk on the other side of the opaque divider wall. Acquainting herself with the various shell programs she'd be required to use for the research they were supposed to be conducting.

Steph's soft chuckle tickled at her eardrum, raising goosebumps along the right side of her face.

"You really do get around, don't you?"

"What can I say? I was raised by people who insisted sex was only for making babies."

Phera's shoulders rose and fell in an absent shrug, mind largely preoccupied with the hallucinographic workspace she was organizing for herself inside the Iotech network.

"Call it making up for lost time."

"Hmmm. I suppose that's fair."

Tucking back a dyed lock of black hair, Steph rubbed at the mesh data plate embedded in ver palm, working out some of the phantom tingles that always followed a prolonged session of direct interfacing with a secure system.

"This research, though... It's something else. And they're using it for... Just. Wow."

"Even more than you were expecting?"

Phera kept her tone breezy and conversational as she asked the question. Obette, in the brief interaction they'd managed to have in the station's cantina the night before, had warned her that every room on the station had cams. Even if each individual cam didn't have someone actively monitoring it at all times, the security algorithm was probably easy enough to trip. So, she made sure to pick her words extra carefully just in case.

"Don't tell me those little seed pod things actually hold the key to eternal life or whatever. You said Alell was just pulling my leg, remember?"

"Not quite, no. We'll talk about it over lunch."

The door to the inner chamber slid open then and Steph emerged, still looking somewhat dazed as ve leaned against its sturdy frame for support.

"In the meantime, I think we'd better get acquainted with the specimens in storage. You're finished here, yes?"

Ve tried to sound stern, but was still clearly distracted with whatever ve'd just seen.

"Of course!"

Ever the dutiful assistant, Phera triggered the sequence required to safely disconnect her neural implant from the terminal she'd been using. Her interface cable disconnected from the port beneath her ear with a satisfying *click*, and as she rolled it back up and tucked it into a pocket beneath her breasts, she nodded toward the half-empty mug of coffee on the table beside her, old instincts kicking in.

"Would you like me to top you off first? I can meet you there if you'd like."

The professor she'd worked for back when she was a lowly PhD candidate had been a real stickler about their coffee always being full, and she'd found herself asking the question without even thinking about it.

"No. That'll react poorly with the, uh..."

Groaning, Steph let ver sentence falter and fall flat.

"Are you all right?"

"I'm fine, I'm fine..."

Massaging ver temples, ve waved away her concerns with a weak smile.

"Let's just say I needed a little extra help thinking really hard, and I'm still coming down from that. So, yeah. I'll pass for now on the stimulants, thanks."

Starting to catch ver second wind, ve stretched ver slender arms above ver head and then set off toward the exit hatch to the room.

"Leave the coffee for now and let's go."

"Right!"

Shooting back to her feet and smoothing down the front of her crisp uniform skirt (she'd found she liked the skirt version a little better than the trouser variant, especially the way it hugged her hips and lifted her butt), Phera gave her multi-hued curls an eager toss and hurried off after Steph's retreating form.

"I'm right behind you!"

—

"So."

Steph stood staring at the array of refrigeration units inside the airtight, maximally-sterile containment compartment behind the five centimeter thick plex barrier running the length of the biological sample storage room. Ve hadn't bothered with putting on a vacsuit and going in yet. That would have to wait for later when they started their extraction plan. But, judging by the look of naked hunger on ver face, Phera was pretty sure ve would've loved nothing more than to go frolicking through the rows of neatly-organized samples in front of ver.

"Third unit from the back, far left side," ve continued, pointing one darkly painted nail at the sample in question. "That's the secret to life, the universe, and everything."

"Wow, really?"

Snorting, Steph rolled ver eyes, hand twitching automatically to swat at where Phera was bending over and squinting through the eyepiece of a microscope in the outer lab, only half paying attention to ver. Ve managed to stop verself just in time, though, and instead smoothed back ver hair again.

"Okay, that's a little bit of an exaggeration," ve allowed. "But, it is *one* of the secrets to a particular kind of life."

"Neat."

Phera, whose only exposure to microbiology had been a class she'd nearly failed in her sophomore year of college, nevertheless made what she hoped were the appropriate "This is fascinating!" sounds as she examined the specimen in front of her. Which, to be fair, wasn't exactly hard. In a small pool of clear fluid in the sample dish, a semi-circular array of threads acted as a sail for a three-armed, crystalline structure that hung beneath it, navigating through liquid methane with spinning, waterwheel-like organs.

"Is this, uh... alive?" she found herself asking, straightening up and kneading her lower back with her knuckles, entirely oblivious to Steph's appreciation of just how well she filled out the seat of her skirt. "Those are colonial organisms on a crystal, right? Or am I misreading this?"

"Who cares?"

Throwing ver arms up in exasperation, Steph took a menacing step toward her.

"That's just some hydrocarbon xenoform- Oh!"

Only for ver hand to stop midway in its discreet journey toward pinching one of her ample cheeks in annoyance as ve got ver first clear look at the microscope's projected display. Dashing in close beside her instead as ve let out an excited squeal.

"Oh wow, it's so *cute*! Is that? Hah! It is! The wheels must be mesosymbiotic prokaryomorphs! Awww, it's like an itty-bitty clown car! I love it!"

Ver hands grabbed for the holodisplay, fingers passing through empty air without actually managing to close around the rolling, sailing creature. Eliciting a comically adorable pout from ver in the process.

"We are absolutely keeping these!" ve declared with a decisive nod, straightening up and planting ver hands on ver hips. "Add them to the list. Even if they're just a distraction from the research, we *have* to keep them!"

"Sure thing, boss," replied Phera, tapping out a note to herself on her wrist comp before pinching her nose twice in quick succession. "Honka honka."

Slipping back into her attentive assistant persona then, she gestured toward the sealed area beyond.

"So... Can I get a look at the key to the universe or whatever it is?" she asked, drawing her interface cable out of her pocket. "Actually, if you give me a lot number, I can call up whatever data is sitting on the local storage for review. Might need your credentials for that, though."

"Uh, yeah, sure. It's not much to look at. Just, uh... Here. You can read the text summary."

Placing ver hand atop one of the data interface pads on the desk, Steph called up the available information on the sample in question, entering ver credentials as ve did so. The holodisplay flickered, replacing the crystalline clown car with a collection of translucent gray spheres holding position in a low-temperature biostorage gel. Inside each sphere, a complicated spread of tightly-packed organelles was annotated and highlighted by glowing arrows.

"They look like bacteria, yeah?"

"Uh... Yes. Totally."

"Exactly! Here's the thing, though. They're not actually put together like it."

"Huh."

The text summary was honestly way too jargon-filled for Phera to understand.

"Yeah, that *is* odd," she still agreed for the benefit of any station sec who might be listening in on them as she eased up onto her tiptoes to squint more closely at the projection. "So, if they're not bacteria, what are they?"

"Well, like it said in the published prelims, they have a *really* complicated system of contingencies that lets them coordinate on big projects. Sort of like what you see with bees, or bone wasps, but no neurology for a monocellular organism, it's all biochemical computing. And, well... Let's just say it's lucky these ones here were frozen on the planet's night side deep beneath the surface. Every single one of those organelles you see has its own complete genome, and a single mutation in any of them would be spotted by the others and cause a chain reaction shut down."

"Oh?"

Again, Phera had virtually no idea what most of that meant, but it did sound interesting.

"Under normal circumstance, it actually *can't* mutate," Steph continued excitedly, oblivious to her lack of comprehension. "It's as safe as the stuff we use for consumer genetics right now. Safer, probably."

Ver face was as earnest as Phera had ever seen it as ve looked up at her then and beamed.

"It's been frozen for a long time. Like, a loooong time. You picking up what I'm putting down here?"

"Oh my gods!"

Phera felt her stomach give an excited lurch as, finally, something clicked into place for her.

"Are you saying this is *precursor* tech?"

"Exactly."

"That's... Wow."

She could see now why Steph had been so excited. Back when humanity and its generation ships had first reached this solar system some three hundred years ago, they'd been shocked to discover that all of the planets in orbit around the Goldilocks zones of the two primaries had already been terraformed some ten million years prior. All that was left of the civilization presumably responsible for that feat of insanely-complicated geoengineering now were a faint scattering of ruins and a handful of habitable planets. The current prevailing wisdom was that they'd experienced some sort of system-wide catastrophe which had necessitated that they remake their ravaged worlds and perhaps flee to somewhere else in the galaxy in the meantime. Where exactly they were now, though, was anyone's guess.

Holy shit. Shi is going to absolutely lose his mind when we tell him about this!

Still staring, something struck Phera then and she very nearly joined Steph in jumping up and down in excitement.

"Wait. You said these things could coordinate on big projects."

She cocked a brow as an eager grin pulled up on the corners of her ruby painted lips.

"Do you mean, like, planet-sized ones?"

"I don't know."

Steph shrugged in a way that made it abundantly clear that didn't bother ver in the slightest.

"I don't think *anyone* knows. Not for certain, anyway. In the tests on record, they've just been able to coordinate things on a much smaller scale. But, um, yeah. Iotech has managed to isolate the organelle-analogues that do the inter-unit communication, and the plan right now is to duplicate them for a new generation of medical nanites. And, heh, well, with a lot of adjustment your software actually might work pretty well with these things, so..."

Ve gave Phera's upper arm a congratulatory pat.

"Good for you!"

"Damn. That would be *so* cool."

Head already spinning with half-formed ideas for an armada of adaptively-coordinating nanites, it took a supreme effort of will on Phera's part to draw herself back to the present.

This tech wasn't theirs just yet, after all.

"So, how many samples do they have on hand right now? Have they managed to actually synthesize those organelle transceivers or just isolate them?"

It was only after she'd asked this last question that it occurred to her that it might sound suspicious for a lowly assistant to be wondering about things so above her pay grade, and she quickly added.

"Or, um, is that what we'll be working on?"

"Early stages," answered Steph briskly, giving the hand still on her upper arm a warning squeeze. "But, just watching how these things operate is opening a lot of new doors."

Taking the hint, Phera gave the faintest sliver of a nod.

"Well now, that's wonderful! So, where do we fit in?"

"Like I said."

Indulging ver eager assistant with an amused chuckle, "Doctor Iris" began steering her out of the sample storage room with a firm hand on the small of her back.

"We'll talk about it over lunch."

CHAPTER TWENTY-SEVEN

CHARGES ACCRUED

Attempted Burglary, Unauthorized Access to Class 1 Biological Specimens, Resisting Arrest, Providing False Testimonya

One thing that Phera wasn't prepared for as she and Steph spent the next week pretending to work for Iotech while they waited for their extraction date to arrive, was that she actually enjoyed herself quite a bit. The knowledge that this whole situation was only temporary did a lot to alleviate her creeping anxiety about being stuck on an isolated corporate station once again. And, even better, she actually liked her coworkers for a change.

At first, she and Steph had done their best to keep to themselves as they worked. But, even so, Phera was a natural social butterfly. On top of that, she looked way too good in her uniform not to attract at least *some* attention when she passed people in the corridor or bent over to pick something up. So much so, that by her third day posing as a research assistant, she'd made friends with what felt like half the staff in their project's cohort. Even going so far as to manage roping grumpy "Doctor Iris" into their nightly games in the company lounge once their work cycle was over.

Part of her actually felt a bit bad about what she was doing there. Had fate been a little kinder, she could very well have ended up on a station just like this one. She doubted she'd have ever made it into management. Even with her Cilaran upbringing, she'd never had the cutthroat competitive streak required for clawing her way up the corporate ladder, but she could've been content spending her days tinkering away in her lab on some cutting edge bit of drone tech and whiling away her evenings flirting with whoever looked cute in the station cantina.

That wasn't about to stop her from doing what she'd come here to do, however.

This station wasn't her home, and these people weren't her crew. Whenever she felt the first stirrings of guilt start to creep up inside her, she would crush them underfoot by reminding herself that she wasn't robbing her friends. She was robbing *Iotech*. The research and its fruits would all be owned by the board, just like everything else they produced. No credit. Little to no acknowledgment for the vast majority of them, and certainly no revenue shares. They were wage slaves living off of whatever scraps their managerial overlords decided to trickle down to them. Pure and simple.

So, while Phera might've felt a *bit* bad about the shitstorm she and her fellow pirates were about to bring down on the station as a whole, she stayed determined. Her conscience doing nothing to stop her as she went about loading up all the samples she and Steph had earmarked for reappropriation four days later.

"Thirteen, fourteen, and... fifteen! All right, that's all of them."

Snapping the lid of her sample carrier closed and securing its latches, Phera dusted off her hands and resisted the urge to dance in celebration. She *was* still on cams, after all. Still, she had reason to be excited. She'd followed Obette's instructions to the letter and managed to avoid triggering any alarms as she extracted each sample canister from its security housing in storage. As a result, she now had enough biological specimens neatly packed up and ready to smuggle off station to have paid off her student loans about twenty times over.

"Hmmm..."

Eyeing the assembly of drop-proof rubber gaskets and temperature control hardware in front of her, Phera pursed her lips in mild annoyance.

"Maybe should've brought a cart or something."

Before rolling her shoulders and popping her neck with a resigned sigh.

"Oh well."

Grabbing a handle on either side of the wide, open-faced carrying case, she hefted it up with a grunt. Suddenly, she was actually glad that Lem was such a hard-ass about making sure she worked out multiple times a week. While the samples container wasn't particularly heavy, its shape was still cumbersome. With her wide hips, large breasts, and not particularly long arms, she was forced to turn and awkwardly shuffle her way out of the storage room's narrow exit hatch sideways while stretching her arms all the way out to either side of her in order to maintain her grip on the container.

The case might be drop-proof, but there was no way in hell she wanted to put that claim to the test.

All in all, though, she was feeling pretty good with how things had gone so far. Now, she just had to meet her "boss" back in ver lab to finish their shift, and then they could be on their way off this station.

"Easy peasy lemon squeezy."

Of course, *that* was when the sirens started going off.

"Eep!"

Jerking to a halt just outside the sample storage room as its reinforced hatch slid shut and locked with a heavy *THUNK!* of bolts sliding home, Phera threw a fretful glance down either side of the empty corridor she was in, trying to decide if she should start sprinting toward Steph's office or the docking ring. That question was rendered moot, however. For no sooner had she heard the rapid approach of footfalls over the wailing klaxon, than a pair of station sec officers decked out in pristine tactical helmets, goggles, and armored vests with Iotech's logo embossed across the chest rounded a corner, barreling right for her.

"Freeze right there-!"

"Drop the case and get down on your-"

Both of them started shouting at the same time, before one gave the other a menacing glare, shutting him up so that he could deliver the rest alone.

"Get down on your knees with your hands behind your head! Er, um, eyes closed!"

These last two words were barked out extra loud and with a slight note of panic, as if he'd nearly forgotten them. The muzzle he had leveled directly at Phera's face, on the other hand, was anything but unsure.

"Okay, okay! I'm going, I'm going!"

Heart hammering and lungs seizing, Phera's words emerged from her as a barely-intelligible squeak as she dropped to her knees like a stone.

"Urk!"

On reflex, her eyes screwed up tight with the hiss of pain that escaped her as her poor kneecaps smacked full force against the hard metal deck beneath her, keeping them closed as she very carefully lowered her container the rest of the way down to the floor in front of her. Only letting go when she felt its rubber feet find purchase there.

"I said hands on your head!"

"Oh, right! Sorry!"

Straightening up with a lurch, her hands flew to the back of her head, fingers interlocking through her dyed curls.

"Done!"

It felt incredibly stupid to say that out loud, but with those coilguns she'd seen still fresh on her mind, she wanted to do whatever she could to encourage the people holding them not to fire. Even set to non-lethal, she'd likely wind up with a concussion when her head hit the deck or the wall behind her. Assuming, that is, that the magnetically accelerated rounds didn't just do that on impact.

"Move away from the samples!" the second officer, the one who'd been cowed by the first, snapped.

This was a rather difficult instruction to follow, given that Phera was on her knees just then, and was further complicated by the first officer shouting at the same time, "Move a muscle and we'll shoot!"

Then, from the other direction, there came a louder set of polymer-reinforced boot soles clomping against the deck, followed by a coilgun slider clicking into position.

"Down on the floor!" commanded a rough female voice this time. "Now! Arms and legs spread out!"

This new voice sounded more confident than the others so far, and nobody seemed to be countermanding her, so Phera decided it was probably safest to follow it over the others. Still, with most of her thoughts preoccupied with repeating the phrase "Oh gods, oh fuck, oh shit!" over and over again, she decided it'd be best to try and follow as many instructions as she could.

So, hands still clamped to the back of her head, she shuffled around on her knees until she felt like she was probably perpendicular to the samples container (hard to know for sure with her eyes still shut), before scooting forward what she hoped was a couple meters and lowering herself to the floor as slowly as she could. Which, given her absolutely abysmal core strength, basically meant that she face-planted. Fortunately, she'd managed to turn her head just in time and her right cheek and elbow took most of the brunt of the impact.

It still hurt like a mother fucker, though.

After taking the briefest of moments to curse under her breath as even more joint pain was added to her already oversized collection, Phera splayed her arms and legs in the worst possible version of a Cilaran snow angel she'd ever done. Wishing very much that she was still wearing slacks and not a stupidly snug pencil skirt.

"This is all a big misunderstanding!" she found herself insisting, if for no other reason than to at least *try* and prevent herself from being arrested. "I don't know why the alarm went off, I swear!"

Which was definitely true.

What had she done to mess things up?!

There came a sudden *whoosh!* above her hair then, followed by an alarming *CRACK!* of something metallic ricocheting off the deck just between her thighs. The man who had instructed her not to move had either just fired a warning shot, or tried to shoot her and missed due to some combination of trembling hands on his end and spasmodic wriggling on hers.

She honestly had no idea which was worse.

Another alarm immediately started going off with the impact, accompanying its fellow in a cacophony of discordant notes that made Phera's teeth clench just a bit harder. She recognized this new klaxon at least, for what little comfort that was. It was the same one that Panorama had used whenever the audio sensors detected coilgun fire outside of the training range and maintenance workshops on station.

"Heads up!"

More footsteps followed from multiple directions then, as even *more* station sec officers converged. This time, though, they were accompanied by the calm, clipped clarity of Obette's voice.

"Firefight in progress?"

He spoke loud enough to silence the half-dozen other yammering exclamations and questions around him.

"Or did I miss all the excitement?"

His voice was coming from right above Phera now.

Oh thank gods! she thought to herself, just barely managing not to say so out loud.

Instead, she drew in a shaky breath, toes curling and uncurling on reflex inside her flats as she squeaked out, "I'm not armed! Please don't shoot! I promise I can explain!"

She wasn't out of harm's way yet, not by a long shot, but she was at least headed in the right direction now that she had some back up.

Probably.

"Situation's under control, rookie," the female voice from earlier grunted.

Then, before she could add anything else, the first officer to confront Phera added, "Just one shot fired. Intruder's been pacified."

"Very pacified!" agreed Phera, going completely ignored save for someone (she assumed Obette, but couldn't be sure since there was no way in hell she was going to so much as crack an eye open without explicit permission) poking her firmly in the ribs with the hard toe of a boot.

"Yeah, well, are you gonna cuff her or what?" huffed Number One's partner, sounding annoyed that he hadn't been the one to get to shoot at her.

"I thought you had the cuffs."

"Fuck. Right. Hold on."

Phera felt several pairs of hands roughly grab for her wrists then, forcing them together behind her back as a pair of metal rings were magnetized shut around them, locking them in place while someone else wrestled off her comp glove.

Oh gods! Oh gods!

There were *way* too many bodies crowding around and pushing down on her now, and not enough air. Seriously, it felt like she had half the damn station sec contingent kneeling on top of her.

"I'll just go ahead and bring this in for inspection," Obette's coolly confident voice came again, accompanied by the sound of the rubber, shock-absorbing feet of the carrying case being pried off the floor. "I think we'd best not open it until we're certain our little thief here isn't the explosively inclined sort."

"Uh, yeah."

This suggestion seemed to sap much of the crackling machismo from the situation, and Phera breathed a literal and figurative sigh of relief as the pressure on her back eased and someone finally silenced the cacophony of alarms.

"That's SOP, private," confirmed the female officer. "You do that. And, you three."

She snapped her fingers, all brusque business now that the action was over.

"Secure the entrance. I'll bring the suspect in. Shakre, you're with me. Keep behind her and make sure she doesn't try anything cute."

"Copy that."

Phera thought she might've heard the woman snort just a little, but then she was barking out another command, at her this time.

"All right, *you*."

There came another, much less gentle, boot-tip prodding at her ribs.

"On your feet. Eyes stay shut."

"Y-Yes ma'am!"

Bringing her knees together, Phera began wriggling her hips back and up until she was in the sort of position the Captain particularly liked her in. Judging by the handful of unfriendly chuckles she heard coming from behind her as she rocked forward and back a couple of times to build momentum and tip herself back up onto her knees, many of the station sec officers appreciated it too.

Humph. Assholes.

Reassuringly, Obette's retreating voice put in just then, "I'm going to go brush up on her personnel file, Sergeant. I think I might just have a question or two I'd like to ask the young lady once she's in lockup."

"Suit yourself, rookie."

Phera could practically hear the security woman rolling her eyes at her overly helpful subordinate.

"Just make sure those samples go to lockup."

"Absolutely, ma'am. Top priority."

*Well, at least there's a chance we haven't totally lost our haul yet. That's **something**, right?*

"Um, okay, I'm up, um, ma'am," Phera mumbled, voice high and strained as she struggled to breathe down an impending panic attack. "I, um, can't really see where I'm going, though, so…?"

In answer to her unfinished question, she felt the cold press of a coilgun muzzle against the back of her head.

"Just go where you feel me pushing," sneered a male voice from directly behind her.

"And follow my footsteps," the woman in front of her added.

Swallowing hard, Phera gave the barest sliver of a nod.

"R-Right…"

—

Despite the nerve-wracking reality of having a coilgun to her skull, Phera still couldn't help but take a small sliver of vindictive pleasure in her station sec escort having to let her open her eyes once they'd reached their offices. Granted, that was only *after* she'd tripped over one chair and banged her shins against two different desks. But, still.

It was the little things.

That small ember of warmth inside her chest was promptly snuffed out, however, when she was marched into an interrogation room and sat down forcefully in an armless metal chair bolted to the floor.

"Nice place," she whispered, sulkily, trying to cheer herself up with some very hollow bravado.

"Shut the fuck up," snapped the older woman, gruffly locking her ankles into the built-in restraints on the chair.

Part of Phera wished she had the nerve to tell the woman to make her. But, with her partner still keeping his weapon trained on her, she thought better of it and instead just mumbled.

"Yes ma'am."

That earned her a pair of snorts from the two officers. Then, almost as bad as the warning shot, they left her alone.

"Oooh... fuck."

Breathing out a shaky exhalation, Phera fought down the urge to vomit as her stomach continued to lurch in a non-stop series of accel shifts.

"Fuck. Fuck. Fuck!"

This was it.

She'd been caught red-handed and arrested.

She was so unbelievably fucked!

Well... Maybe.

She'd been apprehended by station sec. They hadn't *actually* called in InterSec.

At least, not yet.

Okay, Phera, just calm down. You're not done yet. All they know is that an alarm went off and you were there when it happened. Just remember you're playing a role here. You're not a pirate to these people. You're just a ditz who fucked something up for her boss.

Closing her eyes, she took in a deep breath through her nostrils.

Hold it for a seven count...

And breathed it out in a thin, controlled stream through pursed lips.

Six... Seven... Eight...

Again and again she performed the breathing exercise, more grateful than ever that her university had such a robust cognitive behavioral therapy clinic on-campus, as she gradually tamped her heartbeat back down to something approaching calm. Her anxiety was still there, true, but it was compartmentalized and pushed out to arm's length now. She could acknowledge its presence, but it no longer had control over her.

"Right then. Guess I just have to sit here and wait?"

The room remained silent to her rhetorical question, and she wrinkled her nose in annoyance.

"Great..."

—

With her comp glove confiscated and no clock on the wall to refer to, it felt to Phera like she was left waiting in that cramped interrogation room for hours. It was a bare room, giving her only a dull metal table and one lonely sunsim panel in the ceiling for company. Despite her best efforts to keep focused on her mission, with nothing else to occupy it, her mind began to wander.

What was going to happen to her?

Would Obette and Steph escape with the samples and leave her behind?

Surely they wouldn't! She was part of the crew!

No. No. None of that. Stay calm. They wouldn't do that to you.

But, even knowing that she had friends looking out for her, how the hell were they going to get her out of this mess?

Now sure would be a perfect time for Straya to show up...

Blowing out what felt like her thousandth heavy sigh of the last twenty minutes, Phera gave her restraints an experimental tug.

They didn't budge.

Maybe if I can just hold out long enough, she and Adri can come kick in the door once the shuttle gets here?

She bit out a bitter laugh.

Oh, yeah sure. I can totally keep whoever comes to question me talking for...

She did some quick mental math.

Four... ish? Hours.

It was a slim hope. But, just then, that was all she had.

"Fuck."

As if in response to her cursing, the door to the room slid open once again. This time, the bald, muscularly-built mountain of a man who she knew from Obette's briefing was head of security for the entire station stepped inside. Unlike his overeager underlings, however, this man just looked exhausted.

Phera perked up at seeing a face that didn't look hostile. "Uh... Hello there..."

He didn't respond.

Uh-oh. Not good.

Over the years, she'd learned that there were basically three different types of corporate security personnel. There were the ones who wanted to be action heroes. The worst of the lot. There were the ones who were always looking to exploit the situation. Just cynically corrupt, but could at least be worked with for the right offer. Then, there were the ones who wished they'd chosen anything else as a career, but didn't have anywhere to go in the foreseeable future.

This salt and pepper bearded fellow, Phera could instantly tell, was squarely in the third category.

"Astra, yeah?"

Moving with the resigned air of someone dealing with a mess that had been dumped unexpectedly into their lap, he settled down against the edge of the table in front of her.

"I..."

The speech about how all of this was just a big misunderstanding that Phera had been rehearsing in her mind fell apart as soon as she opened her mouth to speak. Swallowing hard, heart hammering and lungs constricting with fresh panic, she managed a stilted nod.

"It's-"

She swallowed again, and did her best to meet the man's tired eyes.

"It's Ast*rid*, actually. Um, Commander?"

She was pretty sure she'd heard people call him that, but she wasn't about to run the risk of inadvertently insulting the man if she could at all avoid it.

"Sure."

The man's broad shoulders rose and fell in a heavy shrug.

"Doesn't really matter from your perspective, does it? Commander. Major. Colonel. I'm just the guy in charge."

Hands dropping to his sides, he fixed her with a ruthless, interrogatory stare that was completely at odds with his fatigued bearing. One that had Phera flashing back to those private quarterly interviews with her local Church of Harmony high elder back when she was growing up on Cilara. He'd almost always been able to tell when she was lying back then, especially when she told him that she'd been diligently reading her scriptures for twenty minutes every morning before school like she was supposed to. Hopefully, this man wouldn't be able to read her quite as easily.

She *had* gotten a lot better at lying since she was thirteen.

Thanks for all the help, I guess, Eminence Raschke…

"So," the security head continued, snapping her out of her mental tangent and making her jump. "Let's hear your side of the story."

Had her situation been any less dire, Phera would've been extremely tempted to fire back with, "You've got it, Colonel Commander Major in Charge!" But, with a room full of station sec officers with itchy trigger fingers just beyond the door, she opted instead for a meek nod and an infinitely safer, "Yes sir."

Even those two words alone were already leaving her winded. She'd never been good at confrontations like these. In an effort not to pass out, she forced herself to take in another deep, steadying breath in a truncated version of her earlier breathing exercise, before beginning her explanation.

"I was gathering samples for Doctor Iris while ve had ver lunch break," she said, before adding in a rush when the man raised one skeptical brow at her. "I know I'm *technically* not supposed to do that, but ve said it would be fine if I just followed ver instructions."

"We found the retrieval list on your comp."

The commander said this in a way that could have either been confirmation that she was saying what he expected her to, or a threat.

"Right! Um, so, I packed up the samples just like ve told me to. Then, when I took them outside the storage room, that siren started going off and then everyone was yelling, and I wasn't sure what was happening, and… and…"

Phera broke off from her explanation then as she gave a sniffle and tried to blink away the tears that were starting to gather at the corners of her violet eyes. The stress and fear were entirely genuine, and she hoped to every god and devil out there that it'd help sell her story.

"Uh-huh."

The security head levered himself up from the table and took a step toward her, sighing expansively and making no secret of the fact that he'd been hoping she would say anything else other than that.

"Doctor Iris," he repeated. "Told you to remove the transponder tags from those canisters? You seriously expect me to believe that?"

"I..."

Oh shit.

Phera had *really* been hoping that nobody would've noticed that. Still, she couldn't exactly just say, "Oh, yeah, you're right. Oops, you got me!" now.

All right, girl, time to lie your ass off.

"Is *that* what those little things were?"

Cocking her head to the side, she let her mouth form a small O of understanding, as if just now getting the punch line to a joke everyone else had already long since finished laughing at.

"Ver instructions didn't mention them, so I thought maybe they were just something extra for temperature monitoring or data recording? I don't usually handle sample storage directly, and I wasn't sure if the canisters were going to fit inside the carrier ve told me to use with them still in place. So... You know..."

Swallowing again, Phera did her best to look like a hapless idiot as she peered up at the commander through her eyelashes.

"Was that... Was that bad?"

Staring at her, totally dumbfounded, the man took in a long, slow, and very deep breath. Eyes turning up toward the ceiling in supplication.

"Are you...?"

He stopped himself before finishing whatever it was he'd been about to say, and instead shook his head in disbelief, one hand rising to massage his temples

"Ve... Oh for the love of-"

Just then, the interrogation room door swished open again, and Doctor Iris came storming in with Private Obble and the security woman from Phera's arrest trailing in ver wake.

"Speak of the devil."

"Astrid," The petite doctor growled, constricting her in a furious, narrow-eyed glare that looked much more suited to Kelt or the Captain than her impish friend. "What the FUCK did you do in there?"

"Oh! Um, hi, Doctor!"

Again, the squeak of terror that left Phera was entirely genuine, and not just because she was intimately familiar with what an annoyed Steph was capable of.

"I... I... I was just following your instructions," she insisted, face going pink. "You said you wanted all the samples from lots I-5 through I-19!"

"I..."

The doctor blinked.

"You... You took the *I*-row?"

Phera could see Steph's mouth starting to turn up at the corners as ve spoke. She knew it was ver "Oh, that's a brilliant idea!" smile, but ve was doing a good job of hammering it back down into Doctor Iris's sardonic "Oh my god, what an idiot" disbelieving one.

"That was a lowercase *L* not an uppercase *I,* you... you...!"

Ve whirled back around and took in several slow breaths, making a show of trying to calm verself down.

"And you *removed* the transponders? What, did you think they were fucking locking clamps or something?"

Even though she knew it was all an act, Phera still found herself shrinking back in her seat, thoroughly cowed by the scolding.

"Um... Maybe?"

Steph wheeled around at that, glaring daggers at her. Ve'd worked every last hint of the complicit smile off of ver face now, and replaced it with bared teeth in a vicious snarl.

Meanwhile, Obette carefully avoided saying, or even revealing via expression, anything as he watched the drama unfold. The female security officer standing beside him looked like she was ready to strangle both of the lab staff with her bare hands. Colonel Commander Sergeant seemed to seriously be contemplating doing the same to himself if for no other reason than to avoid having to deal with this colossal clusterfuck any longer.

"Did I fucking *tell* you to do that, Astrid?"

"Um, not really, no..." admitted Phera, slipping back into her role as Doctor Iris's ditzy research assistant. "But they weren't going to fit inside the case you told me to use."

She heaved out an annoyed huff, sending a few strands of blue and purple hair flying away from her nose.

"How was I supposed to know those things were important? They were attached to the OUTSIDE of the canisters!"

"You!"

Steph took two quick steps straight toward her, reared back, and slapped her full across the face like a jilted soon-to-be-ex from some cheesy romcom vid.

SMACK!

A bright pink handprint lit up across Phera's cheek as her head jerked to the side in a flash of white hot pain.

"Did you spend last night with your head in the nitrogen freezer?!"

"Now, now, Doctor…"

Stepping forward to intercede, the commander put his arm out to keep the thoroughly irate Doctor Iris from assaulting his suspect any further. All while Steph made to grab ver restrained assistant by the lapels, looking and sounding for all the world like ve was actually going to strangle her.

"Please try to calm down," the commander sighed. Then, more quietly, "Please?"

Private Obble took this as his cue to interject.

"I suppose we'd best report to the administrator about young Astrid's continued prospects with Iotech then?"

He sounded disappointed. Though, mostly in an "Oh darn, the hot bimbo might be leaving early" sort of way.

Steph, in turn, loosed another exasperated growl.

"Please don't bother administration with this. Fuck. I do *not* want to have to deal with the fallout over this."

Ve looked back toward the others then.

"Do any of you?"

"Fuck no," snorted the security woman, while Obette chimed in with a bemused, "Not particularly."

The commander, though, just gave his bald, bearded head a fatalistic shake.

"No choice I'm afraid, Doctor. It's protocol."

"Of course it is," pouted Phera, huffing petulantly.

Earning herself yet another sharp glare and a pointed "Shut it!" from Steph in the process.

"Well," ve finally said after a tense moment or two of cradling ver head in an obvious attempt to stave off an impending migraine.

"Are you going to at least let my dumb fuck of an assistant out of that chair?"

"Please?" piped up Phera hopefully, tossing her hair and doing her best to positively exude apologetic energy from every pour. "I promise I'm really, really, *really*, sorry."

Squirming in her restraints, she tried to look back toward where the exhausted security head stood. Knowing she still needed to sell this.

"Also, um, could you maybe please not report this, sir?" she wheedled. "I already told my parents about this transfer, and I really can't afford to get fired now. Pretty please?"

Well, she managed to hit pleading. Unfortunately, she also hit childish whining in her attempts to convey her sincerity. Still, it was too late to back down now.

Fortunately, her appeals got exactly the reaction she'd been hoping for.

"And what am I supposed to tell the superintendent? That we had an alarm malfunction and forgot to record any repairs in engineering?"

"Oh! That would be *perfect*!"

The commander shook his head, still frowning, and looking more than ever like he wished he'd chosen to do absolutely anything else with his life.

Seeing that she'd get no help from him, "Astrid" turned her attention back to her supervisor.

"No really, though. I'm sorry, Doctor," she continued, cheek still smarting where ve'd slapped her. At least ve didn't wear ver nails long and pointed like the Captain did. "It won't happen ever again, I swear."

"I…"

Steph was clearly struggling to decide what to say here. Ver pixie-like features were tense, and ve wasn't making eye contact with anyone else in the room. Phera could tell ve was starting to panic as ve hit the limit of ver improvisational skill. Which, in turn, was causing her own panic to begin to spike once again.

Thankfully, Obette spoke up before any of the others could.

"You know, boss, there *is* the matter of our new geneticist's support staff to consider," he pointed out. "How long is it going to take for a replacement for the miscreant young lady here to arrive?"

Obette turned back toward Steph.

"How much would the manpower shortage slow you down until then?"

"That's a good point!" agreed Phera quickly, moving to raise her hand only to remember that they were both still locked behind her back when they refused to budge. "It's going to take at least a week for someone to arrive from Konnara, assuming they leave tonight. And, not to brag or anything, but Doctor Iris definitely needs me."

In lieu of gesturing with her hands, she thrust out her chest with all the insufferable low-level underling pride that she could muster.

"Ve's a very capable researcher, I'll give ver that, but..."

Rolling her eyes, she made a small, disappointed noise in the back of her throat.

"Ver bookkeeping and note taking are an absolute mess. Ve'd be completely lost without me."

SMACK!

"Ack! Hey! Come on, it's true!"

SMACK!

"Shut UP!"

Phera knew she'd been asking for it that time. But, still, those slaps hurt! Jerking her head to one side and then the other, as Steph left two more bright pink handprints across her fair cheeks.

"You," ve ground out, voice low and menacing. "Do *not* get to tell *me* I'm making a mess of things. Not right now. After this, maybe not ever."

Ve backed away again when the gruff security woman started lowering her hand back toward her coilgun, and sighed in bone-weary exasperation.

"But, well, I suppose she does have a point," ve allowed, pointedly refusing to look at ver assistant. "Unless the superintendent wants me to wait another two weeks, I'm going to need her here. Besides, as *fucking stupid* as she is, I'd really rather not have to train a new assistant from the ground up."

"I understand that, Doctor," the commander attempted to placate. "However, I'm afraid my hands are still tied here."

"Oh, very well."

Steph gave ver slim shoulders an irritated shrug.

"Make your report then, I suppose. Just... Can I at least attach a request for leniency when you do? In the interest of keeping my project on schedule."

Private Obble spoke up again at that, smirking.

"Better make that one convincing letter, doc."

While the security woman added, "And your little minion here had better watch her fucking step."

Her glare was narrow-eyed and suspicious. As if she, unlike the commander, wasn't quite buying this story yet.

"You know, we don't *have* to report this as a mess up on my end," put in Phera, trying her best not to pout as she poked at the inside of her freshly smarting cheeks with her tongue. "Maybe we could just say I was, uh... helping test security by performing a surprise drill?"

She cast a hopeful look around the room, but her "boss" still looked beyond done with her shit.

"It's not like anything was actually, um-"

She'd been about to say "stolen", but that seemed like a very bad idea all things considered. Even by her standards.

"The more *important* samples were secured almost immediately. So..."

Putting on her most dazzling smile (the one that sometimes even worked on Straya), she batted her eyelashes at the head of security and his still miffed officer.

"No harm no foul? I promise you've absolutely scared me straight."

She very nearly added, "Well, almost," along with a flirtatious wink at the still scowling security woman, but stopped herself just in time. She wasn't sure if she was her type for starters, and something told her that the tactics that usually got her what she wanted among the Blazar Bitches probably wouldn't fly with corporate security.

As if reading her thoughts, the woman set her jaw and gave her a look. It wasn't wholly unlike the ones she sometimes got from Lem or Kelt back on the ship. Albeit one that was a lot less friendly.

After a moment's silence, the commander groaned in defeat.

"Protocol says we hold her at least until the boss makes a judgment call. So, we'll keep her in a cell for now until I can get a meeting. Doctor, I suggest you start working on that letter. Private?"

"Yes sir."

Stepping forward, Obette thumbed a button on the back of Phera's chair that released her ankles.

"I'll escort her then?" he asked, helping her up, wrists still cuffed securely together behind her back.

"I'll give you a hand," the station sec woman put in.

"Great."

Obette did a good job of hiding the "oh shit" reaction Phera felt ripple through his grip on her upper arm as the woman took up position on her other side, seizing an elbow.

"Three should be more than sufficient to handle this one, aye."

In response to this, the woman looked at him, clearly confused.

"Pardon?"

"You're lending me a hand," he elaborated, waving one of his own for emphasis. "I have two of my own. So, three hands."

Everyone was staring at him now.

Obette breathed out a wounded sigh.

"Comedy is a dying art, I see."

"Only because you killed it," Steph spat.

For a moment, things felt more natural, like they did aboard the Mayhem.

The two locals grunted.

"Well," the commander replied, weary, but clearly happy to put this whole thing behind him. "Put those hands to work, however many of them it takes, and get her into holding. Doctor, please have that letter to me by 16:00. That'll be all. I hope?"

He really, *really* looked like he hoped that would be all.

"Of course," nodded Steph, curt and professional as could be.

"Great. You two get her out of here."

"Understood."

"Yes sir."

"I thought your joke was funny," Phera mumbled, as she was led away by far too many hands as far as she was concerned.

Obette gave her shoulder a brief, reassuring squeeze, while keeping his face even and vaguely disapproving.

"You're too kind. Really."

The fact that she and her crewmates had managed to deescalate things from "let's shoot at the scary thief" to "wow, this girl sure is an idiot" was doing a lot to restore the spring in Phera's step. Having her ankles released from her shackles also helped with that. Now she just wished they'd let her hands loose too so that she could smooth down her stupid skirt. Iotech's employee uniforms weren't exactly what she'd call daring, but between all of her squirming on the corridor floor earlier and being shoved into that seat in interrogation, it was riding halfway up her thighs now.

"Are you sure you can't just confine me to quarters instead?" she wheedled as the three of them stepped out into the security station's main office. "I'm not really a fan of closed in spaces."

Besides, the barracks would be far easier to sneak out of, she was sure. Their ride out of here *was* still on schedule as far as she knew, after all.

"Do you seriously," Private Obble began to reply with a stern look. "Think that you're in any sort of position to negotiate here?"

Then, after a moment, before they could reach the end of the office, he seemed to be struck by an idea.

Giving the back of his fellow officer's head a shrewd look, he added, "You wouldn't want to make a scene in the middle of security HQ, now would you? We have important things to do, you know."

Phera had spent enough time cooped up on the Mayhem with the infiltrator to have a pretty good idea where he was headed with that remark. Just *how* exactly he planned on making use of it she wasn't exactly sure, but if Obette wanted a scene, she'd be only too happy to give him one.

"Oh, yeah, tooootally."

Snorting in derision, she gave her dyed curls a contemptuous toss that managed to catch both of her escorts in the face.

"This station is just soooo dangerous. I shudder to think what might happen if some other tech happened to run in the halls too fast or something. It could be a disaster!"

Despite her plan to just act the part of an annoyed employee free-falling into a probable firing, Phera couldn't help but feel more than a little genuine contempt for the station sec officers who'd been so eager to shoot at her.

"Then again, I guess you goons have to find *some* use for all that time you put in at the gun range, don't you? Pushing around innocent women doing their jobs must make you feel so big and tough, huh?"

"Excuse me?!"

Coming to a sudden halt, the female officer wheeled on her with a snarl.

"Is that really what you want? Really?"

Her hand had drifted back down to the grip of her holstered coilgun as she spoke, and her thumb was primed on its release catch.

"Because, I'd be thinking *really* hard about what I just said, if I were you."

Holy... Is she actually serious?

Phera was saved from having to answer her, though, by Obette stepping in between the two of them.

"Actually," he said, turning his head back to stare down at the prisoner with open malice. "I'd say it's my time on the station's racquetball court that you should be most worried about, young lady."

Looking back to the other woman, he favored her with a cruel, conspiratorial smile while she just looked confused.

"Pardon?"

Obette snickered.

"Guess you haven't heard the rumors about this one and Iris, huh?"

Sighing to himself, he made his meaning far clearer by grabbing Phera by the hair and shoulder and suddenly yanking her toward an empty desk.

"Ack! Hey! Let-! Ow-! Let me go!"

Oh gods, please don't tell me he's about to do what I think he is...

He was.

"Noooo, don't think I will. Not after all the grief you've been giving us."

"But... but...!"

As the front of her skirted thighs were shoved roughly up against the edge of the desk before her, Phera's tone turned decidedly more pleading.

"Please?"

SMACK! SMACK! SMACK!

In response to her question, Obette delivered three hard swats in quick succession against the snug seat of her skirt as he shoved her over the desk. Angling her backside up and out in the process.

"I believe I already answered that question."

SMACK! SMACK! SMACK!

These weren't the worst swats that Phera had ever endured, but the infiltrator hadn't been joking about his arms. While not as bulky as Straya or Adryel, he still managed to almost keep up with their workout routines on the Mayhem. Phera knew from personal experience that under that uniform and tactical armor he was still wearing, his body was lean, toned, and more than muscular enough to leave her howling and unable to sit down if he decided that's what he wanted to do.

SMACK! SMACK! SMACK!

"Owie, ow, ow!"

Which, apparently, was exactly what he intended.

"Little overeager there, private?" the security woman asked, sounding more amused than disapproving now that she saw what her partner had been getting at.

"Very!" squeaked Phera in agreement.

Obette just stepped aside and gestured at his captive target.

"You can go first, if you'd prefer. It *was* you she insulted, after all. At least primarily."

Moving around to the opposite side of the desk, he continued holding Phera's ample chest in place as, behind her, heads began to peek out of doors to see what all the commotion was about.

"Oh come on! I thought you were supposed to be the good cop?"

Thoroughly blushing cheek pressing against the paperwork beneath her, Phera blew out a disgruntled harrumph and raised both middle fingers at the woman and any gathering onlookers.

"Pretty sure pinning me to a desk isn't what your boss meant when he told you to escort me to 'holding', you know."

Ignoring her entirely, Obette continued addressing his partner.

"What do you say, bad cop? Want to help adjust this miscreant's attitude a bit before we tuck her away?"

"You know what?"

A grim chuckle rose up from the woman as she stepped into place where Obette had been standing just a moment earlier.

"Why the hell not?"

SMACK...! SMACK! SMACK!

Her hand hit Phera's backside full force then, as if performing martial arts attacks. Off-center. Uneven. Clearly unused to doing this, but with an enthusiasm that perhaps indicated a curiosity. Unfortunately for the engineer currently being targeted by her inexpert striking, though, she was mostly hitting the bonier spots around the outer edges of her rump. The spots with much less padding.

"Hey- Ack!" Phera yelped in real distress this time, automatically angling her inviting hips more toward her right in an attempt to stop the woman from smacking the sides of her hips quite so much. "Not- Oh! Not fair!"

This all seemed to be gathering her and Obette *more* attention rather than less, but she had to trust that he knew what he was doing. And so, playing her part, she worked to roll over and right herself as she sent a bevy of curses at the station sec woman.

"What the fuck, lady?" she demanded, glaring at her with a mixture of petulance and disbelief through her disheveled hair. "Don't you have other shit to do?"

"You kinda cleared my afternoon schedule," the woman countered, shoving her back over and nodding toward Obette to hold her steady. "Do you have any fucking idea how much paperwork I'm going to have to deal with tomorrow because of your bullshit?"

She resumed her assault then, pouring real anger into her movements this time as she made Phera yelp and howl. It wasn't that she was swatting her harder than Lem did when she was annoyed. It was more the attitude behind it that was staggering.

She was *pissed*.

SMACK! SMACK-SMACK! SMACK!

Well, that, and she was also going at her captive cheeks pretty damn hard.

"Good cop's turn?" Obette eventually prompted after a dozen more vigorous swats.

"No, no," waved away the other woman, panting slightly. "Think I'm finally starting to get the hang of this."

She definitely wasn't. Her impacts were uneven, way too hard, and inconsistently applied. Phera's right cheek was stinging way more than her left. Even so, she was definitely doing her best to make up for it through sheer determination.

SMACK-SMACK! SMACK! SMACK!

"It's not my- Oh! Fault- Ack!" the pirate protested, actually hopping a little now as her weight shifted from foot to foot in time with each hip-rattling **SMACK!** "Can't you just- Ow! Say it was a false alarm or something?"

SMACK! SMACK! SMACK!

"Oh, for the love of- Just SHUT THE HELL UP!"

"Just shut the hell up!" Phera parroted back in a mocking cadence undercut by high-pitched yelps.

"Why you little-!"

SMACK-SMACK-SMACK-SMACK-SMACK!

The woman's arm started pistoning blindingly fast then. Which, while definitely not pleasant, at least had her hand mostly hitting the centers of Phera's cheeks this time. Though, still unevenly.

She definitely seemed to favor her right cheek. That was for sure.

SMACK-SMACK-SMACK-SMACK-SMACK!

This change in tempo was met by a chorus of appreciative whistles along with some shouts of encouragement from their gathered audience around the security office. All eyes were fixed squarely on Phera's shapely backside as her cheeks rolled and bounced beneath the taut embrace of her navy blue skirt.

Meanwhile, Doctor Iris just shook ver head in mild disgust as ve strolled off with the confiscated samples container. Going completely unnoticed as ve let the automatic doors to the security office slide shut behind ver.

"I swear."

Obette snorted.

"It's as if she really doesn't care if she retains her employment at all, isn't it?"

However, before the fuming station sec woman could respond to that, Colonel Commander Sergeant whatever-his-name-was came storming into the room.

"What in the ever loving fuck is going on out here?"

"Oh! Uh, Commander!"

Her hand coming to a stop mid-swing, the security woman stiffened to attention, releasing her hold on the small of Phera's back.

"She was, um... She was resisting-"

She cast a look about for Obette to back her up, but the man had somehow managed to blend into the crowd of onlookers, completely out of the line of fire of the commander's glower.

"Then drag her to the damned cell! Actually, no, I take that back. Vence!"

He jabbed a finger at a portly officer who immediately jumped to attention.

"*You* escort her to holding. And, you, Jaeve!"

His finger stabbed at the woman this time, before he hooked a thumb over his shoulder.

"Get your ass in my office. Now!"

With that done, he sent a truly furious glare around the room.

"The rest of you get the fuck back to work."

"Yes sir!" came the crisp reply of a dozen people all at once while the woman, Jaeve, glared absolute venom at Obette.

Ignoring her, the infiltrator leaned in and murmured to Phera in passing, "Just do what they say and I'll be by to collect you later."

Phera nodded as she was hoisted back up by another guard, arms still bound together behind her back.

"Bye, Jaeve," she called over her shoulder with an exaggerated singsong as she was marched away, blowing the scowling woman a kiss. "Call me sometime, yeah? I'd be more than happy to show you how to *actually* work this ass."

—

The holding cell Phera was parked in to await her firing wasn't all that different from the interrogation room. Just smaller, with a cot bolted to the back wall, and a discreet toilet-sink combo shoved into one corner. It wasn't exactly dreary (it actually had pretty nice lighting all things considered), but she'd be lying if she said she wasn't starting to go just a little stir-crazy by the time her first hour was up. Again, without her comp, she couldn't actually tell how much time was passing. But, when the door to her cell eventually slid open, she was willing to bet half a dozen trips across Lem's lap that she was well into her second hour of confinement, if not her third.

"Fucking finally!"

Jumping to her feet, she took a petulant step forward.

"Are you going to let me go now, or-?" she started to demand, before actually seeing who it was on the other side of the door. "Oh thank gods!"

Never had she been happier to see Obette's trim figure and roguish grin.

"I wouldn't go thanking them just yet," the man teased, still smiling as he tossed her comp glove and a pair of station sec uniform pants onto her cot as he stepped into the cell. "Word on the street is there's about to be a major biohazard containment breach."

"Is that right?"

Phera smirked.

"Sounds dangerous."

"Mmhmm. Very."

As he spoke, Obette got to work on her handcuffs.

"I really would love to leave these in place as they suit you rather well, but…"

He favored her with a wink as her cuffs sprang open and fell to the deck behind her with a dull *clank* of metal on metal.

"The ventilation systems between Freezer C and the secondary docking ring access are about to be thoroughly contaminated. So, we'd best evacuate."

"You know, I was *just* thinking that."

Phera, grinning from ear to ear now, could feel a fresh sense of giddy anticipation rushing in to fill her stomach. She pulled on her comp glove and gave her finally freed fingers a celebratory wiggle.

"Oh, before I forget," continued Obette, hefting a small hypo-injector. "I brought you a present from the good Doctor Iris."

"Awww, that was sweet of ver."

Phera was only half paying attention as she reached back to draw down the zipper on her uniform skirt.

"What is it?"

"Special chem cocktail just for you, my dear."

"Nice!"

"Tell me about it."

Obette made absolutely no attempt to look away from her bobbing hips as she bent over to wrestle her practically painted on skirt and sheer tights down to her ankles. Instead, taking a moment to admire her creamy cheeks and the delicate bit of black lace threading between them as they wobbled with her movements.

"We're about to do quite a bit of running, and ve thought you could do with a little something extra to help you keep up."

"Huh. Good thinking- Ah!"

Phera jerked upright with a sharp, high-pitched yelp as Obette jabbed her right in the meatiest part of her left cheek with the handheld injector.

"Geez, what the hell, Ob?" she demanded, one hand flying back to rub furiously at where she'd just been stuck.

Before yelping again when he repeated the process with her right cheek.

"Apologies," he said in response to the death glare she sent his way. "MitoStims tend to work fastest when applied intramuscularly at the area you wish to augment. And, well, since you don't have a distribution port..."

He shrugged and flashed her one of his more rakish grins as he tossed aside the spent injector and reached into his pocket, producing a hair tie for her.

"Uh-huh. Sure."

Phera, face flushed but still smiling, rolled her eyes as she accepted the springy loop and pulled her curls into a messy ponytail while simultaneously kicking off the tangled mess that was her skirt, tights, and flats. She could already feel the stims starting to take effect as she hurriedly tugged on the pants the infiltrator had brought for her. Heart rate picking up fast as the muscles in her legs and glutes began to tremble with barely-coiled energy.

"Whoa, damn. This stuff is, uh… kinda intense."

It took her a moment to realize that she was bouncing on her toes, feeling just then like she could sprint an entire marathon without breaking a sweat.

"I should hope so. That was two full doses I just stuck you with," chuckled Obette, poking his head back out into the corridor outside her cell, looking left and right with his hand on his coilgun. "You're going to be wired for quite a while, I suspect. And, uh, apologies in advance for the hangover and jelly legs tomorrow. And the lactic acid buildup; you're going to be even sorer than usual around the injection sites."

"That's fine. We make it out of this in one piece, and I'm sure the Captain won't mind giving me the day off."

Obette snorted gently.

"I'm sure Straya will appreciate the easy access too."

The mention of the other woman's name touched off a bundle of fireworks inside of Phera's chest as she clapped excitedly and twirled in place.

"Ooooh, I can't wait to see her again! It's been way too long!"

Holy shit, Steph. These stims are no joke.

Attempting to calm herself, she tried to focus on her breathing as she watched her fellow pirate squat down just outside the door to her cell and start tugging at something.

"Here. These ought to fit you."

With that, he tossed first one boot and then the other back to her. And, by some small miracle of hand-eye coordination, Phera actually managed to catch them.

"Thanks! Um… Is she going to be alright?" she asked, nodding toward the currently unconscious (and barefoot) security officer Obette was dragging into her cell as she flopped down onto her thin cot and began wriggling her toes into her new pair of boots.

"Oh yeah, she's fine," he reassured her, snapping her cuffs onto the other woman's wrists before attempting to make her as comfortable as he could while she was lying on her side. "Just hit her with another little something from Steph. She'll be out for about an hour and wake up with one hell of a headache, but that's about the extent of it."

"Ah, phew."

Just then, an alarm began to sound and Phera sprang back to her feet with a startled squeak.

"Time to go?"

She grinned, almost manic with surging adrenaline.

Obette matched her smile with one of his own as he nodded, unholstering his coilgun.

"Time to go."

CHAPTER TWENTY-EIGHT

CHARGES ACCRUED

Unauthorized Consumption of Class 1 Stimulants, Evading Arrest, Accessory to Assault, Grand Theft, Aiding and Abetting Unauthorized System Access

"Hitting station space in five."

Adryel's voice on the comm snapped Straya back to the present with a start.

"Copy that," she responded, switching the displays inside her ulfsark from internal diagnostics to the hull feeds of the shuttle she was currently hanging off the side of. "Begin final weapons check and prepare for insertion on my mark."

"Ma'am, yes ma'am," came the crew cook's easy reply from inside the shuttle. "Feeling a little tense there, Stray?"

It was a fair question. They'd done three weapons checks already. One before leaving the Mayhem, one when they boarded the shuttle, and one only an hour ago. But, if there was one thing that had been drilled into her brain in her time with Gilgamesh, it was that you checked your damn gear before a mission.

"I'm *fine*."

"Uh-huh."

Adryel did not sound convinced.

"Look."

Straya felt a snarl catch in the back of her throat, and had to force herself to ease her clenched jaw before she cracked a molar.

"I just don't want these fucking cum garglers getting the drop on us because we half-assed our prep is all."

"Fair enough," conceded Adryel, sounding not the least bit convinced by her explanation.

Rather than probe further, though, they just let the silence between them grow.

Straya could just picture them sitting inside the shuttle balancing their knife on the tip of one finger as they waited for her to crack. Which she did. Blowing out an aggressive sigh that lifted the loose curls hanging over her forehead.

"It's been nearly a MONTH," she spat into her comm, unable to stop herself now that she'd started. "*I'm* picking the damn raid next time. Something quick and dirty, like knocking over a cargo transport. None of this cloak and dagger shit."

"Easy there, Stray…"

While her voice was tensely coiled, Adryel's remained calm and soothing.

"I'm sure we'll be doing all sorts of nice and boring work once we sell off this haul. You'll have time to get your hands all over your favorite pair of sweet cheeks, I promise."

"Uh-huh."

Despite her best efforts to stay annoyed, Straya could feel a reluctant half-grin tugging at the scarred corner of her mouth.

Adri *did* have a point, she supposed. As much as she hated to admit it, she'd been more of a mess than usual while Phera and the others had been gone. For the first few days everything had been fine. She'd actually enjoyed the peace and quiet (that was mostly down to Steph's absence, specifically), and the extra elbow room on the hab cylinder hadn't hurt. As those days started stretching out into weeks through, she'd begun to worry, and that worry had festered into a near-constant coiled tension deep in her gut.

Maintenance on her suit could only take up so many hours in a day, and Kelt had made it pretty damn clear that she wasn't going to keep putting up with her taking out her pent-up anxiety on Shi's bouncy ass by the end of that first week. She might have a whole head's worth of height and a good twenty or more kilos of hard muscle on the woman, but she still knew that was a fight she'd lose if push came to shove. You just didn't fuck with the lady who controlled your enviro, and the last thing she needed was Adryel roasting her over the rump roasting she'd have come away from that confrontation with. So, instead, she'd turned her attention to dragging Adri into the rec room with her for longer and longer workouts in preparation for their upcoming extraction mission. Being absolutely merciless with the amount of klicks the two of them put in on the Mayhem's two aging treadmills, along with the number of reps she demanded from their free weights, in between finding excuses (or foregoing them entirely when she couldn't be bothered) to shove them over whatever happened to be convenient to go to town on them in lieu of Phera.

She had to admit, that heavy belt Adryel wore for their thigh holster did leave some *very* nice stripes.

No matter what she did to distract herself, though, her thoughts would inevitably be drawn back to that damn bubbly redhead she'd come to care about. What was she doing? Was she safe? Had she been caught and whisked away into an InterSec prison cell without any of them finding out? Straya knew she had Obette and Steph watching her back, so chances were pretty low that things would actually go full on tits up.

But still.

Lying alone in her bunk late at night, her belly warm with the one glass of whiskey the Captain was rationing her to and her arms wrapped tight around Phera's pillow, she just couldn't stop herself from worrying.

Somehow her brain, asshole that it was, even managed to make the thought that she was doing totally fine even *more* stressful than if she were in trouble. For as much as she liked to joke about her acting ability, Phera played the role of a corporate cog exceptionally well. What if she decided that she actually liked working for Iotech and never came back to the Mayhem? Straya understood on an intellectual level that this was a totally baseless fear. That there was no way for her to keep working for the corp, even if she wanted to. Never mind the fact that the woman herself had told her personally that she'd left that part of her life behind. She knew that Phera wouldn't willingly choose to abandon the crew.

But still.

Try as she might to smother her gnawing worries, her mind kept coming back to those two damn, seemingly unconquerable words.

"Hey, hey, come on now, deep breaths."

Again, Adryel's steady voice broke into her circling thoughts.

"Shit. Sorry."

"No worries," they reassured her. "Seriously, though, it'll be fine. This is gonna to be a total cake walk. In and out. Five minutes, tops."

"God damn it, Adri."

Straya snorted out her first genuine laugh in what felt like way too long, some of the tension in her shoulders easing beneath the weight of her power armor harness.

"What?" demanded the enby, feigning innocence.

"You know what."

"I most certainly do not!"

She could feel her cheeks actually starting to hurt a little with her smile now.

Adryel was a treat.

"You just *had* to go and say that, didn't you?" she demanded, cutting loose with another long-suffering sigh.

"Heh. Got you to stop worrying about your girlfriend for a bit, didn't it?"

"Fuck you."

"Three way with Phera? Count me in."

Adryel laughed at their own joke, and so did she.

"Thanks."

"Any time, cupcake. Now, look sharp, you're up."

"Damn fucking right I am."

Brain snapping into combat mode, shoving all other thoughts aside, Straya locked in her vector calculations and prepared to jump from the side of the shuttle.

"Breaching air lock in three... two... one!"

Her ulfsark sprang into action. Launching from its perch on their commandeered transport shuttle and slamming shield first into the sealed exterior hatch of the docking bay berth they'd been assigned before Epiphany Station had gone into quarantine lockdown.

Of course, with all the boarding control workers scrambling for vacsuits just then, nobody was actually there to open the hatch for them, but that was fine.

She had a key.

Well, to be more precise, she had a plasma torch.

In less than a minute, she had a hole in the thick metal of the exterior hatch large enough for one leg to reach inside and trigger the emergency override for cycling the airlock. Slipping inside just as the shuttle carrying Adryel matched velocity with the docking ring and began mating its own airlock passthrough to the newly created opening.

"Ready?" she asked over the comm, the armored hand of her suit primed on the inner-hatch's manual release.

"My weapons have been quintuple checked and my suit reads one hundred percent integrity. Your rear guard's about as prepped as it can be."

"Copy that," replied the former soldier, switching her comm over to the frequency the Blazar Bitches used for general communication during a raid. "All right, kids, pack it up. Your ride's here."

The comm remained silent for a few nerve-wracking seconds, before crackling to life.

"Oh fuck, is that you, Straya?" came Phera's voice in a hurried rush, instantly filling her gut with a fresh burst of warmth. Warmth that cooled to a leaden ball of ice as she heard the all-too-familiar *CRACK! CRACK! CRACK!* of coilgun fire through the open comm.

"Sure is. What's your status?"

"Shit!" Steph's voice came over the line to answer for her, shouting loud enough to be heard over the din of combat. "We're pinned down in a supply closet outside the entrance to secondary grav acclimation, and Ob's the only one with any fucking armor!"

"Ve's right, I'm afraid," confirmed the infiltrator, cadence even as ever. "We had a small hiccup before you got here, and the superintendent decided to take the precaution of stationing squads at all docking access points. We've got four…"

CRACK! CRACK!

"Scratch that, *three* well-armed hostiles dug in where we need to go."

"Understood."

Straya slammed the manual release to the airlock and went storming through before it finished cycling open.

"Sit tight and don't get shot. I'm on my way."

"Oh thank gods!"

CRACK!

"We'll be here," Obette all but singsonged. "They seem content to keep us in place for the time being until their backup arrives. Too bad for them then that I disabled the cycling mechanisms for the hatches behind us."

CRACK!

"Hell yeah!" cheered Phera amid the chaos of a heavy-sounding equipment shelf being toppled over. "That one almost hit me!"

"It sure did," agreed Steph, sounding surprisingly exasperated for someone caught up in the middle of a firefight. "Now get back down here like I told you to before you actually do get hit by something."

SMACK!

"Fine, fine... Spoil sport."

"What the-?" Straya started to ask, before being cut off by Obette.

"You'll see when you get here. It's... fine? It's fine, right, Steph?"

"Tooootally."

Yep. Next time we're doing a regular god damn ship-jacking.

"You get all that, Adri?" Straya bit out into her comm pickup, toggling back to her private channel with them as she sprinted through the empty docking ring as fast as her suit-augmented legs could carry her. The auto-magnetizing soles of her ulfsark's feet producing a reassuring *CLONK! CLONK! CLONK!* that confirmed the place hadn't been vented of atmo when the containment breach alert had been issued.

"Sure did," answered the crew cook, following after her as fast as they could while staying behind cover wherever possible. "Sounds like a real *blast*. You want me to tag along?"

Straya snorted at the joke.

"Negative. It's going to be a tight fit with this damn suit as is, and there's no guarantee they won't have any armor of their own waiting for us." Toggling back to the general crew channel, she asked, "Any heavy ordinance or suits waiting for me, or is it just station sec?"

Obette took two more shots before answering her question. "Just well-armed personnel with repeating rifles."

"Good. Sit tight, I'm on my way."

As if on cue, just as she reached the broad, circular hatch that led into the secondary grav acclimation tunnel for the station's habitation cylinder, two automated turrets rose up from the floor and began showering the back of her ulfsark with a hail of magnetically-accelerated pellets.

"FUCK!"

The word was practically knocked out of Straya as she dove for the tunnel entrance, coming up with her shield at the ready.

PING-PING-PING-PING-PING!

Another dozen shots ricocheted off of its semi-translucent, carbon-reinforced surface, jarring her inside her suit. She felt the air drag of her ulfsark go off balance, and she heard the hiss of expanding ferrofoam as it spread across her back. Every third or fourth of those bullets must have been foam capsules, and a couple had hit her back before she could turn. She was damned lucky one of them didn't get into a shoulder joint and disable an entire limb.

"Okay, that's going to be a problem," she said to Adryel as she backed into the spiraling tunnel as quickly as she could while keeping her shield braced in front of her. The shield, too, was now sprouting a number of growing foam patches on its front.

Pulling up a status report on her suit's integrity, she let out a small breath of relief when she saw that the damn turrets had only managed to add a couple new dents to her already scuffed and faded power armor, and none of the servomotors were obstructed. She might not be as pretty as she had been back at Midway. But, just then, Straya was feeling incredibly vindicated over pouring as much of her crew shares into keeping her as functional as she did.

"A problem, a snag, a hitch, a stumbling block, and a big fucking issue," agreed Adryel from behind cover, their voice helping to center her thoughts on the problem at hand. "I thought Ob said this corp was hemorrhaging money. Where the hell did they get the cash for something like *that*?"

"Must be their mysterious benefactor."

"Humph. I want a rich investor sugar daddy."

"How about you make do with finding out where those turrets are being controlled from and shutting them off?" suggested Straya as she turned and began to speed ahead through the tunnel, a bit more clumsily now thanks to the bulging adhesive globs hanging off of her back and shield.

She was thoroughly in her element now, foamy bits aside. Teeth bared in a vicious snarl as her organs shifted inside of her with the gradual increase in pseudograv.

"If I had to guess, there's probably someone in boarding control who decided they wanted to try out their new toys."

"Good thing we found them first then."

"Fuuuuck. No kidding."

The thought of Phera sprinting into the docking ring, only to be mowed down by automated turret fire was enough to have Straya's stomach compressing into a black hole, and her vision going red.

"Find whoever is controlling those damn turrets and stick a knife in them."

Her voice was as cold as the void now, and exactly as unforgiving.

"That's an order."

"Heh."

Adryel's grim chuckle carried through their private channel. Straya could hear them taking several deep breaths, psyching themself up for the sprint across the largely exposed docking ring to reach the lift that would lead up to the observation office where their target would most likely be hiding.

"It would be my pleasure."

—

The deafening **CLANG!** of metal on metal as Straya's ulfsark dropped into the station's hab cylinder proper was extremely gratifying. Especially when the contingent of station sec officers that had up until that point been keeping her fellow pirates trapped behind cover with suppressing fire all but shit their pants at the sight of her, half of them nearly dropping their weapons in their haste to whip around and face this new threat.

No rear guard? Seriously?

Unfortunately, while their tactics might have been woefully amateur, the military-grade repeating coilgun rifles and armored vacsuits they were sporting were anything but. The fact that Obette had managed to drop one of them with nothing more than a sidearm was honestly pretty impressive. A high-powered shot to a target's faceplate while they showered you in automatic gunfire was no mean feat.

PING-PING-PING!

Speaking of...

Gritting her teeth, Straya crouched down behind her shield, angling herself to present the smallest target possible and hopefully avoid sending any shots ricocheting back toward Phera and the others as station sec opened up on her.

Those vacsuits were going to be a problem. She'd armed her ulfsark with a chem launcher and a ballistic shield in order to minimize fatalities during the extraction as per the Captain's orders. Adryel was the one with the damn rifle.

"Fuck."

She could tell just by looking that the filters on those suits were going to be more than up to the task of straining out the irritant payload she'd brought with her.

For the briefest of moments, Straya considered just wading into the group of toy soldiers and using her power suit's mechanical strength to kick their asses the old fashioned way. Two and a half meters of hardened ceramic and armor-plated fuck you was a pretty good way of settling an argument, after all. But, fun as that might be, the corridor they were dug into was narrow, and doing that would require her to expose her back. She and Kelt had done a decent job of keeping the plates there well-maintained, but she didn't want to risk one of those corporate fucksticks getting a lucky shot off on her when she wasn't looking. Plus, she had to admit she'd really rather avoid giving Phera nightmares by exposing her to the sight of nearly half a dozen men and women reduced to bloody smears and broken bones if she could.

Fortunately, she had one other trick up her sleeve.

"You still alive, Ob?" she sent via suit comm.

"And kicking," the infiltrator confirmed. "What's the play here?"

"Brought one of Steph's toys with me. Standby to fire."

Straya heard the petite doctor's delighted gasp over the comm, while Obette snickered.

"Oh my, that is *ruthless*."

It wasn't a criticism.

"Just give the word."

God. It was so nice working with professionals.

"Copy that. Stand by…"

Straya felt a predatory grin spread across her face as she toggled her chem launcher over to the special backup payload Steph had been developing for the last few months. With one hand braced on her shield, she angled the barrel of her weapon up and sent a pressurized canister of bone wasp larva enzymes arcing over the heads of the station sec officers.

"Now!"

CRACK!

At her order, Obette sent a single shot drilling straight through the canister, causing it to explode in a burst of rapidly condensing mist that poured down all around the armored targets.

"What the-?" she heard one man begin to demand, pausing in firing at her to wipe a hand over his suddenly wet faceplate, before letting out a horrified shout when he saw the polymer palm of his vacsuit glove dissolving right before his eyes, leaving a thick, gooey residue behind on his faceplate. "Fuck!"

Straya didn't give him time to say anything more than that. Instead, toggling her chem launcher back to its primary ammunition cartridge with a flick of her thumb and nailing him directly in the chest with another canister that exploded on contact. Engulfing him and the people around him in an orange cloud of synthetic capsaicin and a non-lethal nerve agent that was absolute hell on motor functions.

"Direct hit. Prepare for evac in thirty."

Obette's appreciative whistle drew out a husky laugh from Straya.

"That was absolutely beautiful," he crooned. "Marry me, Straya?"

"Sorry, stud," she snorted, toggling her visual feed over to her recently repaired infrared spectrum mode to keep an eye on things. "I prefer my partners with a bit more meat around the hips."

"Alas, such is life…"

The infiltrator's melodramatic sigh filled her cockpit as she watched the last of her targets succumb to the gas she'd just hit them with. With their vacsuits' softer components compromised, they'd dissolved into a fit of coughing and retching mixed with howls of pain as the irritant flowed in through the half-melted filters and went to work on their eyes and lungs, burning both mercilessly as they tripped over one another and fell to the floor unable to move.

Twenty-eight, twenty-nine, and… thirty.

As her mental count wound to a close, Straya strode through the already dissipating cloud of chemical fog. She'd deliberately chosen a composition that was heavier than air, so that she wouldn't have to worry about Phera or the others needing vacsuits should she have to deploy it ahead of them. And, as she clomped her way over to the half-open hatch Obette was peeking out of, she was feeling pretty damn pleased with herself.

"Oh my gods, Straya!"

A blur of purple and teal curls accompanied a deluge of additional exclamation points as Phera shoved her way past the infiltrator and sprinted over to Straya's ulfsark.

"Hey, hi, hello! Oh my gods, it's soooo good to see you! How have you been?"

"Um, hey there," the older pirate responded, suddenly feeling a bit tongue-tied as she angled her shield, still half-covered in foam patches that now sported bullet holes themselves, to cover the engineer while she jogged in place. "You, uh… You good?"

Phera ignored her question entirely.

"Holy shit that was so COOL!" she exploded with instead, pupils blown wide as saucers as she started pantomiming combat maneuvers, complete with sound effects. "You were, like, SCHWOOM! And they were all, like, 'Oh fuck!' And then you fired that thing right at that one guy and he was, like, 'Grah!' And then-"

Despite still being asshole deep in enemy territory, Straya couldn't help but loose a genuine, deep belly laugh as a surge of affection welled up inside of her.

"Okay, which one of you dosed sweet cheeks here with stims?"

"Ob!" Steph immediately asserted, jabbing an accusatory finger at the infiltrator and basically confirming Straya's suspicions for her.

"Steph *may* have overestimated Phera's tolerance just a touch," the silver-haired pirate allowed with a bemused shake of his head.

"Hey!"

Steph whirled on him, looking utterly betrayed.

"It's not my fault I overshot her weight!"

Before waving one hand back toward Phera as she continued her reenactment, oblivious to their discussion.

"Do you *see* those tits and ass? Anyone could've made that mistake!"

"So, you admit you made a mistake then?"

"I- Don't go changing the subject. We're talking about Phera!"

"Of course."

The look Obette gave ver made it abundantly clear exactly what he planned on doing with *ver* ass and tits once they were all safely out of here.

"Ahem."

Attempting to get things back on track, Straya poured some steel into her voice.

"She's not going to have a heart attack or anything, is she?"

"Heart attack?" piped up Phera, dancing over to where Steph stood glaring up at Obette and lifting ver tiny frame up in a bear hug, spinning ver around. "I feel great!"

"S-See?" wheezed Steph, kicking at the engineer's shins to get her to let go. "She's just having a good time is all."

When Phera dropped ver, ve did ver best to resume a dignified stance, but couldn't quite hide ver amusement.

"She's going to need a *lot* of water once we're back on the Mayhem, though."

"Speaking of..."

Passing his coilgun off to Steph, Obette turned around and picked up a complicated looking carrying case. Hefting it up in both arms and moving toward the entrance to the grav acclimation tunnel now that the last of the irritant fog had settled on the deck around the twitching, whimpering guards.

"Shall we get going?"

"Definitely."

Taking the lead once again, shield at the ready, Straya opened up a comm channel to Adryel as she began moving at a steady clip while the three others jogged behind her (Phera literally sprinting circles around Steph and Obette).

"Heads up, Adri, we're on our way back. You take care of those turrets yet?"

"Turrets?!" squeaked Phera, immediately being shushed by Steph.

"Never you mind, party girl. Just stick close to Straya and do what she says, yeah?"

"I can do that!"

"Oh, I'm well aware, sweet thing."

Ignoring their banter, Straya's pursed lips twisted into a frown as her comm continued to remain silent.

"Adri. Come in. Repeat. Come in."

Come on... Please don't tell me you let some nerd with a pair of toy guns take you out...

Thankfully, this time the enby responded.

"Agh, fuck-" they gritted out, breathing heavy enough for their comm to pick it up. "I'm here, I'm here..."

Rather than relax, Straya felt her chest tighten and her palms go clammy.

"You okay?"

"Uh-huh. Took out the... the turrets."

They groaned out several more curse words before rasping in another ragged breath.

"And got tagged in the process."

"Fuck."

Hearing this did absolutely nothing to ease Straya's stress.

"How bad is it?"

"Oh, you know..."

Even through their haze of pain, Straya could still hear Adryel's usual good humor shining through.

"In and out a few centimeters above my right hip. Hurts like a motherfucker, but I'll be fine. You've got Steph with you, right?"

"Yep."

Straya allowed her attention to flick for a split second over to one of her rear camera feeds where she could see the petite doctor and Obette were now sharing the load of the carrying case.

"Hang tight. We'll get you patched up as soon as we're out of here."

"Take your- Ack. Time. I'm just bleeding all over my favorite suit is all. Maybe I'll do a couple laps around the docking ring or something while I'm waiting."

"Smartass."

"Bitch."

Adryel's laugh, though pained, still managed to make Straya smile.

"See? What'd I tell you? Total cake walk."

CHAPTER TWENTY-NINE

Much as Phera wanted to celebrate their latest successful raid by getting absolutely shitfaced with the rest of the crew (minus Straya, who she was pleased to see was trying to cut back on her liquor, and Adryel who was laid up in medbay on a much-deserved painkiller drip), Steph wouldn't allow it.

"I know this is largely my fault."

Ve paused just long enough in ver dramatic reenactment of Phera's station sec interrogation to shoot a playful scowl toward a very smug looking Obette.

"But, let's give your kidneys a break for tonight, sweet thing," ve ordered, pressing yet another bottle of water into her hands. "You're already crashing as is. There's no need to make things any harder on yourself than they have to be."

"Humph."

Accepting the drink with a pout, Phera made a show of taking a long, deep pull from it.

"Yes *Mom*."

Steph giggled.

"I mean. That's really more Kelt's thing…"

Before adopting an admonishing, hand on hip posture, and waggling a finger at her.

"But I'm sure I can do a passable job if you want to keep on sassing me, young lady."

"All right, all right, you win," Phera laughed, bringing up her hands in mock-surrender. "No need to go threatening to send me to my room or cut my allowance."

This last bit of blatant brattery managed to draw out a snort from the actual Kelt. Who, had she not been busy cuddling Shi on her lap, she had little doubt would've already been halfway through seizing both her and Steph by the ear on principle alone.

"Now that I think about it, though, going to my room *does* sound pretty nice right about now..."

Stifling a yawn, Phera drained as much of her water bottle as she could and then disentangled herself from the arm Straya had wrapped around her. And, after sharing a quick kiss with the woman (which turned into a much longer one with just a hint of hair pulling and tongue tangling), dragged herself back to her feet.

"You gonna be okay on your own?"

Straya's look was part concern for her well-being and part admiring appraisal at the impressively snug seat of the station sec pants she still had on.

"As long as I don't have to race anyone there, should be."

Phera took an extra-long time stretching her arms above her head, making sure the other woman (and anyone else watching) got an equally good look at the downright provocative way she filled out the chest of her Iotech uniform top.

"You sure? I can walk you back-"

"No, no, it's fine."

"Well, if you're sure..."

"I am, don't worry."

Leaning in, Phera planted a quick kiss on Straya's scarred cheek.

"You go ahead and have fun for the both of us, yeah?"

Straya smirked.

"Guess that means I get her share of the rum then, Cap?"

The Captain just rolled her eyes.

"You can have *one* extra glass."

"Works for me."

"Hehe."

Unable to resist those hard, severe cheekbones and the little dimple that peeked out whenever Straya smiled just so, Phera leaned back in for one more kiss.

"I'll see you later, babe," she said, briefly interlacing their fingers before letting go with another yawn.

Straya, in turn, gave her backside a firm pat.

"Sleep tight, sweet cheeks."

"That's the plan."

That last remark earned her a slightly firmer pat and a snort of amusement, and then Phera was moving off toward the exit hatch of the mess. Had she been any less tired just then, she probably would've picked up on the very obvious hints Straya was giving her. But, despite her insistence that she was totally fine, she really was pretty exhausted.

She'd started coming down from her chem high right about the same time as their borrowed Iotech shuttle had rendezvoused with the Mayhem. At the time, she'd thought she had herself more or less under control. She no longer felt like running around in circles and her hands and feet had stopped trembling, at least. But, she must've still been pretty out of it, because the Captain had gotten one good look at her and then let loose with a delighted cackle.

"First time on stims I take it, swabbie?"

"Why, *Captain*!" she'd gasped theatrically in response, hand to her still fluttering chest as she hopped forward into the other woman's personal space. "I can't believe you'd even think to ask me that! A virtuous Daughter of Harmony such as myself would never partake in such wickedness."

"Oh, dear. How presumptuous of me."

Gliding the tips of her pointed nails along the line of Phera's lightly clenched jaw, the Captain licked her lips.

"Remind me to pick you up a habit the next time we're in port. I've always wanted to fuck a nun."

She'd seized hold of her chin without warning then, staring deep into her dilated pupils as her face went blank and her mouth dipped down at the corners.

"Go with Steph to medical. Ob can handle debriefing us on his own."

"Awww, nobody said anything about a post-mission sex party!" Phera had whined, which at least managed to crack the Captain's dispassionate mask as her lips twitched back up into her usual "I am *this* close to fucking and/or punching you" half-grin.

"You ought to know by now that that part comes *after* we've inventoried the booty."

She'd kissed her roughly then, seemingly just to remind her that she could.

"Now, get going before I have Lem bring me my belt so I can do something about yours."

"Aye aye, ma'am!"

Despite the pleasantly sharp increase in her already elevated heart rate that the prospect of the Captain and her way too heavy, genuine leather belt produced within her, Phera had wisely chosen to do as she was told for the time being. Besides, the chance to play doctor had sounded like a lot of fun. So, after flashing the lean and leering woman and her first mate a crisp salute, she'd danced off down the corridor after Adryel and Steph. Who, once they were inside ver lab, had stuck her with something ve said would help ease her coming crash before shooing her out with orders to find something to eat.

"Oh, and maybe bang on the table or yell or something if you think you're about to have a heart attack. You *should* be fine now, but you never know!"

The mention of food had made Phera aware of a gnawing hunger deep in the pit of her stomach that she hadn't noticed until just then. She'd spent her lunch break in a holding cell, after all, before then kicking her metabolism into overdrive with a chemical cocktail that was no doubt very illegal without a prescription. And, by the time she was halfway through her third reheated plate of Adryel's absolutely orgasmic spicy protein paste curry and rice, and people started trickling into the mess to keep her company, her energy levels had started to plummet and her legs had begun to feel about ten times heavier than they had any right to be.

So, yeah. Sleep sounded like just the thing.

Waving goodnight to the rest of the crew and receiving a deadly serious warning from the Captain to make sure she washed and pressed her Iotech uniform because she expected to see her in it in her cabin a few nights from now, Phera shuffled off in search of her bunk.

Of course, once she'd actually managed to get there, strip off her clothes, pull on the long white shirt Straya had given her that first day after joining the crew (well, thrown at, same difference), and climbed beneath the covers, she'd found that she wasn't all that tired after all. Or, to be more precise, her body was exhausted, but her brain was still stubbornly active. As a result, she found herself running through all that had happened in the last twelve hours over and over again as she stared at the dozen or so photo projections of her and the other Blazar Bitches she'd affixed to the wall and ceiling above her.

She'd learned from Obette on their way back to the Mayhem while Steph had been busy patching up Adryel's latest rugged-scar-to-be and administering Vernie's "antidote" (which turned out to be an injectable saline solution, though she wasn't about to tell him that), that Iotech had applied an invisible, infrared registration tag to all of its high-security specimen canisters that was scanned whenever they were removed from storage. Apparently, *that* was what had wound up triggering the alarms on her. Which, while definitely frustrating, had at least made her feel a whole lot better about her end of things. It was nice to know that she hadn't actually messed anything up like she'd originally feared. They'd just gotten unlucky was all.

"Should've been *your* ass getting it in front of all those station sec jerkoffs," Phera had pouted, fidgeting in the crash webbing harness the infiltrator had insisted on strapping her into upon boarding the shuttle.

"Ah, but yours is so much more captivating," Obette had countered, looking not the least bit sorry for his role in their impromptu distraction plan. "Not to mention you were being an absolute brat while Jaeve and I were escorting you to holding."

"Because you told me to!"

"I hardly see how that's relevant, my dear."

"I'll show you 'relevant' you-!"

"Oh please. Don't even pretend like you didn't love every second of that," Steph had chimed in then, cutting off her building tirade with a knowing giggle. "I bet if Ob had managed to talk that lady into dragging up that tight little skirt of yours, you'd have been soaking your way through your tights, you slut."

"No comment."

Phera's pouting had only made Steph smile all the wider.

"Besides, if he hadn't gotten you over that desk, I probably would've."

"Wh-What?! Why?"

"Can't have my assistant disrespecting me like that in front of everyone, now can I?"

That had managed to make Phera giggle much more than she usually would have. The stims Obette had stuck her with were making everything a *lot* more entertaining just then.

"Awww, you say the sweetest things, doc."

Steph had blown her a kiss in return, and she'd seriously considered pouncing on ver right there and then just for the fun of it, assuming she could disentangle herself from the safety straps she was cocooned in. Now that they were out of immediate danger and had managed to escape with everything they could've possibly hoped for, her lingering adrenaline and a whole bunch of other hormones she didn't know the names of but assumed were being secreted way more than they should be, had her feeling decidedly horny.

Well, hornier than usual.

Steph had been busy making sure Adryel didn't bleed out, though, and Obette had been keeping an eye on their pilot. So, she'd had to make do with imagining all the fun things she'd get up to with Straya once they were back home while trying not to think too much about how damp her crotch was.

Too bad Straya was stuck on the hull that whole trip, I bet Vernie would've enjoyed the show. Hope he manages to get over the whole "threatening to make your cock fall off" thing...

Smiling to herself, Phera rolled over and tried to get more comfortable. She was so unbelievably happy finally being back in her bunk on the Mayhem, and not just because her pillow smelled so much like Straya. It had been way too long since she'd been able to just curl up beneath her blankets and be lulled to sleep by the constant, low thrum of the negdrive and air scrubbers. The hotel bed she'd shared with Steph had been fine and so had the Iotech employee barracks, but there was just something about sleeping in her own bunk that made relaxing that much easier.

Plus, it didn't hurt that the worst thing she had to worry about happening to her while on board the Mayhem was someone deciding to jump her from behind for some surprise fun.

I'll take a horny Lem on the prowl for something soft and jiggly over getting shot at by trigger-happy station sec any day, thanks.

Beyond the simple joys of being back in familiar surroundings, Phera was also just plain glad to be back to her "regular" life. Glad to be back to the comforting rhythms of working with Kelt on keeping the Mayhem running smoothly in between coaxing out her oh-so-endearing motherly scowls and tuts, and fiddling with her projects in the workshop. If anything, these last few weeks had confirmed for her over and over again that she really was a pirate now. There was absolutely no way she could ever go back to living as a respectable corporate wage slave ever again. Though, that being said, with how tumultuous those last few hours on Epiphany Station had been, she was also ready for a vacation from action-packed swashbuckling for at least a few days.

Then again...

Much as she might be craving a break from the action, Phera also knew too there was no denying that she was totally and completely hooked on the adrenaline rush that went hand in hand with piracy. Putting some literal and figurative distance between her and the Iotech raid had managed to polish the hard edges off of the fear and anxiety from her being arrested and shot at so that only the heady thrill of adventure remained. Now all she could think about was how it had been *so much fun* fucking over a giant corporation while causing a bunch of property damage along the way. Hell, if they were lucky, Iotech might have to fold completely! At the very least, their investors were going to be *pissed*.

Oh yeah. She was definitely hooked.

Just as hooked as she had been after that first time back in college when she'd called her roommate's bluff about doing something if she didn't start pulling her weight cleaning up their dorm. She'd barely gotten the words "make me" out of her mouth, when she'd snapped and dragged her over her knee for what was easily the most fun thing either of them had done all semester.

I really should shoot Gideon a message one of these days. See how she's doing working for... Caldera? Cayne?

Yawning, Phera rolled over again and wriggled forward so that her forehead was resting against the cool metal where her bunk met the cabin wall.

She was just beginning to feel that heavy, all over tug that meant sleep was right around the corner, when she heard the hatch to the room slide open and someone pad their way inside on a pair of bare feet. Had she been more awake, she might've peeked over her shoulder to see who it was. But, that question was answered for her, when she felt her bunk creak and Straya's familiar form settle in behind her beneath the covers.

"Hey there…"

Sighing contentedly, Phera relaxed back against her favorite set of soft breasts and firm thighs.

"Hey yourself."

She smelled fresh and clean, apparently having just taken a shower. Her spacer body heat biomod made the residual moisture clinging to her skin practically steam away, and Phera could feel through the back of her thin shirt that she hadn't bothered with getting dressed before getting into bed with her.

Straya draped an arm over her torso and pulled her closer.

"I missed you," her brassy alto murmured into the back of her hair as she paused to breathe her in.

"Me too," Phera whispered softly in return, snuggling more fully into her.

She felt a low chuckle rumble up through her lover's chest behind her as she reached beneath her top, casually fondling one plump breast in a calloused palm.

"I also missed these."

"Mmmm…"

A tingle crept up Phera's spine as it arched on reflex, pushing her chest more fully into the other woman's groping hand.

Taking the hint, Straya's fingers found her nipple and gave it a gentle squeeze. Rolling it between her thumb and forefinger while she chuckled once again at the breathy moan it produced from the engineer.

"Oh… Oh gods, Straya."

"Yes?"

Keeping up her attentions on her breasts, Straya leaned in and kissed the side of Phera's neck.

"N-Nothing, just-"

"It didn't *sound* like nothing," the pirate taunted, pinching one thoroughly erect nipple hard enough to make her yelp.

"Ah!"

Straya kissed her again.

"I have ways of making you talk, you know," she purred directly against her ear, her voice pure sex and honey as she returned to rolling Phera's hyper-sensitive nipple between her long, clever fingers.

Phera couldn't see the look on her partner's face, but she had a fun time imagining it.

"Do your... worst," she panted, pushing her hips back with a defiant wiggle, reveling in the feel of Straya's pelvis cradling her ass.

"Hmmm, I suppose I could."

Straya returned to playing with her nipples, apparently not affected in the slightest by her attempts to intimidate her with her curvaceous wiles.

"But, I'd much rather just do this."

Suiting actions to words, she shifted a thigh between Phera's leaden legs, discovering for herself that she wasn't the only one who'd foregone putting on any underwear before getting into bed that evening.

"Well, well, well, would you look at that?"

She shifted her leg further up as she spoke, grinding the top of one bare thigh against the slick heat between Phera's parted legs.

"You know..."

A light flick against her right nipple had the younger woman biting down on her lower lip to stifle a gasp.

"If I didn't know any better, I'd say you *like* my very scary interrogation techniques."

"Y-You think so?"

Phera's attempts to sound obstinate only succeeded in earning her some really rather cruel thigh bobbing and nipple pinching.

"I really..." Straya began.

More thigh bobbing. Lightly grinding her aching clit against smooth, firm skin.

"Really..."

More nipple pinching. Just hard enough to make her grit her teeth and squirm.

"Do."

Then, cruelest of all, Straya withdrew her leg and let her hand dip down to rest along the gentle curve of one of Phera's love handles.

"Or am I wrong?"

"Ugh."

Rolling over with an affectionate glare, Phera kissed the tip of the extremely self-satisfied woman's nose.

"Maybe."

"Maybe, huh?"

Straya leaned in, gently pressing her lips to Phera's own, deep and slow. Exploring. Reconnecting. Pulling her back into the familiar orbit of her commanding presence and reassuring warmth as their tongues danced with one another. She tasted just as delicious as Phera remembered. All coiled violence and buried gentleness, mixed with just a hint of rum and some spice she could never quite put her finger on.

Ugh. I love her so much…

Absence had only made her heart grow fonder, and it almost hurt just how much she needed her then.

When Straya eventually tried to draw back, Phera caught her behind the neck and tugged her in for yet another kiss. In retaliation, Straya glided one hand down over her soft stomach and between her legs. Causing her to moan into her mouth as her fingers slid inside of her with possessive ease.

"Oh gods!"

Head twitching back and chest thrusting forward, stars exploded behind her half-lidded eyes as Straya began to casually fuck her.

"Just me, sweet cheeks, but thanks for the vote of confidence."

"Wh-Whatev-"

"Shhh…."

Straya pressed a finger to her lips before she could finish firing back with something sufficiently sassy. Fixing her with one of those secret smiles she only shared with her.

It had been way, *way* too long since they'd been able to just be alone like this, and Phera offered no resistance as Straya removed her silencing finger and buried her face against the side of her neck. Biting down hard enough to make her cry out while her thumb found her clit beneath the sheets and went to work in time with her rhythmically pumping fingers.

"Mmph! S-Straya, I... I...!"

The power of speech was rapidly fleeing Phera as the other woman curved and twitched her fingers inside of her, beginning to take her faster. She wasn't being gentle now, and the panting engineer loved her all the more for it as she surrendered herself entirely to her touch.

"What did I *just* tell you?"

With a low, husky growl, Straya shoved her roughly up against the wall. Her fingers still deep inside of her as she seized a fistful of dyed curls with her free hand and captured her lips once again in a savage, primal kiss.

"Now, you're going to come for me, you little brat, and you're going to do it right fucking now. You hear me?"

"I... I...!"

"Right."

In and out. Fingers pounding hard enough to shatter any attempts she might've made to defy her.

"Fucking."

Round and round. Straya's thumb tracing out brutally sensuous circles against her aching clit.

"*Now.*"

She bit her again then, sucking hard enough to leave a mark that would be visible to the rest of the crew for the next couple days as Phera toppled violently over the edge into oblivion.

"Oh my godssss!"

Straya didn't stop pumping or kissing as her body was racked by wave after wave of orgasmic fury. Ruthlessly continuing to take her over and over again as she convulsed around her fingers. Drinking in her moans and squeals of pleasure as she sought out her tongue and thrashed it with her own. Doing her damnedest to take her as fully and completely as she could. As if making up for lost time.

It.

Was.

Bliss.

"O... Okay, *damn*."

Phera was sprawled out on her back, sheets kicked back and sweat-matted hair clinging to her forehead as she rode out the last few aftershocks of her climax once Straya had taken pity on her enough to let her go.

"I know you said you missed me, but... Damn."

Rolling over onto her side to face the older pirate who was watching her with her head propped up on one elbow while she sucked arousal off the tips of her glistening fingers, she smirked. Her kiss-swollen lips making her look all the cuter in the muted, blue-hued amber light of the cabin.

"Maybe I should leave more often if this is the kind of welcome back I can expect."

In response, Straya reached over and pinched her ass.

"Owie!"

"Don't go getting cute on me now."

Phera pouted back at her.

"I thought you liked it when I got cute?"

"I do..."

Straya's lazy drawl was utterly content as she palmed the round, full cheek she'd just pinched, making it wobble and bounce against its fellow.

"But, I'm also way too tired to turn you over my knee for it."

"Oh really now?"

A smirk returned to Phera's lips, before just as quickly being replaced by another pout as Straya pinched her again.

"Really."

"Womp womp..."

Phera's pout gave way to more giggling as she pushed Straya onto her back. Straddling her, she leaned in for another kiss (one that was much more gentle this time), before beginning to work her way down the column of her throat to her absolutely perfect collar bones. Trailing kisses across the muscular woman's freshly scrubbed skin. Pausing to lick at each small scar and nick she came across along the way as she gradually drew closer and closer to her chest.

"Fuck, I've missed you."

Proving just how much she'd missed her lover, Phera took one dark brown nipple between her eager lips and began to suckle and tease at it with her tongue. Gently rasping at her areola with her teeth just the way she knew Straya liked it, while her free hand kneaded its twin.

This time it was Straya's turn to arch her back, a stirring of pleasure that was part growl and part sigh rising up from deep within her as she did so.

Mouth still hard at work teasing out further gasps and throaty moans from the bigger woman, Phera worked Straya's legs apart with a knee. And, slipping between them, began trailing still more soft, lingering kisses along her flat, firm stomach and the shallow valley between her well-defined abs. Circling her tongue around the bowl of her navel before drawing down between her raised, muscular thighs.

"Missed that too?" teased Straya, one hand resting fondly atop Phera's curly hair as she peppered kisses up and down along the insides of her thighs.

"Like you wouldn't believe."

Phera's laugh was warm against Straya's arousal-slicked vulva. Drawing out an involuntary shudder from the woman as her head fell back against the pillows and her eyes drifted shut.

"Want me to prove it?"

In response, Straya tightened her grip on her hair and drew her smart mouth down against her swollen lips.

"Get to work, brat."

Had her mouth not been so full of Straya just then, Phera would've most definitely fired back with something sassy. But, again, considering that her lips were currently locked in a passionate embrace with the pirate's own, she decided to just do as she was told for a change.

Honestly, it wasn't that hard of a decision.

"Mmmm… Yeah, just like that…"

Especially when doing so had Straya groaning her approval so openly.

Phera knew she could've pushed her over the edge pretty much immediately if she used her fingers. But, despite the insistent grip on her curls making sure she didn't wander off, she really wasn't in any sort of rush. She'd been dreaming of having these long, thoroughly muscled legs over her shoulders, rhythmically tightening around her head in time with their owner's low moans, for way too long to let her off that easily.

Oh no. She was going to have Straya *begging* her to stop before she was finally through with her.

Dipping her tongue between her folds, Phera lapped at her again and again. Determined to drink up every last drop of arousal at her core in between shifting her attention up to her clit. Spelling out her name against the swollen bud again and again before dragging her silky tongue up and down along her smoldering mound, eventually pausing at its base to part her folds before slowly but surely working her way inside of her.

Again, she tasted absolutely delicious.

"Ohhh... FUCK! Don't you dare stop!"

And, judging by the way Straya's fingers had tightened in her hair while her hips rolled and bucked against her eager mouth, she was enjoying herself quite a bit too.

Gods. It was so good to be home.

—

Floating along in a haze of warm bliss from her third? Fourth? orgasm while her partner continued to eat her out, Straya was just considering dragging Phera back up so that she could catch her breath and maybe make good on her earlier threat to spank her after all, when she noticed the hypnotic bobbing of purple and teal curls between her legs had suddenly stopped.

"Uh... Phera?"

In response to her question, she half-heard and half-felt a faint snore against her still very sensitive lips.

"Ah."

Steph *had* said she was in for a stim crash.

"Oh well..."

Rolling her eyes, she blew out a long-suffering sigh and very carefully eased herself back from the younger woman's mouth. Then, mindful not to wake her (though, given how she'd literally just passed out on top of her, she doubted that was much of a worry), she muscled her back up to their pillows and pulled her in close; petting the back of her head affectionately as she drew the covers over the two of them.

"Sleep tight, sweet cheeks. I love you."

CHAPTER THIRTY

CHARGES ACCRUED

Accessory to Extortion, Accessory to Assault, Accessory to Kidnapping

As it turned out, unloading ultra-high-end medical research data built on top of eons old precursor tech was slightly more complicated than selling off the premium, planet-raised meat the crew had stolen from the Altona during their last raid. Sure, there were plenty of people who'd *love* to get their hands on what they'd taken. The trick, though, was finding someone who was willing to pay what it was actually worth.

Which was quite a bit.

Granted, splitting the take nine ways (after setting aside a big enough chunk to cover general crew expenses and ship maintenance for at least a couple months) meant that neither Phera nor any of her fellow pirates would be retiring to a luxurious villa staffed by attractive servants in preposterously slutty outfits any time soon. But, their shares would still be more than enough to cover a truly decadent amount of partying on Marcos Station, along with that one pair of lace-up, knee-high boots with all the elaborate straps and buckles Phera had been drooling over the last time they'd been in port.

Of course, before they could do any of that, they had to actually sell the damn haul first. Fortunately, that was the Captain's forte. And, after spending the next few weeks running surplus loads of graphene and hydrocarbons all over B-Sys while the Captain ran down her contacts, they had a meeting.

—

Phera had fully expected to stay on board the Mayhem helping Kelt recalibrate the port side particle spectrometers while the Captain and the more intimidating members of the crew (minus Adryel, who was in the final stages of recovery for their gunshot wound and still confined to the ship by Steph) met with their buyer. As such, it came as a bit of a surprise when she was informed the night before their meeting that she would be accompanying the Captain, Lem, Straya, Obette, and Steph when they went into the station that following afternoon.

"You helped bring this together, swabbie, which means you're coming with." the Captain explained, using the auburn-haired engineer's shoulder-length curls to yank her head back as she energetically took her ruby red ass from behind with one of her more menacing strap-ons. "So, clear your schedule."

At that particular moment, Phera's mouth was gagged by her own wadded up panties, but her muffled yelps and moans of pleasure seemed to register as acquiescence for the older woman.

"Great!"

Who gave her still sizzling handiwork a hard swat with her free hand.

SMACK!

"Ackth!"

"I know! I'm excited for you to pop your cherry too. It's about time you came along for one of these meetings."

SMACK!

"Oh, and make sure you wear something cute and intimidating. I have a reputation to maintain, you know."

—

Striding with her fellow pirates through the sunsim-lit corridors of Marcos Station that following afternoon, Phera wasn't so sure she'd quite managed to hit intimidating with her choice of outfit, but she was at least reasonably confident that her flatteringly snug synthleather pants, LED-bedazzled boots and belt combo, low cut top, and cropped jacket more than fulfilled the cute requirement. To be fair, she felt a lot more like a party girl on her way out for a night of dancing than a dangerous swashbuckler heading to a shady meetup to unload illicitly-acquired medical goods. But, with the Stinger Mark 12 stun gun strapped to her right hip, she at least looked like a party girl you should probably think twice about fucking with.

Granted, that hadn't stopped Straya from doing just that over one of the tables in the mess after breakfast that morning. But, still. She couldn't stop herself from swaggering just a bit as she walked.

"The Velvet, huh?" asked Straya as they all squeezed into one of the narrow, exposed rock wall lifts that would take them deep into the heart of the mined out asteroid.

"Mmhmm…"

The Captain sounded almost bored as she buffed her freshly painted fingernails against the front of her knee-length (and extremely formfitting) coat. It happened to be the very same one she'd worn that first day when Phera had met her. And, with the way the older woman's hips rolled beneath its armored folds in time with her impatiently tapping bootheel, she was having a surprisingly difficult time keeping her attention focused on the task at hand.

"Even with B-Sys worker collectives, business is still business," the Captain sighed, sifting a hand through the ice white swoop of her bangs with a flourish. "Which means you make shady backroom deals in shady backrooms."

Lem snorted.

"Seems a bit on the nose, don't you think?"

"Tell me about it. I would've much preferred to do this via dead drop, but our buyer was *very* insistent that we meet in person."

One corner of the Captain's mouth twitched up as the doors to the lift creaked open and they began filing out.

"Fortunately, the Velvet has top-shelf refreshment and ample entertainment. We can get straight to celebrating as soon as we're done fulfilling this idiot's action vid fantasies."

She draped an arm around Phera's shoulders then.

"What do you say, swabbie? Feel like stripping for us? They've got a stage with a pole and everything, you know."

"I, uh... Maybe?"

That question did absolutely nothing to help Phera's focus as her nipples tightened beneath her top.

"Yes, yes, yes!" cheered Steph, while Obette chimed in with a no less excited. "Oh, you simply *must*!"

"Heh. Well..."

Phera was starting to regret choosing to wear a jacket just then as the temperature in her face ratcheted up several orders of magnitude.

"Put enough drinks in me, and I'm sure I'll be more than happy to," she eventually conceded with a self-deprecating laugh. "Though, fair warning, I haven't tried to do a striptease since I was in college. I don't know how good I'll actually be."

This admission prompted Straya to reach over and draw her away from the Captain with a possessive squeeze to her thoroughly well-outlined seat.

"I'm sure you'll figure it out," she chortled, fingernails digging into her thong-exposed cheek through the practically painted on material of her pants. "Though, you start losing your clothes and I can't guarantee that drinks are the only thing that's going to wind up inside of you."

Blushing even harder now, Phera nevertheless pushed her round hips further into the taller pirate's grip.

"Promises, promises..."

SMACK!

Before jumping ahead a full two steps with a startled yelp when Lem caught her other cheek with a frankly unnecessarily hard swat.

"Focus on getting laid *after* we're done with the hand off."

"Ugh!"

Spinning around and walking backwards, Phera stuck her tongue out at the perfunctorily scowling first mate.

"You're, like, a total fun suck. You know that, right?"

"I'm a professional," the other woman countered, unaffected by her glower in the slightest. "Now, try and look like you know what you're doing. We're almost there."

"She's right, you know," agreed the Captain, completely ignoring the fact that she'd been the one to start everything. "Look sharp, swabbie."

"Humph."

Unable to stop herself, Phera directed a petulant pout toward her, all the while still walking backwards.

"How about you fucking make m- Ack!"

Before the words had fully finished leaving her mouth, the Captain had closed the distance between the two of them. Seizing a fistful of copper curls and yanking her up onto her tiptoes so that they were suddenly eye to eye.

"Care to repeat that?"

"Ow! Hey! I was being rhetorical!" protested Phera, her suddenly diamond-hard nipples pressing roughly into the lapels of the Captain's coat as she grew decidedly wet.

"Suuuure you were."

The Captain did not sound the least bit convinced, but she at least eased her grip enough so that Phera was able to ease back down onto her heels without feeling like her hair was about to be wrenched free at the root.

"You're lucky you're cute, hon."

"Awww, thank you, ma'am. You're not so bad yourself."

Rolling her eyes good-naturedly, the Captain looked over to Straya and gave the engineer in her talons a firm shake.

"Spank this one absolutely raw once we're finished."

Before focusing her slightly unsettling amber gaze back on Phera, her full lips pulling back in a cruel grin.

"On stage. In front of everyone."

"Hah!" exclaimed Steph, while Straya cracked her knuckles.

"Works for me."

"Oh come on! Don't I at least get a say in any of this?" whined Phera, thighs squirming together at the prospect of yet another very public spanking.

Upon receiving five simultaneous permutations of "No", "Fuck no", and "Hell no" in response to her question, she stomped a foot.

"Ugh! Fine."

"Fine?"

Once again, the Captain's voice dipped low and dangerous, and Phera found herself suddenly grateful for her supporting hand in her hair as her knees went to jelly beneath her.

"Er, I mean- Aye aye, ma'am!"

"See?"

Yanking her in closer, the Captain brought her lips right up to her burning ear and nipped the lobe, making her shudder.

"That's what I *thought* you said."

—

The Velvet, Phera soon discovered, was very much the sort of establishment she'd always pictured being on a seedy Proxward station when she was younger. Half strip club and half brothel, it was made up entirely of dark interiors lit by garish pink and purple neons, pounding synth rhythms, underlit tables, and the sort of clientele you didn't maintain eye contact with for very long if you weren't prepared to get into a fight.

Needless to say, the Captain fit right in.

"Ahhh, memories," she sighed wistfully, eyes lingering on the intricately tattooed thighs of a woman eating out a customer lounging in a booth as she in turn did her best to ram her tongue down her companion's throat. "Right then, girls. Quit ogling and let's get to work."

Slicing through the raucous crowd of dancers, drinkers, and the casually fucking like an ultrasonic knife through protein paste, the Captain led Phera and the rest of the crew to a secluded VIP lounge that was, in fact, nestled into the back of the club.

"Linus!" she exclaimed with the sort of false brightness Phera had never heard her use before as the door to the lounge slid open to reveal the other half of their meetup. "So good to finally see you in person."

"Ah, Captain. Welcome."

Inside, a well-dressed man in his late forties with neatly swept back hair sat in the middle of one of a pair of half-circle leather couches arranged around a low table, looking bored and just a bit disgusted by his surroundings. The haughty, upper-class Alpha System bearing he carried himself with instantly reminded Phera of her father, and she found herself taking an immediate disliking to him.

"Please."

The man the Captain had addressed as Linus gestured to the couch across from him, the material of his expensive looking suit swishing quietly with his movements.

"Have a seat."

The Captain, who'd already been doing just that before he'd even spoken, favored him with a tolerant quirk of her right eyebrow.

"You're too kind."

Meanwhile, Phera, on instinct, had been moving to join her. Only to realize as she was lowering herself onto the cushions beside the older woman that nobody else had done so. Lem and Straya had taken up positions to either side of the Captain behind the couch. Steph had found a comfortable looking bit of wall to lean against with ver hands stuffed into ver pockets. And, Obette was just plain gone.

Smooth Phera. Real smooth.

Attempting to cover her minor misstep, she made to straighten back up again, only to feel a pointy-nailed hand slip inside the partially sagging back waistband of her pants with an insistent tug.

"Oh no you don't."

The next thing she knew, Phera found herself plopping down onto the Captain's lap. Her long legs and lean thighs making an excellent perch for the engineer's full hips as her booted feet dangled a handful of centimeters above the floor to the left of her knees.

"These sorts of meetings tend to be much more fun with a bit of lap candy," she explained while Phera did her best to fight down a sudden flush creeping up her neck.

"Um, are you sure? I can always just-"

"Shhh..."

Pressing a fingertip to her lips, the Captain hit her with a look that warmed her in several places all at once.

"I'm sure."

Before winking as she drew that same finger down along the bow of her lower lip.

"You just keep that pretty mouth shut until someone asks you a question. Yes?"

The hollow of Phera's throat bobbed up and down as she swallowed. Doing her best to ignore the smirk on Steph's face and the pair of amused snickers coming from Lem and Straya off to her left.

"I, uh…"

She nodded.

"Aye aye, Captain."

Which earned the upper curves of her chubs a fond pat.

"Perfect."

Just then, the door behind them slid open and a petite woman in a way too short dress that showed off that underwear wasn't part of the employee uniform for this establishment appeared holding a tray with a helical glass set atop it.

"Compliments of the management, ma'am."

"Oh? How sweet. Do tell Nona thank you for me, won't you?" crooned the Captain, accepting the luminous beverage with a wolfish grin while giving the server a blatant once-over. "And don't *you* go wandering off too far either, sweet. I'm going to need someone to keep Phera's spot warm while she's showing off the goods once our business here is concluded."

Rather than make her blush like it very much did for Phera, the younger woman instead just rolled her eyes at the Captain's shameless propositioning. Though, judging by the small twitch at the corners of her mouth and the lingering once-over she gave her in return, she seemed to be giving the pirate's invitation/order some serious consideration.

"Enjoy your drink, Captain."

As she busied herself with bustling out of the room, the Captain did just that. Draining a full third of the liquor inside the complicated glass and smacking her lips in satisfaction.

"Ahem."

The man in the suit pointedly cleared his throat.

"Are you quite finished?"

"Just about."

Unhurried by his impatient frown, the Captain made a show of giving Phera's ass (which was still fairly tender from its rough treatment the night before) a hearty squeeze that made her squirm before settling more fully against the back of the couch.

"Now then, let's get down to business."

"Yes. Let's."

Straightening up in his own seat with an officious huff, as if matching postures with the pirate across from him was a personal affront to his dignity, Linus adjusted his tie and cast an expectant look toward the sample container at Steph's feet.

"Is that it?"

"Sure is."

The Captain took another languorous pull from her drink before nodding toward the blonde.

"Steph? If you'd be so kind."

"You got it, Cap."

Bubbly as ever, Steph hefted the broad container off the floor with a grunt and muscled it over to the table between the Captain and the suit.

"Help yourself," the lean pirate offered, one hand still idly fondling the seat of her favorite cabin girl as she kept her attention focused on the man in front of her. "That's three years' worth of prototype tech. And, from what the good doctor here tells me, some truly astounding precursor biological specimens."

"So you say."

Phera, who'd been doing her best to look serious and competent while perched atop someone's lap being groped, felt her lips pinch in annoyance at the man's casually dismissive attitude. That changed soon enough, however, as he popped open the lid of the container and selected a canister at random. As soon as he'd attached it to a handheld scanning device he'd produced from a small case beside him, his bushy eyebrows went rocketing up toward his receding hairline.

"My god! But, this is…"

"Incredible? Fantastic? Some of the most valuable shit you've ever fucking seen?" suggested the Captain, her own expression growing steadily more predatory.

"Er… Ahem. Yes. Quite."

Clearing his throat once again and very carefully returning the sample canister back to its shock-proof gasket inside the case, Linus met the Captain's amused eyes a lot more eagerly this time.

"And the research data?"

"Right here."

Passing her drink off to Phera with a silent order not to spill any, the Captain dipped a hand into an inner pocket of her coat and produced a slim data chip with a flick of her wrist.

"The keys to one of the biggest technological innovations in at least a decade. Plus, a metric fuckton of office gossip, memos, and inter-department sniping and passive aggression for good measure. Just like we discussed."

She tucked the chip into the cleft between Phera's breasts then, giving them a pat.

"Now. I've shown you mine. Let's see yours."

Her hand dropped to Phera's thigh as she spoke, while the suit's hungry gaze remained locked squarely on the engineer's ample chest.

"Where's our payment?"

"Ah, yes. As to that..."

A wave of truly face-punching smugness washed over Linus then as he eased back in his seat and plucked up a half-finished tumbler of whiskey. Phera had only a passing moment to indulge herself in imagining the look on his stupid face if she knocked that tumbler out of his hands, though, before she was sent toppling onto the floor as the Captain sprang to her feet; shoving her down as she went.

"Wha-?"

The rest of the curvy pirate's words were cut off in a startled gasp as she watched from her prone position on the floor as the Captain vaulted over the low table in front of her and drew an intricately-filigreed coilgun from a shoulder holster beneath her coat, pressing its octagonal muzzle against the center of Linus's forehead in one smooth motion.

In the next moment, just as Straya and Lem were diving for defensible positions in front of the couch their boss had just abandoned, the door to the lounge slid open and half a dozen mercenaries decked out in matte black combat armor and reflective faceplates flooded into the room. Each held a wicked looking coilgun rifle at the ready, and the sight of them immediately had Phera going stock-still on the floor, completely ignoring the fruity liquor soaking through her top. This definitely wasn't the kind of situation where you made any sudden moves, she knew, which was a bit of a problem since sudden moves were basically the Captain's whole thing.

At least *she* wasn't panicking, though.

Instead, her face had gone abruptly blank, and Phera felt the hairs on the back of her neck stand on end as she watched the older woman's air of wry menace fall away to reveal something that was just plain menacing.

"Tolonine CX-4's, eh?" she mused aloud after several extremely stressful seconds of silence, her own coilgun remaining unwaveringly still against an equally stressed looking Linus's forehead. "Aren't you girls a bit far from the Victoria Group's usual territory?"

"Shut the fuck up, bitch," barked a distinctly unfeminine voice through an external vocaster mounted to the helmet of what Phera had decided to think of as the lead mercenary. "Drop the gun and get on the floor before I plaster your skinny ass all over the upholstery."

"Hmmm... No. I don't think I will."

Completely unfazed by having several heavily-armed people holding her and her crew at gunpoint, the Captain kept her voice light and breezy while her amber gaze hardened to tungsten.

"I take it then that since you haven't started perforating me and my associates, that this worthless piece of shit..."

At this, she shoved the muzzle of her coilgun harder against Linus's forehead, making him whimper as he was forced to tip his head back against the couch.

"Is the one paying you, rather than being the bait for this little surprise party?"

Again, her question was met with clipped profanity and hard scowls from the mercenaries. Well, Phera *assumed* they were scowls. She couldn't actually see any of their faces behind their helmets' reflective faceplates.

That didn't seem to bother the Captain, though.

"Linus, be a dear and tell your friends to go home before one of them does something stupid."

"Er... I... That is..."

"*Now.*"

All the levity had drained away from the Captain's voice, leaving it eerily flat and deadly.

"I'm not going to tell you again."

"Uh- Ahem. R-Right!"

Despite looking as if he was about to piss his pants, the corporate suit still did an admirable job of gathering himself and what meager sense of authority he still had left.

"Sergeant, please. You and your men are no longer needed here. You may go."

"Sir?"

The lead mercenary's helmet cocked ever so slightly to the side.

"Are you sure?"

"Yes. He is," intoned the Captain, while Linus nodded as best he could without jostling her trigger finger.

"I... I'm sure," he managed to get out around a very tight sounding throat. "You and your men will still be compensated of course. Return to your shuttle for now, and I'll..."

He swallowed.

"I'll be in touch."

"There's a good boy," crooned the Captain, all saccharine sweetness now, before leveling the sort of stare at the mercenaries that made Phera want to dive for cover. "You heard him. Get the fuck out."

"Understood."

Immediately, all six mercenaries lowered their weapons and withdrew in quick order. And, just like that, the Blazar Bitches were once again left alone with their buyer.

Well, not really a buyer, I guess? Phera amended silently, levering herself back up onto the couch as her legs trembled beneath her.

"Easy there, sweet cheeks. It's just combat rush, it'll pass," Straya soothed, one hand dropping reassuringly onto her shoulder while she kept her own (far more utilitarian) coilgun trained on the suit. "Just keep your eyes on Steph and focus on your breathing."

As if summoned by her words, Steph popped up from where ve'd been hiding behind the couch Linus was sitting on with a little wave as ve holstered ver coilgun.

"Hi Phera!"

"Uh, hey…"

"See?"

Straya gave Phera's shoulder a quick squeeze.

"You're good."

"Th… Thanks," the engineer managed around her shortened breath, sliding the taller woman a grateful smile before returning her focus to Steph's mother of pearl gaze.

"You two are just *precious*, you know that?" cooed the Captain, before dipping her chin against what Phera guessed was some sort of hidden comm switch embedded in the collar of her coat. "Ob, honey, are there any squads of heavily-armed people on their way to kill us right now?"

"Not at the moment," came the infiltrator's tinny reply through a small speaker also in the Captain's collar. "There were three people with some rather impressive looking rifles loitering near the rear entrance to the club, but they just pulled back."

"Excellent. Continue monitoring vid feeds for the time being."

"Already on it. I'll ping you if anything starts heading your way."

"That's what I like to hear. Double dessert for you tonight."

Cutting off her comm with another dip of her chin, the Captain redirected the full force of her very unamused attention back to the suit she still held at gunpoint.

"Now then, as for *you*."

"Holy fuck, lady! Are you out of your mind?!" he demanded, seeming to have finally found his nerve once again.

Along with a sizable reserve of indignation.

"Who me?"

The Captain looked almost hurt by the accusation.

"Not at all."

Drawing back her coilgun, she twirled it several times around her finger before shoving it back into her shoulder holster.

"Incidentally, you really should have just made the trade. You would've had a much better chance shooting us in the back as we were leaving."

She adopted a pensive pout then, and let her shoulders rise and fall in a casual shrug.

"Oh well. Live and learn, I guess. Anyway…"

Her face once again adopted a look that was simultaneously teasing and threatening.

"Let's take another crack at negotiating terms, shall we?"

It wasn't a request, but Linus still very wisely chose to nod his agreement.

"Good boy."

The Captain gave the sweating suit's cheek a patronizing pat.

"Now, I want to know who hired you to carry out this very ill-advised robbery attempt. And, before you say anything, let's just go ahead and skip past the part where you try and convince me it was Terramen or LDH. If an *actual* B-Sys group had hired someone to kill me and my crew, they would have done a far better job of it."

"Plus, none of them are willing to fork over the kind of cash you'd need for that many mercs," added Straya.

"An excellent point," agreed the Captain with a contemplative purr. "Which means that you, my friend…"

At this, her lips twitched.

"Well, not *friend,* but you know what I mean."

She waved away the label.

"Either way, you, Linus, are clearly a tourist with a wealthy backer from somewhere toward the primary. A backer who I would very much like to introduce myself to. So…"

The Captain's grin seemed to gain an extra couple teeth then, causing both Phera and Linus to shift uncomfortably in their seats.

"You're going to tell me exactly who hired you and why. And, in return, I won't have Straya here shoot you in the face. Deal?"

Again, it wasn't a request.

"Are you… Are you serious?" croaked Linus, seeming to be caught somewhere between disbelief at how badly things had gone for him and sagging relief that he'd just been tossed a lifeline. "You expect me to screw myself over just like that?"

"Yep, sure do. I think we both know that your boss's identity isn't worth your life."

The Captain cocked an almost playful brow at him then.

"Unless you're actually going to tell me you're a true, dyed in the wool corporate loyalist?"

"Hardly."

Scoffing, Linus seemed to find his footing once again.

"As you so succinctly surmised, no paycheck is worth my life."

"Excellent," crooned the Captain, before darting her hand out quick as a striking bone wasp and roughly seizing hold of the man's face by the chin. "Now *talk*."

"Well… Ahem. As to that."

Somehow, Linus managed to sound both apologetic and smarmy with the Captain's long fingers squishing his pallid cheeks together.

"Walking away from this meeting with my life alone isn't exactly the best bargain for me, now is it? Perhaps you'd be willing to throw in something extra in return for my cooperation? I'm going to need funds to tide me over while I find a new career after this, you know."

"I'd say leaving you alive and kicking is more than generous," countered the Captain. "Considering, you know… The whole attempted murder thing."

"But- That's- You can't just-!"

"You seem like a smart fellow, Linus," she cut him off by saying, leaning in so that they were practically nose to nose. "Well, again, maybe not *smart* given what you tried to pull here, but I'm sure you'll still find something to occupy yourself with."

Her face grew cruelly teasing then.

"I know Nona is always looking for new dancers. You've certainly got the legs for it."

"I don't think-"

"I'm not fond of repeating myself, so I'm only going to say this one more time," interrupted the Captain once again. "Boss. Name. Now."

Before tipping her swoop of icy bangs back over her shoulder toward Lem, the material of her partially-exposed neural implant sparkling in the recessed lighting of the lounge.

"Or else I'm going to have to ask my first mate here to 'encourage' you to cooperate. And, well, like I said… Cute legs."

She let him go then, straightening back up with a wink that very nearly dissolved Phera into a fit of hysterical giggles.

"So, let's keep this civil, yes?"

"Er… Right. Point taken."

"Great. So...?"

"So..."

Linus took in a very long, very deep breath to steady himself, before abandoning that tactic altogether and shotgunning the remainder of his whiskey instead.

"I'm a fixer for Panorama-" he wheezed around the burn of alcohol in his throat.

"Panorama?!"

Going rigid where she sat on the other couch, Phera let out a startled squeak.

"Yes, Doctor Sinclair. Panorama," confirmed Linus, his earlier smugness returning with a vengeance as he turned a leer on her. "Thanks to you and your new associates' proclivity for public displays of... Ahem. Percussive disciplinary measures."

At this, his gaze dipped toward Phera's plunging neckline and the impressive bit of (now slightly sticky) cleavage she had on display.

"We were able to plot a loose outline of your movements since you abandoned your contract with us. For those who know what to look for, you've managed to leave quite a trail of video evidence depicting your more, shall we say, *submissive* activities from Marcos, to Excaden, and even your brief stay on Epiphany Station. That last one in particular was one of my personal favorites."

He actually, honest to gods, clucked his tongue at her then. The very same way her father so often had whenever she'd brought home a bad report card.

"You do get around, don't you, young lady?"

"Oh, you have got to be fucking kidding me."

Utterly mortified, Phera buried her smoldering face in her hands as the meaning behind the stuffy corporate suit's thinly veiled taunting became all too clear.

All those times she'd wound up getting spanked in public over the last few months. In Tortuga on any number of occasions, on Excaden when she and Straya had had to distract the docking inspector, in the station sec offices on Epiphany. Hell, probably even that one time when Lem had decided she'd gotten just a bit too mouthy (and looked way too good in the leggings she was wearing at the time) while they'd been walking to dinner during their last shore leave. All of those occasions of public humiliation had been recorded by whoever happened to be around to see them at the time. And, in turn, had been used as data points to track down her and the rest of the Blazar Bitches so that they could be lured into this ambush.

Which, thankfully, had failed spectacularly because the Captain was scary fast on her feet.

But, still.

Fuuuuck.

Her former bosses (and gods only knew how many other techs and temps doing the actual grunt work of sifting through social feeds and security recordings to piece that information together for them) had seen her being dominated by her crewmates over and over and *over* again. Which, honestly, would have been really fucking hot if not for the fact that her body was still flooded with fear and adrenaline from almost being murdered by a pack of mercenaries hired by those very same bosses who she *still* had nightmares about going back to work for on a semi-regular basis.

"Now, now, you have only yourself to blame, you silly girl," chided Linus, snide as could be. "Incidentally, I must say it is rather a shame that we weren't aware of how well you responded to your current employer's managerial style before you left us. I'm sure we could have found a way to accommodate you if we had. I know I'd have gladly done my part to ensure that impertinent little ass of yours-"

CRACK!

A single, precisely placed coilgun shot punched a fingertip-sized hole straight through the plush upholstery three centimeters to the left of the leering man's head.

"One more word about her ass, and you'll have a brand new hole to shit out of yours with, you cum guzzling fuck stain," Straya growled, coming to Phera's rescue in just the most Straya way possible.

Gods. I love her.

Immediately, Linus's smug and vaguely condescendingly horny attitude dissolved back into barely suppressed panic as it once again dawned on him that he was still trapped in a room full of very pissed off pirates. Pirates that, unlike Phera, hadn't been raised with any sort of deeply ingrained deference for corporate officers and authority figures.

"Ahem. Point taken," he managed, his strangled voice coming out several octaves higher than it had just a moment ago.

"My apologies, Doctor," he hastened to add, before hurriedly turning his attention back to the Captain. "But, um, yes, as I was saying, I was dispatched at our chief executive's order to deal with a pirate problem."

"That problem being us?" surmised the Captain, sounding skeptical. "I had no idea Panorama would take the loss of one scientist and a shuttle's worth of drones so personally."

"Yeah, just write it off and collect the insurance money, damn," grumbled Phera, pouting out her lingering embarrassment.

"Well, as to that..."

Again, Linus looked to her with the ghost of a sneer, before noticing the snarl still plainly visible on Straya's scarred face and quickly focusing back on the Captain.

"While I'm sure Doctor Sinclair's talents are sorely missed back on The Bin, I was given to understand that that wasn't what finally forced my employer's hand."

"Ahhh, I see," nodded the Captain, understanding dawning on her sharp features. "Panorama was the one funding Iotech."

"I... We were?"

Linus actually seemed to be taken aback by that.

"Well, *duh*," scoffed Phera, gleefully seizing the opportunity to send some sneers of her own back at the obnoxious man. "It doesn't exactly take a genius to figure out that not just anybody would have access to secure cam feeds from a privately owned corporate research station."

"Especially not after the absolutely spectacular job we did robbing them blind," added Steph, all but cackling from ver perch on the arm of Linus's couch.

"Hell yeah we did!"

Leaning forward, Phera high-fived the crew doc with gusto.

"Yes, yes, we're all very impressed by your proclivity for pilfering," dismissed the Captain with a genuine smile for her self-hyping techs. "Now then, I-"

Just then, the door to the lounge slid open *again* amid a burst of pounding synth rhythms. And, in the very next moment, the

Captain, Steph, and Lem all had their coilguns aimed at the opening before it could even occur to Phera that maybe she should draw her own weapon.

"Easy now, it's just me," called a woman from somewhere around the corner of the door frame. "You still alive in there, Cap?"

"Oh, hey, Nona. Yes, we're fine. Though, not for lack of trying," called back the Captain with a laugh, once again holstering her pistol as the woman who Phera assumed must be the club's owner stepped into sight with her hands on her hips. She looked to be about the same age as the Captain, though about a head shorter and twice as plump, wearing a sort of strappy, full-body bondage harness that managed to cover absolutely nothing on her.

Phera immediately took a liking to her and her myriad facial piercings, seriously starting to consider the merits of a lip ring or maybe a nose stud.

Those nipple barbells aren't so bad either...

"Ah, a lot less bloody in here than I was expecting. That's good."

"Yes, we were able to reach an amicable arrangement with this dipshit's babysitters before things could get out of hand."

"Phew! I was starting to worry when I saw those goons storming through my club. Glad to hear you're fi- Oh gods damn it!"

Instantly, the woman's demeanor went from relieved to positively peeved as she jabbed an accusatory finger toward Linus's left shoulder.

"Which one of you idiots shot my couch?"

"He decided to fuck around," Straya replied, not sounding the least bit sorry as she kept her attention (and weapon) fixed squarely on Linus's forehead. "And he found out."

"Damn right he did," grunted Lem, watching the open entrance of the lounge for any more unexpected visitors.

"Of course he did..."

Sighing, Nona scrubbed a hand over her stud-studded face and cast a supplicating glance up toward the ceiling.

"You're paying for that, I hope you know."

"Yes, yes," soothed a just as unapologetic Captain. "Put it on my tab, grumpy cakes."

This seemed to mollify Nona, who drew herself back up to her full height with a huff and a soft jangling of metal on metal. Despite looking like she'd just come from being handcuffed to the rafters for a prolonged and decadent play session that Phera was very disappointed she hadn't caught sight of on their way in, she still managed to make herself appear serious and dignified.

"I take it then you won't be needing Seska's services after all?"

"Afraid not," pouted the Captain, clearly put out by not being able to get her hands on the serving girl she'd been lusting after earlier. "We're going to have to pull out of Marcos for a bit after this. Business."

"That's a shame."

Nona actually looked disappointed to hear that, before shrugging and turning to go.

"Well, we'll be here when you get back. Don't go getting yourself killed, you hear?"

"If you insist."

Snickering, the Captain blew the departing woman a kiss.

"Tell Lucia I said hello."

"Stop trying to seduce my wife, you slut," snorted Nona, flipping the Captain off with a wink as the door slid shut behind her.

"Right then, where were we?"

Giving her hair a dismissive toss, the Captain turned back to the quietly sweating suit who'd been doing his best to disappear into the couch while she'd been flirting with the club's owner.

"You were saying something about how you were dispatched to deal with a very attractive and charismatic pirate problem?"

"Er... Yes, that is correct."

Seemingly unsure what to do with his hands, Linus took several moments to adjust the knot on his tie before continuing on in a rush.

"My orders were to meet with you, retrieve the property you'd stolen, and return with it, along with you, Captain, to our corporate campus on Cilara. And, before you ask, no, I don't know why I was told to collect you as well. I was just told that you were to be delivered alive and undamaged."

"Me personally, huh?"

As he'd spoken, the Captain's face had fallen back into its blank state of what Phera had come to associate with hyperfocus.

"How flattering."

"That's certainly one way of putting it," grumbled the engineer under her breath, folding her arms beneath the swell of her breasts to stop herself from fiddling with the clasp on her stun gun holster. "They probably want to make an example of you on the news feeds or something."

"Like I said. Flattering."

The Captain spared just a moment to flash Phera a look of rough affection that seemed to communicate that she wouldn't let anything happen to her, before redirecting her attention back to Linus.

"I take it you were expected to report back via secure comm once you'd finished killing my crew and taking my things?" she pressed, her face once again growing eerily impassive.

"That's right. My supervisor and a personal aide to the chief executive accompanied me to our satellite office in the Midway Cluster where we made arrangements to contract the Victoria Group. While there, I was given an encryption key and an address that routes directly to my supervisor's personal slate to make periodic status reports with."

At the mention of Straya's old (skull) stomping grounds, Phera cut a questioning look toward the taller woman behind her to make sure that she was all right. Linus hadn't mentioned anything about the Dornu Republic, but it sort of went without saying that that would be where Panorama's offices would be located. When Straya met her eye, though, she just flashed her one of her usual sardonic half-grins and gave a minuscule nod, wordlessly communicating that she was fine but appreciated the concern.

"Direct, you say?" continued the Captain, while the two of them made googly eyes at one another. "Are there any key phrases I should be aware of in these communications? Something to convey if you're under duress for example?"

"No?"

Linus sounded genuinely confused (and perhaps a bit snidely bemused) at the question.

"It's a secure channel. Why would I need something like that?"

Which had the Captain, Straya, Lem, *and* Steph all snorting.

"Fucking amateurs," the first mate growled in disgust.

"Too much cash and comfort tend to breed a sense of invulnerability, lemon cakes," chided the Captain in a teasing singsong, wagging an admonishing forefinger in her direction, which managed to raise an actual blush in the muscular woman's chiseled cheekbones.

At least, Phera *assumed* it was a blush. Lem turned back to guard the door so fast that she only managed to catch a split-second view of her face. In that split-second, though, the Captain seemed to have reached a decision.

"All right, Linus. Slate. Now. We're calling your boss."

"Er... What?"

"Straya?"

CRACK!

Without so much as a second of hesitation, Straya sent a second shot straight through the hole she'd already made in the couch, causing the suit to let out a profoundly satisfying squawk of terror.

"I've already made myself abundantly clear about repeating myself," crooned the Captain, her voice absolute poison as her amber eyes narrowed in the subdued light of the lounge. "And I am absolutely out of patience for your bullshit. Instead of spending this evening fingering a cute girl on my lap while watching my roboticist get her delightfully bratty ass beat by her very capable partner, I get to deal with *you*. So, either sprout some tits and start giving me a lap dance, or else get out your *fucking* slate and call your *fucking* boss. *NOW!*"

Unsurprisingly, a loaded coilgun and a fuming pirate captain made for a powerful negotiating position, and Linus's trembling right hand immediately went for the inside of his suit jacket.

"Right! Of course!"

For half a heartbeat Phera was worried that he was about to draw a weapon of his own for some sort of profoundly stupid last stand. But, when he only produced a high-end slate in an expensive leather case, she released the breath she hadn't realized she'd been holding.

Fuck, I'm jittery. Okay, just look at Steph and focus on your breathing. Everything's fine, everything's fine, everything's... fine...

"I, um, I can't guarantee he'll pick up," Linus mumbled as he thumbed the device in his hand to life. "It's local night on the Aphrodite subcluster right now."

"Oh, he will."

The Captain sounded utterly confident as she impatiently tapped her foot.

"He's no doubt been sitting on pins and needles waiting to hear back from you about your little kidnapping mission."

As if on cue, the slate in the man's hand chirped with an alert for a new incoming message.

"Speak of the devil," observed the Captain with a wry smirk, before switching back to a dangerous deadpan. "Play it."

Nodding stiffly, Linus tapped at his slate a few times, and then set it on the table in front of him.

"Linus! What the fuck? *Please* tell me you've dealt with that bitch," a reedy voice echoed up from the device. "The big man's been breathing down my neck all god damn day about this pirate shit!"

"Uh-uh."

The Captain batted away Linus's reaching hand and snatched up his slate before he could start recording his reply.

"Not quite," she crooned into the device's mic pickup for him instead. "This is the *Blazar* bitch your little underling here just tried to fuck over. Isn't that right, Linus?"

The Captain's tone was no less dangerous than it had been just a moment earlier, but it had now gained the sort of low purr to it that Phera knew from a great deal of personal experience spelled trouble.

Her intuition was immediately proven correct as she watched the Captain kick the pale-faced Panorama employee in the calf as hard as she could.

"Ack! Hey!"

Letting out a pained grunt, Linus hunched forward to massage his no doubt bruised leg, before squawking out a hurried reply when the Captain drew back her boot for another kick.

"I mean, yes ma'am! That's right!"

"Good boy."

Chuckling, the Captain gave Linus a playful tap with the toe of her boot before continuing on with her recording.

"Now, you listen to me, you little go between pissant. I've got a message for that management puke that's tagged along to oversee things," she snapped, all business now. "You tell him that the price for the goods has just doubled, and *he* is going to meet us in person to pay for them and collect his dumbass fixer while he's at it too so that we can sort out this whole 'let's kidnap the hot space pirate captain' thing like adults."

With an annoyed huff, she stabbed one of her blunted talons at the screen and sent the message off, before tucking the slate into an inner pocket of her coat.

"It's going to take at least twenty minutes for a response to reach us from Midway. So, in the meantime, Phera?"

Still keyed up on adrenaline and anxiety, the engineer immediately sprang to her feet.

"Yes, Captain?"

"Go get us some drinks. You can tell the bartender to put it on my tab."

"Oooh!"

This pronouncement had Steph dancing in place on ver perch at the end of Linus's couch.

"Does that mean we can order the good stuff?"

"Hmmm..."

The Captain made a show of pursing her lips in thought, before eventually nodding her agreement.

"You can have *one* star cruiser," she conceded with false-annoyance. "You're still on duty, you know."

"Yeah, yeah."

Popping back up to ver feet as well, Steph proceeded to propel Phera toward the door with a series of not particularly hard swats to her leather-clad seat.

"You heard the boss. Go on, shoo! And bring back some peppers too while you're at it. I'm starving!"

—

As the door to the lounge slid shut behind her, Phera's shoulders sagged and she eased her back against the cool metal behind her with a long, weary sigh. It occurred to her then, that she *really* needed some time to clear her head before she went back in there. Being confronted so suddenly by someone from Panorama like that had rattled her a lot more than she'd thought, even with Straya and the others there to back her up.

With that one damnable word, her entire world had been put on tilt. Suddenly she wasn't the (mostly) confident space pirate she'd worked so hard to become. Instead, she was back at home with her parents as a preteen, keeping an ear out for one of her dad's angry surprise storm-ins while she chatted with her friends from school instead of doing her homework. She was back in the office of High Elder Raschke, lying through her teeth about obeying the laws of chastity and temperance while doing her best to not let on how nervous he made her feel. She was back in her sophomore year of college staring down the barrel of her scholarship running out, trying to decide if it was worth joining the military and potentially dying in some foreign war just so that she could finish her degree. She was back on The Bin, trapped in an endless cycle of monotony and shitty office politics with the looming shadow of crippling debt just over her shoulder to remind her that she was there forever. She was-

"No. Stop it."

Phera gave her cheeks a couple of bracing slaps and forced herself to run through the breathing exercises her therapist had taught her as she tipped her copper curls back against the smooth, cold metal behind her, letting it ground her to the present.

"You're fine... You're fine. Just... *breathe*..."

Fortunately, The Velvet was chock full of unique and interesting things to distract oneself from an impending panic attack with. Rough and tumble B-Sys stationers in various states of undress dancing and fucking Phera could absolutely handle. Smug corporate enforcers throwing her past back at her out of nowhere? Not so much. But, again, fuck Linus. She was a badass pirate who lived life by her own rules and had an amazing found family to rely on, and he was just some sad middle manager who'd totally shit the bed on what was probably supposed to be his big break assignment in the company.

"Heh. Couldn't have happened to a better guy."

So, hands stuffed into the pockets of her cropped jacket to keep any residual trembling at bay, Phera set off at an unhurried pace to make a circuit or two around the club, quietly hoping that she might run into Nona and whatever fun she was getting up to before she got around to playing barmaid for the rest of the crew.

Things would be fine.

They would...

They had to be.

—

By the time Phera returned to the lounge, teetering beneath the weight of nearly half a dozen drinks and an array of snacks she thought sounded good arranged on top of a platter, a reply from Linus's supervisor had arrived.

It was not encouraging.

"I... Are you serious, lady?"

"Do I *sound* like I'm joking, little man?" the Captain snapped into Linus's slate, her hand cutting through the air beside her with her irritation as she stalked around the tiny room. "Tell your boss that he either takes the deal, or I swear to fucking god, and any of the other gods Phera here may or may not believe in too for good measure, that I'll open source this damn project so fast it'll make his tax-evading head spin. You hear me?"

Phera, who'd been taking an almost erotic thrill in watching the older woman tear her former employers a new one let out a startled squeak at hearing her name being mentioned, nearly dropping her tray in the process.

"Careful there, sweet cheeks, I only get one of these a day."

Thankfully, Straya was able to multitask. Steadying her before she could fall and plucking up her rum from the tray without spilling so much a drop. All while keeping her coilgun trained unerringly on Linus's heart.

He'd since slumped in defeat against the couch cushions behind him and was now picking despondently at his meticulously manicured fingernails, but Phera supposed you couldn't be too careful when it came to dealing with someone who'd tried to have you killed.

"Oooh, those smell great!"

Hitting send, the Captain let her indignation roll off of her shoulders all at once and tossed her pilfered slate onto the couch across from the self-pitying Panorama employee as she sauntered over to where Phera stood. Swiping up a fresh helical glass of luminous liquor and one of the breaded and fried hydroponic peppers Steph had asked for, she eased down onto her couch and crossed one long leg over the other as she munched contentedly.

"Shi, are you at the ship?" she asked aloud around her mouthful of food.

Blinking, it took Phera a moment to realize the Captain had activated her personal comm again. She hadn't seen her head move this time.

"Shi...?"

"Yes ma'am!" came the pilot's breathy reply almost half a minute later. "Sorry about the delay, Kelt and I were just-"

"You can finish sucking your mommy's titties later, hon. Right now, I need you to start prepping the Mayhem for takeoff."

This declaration was met with a truly adorable strangled yelp from the other end of the connection, coupled with the unmistakable sound of Kelt cracking up.

"Trouble, Cap?" her semi-muffled voice called out.

"Buyer decided to try and double cross us. We're pulling out of Marcos for now while I sort a fix."

"Shit. Do I need to start prepping Straya's ulfsark?"

"No, no, we've got a hostage to keep the hired muscle at bay. Just don't let in any strange men in combat armor while I'm out."

"Pretty sure I can handle that," chuckled Kelt, before slipping back into consummate professionalism. Phera was pretty sure she could actually hear her pulling her salt and pepper hair back into its usual no-nonsense bun. "The negs are still offline for maintenance, but I can have them back up in thirty. Twenty if we absolutely have to do a cold start. Is that going to work?"

"Thanks, babe, that'll be fine. I'm still negotiating with someone higher up right now, so take your time and do it right."

"Have I ever done otherwise?"

"Hah. Fair."

"Damn straight."

"Smartass."

"That's why you pay me."

There came the tinny sound of a hard *SMACK!* on the other end of the connection then, coupled with a fresh yelp from Shi.

"You can find your other boot later. Get your butt back to the bridge, kiddo!"

"Ah! Yes ma'am!"

"See you when you get here, Captain. We'll be ready."

—

Phera had never been particularly good at waiting around, and that afternoon was proving to be no exception. By the time the next reply from Linus's supervisor arrived, she'd just about worn a ring into the floor of the lounge from all her pacing, and had caught a collective two dozen hard swats from her various crewmates.

Thankfully, though, the reply from Panorama this time around was a positive one.

"Your terms are acceptable," intoned a totally different masculine voice from Linus's slate, one that was oddly lacking in affect in a way that had nothing to do with the device's tiny speakers. "Provide a time and location for our transaction to take place."

"Now that's more like it," snorted the Captain, all the while smiling from ear to ear in profound self-satisfaction. Which was totally deserved. She'd managed to coax the one person with actual decision making power in this situation onto the comm, after all. "We'll rendezvous with you on the border of B-Sys, three AUs outside of Excaden's orbit ten days from now. You and no more than *five* bodyguards are to come in a shuttle and dock with us for the handoff. I'll send along specific coordinates and a meeting time in the coming days."

She paused for a moment to catch her breath then, before adding with an air of finality.

"Also, I can tell you right now that if you're thinking about trying to get cute like Linus did, I am deadly serious about releasing everything we stole to the public. If I smell so much as a *hint* of betrayal from you, everything is going out from as many data beacons my infiltrator can get his extremely capable hands on between now and our meeting."

And, just like that, she was done. Sending the message with a roll of her eyes before thumbing off the device and shoving it back inside her coat.

"Damn, Cap."

Bobbing ver ankles back and forth in front of ver as ve leaned back on ver palms, Steph whistled appreciatively.

"I can't believe that actually worked."

"No shit," agreed Straya while Lem just shook her head.

"It was either that or haul ass out to the furthest asteroid we could find and lie low for who knows how long."

The Captain gave her hair the sort of devils-may-care toss that always made Phera's stomach lurch with giddy anticipation.

Gods. How is she so good at that? She must practice in the mirror or something.

"Figured threatening to hit them where it hurts most was our best shot at getting out of this in one piece while making some cash along the way."

"Have I ever told you how much I love you?" snickered Lem, relaxing seemingly for the first time since they'd entered The Velvet.

"Awww, music to my ears."

Pressing a hand to her cheek, the Captain feigned a swoon before dusting off her palms and abruptly pushing herself back to her feet. Making a beeline toward the exit of the lounge in a whirl of armored coat and glinting neural implant.

"Right then, girls, let's get the fuck out of here. We've got guests to prepare for, and Phera still owes us a show."

"What?"

Jumping back to her feet with a disbelieving (though not entirely all that surprised) yelp, sloshing alcoholic slush over the rim of her half-empty glass in the process, Phera shot an indignant pout at the back of the Captain's retreating form.

"Did you think I'd forgotten?" she asked, turning back to her with a wicked grin.

"I was kind of hoping so, yeah."

"Well think again, swabbie. I said *raw*, and I meant it."

Phera nearly parroted that last line back to her in a mocking cadence, but some lingering self-preservation instinct managed to catch her at the very last moment.

"Fiiiine," she groaned instead, pouting even harder in a futile attempt to distract herself from the unmistakable moisture soaking through the front of her panties.

"I know, I know," the Captain soothed, her painted lips pushed out into a mocking moue. "It's no stage with a stripper pole, but the rec room on the Mayhem will just have to do."

Before clapping her hands twice in quick succession.

"Come along now. Chop, chop! Lem, help Steph with that case, ver arms were starting to shake when we got here and I don't want ver tripping with the goods on our way back. Straya, you escort our shiny new hostage. And, Phera, hmm... You start thinking of interesting things Straya can do to you while we all watch. I'm expecting at least five ideas by the time we're back to the ship, and they'd better be creative."

"I... Yes ma'am."

Phera, flushing nova bright, didn't bother trying to hide her chagrined smirk. Even neck deep in the swirling chaos of betrayal and unseen megacorporate enemies striking at them from the shadows, the Captain remained steadfast and unflappable as ever.

And undeniably horny.

She wouldn't have had it any other way.

CHAPTER THIRTY-ONE

CHARGES ACCRUED

Accessory to Extortion, Resisting Arrest, Assault With a
Deadly Weapon, Unauthorized Use of Company Property

"We've got a port side shuttle contact on active sensors, Captain.
ETA to intercept, seven minutes twenty-three seconds. And... yeah,
they're hailing us now to say they're from Panorama."

As per usual, Shi's light, masculine tenor was clear and confident
as he made the announcement over the Mayhem's general shipboard
comm.

"Acknowledged," came the Captain's reply from inside the cargo
hold where she was overseeing Lem and Straya's final preparations
for their guests. "Let them know we're ready for them and continue
monitoring for additional contacts."

"On it."

"Oh, and keep the negdrive hot just in case we need to beat a
hasty retreat. If InterSec decides to come sniffing around, I want us
gone."

"That means eighty percent, max," Kelt's no-nonsense voice
immediately cut in, her crisp reprimand brooking no argument in
stereo as it carried over both her comm and the pilot's mic pickup
inside the bridge where she was presumably leaning in to waggle
an admonishing forefinger at him. "I'm not about to do another
mid-flight coupler bypass just because you decided to redline the
engines."

"Oh come on, that was one time!"

"Which was one time too many, young man."

"But-"

"Oh shit, I remember that!" exclaimed Adryel over their own comm from inside the hold. "Wasn't that when you tried pulling a rolling scissor *and* Immelmann turn at the same time? What'd you call that again? A knife spiral?"

"Razor vortex..."

"Uh-huh."

Despite her unimpressed grunt, Phera could tell that Kelt was fighting back a smirk. She'd had enough experience winding the her up by now to pick up on her little tells, even if it was just over audio.

"Either way, *I* seem to recall a very remorseful little boy promising to watch his power consumption by the time I was through with him. Are we going to need to repeat that discussion, Shi?"

"No ma'am!"

"That's what I thought. So?"

"Eighty percent?"

"Eighty percent, *max*."

"Right. Max. Got it!"

Phera couldn't quite stifle a snicker as she heard Steph snort into ver comm. Strapped into a jump seat on the bridge (on standby in case ver medical services were needed), ve had a literal front row seat to the flawlessly executed dressing down Kelt had just finished delivering to her easily flustered boy toy.

"Er..."

Rather than further risk the ire of his very capable mommy-domme, Shi instead turned his attention back to the ship's active sensor suite.

"Six minutes fifteen seconds, Captain."

"Thanks, hon."

The Captain's amusement carried over the comm like a caress, sending a shiver down Phera's spine as she shifted on her maglocked feet beside her in the hold.

"And, yes, follow Kelt's orders on power consumption. Those couplers aren't cheap."

"Aye aye!"

"At least these people are punctual," quipped Obette from where he'd set up shop inside the mess hall, monitoring data transmissions within range of the Mayhem for anything suspicious.

"You have noooo idea," agreed Phera around a slightly jittery giggle, her voice sounding oddly muffled to her own ears inside the confines of her secondhand (though, thankfully, properly sized and armored) vacsuit. "I got written up *so many times* for clocking in late back on The Bin."

"Oh, I've seen your records, my dear. I have to say, fifty-two times in less than two years is rather impressive."

"What? No way. It wasn't *that* many. Um... Was it?"

"Yes, it was," deadpanned the Captain, expression turning serious behind her faceplate as she cut a glance down and to her left toward the fidgeting engineer. "Now, stop trying to assert your credibility as the biggest brat on the ship and double-check your suit seals."

"Gaskets *and* filters," Straya barked over the comm, all rigid, military precision as she began stomping her way across the hold toward them from where she'd been conducting a final weapons check with Lem and Adryel. "A faulty filter is a great way to choke to death on a gas grenade, and there's no guarantee these fucks won't just start shelling us as soon as the airlock cycles."

"Uh, right! On it!"

Hands fumbling and heart racing with that ominous visual, Phera hurriedly moved to do as she was told. She could tell that Straya still wasn't happy about her being there. She'd literally threatened to tie her to a jump seat on the bridge the night before when she'd asked to be present for the exchange that was about to take place, and it had only been through the Captain overruling her that she'd been allowed to join her and the other combat-ready members of the crew inside the hold. As such, the need to impress the former soldier turned pirate bearing down on her churned at Phera's insides like a particularly antsy black hole.

"Well?"

"Just a second, I'm checking them now."

Licking her suddenly dry lips, Phera felt her eyes start to glaze over as she scrolled through a dizzying array of diagnostic and status report feeds for her vacsuit, wishing that she'd paid closer attention to the pre-combat crash course her partner had ran her though the night before.

"Wait, is it filter capacity or particulate flow that's supposed to be the low one?"

"Remember, I told you. It's 'Flow is low, you're good to go. Capacity high, or else you die.'"

"Ah. Okay, yeah, that makes sense. Let me just-"

"Ugh. Here, let me help you…"

Sighing with the sort of long-suffering exasperation she reserved only for her, Straya released the locks on her magboots and pushed off the deck. Executing a picture perfect null-grav tuck and roll before activating her boots once again and landing with a muted *clomp* behind Phera.

"Thanks," mumbled the auburn-haired pirate, tension draining from her shoulders as she blinked twice into the hallucinographic heads-up display her neural implant was providing for her via the data cable threaded up her sleeve from her wrist comp and into the side of her neck, switching over to a private channel with the woman behind her. "Let's see… Gaskets say they're at one hundred percent, and all the filter status things are green."

"Good."

Straya's voice was still clipped and brusque, but her hands moved with a deliberate tenderness that belied her annoyance as she trailed her fingers up and down along each visible joint and seal on Phera's vacsuit, manually confirming what the diagnostics were reporting.

"It's still not too late to bail, you know."

Draping her motor-assisted arms around Phera's waist from behind, she pulled her in close after giving her thighs and calves a quick but thorough once-over.

"You could fall back to the mess and keep Ob company."

"No."

The back of Phera's helmet made a muted *clack* as she tipped her head back to rest against Straya's chest. The vacsuits they were both wearing prevented the gesture from being quite as comforting as she'd have preferred, but she still appreciated the brief moment of intimacy.

"I have to do this, Stray. I can't just let you and the others face this jackass alone while I hide and pretend nothing's going on. If I don't look him straight in the eye and show him that I'm not afraid, I'm going to feel like I'm running away from Pano for the rest of my life."

It was her turn to sigh this time, letting her eyes drift shut as she cycled through an abbreviated version of her breathing exercises.

"I know it's not rational, but-"

"Nah. It's okay, I get it."

Straya gave her broad hips a firm pat that manifested for Phera as a reassuring rumble from her suit's haptic feedback system.

"Just... Stick with Cap, yeah? She's a damn good shot."

"Better than you?" Phera couldn't help but tease, her violet gaze drifting toward the coilgun holstered to the thigh of the Captain's ostentatious black and crimson vacsuit.

"Heh."

She could feel some of Straya's tension ease out of her as she scoffed.

"She wishes."

"Well, I'll make sure to follow her lead anyway if something goes wrong."

There came another vibration against her hips then.

"Good. I love you."

"Me too."

With that final exchange, Straya's walls went back up and she pushed off the deck to take up her position forming a flanking pincer with Lem and Adryel around the Captain, Phera, and Linus (who was the only person in the hold not wearing a vacsuit just then).

"Look sharp, people," she snapped over the general crew comm. "Remember, if shit goes down, short bursts, aim for center mass, and fall back to grav acclimation."

"Got it," came Lem's equally brisk reply as she made a minor adjustment to the power settings on her coilgun rifle.

While Adryel opted for an irreverent, "Ma'am, yes ma'am" as they flashed her a two-fingered salute off the top of their scuffed helmet.

Right on cue, Shi's voice came back onto the comm.

"Mating airlocks now."

A heavy *THUNK!* echoed through the mostly empty hold then, followed by a teeth-grating whirring noise as the two ships' airlocks came together to form a single umbilical passthrough.

"This is Panorama Administrative Aide 668-B, here to exchange goods with the captain of the Blazar Bitches as per our earlier communication," the same affectless voice from back at The Velvet intoned over the comm channel they were all using, pronouncing the crew's hard-edged name with the same level of even precision as he had his own employee identification number. "I am hereby requesting authorization to board."

"Yeah, yeah. Come on over and let's get this done. I've still got things to do today."

"Understood."

No chemical grenades or hails of coilgun fire followed the inner airlock cycling open, which Phera chose to take as a good sign. Instead, a man who looked to be somewhere in his early thirties and dressed in expensive corporate officer attire drifted forward at a leisurely pace while five darkly-armored people flanked him to either side. Eating up distance with long, graceful strides, their magboots set to minimum power for maximum maneuverability as they used their elongated spacer's toes to make minor adjustments to their trajectory with each step they took.

"Well, well, well, if it isn't the Vicky Brigade," crooned the Captain from where she stood watching the group's advance, one hand on her hip (centimeters away from the grip of her coilgun) while the other held Linus by the rumpled scruff of his suit jacket, preventing him from floating away in the null-grav. "Still hard at work wiping your boss's ass, I see. What? Were there no labor unions that needed busting?"

This time around, the mercenaries were professional enough not to rise to the Captain's taunting. Instead, taking up positions mirroring Straya and the others with their weapons not quite raised (but still raised enough to make it clear they had no problems using them) as the suit they were escorting came to a stop a couple meters away from where Phera and the Captain stood.

"Come now, Captain, there's no need for such ribald antagonism," the man who'd requested boarding access chided lightly.

His earlier affectless cadence had been swapped out for the sort of easygoing, patronizing demeanor that immediately raised Phera's hackles, reminding her all too well of the recruiter who'd roped her into her original contract back during college. He was young, impeccably dressed, and full of the sort of upbeat, charismatic false-sincerity that could easily trick someone into thinking he actually cared about them and their well-being if they didn't know better.

"See, considering what these assholes were planning on doing to me and my crew the last time we ran into each other, I really think it is," countered the Captain, matching the aide's condescending tone beat for beat.

"Ah, yes, I suppose that's fair. In that case, shall we dispense with the formalities and get straight to the matter at hand?"

"Works for me."

Shrugging one shoulder, the Captain nodded toward the sample container Linus held in a white-knuckled grip in front of him.

"Data chip's in there along with everything else. You got our money?"

"Your funds have been prepared, yes. However, double your original asking price has been deemed unacceptable. After consulting with our actuaries on the matter, I am prepared to raise your compensation by an additional twenty-eight percent."

"Cute."

The Captain did not, in fact, sound like she thought the counter-offer was cute. Though, to the administrative aide's credit, he didn't flinch as her eyes narrowed at him behind her transparent faceplate.

"Let me put this another way since you seem to be having a difficult time understanding a straightforward deal when one's being presented to you. Double is our 'you tried to kill us and I'm still fucking pissed about that' price, and it's *non-negotiable*."

"Be that as it may, twenty-eight percent is still more than-"

Rolling her eyes, the Captain activated her comm.

"Ob, honey, what's the status of those data relays?"

"Thirteen primed and ready to go with thirty-six hour trigger delays. Want me to send out the transmission order now?"

"We'll see. Stand by."

"Captain, I- That's really not necessary-" spluttered the aide, face blanching and hands gesticulating in front of him.

Huh. Well, would you look at that.

His hurried movements caused the bright lights inside the hold to reflect dully off of the metallic hardware embedded in the side of his head. Hardware that looked awfully similar to the Captain's own cranial implant now that Phera got a better look at it.

Maybe he uses it for stock trading or something?

"You heard the man."

The rough shake the Captain gave Linus to emphasize her point yanked Phera's attention back to the present.

"I'm serious about dumping that data if you keep trying to jerk me around. So, last chance. What's it gonna be? Pay up, or get fucked?"

"One moment please."

The face of the aide (Phera had decided to think of him as "Six" since he didn't seem like he planned on offering up his actual name any time soon) went totally slack in an eerie parody of the Captain's own hyperfocus countenance. Remaining blank for a full two seconds before resuming its original vaguely smug expression.

"Well?"

At the Captain's impatient bark, he gave a slight nod.

"Ahem. While I appreciate that Mister Cendeno appears to still be on remarkably amicable terms with members of the Silver Nations' Intelligence Service, there will be no need for those transmissions. Double your original asking price will be acceptable, provided you no longer target Panorama Inc. or its subsidiaries in any of your future... endeavors."

Oh my gods, I knew it!

A short laugh of surprise burst out of Phera with that. Not at the suit capitulating to the Captain's demands, she knew there was no way in hell a megacorporation as pathologically profit-driven as Panorama would ever let their competitors get a leg up on them, but rather that Obette was apparently some sort of spy. She'd always thought he'd been just a little *too* good at his job, not to mention way too calm under pressure. No wonder, though. He'd been an honest to gods secret agent! Or, at the very least, some sort of shadowy intelligence officer.

Geez. Shouldn't he be back home plotting coups or something? Oh! Maybe his cover identity got burned so he had to run away and become a pirate?

She'd definitely have to probe him further about his mysterious past later (ideally while he was doing some probing of his own to her). Regardless of how the suave, silver-haired man had come to join the crew, however, this new bit of information made a lot of things about him make a lot more sense.

And made the man himself about ten times more attractive.

Kinda shitty for this guy to just go and out him like that, though...

Apparently, the Captain agreed.

"And, while *I* appreciate your heavy-handed attempt to rattle me and my crew by showing off how much information you've managed to dredge up on us, it's really not necessary either. I wasn't planning on going after you assholes again anytime soon as is. So, sure. You pay up and fuck off, and we'll do the same."

"Very well. Initiating funds transfer now."

"Great. Ob?"

"A deposit with a whole lot of very lovely zeroes just popped up in the local account. I'll start breaking it up and routing it through the usual blockchain proxies and into general crew funds now."

"Wait, really? That's it?"

The words were out of Phera's mouth before she could stop them. She'd long since learned that her childhood upbringing on action vids and corporate dramas wasn't exactly the most accurate representation of life outside of Cilara, but she still couldn't help being a little bit shocked at how abruptly things had come to an end. She'd been expecting at least a little more haggling, or threatening, or *something*.

"Just like that," confirmed the Captain, sending a wink in her direction before returning her focus to the aide. "Well, gents, wish I could say it's been a pleasure, but..."

With a huff, she sent Linus and his payload of medical research data sailing ahead of her.

"Kindly get the fuck off my ship."

Sidestepping the human missile heading his way, Six nodded absently.

"Dorst, you may await me in the shuttle."

"Yes sir! Right away, sir!"

That curt dismissal seemed largely unnecessary to Phera, considering that Linus was already in the process of tumbling away in an awkward tangle of arms, legs, and a small fortune's worth of research specimens in the general direction of the cargo hold airlock. Meanwhile, though, Six remained right where he was, staring straight ahead at the Captain expectantly.

"Got something else you need?" she asked, the hand on her hip shifting slightly closer to her coilgun as Straya and the other's made a point of adjusting their grips on the rifles they held at the ready across their chests in a not so subtle reminder that he wasn't the only one with an armed escort.

"I do indeed, as a matter of fact."

Crossing his hands behind his back, Six gave no impression of being the least bit intimidated by the pirates surrounding him.

"I'd like to broker the return of the other piece of Panorama property you are still in possession of."

He swept his gaze up and down over Phera then.

"Who? Me?"

It was a dumb question to ask, but it was the only one she had just then as she pointed toward her helmeted head, fighting a sudden rush of vertigo that sent her stomach plummeting to her ankles as if Shi had just cranked up the engines without warning.

Ignoring her entirely, the man from Panorama directed his gaze back to the Captain, who snorted out a derisive laugh.

"Are you serious?"

"Of course. Doctor Sinclair has yet to fulfill her obligation to us for the investment we've made in her," Six replied evenly. "Factoring in for the loss of productivity her absence from Asteroid Mining Facility F6C-8 has produced, with an additional thirteen years and nine months of committed labor under our standard penalty pay scale, she will once again be generating a positive ROI for the company. As such, I am prepared to offer you a sum that I believe we can both be comfortable with for her return."

He quoted a number then that was barely a fraction of the price he'd just paid for the Iotech data. Leaving Phera unsure if she should be insulted or not. Mostly, she was just terrified that she was about to be bundled off back to The Bin.

"What?! You can't just-"

"Uh, yeah. How about no?" Straya growled over her indignant splutter, bristling in her armor as she pivoted toward Six, glaring daggers at where she aimed her rifle at the back of his head.

"Definitely gonna have to side with Straya on this one," agreed the Captain, all levity draining from her as her hand settled on the grip of her coilgun with an air of finality.

"Are you... certain?"

Six appeared to be genuinely taken aback by this. Though, again, he was also far less intimidated than Phera would've preferred. And, for another second or two, his face went blank.

"If it's a matter of compensation," he eventually continued, head angled to the side and eyes focused on the Captain with an intensity that was at odds with the rest of his dispassionate demeanor. "I am willing to raise your compensation by an additional-"

"Look."

The Captain cut his revised offer short with a raised hand.

"I'm not in the habit of buying or selling people. And, even if I was, Phera's one of mine."

At the Captain's acknowledging nod, Phera felt a surge of savage pride that straightened her spine and beat back her anxiety.

"Damn right I am."

Unfortunately, her newfound sense of aggression had absolutely no effect on Six and his placid arrogance.

"Your consent in this matter is irrelevant, Doctor," he replied, not even bothering to look at her. "Your contract remains legally binding. And, as such, I am well within my rights to compel your return. By force if necessary."

No sooner had those words left his mouth, than five simultaneous *SNAPS!* echoed through the hold as what Phera had taken for decorative pieces of bulky shoulder armor exploded out from each of the mercenaries. Time slowed to a crawl for her then as she watched in numb horror as one after another each projectile punched straight ahead with unerring precision into the chests of her, Straya, Lem, Adryel, and the Captain all at once.

Oh my gods, oh my gods, oh my gods!

However, rather than shattering her torso in a nightmare eruption of gore and armor fragments like she expected it to, the projectile instead burst into a semi-translucent mass of... phlegm?

"What the?"

It certainly felt viscous and sticky enough to be phlegm to her as she dragged two fingers experimentally through the goop covering her from shoulders to ankles. Only realizing after it started hardening into an oddly organic concrete just how screwed they all were.

"Son of a mother fucking bitch!"

Snarling, Straya's suit creaked and whirred as her motor-assisted joints tried and failed to break free from their sudden confines.

"God damn shit fucking snot rocket mother fuckers!" added Adryel at the same time, the knife they'd managed to draw the moment before the goo had solidified over them and their rifle angled uselessly up by their shoulder where they'd been poised to throw it.

The Captain and Lem, meanwhile, just sighed.

"Damn it."

"Shit. I'm sorry, boss."

"Not your fault, lemon cakes," the Captain soothed, her own coilgun uselessly trapped against her side, half-drawn from its holster. "They got the drop on us fair and square."

Rolling her still free head around her hunched shoulders, she leveled an exasperated look at Six.

"All right, you have my attention. What do you want, aside from Phera that is, to make this go away?"

"I have already made my desires in this matter clear," intoned Six, voice still flat and distant as his mercenaries began making a beeline toward the grav acclimation tunnel at the far end of the hold. "My associates and I will now be relieving you of Doctor Sinclair, as well as your freighter."

"Like hell you are!"

Any lingering facade of good humor went up in the flames of the Captain's furious exclamation.

"Kelt! Cut habitation grav and prepare for incursion! If these mother fuckers want the Mayhem, you make them *bleed* for it."

"On it," came the senior engineer's immediate reply, the hatch to grav acclimation irising shut with a surprising (and decidedly un-Kelt-like) amount of violent force as she spoke, cutting off the mercenaries just before they managed to reach it.

"I assure you that such hysterics are entirely unnecessary, Captain. Sergeant Briggs and his men are more than capable of breaching a sealed hatch," tsked Six, observing his mercenaries with cool detachment. "Further resistance is futile."

"Further resistance is futile," parroted Phera in a mocking falsetto before the Captain could reply, drawing Six's attention to her fully for the first time since his arrival.

To her mild surprise, her voice didn't shake even slightly as she issued that challenge. Within the span of one moment to the next, she'd reached a level beyond fear that brought with it a numb sort of clarity that left no room for fear or doubt. Straya had once tried to describe the sensation to her when she'd worked up the nerve to ask her about her past experiences in combat, but it was only now as her options had dwindled to either fight or die, that she finally understood.

"Are you... mocking me, Doctor?"

A bloom of vindictive satisfaction lit up inside of Phera's pounding heart as Six's look of blank indifference crumpled into confusion, his brows drawing together in consternation.

"Are you mocking me, Doctor," she echoed back, pouring even more obnoxious sass into her tone as she hurriedly cycled through command sequences inside of her hallucinographic workspace.

"I really would advise against further acts of bravado. You are already in quite enough hot water as it is. Defiance will not do you any favors."

"You really think so, huh?"

"I do indeed," replied Six, his mask of polite amiability starting to slip, revealing a hint of the fury her utter lack of respect was stirring up inside of him. "Your time playing pirate has come to an end, and you will now return to where you belong and face the consequences of your actions."

"Uh-huh. Sure."

"Sure? Really? Do you think I'm joking here, *girl*?"

"Ooooh, *girl*. So scary. Wow."

Phera gave her eyes the hardest roll she could.

"And, for the record, of course I think you're a joke. Those expensive clothes don't make you any less of a glorified errand boy, you know."

"Errand boy?!"

Her continued noncompliance had the executive positively fuming now, unused as he was to his underlings refusing to bend to his will. After all, who was she to be so defiant? She was Cilaran born and bred. She knew her place. He was an *executive*, and she was just a lowly tech. And worse, a lowly tech who was also a contract breaker. She should be on her knees begging for a second chance with the company! (Assuming she could actually move her knees, that is.)

Jaw clenched and hands balled into fists at his sides, Six drew in close enough for his breath to fog the front of Phera's faceplate.

"Allow me to disabuse you of that notion," he ground out, biting off each word with barely-suppressed anger.

"Oh, please do. I'm all ears, really," drawled Phera, blowing a few stray curls out of her face for added annoyance. "Though, fair warning, you're going to have to try pretty hard to out intimidate my crewmates. Lem does this thing with her eyebrows that knocks my knees out from under me pretty much every time she uses it. So, you know, big shoes and all that."

"Very well. How's this then?"

Breathing out his anger in one long exhalation, Six straightened back up to his full height as a brittle simulacrum of his earlier sneer reasserted itself.

"In spite of your obstinate attitude, you will still accompany me back to Cilara for a disciplinary review and reassignment. And, unlike your little crew of ruffians who will at least be given the opportunity to return their shares of the funds I just transferred in exchange for their freedom, *you* will never see the outside of whatever remote facility we wind up dumping you in ever again.

There will be no escape. There will be no rescue. You will fulfill your contract with all due diligence until *we* decide you are no longer of any use to us, and you will be grateful for the opportunity."

"Hmmm… Not bad. I'd say that was a solid six out of ten."

Hot on the heels of that taunting came Phera's first truly piratical grin. Stealing across her usually soft features, it drew her lips back into a feral snarl that was three parts threat and ten parts challenge as her body flushed nova bright with fresh adrenaline and hate. Even frozen in place, in that moment she knew without a shadow of a doubt that she was the most dangerous thing on board the ship.

And, blinking out a transmission order through her HUD, she proved it.

"Here, let me show you how it's done."

THUD…! THUD…! THUD…!

"What the?" demanded one of the mercenaries, whirling to point their weapon at her as a rhythmic series of bone-jarring impacts began to reverberate through the hold.

THUD…! THUD…! THUD…!

"What the fuck did you just do?"

THUD…! THUD…! THUD…!

"Oh, nothing much."

THUD…! THUD…! THUD…!

Phera forced herself to count to three before she spoke again, never letting her gaze waver from Six as she willed his heart to explode inside his chest.

"Pardon me, *sir*," she continued in a poisonous inversion of the tone she'd so often used with her superiors back on The Bin. "But, I believe you've forgotten about one other bit of Panorama property we've been holding onto."

"Explain. Now."

The aide's level tone had sharpened to a micron-thin knife's edge as his nostrils flared. But, rather than crush her confidence as it might have in the past, Phera instead fed on it. Using his simmering rage to fuel the reactor of her own reckless daring as she made a show of licking her lips in a naked display of aggression.

"It would be my pleasure."

THUD…! THUD…! THUD…!

"Right now there's an entire mining shuttle's worth of ore excavators affixed to the exterior hull of this ship that are slowly but surely working their way inside to say hello."

With the sort of dramatic timing only achievable via direct remote control, a sharp **CRACK!** of plex and metal being thoroughly abused by multiple Pendragon Gatecrashers echoed back from the ship mated to the Mayhem's cargo hold airlock, along with Linus's cries of terror.

"Well, the hold, and your shuttle."

THUD-CRACK!

"Why, Phera! That's so *devious*!" exclaimed the Captain, feigning a sniff. "I'm so proud."

"What can I say? It worked pretty well for the Excaden job. Figured it was worth a shot now."

Despite her best efforts to pretend otherwise, Phera's anxiety was definitely starting to gnaw away at her insides, but the Captain's praise did a lot to help bolster her front of unshakable confidence as she glared at Six. Who, rather than fold immediately like she'd been hoping he would, instead loosed another breath and let his face fall slack. Looking serene and unperturbed while his mercenaries frantically pinged him for orders.

"My point defenses are more than capable of dealing with any errant drones, Doctor Sinclair."

The unmistakable **WHUMPH-WHUMPH!** of a micro-meteor cracking laser opening fire from the mated shuttle punctuated this flat dismissal, drawing out a derisive snort from Phera in its wake.

"Doubt it."

THUD-CRACK!

Phera's voice picked up a growl to it then as her connection to her drones fizzled out amid a burst of signal jamming static. Apparently, the Captain wasn't the only one who'd thought to bring along someone with digital countermeasures experience to the party. Not that it mattered now.

"You might take out a few of them, but that's all you're going to get. Those aren't normal drones out there. They're running the completed version of the mesh communication system I was working on before I left Pano. And, trust me, *they're* more than capable of adapting to scenario changes all on their own."

THUD-CRACK!

"Soooo, I'd definitely start thinking about cutting my losses before they breach and decide to start mining *you* for resources."

WHUMPH-WHUMPH!

"Sir! I have a shot! Just give the order to fire!"

Phera only snorted again at the distinct note of panic in the mercenary's voice.

"Yeah, go ahead and pull the trigger. See if I care," she taunted. "You'll be following right after if you do."

THUD-CRACK!

"I see."

Six's features remained slack and unfocused while Phera's heart pounded in chest-tightening time with the encroaching death just on the other side of the suddenly way too thin seeming hull. She'd made sure to account for negotiation time when she'd been preparing this backup plan last night, but she'd forgotten to set up a time tracker when she'd issued the start order. So, it was anyone's guess just when the drones would finally breach and take the choice out of Six's hands.

THUD-CRACK!

Come on...

WHUMPH-WHUMPH!

Come on...

THUD-CRACK!

In that moment, seconds stretched out for an eternity, pulling her awareness of herself into stark hyperfocus. Her perceptions shrinking in until all she could sense was her stomach rolling with each breath she took, the lingering hint of syrupy sweetness on the back of her tongue from the coffee she'd had before suiting up, the thin rivulet of sweat tickling its way down the small of her back, the-

"Very well."

With those two words, Six popped the bubble of tension that had been gradually strangling Phera.

"We shall nullify your contract and write off your remaining debt to us in exchange for a cessation of hostilities and the guarantee of a safe departure."

"I... Uh, yeah. Sure."

Swallowing, she did her best to get a grip on her frazzled nerves, wishing that she was capable of properly shaking her head to clear it.

"Just, you know, kill the jamming and I'll call them off."

"Done."

Phera very nearly spoiled her front of suicidal indifference by spluttering, "Wait? Really?"

Somehow, it all felt too easy. But, again, sudden decisions and decisive action seemed to be this guy's whole MO when he wasn't being an obnoxious Alpha-sider prick.

Well, to be fair, I guess I did just threaten to take us all out in a blaze of drone-powered glory, she mused, issuing a pause order to what remained of her automated attack force as soon as the jamming static had dissipated. *Still...*

She couldn't believe her bluff had actually worked.

In the deafening silence that rushed in to fill the void left behind by her drones, she and Six fell into another impromptu staring contest. Phera not knowing what to say next, and Six seemingly mulling something over before abruptly returning his attention to the Captain and slipping back into his role as a high-energy corporate go-getter.

"Well, Captain, this has certainly been an eventful meeting."

"It sure has," agreed the Captain, rolling her eyes. "Let's never do it again."

An easy, self-deprecating chuckle rumbled up from Six as he gave the cuffs of his sleeves a couple of perfunctory tugs.

"I suppose only time will tell. For now, I wish you all smooth sailing."

With that incongruously cordial goodbye, he disengaged the locks on his magboots and gently pushed off back toward the airlock behind him and his waiting shuttle.

"We're finished here, Sergeant."

"Sir!" came the immediate reply of all five mercenaries in unison, abandoning their attempts to breach the grav acclimation hatch and instead falling back to form a protective screen of armor and raised weapons around Six as he slipped back through the airlock umbilical.

And, just like that, things went from "Oh fuck, we're all going to die!" to "Well, that was certainly something." The airlock cycled shut, the sounds of the two ships disengaging from one another echoed through the hold, and then Shi was back on the comm announcing amid what sounded like barely held back tears of relief that the Panorama shuttle was pulling away without incident.

"Good fucking riddance," grumbled the Captain, before breathing out her own sigh of relief. "Steph, get your cute ass in here and help us out, would you?"

As if ve'd been waiting for just such a summons, the acclimation tunnel's hatch irised open once again to reveal a broadly beaming crew doc with a bulky chem launcher and a frankly distressing number of cryptically labeled canisters nestled into a bandoleer across the chest of ver vacsuit.

"All right, who's bleeding, and who's just bruised?"

"Wow, that was fast," marveled Phera as the slim enby glided effortlessly toward her and the others, head swiveling to assess each of the crew in passing as ve went.

"Oh, yeah, I was actually just down the tunnel prepping to give those mercs a taste of bone wasp enzyme and potassium chloride when they breached."

"I, uh... I see."

Shivering, Phera did her best not to dwell too long on that particular visual as it hit home for her once again just how dangerous dismissing the petite doctor as harmless could be.

At least ve only uses ver powers for evil on me in fun ways...

"Thank you for not poisoning the atmo on my ship," snorted the Captain, dragging Steph away from ver menacing of Phera with a smirk. "Now, do you think you could do something about this shit we're all covered in?"

"It's a low-density niobium foam," clarified Straya, still sounding pissed at herself for letting Six's mercenaries get the drop on her.

"LDN, huh?"

Sucking in a breath through ver teeth, Steph gave ver helmeted head a rueful shake.

"That's definitely going to be a pain in the ass to scrub out later."

"Steph."

The Captain's voice was starting to fray at the edges.

"My nose has been itching me like crazy for the last I don't even know how long, and I'm about to lose it. Get to work!"

"Ah, right, wouldn't want to have to reattach that."

Flashing ver boss an impish look, the crew doc pulled out a canister from ver bandoleer, squinted at it for a second before swapping it out for another, and then twisted an aerosolizing adapter onto the end of it.

"Hang in there, Cap. I'll have you loose and scratching in no time."

True to ver word, as soon as Steph began to mist the hardened, apparently not-phlegm with ver chosen counter-agent, it began to bubble and dissolve into a runny sludge that dribbled down onto the deck plates; inert and viscous.

"Oh. My. God. *Yes.*"

With her arms were free, the Captain wrenched off her helmet and went to town on the side of her nose, sagging in relief while Steph turned ver attention to Phera next.

"You know, it's too bad I don't do paychecks," she mused after sorting out her various itches, focusing now on scraping off great globules of half-dissolved goop from the front of her vacsuit with a mild look of disgust. "You'd definitely have earned yourself a raise after that stunt, swabbie."

"No kidding, you little psychopath," agreed Lem with a booming laugh, slapping Phera hard enough on the back to knock her face-first into the Captain's semi-sticky front after Steph had finished spraying her down as well. "I still can't believe you managed to chase off an entire squad of mercs just by banging a bunch of pots and pans together. I'm definitely taking you out to play cards the next time we're in port."

"Excuse me, but those were some *very* big pots and pans, I'll have you know."

Phera's accompanying giggle with that mock-affronted declaration was definitely more than a little on the manic side as she too started stripping off her helmet. It had suddenly grown claustrophobic inside her vacsuit, and she needed to breathe some (relatively) fresh air before she had a total breakdown now that the reality of what had just happened was finally catching up with her.

"Pots and pans that definitely would've cracked the hull if push came to shove," she continued, complexion going pallid as her fingers fumbled with the data cable still plugged into the port below her ear. "I mean, I didn't *want* them to, but I wasn't about to let them just have their way, and I-"

"You know..."

The Captain's words and the steadying arm she draped across Phera's trembling shoulders were both uncharacteristically gentle as she popped the cable free for her.

"I'm starting to think we might be a bad influence on you."

"Heh. Maybe just a little," allowed the engineer, grimacing her way through the electric tingles jangling their way up and down her nerve endings with the sudden loss of her neural link to her wrist-comp. "Pretty sure I never tried to murder someone with a drone before I met you, Cap."

"Ahem."

Straya very loudly and very pointedly cleared her throat.

"You sure about that one, sweet cheeks?"

"Okay, I never tried to murder someone with more than *one* drone," amended Phera, sticking out her tongue at the (for the moment) still safely trapped in place raider. "Pedant."

"Brat."

"Army of killer drones or no, you're still going to be the one to break it to Kelt about what you did to the hull," piped up Adryel as Lem finished scraping off the last bits of gunk around their knee joints, sheathing their knife at the small of their back with a liquid whisper of ceramic on plex.

"Oh... Yeah."

Truth be told, Phera hadn't quite thought that particular part of her plan all the way through.

"Um, I'm sure she'll be fine. The drones were *barely* powered up to forty percent. At worst, we've got some interesting new dents and plasma scorches."

"And an entire cargo hold's worth of welding seams to check for stress fractures," added Kelt over the comm, making Phera jump despite the note of amusement in her voice. "We'll definitely be discussing those later, young lady."

"Awww, come on. Don't I get a free pass for saving all our asses?"

"Afraid not, swabbie."

Dragging a hand through her sweat-matted hair, the Captain sent Phera a wink.

"She outranks you."

"Damn right I do, *and* I've got plans for a carbon fiber paddle I've been meaning to print for a while now."

"Oooh, that sounds like fun!" cooed the Captain with a stomach-churning amount of enthusiasm. "Print me one too, Kelty."

"As soon as I've finished stress testing the prototype on Phera, I'll gladly whip up one for you and anyone else who wants to use them on her."

"Fantastic! I'm looking forward to it."

"Ditto," added Adryel.

"Same," agreed Straya.

While Steph and Shi both just snickered and chimed in with matching, "Count me in"s.

Obette, chivalrous rogue that he was, responded with a lilting, "I'll stick to my belt, thank you very much."

While Lem just rolled her eyes.

"I'll just borrow Cap's."

"Humph."

Phera did her best to pretend she was miffed at the promise of what would no doubt be an extremely memorable series of spankings at the far-too-capable hands of her crew, but it was kind of hard to be grumpy when she was smiling so hard it made her face hurt.

"This is *so* unfair. You know that, right?"

"Sorry, babe."

Straya's magboots sealed to the deck in front of Phera with a heavy *clomp* as she dragged her into a rib-crushing hug without warning.

"But you know the deal."

"Let me guess," the auburn-haired younger woman managed to mostly deadpan around a wheeze, head tipping back to meet Straya's iron gray eyes and choosing not to mention anything about the hastily scrubbed away tear tracks still evident against her scarred cheeks. "Pirates?"

"Pirates," she confirmed, kissing the faux-pout from her lips. "Besides, you're the one hoarding all the booty."

There came a twin rumble from Phera's vacsuit in the area of said booty then as Straya gave it a possessive squeeze, crushing her lips to Phera's own for a much more rigorous kiss this time.

"Right then. Shi, set a course for Marcos," ordered the Captain while her lead raider and her favorite cabin girl made out in the null-grav with reckless abandon. "I think it's safe to say we've all earned ourselves a few days shore leave."

"Already got a slingshot lined up and ready to go. Getting us underway at eighty-five percent."

"Shi…" warned Kelt.

"Kidding, kidding!"

"You'd better be, mister."

"Looks like Phera isn't the only one who's been getting exposed to bad influences," observed Obette dryly, drawing out a chuckle from the Captain.

"Positively *rebellious*," she agreed. "Speaking of…"

Distracted as she was by Straya's tongue inside her mouth, Phera didn't notice the nod the Captain gave Lem and Adryel until it was too late. Only realizing that she'd been lured into a trap when she felt Straya toe the release catch of her magboots off for her while the other two hoisted her up so that her feet dangled uselessly above the deck.

"While I appreciate your daring and ingenuity, Phera, dear," continued the Captain, advancing on her with all the slinking, languorous menace of a predator cornering its prey. "I simply cannot abide such wanton disrespect of crew property. That's *everyone's* hull, after all."

"But I-!"

"Uh-uh-uh…"

Clucking her tongue, the grinning pirate cupped the engineer's chin and leaned in so that her soft lips brushed against the side of her rapidly heating ear.

"I hope you're ready to make the trip back to port standing up," she murmured in a husky purr before kissing her cheek and stepping back, hands on her hips. "Assuming Kelt doesn't just space you first, that is."

"Heh."

Bookended by her snickering crewmates as her stomach roiled with a familiar mix of anticipatory dread and lust, Phera's face broke out once again into a piratical smile; matching the Captain hungry grin for hungry grin.

In that moment, there was no place she'd rather be.

"Aye aye, Captain."

THE END